An Omnibus of
Short Stories

OTHER BOOKS BY JAMES T. FARRELL

STUDS LONIGAN

A trilogy comprising "Young Lonigan," "The Young Manhood of Studs Lonigan," and "Judgment Day"

The Danny O'Neill Novels

THE FACE OF TIME

A WORLD I NEVER MADE

NO STAR IS LOST

FATHER AND SON

MY DAYS OF ANGER

THIS MAN AND THIS WOMAN

BERNARD CLARE

THE ROAD BETWEEN

YET OTHER WATERS

THE SHORT STORIES OF JAMES T. FARRELL

Comprising "Calico Shoes and Other Stories," "Guillotine Party and Other Stories," and "Can All This Grandeur Perish and Other Stories"

FRENCH GIRLS ARE VICIOUS

AN AMERICAN DREAM GIRL

THE LIFE ADVENTUROUS

WHEN BOYHOOD DREAMS COME TRUE

TO WHOM IT MAY CONCERN

$1,000 A WEEK

GAS-HOUSE MCGINTY

ELLEN ROGERS

TOMMY GALLAGHER'S CRUSADE

A NOTE ON LITERARY CRITICISM

THE LEAGUE OF FRIGHTENED PHILISTINES

LITERATURE AND MORALITY

REFLECTIONS AT FIFTY

An Omnibus of
Short Stories

by

JAMES T FARRELL

New York

THE VANGUARD PRESS

TO MARYA AND HORACE GREGORY

Contents

$1,000 A WEEK

TO WHOM IT MAY CONCERN

THE LIFE ADVENTUROUS

$1,000 *a Week*
AND OTHER SHORT STORIES

Not knowing when the dawn will come

I open every door

EMILY DICKINSON

$1,000 a Week

I

ON A SUNNY Monday morning Tom Lambert reported for work at the studios of Grandiose Films, Inc. He went to the office of Sidney Klem, producer, and introduced himself to the secretary, Miss Kennedy.

"Mr. Klem usually works late and so he doesn't get in early. I don't expect him until eleven o'clock. But, Mr. Lambert, would you like me to see that an office is assigned to you and to make the other arrangements for your work here?" she asked.

"Yes, thanks."

"Well, now, first of all, your secretary. Of course, you want a secretary, don't you?"

"Yes."

"We always like to get the right secretary for our writers. If a writer has the wrong secretary, it can be very unpleasant, and he isn't able to do good work. Tell me, Mr. Lambert, would you like a girl who is efficient and impersonal or would you prefer one who is more personal?"

"I'd like one who is efficient but human."

"I have just the right person in mind. I'll see if I can get her. But, Mr. Lambert, if she isn't satisfactory, you just let me know, and I'll get you another one. We try to make everything as pleasant and comfortable as we can for writers in our unit."

"Thank you."

Tom puffed on a cigarette while she made several inter-studio calls, arranging for his secretary, his studio pass card, and other such matters.

"Now everything is settled. And, Mr. Lambert, I want to say that we're very proud to have a writer like you here with us. I've read your books and I think that . . . that they're just wonderful."

"Thank you," Tom said; he was usually embarrassed and at a loss for a reply when his work was praised to his face.

"I mean it. I think they're wonderful. Now, if you want to, you can wait here for your secretary to come and show you over to your office, or if you like, you can look around the lot. I am sure that Mr. Klem won't be free to see you until sometime this afternoon."

"I'll wander around for a while and be back later."

Tom left the office. It was in the general administration building, which was a low stucco structure; its long corridors were painted blue and gray. He walked aimlessly up and down the corridor, reading the names of producers and writers on the successive doors. He had never heard of most of the writers. He went into the office of Allan Storres, a former newspaperman who was now a highly paid writer-producer. Tom found Storres seated at his desk and poring over a script. The office was large and comfortable.

"Hello, there, how are you?" Storres said cordially.

"Pretty good. I'm starting to work here this morning and I thought I'd drop in and say hello."

"Congratulations. I'm glad to hear it. Whom are you working for?"

"Sidney Klem."

"I wish you luck, fellow," Storres said, frowning.

"I don't really know him. I only met him twice, and he was in a hurry each time. He seemed anxious to get me here, but my contract gives only a two-week guarantee. Then if Avilov likes what I do, they give me a longer guarantee."

"I hope things work out well for you. What are you working on?"

"A re-make of an old play, *The Human Element*. It was

originally written about twenty-five years ago, and I've been told that the author made about a million bucks out of it. Then he retired, bought himself a farm, and never wrote another line. He's now supposed to be a very happy and contented old gentleman."

"Yes, and every time they do a re-make of that thing, I discover I have an inescapable obligation that prevents me from seeing it. It's necrophilia to make another picture out of that turkey."

"It's a Cinderella story," Tom said apologetically.

"The dame gets knocked up, doesn't she?"

"But not in the picture. She's got to get married first before that happens."

"Well, it's the censorship. But then, there're two sides to that question, and there's something to be said for voluntary censorship. You know, there are just some things you can't show people on a screen. Take that last book of yours. God, what a book! I liked it. I've been a Lambert fan from way back. But how are you going to put your books on the screen? If I thought you could, I'd have done it long ago."

"Well, I'm going to try and make a go of it out here. If I do, I won't have to work at the same intense pace I've had to in the past. I came out here to get something to do, you know, because a writer can't live on fame. And I've got to do something because my books don't make enough. I've been terribly overworked, and after I finished my last book, I almost had a nervous breakdown. So I'm going to do the best I can out here."

"I wish you luck and think you deserve it. And, Lambert, I don't like to give advice. It's not in my line. But since you're just starting out here, let me say this much. Every time I do a picture, I keep this in mind. I know the folks back home in my little home town, Squireville, Ohio. I know them from A to Z. When I make a picture, I ask myself: 'Now, will these folks walk out of the theater liking this picture or not? Will they send their kids and the neighbors to see it?' If not, I don't see any use in making the picture. For then I'm pretty sure that it will be a flop. Whether you like it or not, that's pictures."

"I take the same attitude toward the folks in Squireville, or toward the people anywhere. I don't assume that they will always go on wanting what they get now. Just as we change our minds and learn, so can they, and I think they will."

"When they do, we'll make better pictures."

"But I think that now is the time to prepare for that change. That's why I wish they'd give me something else to do out here, something better than *The Human Element.*"

"No matter what you do in pictures, it's got to gross at the box office. That's an infallible law of pictures. Many writers don't like it, but it's the fact. Still, there's something to be said for writing in pictures. Suppose you do a script and the picture is a flop. The writer is the last one who's likely to be blamed. The other fellow takes the rap: the producer, the director, the stars. And the writer goes on getting his pay check every week."

"I hope I can do something good and learn a little about the whole industry."

"Well, Tom, I hope you click. You know, I'd have been damned glad to have you work for me if I'd've had anything that was really worth your doing. I don't think a writer like you should be put on just any story that comes through the mill. That's why I don't understand why they asked you to work on the one you've got. But anyway, the best of luck, and I'll see you around the lot."

"Thanks. I'll go along now and get myself organized."

"Good luck."

II

Tom was introduced to his secretary by Miss Kennedy. Miss Solomon was a tall thin girl with black bobbed hair and angular features. She had a friendly manner and a pleasant face. She guided him out of the building, down a street lined with stucco structures, then past some bungalows which she told him were used by the stars, and finally into another short street. This

was lined on either side by trees, and in front of a row of three
bungalows there was a patch of grass.

"The first of these bungalows is ours," Miss Solomon said,
pointing.

They crossed the grass, walked up the steps, and entered
the bungalow. It was divided into three offices. The central
one was for Miss Solomon, and the others were for writers.
Tom's office was on the left; the other one was unoccupied.
Miss Solomon explained various details of studio routine to
him, and then she looked into the cabinet and desk drawers
in order to check on the supplies.

Tom entered his office. It was quiet, light, and cheerful. By
a window looking out on the lawn there was a couch uphol-
stered in blue; near it stood a comfortable easy chair with the
same upholstering. Opposite, there was a large, plain office
desk, a swivel chair, and a small table on which a typewriter
rested. He suddenly noticed that the carpet also was blue, and
then he remembered having heard that Avilov, director of all
production at Grandiose, was singularly fascinated by the color
blue. All of Avilov's offices were decorated in blue; his cars
were painted in different shades of the same color; he generally wore blue ties and blue suits; blue was a predominating
color everywhere on the Grandiose lot.

Tom sat by his desk and looked vacantly at the desk blotter.

"Mr. Lambert, what kind of paper do you like to use when
you work?" Miss Solomon asked, appearing in the doorway.

"It doesn't matter."

"Well, I can order yellow paper or white paper. Or do you
want both kinds?"

"Order both, please."

"And do you like soft lead pencils or hard ones?"

"Soft."

"And do you ever use scratch pads?"

"Yes, get some. Order whatever you think we'll need."

"All right. And is there anything else I can do now?"

"No, thanks."

She went back to her desk. Now he was at work. What

should he do? There was nothing to be done until he saw
Klem. He found stationery in one of his drawers and wrote
some letters.

III

The main room of the commissary was noisy and crowded.
Tom sat having lunch with Miss Solomon at a small table. All
about him he saw studio sailors, cowboys, butlers, gentlemen
and ladies, pirates, Indians, and pioneers. Miss Solomon kept
pointing out various studio personalities, stars, stars of the
silent days who were now extras, writers, producers, executives,
agents, ex-policemen who were technical advisers, animal
trainers and others. After lunch he returned to his office and
waited for a telephone call from Klem. It came at three o'clock.
Tom picked up the notes he had made in preparation for the
conference and hurried over to Klem's office.

"Welcome to Grandiose, Tom," Klem said as Tom entered.
They shook hands.

Klem's office was large and pleasant, carpeted in blue, with
bookcases and books, conventional water colors hung about
the walls, telephones, cabinets, and a large and expensive ma-
hogany desk. Tom sat down and glanced at Klem. He sensed
that Klem was observing his clothes. Klem was about twenty-
eight and just beginning to get stout. He had very soft skin
and light wavy hair. He wore blue trousers and a loud, gray-
checkered jacket, with a gardenia in his buttonhole. Born in
Brooklyn, he had been an office boy, a reader, a Hollywood
scenarist, and, for the last year, a producer.

"Just a minute, Lambert, and we'll have our conference,"
Klem said.

He pushed a button and asked his secretary to come in. She
appeared immediately, notebook in hand. He stood over his
desk, handing her letters and bills and giving her instructions
concerning each item. When she left, he dropped into his chair
and sighed.

"I've been so rushed that I don't know if I'm coming or
going," he said.

"Yes, I guess you must be busy," Tom said, merely to make conversation and feeling a bit embarrassed.

"Busy? It's hectic here. And with my temperament, I was never cut out for such a hectic career with so many responsibilities." He lit a cigarette and leaned way back in his chair. "Tell me, Lambert, have you any ideas on how we'll lick *The Human Element?*"

"First of all, I don't think that the heroine should be a servant girl."

"Why?"

"Well, the story about the servant girl and her rich master has been done to death. I'd like to do something fresh and original."

"We don't have to worry about that. You will. With the situation we got in this story, we can get a lot of schmaltz into our picture."

Schmaltz? Tom suddenly recalled having been told what this word meant. It referred to lachrymose scenes which moved an audience to tears.

"Just a minute until I make a call."

Klem picked up a phone.

"Yes, we have something that's going to be terrific, if we bring it up to date," Klem said.

He took up his phone and told his secretary to get him someone named Jack Spiegel. He waited until the call was put through.

"Hello, Jack? This is Sidney Klem. You know at that party last Saturday night, well, my wife got the wrong lynx coat. . . . I don't know how it happened, but we know that it isn't her coat because it's too short—comes up to about her knees. Mabel isn't as tall as Kitty, so we both thought that perhaps Kitty had taken Mabel's coat by mistake. . . . You don't know? Well, will you speak to Mabel and find out? . . . Thanks, Jack, and let me know. I'll see you soon, and oh, yes, Chaplin can't come to dinner this week. I'll let you know later when he can come. So long, Jack."

Klem turned an expressionless face to Tom. There was a knock on the door, and suddenly a gross head appeared.

"Oh, Max, come in."

A stout bald-headed man entered.

"Max Lozovsky, shake hands with Tom Lambert. You ought to know who he is, he's a damned swell writer, and he's just started working in my unit."

"Yes, yes, of course. Glad to meet you," Max said, shaking hands. Then, ignoring Tom, he turned to Klem. "Of all the goddamn four-leaf clovers!"

"You lost, didn't you?"

"The Bums had the game won yesterday. Henrich struck out. It was the last out. And then the Yankees go on and win the ball game."

"The best man always wins."

"Horseshoes. I'll get my nickels back from you, boy. What's your team for the football game Saturday?"

"Oregon," Klem said.

"That's my team. Why do you want Oregon?"

"Why did I want the Yankees?"

"Then it's no bet. I'll place mine with my bookie."

"Better luck next time," Klem said, smiling.

"They had the game won. And you call that baseball? Baseball, my aunt's crabapple," Max said, leaving the office.

"Lambert, that fellow is a genius in the field of picture exhibition. But let's get going on our story," Klem said, sinking back in his chair.

Lambert leaned forward hopefully and said:

"My idea is this—to tell a human but ironical story, a comedy. We'll reverse the Cinderella pattern and tell the story of a girl who refuses to be a Cinderella."

"Just a minute, Tom. I'm sorry you find me so rushed, but everything is happening today," Klem interrupted, pressing a button.

Speaking into the phone, he told Miss Kennedy to get his wife.

Tom lit a cigarette. He glanced at his notes. He shoved them into his pocket.

"Hello, darling. . . . How are you? . . . Good. . . . Say, I talked with Jack, and he's going to find out if you got Mabel's coat. . . . The luncheon that Mr. Avilov gave today here for Lord Wisthaven? Very good. I enjoyed it. You must meet Lord Wisthaven. He's very witty. He told a number of good jokes. He's really terrific as an after-dinner speaker. His best joke was very clever. I'll tell it to you. He said Hitler claims that the Nazis will establish a New Order for a thousand years. Even if they could do that, he said, the Germans in that time couldn't make the Italian navy come out and fight once. Isn't that good?" Klem laughed. "He gave me a good idea of the King. The King must be just like Lord Wisthaven. After seeing and meeting him, I felt as if I'd known King George all my life. . . . Who's coming to dinner tonight? . . . Good. . . . Good-bye, darling, and take care of yourself."

Klem swung around in his chair.

"Tom. I don't think we've got the right line on this story. Perhaps we ought to make the gal an upstairs maid in this rich home. Her family is poor. She's living at home, you know, the kind of stuff you give us in your books. The old man is a dock worker, and he gets killed in a strike. She's got to find work and she gets this job as a maid. The son is a jerk, a jazz-age college boy with a turned-up hat, a raccoon coat, and no brains—just a jerk in the dizzy twenties. He comes home boiled one night and he sees her. He goes for her. In real life, of course, he lays her. In the picture, that's what we mean, but what we got to have them do is to go off, and after a wild midnight ride in an automobile in the rain, they get a justice of the peace out of bed in his nightshirt. After they get married, she finds out that she's knocked up. The family won't accept her. They're snooty, snobs in the Social Register, and all that crap. So he and the girl go off. Now, here's the problem. He's a jerk, and he can't take it. But do we want her to divorce him and marry another fellow? But on that, now let me think a minute."

The telephone interrupted Klem's processes of thought.

"Yes, send the manicurist in and get me the shoeshine boy if he's around."

He turned to Tom.

"Tom, I'm rushed, and we'll have to finish this discussion tomorrow afternoon." He wrote something on a slip of paper and handed it to Tom. "Here're the titles of two pictures I want you to look at in the projection room. When you go out, speak to Miss Kennedy. She'll arrange for you to see them. You can catch one this afternoon and the other in the morning."

Klem saw him to the door.

"And I want you to know, Tom, that I'm damned glad to have you working with me. We'll lick this story, and what we do is going to be really terrific."

IV

Tom returned to his office from the projection room at about eleven-thirty the following morning. He asked Miss Solomon to call up Klem's office and to tell Miss Kennedy that he'd seen the two recommended pictures and was waiting for another conference. He sat at his desk. This was his second day of work. Until the line of approach to the story was settled with Klem, there was nothing for him to do. He lit a cigarette, and sat thinking.

His story conference yesterday had lasted exactly forty-five minutes. He knew that Klem's salary was the same as his—a thousand dollars a week. How much had each of them earned yesterday for the work they had done conferring?

He calculated, assuming that each of them worked a thirty-two hour week. On the basis of that assumption, they earned $31.25 an hour. He made additional calculations and discovered that he and Klem had each earned $23.43¾. This meant that the conference had cost American economy $46.87½.

He tore up the sheet of paper on which he had made the calculations and tossed it into the wastepaper basket. He called in Miss Solomon and asked her to telephone the Script Department to get him some representative story treatments and screen plays, so he could see what kind of writing was done at Grandiose.

v

Tom put down the treatment he had just read and looked at the notes he had made about it. He read a quotation he had copied from the treatment.

When a man and a woman love one another, the four horse-men of Cupid ride down into their hearts, blowing songs like gentle winds of Heaven.

He tore up his notes. He looked at the front page of the treatment and observed that it was written by someone named Alvin Dunwiddie. He went out to Miss Solomon's office.

"Is Alvin Dunwiddie a successful writer out here?"

"Oh, yes, he just got a three-way contract at one of the other studios."

"You wouldn't know what he earned when he did this treatment I've just read, would you?"

"He's tops. He must have made twenty-seven hundred and fifty dollars a week."

"And you wouldn't know how long it took him to write it here, would you?"

"Yes, I do. His secretary is a good friend of mine, Peggy Baker. He worked on it eight weeks. If you'd like to meet him, I could have Peggy arrange it. He liked her work."

"No, that's all right. I was merely curious."

"It's a good treatment, isn't it? It made a swell movie. And I was told that when Mr. Avilov read it, he raved about it. He was sore when Mr. Dunwiddie left us for another studio."

"How did you hear all that?"

"Oh, when you work on the lot here as long as I have, you hear about everything that goes on."

Tom went back to his office. He picked up a screen play, but flung it aside, bored after having read five pages. He lit a cigarette, and sat thinking. It was quiet and pleasant in the bungalow, and he had the illusion that he was in a small country town. He could see the sun slanting through his window, and outside, the grass and the sidewalk of the deserted little street.

The telephone rang. He thought it would be Klem, but it was a friend of Miss Solomon's telephoning to while away the minutes chatting.

VI

Tom waited while Klem concluded a telephone conversation with his tailor.

"Now, let's get going, Tom," Klem began, pacing the floor as he talked. "The first question is this: Do we want to have the time in the picture run over a short period in the present or do we have to carry along over a number of years running down to the present?"

"What do you think?" Tom asked.

"That's the question."

"Since we begin it in the jazz age, we'll have to plan it over a period of years."

"For the moment, we'll plan it that way."

"I still think we don't have to make the heroine a maid," Tom said.

"Forget that. She's a maid."

"How about the end?"

"We don't want her to become a great actress or an opera singer. That's been done. We don't want anything corny in this picture." Klem paused and thought. "But, of course, if we make her an actress at the end, our star can wear some swell clothes. We can have some shots of her all dolled up to kill, and we might even pull in some shots of a Hollywood première. That's a good angle. The public likes to see the stars dressed up."

"What about the fellow in the picture?"

"She gives him the air. That's settled. This guy is a heel. You can characterize a heel. I was looking through your books last night. God, your characterizations are so true to life. I want you to get the same true characterizations in this picture."

"I think I can do better with the characterizations if you take my original idea—that of reversing the Cinderella pattern."

"Drop that for the minute. Now, here is what she does. She divorces this jerk." Klem again stopped talking; he stood reflecting. "No, she better not divorce him. I'll tell you what to do. Just bring the old play up to date. Let her end up a famous actress. Make the guy a heel, but a lovable heel, the kind the gals go for. He is redeemed and regenerated because she leaves him. She sends him home to his parents. She has her baby alone and makes a terrific fight to succeed. And when she makes the grade, she meets him at a swanky reception his mother gives. He's now regenerated, and she's a different person, and there's your final clinch. Here's what I want you to do, Tom—tell that story and make everything flow out of character."

"I can't do that in two weeks."

"I know. I just want the outline first."

"With everything you said kept in the story?"

"Yes, Tom. I think I've given you everything. All you have to do is write it."

As Tom began to say something, Klem picked up the telephone. That was the signal for Tom's departure. The conference was finished.

VII

Tom got to his office at nine the next morning and pitched into work on his story, writing desperately. When Miss Solomon arrived at ten o'clock, he stopped writing and dictated to her. He dictated the story continuously, except for the halt at lunchtime, until five o'clock, and then he stopped, feeling that he had worked his secretary enough. He went to his hotel, ate hastily, and continued on his story, picking up where he had left off in his dictation. He was at his office early again the next morning, and by the time Miss Solomon got in he had finished a twenty-five-page first draft. He set her to work immediately typing out clean copies. While she was typing, he had nothing to do. He felt utterly empty. He had strained his eyes and he couldn't read. He sat at his desk. He rested on the couch. He looked out the window. He walked about restlessly.

The manuscript went to Klem right after lunch on Thursday. Klem had promised to read it immediately. Tom waited all of Thursday afternoon and all day Friday for a conference with Klem. On a sound stage behind him, a picture was in production. A group of Hawaiians were kept busy all day practising one boom on a drum. Over and over again he heard this same boom. The monotony of the day, punctuated by the drum, was relieved only by a series of telephone calls. The news that he had been hired at Grandiose had been printed for two days successively on the front page of the trade papers, and this made him fair game for salesmen. He received calls from tailors, salesmen representing houses dealing in English tweeds, real-estate agents, furniture dealers, automobile salesmen, book dealers, and others, all trying to sell him something. At five o'clock on Friday Miss Kennedy informed him that he could see Mr. Klem at eleven o'clock the next morning. At twelve on Saturday he got into Klem's office. Klem said that Tom's script lacked true and real characterizations. Tom replied that it was an embodiment of Klem's own instructions. He proposed that on the basis of his draft they begin a precise and detailed discussion of the story. Klem yawned. He started to outline a completely new story, acting it out as he talked. Suddenly he stopped and said that the conference would have to be continued on Monday. He invited Tom to have lunch with him at the commissary. When they arrived there, Klem suddenly excused himself, pleading a forgotten engagement; he ate with several executives and a male star.

Tom had lunch alone. He felt disheartened. Hollywood was a very lonely place. And now he had the week end to get through. He wished he were home with his family. Working for one thousand dollars a week was decidedly less pleasant than living in his three-room apartment with the noise of the elevated in the distance, the dirt of New York, the pressure under which he had to write. All about him he heard people talking about pictures. He hurriedly finished eating and left the lot.

On Monday he was able to see Klem at four-thirty.

"Tom, I've got to work with you this week. I'll stick with you on this story and we'll lick it. We'll have something damned good to show Avilov by Saturday. I want to keep you here. I feel that you have a positive contribution to make to motion pictures."

"I would like to get this story settled so that I can really get to work."

"We have a week. Avilov understands that you're not to turn out a finished treatment in two weeks. He merely wants to see something that will show him if you can write for pictures. And we'll prove that to him. By the way, where are you living?"

"I've got a little hotel room for ten bucks a week. It's dreary, but then it's clean and adequate, and I can walk to the studio from it."

Klem said nothing. Tom caught a look of pity and contempt on his face. He knew immediately that he should not have said this to Klem.

"You're going to plan on staying here and bringing out your family, aren't you?"

"Yes, if this deal goes through."

"Don't worry about that. Now, about this story."

Klem sat back in his chair, silent.

"Wouldn't it be a good idea if I watched some shooting? I think I might learn something. I'd like to watch various directors at work. I'd like to see how they work, what they want in their scenes. I think that way I might get a better sense of pictures."

"That'll come later. We're not ready for that yet. Tom, tell me, do you like writing for pictures?"

"If I can get my teeth into it and do something, I will."

"You will. All right, here's your story." Klem paced back and forth, gesturing as he talked. "The guy isn't a heel. He's a nice guy. His family is nice, too, liberal and tolerant, noth-

ing snobbish about them. The girl is no good. She's on the
make, just a tramp. We begin with her and her girl friend—
call her Tillie, that is, the friend—working as taxi dancers in
Florida. That way we can get in some swell Palm Beach shots.
The gals are just hookers, working in a joint where they roll
sailors. Now we see these two hookers at work on two sailors . . ."

Tom sank back in his chair and sighed to himself. Klem
paced back and forth, talking endlessly, improvising a story
which resembled almost all the motion pictures Tom had ever
seen.

VIII

Miss Solomon handed Tom several copies of a neatly typed
twenty-four-page manuscript.

"Thank you. I'm very sorry that I had to make you work
so hard again this week, but Mr. Klem changed his mind and
outlined a totally new story. And I must have something to
show Mr. Avilov by Saturday."

"Oh, I don't mind it at all. It gets monotonous here sometimes when there isn't much to do. And I like your story.
Except that I don't think the girl should be an actress. But
it'll make a good picture, especially with Mr. Klem producing
it. He's done two pictures here, and they've both been terrific
successes. Only I think you're giving them too much work.
Most writers would take five or six weeks to give them what
you're giving them in a few days. They don't appreciate what
you do if you give it to them too fast."

"It's done now. I'll glance over this story; then will you
send it over to Mr. Klem?"

Tom began reading his treatment. He had hammered it out,
working with the same desperation as that of the previous
week. It was agonizing to read this story. The words were his.
The ideas belonged to Klem. But he needed money. He needed
it badly. He needed the rest it would give him. But now, despite this need, he no longer cared whether or not Avilov
approved or disapproved of his work. He forced himself to

concentrate; he read his manuscript closely and gave it to Miss Solomon to have it delivered to Klem. He went out to lunch.

It was Thursday. Again he waited all afternoon, but he received no word from Klem. On Friday Miss Kennedy called him three times to postpone appointments, and at five o'clock he was told that Mr. Klem couldn't see him until the next morning. When he saw Klem on Saturday, the producer was dressed in sports clothes, prepared for an afternoon of tennis.

"I'm sorry I had to push you around this way, Tom, but I've been so busy that I couldn't help it," Klem said, looking up from a script.

Klem let Tom sit, and he went on reading. Then he slapped the script down and picked up Tom's manuscript.

"I like your treatment, Tom. The only thing that worries me is that I'm afraid the girl is too much of a tramp."

"You said that you wanted her to be one."

"Yes, I did, but I wasn't thinking of her as such a tramp. However, there are a few small changes I want to make, and then I'll have this mimeographed and sent down to Avilov. He won't read a script unless it's mimeographed."

"What are the changes?"

"I'll read it."

Klem began reading Tom's treatment aloud. There was neither interest nor expression in his voice. Tom was embarrassed. As far as movie writing went, there was nothing to be ashamed of. But, yes, it was embarrassing, humiliating. Klem read on, stopping now and then to make minor changes and unimportant cuts. After the eleventh page, he looked up at Tom, bored.

"The rest is all right."

Tom did not miss observing Klem's boredom. It was more than a forewarning. There was no relief, no rest to be gotten from this venture. But what was the use of being angry with what had happened? Were he to say anything, Klem would not understand it. At all events, his contract was up. He was not interested in indulging in gestures. He just wanted to get away.

"Say, can I get a plane reservation through the studio for New York tonight?"

"Yes, but don't you expect to go on with us here?"

"I can come back in a day, if Avilov picks up the option on my services. And a decision won't be reached on this treatment for a couple of days."

Klem called in Miss Kennedy, and she arranged for the reservation. While Tom waited, he talked banalities with Klem. He wrote out a check to Grandiose for the cost of the plane trip, part of the money he had earned in these two weeks. He and Klem shook hands.

"It's been good working with you, and I think that we'll go on with it. I'll be seeing you next week, Tom."

"Yes, next week," Tom answered, leaving.

He went to his office and cleared it out, ordered a cab, and left the Grandiose lot for the last time. Stepping into a cab in front of the administration building, he felt free, liberated for the first time since he had been in Hollywood. He was impatient to get away. He thought of his family, his apartment, his desk where he would begin a new book as soon as he returned home. It was better to be overworked on his own books than to be underworked for Mr. Avilov whom he had never seen, and for Klem, whom he never expected to see again.

At his hotel he packed his belongings and then he whiled away the afternoon, smoking cigarettes, watching two old cronies play checkers, standing out on the porch looking absently at the famous sunshine of California. He was anxious to be gone. Heretofore, he had felt a certain regret in almost all departures. Once he came to a place, he disliked leaving it. Now he was making a departure without regret. His last afternoon in Hollywood passed slowly.

1941

The Sport of Kings

I

THE HOTEL LOBBY was crowded with guests listening to the broadcast of a long, extra-inning game that the Cubs, in the thick of the pennant fight, were playing with the Phillies. The hotel was one of a chain on the south side of Chicago. It was fairly cheap, clean, comfortable and, in the main, respectable.

Harry entered, feeling rather low and tired. Sonny romped to him and held out a pair of small, chubby arms, waiting to be swung onto his father's firm shoulders. After Sonny was kissed and swung in the air until he giggled and shrieked with glee, he was set down. He held his father's hand, looked up at him. The mother, a tall, fleshy woman with soft dark hair and regular features, smiled at both husband and child. She looked attractive in her summery blue dress.

"Daddy," the child called.

"Yes," Harry said, turning his eyes from wife to child and smiling down at his four-and-a-half-year-old son.

"Daddy, she lost money on the races again," Sonny said so loudly that many strangers heard and glanced at the family.

Sarah laughed, a slight laugh of embarrassment. Harry's face colored. Then he frowned. He looked at her, his moon face set grimly. He said nothing. He slouched into a chair beside her and listened to the broadcast, but he couldn't keep his mind on the game.

She had promised him!

Sarah sat gabbing with her friend, Mrs. Ross, the fat woman

21

who managed the hotel. Mrs. Ross played the races regularly and seemed to lose a lot of money. He hated that goddamn fatass of a woman. He held her responsible for what Sarah did. Sarah was sitting there calm, not minding anything. There she was, jabbering away about horses. She knew how he felt. They had quarreled bitterly over this matter only last week. She had given her word. But what good was her promise? What good? He slouched down further in the chair. He watched Sonny run about the lobby, playing with the guests, talking, pretending that he was riding a horse. If only he didn't have Sonny! No, he loved Sarah. But she just had to reform, that was all. There was Sonny now, talking with Sam, the colored bell boy. Sonny left Sam and ran outside. Harry sat and tried to listen to the broadcast. He couldn't keep his mind on the ball game. Damn that woman! Damn her! Why couldn't she play according to Hoyle? She'd given her word, and here she was, still gambling.

Suddenly Sonny rushed into the lobby crying. He had fallen and skinned his lip. Sarah picked him up and coddled him. Harry got up and walked beside her while she carried the child to the elevator to take him up to their two-room suite.

"Take care of your son!" he said just before she got into the elevator.

He returned to slump in a chair and listen to the broadcast. The Cubs lost to the Phillies in the twelfth inning. He got up. He was sore, and he was disappointed about the game, too. He went upstairs. Sonny hadn't been seriously hurt and now he was sleeping. Harry scarcely talked to his wife. They went out to supper.

"You didn't even wash for dinner," she said, walking beside him toward Sixty-third Street.

"Keep still!"

He knew her tactics. She always did this, lit into him for something, anything, whenever he had the goods on her.

"A fine way to talk to me! Oh, well, I guess that's what happens after you're married and the novelty of sleeping together wears off," she said with a kind of feigned and overdrawn weariness.

"Isn't that a delicate and refined way for a man to hear his wife and the mother of his child talking!"

"What do you mean?" she asked aggressively.

"Isn't there a more elevating subject to talk about?"

"You sleep with me, don't you? Why do you mind it being mentioned?"

"You could talk about something else," he said.

"Oh, well!" she exclaimed with a weary shrug of the shoulders.

"Why did you bet on the races?" he asked.

"I knew that was coming," she said, bored.

"That doesn't answer my question."

"Can't you talk about something else . . . something more elevating?"

"No," he said.

"Well, then, let's not talk."

They turned the corner to go eastward on Sixty-third Street just as an elevated train passed overhead.

"You're not going to get away with it, do you hear me?" he said, raising his voice.

"You're talking so loud the whole street can hear you."

"I don't care who hears me," he said.

"I just found that out."

"You promised me, didn't you?"

"Oh, Harry, please! I'm sorry and I won't do it again. Mrs. Ross at the hotel told me about a horse that looked like a sure thing."

"Mrs. Ross did?"

"What do you expect me to do all day? I have to do something. Or do you just want me to sit sucking my thumb, waiting for my hubby to come home at night and be sarcastic and nasty?"

"You promised me that you wouldn't play those goddamn races any more, didn't you?"

"Yes," she said brazenly.

"And you lost money on them today, didn't you?"

"Yes."

He grunted. He looked sidewise at her in hostility and triumph.

"Now what have you got to say?" he sneered.

"Well, what are you going to do about it?"

He glared at her. He clenched and unclenched his fists. She smiled at him, sarcastically curling her thick, heavily rouged lips. He was silent.

They entered a crowded cafeteria. As they pushed slowly along with trays on the rail, selecting their food, he felt disgusted and uncomfortable. He had nothing to say to her now. He felt injured. She'd promised him, and then she'd broken her promise. And as if that wasn't enough, she'd asked him what he was going to do about it. He hated to admit it to himself, but he had to. She was a woman without honor. If she had any, she wouldn't be so brazen after she'd broken her word to him. Oh, Christ, he felt like socking her, right square between the eyes!

They set their trays down at an empty table. In his anger and dismay, he had forgotten to get an evening newspaper. He had nothing to read. He ate quickly. They were both silent. He was finished with his entire meal by the time she began to eat her meat and vegetables.

He sat frowning. She got up from the table and went to the long counter. He knew what she was getting. Dessert. She was taking on weight. Well, he wouldn't say anything. It was her funeral. If she wanted to look like a pig, let her! He wouldn't say anything. He'd never again even ask her a question. She returned to the table with a piece of strawberry shortcake that was smothered with whipped cream. Still frowning, and quite nervous, he watched her eat it. She ate with complete casualness, as if she were totally unaware of his mood.

"Why did you eat that?" he snapped when she had finished.

"Because I like it." She looked him squarely in the eyes.

"Because you wanted to! You know it isn't good for you."

"Oh, I forgot that. Thanks for reminding me. I'll remember it next time."

"Things aren't joking matters with me."

"Oh, aren't they, dear?" she said, leaning across the table toward him.

"No, they aren't, *dear!*" he snapped.

"Why, gee, my little lamby hasn't got his sense of humor with him tonight, has he?"

"When you eat enough sweets to make you look like a pig, you won't have your sense of humor either, will you?"

"But you'll love me then, won't you? You'll always love me like you used to tell me you would before we were married, won't you . . . *dear?*"

He frowned. Then he blushed. His lips compressed with anger. He struggled to maintain his self control.

"My little sweet hubby is angry. He's growling and frowning."

"Let's go!" he ordered, getting up and taking the checks from the table.

He walked hurriedly to the cashier's desk by the door. She followed, pointedly taking her time. Outside, he stood waiting for her.

"You're disgusting," she said, joining him.

He didn't answer.

"You'd just like me to get fat as a pig, wouldn't you? You'd gloat over it, wouldn't you?"

In hostile silence, they returned to the hotel.

II

Harry stopped fiddling with the radio and gazed over at her. She was sprawled out on the bed, reading an issue of *True Confessions*. It was raining outside and the room was cool enough for them to remain in it.

"Sarah, dear, I'm sorry," he said.

She went on reading. He watched her sheepishly.

"Sarah?" he said.

Casually, she glanced up from the magazine.

"Sarah, I'm sorry," he said.

"You are?"

"Sarah, we've hardly spoken to each other for three days now," he said.

"It wasn't my fault. I didn't start it."

He went over to the bed, took the magazine from her hands, and dropped it on the floor. He drew her to her feet. He embraced her, their lips meeting passionately.

III

They lay together, tired, fatigued.

"You do love me, don't you?" she asked softly.

"Of course I do," he answered with tenderness.

"And you are sorry you quarreled with me?"

"I'm sorry we quarreled," he said, and then he kissed her.

"But you did say mean and cutting things to me."

"You said them to me, too."

"But what I said to you didn't hurt like the things you said to me."

"Maybe they did."

"I didn't say you were becoming a pig," she said.

"I didn't say you were."

"But, honey, you did."

"No. I said something like you might become a pig if you didn't stop eating sweets."

"You said I was going to be a pig."

"I didn't. I said . . ."

He was seeking to remember the exact words he had used during the restaurant quarrel. She kissed him unexpectedly.

"I love you," he said, and he followed his declaration by kissing her.

"And I'm not going to bet on the races any more."

"I knew you'd come to your senses."

"My darling husband brought me to my senses. And do you know what else?"

"What?"

"I haven't eaten a sweet or a piece of candy in the daytime since our quarrel."

"But you did at supper."

"You boob! I did it only to make you angry. You look so funny when you frown," she said.

"I didn't know that."

"Frown for me."

Trying to frown, he looked ludicrous. She laughed. She kissed him again.

"I love you and I'm not going to quarrel with you any more," she said.

"I don't get any kick out of fighting with you."

"And you're not going to do it any more, are you?"

Grinning, he shook his head from side to side.

"You're going to boss me, too, aren't you?"

"I don't want anyone to be the boss in this family," he said.

"Say you're going to boss me," she urged.

"I don't want any boss in our family."

"Say it!"

"But, darling . . ."

"Say it!"

"I'm going to be boss," he said without conviction.

"And say this—'Sarah, you must never play the races again.' "

"Sarah, you must never play the races again."

"Tell me to promise you."

"Promise me you won't play the races again."

"I promise you I won't play the races again."

"And make me promise to cut down on sweets."

"Promise me you'll cut down on sweets."

"I promise I'll cut down on sweets."

He kissed her and stroked her hair.

"I cried after you fought with me," she said.

"I felt lousy myself."

"You ought to have felt a little bad."

"I did."

"And so did I."

"It's over now," he said.

"And it isn't going to happen again," she said.

They kissed, and their passion was rekindled.

IV

Sarah had intended to keep her promise to Harry. She really tried to. But her life was rather dreary in the daytime. She didn't have much to do. They had decided to forego the trouble of housekeeping and they had lived in a hotel since their marriage. After their child was born, they had continued living in a hotel. They were saving money. Harry was a good salesman, and he usually earned fifty dollars a week and sometimes even seventy-five. But the days were so dull for Sarah. She didn't seem to know precisely how they passed. They all seemed long. She got up as late as she could and dawdled over breakfast. She played with her child. She sometimes went to the beach. She took walks. She went to the movies. She played solitaire. She read cheap magazines. It was a slow, dull summer. After kindergarten opened in September, she had a longer day. She took Sonny to kindergarten in the morning, returned to the hotel, and had little to do for the greater part of the day.

Mrs. Ross constantly talked to Sarah about the races and continually asked Sarah if she was betting. Sarah talked about the races, but did little betting. She thought the world of her husband, but Harry just didn't seem to understand. What was she going to do? She started playing the races again. She began with small bets on one or two races and gradually increased them. She had a streak of luck and won a hundred dollars on a hundred-to-one shot. She put her winnings in a separate bank account, unknown to Harry, and drew from it daily for her bets. Everything was more exciting when she played the races. Life seemed different to her. And as long as Harry was ignorant of it, what he didn't know wouldn't hurt him.

V

One night late in September, when Harry came back to the hotel for supper, they went out as usual. He seemed to be in a good mood. However, he was wondering to himself, was she doing it, or wasn't she? He didn't want to know, and he wanted to know. Their life had been so smooth and good since that bitter three-day quarrel they had had in August.

"What did you do today?" he asked.

"Oh, nothing much," she answered warily.

"What's nothing much?"

"It's just nothing much. That and nothing else."

"It's not very clear to me," he said, forking a piece of apple pie.

"I suppose it isn't. It isn't even clear to me. I don't have anything to do all day."

"You can go to the movies."

"But we go so often. I can't be going to the movies every day. That's too much. And I'd have to be touring new neighborhoods and half of the city to find new pictures that I haven't seen before."

"You can be with Sonny more," he said.

"Sonny is better off at the kindergarten, and it's better for us to let him eat at the hotel than take him out with us. When I put him to bed, he cries. When the maid does and I'm not there, he goes to bed quietly. We don't want to spoil him."

"He's not being spoiled."

"I'm seeing to that."

"You don't mean that I spoil him?"

"All fathers spoil their children."

They lapsed into silence, and then he said:

"I don't know. If I had my time to myself, I guess I'd know what to do with it."

"What would you do?"

"Oh, all kinds of things."

"What kind of things?"

"Lots of things."

They were finished eating. He didn't know what to say now. He got to his feet and led the way out of the cafeteria, paying the checks at the cashier's desk. They went to a movie.

VI

He kissed her tenderly when they got back to the hotel after the motion picture. They started undressing, yawning as they removed their clothing. He noticed a slip of paper under the desk in a corner. He picked it up and looked at it. It was a receipt for a bet made at a bookie's. He looked at it intently. He was shocked. His mood changed completely; he felt hurt and betrayed.

"What's the matter?" she asked, noticing his changed expression as she let down her slip.

She watched him frowning as he stood in his underwear, still looking at the slip of paper he held.

"I thought you promised me," he said.

"Promised you what? I promised you lots of things in my life."

"You know what I mean."

"Honest, darling, I don't. Now don't be getting so angry with me. Tell me what's on your mind," she cooed.

"You've been playing the races. I'll bet you've been doing it right along. And after you promised me solemnly that you wouldn't."

"Why, how can you accuse me of such a thing?"

"And now, when I got the goods on you, you deny it," he said in growing anger.

"What do you mean? You men, you're so suspicious, and all the time you're suspicious over nothing at all. I suppose. if a woman did do something really awful, you wouldn't even suspect it."

"What do you mean?" he asked anxiously.

"I mean that you're great big suspicious boobs. Now, just wipe that frown off your face and stop accusing me after I've kept my promise," she said in a mock, scolding manner.

"You didn't keep it! And you stand before me like that and lie," he countered in a storm of self-righteous anger.

"Stop it!" she cried.

"Look at this and tell me if you haven't broken your word," he said, flashing the slip of paper at her.

She took the ticket and looked at it.

"It isn't mine," she said positively.

"Well, how did it get here?" he asked in an insistent voice.

"I don't know."

"You ought to."

"Not any more than you ought to."

"Why?"

"You live here just as well as I do. I don't know anything about it."

"You mean to insinuate that it's mine?"

"I don't know. I know I had nothing to do with it," she said.

"You accuse me of playing the races in order to squirm out of it yourself when I've caught you hands down."

Suddenly she started laughing.

"A fine time to laugh," he said.

She continued laughing.

"You break your solemn promise to me and then you laugh at me, do you!"

"I know what it's all about now," she said, ceasing her laughter, but smiling at him.

"What?"

"Mrs. Ross. She was up here. It must be hers. She was up here about five o'clock, and I know that instead of phoning her bets in today she went down to the bookie's and placed them direct."

"Well!" he said, starting to talk but finding himself with nothing to say; he stood before her, suddenly abashed.

"So you see, your suspicion was wrong," she said.

"I'm sorry," he said, sheepishly.

"You should be sorry," she said flirtatiously.

"I am."

"Promise me you'll never be suspicious again."

"I do," he answered.

Riding downtown in the elevated train the next morning, he wondered about last night. Her excuse had seemed so simple and so natural when she had told it to him. But now, he wondered. If Mrs. Ross had lost that receipt, why was it under the desk? That was a question he couldn't answer. He tried to concentrate on his morning newspaper. But he couldn't keep that question out of his mind. How did it get under the desk? Mrs. Ross could drop it and it could get kicked under the desk just as well as if Sarah had dropped it. No, he guessed he didn't have any reason to be suspicious of her. He was sure she was telling him the truth. Only she had lied to him before and broken her promise. He guessed he was just a sap. That's all. He was just a sap. She lied to him like a trooper, and he fell for her lies. She thought he was nothing but an ordinary common garden variety of sap, and nothing else. He was nothing else but that. She knew he was. She curled him around her little finger with lies. Well, he wasn't going to be made a fool of any more!

Tonight when he got home he'd walk in as if he were not in the least suspicious.

Hello, dear, he would say.

He'd kiss her, and sit down, and just ask how things had gone today. And he'd ask what she'd done. She'd say something, seen a movie, something. He'd say he hoped that she'd had a good time. Maybe she'd say that she was bored and that she'd had a rotten day. If she hadn't had a good day, it was probably because she'd lost money on the races. He'd say it to her, point blank. If she protested, then he'd just start talking cold turkey.

Listen, you, don't think you can fool me any longer! Don't try it, because I know better.

What do you know? she'd answer, asking him this question because she'd be suddenly afraid that he knew too much.

That was the way he'd catch her in a trap. He'd pretend to have the goods on her.

What do I know? I know plenty, and you know just what plenty is.

She'd maybe pretend that she didn't know what he was talking about. And he wouldn't fall for that game.

Listen! he'd say. Listen, I know enough! You know what it is as well as I do. You think you've been pulling the wool over my eyes, don't you? You think you've been putting fast ones over on me, don't you? Well, you haven't. You know what I know. You thought I fell for that stall about Mrs. Ross last night, didn't you? You thought I was a chump, didn't you? You thought that your lame excuse fooled me, didn't you? Well, it didn't.

If he really took a firm and knowing attitude, and if he didn't back down, why, then, he'd trap her and drag it out of her.

And after he dragged it out of her, what would he do? How would he act then?

He'd caught her before and done all that, and what good had it done? Why should he think that this time it would do more good? Why should he think that this time he'd made a bigger dent in her? Yes, why?

He would, if he stood firm and didn't let her bluff him, wheedle him, coo his determination out of him. If he was really firm, if he really convinced her that he meant business, maybe he'd impress her and make her fearful of losing him, or something. Then, why, maybe she'd change.

But goddamn it, why did a man have to have a wife he couldn't trust?

He tried to keep his mind on his newspaper but couldn't.

VIII

Twenty dollars lost today. She was doubling her bet on the last race, just to get it back. Maybe she was a fool. No, she wasn't. Lily Ross was playing Speed Demon, too. If Speed Demon would only win! Sarah leaned back on the bed and started reading another story in *True Confessions*. She reached to the table beside her and took another piece of candy. She couldn't keep her mind on the story. She had to get the results of the race. She was damn nervous. She reached over and took the phone.

"Mrs. Ross, please."

She waited.

"Hello, Lily! Any news yet? . . . No? Well, you'll be sure to ring me up as soon as you get it, won't you? Be sure and do it because I can't stand the suspense. You're a darling, Lily. And certainly we'll celebrate if we win. We're going to win, aren't we? Don't think of the chance of losing or it might make us lose, Lily."

She hung up. She strode back and forth across the room. She lit a cigarette. She turned on the radio and listened to some popular songs. The phone rang.

"Hello! Oh, tell me quick, Lily! . . . Lost? I'm crushed. I'm crushed, darling. Sixty dollars today. . . . You lost as much? Darling, we'll have to have a funeral instead of a celebration."

After hanging up the receiver, she paced the room, wringing her hands.

That goddamn horse!

Suddenly the door opened.

"Why, Harry, you're home early!" she said, surprised at seeing her husband, striving to smile pleasantly but achieving only a strained grin.

"What makes you so nervous? You look worried," he said.

She kissed him perfunctorily.

"What's on your mind? Tell me, darling?" he said.

"Why, nothing."

"There is, too. You're worried. I can tell. I saw the look on your face when I came in."

"I was just surprised. I didn't expect you home so early, that's all," she answered.

"You're not sorry I got home early, are you?"

"You goose, you know I'm not," she said.

"Where's Sonny?"

"He's out playing. I left him at the playground and I'll have to be going for him soon."

"I had a good day today," he said.

"That's wonderful."

"That's why I knocked off early."

"I'm glad."

"Tell me, Sarah, why did you look so worried when I came in? What was on your mind?"

"Say, is this a schoolroom?" she asked.

"Forget it," he said, but he eyed her closely, seeking to get her reaction.

"Yes, it wouldn't be a bad idea if we did. School's over for today."

"I don't think you're so glad to see me home early," he said, still watching her intently.

"Of course I am. Sure I am. I'll get up and sing," she said, raising her voice and jumping to her feet.

"Sarah, darling, calm yourself."

"I'm just happy," she said in an almost neurotic anger, dancing around the room as she spoke.

"A funny way to be happy," he said, not really knowing what to say to meet the situation.

There was a pause.

"Well, I'm sorry I intruded on you before you expected me home," he said.

"Why, you didn't intrude. I'm happy. Can't you see from the way I talk that I'm happy. I'm overjoyed. I'm dancing with tears in my eyes. I'm singing in the rain. I'm shouting in the bathtub. I'm happy that you came home at a quarter to five instead of at six o'clock. Doesn't that satisfy you? Doesn't that make you believe me?" she asked in a rising voice.

"Please! Please!"

She flopped down on the bed.

"What's the matter, Sarah?" he asked, his voice now sympathetic, seemingly bathed in the desire to be understanding.

"Nothing. I was just nervous and upset. You looked at me

in such a funny way. And you seemed to be putting me through a question-and-answer test."

"Why, I wasn't at all. I wasn't at all. I came home expecting to surprise you. That's all."

"Well, I'm sorry."

"You haven't anything worrying you that made you nervous and caused you to act this way?"

"No! No! No! I say no! I'm just tired of these questions of yours. Please let me alone!" she said curtly.

"All right, I'm sorry. I guess I just don't know what to say or do around here. I feel superfluous," he said, getting to his feet and walking slowly back and forth across the room.

"I'm going to get Sonny now," she said, jumping up after they had both been silent for a little while.

"Want me to go along?"

"No, it's all right. I'll be right back," she said, going to the closet.

She put on her hat and coat.

"I'll be right back," she said.

He sat perplexed for several minutes after she had gone. Then he carefully searched the room to see if he could find any evidence that she had been playing the races. He found nothing. Still, he was sure that she had been. But he didn't know how he was going to trap her.

He stood in the center of the room and raised his hands pleadingly toward the ceiling.

Goddamn it, why did he have to have this suspicion? Why?

IX

Harry noticed the box of candy by the table near the bed. How had he missed seeing it all the time since he had come home? And he had just searched the room. He examined the box of half-eaten sweets. So she was eating candy again. She'd promised him not to. If she told him one lie, why couldn't she tell him another? No reason at all. Now he was sure that she was playing the races.

He paced the room thinking of how he might use the candy

to trap her. But suppose he did? He couldn't leave her. If Sarah would only be truthful with him. And then, there was Sonny. Goddamn it, this business was driving him nuts. What was he going to do about it? Every day he had it on his mind. It kept popping up when he was selling, sitting in the movies, all of the time. If he only knew and could settle it with her once and for all. He made another quick search of the room and found no evidence.

Gloomy, he sat down on the bed. He unwittingly picked up *True Confessions*. His mind on his wife, he thumbed through the magazine. Some papers fell out of it. He picked them off his lap. One was green, a dope sheet with selections for races that had been run this very day. The other piece of paper was scrap paper with her writing on it. He found figures, calculations of odds, lists of horses, and sums of money after one name on the list. Obviously, she had bet. Now he knew. Now he had her. After her promises, he had the proof in his hands. Now he knew. And he asked himself suddenly, what was he going to do? His mind went blank. Spiritlessly, he looked at the pieces of paper. He carefully put them in the magazine and laid it on the bed where he had found it.

After he exposed her, what? Would she promise again? If she did, what was her promise worth? Just what was he going to do? Leave her? And if he did, what about Sonny? And himself, living alone in some rooming house or hotel, eating alone every night, missing his boy? Could he divorce her and take the boy with him? How could he decently support two households? How could he raise the child? A child needed a mother.

He sat there, acutely aware of his own helplessness.

X

When Sarah returned, Sonny ran to his father. The sight of the child changed the set, grim expression on Harry's face into a smile.

"Daddy, Mommy pushed me in the swing and I went so high. I want you to push me in the swing."

Harry picked up Sonny, kissed him, and listened to him babble. Sarah watched them, smiling as if there were nothing to trouble her, nothing to disturb her conscience. Harry wondered how she could be that way. Even if she didn't know that he knew. . . .

"He talked about you all the way home," she said.

Harry set Sonny down. The child ran about the room and then into the adjoining one. Soon he was talking to himself as he played on the floor with a set of building blocks.

Harry dropped into a chair and waited for her to speak. She took off her coat and hat, hung them in the closet, and sat on the bed. Neither of them spoke for a moment. Harry stared at her, his gaze making her uncomfortable.

"It's too early for supper."

"Uh huh," he muttered.

"Are we going to the movies tonight?"

"I don't know," he said.

"There's a new Joan Crawford picture at the Tower and I'm specially anxious to see it," she said.

"All right."

Another pause. She watched him. He seemed depressed.

"Are you feeling all right, Harry?"

"Oh, I'm all right," he said slowly, and casually drew out a cigarette and lit it.

"I notice you're eating candy again," he said noncommittally, after a pause.

"Oh!" she exclaimed, startled. She looked at the box of candy on the table. She blushed and added guiltily, "Yes, I . . . I'm sorry, but I was weak."

"Don't you care what you look like?"

"Oh, Harry, now do be sensible. I look all right, and these few pieces of candy aren't going to make any difference."

He didn't answer her, but continued to fix his gaze upon her.

"Why do you keep staring at me? What's the matter?" she asked, uncomfortable because he would not take his eyes off her.

"Nothing."

"I come in and find you with your jaw so long it's almost hitting the floor, and there you sit looking at me as if I was guilty of murder or something. What is this, a game?"

"I don't understand you."

"Well, do you think I understand you?"

"No, I guess not," he said with double meaning.

"Now, what's that mean?"

He shrugged his shoulders. She nervously walked around the room.

"Why don't you sit down and take it easy?" he said.

"I'm all right. I can walk if I please, can't I?"

"Sure you can."

"I must say you're acting awful queer," she said, still pacing back and forth.

He was silent.

She stopped to look out the window. She turned from it, found a cigarette, lit it, and puffed rapidly.

"I must say your behavior is curious. Have you got something troubling you, bothering your conscience?" he asked.

She looked at him with wide eyes. Then she smiled sarcastically.

"I know it now. You think I've been playing the races."

"Who said a word about the races?"

"Well, you must have them on your mind. You came home with a grouch on and got in early to try and trap me. And right away you started that question-and-answer business. You think I've been playing the races again, don't you?" she said, growing aggressive and hostile.

"I don't know what makes you think I think you've been playing the races."

"Oh, yes you do," she challenged.

"Skip it."

"Harry, listen to me!" she began melodramatically. "Listen to me! Harry, I swear to God that I haven't played the races since last summer when I promised you I wouldn't."

"I'm glad of that."

"You believe me, don't you?"

"Yep."

She went to him and stroked his head. He sat there, thinking of their past life, their early days, thinking that she was now a different woman from the girl he thought she was when he had married her.

She bent down and kissed him. He was unresponsive.

"You go and wash Sonny for his supper, and then we'll take a walk before eating," Harry said.

Again she caressed his head.

"All right, I'll tend to Sonny, and then we'll take a walk. It's nice at this time in the fall. Remember how we used to walk in the fall when we first met?" she said.

"Yes. It seems a long time ago."

"It does. But days like this make me remember it."

She went to Sonny. Harry looked at her with utter contempt. His eyes were full of hatred. He got up and turned on the radio. He could hear the child babbling and gaily talking to its mother as she washed him. He turned off the radio and sat there waiting until they would take their walk. Then they would eat supper, see another moving picture, and come back to the hotel.

1930-1938

Sorel

I

JACQUES SOREL was a handsome young fellow. Husky and broad-shouldered, he was taller than the average Frenchman. He had been a schoolboy during the First World War. In after years, he spoke of wartime Paris light-heartedly, describing events and scenes of these days almost as if they belonged in an Offenbach opera. He told many stories to illustrate the *sang-froid* of the Parisians while they were being bombed and shelled. When they had gathered together for shelter in the Metro stations, it had always been a gay occasion, an invitation to flirtations, lechery, and wine-drinking. But the war had left a profound impression upon him. The chauvinism of those days, learned in the classroom and absorbed in the press, the streets, and in his own home, was stamped permanently upon his mind. And the war had filled him with a despair which conditioned his recurrent fits of recklessness.

Sorel had received an excellent education. His first love was literature, and as a youth he had dreamed of himself as destined to become a modern Baudelaire or Rimbaud. He had also studied history, philosophy, science, and mathematics. As a student he had been as brilliant as he was rowdy. A young royalist, he had participated in many street demonstrations; he had fought with radical students and with the *flics* in the district surrounding the Boulevard Saint Michel. Sorel did his year of service in the early twenties, and he was promoted to the rank of lieutenant. When the French Army occupied the

Ruhr, he was called to the colors and was an officer of the invading forces. His contact with the Germans did not lessen his hatred of the Boche. He claimed that the German people themselves caused the inflation by speculating on foreign exchange against their own currency; this, he held, was an unpatriotic act. He also believed that the Germans deserved to have their soil occupied by Senegalese troops.

His parents were shopkeepers from Normandy, but he usually claimed that he was descended from pre-revolutionary French nobility. During the early twenties his father suffered a series of business reverses. When Sorel came out of the army, he had to earn his own living. This was a disappointment to him, because he had planned to dedicate himself to poetry and live off an income from his father. He became a reporter on one of the leading dailies of Paris. Although it was a reactionary paper, he was opposed to its policies; he was on the extreme right. In a short time he was given important assignments, covering political events in Paris, London, and Geneva. His reports from Geneva were particularly vitriolic; he thought the League of Nations was all nonsense, a scheme devised by Woodrow Wilson and others to cheat France of the fruits of her victory. On one assignment he was sent to report a mine strike in France; his articles cost him his job. He expressed sympathy for the miners and vividly described the conditions under which they lived; but at the same time he condemned their leaders as Marxists and castigated their employers as fat and greedy bourgeois.

By this time he had already married a girl from Normandy, the daughter of a family of horse dealers. He chose to believe that her ancestors were among the oldest families of the French nobility. She was a beautiful but erratic girl, a spendthrift, and irascible. They had one daughter. After a series of quarrels—due to money matters and love affairs—which became increasingly bitter, they separated. He was saddled with the necessity of contributing to the support of his wife and child. She dogged him, bullied him, threatened him. But once he lost her, he wanted her back; she would not return. Dis-

charged from the newspaper, he was forced to do a number
of hack jobs, mainly translations. He also wrote poems in
avant-garde magazines and contributed political diatribes to
the royalist press. He was engaged in riots and fist fights concerning literature, once knocking out a man who had criticized the poetry of Guillaume Apollinaire. In 1930, after a
period of hard luck and dreary work in the Parisian Grub
Street, he got a job with the publishing firm of Dubuisson
Frères. They were the largest publishers in Paris; their reputation was world famous and they published most of the illustrious literary men of France. It was an excellent connection.
He was hired as editor of a series of detective stories. He had
authority to select books, to make deals for foreign works,
and to arrange for translations. Besides his salary, he was given
a small percentage on the sales of the books in his series, and he
received extra compensation for the books which he himself
translated. He had not been long at Dubuisson Frères before
he learned how carelessly this firm conducted its business. Its
accounts were never kept up-to-date. The two Dubuisson
brothers never seemed to know whether or not they were
making or losing money. They contracted for every book they
could get their hands on, and then they often stored these contracts away and never bothered to publish the books. Except
for a few famous French authors, none of their writers was
sure when he would receive a royalty statement. The business
was run without any real system. Sorel saw a great chance to
make money in such a publishing house, and he missed no
opportunity to do so.

However, with the betterment of his material circumstances, he spent more money. He lived more comfortably,
gambled, and had to give more to his wife. Recurrently, he
had sentimental moods and sought to restore his home life. His
wife took advantage of these moods to get money out of him.
He was constantly in financial trouble, and the more harassed
he became, the more complicated grew his accounts at Dubuisson Frères. He pretended to hire translators for his books and
pocketed the money. He was always paid up for five or six of

his own translations in advance. Whenever he was asked about the progress of the translation of overdue books, he contrived ready and suitable excuses. He exploited translators who feared to protest lest they lose the source of a miserable existence. His bills were always in arrears, and he had been evicted from more than one Parisian hotel. He owed money to merchants, to friends, and to anyone else who had been willing to become his creditor. His problems and troubles seemed to be endless.

His real name was not Sorel. He had adopted this name as a pseudonym from Stendhal's character, Julien Sorel. Among French novelists, he admired Stendhal more than Balzac or Flaubert. He looked upon himself as a twentieth-century Julien Sorel. In the novel, *The Red and the Black,* Julien had cried out to himself, asking what would poor wretches such as he do for a career inasmuch as Bonaparte was gone? Often Jacques Sorel cried out in the same vein; for Napoleon, however, he substituted a King. For a while he had moved on the fringe of the *Action Française.* Quarrelsome by nature, he had had bitter personal disagreements with all the men with whom he was in closest political agreement. He dropped his political affiliations. He also mixed in various literary and artistic groups, mainly of the *avant-garde.* His experiences here were a repetition of those in royalist groups. He was unable to remain long in any one circle. His friends generally learned not to trust him, especially in financial matters.

Sorel was a literary young man, living by his wits.

II

In the autumn of 1931 Sorel shared an apartment on the rue Guilleminot with a taxicab driver named Cochineau. Their quarters were roomy and comfortable. He had tacked on the door of the apartment an engraved card with his name, and under it the words *Homme de lettres.* Cochineau's name was not on the door.

It was an unusually lovely autumn. The days were mild. Paris was beautiful, and its streets were gay. But Sorel was miserable most of the autumn. Once again his wife had re-

pulsed his advances. And he had speculated disastrously on
foreign exchange. The American dollar had been declining in
ratio to the franc, and gold was flowing from New York to
Parisian bank vaults. Sorel, certain that this tendency would
be reversed, had scraped together every franc he could and had
bought dollars. But the dollar had continued to decline, and,
caught short, he had been forced to sell at a loss. The future
looked unpromising for him, despite his connection with
Dubuisson Frères, and he saw in his own mood the gloomy future of the world. He was particularly enraged because of certain members of the Senate and the Chamber of Deputies;
he claimed to have absolute proof showing that they had been
bought with American gold to sell out the interests of France
during the period of the Hoover moratorium and the Laval-
Hoover conferences. He bewailed the lack of patriotism in
France.

He was then in his early thirties. He felt that he had accomplished nothing in his life. He who had dreamed of himself as a twentieth-century Baudelaire was forced to do hack
work for miserable francs. As an artist, he believed he was being destroyed; he believed that since the Great French Revolution every great French writer had been destroyed, killed by
democracy. Many times in this period he would sit at his desk
at home, plodding over the translation of an American detective story. He would stop work and bring out the sheaf of
poems he had once written. He would read some of these aloud,
intoxicated with the sound of his own words, and he would
try to convince himself that these youthful poems were not
ordinary, immature, imitative. He would put aside his poems,
take the books of Rimbaud and Baudelaire from his shelf, and
read aloud from them. At such times he was most sincere. Filled
with nostalgia, he would recall how as a youth he had vowed
to dedicate himself to the search of *"la vision de la pureté."* A
sense of defeat would overpower him. Self-disgust would well
up. He would even wish for death. He would hate the entire
world. Although he preferred many other poems of Baudelaire
to *Les Litanies de Satan,* he enjoyed reading this poem in such

moods; it seemed to fit his own mood. He would change the
word God for that of Satan, and he would cry out endlessly
to the walls of his room:

Oh, Seigneur, prends pitié de ma longue misère.

Sometimes he would force himself back to his dreary work.
Other times he would go out to tramp the streets. On one mild
morning, in such a mood, he stood before the tomb of Baudelaire.

*—Ah! Seigneur! donnez-moi la force et le courage
De contempler mon coeur et mon corps sans dégoût!*

In self-pity he recited these lines many times.

He lit a cigarette and recited whole poems from *Les Fleurs
Du Mal*.

This action had a purgative effect upon him. His agitation
calmed. He left the cemetery and walked about aimlessly. He
stopped at the window of an art shop near the Luxembourg
Gardens and looked at some lithographs of Daumier which
were on display; these were portraits of obese politicians. He
admired them tremendously, and reflected that here were portraits of the men who had ruined France—the politicians. He
told himself that these men were no different from those who
were now in the saddle in the Third French Republic. And
what was he but the child of a ruined France? No wonder
he could write no poetry.

He stepped in at a little bistro and had a hard-boiled egg and
a glass of black coffee. He paused idly to talk with the fat
woman in black at the cash desk. They discussed the time at
which the bistro opened and closed, the way in which the
floor of the bistro was swept every morning, the weather, the
crise, and the evil influences at work in the red zone of the
working-class suburbs surrounding Paris. He left the place. It
was a misty day, and when he came to the Seine he saw the
cathedral of Notre Dame, dreamlike and heavenly in the distance. Crossing the river, he walked on and stood before the
portal of Saint Anne. He wished he had been born in the

France of the middle ages, or else during the time of Louis XIV.
But he was annoyed by American tourists. He watched a
famous American movie star spend three minutes studying and
admiring the cathedral, and he walked off feeling that he had
witnessed a sacrilege. He wandered along the quays, and the
past thronged into his mind. Idly, he examined some books in
the stalls. Suddenly his eyes lit on two pictures which were for
sale: one revealed Camille Desmoulins addressing a crowd at
the Palais Royal on July 14, 1789; the other was a lithograph
depicting Marie Antoinette on her journey to the guillotine.
His anger returned. He saw in the Desmoulins picture the reason for all of France's troubles and agonies and, consequently,
of his own frustrations, miseries, disappointments, failures.
The Great French Revolution! He cursed it. He suddenly felt
as if Marie Antoinette had died only yesterday, and as if the
Jacobins and the *Enragés* were his own bitterest enemies. All
the way home he raged to himself against them. Back at his
desk, he lit a cigarette, picked up his pencil, and determined to
work. He threw his pencil on the floor. Bah! It was all beyond
disgust. He returned to his desk and worked for a half hour.
Then, after glancing at his watch, he got up to go to the
Dubuisson office. He had to get money for his wife by this
evening.

III

Sorel's roommate, Cochineau, was a small swarthy man in
his late thirties. He had a comfortable paunch and was beginning to get bald. He was the son of a French provincial
café owner who had made considerable money during the
war. He had fought through four years of the war on the
Western Front without even catching a cold and he had been
a hero at Verdun, winning the Croix de Guerre. He spoke of
Marshal Pétain familiarly, calling him "Papa." Shortly after
the Armistice, Cochineau's father had died, leaving him a size-
able fortune. Restless and thirsting for adventure, he had gone
to South America. In Rio de Janeiro he had fallen in love with
a prostitute. He had spent all his money on her and had given

her his decoration, which she had promptly handed over to a pimp. When he went broke, she left him. He had then managed to earn another fortune, but he was never clear or precise about just how he had gained it. He had found a second girl, blown his money on her, and again had been abandoned. Disillusioned and penniless, lonesome for France, he had returned to Paris, where he had become a taxicab driver. He managed to scrape out a living, and he dreamed of how he would one day become one of the eternal glories of French letters. One day, he had gone to Dubuisson Frères with the manuscript of a lurid detective story. There he met Sorel, who read his manuscript. Sorel praised the novel and said that he would like to publish it; however, it was very hard to get his Philistine bosses to agree, because the book had merit. They had a congenital hatred of merit. However, if an *arrangement* were made, he could grease the palm of a secretary and swing the deal. Cochineau, hungry to see his name in print, agreed. Sorel pocketed the money decided upon in the little *arrangement*. The book was published, but it received little notice. Only a few copies were sold, but Cochineau saw in Sorel a man who could aid him in his career. They agreed to share an apartment, and often Cochineau had to pay more than half of the expenses. Sorel read Cochineau's manuscripts, mingling criticism with encouragement. Sorel continually urged him to quit writing detective stories and to do a book on his South American adventures, or else a Paris novel written in the racy argot which he spoke. But Cochineau stubbornly persisted in working on his lurid tales.

In Paris Cochineau felt differently about women than he had in South America. Having wasted two fortunes on Latin beauties, he was now determined to spend the fortune of an American heiress. To realize this ambition, he believed he merely needed to meet the right heiress. Since Sorel spoke English so well and saw so many Americans, Cochineau hoped that through him he would meet the right American woman. In fact, at this time Sorel's mistress was an American, a former tennis player who lived on an income. She was attractive enough to satisfy Cochineau's taste, but he thought that her income was too small. He always twitted Sorel for not having found a richer American mistress. Waiting for his heiress, Cochineau collected an odd assortment of mistresses who revolted Sorel's sensibilities. They were uniformly drab. On many mornings Sorel would wake up to see Cochineau wandering about in long underwear, with his belly sagging; trailing him would be one of these women, whose bathrobe, as if by pre-established harmony, was dirty. After such incidents, Sorel and Cochineau often quarreled, but these quarrels were never serious. Nothing in the world caused Cochineau to become seriously angry except rival taxicab drivers, a policeman who asked for his papers, and the Russian people. Of these, the Russians disturbed him the most. He thought that almost all Russians were crazy. At any minute they might invade Europe. If they did, he would have to take up arms and defend the frontier of civilization on the Vistula, and then his literary career would be interrupted.

One of Sorel's friends was an American artist named Cambry. Sorel had met him in the Café du Dôme; although Sorel claimed to detest this place as a tourist hangout of people who didn't belong in France, he was often to be found sitting on its terrace. While Cambry scorned Kisling, his own mediocre pictures were imitations of that artist. When they first talked, Sorel got the false impression that Cambry was rich. Actually, Cambry lived on a small allowance supplied by a patron in New York. Cambry took Sorel to his studio. Sorel studied his pictures and praised them, concluding with the statement:

"My dear chap, you paint like a Frenchman, not an American."

Cambry was starved for recognition and anxious to free himself from patronage. Also, because of the depression, his patron was cutting down his allowance and beginning to hint that Cambry ought to return to New York. He had sold no pictures in Paris. His hopes were aroused when Sorel promised to help him. Shortly after they had become friends, Sorel needed money, and one day when Cambry's allowance arrived, he borrowed a thousand francs, promising to pay back the sum within a week. When the week elapsed, he handed Cambry fifty francs and complained about his bad luck. From time to time, Sorel gave Cambry handouts of twenty-five and fifty francs against the debt. Cambry was charmed by Sorel, entranced by his praise, and convinced that Sorel would succeed in launching him in Paris. They became good friends, despite Sorel's negligence about the loan, and Cambry often visited Sorel.

Cochineau enjoyed Cambry's visits; he hoped that Cambry might find him a rich American woman.

One evening when they were having a spaghetti supper which Sorel had cooked, Cochineau introduced his favorite subject.

"When I meet Mrs. American-Twenty-Million-Bucks—*Oo la la*," he said.

"You better find her quick. Women like that aren't going to be in Paris very long now. There is *la crise* in America. We have many more *chômeurs* than you have," Cambry said.

"Look at him. With that belly of his he thinks he can charm an American woman," Sorel said.

"Hah, hah, when I find Mrs. American-Twenty-Million-Bucks—she will make me—hot," Cochineau said, his greasy face lighting up in a childlike smile.

"Wouldn't a midinette be better for love, for *l'amour?*" Cambry asked.

"*Pour l'amour, oui,* yes. But for me, hah, hah, Mrs. American-Twenty-Million-Bucks."

"If you did by the grace of God meet her, you'd probably lose all her money for her on the Bourse," Sorel said.

Cochineau shook his head confidently from side to side and smirked.

"Ah, no, I will pinch the money," he said.

"See, he's a real Frenchman—what you call—tight," Sorel said.

Cambry changed the subject, hinting that he needed money.

"You know, my dear fellow, these Dubuissons, they are such

damned lice. They won't give me what they owe me. They put everything they can in the sock. Do you know, I think that they are so cheap that they lock up their salt at home because they are afraid that their *femmes de ménage* will steal a pinch. Today I couldn't get a sou out of them. All they did was belly-ache about the *crise*, the *crise*, the *crise*. But don't you worry, old fellow, everything is going to turn out for us, what you Americans call, jake."

"With Mrs. American-Twenty-Million-Bucks—ah, it will be hotsy-totsy," Cochineau interrupted.

"You trust me. I will introduce you to people in Paris who count. They will recognize your genius. You will be put on the map. You belong here in Paris where there are Frenchmen to appreciate you. And when you succeed, you can forget about that slobbocracy of yours in America. It is full of Protestants, morons, Mormons. What is America? A *dérivé* of our decaying Europe, that is all. You just wait. In Paris, we don't do things with the speed and efficiency of your Babbitts. Here, everything takes time. But I will launch you, and then the Mormon yokels in America will have to recognize you because Paris will buy your pictures."

"Did you see that chap who owns the gallery?" Cambry asked.

"I stopped in there this morning, but he was out. I will see him, and we will manage him. He will give you an exhibition. And tomorrow I will see these Dubuisson lice again and get some shekels from them. Do you know, they are lunatics, megalomaniacs! They want to publish as many books as they can. And the fools won't advertise or push most of their books. So they collect in warehouses, and it is all idiotic. And these imbeciles think that they are the guardians and patrons of French literature. Yesterday, it was funny. Morceau, the distributor, came to see them, and he raised the devil with them. He told them: 'I have one warehouse full of your books that have not sold. From now on, you must not publish so many because I cannot afford to build a new warehouse just for your

books.' I tell you, they are megalomaniacs. And they are the
people I must work for. It is enough to make me vomit."

"My friend, you meet me Mrs. American-Twenty-Million-
Bucks and then—it is jake," Cochineau said.

"He really believes what he's telling you. Every morning he
gets up and says to me, 'Today I will find Mrs. American-
Twenty-Million-Bucks,' " Sorel said.

Cochineau grinned.

Cambry was disappointed that Sorel had no money for him
and, also, because Sorel had been unable to introduce him to a
gallery owner who would arrange for an exhibition. Sorel
promised to attend to these matters, and he was most convincing. They had Turkish coffee. Cochineau took his cup over
to a couch. Sorel and Cambry talked about painting. Cochineau curled up on the couch and fell asleep, with his head over
the coffee cup. He snored. Interrupted by the snore, Sorel and
Cambry glanced at him. They laughed.

"You know, he's a decent fellow, very droll. But he's a fool.
For the last six months he has come to me and bragged that
he knows some bigwig with influence with the police. So he
doesn't bother to put his papers in order. He has moved several
times without notifying the police. Every time I tell him that
he had better put his papers in order, he tells me: 'It is nothing.
I will see my friend, and he will fix it up for me if I get in
trouble.' I know the fellow is lying. Some day the police will
get him, and then he will come home with a long face and
bellyache about the fine he has to pay. But he's droll. He
lies all of the time, but he is amusing, and he has talent."

"Listen to him snore," Cambry said.

"And look, he sleeps and doesn't spill his coffee," Sorel said.
They both laughed.

IV

Sorel had bought a detective story by an American writer
named Alvin Dunwiddie. In the late fall, Dunwiddie turned
up in Paris. He was a well-groomed man in his early thirties,
tall, slender, pompous, and he sported a small mustache. He

went to Dubuissons' and there he met Sorel. He suggested that Sorel have a drink in a café with him and his wife.

They met late one afternoon at the Café Select. Sorel liked Mrs. Dunwiddie on sight. She was tall, voluptuous, and had charming brown eyes. They drank *apéritifs*. Sorel did most of the talking, and he continually fixed his gaze on her. He praised Dunwiddie's books and predicted a great future for them in France. Dunwiddie seriously discussed his work; he explained how he filled many notebooks before he even began a novel; he told how he slaved over his style; he complained that serious American critics didn't recognize him because he wrote detective stories instead of the pretentious and socially conscious junk that Americans were now starting to write.

"We'll publish you in France. You will be received well here. And we'll make plenty of shekels out of your books, too."

Sorel continued in this vein, using the word "we" many times. Dunwiddie became suspicious, and Sorel didn't miss this reaction. He explained that inasmuch as he was the editor of the series in which Dunwiddie's book appeared, he got a little cut from the sales. Dunwiddie's suspicion vanished.

"You say there's a good market for my work in France?" Dunwiddie asked.

"You can take my word for it. I know. If we manage this right, we'll make no inconsiderable amount of shekels. It is important that we get a good translation, but if I have the time, I will translate your book myself."

"I wish you would. I'd trust my work with you."

"Yes, because you seem to speak English so well, and you know so much American slang," Mrs. Dunwiddie said.

"I learned it in school, and as a journalist I was often in London. And I have learned your argot from your books and from Americans in Paris. It is my business."

"How do you like London?" Mrs. Dunwiddie asked.

"It is idiotic. All the restrictions of the English—they are idiotic. After you know Paris, what is London?"

"We're dying to see Paris," she said.

"Let's all have dinner together and take in some of the hot spots," Dunwiddie said.

Sorel agreed. His first impulse was to take them to a very expensive restaurant, but he changed his mind and took them to the Restaurant Sainte Cécile on the Boulevard Montparnasse; it was not too expensive. He had plans with these Americans. If he worked it right, he might get some money out of Dunwiddie for translating his book, and on future books he might even talk this boob into giving away part of his royalties. And he planned to manage a rendezvous with Mrs. Dunwiddie.

They liked the food, and Sorel ordered fine wines. He believed he was making excellent progress. But at the same time he was getting disgusted, and he had to repress his feelings.

They went to a *bal* where they drank and danced. The music, provided by a Senegalese orchestra, was good, and it seemed to fascinate Mrs. Dunwiddie. Dunwiddie, realizing that he had had enough, stopped drinking. Mrs. Dunwiddie drank cautiously, but when she danced with Sorel on the small and crowded floor, her cheeks were flushed, and she permitted him to press her body close to his. He was sure of himself, and he knew that he was talking well. He was exhilarated, and he began drinking Pernod. The disgust which he had felt at dinner led him to become sarcastic. He gazed about the small *bal*. The noise had reached a veritable din. The air was foul. A cloud of cigarette smoke hung down from the ceiling. He began to get bleary-eyed. The customers all seemed foul to him. Stupid Frenchmen. Rich American Babbitts. Red-faced Englishmen. Kept women, whores, damned wives. And in one corner there was a tall, stiff, healthy-looking German. They all came to Paris to have a good time, to see depravity, and to be depraved. And here he was getting drunk with two foolish Americans. Ah, it was all *merde*.

Suddenly he leaped onto the table, upsetting glasses and spilling his Pernod on Mrs. Dunwiddie's black dress. He began a speech in French, eloquently launching into a defense of human dignity. The Dunwiddies gaped at him, dumbfounded, frightened. They hurriedly left the table. Dunwiddie paid the bill at the door, and they fled. Sorel went on speaking: He told everyone present that they were pigs. Two Senegalese waiters hurriedly dragged him off the table. He jerked himself free. He rushed at an American who had laughed in his face and knocked him halfway across the dance floor. Blinded with drunken fury, he wanted to punch everyone in sight. The American regained his balance and came back at Sorel, slugging with both fists. Women shrieked. Frenchmen began talking, gesticulating, quarreling. Some of the customers ran off. Other fights broke out. The waiters separated Sorel and the American. Three Senegalese waiters slugged him. In a coma, he was dragged to the door and tossed out onto the sidewalk. Dazed, he struggled to his feet. Amused Parisians looked at him. A quarrel broke out on the sidewalk. Sorel staggered off. His face was battered. His left eye was rapidly swelling. He turned a narrow corner, flung himself into a cab, mumbled his address, and was driven off just as the *flics* arrived at the *bal*.

v

Sorel did not see the Dunwiddies again. He telephoned their hotel three times, but they were always out and ignored his messages suggesting that they should get in touch with him. He farmed out the translation of Dunwiddie's book.

He found a new mistress, a gay and vivacious little midinette. She seemed to be very fond of him, and her company was most enjoyable. Often, after having spent a delightful evening with her, he would lie in bed satiated, contented, recreating his sensual experiences in memory, reflecting upon her charms, thinking how she proved to him that the French were more civilized than the Americans. She was so much more desirable than the American tennis player of whom he had recently tired. Yes, she was an additional proof of the superiority of French civilization.

But Sorel was not satisfied to regard his new mistress as a mere midinette. He put her through a series of veritable cross-examinations about her parents, her relatives, her past, her

ancestry. At first she was bewildered. But gradually sensing
what he was driving at, she gave him the kind of answers he
wanted, and helped him prove to his own satisfaction that
she was descended from the true nobility of France.

Having established this proof in his own mind, he told
Cochineau about it. Cochineau then began to believe that he,
too, was a man in whose veins there flowed the blood of nobility. When Cochineau talked of his own nobility, Sorel was
not interested. He would change the subject, talk about his
midinette, and soon he would break forth in rages against the
Jacobins. For they were the scoundrels responsible for the
Great French Revolution, and for democracy. They had sub-
verted the moral order of the universe, the laws of God and
of nature; they had degraded the glory of France; they had
undermined tradition; they had created the foul society of
men which ended in the declining France of the twentieth century. Even down to the present the descendants of the best and
noblest people of France continued to suffer because of the
dirty work of this pack of scoundrels. And his little midinette
was one of the innocent victims of all this. Thanks to democracy, she, a girl of spirit, a girl who deserved the education and
respect due a princess, was forced to sell lingerie in a department store owned by men who were not only bourgeois, but
also Jewish.

On three successive evenings his midinette did not show
up. When she did come around, she said that she had had to
take care of a sick uncle. Her excuse seemed plausible to Sorel
because he could not think of her jilting or double-crossing
him. But then she did not appear again for a rendezvous. That
night, Cochineau, cruising around in his cab, saw her hugging
a man on a street corner in the Montmartre district. Sorel refused to believe Cochineau's story. But he was finally forced
to, because the midinette deserted him. He decided that she had
lied to him about her ancestry. After all, she was only a slut,
a girl of the people. Why should a man of letters be disturbed
by the conduct of such human trash?

At the same time, he learned that his wife had fallen in love

with a duke and he suffered from severe fits of melancholia.
He was unable to work. Manuscripts and translations piled up
on his desk. He brooded continually, and Cambry seemed to
be his only friend and confidante. He saw the American artist
often and poured out his soul in their conversations.

"I am wifeless and I am childrenless," he told Cambry again
and again.

When Cambry's patron cut off his allowance and demanded
that he return to America, Sorel promised to repay the balance
of his debt. But he speculated again on foreign exchange and
lost. He couldn't repay Cambry. He had not launched the
artist in Paris. They parted with harsh words. Christmas came.
On Christmas eve, Sorel walked the streets of Paris in the cold,
looking in at the lighted restaurants where Frenchmen gorged
themselves at family parties. The new year came. He was
lonely and miserable. A long, hard winter had set in.

VI

When he was most depressed, Sorel talked often of the
coming war. He blamed the politicians, arguing that if they
did not think up a war, they would have no work to do, and
everybody would get wise to the fact that they were parasites.
His assertions and opinions were a mirror of those held by
the most reactionary and chauvinistic groups in France. Although he detested the newspaper *Le Temps,* he often talked
like an editorial from that daily. At the time, French reaction
was sympathetic to the Japanese in their war upon China; so
was Sorel. And while he hated the coming war and blamed the
politicians, he agreed with the reactionary groups that put up
posters on the billboards filled with ringing war slogans and
often including maps outlining a prospective invasion of Germany. Whenever he saw posters put up by pacifists or leftist
groups, he spat at them.

He had met a young graduate student from the University
of Chicago named Morton Brooks; Brooks was studying at the
Sorbonne. He was idealistic, eager to learn, filled with the
curiosity of a good student, anxious to see a better world. He

lived frugally and had no money to lend Sorel. It was strange that Sorel should have been interested in seeing Brooks, but every so often they met and discussed history and politics. They always argued and disagreed. Brooks was eager to know every type of Frenchman and welcomed his meetings with Sorel. He was studying French history very assiduously, and he followed the French press closely. He had come to the conclusion that Léon Blum was the ablest political leader in France, and he constantly defended Blum against Sorel. Sorel always laughed at him, but Brooks was so intent on the pursuit of ideas that he did not become angry at insults or ridicule.

"But you don't have an open mind," Brooks charged one day in late March, when the two of them sat over coffee at a small café on the Boulevard Saint Michel.

"You liberal-minded people—your idea of an open mind is that of an incinerator. An incinerator has an open mind for every kind of garbage. But I am a Frenchman, not an incinerator. I wish I could say the same thing for many of my alleged fellow countrymen."

"That's unfair and irrelevant."

"Yes, it is unfair to the garbage to compare it with Léon Blum."

"You still haven't told me what is wrong with his ideas and his policies. You haven't given me any reasons."

"Do I need to tell you what is wrong with Socialism? It is heresy, folly, sentimentality—especially when it is practised by a Semite."

"That has nothing to do with the question. Blum's origins don't discredit his ideas. And racialism only poisons the world. You always use the argument *ad hominem*."

"So now you will give me a lecture on philosophy, one on which you probably took notes yesterday when you listened to some old fool at the Sorbonne."

"On the contrary, I'm not trying to lecture, but to convince you. If we don't introduce reason in the world, we can't have a better world. Then the war everybody talks of is certain to come. Frankly, I don't understand you."

"My dear young fellow, that is self-evident."

"What is self-evident?"

"It is self-evident that you cannot understand me."

"You never stick to the subject. And you always make all kinds of assertions, but that isn't proof."

"Listen, my dear chap, we Frenchmen have lived history and we have made history. We don't require lectures on history."

"But the trouble with you is that you don't like the history you have made."

"What?"

"For example, you even speak with scorn about France's greatest modern historian, Mathiez."

"He is no more. I shall be a Christian. I shall not speak with disrespect of the dead, even when the corpse is an old fool like Mathiez."

"I studied under him. He was very stimulating and profound. Why do you call him a fool?"

"I studied under him, too. He was an old fool. He wrote so abominably that he made me ashamed of the French language."

"Is that why you disapprove of him?"

"I look at you, and I think that you are very young. Pardon me for saying so, but, yes, you are very young. You mean well. But all you do is to parody that old fool's lectures and books. And whom did he defend? A despicable little lawyer from Arras, a bloodthirsty monster named Robespierre. Ah, what is there to say? You are infatuated with the people. The people always get the government they deserve."

"De Maistre said that."

"Why do you need to tell me what De Maistre said? Do you think that I don't know what he wrote. It would do you some good if you would read his books instead of the bilge of Mathiez and Aulard."

"I have read De Maistre."

"Then it is a pity that it has done you so little good."

"Let's discuss it and see. For example, let's take De Maistre's conception of government."

"All right. I believe in it. I assure you that I do. Man, the people, cannot undertake what is only God's work. Man can only produce a defective and bloodthirsty government. If you destroy the government ordained by God, then you get one influenced by swine like Rousseau. Only God can give us a good government under a king."

"Did God tell you that?"

"Don't profane God, even if you are a Protestant."

"I'm not a Protestant. My religion is man."

"I know that's what you think. It's sentimentality. For example, the last time I saw you, you were full of tears for a million Chinese coolies. You don't know them. You never saw a coolie. But you weep for them. I'm a Christian. I have charity for my fellow man, but I don't weep crocodile tears for a million coolies I have never even seen. They're inferior to the Japanese. They deserve to be ruled by the Japanese, just as the Hindus deserve to be ruled by English policemen. Any other view is sentimentality."

"Why is it sentimentality? Aren't the Chinese men? Doesn't every one of them possess a consciousness of his own? Doesn't a coolie want to live a decent life?"

"You talk about *men*. Never, never are there many *men*, real *men*, alive in this world. Ah, I tell you, when you get older you will understand that man has made a damnable mess of God's creation."

"That's snobbery."

"Of course it is. What man worth his salt isn't a snob?"

Brooks stared at Sorel, utterly speechless.

"I can't stand this sentimentality about the people. The people! Look at them filling Paris with their garbage! They gorge themselves with food and blood! They fill the world with their little lusts and their small emotions! What are they? They are nothing but walking aggregations of appetites."

"What differentiates them from you?"

"I'm a man, a human being. But I aspire to believe in something that is more noble than all this nonsense."

"How do you know others don't?"

"What—the rabble?"

"I can't agree with you on any question. I don't see why one man should assume that he is better, more noble, than any other man. Not even if he does call himself a Christian."

"Some men are more noble. The artist is more noble."

"An artist should put his talents at the service of other men."

"If he does—what? You will get your Russia. Instead of Chartres, you will have all this idiocy of collective farms and factories. And the people will destroy the artist. They will drag him down to their own level. They will kill him."

"No, he might raise the level of the people. That is what the artist should strive to do. He should strive to do it without compromising his beliefs or his art."

"If you were an artist, you wouldn't say that."

"Why wouldn't I?"

"An artist doesn't talk that way—by definition."

Again Brooks looked at Sorel, perplexed. Sorel pulled out his watch. He had to leave to keep an engagement with a new mistress.

VII

Sorel had met many people in Paris and despite his endless quarrels had numerous acquaintances, but he actually had very few friends. One of his friends was a Russian named Karzov. Karzov was sales manager at Dubuisson Frères. He was a thin man who had contracted tuberculosis in Russia during the period of the Civil War. For a while after the Revolution he had worked at his profession; he was an engineer. Despite his Czarist sympathies and his belief in the doctrines of the Greek Orthodox Church, he had managed to get work. But then he had had some trouble with a commissar whom he always described as a raving lunatic. He fled Russia, and in his flight he had wandered through forests in bitter cold, constantly in danger of his life. He had managed to get across the

Polish border, but he had been picked up by the soldiery. They
were planning to send him back to the Soviet Union. He was
questioned by an officer, who recognized his name. The officer
had known Karzov's father, a merchant who had been accidentally shot in the fighting between the Reds and the Whites.
The officer helped Karzov get to Paris. Karzov was very unhappy because he was in exile and because he believed he would
never again be able to practise his real profession. He was a
sad man with gentle eyes, quiet and kindly; the only time he
became angry was when he spoke of the Bolsheviks.

Karzov and Sorel dined together frequently. One night in
March they sat over their dinner, drinking wine and talking.
The situation in Germany was very tense and it disturbed
Karzov to the depths of his being. If there were a workers'
revolution in Germany, there would be a bloc between Germany and Soviet Russia, and then all hope for civilization
would be crushed. He read the press daily for German news,
and his fears grew by leaps and bounds.

"My dear fellow, you are like us French. You have nothing
in common with the Germans," Sorel said as they sat in the
corner of a little restaurant on the Rue Saint Benoit.

Karzov agreed.

"If the Germans get this maniac, Hitler—well, I say that
they deserve him. He will be their penalty, their cross, and
they must bear him. They wanted Bolshevism, and so they will
get the lunatic they deserve. That man is stark mad, but he is
a good antidote for Bolshevism."

"If Hitler becomes Chancellor of Germany, what do you
think will happen?"

"It is the war."

"Can France win?"

"France must win. But this war will be filthier than the last
one. And look at the politicians we have to lead us. They
would sell their shirts for a portfolio. They have corrupted
France and they would sell France, too."

Karzov stared gloomily into a glass of red wine.

"Yes, the Germans are lunatics. But we will fight when it

comes. I hate the bloody business. I wash my hands of it. But I am a Frenchman. I will do my duty.

"Isn't Hitler better than the Bolsheviks?" Karzov asked.

"What—one lunatic is better than another? The civilized world ought to put a wall around Germany and Russia and hang up a sign at the gate: lunatic asylum. There is no other solution than this one, except the bloody war they are going to give us."

"The situation is very dangerous. I am worried."

"I tell you, Vladimir, the world is going to the dogs. And I say, the devil with it. It is the filthy politicians and their false love of the people. These ignorant fools will not be satisfied until they have reduced everything to a shambles."

"The last hope for civilization was an alliance between France and Russia. But Lenin and Trotsky—what dogs!" Karzov said with violent emotion.

"I think it is too late. Civilization will go to the devil. If we don't get the Bolsheviks, we will get the Americans. America will come here and own us with all her Babbitts. We will have to look at these children, these juveniles, these Americans who have no traditions. They have never suffered. What do they understand? Ah, I have seen them in Paris here, lighting cigars with our franc notes, thinking it was a joke, a fine exhibition. Yes, the Americans with their dollars and their machines will own us, body and soul. And our great civilization, our culture, will crumble into the dust."

"But Russia will rise again," Karzov said, a gleam lighting up his eyes.

"We must be true to our traditions and to our Christian feelings," Sorel said. He poured more wine for both of them. "But why should I care? I have no part of this so-called civilization of today. How the fools pollute the very word! Yes, Vladimir, we live at the end of something noble, and the future belongs to the Americans. This is the kettle of soup they have cooked for us, these believers in Marxism, democracy, the people."

"France and Russia must save civilization," Karzov said gloomily.

"It is too late. It is finished, absolutely. I tell you we are looking on death. Tear the masks off almost every face you see on the streets of Paris, and what will you see? Death!"

"And it is Russians, my fellow countrymen, who have done this to the world with the murder of our Czar."

"Most of them were Jews, and the others were traitors, bought by the Germans. And we Frenchmen, we, too, murdered a King. We are still paying the price of that folly down to this very day."

"But in those days we had a great Czar, Alexander, to save Europe. Now there is no King, no Czar to save us."

Karzov was suddenly embarrassed. He glanced aside shyly, remembering that he was speaking of the Napoleonic invasion of Russia and fearing that he had hurt Sorel's feelings by referring to a French defeat. But Sorel showed no offense.

"The English double-crossed us. I tell you, they are with the Germans. And so, what will happen to them? They, too, will be the victims of the Americans. But then, an Englishman is not civilized. He is a policeman. His only service to civilization is that of the cop. He knows how to police these Africans and Hindus and keep them from getting into trouble. Only we French and Russians have a real civilization."

Karzov drained his glass and poured more wine. The two friends sat sipping wine, their countenances gloomy, their spirits depressed.

"The devil with it. I wash my hands of this damned mess," Sorel said.

Karzov burst into a fit of coughing. He gulped down a glass of water. His face was pale.

Karzov nodded. They were silent for several moments.

"You know, I often look at Cochineau and I wish I could be like him. That man has no soul. He is primitive," Sorel said.

"Last week he said to me, 'Don't you worry. We Frenchmen will march across the Vistula and we will save Russia. We will redeem you, and watch what we do to those Bolshevik vermin. Then we will drink vodka,' " Karzov said.

"He is a good soldier. But we French are good soldiers. If the Germans want their lunatic Hitler, then it is the war. We will give them what we have given them many times before."

The waiter served them coffee.

"But France is old. We are too old. We have too much good sense, too much tradition. We understand too much. We are cursed by our good sense, our intelligence, our great and our noble tradition. We have saved the human race from being ridiculous. But now we are ridiculous, thanks to the politicians."

Suddenly Karzov had a violent fit of coughing. Sorel had to take him home in a cab and put him to bed. He was feverish and talked incoherently, continually saying that he would never set foot on Russian soil again. After he had calmed down and gone to sleep, Sorel left. He walked the streets, cursing to himself. It was a fine spring evening.

VIII

At the offices of Dubuisson Frères, Sorel was always guarded in his remarks. There, he felt isolated because of his youth and lack of literary reputation, and also because of his opinions. The two Dubuisson brothers, sensing the probable direction of political currents, began to profess an interest in Marxism and planned to publish some Marxist books. Hearing them outline this plan, Sorel sat in silent hatred. And the editors approved of this plan. They were illustrious literary men. One of them, a world-famous man of letters, was enthusiastic, and he himself was showing signs of interest in Marxism and of sympathy for Russia; another, a famous literary critic, was beginning to espouse liberal political and sociological interests. Seeing these men regularly, listening to them in the offices and during the editorial conferences, Sorel's mind filled with invectives which he dare not utter. He asked himself, would his revenge ever come? He wanted to scream at them, insult them, and he was only the editor of a series of detective-story novels

who needed this connection badly. They talked rot to him, and
he would constantly remind himself that this was the state to
which French letters had descended. But his series of books did
well, and his prestige rose at the firm. His material situation
improved again, and this time he did not speculate on foreign
exchange. But he made still one more vain effort to effect a re-
conciliation with his wife. If he had a home life, he was certain
that he would now be able to write. But his wife dunned him
for more money. And though it was spring in Paris, he was
as miserable as ever. He walked the streets as he had when he
was a younger man and his dreams of literature and poetry
had been new and fresh. He was not a poet. He couldn't write
poetry any more. He was a failure. On late afternoons he often
would leave the Dubuisson offices and walk down to the Seine
to look at the sunset. He would reflect that there was something eternal in France and in her traditions. There was something that must live, and that would live. And yet it was
dying. He was convinced that it was dying. He believed that
in the future, there were only two alternatives: Karl Marx,
or else the rise of Hitler, the war, death by a shell, death by
poison gas. He, a young man in his early thirties, would die
with no accomplishments, no achievements. He would leave
this France, this Paris, and who would care? And when would
it come? Next year? What year? He would walk off and go
home, or else go to dinner with someone. His feelings would
fill to overflowing, and then he would get drunk. And the
cycle of his feeling would repeat itself.

In May, the President of France was assassinated. On the
day of the murder, Sorel went to the office. The telephone girl
in the cubicle at the entrance was nervous and excited. He
glanced at her with contempt. He went upstairs, telling himself that all of Paris was enjoying the spectacle of another
French President assassinated. He remembered ironically that
Clemenceau had once said that there were two useless things
in life: the vermiform appendix and the President of France.
What did the excitement of this girl, and of others, mean?
He knew. It was proof of the blood lust in the beast—humanity.

He entered the office where an editorial conference was being
held. It seemed to him as if everyone present was keyed up; he
thought he saw their eyes gleaming. He was convinced that
these men, too, were all enjoying this murder. He reflected
that the incident proved to him precisely where all these intellectuals stood—they were only broadcasting stations for the
people, and they were dangerous because they were possessed
of a fatal *amour pour le malheur*. That was why they seemed
happy now. He sat silent during the conference. Dubuisson
Frères decided to publish a weekly magazine, and the editor
selected for this task had Marxist sympathies. Again Sorel
asked himself—would he ever get his revenge?

That night he dined at a restaurant near the Place de l'Odéon
where he was known by the *patron*. The place was crowded,
and the customers were talking loudly. The *patron* introduced
him to the guests as a journalist, a man who knew what was
happening in France, and who, because of his many connections, could explain the meaning of the day's event. Sorel began
making a speech. He declared that the assassination was of no
political importance. France had plenty of political old men
to spare, and this murder would lend glamor to a name that
would otherwise have been forgotten. He declared that all
Paris was excited over this event because all Paris enjoyed it;
all Paris was happy tonight. Why? It was filled with the blood
lust that motivated the people; it enjoyed murder and assassination. Every so often such a murder occurred in France, and
when it did, the people were happy. And what had unleashed
these feelings in the world? He could answer this question.
He said that nearby there was a statue in honor of one of the
men responsible for such lusts in the people; it was the statue
of Danton. He got no further. The restaurant was in an up-
roar. Everyone talked and shouted. Some applauded "bravo"
for Sorel; others yelled at him. One man flung the name of
Charlotte Corday in his face, and he answered that she should
be canonized. He left the restaurant in the midst of the furore
and while the customers were gesturing wildly, shouting at

one another, hurling insults, as the worried *patron* vainly tried
to restore order.

Sorel ate alone at another restaurant, and then he went
home. He found Cochineau sitting with his chin in his hands.

"What, have you gone into mourning because of this meaningless assassination?" he shouted at Cochineau.

Cochineau looked up. There was a far-off expression in his
eyes. Sorel argued with him excitedly. Then Cochineau explained the reason for his low spirits. All that he had said about
having an influential friend had been nonsense. The police had
been tracing him from address to address, and they had finally
caught up with him. Now he would have to pay a big fine
because his papers weren't in order. Sorel laughed. He scrib-
bled a note of introduction for Cochineau to take to a newspaper friend who could fix it up. Cochineau's mood changed.
He went off to work, gay, singing a ribald song.

At the moment Sorel had no mistress. He didn't feel like
reading or working. He went off to a café in the Montmartre
district. There, as in the restaurant, he observed that there was
a suppressed air of excitement, a tension that could be felt in
what everyone was saying. On all sides he heard conversations
concerning the assassination. Near him someone was bragging
that he knew someone who knew someone else who had the real
truth about the murder, but he couldn't divulge this story. To
his left he spotted a French girl sitting with a Negro. She
gave him the eye. He told himself that he wasn't interested in
her. He sat over his glass of black coffee, reveling in his contempt of everyone about him. No, he was not interested in
the girl. Her Negro escort went inside to the lavatory. Sorel
signaled to the girl. They rose simultaneously. He left the
money for his drink by his saucer. They walked off, got a cab,
and went to Sorel's home.

The next morning he woke up disgusted with himself. A
common prostitute! Another day gone by. Another night
wasted. He telephoned his wife. A man answered the phone.
He hung up. At the office he ran into Karzov. They went out
for a drink. Karzov was also depressed. He had been going

around with a big Russian blonde and he had just learned that
she had jilted him for a renegade White Guard who now spoke
favorably of the Bolsheviks. They sat with glasses of *vin chaud*
before them and lamented the state of the world.

IX

Sorel's life went on with no essential change in its pattern
for over a year. In the fall of 1933, the Dubuissons dismissed
him, and after he had gone they learned that he owed them
thousands of francs for translations which he had never begun.
He did hack work. Since he was now poor and without influence, Cochineau found no use in him and cleared out. He
moved to a cheap hotel. He joined an organization of fascists
and, changing his name, wrote for their paper. In February,
1934, he was on the streets at the Place de la Concorde, charging the *Garde Mobile*, shouting fascist slogans, crying out "au
voleur," hoping that the riot would lead to a change of government. He had drifted away from the literary world. Suddenly he left Paris. He was next heard of in Italy, where he
was living quite comfortably. He spoke enthusiastically of
Mussolini, and he no longer called Hitler a lunatic. He told
an acquaintance that the Jew Blum was ruining France and
that unless Franco won in Spain, Europe would be overrun by
bandits. Shortly before the Munich crisis, he again turned up
in Paris, and he seemed to have ample funds. During the war
he was called to the colors. His regiment was stationed on the
Italian frontier, and he saw little fighting. After the Armistice
with Germany, he was mustered out of the army and he went
to Vichy. He is now a successful journalist in Vichy. He writes
with a vitriolic pen, demanding the regeneration of France, the
punishment of the criminals who caused her collapse, and the
establishment of a new order in Europe.

Such is the history of Jacques Sorel, a literary young man
of the postwar generation in France, who lived by his wits.

1934-1942

Monday Is Another Day

I

"WELL, the Lord granting, we'll have many more fine and happy Sunday dinners like this one, Ma," Mr. Malone said, pushing his plate from him. He was a lank man with graying temples, sunken cheeks, a face which seemed to be growing more and more set with lines of worry. There was something absent-minded and beaten in his expression.

Tom, the small, twenty-two-year-old son, tossed a look of contempt at his father.

"Now, what's wrong with that?" Marie said. She was twenty, pug-nosed and blue-eyed, with attractive bobbed-hair.

"I didn't say anything," Tom said crisply.

"But you looked it. I saw your face. You're always criticizing around here, and I'm just sick and tired of it," she said, and the father looked from son to daughter, pained.

"You're getting quite brilliant. All you have to do is to look *at* a person's face and you can see what's in their mind," Tom told Marie.

"That's like taking pennies from babies when the person is as superficial as you are," Marie retorted.

"Do we have to have another argument at the Lord's table?" Mrs. Malone asked. She was plump, ruddy, a genial-looking woman whose hair was turning gray.

"Sunday's a day of rest. We're all here together, and we've got our health. We can forget the troubles of the world for this one day and be happy, can't we?" Mr. Malone said, with almost a whine in his voice.

"There isn't any need to stop thinking on Sunday, is there?" Tom asked.

"There he goes again with his damned crack-brained communism. If you want to talk about your damned communism with those bum friends of yours, I don't care. But don't be shooting your mouth off about it here in our home," Bill, the twenty-five-year-old bespectacled brother said, his voice dripping bitterness.

"I hardly opened my mouth. She doesn't like my face, that's all, and it seems to me that's just what's eating everybody here," Tom said.

"You were thinking it just the same," Bill said.

"You know so damned much, tell me, what was I thinking?" Tom asked.

"Your damned communism, that's what you were thinking. You're always trying to get into an argument with us. Well, you ain't gettin' no argument from me," Bill shouted.

"It's a self-evident impossibility that I could get no argument from you," Tom shot back at his brother.

"See, there he goes again," Marie said.

"For God's sake, let's have quiet at the dinner table," Mrs. Malone pleaded.

They stopped talking. Mrs. Malone went to the kitchen to get the coffee and dessert; her daughter followed her. Tom and Bill glowered at one another.

II

"Now I suppose you'll be going out and seeing those bum friends of yours to let them fill you full of communism and atheism, so you can come home and spring some more of it on us," Bill said after they had eaten their dessert in silence.

"What the hell do you know about communism?"

"This much! That's it's all boloney—that, and just that," Bill answered.

"Well, what do you know about it? Tell me," Tom demanded.

"Listen, I don't need to tell you. I know all about your

Lenin and Trotsky and the rest of those bums who didn't want
to work for a living."

"What about Lenin?"

"Look what he's doing to Russia. The best thing Russia could
do would be to get him out of the country. Put him in Siberia,
shoot him. He's ruining the country and blowing up churches,"
Bill said.

"Lenin isn't in Russia," Tom said.

"He ain't!" Bill turned to his father, gloating. "See, he
doesn't even know his damned communism. He says Lenin ain't
in Russia. Didn't I tell you he was all hot air?"

"Lenin's been dead for about seven years," Tom said.

"Well then, Trotsky. I haven't got the time to be keeping
track of those bums," Bill said.

"Trotsky was kicked out of Russia," Tom said.

"Well, that's the first sensible thing the crazy Russians ever
did—and anyway, what the hell do we Americans care about
it? Why don't you interest yourself in America?"

"You brought up the subject of Russia, not I," Tom said.

"Tom, the trouble with you is that you read more books
than you've got the experience to understand. For your own
good, I'm telling you to watch yourself," the father said.

"It ain't human, reading books the way he does. And such
awful books. I looked at some of them he brought home from
the library. I'd be ashamed to let my friends know I have a
brother who reads such books. They're awful," said Marie.

"Tom, the least you could do is go to mass on Sunday," the
mother said.

"Yes, Tom, it wouldn't hurt you to give religion a trial and
spend one hour a week in the Lord's House," the father said.

"If you went to mass on Sunday, Tom, perhaps the Lord
would find you a job," Mrs. Malone said.

"He doesn't find her one, and she goes to mass," Tom said,
pointing at his sister.

"Now, keep God out of this," Bill demanded.

"Look at all the years the whole bunch of you have been

going to mass and putting money in the collection. What's it gotten you? What's God done for you?" Tom asked.

Mr. Malone plainly winced because of Tom's indirect reference to his own failure in life.

"I told you to keep God out of this," Bill repeated.

"Tom, I tell you, it isn't God that's responsible. It's the rich guys and the Jews," Mr. Malone said.

"Oh, hell, what's the use of talking to you? You're all saps. I tell you, it's the system that's got us all where we are," Tom said.

"It seems to me that in times like these, a person has enough to do and think of with his own troubles without starting to think about what's wrong with the world," Mrs. Malone said.

"He calls us saps, and he thinks that the world owes everybody a living," Bill said.

"Well, it does," Tom told him.

Bill and Marie laughed at their brother sadistically. The father and mother looked at each other perplexed.

"What the hell are you laughing at?" Tom asked.

"He thinks the world owes everybody a living," Bill said scornfully.

"Tom, you're never going to get anywhere in life as long as you have such a slant," the father said.

"Well, where the hell has your slant and Bill's slant gotten either of you?" Tom replied.

The father winced again. All of them became tense and silent.

"You needn't be insulting your father. He's always taken care of every one of us and paid his bills like an honorable man. If you become as good a man as he is, you'll not be a disappointment to any of us," the mother said, breaking the silence.

"I'm not trying to insult you. I'm just trying to make you all get wise to yourselves, that's all," Tom urged, regretful that he had hurt his father's feelings.

"Well, it wouldn't hurt you to get wise to yourself. Talking about the world owing him a living, and he hasn't been able to find a job in four months," Bill said.

"If people would get wise to themselves and raise some hell, things would be different in this country. There's no reason why so many people should be out of work and everybody should be trembling in fear that he might lose his job. If the world was sensibly organized, we wouldn't have this state of affairs. That's all I'm trying to tell you," Tom said.

"See, didn't I tell you he's a communist?" Bill said.

"Oh, forget your damned labels. I'm just trying to tell you why there's such a depression in the richest country in the world," Tom said.

"You know it all, don't you? All the answers. You know why there's a depression," Bill said.

"Sure I do," Tom said.

"All right, wise guy, let us in on the secret," Bill said.

"It's the capitalist system," Tom said.

"Ah, you make me sick. And some day you're going to sprain your tongue with long words," Bill said, getting up from the table, pushing his chair back, and leaving the room.

"Tom, it's really about time that you settled down and made something out of yourself. I'm serious," Marie said.

"For example?" Tom asked.

"Something! Some fellows make something out of themselves. You could do it if you'd forget these . . . these crazy ideas of yours. Why, do you know that if any of my friends heard you talking the way you do, they'd say you belonged in the booby hatch," Marie said.

"You and your dopey friends! All the girls you go around with aren't any better than harlots," Tom said.

Both father and mother looked aghast at Tom.

"Why, goddamn you! You no-good bum, go out and get a job. If I ever hear you say another word about my friends, I'll . . . I'll kill you!" Marie shouted.

"Tom, this is our home, and we're not going to hear any more of your talk here, get me!" the father said sternly.

"What the hell's he saying now?" Bill asked as he rushed back into the dining room.

"He's insulting my friends," Marie said.

"Don't pay any attention to him. He's nuts," Bill yelled.

"I'll never speak to you again!" Marie said, and then she stamped out of the room.

Tom shrugged his shoulders.

"What's the idea, Tom?" the father asked.

"Oh, drop it," Tom answered, annoyed.

"That's no way to talk to your father," Mrs. Malone said.

"I'm going," Tom said.

"Sit down and explain yourself. What's the idea?" the father asked.

"There's nothing to explain except to tell you that the world's changed, and you've all believed in lies all your lives," Tom said.

"Give him a soapbox, Pa, and let him tell it to the squirrels," Bill said.

"I've got to go," Tom said, leaving the room where his father and mother sat, bewildered.

"Whoever thought he'd turn out this way?" the father asked.

"It's the influence of bad companions on him," Mrs. Malone said.

III

After leaving the apartment, Tom walked toward Jackson Park. The argument seemed to him to have been so stupid and futile. And he realized that he had not talked correctly to his family. He should have kept his head and explained to them. Everything seemed so simple to him, and yet when he tried to explain it, he argued, and he couldn't frame what he meant in simple words that would be clear to them, that would convince them. He felt that he should explain more and quarrel less with his family. And then, he wondered whether or not it would do any good. They were the dupes of the system; he wanted to explain this to them so that they wouldn't go on being dupes. He told himself that his family was just hopeless.

He lit a cigarette and, walking on, he thought of his sister.

She was just a flapper born a few years too late. She was an
echo of a lot of silly conventions, foolish dreams, Hollywood
snobberies, desires and hopes in life that she borrowed from
what was around her and that would play her false. She was
out looking for some guy she could hook who would have
enough money to keep her in style and make her life seem as
if it were being lived in a moving picture. And there were
just thousands of other girls looking for the same thing. And
the only place where they would find it would be on Sunday
afternoons in a fog of dreams when they sat in the movies.
Her only ambition in life was to be a parasite. And society
sanctioned that ambition in her. If she succeeded in realizing
it, society would congratulate her as a success. She'd been going with Ted Mooney, a nice guy but a dope. As soon as he'd
lost his job, she'd given him the gate in double-quick time.
Yes, his sister was no good, no better than a whore, and he'd
told her the truth. Most of the girls he'd grown up with were
the same.

And look at his brother. The guy was asleep on his feet. If
ever there was a mutt, it was Bill Malone. He'd be a twenty-
five-dollar-a-week clerk all his life, thanking the world for being so kind to him. And the old man, with all his savings gone
except the life insurance policy. Now, wouldn't there be a
touching scene of filial devotion and family loyalty when the
old man died and Marie and Bill went at each other's throat for
some of that money! How many more men were there like his
father; how many more families like his were there in America,
sitting today in crumbling homes, licked, living in dreams that
had turned to vicious lies?

Wandering on, he came to the park. The day was chilly, and
the leaves had already turned and died. They were now stiff,
and a drab tan. The wind cut them from the branches, swirled
them, settled them on the hard earth. The park was almost deserted and he walked on, kicking and stamping through the
dead leaves, feeling very much alone in this world. He belonged to a new generation and he told himself that his generation must go out and fight. Society, he felt, was offering

little to his generation, little except the historic task to march
forth and fight to make a better world. But that was enough.
He asked no more. Yes, his generation could not ask that faith,
hope, and charity would give it a sou or get it anywhere. He
strolled on in the dismal autumn park, the wind strumming a
sad tune in the bare trees, a sadness that suddenly filled his being. He paused and looked about at the leafless shrubbery. He
lit a cigarette. As quickly as he had been precipitated into sadness, he was flung aloft into exultation. Yes, history might give
his generation great tasks. Perhaps, he told himself, history
would give his generation the chance to be like that of 1917 in
Russia.

He walked on aimlessly, full of his own thoughts. The sky
was lowering. Would he be man enough to be a revolutionist?
He remembered how as a boy he had often dreamed of martyrdom for the Church. He had looked backward to the age when
many gave their blood for the religion of Christ. Today, there
was a new martyrdom awaiting his generation. There was a
new faith in the world. There was the Revolution.

IV

"Tom's still young. He'll outgrow it all," the father said
dully.

"When I was his age, I wasn't like him," Bill said.

"It's those bad companions of his. The Lord knows who he
sees when he goes out," Mrs. Malone said.

"I tried to get him a job at the office, but there was nothing
doing. There's Joe Keene. He's been in the office fifteen years,
and last month he was let out. Mr. Dugan said it was only temporarily, but then who knows in days like these? Everyone in
the office is afraid of being let out. Mr. Dugan did say, however, that if things picked up, he might find a place for Tom,"
Mr. Malone said.

"Even if he did, Tom wouldn't want it. It wouldn't be good
enough for him," Bill said.

"On my soul, I never thought that my boy Tom would be

growing up to say things like I heard him say right here today,"
Mrs. Malone said.

"Half the time I don't know what the devil he's talking
about, do you, Bill?" the father remarked.

"He doesn't know himself," Bill said.

"Well, I hope he gets straightened out," Mrs. Malone said.

"Mother, do you give him any money?" Bill asked.

"And where in the name of God would I get the money to
give him? I give him carfare and a few pennies to look for a
job and have a bite to eat, and that's all he gets. He never asks
for money. I can't say anything against him there. And when
he was working, he always gave me the money agreed on every
week with never a complaint," the mother said.

"Well, if he asks for money, he doesn't get it," Bill said.

"All we can do is trust to God," Mrs. Malone said.

"Bill, you going to stay in and listen to Father Moylan this
afternoon?" Mr. Malone asked.

"I'd like to, Pa, but I got a date with Elsie," Bill said.

"Too bad. There's a fine man, and damn smart, too. I'd like
to see Tom stand up to a man like Father Moylan and try to put
across his crazy ideas. But he won't even stay home and listen
to Father Moylan's radio sermons," Mr. Malone said disap-
pointedly.

v

Mr. Malone was nervous. He had read his Sunday paper and
he'd taken a nap. It was still twenty minutes before he could
hear Father Moylan, the radio priest, deliver his weekly sermon
from the Shrine of the Rose of Jesus Christ. Day after day,
worries dogged him, and he couldn't throw them out of his
mind. That was one of the reasons he felt so badly that Tom
had started an argument today at the dinner table. He wanted
Sunday to be a day of rest, not only from work but also from
worry. Tom had spoiled his whole day. Each week he didn't
know but that it would be the last at the office. And he had
been there twenty years. Ah, just to think that a few short
years ago he'd been earning seventy-five dollars a week and had

had no worries for the future. He had been putting Tom through college with great hopes for the boy. And then this depression had come. He was now down to forty dollars a week, and Tom had had to quit college. Yes, times had certainly changed. They really couldn't afford to keep on living here. Sixty-five dollars a month rent was too much for them to pay. But when they'd talked of moving, Marie had put her foot down. She'd asked how could they expect to have any friends, and how was she ever to get a decent fellow and marry him, if they had to live in a dump? So they'd signed the lease for another year, and they were feeling the pinch of it now. Bill and he had to carry the whole burden, and that with sixty-five dollars a week coming in. It didn't go as far as it should with five mouths to be fed. He and Bill had to have carfare and lunch money every day. Tom and Marie had to have a little change so they could go out and look for work. And rent, gas, food, electricity, clothes, a movie now and then, all of the little odds and ends that added up to a hell of a lot when you were running a home. And, yes, how long would he keep his job with conditions the way they were? And even if he did keep it, would his pay be cut any more? They were still fairly comfortable, but could they count on going on this way?

But here he was worrying again. And he had twenty minutes to wait for Father Moylan's broadcast. He could turn the radio on now, but that wouldn't stop him from worrying either. He would start in listening to music, and soon he wouldn't even know that the radio was on, and he'd be mulling the same old story over and over again in his mind.

He got out an old deck of cards and sat down to play solitaire. That took his mind off troubles like nothing else could. With his watch before him, he kept an eye on the time so that he wouldn't miss a word of Father Moylan's. He shuffled the cards and played solitaire.

VI

The voice of Father Moylan, rich, melodious, unctuous, filled the Malone parlor. Now Mr. Malone was hearing the words he had been waiting all day, all week, to hear. He and his wife sat frozen in attention, their eyes far off.

And, my friends, verily, we are glad to put the depression from our minds for a little while—a depression that has come upon us like a plague because the false and idolatrous gods of materialism have betrayed us; a depression that is more than economic because in it we have learned the extent to which the principles of Christ and of the kingdom of Christ have been betrayed and abandoned. Is it thus any wonder to any Christian man or woman that we want to forget this depression and turn our minds to the Lord of the Heavenly kingdom, the one and only true hope, the sole beacon light that will reveal to us the road we must take for our personal salvation and for our national salvation? Nothing else can save us. My friends, as a man of God, a priest as well as a man, I say to you in all sincerity of heart and in all conviction, I say that only Christ can save us; only Christ, with His words, His policies, His faith can save us.

Mr. Malone leaned slightly forward and constantly nodded his head in agreement with what the priest was saying. Father Moylan was explaining how the false gods of materialism had disarmed the Christians of America, leaving the path open for the international bankers to bring this crisis upon the nation. He was giving expression to the feelings which Mr. Malone himself had never been able to formulate as he would like. He nodded forcibly to his wife to tell her that he agreed. The priest continued.

We hear these days of communism. Communism is made. There would be no communism if conditions did not make it. If we would avoid communism we must correct the conditions which cause it to appear. And that we must do under the banner of Christ. My friends, Christ does not want his flock to starve and to suffer, to worry because of the pangs of hunger and the cancer of doubt and fear, and of the ravages of that feeling of insecurity.

"The ravages of insecurity." That was just what he felt. Just that! Father Moylan showed such wonderful understanding. The priest went on to say that communism would rear its ugly head in many American Christian homes if the rulers of this nation did not take heed. Mr. Malone thought of his son. Was this happening in his own home? God forbid! The priest said that people must not starve. There must be security and social justice, and it must be administered and established in the Christian way. The laborer must be worthy of his hire. And property must be preserved, but the owners of property must accept their responsibilities. Everything that was being said was finding its responsive chord in Mr. Malone. Why could not these words be heeded, he asked himself. Why, almost two thousand years after Christ died, was there not more Christianity?

And whose ears are the ones that are closed, yes, deaf and dumb, my friends, to the pitiful cries of agony and anguish in these sad and suffering days? I am not afraid to say so. It is the money changers. It is the international bankers, Jewish and Gentile, who have turned deaf ears on human agony and misery for their paltry profits in the gold of this world. Last week in my radio sermon, I asked a question which I shall ask again today, a question which I propose to ask until an answer is given, an answer not to me, my friends, but to the poor and lowly of this great nation. Why does President Hoover close his ears to the pitiful cries of an anguished nation? Is the President of these United States the servant of the people, or is he the servant of the international bankers, the money changers both Jew and Gentile?

Mr. Malone liked it, giving hell to the greedy big fellows. And he reflected that things wouldn't be the way they were if the bigots hadn't licked Al Smith in 1928. And now, another good question that Father Moylan was asking. Why didn't the foreign governments pay their war debts? America was suffering while money owed to us was spent by foreign governments to arm for war.

I ask, is this Americanism?

Malone was sure that there would be Americanism in the
country, a strong and powerful Americanism, if Al Smith were
President. But the bigots had done that. He wished Father
Moylan would now lace into the bigots. He felt that they, the
Ku Kluxers, were with the communists. He listened on, feeling that Father Moylan was pulling no punches in lashing
against greed and speaking in defense of the little fellow, the
man like himself. And, yes, let Tom answer this sermon. Tom
was proud, that was Tom's trouble. And Mr. Malone was sure
that all of his son's friends were Jews and that the Jews were
making a radical out of the boy.

Mrs. Malone also liked the sermon, not missing a word. She
didn't understand all that the priest said, but she was convinced that what he said was right and good and should be
heeded. She it was who was struggling to keep their home together, who was getting gray with worry, with debts mounting,
and less money coming in, doing the shopping and pinch-
ing to save a penny here and a penny there, answering the credi-
tors who came to the door, washing, ironing, cooking, doing
everything she could for her family. Yes, she knew that the
priest was right. And if only her erring son could be gotten
to listen to him, and to abide by his words.

Father Moylan continued, his words inspiring a mounting
curve of hope and confidence in these two listeners. He was
giving them the courage to go on another week, to continue to
hope for something better in all their fear and worry. They
told themselves that he was right, and right would win out in
the end. They wanted the radio sermon never to end, but Father
Moylan, after a ringing set of denunciations, repeating all
that he had said, concluded:

*We must forsake the towers of Babel. And with the help
and grace of God and of His True Faith, we will, my friends.
In the name of the Father, and of the Son, and of the Holy
Ghost, Amen.*

Religious music followed the sermon. Malone turned to his wife.

"I wish Tom could hear him," he said.

She nodded agreement.

"You know, if the country would listen to Father Moylan, the same as I always said that if the bigots hadn't kept Al Smith out of the White House, things would be different, and everyone would be better off," Malone said.

"Well, maybe the boy'll get a job tomorrow and put away all this trash. I pray every day that he will, and I'm sure that the Lord will answer my prayers," she said.

After Father Moylan had closed with a prayer, Malone went to his room. He took out a dollar bill, put it in an envelope, addressed it to Father Moylan, and put on his hat and coat.

"I'm going out to mail a letter and take a walk, dear. I'll be home for supper," he told his wife and, kissing her on the forehead, he left. He wanted to think over what Father Moylan had said.

VII

Tom had seen friends and students down near the University, and they had had a long discussion. He had broached the subject of joining the Communist Party, and they had talked of it. His friend Jake was reading Trotsky's *My Life* and wasn't so sure that was a good course. He had doubts about the Party. Tom didn't know. All he knew was that he was fed up, and that the society he lived in was rotten. He wanted to work for a better one. There had been many things said, and many arguments. One fellow had asked whether or not dialectical materialism was a real description of scientific method, and they hadn't been able to decide. And then when they had talked about getting jobs after graduation, the ones still in school had been gloomy. They would have to do what he was doing. Pound the pavement and look for a job, see the long lines of men, young and old, streaming from place to place each day seeking work where there was none, hear the stories of men looking for work, see the lines of worry on their

faces. The whole damned business was crazy. But he was sure
that there were others like those he had been with, and there
might be enough of them to fight and change the world.

The gathering had broken up at about nine-thirty, and Tom
had walked home thinking of what had been said. Tomorrow
was Monday, and Monday was another day of looking for
work. And it would probably be the same old story. But then
maybe he would get a job. And if he did, it wouldn't be any
good. Well, there was one thing that he was determined on.
This damned business was not going to break him. He was going to fight back.

When Tom got home, he found his father in the parlor playing solitaire. His mother was in the back of the apartment
darning socks. Bill was evidently out at a movie with his girl,
and he guessed that his sister had a date with some clown or
other.

"Tom, you should have heard Father Moylan today. You'd
have liked what he had to say," Mr. Malone said.

Tom couldn't understand his father. He couldn't make the
old man understand that he had sincere convictions. His father
had no sense of him. He guessed that he might just say that his
father had no sense—period.

"He was good. He's a great man," the father said.

"That unctuous hypocrite!" Tom said, angry both because
of his father's estimate of the radio priest and his father's lack
of perception of him.

"Now, Tom, he's a priest," the father said.

"And I still say that he's an unctuous hypocrite trading in
shameless demagogy," Tom said.

"You didn't hear him today. How do you know what he
said?"

"I've heard enough of his sermons to know what he is," Tom
said.

"What?"

"He's an economic, political, and historic illiterate. If he
doesn't lie, then he's an ignoramus. He doesn't tell the people

the truth about the depression and its causes, about Russia, or about anything," Tom said.

"Tom, you're just a goddamned fool," the father said.

"Listen, Father, why in hell do you have to tell me about that guy? I'm not interested in him. I don't believe him. I know that he is wrong," Tom said.

"Tom, you better stop reading those damn fool books of yours."

"Thanks for the advice," Tom said ironically.

"You don't have to be so snotty. After all, you know, you're only a kid. There's a lot of people in the world that know more than you do," the father said.

Tom looked at his father in disgust. He didn't know whether to hate his father, laugh at him, or pity him.

"I mean it," the father said.

"Listen, I'm telling you Father Moylan is dangerous and misleading."

"You don't need to be an insulting pup," the father said.

He got to his feet and, trembling with anger, faced his son. Tom thought that the old man was going to take a poke at him. If he did, what would he do? He didn't want to hurt his father. Mr. Malone looked at Tom with undiminished anger. Then his anger seemed to change into bewilderment. He sat down again.

"I don't understand you," he said hopelessly to his son.

Tom left the parlor and went to the bedroom he shared with his brother. As Bill was out, he could stay here and read a little while. He heard the old man going by in the hallway. Then, a mumble of conversation. He knew that his father and mother were discussing him. He might as well give up as far as the family was concerned. You couldn't put ideas into their heads. His family would become only so much more slag thrown aside by this system. Well, it wouldn't do that to him.

He lay on his bed and read Karl Marx's *Capital*.

1938-1939

After the Sun Has Risen

IN PARIS, Colonel Leonard, director of the Aid Society, told us that he was sending back an invalid American woman, a writer. He asked us to look after her during the trip.

We did not see Agatha Stallings until we were on board. A paralyzed woman was carried up the gangplank on a chair. She screamed and moaned. I had only a passing glance at her, and she seemed to me to be old. Stewards hustled her into a third-class stateroom. I was certain that this was the woman of whom Colonel Leonard had spoken.

The prospect of our voyage immediately became gloomy. I felt that no one could leave Paris without a feeling of sadness and regret—even though the crossing had promised us a brief respite between one period of poverty and worry and a new one we must face in New York. The voyage was scheduled to last seven days. During that time I could eat without worrying where I would get the money to pay for it. I would face no landlords nor hotelkeepers. I would not have to run past grocery stores because of unpaid bills as I had had to do when living on the Rue de la Glacière. I would not even worry over the crisis in America. I would have one week of good food, work, and forgetfulness. Such hopes had seemed like a compensation for our departure from Paris. Then I would land in New York with scarcely enough money for one week's lodging, and the same old problems would have to be faced.

And now I feared that we would be saddled with this poor woman.

II

We had been assigned to a stateroom next to her. When we settled in our room, we heard her moaning. We made inquiries and learned definitely that she was the woman whom we were to look after. We did not see her the first day out. She was ill, and it was inadvisable for anyone to visit her. During the first night at sea I was awakened several times by her shrieks. The second day was Sunday, and we visited her after breakfast. After we had introduced ourselves, she told us her name, said that she was glad to see us, and remarked that at one time she had written a great deal for women's magazines. She mentioned the name of her divorced husband, a well-known popular painter of whom I had heard. He took care of their twelve-year-old son, but contributed nothing to her support.

She was in her late thirties, or possibly her early forties. My first impression of her had been false. Her face was plain and round. She was pug-nosed. Her straight brown bobbed hair fell over her forehead in bangs. The left side of her face, especially around the mouth, was twisted by paralysis. Her left arm and left leg were like dead things attached to a living body. Looking at her, I reflected that while she had never been pretty, she must have been attractive before she had been stricken. She had gentle, soft brown eyes. And she had no teeth.

From the first moment that she had arrived on board, she had difficulties with the stewardess and the stewards. Her stewardess was a tall, gawky Dutch woman who was suffering from a cold and who became seasick from the moment the boat left the harbor of Boulogne-sur-Mer. She spoke only Dutch and understood no other language. Agatha tried talking to her in English, in French, and in German. It was in vain. Her difficulties with the stewardess made her the more fretful. Nothing satisfied her. She was cooped up in a narrow cabin. The light was so bad that she could scarcely read. The ship

rolled too much. She was tortured by fears and obsessions. She
was being mistreated and neglected. In Paris she had been confined in a hospital for one year, and she claimed that she had
been treated badly because she had no money. She had had several attacks of brain fever, and two strokes. The last had been
severe, and she was a permanent cripple. She had hated
the hospital where she had been confined and now, returning
to America, she was put off in this dingy inner cabin on D
deck. She feared that the boat would sink, and that if it did,
no one would come to save her. She would die, trapped like a
rat on a sinking ship. And even if she did survive the voyage,
she was returning to a family she hated and with whom she
had had little contact for over two years. What would be her
fate in America? She spoke of these matters on the first morning we visited her. And because she was so nervous, so upset,
so obsessed, she poured forth all her wrath on the stewardess.

Whenever Agatha wanted any attention, she rang the bell
incessantly. The stewardess would answer the call as promptly
as she could, but Agatha was impatient. The stewardess would
struggle to understand what she said. Agatha would scream
in three languages. Often she would ring merely because she was
lonesome and afraid. Then she would complain that she
was uncomfortable. If she were sitting up, she wanted to be
put back in her berth. If she were in her berth, she wanted to
be put into a chair. If her arm were strapped, she wanted it
unstrapped; if it were unstrapped, she needed it strapped. She
wanted the bedpan. She was hungry. She was ill. She wanted
to know what time it was. She wanted to know why the boat
rolled and tossed so much. Agatha had ceaseless needs, real and
imaginary. Hating the stewardess as she did, unable to talk
to the woman in a mutually understandable language, she often
rang for her merely to have a human being in her stateroom
for a few moments.

Agatha's condition constantly grew worse. The voyage
seemed like an eternity to her. The seven hopeless days of ocean
travel she faced seemed like seven times seven. She was always
asking what time it was. And then, on being told, she would

moodily calculate how much longer she must be on the ship. She became more and more obsessed with the fear that she would die on board, or else that she would be drowned. She was most obsessed at night. Every night she screamed, awakening all passengers within hearing distance. And during the night she would call for the stewardess again and again. Rubbing her sleep-filled eyes and sniffling, the Dutch woman would rush to Agatha. Agatha really needed nothing. She would talk. The stewardess would look at her, puzzled. Sometimes the stewardess would bring the bedpan. Agatha would fling it aside with her good arm. She would point to her suitcase. The stewardess would lay it on the bed. Agatha would search through her few belongings, trying to find something that would serve as an excuse for the call she had made. For the nights were unbearable to her. She would lie alone in the darkness, trying to sleep. The humming motors, the rolling ship with its many noises added to the imaginary terrors that assailed her. Finally, after screams, visits, disturbances, she would demand that her light be left on. She would lie awake, trembling and alone.

The stewards spoke English, and Agatha was continually pestering them. They were forced to listen to long complaints. Nothing was right. She demanded that the purser come to see her. She complained to him. At night there was too much noise in the corridor and she couldn't sleep. Her calls were never answered promptly, and sometimes when she needed immediate attention she was forced to wait fifteen minutes or longer after she had rung the bell. Everything was done to make her more uncomfortable. And here she was, a poor sick woman treated worse than dogs usually were. When she got to New York she was going to report all the employees on the ship to the Society for the Prevention of Cruelty to Animals. Suddenly, in the midst of these scenes with the purser, she would break down and cry like a baby. He would stand over her, embarrassed, fingering his hat, hopelessly trying to calm and console her. She would shake with sobs. He would stare at her, not knowing what to say or what to do. He would promise her that all her complaints would be investigated, and he would get out of her presence as quickly as possible. The next day she would demand that he return to hear what she had to say, and she would raise such a rumpus that he had to come.

III

Agatha often told us about the hospital where she had been confined in Paris. She hated it and said that she had been treated as badly as she was being treated on the boat. Her bed had been too small. She had been forced to lie on an uncomfortable bed for an entire year. And whenever the nurses had come to change her sheets, they had left her lying exposed, often for hours; she did not understand yet how she had not contracted pneumonia and died because of these exposures. She could have stood the negligence, but there had even been a plot against her. People in the hospital had been planning to kill her. When she had learned of this, she had gotten in touch with the Aid Society and demanded that they arrange for her immediate return to America. Had she not done this, she claimed that she would already be dead. But who wanted her in this world? She asked this question many times, and whenever she did, she broke into tears.

She felt that her return to her family was the final humiliation of her life. She had gone abroad several years ago despite their strong disapproval. Soon they would have their revenge on her. They would rub it into her. Her brother-in-law was self-righteous and conventional. He had warned her against going to France. When she was back home, he would remind her, every minute of the day, of the warnings he had given her. He owned a profitable shoe store in New York, and she talked as if he were very well off. She said that he could afford to take care of her. He had to do it. She would return and allow herself to be dumped on him, and if he didn't like it, he could lump it. She was not sorry that she had gone to France. She had first sailed in 1922. For a while she had made pretty good money writing. And she had had a wonderful time. She was pitiful when she talked of her days in Paris. the parties that had lasted until dawn and sometimes longer, the crazy things that she and her friends had done, drunken escapades, the fun of meeting new people as Americans were constantly coming and leaving, the endless round of pleasures. Every day had been like a holiday; for a while, every day had seemed like the 14th of July. She remembered most fondly trips she and friends had taken in the early morning to the markets at Les Halles; they would all be drunk and they would go around looking at the fruits and meats and vegetables, talking to the workers and peasants, singing ribald songs, getting into arguments with the *flics*, and then they would end up having onion soup in a little restaurant. Yes, she had always loved the cool sharp dawns of Paris, especially when she had had a little liquor in her. And her love affairs. She did not regret these either. And the long days sitting in the sun in front of the cafés of Montparnasse. And the wild trips about Europe when the exchange favored the American dollar.

"You know, I had a grand time," she said repeatedly when she talked of these times.

While she talked, I would look at her, watching her poor face, observing her broken body. There would be little for one to say. All one could do was to try and cheer her up, to help her pass the hours which seemed so long and so monotonous.

We used to see her several times a day, and we would tell her about everything that happened in third class. We described the passengers and recounted what they did and what they said. Our anecdotes would sometimes amuse her, but not for long. She could not keep her mind off herself. She could not forget the fears that worked like moles in her mind. She tried to gain a vicarious sense of participation in life from the gossip we carried to her and she would seem to enjoy herself, but then, without warning, she would shake with sobs.

We ate at the same table with an old Dutchman, and we told her about him. At every meal he would glance about the dining salon and count the number of vacant chairs. With a twinkle in his eye he would remark on the number of passengers who were seasick, and then he would tell us that he

had made forty crossings and had never once been seasick. He
thought that I was a man because I, also, did not suffer from
seasickness. His appetite was prodigious, and Agatha always
wanted to know what he ate. She was particularly amused
when I told her of the night at dinner when he had put away
six bowls of pea soup, one after the other. I also described the
stolidity of most of the Dutch passengers. They would eat
enormous meals, and then they would sit, rarely even talking.
She detested the Dutch, because of her experiences with the
Dutch stewardess. On board there was an old Roumanian
woman who wore native costumes. No one else could speak
Roumanian, and she flitted about like a bird, suspicious of
everyone. At first she had been afraid to enter the dining
salon, and then, to eat. With the help of sign language, the
waiters had finally convinced her that she could eat as much
as she pleased, at no extra cost. And there were two buxom
Lithuanian orphan girls who were going to live with an aunt
in America. They were both convinced that they would marry
rich Americans as soon as they landed. Two callow Lithuanian
boys, en route to cousins in New Jersey, followed them around
the deck like faithful dogs. The two lads had no money, and
always looked wistfully at anyone smoking a cigarette. Once
they asked the girls to buy them cigarettes, and the girls had
answered them so salaciously that the boys had blushed from
ear to ear. Another passenger was a fat forty-year-old Lithuanian who had been a bartender and apparently the keeper of a
brothel in America. He had returned to the old country with
his pockets full of money. In his native village he had married
a pretty girl who was returning to America with him. Married eight months, she was already six months pregnant. Her
husband was worried, lest her condition affect their marital
life. He solicited the advice of every man on board about what
he should do. Agatha laughed when I quoted what he had said
to me:

"Jesus Christ, if we have to stop, then she will have to have
one room in New York and I will have another room. Jesus
Christ, we can't stop."

Another Lithuanian woman always talked about child-bearing and she boasted many times:

"Every nine months I lay a child just like a chicken lays an egg."

But after we had regaled Agatha with ship gossip, she would grow sad. A far-off look would come into her eyes. Once, in such a mood, she said:

"So different! So different from my first trip across. I went first class. We never went to bed until dawn. We had a grand crowd. Because of that trip there must have been at least three divorces."

She talked about that voyage, describing how they had all been gay tourists, drinking, dancing, carousing, without a care in the world, while before them had been France, Paris, a magic city of freedom, of dreams and joys they couldn't know in America. She stopped talking. She stared past us at the wall, moody.

"And now I am going home to my family," she said ironically.

IV

From the second day out, Agatha had begun worrying lest her brother-in-law fail to meet her at the pier. Colonel Leonard had sent him a cable, describing Agatha's condition and naming the ship on which she would arrive, and the brother-in-law had cabled back that he would meet her. But Agatha did not believe it. No sooner would we seem to have convinced her that this fear was groundless than she would again give way to it. She fretted and tormented herself until it became an obsession. Dwelling upon her fear, she would sometimes let out a piercing scream. Someone would go to her. She would be in tears. She would ask what could she do if no one met her. She might be left deserted on an empty ship, and there would be no one to bring her food or the bedpan.

In Paris she had had a young French lover, and she spoke of how kind, how wonderful, how loyal he had been to her. When she had been deserted and forgotten by almost all other friends, he had visited her in the hospital regularly, often bringing her flowers. Every morning she scrawled out a letter to him. Invariably she would remember, after sealing the envelope, that she had forgotten to say something in the letter, and then she would write an added message on the back of the envelope. She put these letters away in her suitcase to be mailed when we reached port. She did not trust any employee on the ship and was convinced they would steal the letters were she to mail them while en route.

The ship's doctor visited Agatha at least once a day. She begged him to arrange to have her transferred to the ship's hospital in the first-class section. Blandly, he said that this was impossible because there were only male attendants in the hospital. She answered that anything would be better than for her to continue where she was. Growing evasive, he said that he would see what he could do. She asked him why it wouldn't be possible to assign a stewardess to the hospital to take care of her. He repeated that he would see what he could do. Nothing was done. Joining with several other passengers, we protested and made several efforts to get her transferred to the hospital. We received the same answers she had been given. The doctor administered morphine to her when she was in pain and unable to sleep. She asked for more. Not getting it, she cried and screamed. After the third day, she called repeatedly for the doctor, and when he did come, she demanded more morphine.   •

All the way across the Atlantic, she complained about the food. Because of her condition, she was on a strict diet and, in addition, there were only a few foods that she could eat because she had no teeth. She was given beef broths, scrambled eggs, soft boiled eggs, ice cream, tea and toast. She complained that her food was not served to her on time and that she even was forced to wait hours for meals while she lay famished. Bored by the monotonous life she lived in her stateroom, she started clamoring for lunch every morning from ten o'clock on. She had no sooner received tea in the afternoon than she would begin ringing and asking for dinner.

During the trip Agatha enjoyed most the times when she talked with us about Paris. Often she would tell us how glad she was that she had gone there. And then, almost in the same breath, she would moan and tell us how sorry she was ever to have gone abroad. If she hadn't, she would not be in the condition in which we found her. Then she would show us a photograph of her twelve-year-old son. She would look at him fondly, and tears would come. She had not seen him for several years. She was certain that the boy's father had turned him against her. She might never see him again. And he was her boy. Suddenly her mood would change. She would dry her eyes and, with defiance in her voice, she would declare that she was glad she had gone to Paris, and that no one could take away from her her Parisian memories and experiences. She would ask us if we knew various Americans who lived on the Left Bank, and she would talk about them. Feebly clutching after these memories, she would ask me to get her suitcase for her. I would set it on her bed. She would bring out little trinkets and show them to us, a crushed dead rose, a menu card from the Café Select, a few picture postcards of Paris scenes. Looking at these souvenirs, she said one day that as soon as she was at home again, and comfortably cared for, she was going to write a book about her life in Paris. She hadn't written for years, but she knew that she could.

As the days passed, she became ever more fretful, ever more obsessed. She rang for service and attention more frequently. She found fresh reasons for complaint. She demanded morphine again and again. She had books sent to her from the ship's library, but she was unable to concentrate on reading. She wrote more letters to her French lover. She asked us more often if we really believed that she would be met at the pier, and she would not believe our confident assurances. Finally she became so obsessed that she demanded that we radio her family from sea. Although I had very little money, I sent the radio and paid for it. We received an answer that she would be met. But still she was not assured. Twenty minutes after the answer had come, she was sobbing in her berth and told us she was sure she would not be met.

As we approached New York, the third-class passengers became excited. A sense of this excitement was conveyed to Agatha by the people who visited her. She was morose. We told her how racial animosities had sprung up among the passengers. A Czech woman on board hated all other Slavs. The Poles warned us not to trust the Lithuanians. The Dutch said we should be careful of the Poles. The forty-year-old Litvak who was taking back two bottles of Lithuanian liquor, asked the purser if he would be allowed to bring it in. When he was told that he wouldn't, he became fearful lest he be arrested for violating the Prohibition Act and decided to have a party on board. He brought out the two bottles of liquor with herbs in it. It was so strong that almost no one could drink it. When I told this story to Agatha, she asked for a drink, but I said that he had thrown the bottles into the ocean. Then I told her how the stewardess had tried to get the Roumanian peasant woman to take a bath. The woman had fled from a bathtub and stood in the passageway near us, her arms folded, her face set with determination. Finally she had been inveigled into the tub, and had emerged from it as happy as a child. Then she had gone about the ship trying to tell everyone how she had liked her bath, and no one had understood her. But Agatha was too troubled to find amusement in anything.

The voyage came to an end. We arrived inside of New York Harbor on Saturday night, too late to dock. The ship rested off Sandy Hook, and all the passengers, except Agatha, lined the decks and looked off at the twinkling lights of New York. Agatha moaned all night. We docked at Hoboken early the next morning. Agatha was met by her sister and her brother-in-law. When she was carried down the gangplank, she screamed.

v

She had given me an address where she would be in New York. A few days after landing, I went to see her. I was told that she had been sent to a city hospital the day after her arrival. She had made the trip across the Atlantic to be transferred from a charity bed in one hospital to one in another, and there, perhaps, she would spend the remainder of her life.

1932-1942

The Fate of a Hero

<hr/>

I

PETERS WAS A HUSKY, almost ox-like young lad from Iowa. After arriving in Chicago, he moved around from job to job, until he was hired as a service-station attendant by the Nation Oil Company. He was accepted in May, too late to attend the Nation's annual school for new attendants. Hence his training was incomplete. Part of it consisted of lectures and inspirational talks delivered to him by Prevost, the Superintendent of Service Stations, and by others with less authority. For more than a half hour he sat in bewilderment while he was told what a large, what a great, and what a humanitarian corporation the Nation Oil Company was. For over ten minutes he listened while he was told how squarely the company treated all of its employees who served it and the public well. For fifteen minutes he sat while an assistant of Prevost told him that the company held its employees more dearly than did the union to which the service station employees and tank wagon drivers belonged. For an hour he was told that he must have vision, imagination, and ambition. Hearing big and unfamiliar words, he sat listening, shaking his head, as if he understood, nodding in acquiescence, adenoidally expressing his agreement in simple language. He sat through twenty minutes of exposition on the values, joys, and virtues of honesty, efficiency, and courtesy as well as the commercial and human value of politeness. His office instruction was finally completed with five minutes devoted to the cursory details of opening and closing a station,

98

to making audits, to preparing the money bag which was collected daily by the well-guarded armored trucks, to the company policy on shortages and other pertinent instructions. He was told:

"And if you ever get held up, offer no resistance. Obey the hold-up man's instructions quickly and to the letter. If he tells you to give him all the money you have, give it! If he orders you to open the safe, open it and hand over to him whatever money there is in the safe. If he says stand on your ear, you stand on your ear as promptly and as efficiently as you can. Obey him to the letter! Nation doesn't want you to incur personal injuries trying to defend its money and its property against armed men. We're properly insured. We lose nothing when our stations are held up."

Peters was sent out to a large and busy station on Marquette Boulevard to be broken in by experienced attendants. He was instructed to report at seven in the morning on his first day. He was down at the station and waiting for it to be opened at twenty minutes to seven. The regular attendants at seven appeared with a key and sleepily opened up. The station manager, Kagan, was on an early shift that morning and he took Peters in hand. He told Peters to warm up by cleaning the crankcase pit. Peters didn't know how to do it, so he was given a can of gasoline and a brush and told to use some elbow grease. He did, for three hours, and the pit was cleaner than it had been in months. He was given kerosene and told to scrub the stone floor of the station. He objected in his drawl voice, saying that he'd been instructed at the office not to use kerosene or gasoline inside the station.

"I'll take the responsibility," Kagan said.

"Well, sir, I can't do that. I was told not to," Peters answered.

"You were sent to me to be broken in, weren't you?"

"Yes, sir."

"All right, go ahead, Peters!"

"Well, sir, now, I was told not to use kerosene or gasoline inside the station."

"Listen, it's my can if anything happens. Nothing will, and this floor's got to be cleaned. Go ahead!"

Peters sulkily obeyed, working on the floor until one o'clock. During a lull in the business, Kagan and Morrisey, the other attendant, watched him, smiling and amused.

"Dumb but earnest," Kagan said.

"No, dumber, more earnest," Morrisey said.

"The hayseeds sure stick out of his ears plenty," Kagan said.

"Out of his ears? His brains are hayseed. If a cow ever sees him, the cow'll come up and start chewing, thinkin' that the lad is new-mown hay," Morrisey laughed.

Peters gulped his lunch in ten minutes. Then, while Kagan sat on a chair eating slowly and Morrisey waited on the customers who drove in, Peters was told where the cleaning rags and the Bon Ami were. He was set to work polishing all the brass in the station. This task kept him busy until three o'clock, when his eight hours were up. The fire guns, the doorknobs, the faucets on the oil pumps were all shining. He left while the attendants were checking up and turning the station over to the afternoon shift.

"Who's the rookie?" asked Kanaly, one of the attendants coming on duty.

"Hiram Hayseed," Kagan said.

"Boy, you sure saved us plenty of worry, breaking him in. I saw the crankcase pit. And, boy, look at them faucets," Kanaly said.

"He's a horse. Before he's transferred from here, he's gonna have our place lookin' like a palace," Kagan said.

On the station grounds, in back of the drive, there was a large plot of grass. On his second morning, Peters worked on it with the lawn mower, and Kagan and Morrisey joked back and forth about how Slicker Peters might think it was home and start calling the cows any minute. They had a good time laughing at him while he plodded back and forth with the mower. After the grass was cut, he was ordered to pull out all the weeds, which he did, slowly, crawling about on his hands

and knees. Then he swept the stone driveway. He scrubbed
the woodwork. He started in cleaning the canned stock and
polishing the tops of the cans. On his third morning he finished
this chore and was told to wash the windows. After window-
washing, he scrubbed the walls and ceiling of the station and
then, the lavatory. On his fourth day, he hoped that he might
be taught how to use the pumps, how to drain a hose properly
when he pumped gasoline, possibly how to pour oil into a
motor, and even how to drain a crankcase. Then, too, he
wanted actual practice in making out an audit. He looked forward to the time when he could act like Kagan and the others,
able to know that he was really broken in and a regular attendant, with a money-changer on a belt strung around his overalls, the uniform cap on the side of his head. Instead of learning how to do these things, he cleaned the pumps. His next
task was to take all the globes down from the posts around the
grounds and to wash them. At one o'clock he finished his
lunch and felt that now he had no more of such work ahead
of him and maybe they'd teach him how to wait on the customers. He was mistaken. Kagan told him to scrub the bricks
on the outside of the station.

As he left for the day, there was a telephone call from downtown and he was told to report the next afternoon at three
o'clock at the station located on Sixty-first Street and Langley
Avenue. He went to his rooming house, pleased. He had been
told that it was a two-man station. He would be alone and a
boss while alone there, just like Mr. Kagan was. He walked off,
smiling. The supervisor drove in just after Peters left. He
nosed around the station and told the boys that they had the
neatest station in the district. He complimented them and said
that Prevost would be told of their neatness.

II

Peters was alone. His partner had made the audit, given him
some hasty, perfunctory advice, and left. He had to learn for
himself. He was alone in a station for the first time. He tried
to feel as sure of himself as Kagan and the other boys did when

they waited on a customer. He was slow in giving service.
Gasoline was nineteen cents a gallon, and he had difficulty in
calculating rapidly the cost of odd gallons, three, four, seven.
He was not familiar with the stock, and on that first day every
motorist wanting motor oil was given Ford oil. He didn't know
what cars took medium, and what ones required heavy oil.
Also, during his first days, he usually spilled oil on the outside
of the motor whenever he poured it. Sometimes he also spilled
oil on the running boards. Many customers got angry with him.
When he drained the hose after pumping gasoline into a tank,
he would often waste half of what was to be drained. One customer accused him of having taken the varnish off his car
with spilled gasoline. When he poured water into a radiator,
he sometimes gave the hood and the metal surface a bath. Several times he forgot to wipe the metal after spilling water on
it, and the customers, not noticing this, drove off. One returned
the next day, complaining angrily, claiming that Peters was
responsible for having rusted the metal surface around his
radiator cap. Three others came back to beef and declare that
he'd sold them gasoline and forgotten to screw the caps back
on the gas tank. He had difficulty in draining his first crank-
cases, and almost stripped several bolts. He was never sure what
wrenches he should use. He learned by blundering, wasting
time, annoying customers who were accustomed to speed and
efficiency. In his daily audits he sometimes gave promise of in-
venting his own system of arithmetic and accounting. And before he had been on the job a week, he was visited by a confidence man, a neatly dressed fellow who looked as if he might
be a businessman, a salesman, one of any number of occupa-
tions. The fellow asked Peters to change a twenty-dollar bill
and light-fingered ten dollars out of Peters during the transac-
tion.

However, these were all the errors and mistakes of a begin-
ner. They were all overlooked by his superiors, all except the
shortage caused by the ten dollars he had been tricked out of.
Peters had to pay that. The company, however, knew its man.
Peters was steady, plodding, honest, hard-working. He pa-

tiently worked to keep his station clean. He learned from his mistakes. He was the kind of employee the company wanted. He could be trained. He gave evidence of being reliable. He obeyed orders to the letter. When he greeted customers, he never deviated from the formula he had been instructed to use.

"Good morning, sir," he would say, approaching a car that had parked by the pumps.

"May I fill your tank?" he would ask next.

The customer would tell what he wanted, and Peters, once he learned to work efficiently, would then promptly fill the order.

"May I test your oil?"

If the customer answered yes, Peters would look at the oil gauge inside the hood, and sometimes, he was able to sell a quart or two of oil. He was scrupulous, and if the oil gauge indicated that the car did not need oil, he made no effort to sell it.

"May I service you with water and air?" he would then say, and since this service was free, he would usually be told to check the radiator and the tires.

He tried to sell as much as possible to every customer. He even tried to sell specialty goods to company salesmen who stopped in the station for gasoline. He became a man to soothe the heart of a superintendent and a supervisor, men who were continuously faced with the problems of handling lazy and dishonest employees, attendants who did not believe the pep talks they were given, attendants who could not sell as much motor oil as they were urged, pressed, driven into selling. Peters wasn't clever, flashy, quick in repartee like the fraternity men from the colleges and universities who were often hired as attendants. But the college men frequently, very frequently, had to be fired for dishonesty. He was just a yokel. He was to receive the regular and standardized pay which, after three months, automatically became one hundred and forty dollars a month. He considered that sum to be very good pay, pay which enabled him to save money. He was satisfied with his job. He was prepared to park at it for the remainder of his life. After the early days when he was learning, he gave no grounds for complaints. He kept his station spotless. By perseverance, he sold oil, and specialties. He did not run shortages. He was caught in no infractions of the rules.

III

One quiet night after he had been working for about five months, two young fellows in a high-powered Marmon drove into the station and parked by one of the gas pumps. They ordered ten gallons of gasoline and got out of the car while Peters prepared to put the pump into the tank.

"Mister, it's against the rules to service you with gasoline while the motor's runnin'," Peters said in his slow, drawling manner.

"Go ahead, buddy!" one of the fellows ordered.

"No, sir, I can't disobey orders," Peters said.

"Come on, we're in a hurry!"

"I'm sorry, sir, but it's against the rules."

The second fellow stopped the motor. Peters pumped in the ten gallons.

"Two quarts of medium oil."

Peters lifted the hood and noticed the gauge.

"I don't think you need oil," Peters said, looking up at them.

"Go ahead and get the oil, buddy. We're buyin'. It's our car."

He walked toward the station house to get the oil. They followed him. Just as he stepped inside the door, a revolver was jammed into his back.

"Get inside, keep your trap shut, do what we tell you!"

He nonchalantly obeyed. He was told to hand over his money. He handed them his money-changer and the small roll of bills which he had in his overall pocket for change. The second fellow pocketed the bills, emptied the money-changer, and then pocketed the silver.

"Open the safe and give us the rest, you dumb sonofabitch!" the fellow with the revolver said.

Peters bent down and dialed the safe, opening it. The fellow

with the revolver kept him covered, and his partner bent down
to grab the money from the safe. Peters noticed the face of the
fellow with the revolver for the first time. He was a kid and
couldn't be over nineteen. The partner took the tin box; he
dallied with it, counting the money before he put it away.

"Hurry up!" the fellow with the gun said.

Peters saw that he was nervous and that his hand was shaking a bit as he pointed the gun.

"One bat outta you, dope, and you get plugged. You was too
wise by the pump. There's heat in this gat, and you'll get it if
you blink your dumb eyes. Hurry up, Mac!" the kid with the
gun said, turning to his partner as he addressed him.

Peters swung quickly, crashing him flush on the jaw with a
powerful left fist. The kid fell, the gun dropping from his
hand. The other bandit was off balance. Peters hastily put him
out with a left uppercut. The first one tried to crawl a few feet
to reach the gun, but Peters barred his way. He arose totter-
ingly, and one more punch drove him onto an oil barrel, helpless. He slipped to the floor, unconscious.

When the police arrived, Peters was sitting on the desk, smiling, gun in hand, casually discussing the incident with a group
of curiosity seekers. The two bandits were on the floor, both
battered with swollen faces, one of them still groggy, the other
sitting with lowered head, whimpering, begging to be let go.
They were taken off in a patrol wagon, and in due time they
received ten years in the penitentiary.

Peters' picture appeared in the morning paper. When he saw
it, he felt like a famous man. He was one of those who, along
with President Coolidge and others, had their pictures in the
paper. He clipped it and mailed it back home to the folks in
Iowa. He was called down to the main office. Prevost congratulated him and told him what a hero he was. Then the
Superintendent admonished him mildly. He reminded Peters
that the company wanted its employees not to resist holdups.
The company money was insured against robbery and burglary. It was too risky for an attendant to resist men with guns
these days when there was so much robbery and killing. It was

particularly dangerous to resist young fellows with guns. They were shaky and nervous, and often they shot and killed out of fear. Peters told Prevost that these bandits had been young, and that the one with the gun had sure been shaky. He had seen that, and had known it was his chance. So he hit him. Peters received a reward of five hundred dollars. Also, the Marmon proved to be a stolen car, and the owner gave him a reward of fifty dollars. Peters privately enjoyed his role as a hero, but he went on working in the same placid, dutiful, conscientious manner.

He was transferred to a larger station where he received better commissions on oil because of the larger volume of business. Several uneventful months passed. He worked day by day in the usual manner. One evening just after he had locked up the station and was walking across the drive, a gang of fellows rushed upon him. They were pals of the two bandits who had been sent up the road because of Peters. They went at him in a gang. He fought back sturdily, determinedly, with courage. He was overpowered, hit over the head with a monkey wrench, kicked, battered, and left lying half-conscious in the drain pit. The next morning he was transferred to another station, and reported there the next afternoon as if nothing had happened. His face was marred with swellings and court plaster. Three more months passed, and again at night after he had closed up he was beaten by the same gang.

He was transferred to the north side. One night when he was alone and there was little business, a bandit came in with a gun. Peters hit him over the head with a stove poker and finished him off with a right to the jaw. Peters' picture was in the rotogravure section of the Sunday papers, and his previous exploit was also described. He received a second reward of five hundred dollars. He was congratulated by his bosses. He was also warned, this time more emphatically. They reminded him of the beatings he had received because he was responsible for having sent those two young bandits to Joliet. He was told that it was very dangerous to take chances with these gangs that were about nowadays. Why had he done it again? The money would have been repaid. Why be so foolish?

"Well, sir," he said to Prevost, "I just didn't think. There he was with the gun, and the stove poker was a-lyin' right beside me. I looked in his eye. He seemed like he was afraid. I just didn't think. I grabbed the poker and I laid it over his head, and then I hit him. He dropped as if he didn't know what had happened to him. Well, sir, I just didn't think of what you told me the last time."

His partner told him he was a sap, and Peters repeated that he hadn't thought. He was unpopular with all the other attendants with whom he worked. He kept the station too clean. He sold too much oil. He was too conscientious, and they claimed that he made it hard for them. Behind his back they called him "the boss's pet."

The third bandit he had beaten up also received ten years in the penitentiary. Peters now had two gangs after him. He was placed in a busy station on Sheridan Road where there was always more than one attendant on duty. A city detective was assigned to the station to guard him from any future beatings. He was sternly told that he must beat up no more bandits. It was too damn risky. He should have learned his lesson. Several times, while he was off duty, he was caught by gangs and beaten. When he reported to work with blackened eyes and court plaster, he said that it had been in a fight over a girl. His partners always smiled at these excuses. They felt that he deserved what he'd gotten, protecting other men's money when it wasn't even necessary. He was just a damn fool yokel. A few more months passed. One evening, around six o'clock, he was alone at the station. His partner had gone down a block to eat. Peters and his bodyguard were caught by a gang and beaten into unconsciousness.

Immediately after this beating, it happened that the Service Station department was reorganized. The stations were divided into divisions of ten, and a supervisor was placed in charge of each division. Peters was promoted to the title of supervisor. He was given a company car to use in his district, and his sal-

ary was one hundred and sixty dollars a month. He seemed to
be headed for further promotions. Despite his foolishness in
taking guns away from holdup men, he was thought of most
highly in the main office. However, he was not really qualified
to be a supervisor. He was on the job sometimes as much as
fourteen hours a day, and he watched his men so closely that
he demoralized them. Prevost liked his supervisors to watch
the men, but he discovered that Peters carried it to an extreme.
It was useless to keep firing attendants and have to break in
new ones. It was useless to drive the attendants jittery. They
were on edge all the time. They were often driven, out of
sheer resentment, to infractions of the rules. One of the best
men, a service-station manager, had even threatened to resign
if he were forced to continue working under Peters. So Peters
was transferred to the main office and put in charge of handling
supplies and the supply vouchers that went to the service stations. He could not do this work. At the end of two months,
two clerks had to be put to work straightening out the mess he
had made of the records. Prevost sent him back to the stations.
He placed Peters in one on West Madison Street, assigned him
to work days only, and an Irish detective protected him while
he was on duty. Six busy months followed. There had been no
attempted assaults made on Peters. It seemed as if the gangs
had decided that they'd taken enough revenge on him. The
detective was withdrawn and sent to the vice squad. Peters
was alone. His station, as usual, was spotless. His partner
silently complained and griped because of the way Peters
worked. He was painfully conscientious. He was never short
in his audits. He never cheated the customers. He always tried
to sell oil. He was a good man. Then, one Sunday morning,
just after he had opened the station, he was held up by four
bandits and found lying on the floor, unconscious.

"I just opened her up when they came in on me. They got
me with my back turned. I knocked one of them down, and
then, well, sir, something hit me on the head and that was all,"
he told the cops, feeling a bump behind his ears.

Prevost called Peters into the office the next morning.

"Peters, you're an exemplary attendant," Prevost said, and Peters felt pleased because of this praise. "You've been honest, efficient, reliable. You have a good record in every way. You're a man with real guts and personality. You're the kind of a man that Nation wants in its service. You haven't one black mark on your record."

"Well, sir, I always just go along and try to do my work as best I can," Peters drawled.

Prevost's face clouded. He said, with emotion in his voice, that despite Peters' fine record, despite his high integrity, they couldn't keep him. To do so would only endanger his own life as well as the company property. Even the insurance company was complaining. Much as he regretted it, Prevost had to discharge him. They had all warned him not to resist holdups. And for some reason he wouldn't take such advice. He persisted in fighting every time he was held up.

"Do you like to fight?" Prevost asked.

"No, sir, I just don't think. It seems they're trying to take something away from me, and so I let them have it. Afterward, I say to myself, 'Now, didn't Mr. Prevost tell me not to do that?' I always feel sorry after I do it, honest I do, Mr. Prevost."

Prevost told Peters that he had never discharged a man with the same feeling of regret. But it had to be done. Peters was too much of a liability. However, he offered to give him the finest recommendation, and he was certain that Peters would find no difficulty in getting new employment.

Peters left the office in a forlorn mood. He thought of going back to Iowa, but instead he looked for a new job. His talents were not left unrewarded. A detective agency which specialized in furnishing strike-breakers heard of him, learned of his record. He was hired by this agency at a better salary than he had received as a service station attendant.

1930-1937

Whoopee for the New Deal!

THE LOHRMANS had come over to see the Robinsons, who lived on the southeast side of Chicago. The two couples were going to have a blowout. John Robinson and Henry Lohrman had been friends for years; before their marriage, in the days when they had been gay blades, and after their marriages the friendship had continued. Kate Robinson had taken a liking to Myrtle Lohrman, and they saw one another regularly. John Robinson was a well-set-up man in his late forties; his hair was gray, but he looked vigorous, healthy, and well fed. Henry was about John's age. He was sandy-haired, youthful in appearance, but beginning to get bald. He spoke haltingly and acted like a man without self-confidence. Kate Robinson was a stringy woman, plain in looks; she had never been pretty. Myrtle Lohrman, the youngest of the foursome, was forty years old. She was chunky, dark-skinned, a hard-looking woman.

"Well, Henry Lohrman, how about a little snifter?" John asked, the four of them sitting in the sun parlor of the Robinson house.

Henry chuckled.

"That's a question. You know me, John," Henry said.

"And the ladies? Ginger ale?" John asked, turning from his wife to Myrtle Lohrman and smiling graciously, showing his fine white teeth.

"Say! Whenever my old man starts oiling his gullet, I'm right there to go along with him. The last time he started snift-

ing his snifters, I drank him under the table and had to drive
the car home. I don't know yet how we got home, but anyway, I got him to bed," Myrtle said in her husky voice.

"Well, having had long experience with Henry, I know how
bottomless his stomach is, so I can guess just about how many
both of you must have had," John said.

Henry beamed with the pride of accomplishment.

"And I drink him bottoms up on every glass," Myrtle
bragged.

"That's the kind of a missus a man should have. Like Kate
here, she's a good wife, a good mother, and a swell drinking
pal," John said.

"I always say a little drink and some fun now and then harms
no one," said Kate.

"Now that the new man in Washington has given us back
our beer, we ought to be gettin' back our whisky pretty soon,
too," Henry said.

"And he's gonna give us times like we had before so many of
us made the mistake of voting Hoover into the White House,"
John said.

"Say, you, here you make my mouth water for a drink and
then you go off and start talking politics. Come on, get busy,"
Myrtle said to John.

"I'll help you fix the drinks, John," Kate said.

"No help needed. There's no unemployment problem in this
house so far as that's concerned. In this house the old man
does that job," John said.

"How about me helpin'?" Henry asked, looking up at John
who had gotten to his feet.

"Say, old man, you and me are going snifter for snifter, and
no sneaking out in the kitchen to get ahead of me," Myrtle
said.

"I wasn't meaning to cheat on you, Myrtle," Henry said,
grinning slyly.

"That's why you're staying put," she said, and she reached
over and patted his cheek. She turned to Kate. "Kate, they

don't come any better than my old man here, but I gotta watch
him."

"Well, everybody keep their shirt on now, and I'll be right
back with something extra special," John said, walking out of
the parlor.

II

"Good stuff, John," Henry said, after having taken a drink
of Scotch and soda.

"Smuggled in from Canada. Good stuff, folks, isn't it?" John
said.

"You can bet your torn socks on that," Myrtle said, and she
drank; Henry's face showed his displeasure with the way his
wife talked.

"You know, Henry, it's too bad we couldn't go away together this year on our vacation, the way we did in other years.
But, then, these are damned hard times, and you feel it, and
feel it plenty, when you've got two kids in high school," John
said.

"Ours starts to high school next fall, and then, old man,
you'll be shelling out for Charlie," Myrtle said.

"Well, the way I look at it is this. You should give the young-
sters every chance you can to have a good time and some fun
while they've got the chance. They're only young once, and I
don't want my kids to be the kind that'll have to say later
on that when they were young they spent their youth getting
dust in their throats from books in a library," John said.

"If they have as good a time as we did, John, they won't
be complaining," Henry said.

"John, Junior, took his girl out to a dance tonight, and you
should have seen him getting ready. And my Sally's only fifteen, but she found herself a beau, a nice boy, and they went
down to the Belgian Village at the World's Fair," Kate said.

"Well, all my Charlie still thinks of is golf," said Myrtle.

"Yes, Henry, you know," John began reflectively, "I was
thinking of this the other day. Now, when you and I were
young, did I carry you home more times than you carried me?"

"Well, judging from my experiences with the old man, I'd say, John, that you did all of the lugging," Myrtle said.

"Say, I hold my liquor pretty good," Henry protested.

"Listen, if you think so, you listen to me, old baldy! Tonight, then, let me do the passin' out for a change, and you drive me home and put me to bed," Myrtle said.

"Yes, and I done that, too, for you," Henry said.

"Nice way for us fathers and mothers to be talking," John remarked, smiling.

"Well, as I always say, we all have only one life to live," Kate said.

"And, old man, remember this—you're a long time dead," Myrtle said, looking at Henry; she drank again, her actions emphatic.

"That's true. You're a long time dead," Henry said reflectively.

"Baldy, the mourner's bench is by the toilet seat. If you want to mourn, go there and mourn alone," Myrtle said.

Henry winced. He turned toward John immediately.

"John, it's almost like old times, isn't it? Except, of course, you've got gray hair, and I'm losin' mine," Henry said.

"He might be gray, but I'll bet he's got stuff left in him, huh, Kate?" Myrtle said, looking at Kate.

Kate blushed.

"This is giving early promise of being a rowdy evening," John said.

"This is mama's night off," Myrtle said, pointing her right index finger at her breast; she drank.

III

"You had a good vacation then anyway, huh, Henry?" John said after they had all gotten fresh drinks.

"Fine! We missed you, but it was fine. Fine!" Henry said.

"Well, business is so bad. But I'm hoping that Mr. Roosevelt is going to make a change. You know, if there's anything I regret in my life, it's that I gave my vote to Hoover twice," John said.

"Well, I don't know what's wrong, but I do know it's something. Many a time these days I say to myself that I'd have been better off if I'd got into something else besides the insurance business," Henry said.

"And, brother, how many times haven't I wished I wasn't a real estate man? Say, Henry, there have been times in the last year when I have looked at truck drivers, and even at coal men, and I've wished I could change places with them. They work every day and get their salary when pay day comes, and somebody else has got to worry about that salary," John said.

"You're both in the kind of business that everybody needs. Everybody has to live in a house, and the man with a family who doesn't take out insurance is a damned fool," Kate said.

"Kate, you know, that's so. I only wish the public would realize it. You know, my salesmen talk to a lot of people about life insurance, and then show them the facts and figures and advantages of being insured, and do you think they'll take out insurance? Not on your life," Henry said, his voice protesting and whining.

"Everybody knows he's got to live in a house, and does. This is my problem: how are you going to collect the rent from a lot of them?" John said. He took another drink.

"And just think! A few years ago John and I didn't have a worry in the world. Of course, we weren't millionaires or anything like that, but we weren't worried about the future and about givin' the best we could to our children. Buildings were going up, times were good, and we never thought about where an extra nickel would go," Kate said.

"Yes, them were the days when people paid rent," John said, smiling.

"A lot of them still do. I know we have to pay rent every month, and ouch, does it hurt! We signed a three-year-lease in good times and now, when you don't get the dollars so easy, we got to pay the same rent. I tried to get them to come down and, say, was I talking to a cold fish when I did! And eighty-five dollars a month rent these times is damned high," Myrtle said.

"You can't blame the fellow too much. Lots of people have gone broke and, you know, real estate men got to live, too. They got families. Look at us. We don't want to hurt any man. We just want to live, get along, have a few of the good things of life, give the best we can to our kids. Well, we got to live. We got to make them pay, or we don't live," John said.

"Of course you're right, John. But I still say my real estate man is a cold fish," Myrtle said.

"I don't know him personally," John said.

"It's the same in my game. If people don't pay on their policies, how are we gonna be able to pay their beneficiaries when they die? It's the old story all over again. You can't get blood out of a turnip," Henry said.

"That's the truth, every word of it," Kate said.

"But there's one thing you don't have to worry so much about in times like these, and that's your income tax," John said.

They laughed and sipped their liquor.

"You know, I was driving back from our vacation and I picked up a young fellow hitch-hiking, and know what he was? A Socialist," Henry said.

"A nut," Myrtle said.

"Well, let me tell you, I never met a Socialist before. I didn't know what they were like. Say, you know what he was? I never quite knew what Socialists were all about before, but now I do. Why, they're morons," Henry said.

"Well, I'm against the Socialists. They don't want private property and the home and religion. Kate and I, now, we're not particularly religious ourselves, but how is the mass of the people going to be kept in place and made to behave if they don't have religion and the fear of God in them? That's why I'm against Socialism," John said.

"They're morons," Henry said.

"I see by the papers that that stuff is being taught in some of the colleges and is affecting the young. Well, thank goodness, none of it is hurting my own children," Kate said.

"And I take credit for it, too. I don't want my kids to be

dunces, but I always say to 'em: 'Don't pay too much attention to stuffing yourself with books. Learn enough to make a
successful citizen out of yourself, and remember, too, that
you're only young once.' Henry and I were never the teacher's
pet, and we've got along pretty good in life," John said.

"You bet," Henry said, smiling.

"Daddy, I never married you for your brains," Myrtle said,
turning to her husband.

Henry frowned, and then looked aggrieved.

"Oh, now, now, daddy boy, don't be getting sad. You know
I think you're smart enough for your old woman," Myrtle
said.

"Aren't you premature?" John said, looking at Myrtle.

"What do you mean?" she asked.

"Calling yourself an old woman?" John said graciously.

"I got to drink to you for that. John Robinson, you're my
idea of a gentleman," Myrtle said; she raised her glass to him
and then emptied it.

"Well, what we gonna do tonight?" asked Henry.

"That's one question I'm smart enough to answer," Myrtle
said.

"Well, what?" asked Henry.

"You know, Henry, our girls are real sports," John inter-
jected.

"All compliments received here. Want a receipt?" asked
Myrtle.

"I mean where we gonna go?" asked Henry.

"We'll drive some place," John said.

"I ain't worried about the driving there. It's the driving back
that gives me the shivers. I want to die on my back and not
lose my maidenly beauty by being smashed against a telephone
post," Myrtle said.

"Well, we ain't had no accidents yet," Henry said.

"Here, lean over toward me, daddy," Myrtle said, stretch-
ing toward her husband.

He leaned forward, looking puzzled. She tapped him gently
on the head.

"I was knocking on wood," she said.

"I say drink up and let's have another," John said.

IV

"Say, John, what you think of this fellow Hitler that's gettin' himself a setup now over there in Germany?"

"Well, I tell you, Henry, I haven't been following what he's doing. I've been so busy and so worried about my own affairs, I haven't followed many things happening in the world the way I once did," John said.

"Neither have I. But I do say that he's giving the Jews what they got coming to 'em. I always said you got to watch the Jews," Henry said.

"Say, old man, if I ever get wind that you're running around with Jews, you'll hear from me," Myrtle said.

"No danger there," Henry said.

"Now, there's a Jewish family living next door to us, the Abelsons, and they are the nicest and the quietest people," Kate said.

"Well, there's exceptions to every rule," Henry said.

"Me, now, I take people as they come," Kate said.

"And that's just what I do myself. But I think this fellow Hitler's going to be a good thing. By putting the Jews in their place over there in Germany, he's gonna make the Jews over here see that they can't be gettin' too forward," Henry said.

"I never was against the Jews. I got a lot of good friends who are Jews, and I like 'em. I like 'em just as much as I do a lot of friends of mine who aren't Jews. But I got to admit it, because it's a fact, yes, I got to admit it whether I like it or not, that there are a lot of Jews in my business who aren't a credit to the real-estate game," John said.

"That's just the way I feel about it. That's why I say that, while I don't know nothing about Hitler, he might do us all some good by putting the Jews in their place. And then, of course, the Socialists, too. I told you already about the Socialist I met and what a moron he was," Henry said.

John looked at his watch.

"You're not getting sleepy, are you?" Myrtle asked him.

"The President is going to be on the radio in twenty minutes and I don't want to miss hearing what he's got to say," John said.

"God! Speeches when we're supposed to be having a party," Myrtle complained.

"We'll go right afterward," John said.

"Then you got to give me another drink or I won't listen. I let my old daddy here do the politics in this family and I don't like speeches," Myrtle said.

"We'll fix you up with a drink, Myrtle, and then the rest of us can hear the President talk," John said.

"Kate, do you like speeches?" asked Myrtle.

"Goodness me, I don't have time to know what it all means, what with my home, and marketing, and taking care of a husband and two children," Kate said.

John got up, collected the glasses, and went out to fix more drinks.

v

They heard the President deliver a radio address announcing the N.R.A., and describing what the N.R.A. would be. They sat for a moment in silence, glasses in hand, now and then taking a drink.

"Well, daddy, tell us about it. What do you think of it?" Myrtle asked, turning toward her husband.

"Me?" he responded like a man brought out of a revery, and not completely aware of the scene immediately about him.

"I don't mean your ghost," she said.

"What you want? What did you say?" he asked.

"What did you think of the speech?"

"Oh, that," Henry said.

"That's it, daddy," she said in a genially teasing voice.

"I think this—the President is going to have us all be like boy scouts. We're going to wear a button on our coat, with a little sign of an eagle on it, like we all belonged to the boy scouts," Henry said.

"Say, I didn't know you could be so funny," Myrtle said, laughing.

"Henry, I think that this speech we just heard was one of the greatest in history. I think we were listening to history tonight," John said.

"What do you mean, John?" Henry asked.

"It's this way. The trouble with this country is that the gears haven't been working right," John said.

"Say, that's just it. The gears haven't been working right," Henry said in a sudden burst of conviction.

"That's it. You see, the business of this country has gotten itself badly geared. Now somebody's got to fix the gears when they're working wrong, doesn't he?" John continued.

"That's true," Henry said.

"Couldn't prove it wasn't so by me," Myrtle said.

"All right then. Who is better able to fix the gears and put the gears of business back working smoothly than the President?" said John.

"I guess that's what he ought to do. We elected him to make things pick up, didn't we?" said Henry.

"And he's the man to do it. Now, things were pretty bad last March. Well, he put the banks back in business, didn't he? And not one of us in this room is out any money. Well, now he's going to put the gears of business in right working order again. You see a couple of things are wrong with the country. For one thing, the psychology of the people is wrong. They are afraid. Take in my business. One phenomenon is this. People are doubling up. Families double up and take the same apartment. They are afraid to sign a lease alone. Take another thing. Young people don't like to get married and set up housekeeping for themselves, because of the rent and other costs. If they get married these days, they'll live with the parents of one or the other so they can split the rents. Well, the same kind of psychology is at work in other lines. And what is it?" John paused to take a drink. "It's fear. And what does the President always say? He said the only thing to fear is fear itself. Now, that's one angle. And I already explained

the other. The gears have to be put right. And my money is
on the line that he's the one to do it, the President. Why, things
are picking up already in some lines. You watch and see if inside of a year we don't go way over where we were before we
got this depression and this fear. I wager that if we're all sitting here one year from tonight, we'll see the change, and
we'll be looking back and wondering why anybody was ever
worried and why business went to hell such a short while ago."

"It may be so, John, but this is a party. What I want to
know is if we are or if we aren't going to go out and make
whoopee?" Myrtle said.

"Yes, let's get going. We'll drive downtown, and I know a
nice lively place to take in," John said.

"You're the boss, John," Kate said.

"Suits me," Henry said.

"All right, come on!" Myrtle said.

"Drink up first. This stuff is too good to be wasted," John
said.

"Now you're talking sense instead of—of history," Myrtle
said.

They drank up.

VI

They left in the Lohrmans' car. Henry drove, and John sat
beside him in front, with the two wives in the rear. They drove
toward Jackson Park.

"Yes, folks, I think we can call this little jamboree of ours
a real celebration," John said.

"You know, I'm always ready to join a celebration even
when there's nothing to celebrate," Myrtle said.

"My missus is a real sport, isn't she, John?" Henry said,
proudly.

"Sure is," John said.

"You know, Myrtle, my John, Junior, is so cute when he gets
ready to take a girl out. You should see the way he spends his
time dolling up, combing his hair, fixing his tie, and seeing
that he looks just right. He's so cute," Kate said.

"Mine'll be that way soon. And say, old man, if he takes after you and your vices, I'm going to brain him. You know, Henry is tamed now, but he must have been a whizzer with the dames in his day," Myrtle said.

"I ain't saying nothing," Henry said.

"Yes, in such a case, folks, silence is golden," John said.

"He doesn't have to tell me. But, say, old man, don't be coming home with any blonde hairs on your coat lapel and telephone numbers in your pockets," Myrtle said, and she laughed raucously.

"Anyway, folks, as I was going to say, we can really celebrate. The man in Washington has fixed us up Jake now. Everything is going to pick up. It's starting to already. Of course, the World's Fair here has helped things along. But even more than that, the man we got in Washington has set the country going. Factories will be booming, people will be working, spending money, and there won't be any more fear. And you won't be going around Chicago like you do now and see 'For Rent' signs in all the windows like a rash," John said.

"You think he's good?" Henry asked.

"I know it. He's already started things humming," John said.

They turned into Jackson Park and drove along the lake front. It was a fine evening, with a full moon over the lake. The water was calm and blue. There were a great many automobiles out, and people were strolling about the park, sitting on benches and on the grass. The Jackson Park beach was crowded. Beyond the fenced-in beach section there were many other people in bathing suits, sitting on the sand, running about, swimming.

"Another thing that's too bad. Too many big apartments and hotels went up all through this section. They were all mortgaged and most of them went into the hands of receivers. Lots of them are full of empty space and only that," John said.

"Come on, no more business from you boys. This is a celebration," Myrtle said.

They drove along the lake front on the outer drive and past
the World's Fair grounds, which were lit up and looked fantastic. They talked about going to the Fair, but then decided
that a speakeasy would be more fun.

VII

They sat in a dingy speakeasy in a basement on Van Buren
Street near Wabash Avenue. The tables were wooden-topped,
with many initials carved on them. There was sawdust on the
floor. The place was noisy and more than half crowded. The
waiters bustled about taking care of orders.

"Well, here's to the man who's gonna make us rich again,"
Henry said, holding up a filled glass.

"To Mr. Roosevelt and the New Deal," John said.

They drank.

"Not as good as the stuff you gave us," Henry said, making
a face after he drank.

"Not on your life," John said proudly.

"I couldn't drink much of this," Kate said.

"I want more noise," Myrtle said.

"Keep on drinking this stuff and you'll be gettin' it," Henry
said.

"Good-natured people come here. They get drunk, but they
never fight. I've been here more than once and I've never seen
a fight," John said.

"Well, it looks like a good place to let off steam. And anybody that's human has got to let off steam sometimes," Myrtle
said.

"You're full of steam, aren't you, Myrtle?" John asked.

"Don't you see it comin' out of my ears?" Myrtle answered.

A bleary-eyed young fellow wandered by their table.

"Know what?" the bleary-eyed fellow asked, leaning on
their table.

"What?" Myrtle asked in her husky voice.

"Pie-eyed," he said.

He staggered away, and they drank again.

"Say, folks, I want you to drink a toast with me," another young fellow said, coming over to their table.

"Sure thing, buddy," Henry said.

"O.K. baby," Myrtle said.

"I want you all to drink this toast with me—to hell with Hitler!" he said.

"Wait a minute," said Henry.

"Shut up, daddy! Drink the toast with my friend here," Myrtle said.

"But . . ." Henry began.

"Be a good sport and come on, Henry," John said.

"I'm a sport," Henry said.

"Now, all of you say it after me," the drunken young fellow said, raising his glass.

They raised their glasses.

"To hell with Hitler!" he shouted.

"To hell with Hitler!" they yelled.

"I thank you, one and all," the young drunk said; he walked back to the bar, erect and with inebriated dignity.

"Daddy, what the hell difference does it make who you drink to or against? Drink, and the hell with it," Myrtle said.

"Sure," said Henry.

Kate yawned. She was drinking less than the others, and she and John were holding their liquor better than the Lohrmans.

"Know something about me, Kate Robinson?" Myrtle remarked, leaning her elbows on the table.

"What?" asked Henry.

"I'm not a lady when I'm celebratin'," Myrtle said.

"Of course you are," said Kate.

"Like hell I am," Myrtle said, and she laughed loudly.

"Say, John, did I tell you about picking up a Socialist who was hitch-hiking when I was driving back home from my vacation? A moron," Henry said.

"Let's yell!" Myrtle said.

Kate frowned.

"Whoopee!" Myrtle shouted.

She picked up her glass and drank, some of it spilling on her chin. She wiped her chin with the back of the hand.

"Whoopee!" she yelled at the top of her voice.

VIII

The speakeasy kept getting noisier and more crowded. Drunks wandered about, talking, shouting, getting in one another's way, crying and sentimentalizing on one another's shoulders, stumbling and foundering about between the bar, the tables, and the lavatories. The Robinsons and Lohrmans talked with strangers and didn't know what was being said, and then they talked with other strangers. Myrtle attracted a crowd about her at the bar. She drank and yelled whoopee, and a number of men cheered her and told her that she was a sport. Henry tried to get her back to their table, and she told him to go sit down. He staggered away from her, fell into his chair, and ordered another drink.

"No, I ain't a lady!" Myrtle yelled at a number of men who formed a circle about her.

"Prove it!" one of the men said.

"Crap!" she yelled.

They applauded her. A man handed her a drink, and she spilled part of it as she gulped.

"Whoopee!" she yelled.

"Come on, girlie, have one on me. You're a sport all right!" an old man said, grabbing her arm.

"Say, foxy grandpa," she yelled at him, pulling herself free, while her audience cheered.

In another corner, a group began singing oldtime songs, and Myrtle staggered over to them. She put her arms around the shoulders of two strangers and joined in the drunken singing.

IX

"We'd better go home," Kate said.

John, half drunk, shook his head.

Henry sang drunkenly:

Git along little doggie, git along.
Git along little doggie, git along.
Git along little doggie, git along.

"John, you better get Myrtle," Kate said.

John got to his feet, staggered to the singers, and touched Myrtle's shoulder.

"Whoopee!" she yelled.

John gently pulled her from the crowd. She looked at him bleary-eyed, her face dirty, her hair falling over her eyes.

"Wanna drink, John?" she asked.

"Come on, Myrtle," he said.

"Drunk my old man under the table," she mumbled, half-walking, half-falling after him.

Henry still sang:

Git along little doggie, git along.

"Hello, daddy," Myrtle yelled, slapping her husband on the back.

Git along little doggie, git along.

John staggered off and returned with the waiter. He paid the bill. They floundered out of the speakeasy. Myrtle stood waveringly in the center of the sidewalk. She flung her dress in the air and yelled at the top of her voice:

"Crap!"

"Come on, Myrtle," Kate urged.

"Crap!" Myrtle yelled.

John took her arm, and Kate, walking a trifle uncertainly herself, inserted her arm in Henry's and struggled with him to the car. John searched through Henry's pockets, found the keys, and opened the door. He pushed the Lohrmans into the rear seat. He helped Kate into the front seat, got in himself, and drove off.

John was able to drive without any mishaps. He didn't talk to his wife beside him, and she suddenly fell asleep. Myrtle, in the back, mumbled unintelligible sounds. Henry was flopped in a corner, and he droned ceaselessly:

Git along little doggie, git along.

John got them home and upstairs to their apartment. The Lohrman boy was awakened by the commotion when they entered, and John told him he was taking the Lohrman automobile to drive home in and would telephone in the morning. Myrtle and Henry fell lengthwise across the bed. Myrtle passed out. Henry lay there, drooling, still singing:

Git along little doggie, git along.

The celebration over, John and Kate drove home. John put the car in his own garage and staggered back to his house. He went upstairs where Kate was already undressing.

"Well, we had something to celebrate," he said, beginning to undress.

1933-1939

The Bride of Christ

I

Sister Bertha, a shriveled corpse, lay in a simple coffin, garbed in the black habit of her order. Her face, with all the wrinkling deformities of old age printed on it, was ashen and hard, almost like stone; there was a bag of skin under the pointed, shrunken chin. Her bony hands were folded over her stomach, and in her stiffened fingers was entwined a pair of rosary beads.

Sister Bertha lay dead before the small altar of the convent chapel, the same chapel in which, these last five years, she had daily heard mass during the school year. Her coffin had been placed in front of the altar rail at which she had so frequently knelt to receive the Blessed Sacrament. And in the front pew of the dim and small chapel, two nuns knelt on watch, their lips moving noiselessly in prayer for the repose of the soul of the departed member of their community. They occasionally lifted their eyes and glanced at the casket, the burning candles, the flickering red altar light before the tabernacle.

The minutes passed slowly and quietly, accompanied only by the occasional rustling of the heavily clothed nuns and by the muffled echoes from other parts of the convent, or from that distant foreign world beyond its walls.

For forty years Sister Bertha had performed the work of a nun, and all during those years death had been almost constantly in her consciousness. For those four decades she had labored in the Master's vineyard so that when she died she

would be united with Him, gaining honored admittance into
the Communion of Saints in Heaven. And now she lay before
His altar, the embalmed remains of a withered old woman.
That goal for which she had pointed her days had been attained: she had died in the state of Grace. She was, if her faith
were justified, now joyous in Heaven.

All memories, all acts of devotion, all thoughts and aspirations, all fears of sin, all prickings of conscience, every impress
of life upon her was wiped out of the decomposing brain within
her skull. All that remained of Sister Bertha lay as a simple
prediction, as a strong and certain prophecy of the destiny of
all living matter. All memory of her was now lodged in living
brain cells and in dusty records. In time, these living brain
cells would be dead. In time, these records would fade into
illegibility. And then, even memory of her would be oblit-
erated.

Thus Sister Bertha lay in death, while two of her sister nuns
kept silent and prayerful watch over her corpse.

Scattered over the world were many men who, as boys, had
been the material, the souls, on which she had worked. As boys
they had sat, straining and awed, tortured into attentiveness
in the classrooms she had querulously ruled with a loud voice,
a frowning sour visage, and a firm ruler. Although these thousands of men had known her at different periods, and in different towns and cities, the majority of them had known essentially the same teacher. They had known a tall nun whose
voice was high-pitched. Some of them had known this nun
when her face had begun to wrinkle. Others had known her
as a middle-aged woman. But wrinkles had only signified that
she was aging, not mellowing. They had signalized no change
in that capricious disposition of hers. These men had, as boys,
known essentially the same woman and the same classroom
routine. She had acquired many nicknames from them in her
forty years of teaching, but over and over again boys in different towns and cities and even sisters in her own community
gave her the same nickname: Sister Battling Bertha.

In this long period she usually had taught seventh- and

eighth-grade boys. She had taught in small towns scattered through Indiana, Michigan, and Illinois, as well as in various neighborhoods of Chicago. But her manner and her method had always been unvarying. She usually had swept into the classroom with an angry frown on her face. As she had grown older, her face had become chalky, and in her last year she had seemed almost ghostlike. Each of her days she had similarly dedicated to Christ, her Master, with hastily murmured prayers. Then would begin her daily struggle with her pupils— catechism, bible history, arithmetic, grammar, history, reading, Palmer Method in writing. Year after year she had taught these subjects from the same textbooks, rigidly following the course, page after page. She would shriek at disobedient boys and at the dunces who could not grasp the lessons easily. Sometimes her voice rose to such a pitch that she disturbed other classes, and her sister nuns would rush to her classroom door to discover whether or not Sister Bertha were having a riot on her hands. She used sledge-hammer methods of teaching. Pupils were required to know the assigned lessons by rote. If not, she bullied them, screamed at them, predicted that they would be failures in life who might even end up on the gallows. Often when boys whispered or threw spitballs in the schoolroom, or when an incorrigible dunce did not know his lesson, she would fling herself from her dais, sweep down the classroom aisle, shrieking, her beads rattling, her habit swishing. She would pound the erring or guilty boy on the back of the neck with her ruler or clapper, and as she administered punishment she would shout in that rasping voice of hers. As she aged, she became increasingly nearsighted, and often, due to this condition, she would strike the wrong pupil. Almost no pupil was safe in her classroom. And when she beat her pupils, a gleam of almost passionate satisfaction would come into those small, weak, watery eyes. She would grab a boy by the scruff of the neck, shake and pound him, and as she did this, the muscles of her face would tighten. Her expression would be that of a fanatic swept with joy. If appearances were not deceiving, the happiest moments of her life must have been those during which she was punishing bad little boys. She terrified her pupils, the innocent and the guilty alike. Few boys ever liked school while she was their teacher. When she was ill, they were happy. When they learned that she had been transferred to another school, they hurrahed. Even the brightest of boys, those who had sometimes earned the nickname of "Sister's pet"—even such pupils were overjoyed when they learned that she would teach them no longer.

Thus for forty years she had taught. During her last years she was half blind. Her memory began to fade. She sometimes showed the symptoms of a person sinking into a second childhood. Her pupils suffered more from the advance of age upon her than she did herself. Her hearing began to fail as had her memory and her eyesight. She screamed more violently, more shrilly, more whiningly. She became, in these last years, like raw energy. She would often suddenly and without provocation descend on a boy and beat him until he screamed for mercy, perhaps to leave him for the remainder of his life smarting under the memory of an unjust, unfair, undue punishment.

She was equally a source of tribulation to her sister nuns who had to live in the same convent with her. She quarreled with them over trivialities. She constantly accused them of being lacking in piety, devotion, and in being lax in the observance of religious duties and obligations. When angered with one of them, she would hurl accusations of impiety and even of heresy. Any sign of simple and harmless levity, any human foible or failing, any little indulgence in gossip which was, almost by necessity, the principal amusement and recreation of the nuns—these led her to offer sharp and curt criticisms and complaints. She would unexpectedly catch two young nuns giggling over some item of gossip and she would sink to her knees and sanctimoniously and melodramatically bless herself and pray loudly to God to save their sinful souls. She would arise from her prayers and even accuse them of having been guilty of a violation of the sixth commandment, a charge, she was convinced, that was true of many of the grammar-school boys and girls whom she happened to be teaching. She would even accuse the young nuns she had caught giggling as having been a bad influence tending to lead pupils in the school to commit the dread sin. She would rant and rage and then go off in a fury to complain to the Sister-Superior to lay charges against the younger nuns. She upset and unnerved the entire convent wherever she was. Life within the convent walls became then a kind of armed truce. She herself stimulated more gossip. She caused dissension. She became the source and inspiration for many an un-nunlike squabble.

Sister Bertha had entered the convent when she was in her early twenties. She had been, at that time, a tall and homely young woman, graceless in stature and mind, awkward in movement, unpopular almost everywhere. She was the daughter of a small-town storekeeper. Shortly before her entry into the convent she had been courted by a middle-aged barber. Her parents, to whom she had become a tribulation because of her carping religiosity, her extreme and rather histrionic piety, had favored her marrying the man. Friends, neighbors, gossipy townspeople had all taken an interest in the prospective match. They had waited in expectation for the news that it had resulted in an engagement. But she had rejected the proposal. She loved Christ, not mortal man. And sex was an ugly cancer in her mind, a hideous unmentionable. Marriage would have meant experiencing this terrifyingly ugly thing. It would have meant sleeping with a man in sinful and disgusting intimacy. It was vulgar, earthly love. Her love was spiritual and Heavenly. She began to pray with an intensified fervor. She devoted long and perfervid hours to God, often remaining on her knees until she suffered pain and physical torture. She made novenas to the Blessed Virgin Mary. She heard mass daily. At length, she became convinced that she had been honored with the call to serve Christ. During a sultry summer evening when she was in bed, her mind became disturbed and distorted. She became feverish with excitement. She was convinced that she was having a vision. She believed that she saw Christ by her opened window, His feet and His hands bearing

the marks of the crucifixion nails, a rent in His side exposing
His bleeding Sacred Heart. He told her that hers was a mission
to go forth in His name, and to teach and guide the little
ones who were beloved by Him and whose tiny footsteps
needed to be guided into the paths of virtue, piety, and holiness.

She entered the convent. At thirty, she began teaching. And
that had been forty years ago. During these forty years there
had been all the little trivialities of the schoolroom, her ex-
plosions, beatings, harsh words, instruction in the so-called
basic subjects, the hearing of lessons, the telling of parables for
the added inculcation of moral lessons, the repetition of the
same distortions and simplifications of American history, the
same problems in percentage, the same answers to catechism
questions, the same sentences to be diagrammed, the same rules
of grammar to be explained, the same routine continuing year
in and year out. She had had few contacts with the outside
world. She had scarcely read newspapers. She had voted twice
on instructions from her bishop. There had been daily prayers
and hours of meditation, and regular confessions. All the
natural impulses of a woman had been canceled in love of and
devotion to Christ. Always, Christ had been in her mind. She
had imagined and relived His life over and over again, His
crucifixion, the vinegar and gall which He had been given to
drink, the wiping of His face by Veronica, the forgiveness of
Saint Mary Magdalen from her sins of the flesh, His Resurrec-
tion and Ascension into Heaven—the life of Christ, her Christ.
How often had she not prayed to Him? How many times had
she not knelt, wishing that she were a Veronica who was wiping blood from the pained, bloody, suffering face of the tormented God! How often had she not visualized Him cruci-
fied, wincing from her vision of the nails piercing His tender
and holy flesh. She had lived with Christ in her mind for forty
years. She had sought to serve Him in her way by teaching the
young to live with Him, and to be worthy of Him in Heaven.

And now she lay dead. Those who had been her pupils were
scattered over the world. Whenever most of them dwelled nos-

talgically and reminiscently on their boyhood days, she became integrally interwoven into their memories. Often, when
they did not image her in such moods, she remained an unseen,
unimaged terror stalking these nostalgic moods and contempla-
tions. Many of them remembered her with resentment, almost
none with understanding. They could not forget her blows,
her shrieks, her rigid classroom discipline, her unfairness. None
of them loved her. And now she lay dead.

II

A solemn high mass for the dead was celebrated over her
corpse. Sacred church music was sung. The nuns in the community knelt in devout attendance. In back of them were the
school children and a few parishioners. The music was slow,
sad, solemn. The parish priest delivered a brief sermon. He
spoke of how Sister Bertha had labored in the Master's vineyard for forty years. She had heard the call of the Master as a
young woman, and she had heeded that call. She had taught
the Truth, inspiring in young hearts the faith and the goodness of Christ, our Lord. Year after year she had taught the
Word to those little ones whom Christ Himself had singled out
as the special lambs who were to be protected above all others in
His flock. Who knew how extensive her influence for good
had been? Who knew on what spot of earth at the very minute
that he was preaching over her poor earthly remains—who
knew but what some one of her many boys was remembering
in the tabernacle of his heart, remembering her teaching, her
inspiration, profiting from that atmosphere of holiness and devotion that had permeated her classroom? Who knew but at
what corner of God's earth, at this very moment, some one of
her former boys was being steered clear of sin and temptation
because of the good example she had set for him years ago in
a little modest classroom?

Yes, hers had been a quiet life, peaceful. It would not fur-
nish the material for even a slender book of earthly drama. No.
But it would for a book of good and holy deeds for the next
world. And how large and bulky that book would be, that

book of the good and holy deeds of Sister Bertha! For daily,
hers had been a life in Christ. It had begun with meditation and
prayers in the morning and it had progressed through the
classroom, to conclude with prayers and meditation before
sleep in the evening. Her first thought in the morning had
always been of God. Her last thought in the evening had also
always been of God. Yes, hers had been a simple and undis-
tinguished life as this world measures a life. But a holy and a
wonderful life, as life is measured in the kingdom of God. A
life of sacrifices here! A life of eternal joys above! And now
in Heaven the angels must be smiling, and there must be the
joy of paradise reigning. One of their own, one of the real
Communion of Saints, had come home. And the joy of Heaven,
it was a consolation for those on earth, sisters, parents, little
boys, who were missing her with heaviness of heart. She was
departed now. Her soul was flown aloft. She was taking her
proper place in Heaven as a true and rightful bride of Christ.

And thus was Sister Bertha buried. All her petty tyrannies,
her unjust punishments, her prejudiced utterances against
those not of the True Faith, her shrieks and shouts, all was of
the past, buried and forgotten; and her thousands of former
pupils scarcely remembered her, scarcely carried with them in
life any example learned in her classroom, scarcely remembered
anything connected with her except the fear that she had
driven like a spike into their hearts. This was the Sister Bertha
who was buried as a Bride of Christ.

1934-1938

A Jazz-Age Clerk

I

JACK STRATTON worked from ten to eight answering telephone calls in the Wagon Department of the Continental Express Company. What he liked best about his job was his lunch hour from one to two. Ordinarily, clerks went to lunch at twelve o'clock, and he believed that people seeing him on the streets between one and two might figure that he was a lad with a pretty good job, because one o'clock was the time when many businessmen took their lunch in order to avoid the noonday jams in the Loop.

One sunny day in early spring Jack went out to lunch. He felt good. He would have felt even better if only his faded powder-blue suit were not so old, and if only it were already the next pay day, because then he hoped to be able to make a down payment and get a new suit on the installment plan. When he had got this powder-blue suit, he'd thought that it was the real thing. All the cake-eaters were wearing them. But it was a cheap suit that had faded quickly. And his brown hat, fixed square-shaped the way the cakes were wearing them, was old and greasy from the stacomb that he smeared on his hair every day. Yes, he would have been feeling much better if he were dogged out in a new outfit. Well, he would some day, he decided. He walked toward Van Buren Street.

It was a narrow, dusty street, with garages, a Continental billing station and terminal, and the rear ends of old office buildings and restaurants. On the other side he spotted a girl,

135

and told himself that she was so hot she could start a new
Chicago fire all by herself. He snapped his fingers and watched
her pass. Daddy! He burst into song:

> *Teasing eyes, teasing eyes,*
> *You're the little girl that sets my heart afire . . .*

Teasing! He expressed his feelings with a low whistle. He
guessed that working in the Loop had its advantages. At least
there were plenty of shebas to look at. He shifted his gait into a
hopping two-step. Self-conscious, he checked himself. People
might laugh at him in the street, just as Gas-House McGinty,
Heinie Mueller, and some of the others in the office laughed at
him. Some day he would like to show them, clean up on a few
of the wise-aleck clerks. And he would, too! They were dumb,
that was all, and they didn't know what was the real thing in
the world today. They didn't have enough sense to be cake-
eaters. And nicknaming him Jenny, like they had. Some day
he would Jenny them! He began walking in a kind of waltzing
dance step, his body quivering as he moved. Another song burst
into his thoughts, *Tiger Rose*.

Sadness and self-pity drove the half-sung chorus out of his
mind. He wanted girls, a girl, and he wanted money to spend on
clothes so that he could impress the broads, and to spend on
dances, dates, going places. But he was only making eighty-five
dollars a month. That was more than he had expected when he
started looking for a job, and he couldn't kick. He knew fellows
who only made their fifteen a week. But his pay wasn't any too
much. And since his old man was out of work, most of his jack
had to go to his mother toward keeping up the home. Gee, he
wished that the old man would find another job, and then he
could have a little more to spend.

He saw an athletically built blonde who was just bow-wows,
the kind to look at and weep. He jerked his shoulders in rhythm
and sang:

> *I'm runnin' wild, I'm runnin' wild,*
> *I lost control . . .*

Now, if there would only be some mama like that in the restaurant, and if he could only get next to her.

The restaurant where he usually ate was owned by a Greek, and was a small establishment with a tile floor and an imitation marble counter. He took a counter seat in the front, several stools removed from the nearest customer. Kitty, the slatternly peroxide-blonde waitress, greeted him with a yellow-toothed yawn, and at the same time she rubbed a fat hand over her low forehead. He looked up at her face; it was crusted with powder.

"Hello," he said.

A customer got up and went to the glass case to pay his check. Kitty left Jack, collected, rang the cash register, deposited the silver in the drawer, and returned. The expression on her face was stupid, bored. Jack snapped his fingers, rolled his eyes, and sang a jazz song.

"What yuh want today, Dapper Dan?" she asked.

"Ham and coffee."

Swinging her head sidewise, she shouted the sandwich order to the chef. Other customers left and she collected. He was the only one remaining in the restaurant. Suddenly he was conscious of his·shabbiness. He reached down to touch the raggedy cuffs of his bell-bottom trousers. He felt the thinness at the right elbow of his coat. Kitty slid a ham sandwich at him, and then she slopped a cup of coffee across the counter.

"Big times tonight!" he said while applying mustard to his sandwich.

"Huh?" she mumbled lifelessly.

"Dance at the South Hall out in Englewood where I live," he said, biting into his sandwich.

"Takin' yours along?" she asked lackadaisically.

"I told her to keep the home fires burning tonight. I like a little variety and change, sister."

His shoulders swung to the singing of a few lines from *The Darktown Strutters' Ball*.

"Cancha sing something that's new," Kitty said petulantly.

"I just learned this one this week at the Song Shop on Quincy Street. Listen!"

No, no, Nora, nobody but you, dear,
You know, Nora, yours truly is true, dear . . .

"Aha!" he interrupted with a leer.

And when you accuse me of flirting . . .

"Like that?" he interpolated with a lascivious wink.

I wouldn't, I couldn't, I love you so,
I've had chances, too many to mention . . .

"Always get chances," he interposed.

Never give them a bit of attention.
No, no, Nora. No! No!

"Nice tune," Kitty said dopily as Jack bent down to drink coffee.

"Fast! And tonight I'm grabbing myself a keen number and stepping myself right up over those blue clouds into heaven."

"You're conceited."

He finished his sandwich. His coffee cup was half full. He looked at the cuts of pie in the dessert case before him. He dug his hand into his right trouser pocket. He swallowed his coffee in one gulp and slid off the stool. He paid Kitty fifteen cents, which she rang up.

"Toodle-oo!"

" 'Bye, shiek," she said patronizingly.

II

Overhead, the elevated trains thundered, drowning out the racket of street traffic. He stood on the sidewalk, hands in pockets, hat tilted, watching the crowd. He decided that today he'd sit in the lobby of a good hotel instead of going to the Song Shop and listening to the new tunes being sung. It would be restful.

If he only had on decent clothes, he could sit in a lobby and seem like a young fellow, maybe, with a rich old man or a good job that paid a big salary. A man in a hurry bumped into him and, hastening on, snottily suggested that he quit taking up the whole sidewalk. Jack looked after him, shrugged his shoulders, laughed. He bent his eyes on the moving legs of a girl ahead of him. He realized that if he got his shoes shined, he would improve his appearance. He hated to spend the dime, though, because when he got home tonight he could shine his own shoes. But his appearance would be improved, and he wouldn't look quite so poor. It was all in accordance with the principles of clever dressing. Always have on something new, outstanding or shiny, a loud tie, a clean shirt, a new hat, shined shoes, and then something else you were wearing that was shabby wouldn't be so noticed. He applied his principle by dropping into a shoe-shine parlor.

A young Negro energetically shined his shoes, and Jack daydreamed about how he would stroll nonchalantly into the lobby of the Potter Hotel and find himself a chair that he could slump into, just so natural. He could spread his legs out so that the first thing anyone noticed about him would be his shined shoes. His thoughts leaped. Wouldn't it be luck if some ritzy queen fell for him! It would just be . . . delicious. Daddy! His mood lifted.

Adventure-bound, hopeful and gay, he hustled toward the new Potter Hotel. His courage deserted him as he passed the uniformed doorman who stood with a set and frowning face, seeming to tell Jack that he wasn't wanted. He paused at the entrance to the enormous lobby, with its gold decorations, its hanging diamond-like chandeliers, its lavish display of comfortable furniture. He told himself in awe that it was like a palace. He noticed men and women, sitting, standing, moving around, talking, reading newspapers, and for a moment he felt as if he were in a moving picture world, the hero in a picture walking into this hotel lobby like a palace fit for the richest of kings or businessmen. He skirted several bellboys and found a chair in a corner, but it was not obscure, because there was a passageway all round the lobby and many people would pass him while he sat. A feeling of awe, as if he were in a church where talking was not permitted, filled his consciousness. He

wished that he hadn't come here where he didn't belong, and
at the same time he was glad that he'd come.

Several yards away from him he noticed a gray-haired man
in a gray suit, whose pleasingly wrinkled face seemed calm,
contented, mellowed. He tried to make himself seem as calm and
as at ease as this man. For want of something to do, he ran the
palm of his hand through his greasy hair; it was meticulously
parted in the center. He sedulously drew out his dirty handkerchief to wipe the grease off his hand. To his right, he heard a
well-dressed fellow discussing the stock market with a friend.
A bellboy wended in and out, intoning:

"CALL FOR MR. WAGNER . . . CALL FOR MR.
WAGNER . . . CALL FOR MR. WAGNER . . . CALL
FOR MR. WAGNER . . . MR. WAGNER PLEASE . . ."

He was unable to chase out his confusion of feelings in this
alien atmosphere of the well-dressed, the well-fed, the prosper-
ous. He wished he could live a life that had as much glitter as
there must be in the lives of these people. He thought how some
day he wanted to be able to sit in a swanky hotel lobby like this
one, well-dressed, and have a bell hop pass along calling out his
name. He tried to visualize himself, a little older, a successful
rich businessman in the lobby with the bellboy droning for him.

CALL FOR MR. STRATTON . . . CALL FOR MR.
JOHN STRATTON . . . CALL FOR MR. JOHN STRAT-
TON . . . MR. JOHN STRATTON . . .

And it would be some millionaire on the wire waiting to close
an important deal that would net him a handsome piece of
change. He'd close the deal and come back to wait for a mama.
Maybe she'd be some hot movie actress like Gloria Swanson who
would be like the sweetheart of the world in her pictures. And
he would be waiting for this movie actress more beautiful than
even Gloria Swanson, thinking how when he had been nothing
but a punk clerk at the express company he'd come to sit in the
same lobby, wearing shabby clothes, dreaming of the day when
things would happen to him.

He watched a tall and handsome young fellow stroll by. Must
be collegiate! Must have had his gray suit made to order and

have paid fifty, seventy-five bucks for it, maybe even more. The threads of his daydream suddenly snapped. All the confidence went out of him, so that he felt shaky, trembly. He wished again that he hadn't come here. He felt as if everyone in the lobby were looking at him, knowing he didn't belong and wanting to see him tossed out on his can. He looked unobtrusively at two snappily dressed young fellows on his left. They were out of earshot, but he wondered what they were saying. They probably had everything they wanted and did anything they cared to do, had automobiles, money on which to date up queens . . . everything. The one wearing a Scotch tweed suit drew out a fat cigar, removed the band, smelled the cigar, bit off the end, lit it like a businessman in a movie. If only his life were that of a hero in the movies! Ah! That was class, the way that fellow in the tweeds had pulled out his cigar and lit it. Yes, when his own dream ship came in and he could afford to smoke four-bit cigars, he would have to remember to light them the way that fellow did.

"CALL FOR MR. O'FLAHERTY . . . CALL FOR MR. AL O'FLAHERTY . . . CALL FOR MR. AL O'FLAH-ERTY . . . CALL FOR MR. AL O'FLAHERTY . . ."

Wouldn't it be the dogs to be paged like that on important business calls! But he had no right even to think of such things. It wouldn't ever be for him. His lot in life deepened his wretchedness. He hadn't had anything to start on. Father and mother with no dough. One year in high school, and that without clothes, no athletic ability, no money, nothing that could get him into fraternities and make the girls go for him. But, gee, in high school there'd been all kinds of hot and classy girls! Only why should they have looked at an unimportant freshman like himself? And anyway, that was all over. Now he was working at a job with no future. Maybe he ought to be glad for what he had, but, gee, he couldn't help feeling that some guys got all the breaks, while he got almost none. All these people, they belonged to a world he would never enter.

A bellboy coming toward him. Gee! He sat stricken in a paralyzing fright. He pushed back the dirty cuffs of his shirt so

that they were invisible. He tried to think up a reason he could
give for being in the lobby when the bell hop came and questioned him. He'd say he was waiting for somebody who was
staying at the hotel. But they could check up on the name. He'd
say he was waiting for a friend coming in from New York who
was going to stay here. The bellboy coming! He wanted to get
up and leave. He had no will. He was so afraid that he began to
sweat under the armpits, and his forehead perspired. Coming!

The bellboy passed by his chair as if no one were sitting in it,
and bent down to speak with the calm-faced man. The man
rose and followed the bellboy across the lobby. Jack again
pulled out his soiled handkerchief, crushed it into a ball so that
it couldn't be noticed, and wiped his forehead.

He watched a slim, voluptuous blonde woman cross the
lobby. She was the dogs, the snake's hips, and the stars all rolled
into something in a black dress. Those lips of hers. She had lip-
appeal, sister, lip-appeal, sex-appeal, and she had it, and she was
like a shower of stars. Looked like a woman some rich bird had
put in the velvet. He followed her tantalizing, sensuous movements with thirsting eyes. She was a trifle taller than he,
he guessed . . . but . . . hot. . . . She sat down beside a
middle-aged man in a conservative blue suit, crossed her legs.
. . . Legs! Wouldn't he like to have the bucks to buy the most
expensive stockings money could buy for those legs. She lit a
cigarette and he bet himself that it was an expensive Turkish
cigarette. Oh, sister!

Tantalizing, he told himself, not removing his eyes from her
legs.

Yes, all he wanted was the money to have a mama like that.
There wasn't a movie queen in Hollywood that had a nickel on
that one. He imagined that she was his woman, seated beside
him, talking to him, saying that she would rather have lunch
at the Fraternity Row today. She was saying she was crazy, just
crazy, about him and didn't care two cents for anyone else in
the world. She was wild for him. . . .

"CALL FOR MR. JONES . . . MR. JONES PLEASE!
. . . MR. JONES!"

The voice of the bellboy was like a jolt, awakening him. He looked at his Ingersoll watch. Two minutes to two. He'd be late, and Collins, his boss, might bawl the hell out of him, and then all the fellows in the office would razz him, call him Jenny, the drugstore cowboy. He placed his hat on carefully and moved swiftly out of the lobby. Hurrying along the street, he fell into a dance step. Then he ran until he pulled up, winded. Four minutes after two. What excuse could he give Collins? He paused to look at a girl in pink. Nice! He unwittingly broke into song.

I'm Al-a-ba-ma bound . . .

He again worried about himself, thought of the things he wanted and couldn't have. He started running, hoping that Collins wouldn't bawl him out. Two seven!

1932

Getting Out the Vote for
the Working Class

I

AL MICHAELSON awoke at eleven o'clock. He yawned, blinked his sleepy eyes, drowsed in bed. He slowly awakened, and then he sat up in bed in the studio. A state of suppressed excitement developed in him because it was election day. Never before had an election caused him to feel like this. Election today was something new. He didn't care whether or not Roosevelt or Hoover were to be elected President. Well, he did, but he couldn't admit it, not even to himself. He wanted to see Roosevelt elected, just as he had wanted to see Smith elected in 1928. But no, he couldn't think that way.

He wasn't going to vote for Roosevelt. He was going to vote for the party of the future, for the working class. He was going to do something today. What he would do would be great, a great gesture. No, it wouldn't be a gesture. It would be a political act. Funny that he should find himself thinking this way.

He got out of bed and put on a dirty bathrobe. He stuck his feet into his slippers. He wished that Lydia was in town. But she was away. She got in only week ends now.

Al lived with Lydia. He was twenty-eight, and Lydia was forty-five. He had met her during the summer of 1928 after he had been flunked out of the University. He had gone around

144

with Pete, the Greek, and that summer Pete had run a little
theater in the art colony. He had been living with Pete in a
basement until he had met Lydia. There were lots of girls
around in those days, but he had never had any luck with any
of them. And then, one night, well, there was Lydia at a party,
and she took him home with her, and since then he had lived
with her, a kept man.

It wasn't his fault that he was a kept man. It was the system.
He had not fully realized it in those days. Now he did. Everyone around the colony, except those few social-fascists who
had joined the Socialist Party instead of sympathizing with
the Communist Party, now at last realized that what was behind everything was the system.

But now he wasn't going to bother about that. He wanted
breakfast. If Lydia were here, she would make breakfast for
him and then, when it was all ready, he would get up, and
there it would be for him on the table. But she was out selling.
He had to make his own breakfast.

He yawned again. Yes, today he was going to cast a vote
against the whole rotten system.

II

The kitchen in Lydia's studio was partitioned off in the
rear. Al set breakfast on the table and sat down. He felt like
having a drink, but hell, it was too early. After voting, he
would have a drink to celebrate. He pitched into his ham and
eggs, ate large slices of buttered bread, and drank coffee.

It was funny—the very idea of Al Michaelson going to vote.
Damned funny. Why, until the last year and a half, he had
never even given a thought to politics. When he had come
from Muncie, Indiana, a freshman at the University, he had
dreamed of being a writer, a new Sherwood Anderson. Just
think, he was hanging out now around the place where Sherwood Anderson and so many other writers had once lived,
written, and attended parties.

He went on eating. He had not even tried to write in over
four years. Well, the system had ruined him. Now, now that

he was a sympathizer of the Communist Party, he would be
a new man, and he would write. If it weren't for his literary
aspirations, he would even join the Party. But he could serve
best with the weapon of the word. In order to do this, he first
had to get experience, experience with the working class. All
of his past experience was petit bourgeois, and he couldn't
write about that. Not such defeatist stuff.

He poured himself a second cup of coffee, lit a cigarette, and
sat thinking idly.

III

He heard the knocker on the front door. Answering it, he
saw Garfield, a man of about forty.

"Come on in and have a cup of coffee," he said.

"All right. How are you?" Garfield answered in a slow
drawl.

Garfield entered. Al slouched back to the rear of the studio,
and Garfield followed him. Al took a dirty cup from the iron
sink, washed it out, and poured Garfield a cup of coffee. He
poured himself another cup. They lit cigarettes and sat facing
each other.

"Voted yet?" Garfield suddenly asked.

"Can't you see I'm not even dressed?"

Garfield looked at Al.

"Yeh, that's right."

"You voted?" Al asked.

"Not yet."

"After we have this coffee, I'll shave and dress and we'll go
out and vote."

"There's lots of time."

"Yeh, it isn't twelve o'clock yet. We still got all day."

They sat, both of them seemingly lost in reverie.

"You got up early today," Garfield said.

"Yes, a little early. Eleven o'clock."

"I got up early, too."

"Well, it's a big day."

"It's a big day. If the whole city was like the Fifty-seventh Street art colony, it would be a big day," Garfield said.

"What do you mean?"

"The colony is going to vote Communist."

"Uh huh! But here, pour yourself another cup of coffee."

"I guess I will," Garfield said, going to the stove.

They dawdled over their coffee in silence.

IV

"Say, I just remembered," Al said suddenly.

"What?"

"I got a little hooch left."

"Al, that would hit the spot."

Al went upstairs to the bedroom; it was partitioned off from the rest of the studio. He got out a bottle of moonshine; it was almost half-filled. He carried it down to the kitchen.

He poured out jiggers of whisky, and they got glasses of water.

"Here's to the revolution," Garfield said.

They raised glasses.

"To the revolution," Al said.

They drank.

"I've drunk worse stuff," Garfield said.

"It's better than nothing. But listen, you, I don't want to get drunk before I vote. This is something solemn, voting for the Party. We got to do it with dignity."

Garfield nodded in agreement.

"We should have done this four years ago when they elected Hoover," Garfield said.

"Here, have another," Al said, pouring out more drinks.

"Oh, thanks."

They drank.

"As I said, we should have voted this way in 1928 when Smith and Hoover ran against each other. Well, it's too bad there wasn't a Communist Party then," Garfield said.

"Sure there was," Al said.

"There was? Running a campaign, too, in the election?"
Garfield asked.

"Yeh."

"Well, why didn't we hear about it?" asked Garfield.

"We weren't politicalized," Al said.

"I remember the election four years ago just as clear as I
remember yesterday or last week," Garfield said.

Al poured out another drink, emptying the bottle.

"Oh, thanks," Garfield said.

They drank.

"Funny, I didn't know a thing about the Party in 1928,"
Garfield said.

"It took the crisis to politicalize us," Al said.

"Well, that's past. Water run under the bridge. Gin poured
from the skillet," Garfield said.

They sat studying their empty glasses. Al lit a cigarette.

"What time is it?" Garfield asked.

"We got plenty of time," Al said.

"Of course. I know it."

"Hell, the polls are open all day," Garfield nodded.

"Give me one of your cigarettes, Al."

"Here, take one."

Garfield reached across and took one of Al's cigarettes.

"Got enough to go in on a bottle with me?" asked Garfield.

"Yeh, but we'll get it after we vote. We'll celebrate."

"That's a good idea."

Al got up and started putting his breakfast dishes in the
sink.

v

"Let's stop in and see Annabelle," Garfield said.

"O.K.," Al answered, locking the studio door.

To their left and above the viaduct an Illinois Central elec-
tric-suburban train rolled into the Fifty-seventh Street station.

They crossed the street.

"I wonder if Annabelle is up yet?" Garfield asked.

"You and she have a night of it last night?"

"We had some fun," Garfield said.

"Doesn't Tom mind?"

"What good does it do him?"

"I don't know. Ask me another."

Annabelle came to the door. She was a husky red-headed girl of about thirty.

"Oh, come on in, boys. Have a cup of coffee with us," she said.

The studio was decorated with velvet drapes, and there were odd-looking amateurish modernistic pictures on the walls. She led them to the rear, where there was a kitchen behind a partition. Tom, her husband, was eating breakfast. He was a plump, ruddy man of about thirty-five.

"Hello," he said nervously; he went on eating.

"Here, boys, sit down and have some coffee," Annabelle said.

They sat down. Annabelle brought coffee to everyone, and they sat around the table.

"Vote yet?" Al asked.

Tom went on eating.

"Tom, can't you hear?" Annabelle asked sharply.

"What, dear?"

"Al asked you, did you vote yet?"

"Oh, no. I just got up a little while ago."

"There's plenty of time to vote," Garfield said.

"Well, things sure are changed a lot around the colony," Al said.

"From when?" Tom asked.

"From two or three years ago," Al said.

"I don't see much change. A couple of young girls from the University are hanging around. Not much else," Tom said.

"I mean politically speaking," Al said.

"Yes, that way," Tom said.

"And, of course, if there have been political changes, that means that we've all changed, and that means that the colony has changed," Garfield said.

"That's right."

No one talked for a while. Tom was nervous.

"Say, got a drink?" Al asked.

"Have we, Tom?" Annabelle asked.

"I don't know."

Annabelle went to the front of the studio.

"Well, we're all comrades now, ain't we?" Tom said, looking nervously at Garfield.

"Yes, sure. We're all voting today for the Party, too. We'll scare the hell out of the petit bourgeois shopkeepers when they see the number of Communist Party votes rolled up in this district. And most of the Party votes in the whole ward will come from the colony," Garfield said.

Annabelle returned with a bottle of moonshine.

"I found this, boys. It must be left from the last party we had," she said.

"We ought to have something to mix it in," Al said.

"Tom, you go get some soda at the drugstore."

"I haven't got my shoes on, Annabelle."

"Well, you can put them on."

He got up, sulky, and went out.

"Tom, get two bottles," she called after him.

They heard the front door close.

"I would have gone, Annabelle," Garfield said.

"That's all right, Tom can do it. He's not working today."

"I would have gone, too," Al said.

"Tom's doing it."

"Well, dear, how is everything?" Garfield said.

"Tom's in bad humor this morning. He knows about last night, of course."

"Did you tell him?" asked Garfield.

"I didn't have to. He guessed. When I'm out until after three, he knows where I am. He was up waiting and was so all-in this morning, he laid off work. He's getting awful nervous these days," Annabelle said.

"Well, what'll we do about it?" Garfield asked.

"Nothing," Annabelle answered.

They heard Tom entering in front, and soon he came in with two bottles of soda. He and Annabelle mixed the drinks.

VI

"Come on, let's vote," Al said.

"There's plenty of time," Garfield said.

"You fellows go and vote now. Annabelle and I will vote later," Tom said.

"We can all vote together," Annabelle said.

"Yeh, solidarity," Al said.

"Let's have another drink," Garfield said.

"You're not crippled. Mix it," Tom said.

"I'll do that, comrade," Garfield said.

He mixed a drink for himself.

"Gimme a drink," Al said.

"Here it is. Fix it yourself, comrade," Garfield said.

"Thanks, comrade. Solidarity," Al said, going to the bottle.

He fixed himself a drink and gulped it down.

Annabelle went over to Garfield and sat on his lap. She glared at Tom. Tom didn't say a word.

"Come on, let's vote," Al said.

"Go ahead and vote, Al. I'll vote later," Garfield said.

"Al, you and Tom go and vote, and we'll be along later and vote ourselves."

"I'll wait until you're ready, Annabelle," Tom said.

"You don't have to. I said go ahead and vote with Al," Annabelle said.

Al had another drink.

VII

"Where the hell are the polls now? I forget. Is it this way?" Al asked, pointing toward Stony Island and Jackson Park. "Or is it that way?" he said, pointing toward Harper, which was beyond the Illinois Central viaduct.

"I'm going to stop in here a minute," Tom said, going to the studio next door to his own; it was an art school conducted by his neighbor.

"They can't stomach me," Al said.

"Well, you go and vote. I'll see you later."

"Oh, we got time for that," Al said.

Tom went inside his neighbor's studio, and Al was left standing alone. His legs were rubbery. He floundered across the street to his own studio and let himself in. His head seemed to be going around. He wanted a drink. He told himself that he was getting drunk and warned himself that he had to vote, so he couldn't let himself get too drunk. He had to remember to stay sober enough to vote. But, hell, he could stand another drink. One more wouldn't knock him out. He had drunk plenty more than he'd put away today without going under the table and passing out. Yes, plenty more. He rummaged about the bedroom and found another partially filled bottle of moonshine.

VIII

"George, I got to vote," Al said, sitting at the counter of the ice cream store at the corner of Fifty-seventh and Stony Island.

"Yeh."

"Yeh, I got to vote."

Al looked into his coffee.

"Today, we're all equal. All equal, all got a vote. I'm going to cast my vote. George, are you going to vote?"

"I'm a Greek."

"Well, when we win, George, it won't matter what you are," Al said.

George didn't pay attention to Al. He was cleaning out the store and he went on sweeping. Al sat before his coffee for a long time. Then he drank it. He almost fell off the stool.

"Put it on the bill, George," he said, and left the store.

He staggered past the row of studios and found Tom in front of his own studio, banging on the door.

"Let me in," Tom yelled.

Al watched Tom.

"Open the door!" Tom yelled.

He pounded on the studio door again.

"Hey, Tom!" Al called.

Tom suddenly turned around and saw Al.

"What's the matter?" Al asked.

"She and Garfield are in there together," Tom said.

"Well, come on and vote, and then when we come back maybe they won't be," said Al.

"I'm a goddamn cuckold. My wife makes me into a cuckold," Tom said.

"Come on and vote against the capitalists. It's the system, that's the trouble," Al said.

"Let me in! Open the door!" Tom yelled.

Annabelle opened the door. She was wearing a kimono.

"Tom, go away. Go and . . . vote. You can't come in yet. Go away," she said.

"It's my own house."

"Tom, go away, or I go," she said.

"But . . ."

Annabelle noticed Al.

"Have you voted yet?" she asked him.

"No. I'm going now."

"Take Tom with you."

Annabelle closed the door. Tom looked at the closed door, disconsolate. He turned to Al.

"I'm a cuckold," he said.

"It's the system that's responsible. Come on and we'll both vote against the system," Al said.

IX

"Where can we bum a drink before we go to vote?" Al said.

"I don't know."

"We have plenty of time. It's only about three-thirty now, and we have until eight o'clock to vote. I think I need another drink before I go around the corner to the damned polls," Al said.

"Well?"

They stood under the Illinois Central viaduct, and they heard a suburban train rolling overhead.

"Let's go see Mort," Al said.

Al staggered down the steep curb and ran drunkenly across the street. He got up on the other side and hurried toward Stony Island, Tom following him. Mort's studio was the last one of a row facing Jackson Park, just south of Fifty-seventh Street on Stony Island Avenue.

"Hello, fellows," Mort said, letting them in.

Mort was medium-sized and in his late thirties. His studio was crowded with old furniture, miscellaneous odds and ends, and it needed to be swept and dusted.

Tom and Al slumped onto a couch on one side of the large front part of the studio.

"Mort, got a drink?"

"Gee, I haven't. I'm sorry, but I'm all out."

"Now, ain't that tough," Al said.

"You look as if you had enough already, Al," Mort said.

"Oh, no, I haven't. I need one more. I need one two more before I go vote," Al said.

"What the hell you want to vote for?" Mort asked.

"I'm gonna vote for the Party," Al said.

"What Party?"

"The Party. Mort, look at me," Al said.

"I am. You're not the most wholesome sight in the world, Al, but I'm looking at you."

"Well, look at me," Al said.

"He's looking," Tom said.

"All right, know what you see! Know what you see! You see sitting before you a revolutionist."

Mort and Tom doubled over with laughter.

"Why don't you join the Party and do some work for it?" Mort asked.

"I would. But I'm not good enough to be a Party member. I'm still only a petit bourgeois intellectual," Al said.

Mort laughed again.

"That's all right, laugh at me. Go ahead, laugh at me. But that doesn't change the situation one little iota. No, sir, it doesn't change the situation even one little iota," Al said with drunken seriousness.

"Say, I'll go buy a bottle of liquor. I need a drink. I'll be right back," Tom said, getting up.

"That's what I say, more drinks. I need one drink, I need one two drinks before I go and cast my vote," Al said.

X

"What did you say you were going to do?" Mort asked, the three of them sitting close together with glasses in their hands.

"I'm going to vote."

"What for?"

"The Party. The Future. The Workers. Humanity."

Mort laughed. He took a drink.

"Mort, don't laugh," Al said.

"Why?"

"Because I mean it. Don't laugh at my dearest and most tender sentiments."

"Dearest and most tender sentiments," Tom said, looking glumly into his glass.

"Say, what the hell is eating the ass of you fellows? Tom there is like a corpse, he's so joyful, and, Al, you're saving the human race," Mort said.

"Let's have another drink," Tom said.

"That's what I need before I go and vote."

XI

Tom lay on the couch, snoring.

"He can't take his drinks," Mort said, his voice thick.

"It's his wife," Al said, wavering badly from side to side.

"What's the matter?"

"She's with Garfield now. She threw him out of the studio to lay up all afternoon with Garfield. If I had a wife like that, know what I'd do to her?" Al said.

"What?"

"I wouldn't vote for her."

"You and your goddamn votes," Mort said.

"What time is it?" asked Al.

"Five-thirty," Mort said.

"Give me another drink," Al said.

"There isn't any more," Mort answered. Mort pointed at Tom, "Well, he won't think of his wife giving it away now."

Al put on his coat.

"What's the hurry?" Mort asked.

"I got to vote," Al said.

"Well, vote for my ass, will you," Mort said, still looking at Tom, who lay there, snoring.

"I can't. I got to vote for the Party," Al said, leaving.

It was dark outside. Al staggered to Fifty-seventh Street. He could hear the wind in the trees in Jackson Park on the other side of Stony Island Avenue.

He stood rubbery-legged on the corner of Fifty-seventh and Stony Island for a moment. He lunged forward and fumbled for the key to his own studio. He let himself in and tumbled onto a couch.

XII

Al woke up still drunk. He didn't know what time it was. He yawned. He heard a ticking noise. It was the clock. He looked at it, squinting his eyes. Ten minutes to eight. He still had time to vote. He got to his feet, put on his coat, left the studio, staggered across the street, and rapped on Annabelle's studio door. She let him in. Her hair was askew, and her opened kimono exposed one of her breasts. He saw Garfield sleeping on a couch.

He roused Garfield, who looked at him with dull eyes.

"Come on and vote," Al urged.

"Huh?"

"Come on, we all got to vote for the Party," Al said.

"Here," Garfield said, holding out his hand. "Here, take my vote, vote it for me."

"We got to vote," Al said, turning at Annabelle.

"We did everything else today but vote," she said, giggling.

"Gimme a drink," Al said.

Annabelle pointed to a bottle on the table.

Al poured himself a drink, gulped it down, and rushed out

of the studio, almost falling on his face. He lunged on to Harper Avenue. The polls were right down the street. He had to vote. He had time. Had to vote. He staggered on. He could see election officials and policemen inside the store which served as the voting place in the precinct. He tried to open the door. A cop motioned for him to go away. Telling himself he had to vote, he rapped on the door.

A cop opened the door.

"Get the hell out of here before I run yuh in."

"I got . . . got . . . gotta vote."

"You're too late. The polls is closed."

"But I got . . . got . . . got . . ."

"Get the hell out of here!" the cop said, shoving Al away.

Al spilled on his face. He patiently fought his way to his feet and wandered off, telling himself that he had to vote for the Party.

1940-1942

The Fall of Machine Gun McGurk

THOUSANDS of fight fans, hungry for thrills and sensations, streamed into the Yankee Stadium to see the big fight between Machine Gun McGurk and Leo Robis. With the exception of the Machine Gun, there was no class in the heavyweight division. Gone were the days of Dempsey and Tunney. Cynical sports writers stigmatized most of the leading heavyweights as bums, palookas, false alarms. Whenever they saw two of these beef trusts falling over each other and fanning the air in what was technically called a prize fight, they wrote of how they yawned through the dreary encounter. Only the radio announcers seemed to take these fights seriously. And the champion was no better than the leading challengers; when he won the title, he and his opponent should both have been disqualified, thrown out of the ring for stalling. The fight fans had had to exist on a poor heavyweight diet. And then the Machine Gun had appeared suddenly, as if from nowhere.

He was an Irish lad, born on the west side of Chicago. For reasons unknown, sports writers had often called him the South Chicago Machine Gun. At other times they said that he had come from back of the Chicago stockyards. McGurk was only twenty-three, but in a couple of years he had suddenly changed the heavyweight picture. He had come up through the Golden Gloves tournaments, winning the heavyweight title in his last year of fighting in that competition. He had been picked up by Tim Malone and Sol Levinson, and they had brought him along fast. His record was one long series of quick knockouts. Few fighters had stayed with him for more than three rounds. No heavyweight had made a more impressive record and showing than Machine Gun McGurk in those pork-and-bean years when a fighter is brought along and prepared to step up into the top class and fight for the big money.

McGurk was a terrific puncher, a murderous finisher, and he looked fine and graceful in the ring. His record was probably as honestly earned as that of many other fighters. But Malone and Levinson were not in the fight game for sport. Every fighter they had had for over five years had turned out to be a bum. They had to get back in the big dough. So they took no chances with McGurk. When they hit the tank towns to give their boy a long list of K.O.'s, they had with them a retinue of three burly chauffeurs. Alternately, one of the chauffeurs would go ahead two or three hundred miles to some town and establish himself there as a fighter. McGurk would arrive in due time, and a match would be arranged. McGurk would fight one of the chauffeurs and add another quick knockout to his record. Then the chauffeur whose turn it was next would go ahead, and there would be a repeat performance. Fifteen of the knockouts in his sensational rise had been produced in this manner. Besides, he had fought worn-out punching bags, Negroes who were forced to take a dive under threats of violence, and others of an odd assortment of human hulks. But his record looked good, and that was what made publicity. Having been nursed through the tank towns, he stepped into a better class and continued his string of knockouts. And the sports writers had been avid for a new heavyweight sensation. They needed one. They were fed up with writing about the clumsy champion, and his equally clumsy challengers. The public was tired of seeing them fight. A new fighter was needed to restore prosperity to the heavy-weight prize-fight business. McGurk filled the need. He had form. He looked like a wonder. He could punch. He appeared to be the best finisher since Dempsey and, once he had his opponent weakened, he went in to kill and slugged his man into the kind of coma that brought the crowd to its feet. He looked good, and he was just what the writers needed.

His build-up had been quick and sensational. Sports writers vied with one another in coining phrases to describe his destructive powers. He was the Machine Gun, the South Chicago Machine Gun, the Dynamiting Turkey, the Irish Cavalcade, the Murderous Turkey, the Assassinating Harp, the Human Dum-Dum Bullet, and, needless to add, he was the greatest heavyweight of them all. Sports writers kept describing imaginary fights in which he put away Dempsey, Tunney, Jack Johnson, Jim Jeffries, Bob Fitzsimmons, Jim Corbett, and John L. Sullivan. He became a big draw, and the only heavyweight fight which could make money was one in which he was a contestant.

Leo Robis was an experienced old war horse of a fighter, among the best of a bad lot of heavyweights. He was the last obstacle in the path of Machine Gun McGurk. After Robis, the title fight, and then a real champion would be born.

II

The crowd kept thronging to the Yankee Stadium. Once again the fight fans could smell blood. All they hoped was that McGurk would give them a run for their money and let Robis hang on for a couple of rounds. Even so, it would be a treat to see McGurk lay the Polack out flat in record time. Perhaps he would cancel Robis in even less time than it had taken Jack Dempsey to flatten Fred Fulton.

The preliminary boys slugged and floundered away in the ring. A big Argentine was mauling away with a Negro heavyweight, and when the Argentine got an adverse decision, there was a round of boos. Then two more gorillas came into the ring. One of them in purple tights came out like a windmill, turned into a dynamo, punched his opponent back and forth across the ring for forty-five seconds, took one punch on the chin, and staggered as his legs caved in. He went down and stayed down, and was carried to his stool amid a chorus of boos and cheers. Another fight, and it was time for the real business to begin.

Now everybody found his or her seat and waited. The excitement and tension mounted. Spectators coming in late hurried to their places. This fight might be over so quickly that they couldn't afford to miss anything. Around the ringside section, people glanced about to see and to be seen. There was the usual brilliant collection of former prize fighters, politicians, baseball players, theatrical producers, slick-paper magazine writers, glamor girls, big-town Charlies, and persons whose babies were born in the gossip columns of the newspapers. Robis was cheered when he entered the ring. Then came McGurk, and the ovation was thunderous. Photographers swarmed about the ring, and former champions began clambering through the ropes to be introduced and to get their hand. Jack Dempsey got a loud and enthusiastic ovation. And then Gene Tunney was introduced, the announcer describing him as an inspiration to the youth of America, and he was loudly cheered. Mickey Walker was introduced as one of the greatest thrill producers, bar none, in the history of the prize ring, and he, too, was applauded. Others came, and then the present champion was introduced. He was booed, and many from the crowd yelled for him to wait until McGurk got him. Finally the ring was cleared. The fighters were introduced and received their final instructions in the center of the ring. They went to their corners.

The crowd waited, keen and alert; eyes were riveted on the green-roped ring. Nervous conversation popped on all sides like firecrackers, and many were asking one another how long the dark-haired Pole could last. They were waiting only to see him stretched out, bloody and unconscious, another victim of the new hero. And the gong! A loud cheer. The Murder of the Century was on.

III

Machine Gun McGurk danced and pranced cautiously about the ring, facing a man who seemed clumsy before him. McGurk feinted with the snap of a trained and perfectly co-ordinated boxer. He had come a long way, this Golden Gloves boy, or so it appeared in those first seconds of the first round. He seemed to be possessed of almost insolent confidence. He maneuvered to let go with that deadly one-two punch that had earned him the sobriquet of the Machine Gun. A left to the body, and a murderous right across to the jaw, and the opponent would be where Dempsey's opponents used to be. That was all that was needed to put the hapless Pole into a state of temporary paralysis.

"Fight, you bums!" someone yelled from the grandstand as they continued to feel out one another.

But they sparred and shifted in a first round which went to McGurk by a harmless margin. The sympathies of many in the crowd suddenly turned to Robis, the underdog. During the one-minute intermission before the second round, many spectators began to coach Leo Robis.

"Get in there, Leo boy. Bob and weave and duck his left."

"Don't stand up straight for him, Robie, old boy!"

The encouragement to Robis brought out counter advice for McGurk. One cynical-faced thin fellow in a checkered suit peered through binoculars from close to the ringside.

"Don't be a bum, Robis. You're yellow. Fighting the kind of a fight the Machine Gun wants you to. Down, there! Bob and weave! Use the right! Bob and weave!"

The second round came up. It was fought cautiously. McGurk boxed, poised and graceful. Robis was still clumsy, a man who seemed to have no right to be in the same ring with this Irish giant.

"Fight, you Polack bum!"

"Get going, Leo!"

"Give him the sub-machine gun, Mac!"

"Make it fast, Machine Gun!"

And still the cautious feeling-out process went on.

"He's giving us a little run for our money," many in the arena said.

"No, a waltz," some wit answered.

Swaying and weaving, Robis moved about awkwardly but carefully, and McGurk sparred. Not one authentic blow was struck during the entire round.

And the gong! The lights going on all over the arena. The

high-pitched conversation. The seconds expertly working over the men. Again the gong!

IV

All lights off except those over the ring. All over the stadium little flares flickering up, going out as cigarettes were lighted. A sudden, loud, and long Oh breaking forth like a collective groan of thousands, and everyone was on his feet. Robis had bounced McGurk's head back with a straight right.

"Oh, what a bum! He's yellow, Leo! Get in there, Leo!"

"Blank-Cartridge McGurk!"

"Polish him off, Robis!"

"Dempsey would have killed him," the gray-suited fellow with the binoculars yelled.

"Get going, McGurk!"

"The Machine Gun now!"

"Cover up, McGurk!"

And Robis relentlessly followed McGurk about the ring. The Irishman was plainly in trouble. The gray-suited fellow with the opera glasses kept yelling that McGurk was mad and swinging wildly now. McGurk was no longer the graceful, panther-like animal, prancing around in certain expectation of a kill. Robis had him, it seemed.

V

When the fourth round started, the crowd yelled for blood. Robis came out of his corner with his eye nicked from a wild punch that had landed at the end of the last round. McGurk seemed refreshed. This was the round. And McGurk was down. Another right. McGurk was up immediately, punching wildly, and the experts about the ringside kept yelling that McGurk was dizzy, didn't know what he was doing, hadn't known enough to take a count in order to clear his head. He swung low and landed with a roundhouse left, and the crowd booed.

"Hey! Hey! Watch it, you!" the fellow with the opera glasses yelled threateningly.

"Kill him, Leo!" a woman yelled.

The crowd now cheered and exhorted Robis. Shaken by surprise at the unexpected turn of the fight, it wanted blood. McGurk rooters showed concern, and either pleaded with their man to come back or were gloomily silent.

And methodically Robis followed McGurk, blocked his floundering punches, steadily punished him with a straight right.

The heart seemed utterly gone out of the hurt, floundering Machine Gun McGurk. Missing punches, he revealed how the Pole's plan of battle was working out. Drawing the Machine Gun to lead with his left, Robis ducked under the blow and pegged in solid right-hand punches, sometimes following up with a choppy left. Now a majority of the crowd yelled that McGurk couldn't take it.

"Oh, you Glass-Jaw McGurk!"

After each round, McGurk wobbled about the ring, scarcely able to find his own corner. Loud and gleeful voices announced that the Irishman was out on his feet. The new superman of pugilism had turned out to be another bum because of one knockdown and a pounding succession of right jabs.

Groggy for two rounds, McGurk seemed to recover in the seventh round. He attacked, and the mob was on its feet, ready to shift its allegiance as he banged at Robis.

"He ain't hittin' Leo! He's hittin' the Pole's gloves! McGurk's face is hamboiger! It's hamboiger! He's a sucker for a poifect right! Go in with the right, Robis, and you'll kill the yellow bum!"

And the diehard McGurk fans kept urging their man on.

VI

For nine rounds Leo Robis punched Machine Gun McGurk into a state of bewildered, rubbery-legged helplessness. McGurk swung wildly, feebly. Before the end, Robis was laughing at him. The Pole continued to fight cautiously, ploddingly, slugging away until he grew arm-weary. Some spectators called the referee to stop it. One fellow by the ringside yelled out that

Robis was a bum because he was taking so much time to knock out a thoroughly beaten man.

From round to round, the roaring grew in volume. From behind, there came petulant, repetitive cries for those in front to sit down. Robis was exhorted to polish off McGurk, to kill him. McGurk, utterly confused and groggy, kept swinging aimlessly. He landed several low blows. He was booed. Then finally, after one minute of the thirteenth round, Robis straightened McGurk up and bounced a last needless right off the Irishman's jaw. McGurk fell into the ropes, relaxed, slid on the canvas, quivered, feebly rolled over. A long and lusty roar acclaimed the end of one superman and the elevation of another superman to supplant him in the sports columns.

The beaten heavyweight was led off, half dragged, half carried, his face smothered in a towel. Some yelled sympathetic words to him; some shouted that he was yellow. He didn't hear. Then there was a last pitying cheer for him. Thunderously applauded, Robis left the ring, guarded by policemen, waving and grinning in recognition of the plaudits which acknowledged him the hero of the evening.

VII

In his dressing room, Robis stood under a spraying shower, surrounded by reporters and photographers. His dark hair was sopped and, after drying, he covered his middle with a towel and crushed his way out of the shower to dress. The reporters clung to him, asking him questions. Photographers clambered onto benches, and flashlight bulbs flared as he was mugged continuously and from all sides. Again and again, reporters asked him how he had won and solemnly copied down his almost monosyllabic answers. He said that McGurk was a good boxer, but could be hit, and that McGurk's punches had not hurt him seriously, except the low punches. He said the nick on the eye was nothing. And the photographers kept working away.

"Hey, Leo, please smile! I want you smiling, and I'm finished," one of the photographers pleaded.

The confusion in the dressing room continued. Policemen

kept barring newcomers, chasing out others, and the reporters continued repeating their questions. All Robis's answers were noted. The experts said that these answers were excellent. Robis spoke of the championship. He accepted more tumultuous congratulations from all sides. A radio announcer kept barking out a description of the scene, promising every moment to put Leo Robis on the air. Robis's manager, a slick-faced, corpulent man, chewed away on a cigar, wiped oceans of perspiration from his brow, and chided the experts who had picked McGurk to win. Finally the sweating radio announcer, a handkerchief around his neck, broke through the crowd and got Robis to say a few words.

"Well, I won like I said I was gonna win. I fought hard, and Machine Gun McGurk is a good fighter and he fought hard. It was a hard fight, but I won it, because I didn't want to let my friends and admirers down." Robis paused. "Yes, it was a hard fight. McGurk fought a hard fight."

"Now what do you plan, Leo?" asked the announcer.

"I wanna fight with the champion."

"Thank you, Leo Robis. You have just heard Leo Robis, the winner in this sensation, thrilling, murderous battle of the century. And, folks, I wish you could see Leo Robis's dressing room. Everybody crowding in here, everybody smiling, everybody talking. I tell you, it's bedlam. Folks, it's bedlam. And, folks, I got to sign off now, and I want to say again, I am sorry that we cannot get a word from Machine Gun McGurk. But remember in hearing all this noise and joy here that the loser fought a good clean fight, trying every minute, fighting with the stoutest heart ever seen in a prize ring and showing us sheer courage like we have never been shown sheer courage before, and we experts have seen lots of sheer courage of the most courageous in our experiences covering prize fights. Again, this is Jack Jackson, your announcer, signing off after carrying to you, through the courtesy of Good-Hearted Candies, a blow-by-blow description of tonight's fight between Leo Robis and Machine Gun McGurk, and then bringing you a description of Leo Robis's dressing room, and the words of Leo Robis himself from his dressing room after he emerged the victor in the greatest and most thrilling fight that anyone has seen in a long, long time. Good night, folks, Jack Jackson, your announcer, and please stand by for station identification!"

"Hey, Leo, please smile! Hey, tell him to smile. I can't get home till I get a shot of him smilin'. Hey, Leo, please smile for just a second!" a photographer pleaded as he stood above the crowd on a bench.

Robis was dressed now, gay and not worrying about his bruised eyes; he grinned stupidly.

"Hey, please, Leo, please get Leo to smile. For Christ sake, I can't go home until I get one of him smiling!"

VIII

Machine Gun McGurk's dressing room was almost deserted. Clad in a loud greenish suit, with a straw hat askew on his large head, Machine Gun McGurk sat bowed. This west-side Irish boy from Chicago, who had never been considered bright, who had been expelled from school in the sixth grade, and who had earned thousands of dollars in the few years of his "meteoric" rise, sat crying on a bench, much like a sickened animal. His managers stood by him, saying little, and one of them now and then patted him on the back. His face was puffed and bruised, almost unrecognizable. He constantly felt his face and head. A trainer massaged his neck. Tears came easily, and he wiped his battered eyes with a towel. His knuckles were bruised. He sat, dazed and stupefied from punishment. There was a rap on the door, and a couple of newspapermen entered. The managers told them that McGurk wouldn't make any statements.

"How about one of you fellows making a statement?" one of the newspapermen asked.

"Over-confidence," Tim Malone said.

"He was trained too fine. We congratulate Robis on his good clean fight. All we ask is another chance, and our boy will knock him out," Levinson said.

The reporters copied down the statement and grinned. They looked at the beaten heavyweight but said nothing.

McGurk sat there. Again he dabbed his eyes.

"Jesus, it's a morgue," a newspaperman said.

Nothing much was said, and McGurk sat there; his managers stood near him, and one of the trainers continued to massage his neck. Photographers stood on chairs and benches, hoping to get a shot of the Machine Gun as he left. They begged Levinson and Malone to let them take a picture of McGurk, and both managers flatly said no. Loud echoes from outside announced Robis's departure. And still McGurk sat there in his stupor. Finally, the managers and trainers got around him. He couldn't walk. He left like a drunken man, surrounded by cops and his retinue, his face hidden behind a straw hat and the collar of his gray topcoat, and the photographers weren't able to get a decent shot of him. Outside, police shoved the waiting crowd back, and the helpless giant was dragged into a taxicab and hustled away.

Machine Gun McGurk had had his day, and that fight was the beginning of a long descent that was to end with him another punch-drunk bum hanging on the edge of the sport world, broke, shabby, with a beaten and battered brain making him the butt of cruel and stupid tricks.

1939

Yesterday's Love

"HELLO, Harry, how are you? . . . You know who this is, don't you? Sure you do. . . . Why, this is me. Harriet. . . . Sure! . . . How are you, Harry? . . . Say, I'm not bothering you, am I? I just thought I'd give you a buzz and say hello. . . . How's all the gang? Tell 'em I was asking for 'em. And how's Marie? She's such a sweet innocent kid. Say hello to her for me. . . . I like Marie, Harry, and I think you pick 'em good. . . . Harry, seen Jeannette lately? She's still goin' with Phil, ain't she? Say I was asking for her, too. I like Jeannette. I think she's swell. . . . God, Harry, but I'm all in. Do I feel lousy! I been tight for five nights in a row. I been tight every night this week. I was so washed up this morning that I couldn't go to work. I slept all day, and I'm still feeling like a wet towel. Gee, am I glad tomorrow's Saturday. . . . Operator, get off the wire. . . . The damn operators are always buttin' in. Well, I hope this one gets her dirty ears full. . . . But did we make whoopee! I tell you, I never had so much fun, never except last summer when we all was goin' together, and I was going with Mark. . . . No, I wasn't out with Jake neither. You ought to know me better than ask me that. Jake's a nice fellow and I like him. He's swell. But he's too old for me, thirty-five. Still, he's been damned swell to me. He gives me anything I want. You should just see the beautiful dark brown suede purse he gave me for my birthday. He'll give me anything I want. . . . Oh, Harry, you got a dirty mind. It isn't that neither, no, it isn't. Jake and I are just friends. . . . You

169

know I'm engaged. . . . Why, didn't you hear about it? . . .
Well, I been engaged for a couple of weeks. . . . No, I was
sober when I consented. And you should see the ring I
got. Diamond, square-cut, and set in platinum. . . . I was
really engaged longer, but I didn't breathe a word about it to
a soul, that is, until two weeks ago. . . . And I didn't get
engaged on account of Mark either. Harry, you know I said
that if Mark and I ever broke up, I'd never be a pest and a
public nuisance like Ann was. But I really didn't get engaged
because of what Mark did. You know me, Harry, and you
know I wouldn't do that. Honest, I didn't. Of course I liked
Mark, but then, well, I'm not sobbing any blues because I'm
not that kind. And when a fellow does to me what Mark
done, well, I just snap my fingers and I say good riddance to
bad rubbish, not that Mark was bad rubbish or anything like
that, but it's just that, well, life is too short to be wearing out
your handkerchief crying. Of course I got to admit that I did
like Mark. He was fine, and good-looking, and—intellectual.
But then, he did play a dirty trick on me, not saying a word
when he went and did what he did. . . . Say, what kind of
a girl is this Fritzie that he married? . . . She's a nice kid,
huh? . . . Well, I'm glad of that. . . . I thought she must
be. . . . No, I ain't sore at him, and I'm not going to squeeze
my tears all over the pavement, like Ann did when Mark gave
her the gate. Like 'em and leave 'em with a smile, that's my
motto every time. . . . 'Course I think he played a dirty
trick on me. Here I was sending him money all the time he
was in Los Angeles. And I sent him shirts, and handkerchiefs,
and candy, too. And, Harry, I sent him the bus fare back to
Chicago. He got in a week ago Tuesday, and he called me up
the next morning, and saw me that night, that was a week ago
Wednesday. We were together, and when I went to work the
next morning, that was a week ago yesterday, he was sleeping,
and when I came home he was gone, and I ain't seen him since.
Now, I think that was a dirty trick to play on me. I was decent
to him and think I have a right to be treated on the square
when I play square. All he had to do was to leave a note saying

it was all over, or else to come out in the open and tell me, and
I wouldn't have been no weeping willow, nor nothing like
that. . . . I'm not sore, Harry, but you know yourself that
it wasn't right or decent. It wasn't fair. . . . And please,
Harry, don't repeat this to Mark. . . . I really think that it
was a dirty trick, and I never thought that Mark would treat
me like this. . . . And, Harry, don't think that I got engaged to get even with him or show that I wasn't affected,
because I didn't. . . . I like Jack. Harry, I want you to meet
him, because he's perfectly swell. He's swell. I want you to see
the diamond engagement ring he gave me. I'll bet he spent at
least five hundred on it. . . . Operator, get off the wire. No,
I won't give you another nickel. I haven't been talking five
minutes. . . . All right then, here's your nickel. . . . Darn
those operators. . . . But as I was telling you, Jack is swell.
Harry, Jack's a prince. They don't make them in any better molds. . . . Oh, Harry, how perfectly awful and dirty-
minded you are to say that! . . . Well, we been all over town,
and I've been getting in every morning at the most ungodly
hours, tight to the gills. The night before last I was so drunk
I can't remember much about it. Well, anyway, we went to
Petrushka, you know, the funny Russian place. And did we
have a grand time! But I know that this bores you and, Harry,
I just don't want you to think that I'm talking about all this
and telling you I'm engaged just to prove that Mark's getting
married like he did hasn't made me feel bad. I feel wonderful.
You know, Harry, when Mark was in Los Angeles, I didn't sit
on the shelf and get dusty like an old package. I was out every
night. And if Mark knew all the things I did, well, his pride
might have been hurt because he was always writing me letters
and asking me to be true to him. I wasn't true to him. Mark
doesn't know it, but I wasn't. . . . Why, Harry, I didn't say
that. All I said was that I wasn't true to him. . . . Of course,
Harry, I know you're Mark's best friend, but I wish you would
do me a favor and not say anything that I just told you to
Mark. Just tell him I said I wish him happiness and congratulate him. I'd like that he and I would remain just old friends.

But, Harry, I'll always like Mark, and remember that I had some of the most beautiful moments of my life with him, but I do think he played a dirty trick on me. It was not that it hurt—well, yes, it did hurt me, because he was so ungrateful and unfair. But I ain't sore. . . . Harry, do tell Mark that I wish him all the happiness in the world. And I'm glad that this Fritzie is a nice kid, and not noisy, or vulgar, or crazy like Ann was. . . . Say, I'm not bothering you talking like this, am I? . . . Why, Harry? . . . But I did have a lot of fun with Mark, and I'm not sorry I met him because we did have a fine friendship, because that was what it really was with me, and that other, well, I did that to please Mark because I really am not the kind of a girl that enjoys it. Well, maybe I did sometimes think I loved him, but anyway, Harry, do tell Mark what I asked you to. . . . Gee, I feel lousy. I got a head that goes round, dizzy like a top. But I'll have to be hanging up in a minute. Got another date tonight with Jack and we're going to the Club Alabam'. Say, Jack and I got awfully plastered at the Drake Hotel, and I was running around laughing, you know, a laughing jag. But now I'm paying for my fun. That's the way it always is, isn't it, Harry? You got to pay dear for your fun. And Monday night at a party, I passed out completely and Jack, he had to take me home with him. . . . Well, ain't that all right if I'm engaged and going to get married in June? . . . You didn't see Mark's wedding, did you? Do you think they're really married, or is he only pretending like he was with Ann? . . . What? . . . You saw the license? . . . Then they are married. . . . Yes, I believe you. . . . Darn this old cold of mine, my nose is running. . . . Well— tell Mark that I congratulate him, and wish him happiness and success. I'm glad he's working, too. But I got to hang up. I got this cold and my nose is running. It makes me sniffle. Yes, Harry—you just say to Mark what I said. Good-bye, Harry.

1930-1942

Counting the Waves

I

He dropped into the stateroom chair and gazed casually at the berths fastened against the wall. He felt less depressed now than he had been in these last few days. He was free of his wife's company for a brief hour or so. She had had some last-minute shopping to do, and he had begged off going with her and had come straight to the boat. Suddenly he began to hope that she would miss the boat and that he would be free to cross the ocean without her. Then, each night he would crawl into the lower berth here alone and he would sleep, if his insomnia didn't keep him awake. He would perhaps lie awake and think of what a dead and hollow relationship his marriage was. But he felt that he was now too old to hope for anything.

He got to his feet and stood for a moment, indecisive, in the center of the stateroom. He was a medium-sized man, corpulent, his abdomen protruding, his face large and rough-skinned, his small brown eyes dull, as if they were not functioning or seeing anything. His hair was graying at the temples, and his expression was a moody one. He pulled down the cupboard basin and thoughtlessly washed his hands. He took a towel and dried them. He tossed the towel into the wastebasket. He had washed his hands just before leaving the hotel, and he had just done it again, merely to be doing something. He sat in the stateroom, his mind in a vague reverie. Outside the door he heard noise and a bustle of activity, people talking and laughing, the farewells and talk of Europe, echoes of gaiety.

After sitting in the stateroom for about fifteen minutes, he went up on deck and leaned against the rail, glancing vacantly at the scene below him. The dock was crowded with people continually moving to the gangplank. There was a square of trunks and valises at which a number of people paused to identify their baggage. White-coated stewards then grabbed the baggage and hustled forward, wending in among the steady flow of people that moved up the gangplank. Soon, he tired of watching this scene and walked to the other side of the deck. Again he leaned against the rail. He watched a bellied ferryboat plough toward Hoboken. He stared up the Hudson River, through mists, to where the Palisades were. He smelled, or believed he smelled, the clean ocean breezes, and he wished the ship were already on the Atlantic, cutting through the waves with no land in sight. But he hoped that he wouldn't be seasick when that happened. And he wished that the sun were out today and shining brightly to make it a lovely April afternoon. At times, a man felt happier with the sun out.

He lit a cigar.

Unhappiness cut into him like a razor. Evil, a catastrophe, might be at least exciting, something better than that vague dissatisfaction he had felt since he had retired from business. Perhaps if the ship sank and he were to be placed face to face with death, he would learn how to live, and to understand more of what life was about—that is, if he survived. Perhaps the liner would hit an iceberg and she'd be dragged down with it. Then he would be free of his wife. And perhaps he would even become a hero in the sinking. Or he might also drown. And if he did, would that be so bad? He asked himself about death, as another ferryboat ploughed in front of him. Was death nothing more than going to sleep without even dreaming? Was death without sorrow? Was it just sinking into nothingness with no remembering? And if it were that, was there any sense in being afraid of death?

But no, no, God, no, he didn't want it. He wanted life. Lots of life.

Perhaps life would sing a different tune for him in Europe.

But how could it? After all, he was over fifty, and what could he expect? Love? Love from some beautiful girl with young white flesh? Hardly, unless he bought it, as he'd often done in Chicago. And then it wouldn't really mean very much. It would probably be the same thing in Paris as in Chicago, even though the girls would be of a different race and would speak a different language. He recalled high-class brothels in Chicago that he'd patronized. What else could that kind of thing in Europe offer him, provided he would be able to sneak away from his wife to go to one of them? Or the meals he'd eat. Food, when it so often gave him indigestion and stomach-aches? New things to see? When they'd gone to Mexico a couple of summers ago on a vacation, he had gotten bored with looking at mural paintings and scenery and Indian villages, and he had been unable to stand the smells of the markets. What was he going to feel like, looking at a lot of pictures, cathedrals, and all the other things his wife called culture?

Now he wished he'd never retired from business. He couldn't understand why he'd been such a damn fool and done it. He felt that he had built up a fine business with his own youth and life, the fruit of his own planning, his own hands, and his own brains. He had started out with a little capital and this idea of his of a wholesale directory distributed free and paid for by the advertising, and it had become a publication with national distribution and offices all over America. He had built it all himself, and it had given him fine rewards in the end. But like a fool, he had sold it and retired. He had always taken such pride in his business, too. How he would sometimes go out selling, go around the Loop in Chicago to offices and see successful men. He had always been treated with respect. When he came in to sell them, they didn't treat him like some cheap jack of a salesman. They knew he was a businessman of standing and they treated him as such. And how he would go downtown to his office every morning. Of course he had worked hard, paying attention to all the details of his business, the copy, the office costs, printing costs, ads and illus-trations, accounts, business conditions, the credit of those he

did business with, everything. But he hadn't been killing himself. And every morning he would walk up to that door with
his name on it on frosted glass, *Avery M. Kent.* That was a
name that had work, credit, reputation behind it. Ever since he
had sold out, leaving himself comfortably fixed for the rest
of his life, he hadn't known what to do with himself. Reading
the newspapers, playing golf, going to baseball games hadn't
seemed so much fun after he found himself with the time to
do anything he wanted. Then everything just got to be dull
and empty. And he'd felt that this trip to Europe would give
him the hold on himself and the interests that he needed. But
would it?

He moved about the deck, now crowded with talkative
people. Passengers and visitors were still streaming on board.
On all sides he could hear fragments of conversation. Most of
those about him, too, seemed so happy. He envied the people
whom he saw about him because of their show of spirit and
gaiety. He noticed young girls, pretty and full of energy, and
he hoped that they would all be fellow travelers. And again he
thought of his wife. He hoped there would be an accident. Accidents happened every day. Why couldn't one happen to her?
She'd be riding to the docks in a taxi, and a truck would smash
into it. She'd be killed. The ship would have left before he
could be reached. He'd never see her again. But if there were
an accident, he would probably be reached in time.

It wouldn't be smart to stand near the gangplank where he
could be easily located. He moved along the deck, seeking
an obscure spot. Finally he settled upon the upper deck on a
bench facing the marked-off space of the deck tennis court. He
waited in anxiety and hope for the ship to sail. Once a steward
passed him and his hand shook. But he wasn't being paged.
Suddenly he found himself believing that she wouldn't reach
the ship in time. He sat thinking of how he would be free.
He heard none of the noises, the talk on the decks below,
the warnings for visitors to leave. He sat smoking and, by God,
he was certain that she wouldn't reach the boat, that there'd
been an accident.

II

He gaped down at the swell lifting away from the vessel as it rocked on through fog banks, head-on for the middle of the Atlantic. Off in the distance were thick masses of fog, and huge waves rolled and heaved into the end of a visible world that was a barren grayness. He bit at his unlit cigar, priding himself that he had survived three days sailing without seasickness. And he told himself that as soon as the boat got out of the fog banks, they would probably have clearer weather and better sailing. Since he had managed to stand up this far without getting seasick, he would probably have no difficulty. He leaned against the railing, looking down at the swelling anger of the waters, gazing out upon the impenetrable wall of fog.

Sunday, when the boat had docked at Halifax, he and his wife had gone ashore, ridden into town on an old trolley, and visited an ancient fort. A small company of soldiers was stationed there, living on in an easy and useless existence. One of them, a very obliging cockney just back from India, had shown them around the fort, pointing out the ramparts, even bringing them down to see the ruined dungeon, miserable little cells that had once been used as prisons. Golly, it had been interesting, and he had looked at everything and listened to what the soldiers had said, forgetting all about his wife. While there, he'd not been so gloomy and silent in her presence. But coming back to the boat, there she was, grim-faced, at his side, and the sight of her had been enough to eat away the pleasure and absorption the visit had given him.

A dash of spray slapped his cheek. His face became meditative. He leaned on the rail and stared at the ocean.

He took several turns around the deck, passing fellow passengers who bowed to him formally. He wished he would find someone to chat with, that that Russian woman would come up for a walk and. . . . But why hope for miracles? And then again, why not? If a man was hoping, why not hope for miracles? But it was no use. She was always with the Canadian eye specialist who'd gotten on at Halifax. He'd hoped to meet some people on board, really meet them, but somehow he hadn't managed to. The passengers had more or less gotten acquainted and used to each other, forming their own groups, and he felt himself out of the picture. There were the bridge cutthroats who sat in the lounge all day, playing bridge as if their lives depended on each game. And the young people who were so jolly and loud. There was a young architect and his wife, a professor of geology from Princeton with his wife who was like a flapper, a taciturn young man from Boston who acted very queer and talked with a high-toned accent. And there was that gay old dog Benson, the gray-haired bastard who played deck tennis, danced, sat up late drinking beer with the young people. And they were nothing but kids, and he'd bet that Benson was old enough to be their grandfather. But there was life in that old dog, Benson. And there were the old fellows who spent so much of their time lounging in the ship's bar, talking about what they should have done before the market crashed. And that general who was such a nice, kind old man, and his wife, a little old dear, the two of them like old folks in a nice movie. Every time he looked at them he thought of the song, *Silver Threads Among the Gold.*

He flung his cigar butt into the ocean. He wished, as he had so often wished these last few days, that he could make up with some fellow on board who'd turn out to be a real friend. A fellow with whom he could be man-to-man and who'd understand him straight when he talked of what he really felt. They'd talk, and he'd explain things, and the friend, well, he'd point out what was the way to make yourself feel happier about life and be able to live so that you could get more out of it. Then this trip would be different, and so would life ever afterward. They could walk the deck together, smoking, talking as men and as friends about such things, now, as is there or isn't there a God, and what does God do to you when you die? And at times they could walk around, then stand and watch the ocean. . . . Or a woman, a young and beautiful one maybe. That Russian woman. After all, fellows his age sometimes did get younger women, and why couldn't he? That

Russian woman now, she probably didn't care an awful lot for her husband, because she was going to Europe alone with her thirteen-year-old daughter. But she didn't look as if she was a woman with a daughter that age, no, sir.

Now she was just the kind for him, and if only the ice were broken, she'd understand him. She'd see how there was something good and big inside of him, if only the right person would touch it off and bring it out. That was just what had been the matter all his life. The right woman had never come along and touched that hidden good in him and brought it out. And that Russian woman, she could be the one that would. He could see that from just looking at her and seeing her around the ship.

He walked around the deck. The Russian woman, dark, small, clear-skinned, with a fine and dignified figure, passed him. She was chatting with the Canadian eye specialist, and neither spoke to him. He met them at the other side, and again they passed him, still in animated conversation.

III

The sun was flashing on the ocean again, and the sky was clear and blue, meeting the waters at the distant horizon. Under the sweeping breezes the waves rolled away, causing a life of breaking white caps to spread across the blue waters. He stood for an indefinite period, gazing out, his elbows on the railing, a cigar in his mouth. He glanced down suddenly at the dirtyish white swell at the liner's sides. He gazed vacantly at the nautical line. He looked out over the ocean again, following one rolling wave with his eyes, then another, and another, feeling within himself a melancholy sense of desolation. He observed the gleaming of colors on the waters, and the ship ploughed onward, sweeping off its blue swell. He stood looking at the colors on the waters, seeing now a deep blue, then turquoise, a deep green and gray, a robin's egg blue. And the waves were endless, rolling, chopping, wrinkling on the waters, turning and churning continuously. Finally, he got bored. He took another turn around the deck. He went up to the top deck and watched

Benson win a game of deck tennis from the young architect. He felt like playing, but no one noticed him, and he felt as if he would be an interloper if he asked to play. And he was getting along in years, too old for such strenuous exercise. He didn't know how Benson could stand the pace. He returned to the deck below and stood by the rail, his eyes upon the ocean.

Last night he had stood at the same spot, looking out on the black waters, while his wife had sat inside in the ballroom, watching the passengers dance. He had known that the Russian woman was with the eye specialist. He had stood looking at the black waters for a long time, pitying himself, letting his mind wander until he had not even been aware of what he was thinking. Once a dash of spray had slapped his cheeks, bringing him to his senses, and then again he had let his mind wander. Finally he had gone inside, but he had hardly talked with his wife, keeping his eyes on the Russian woman most of the time. Then he had gone to the bar and sat alone drinking. He had gone to bed late, feeling damned low.

Now it was another day. Each morning during this trip he got out of bed with a feeling of hope, a feeling that something was going to happen, and that it would be of great importance to him. And so far, nothing had. He stood by the railing. He let his eyes drift over the ocean. He kept telling himself that if he could take his hands now and build something out of the rest of his life. . . . Or if he could have this Russian woman and the two of them could make a new life. . . .

He stood sleepy-eyed at the railing, listening.

IV

A man wrapped in thoughts about himself and his troubles didn't always realize that other people carried their own crosses. But when he suddenly did realize this, it made him feel less lonesome, at least for a little while. His wife had been picking up all the gossip on board and telling it to him. He realized that he wasn't so badly off. If he was unhappy there were many others in the same boat as he, and they were traveling with him right now. The rough-faced man who hardly ever talked, and the frail and sallow little woman who sat at their table were not man and wife, but brother and sister. The man earned his living carving wooden models of ships, and he was taking his sister home because she was a consumptive, and she wanted to die in the house at Plymouth in which she had been born. Her time was pretty short. And Benson had his troubles. He wasn't going to Europe on a vacation. His daughter had married an Englishman who'd turned out to be a swindler. He had been sent to jail, and Benson's daughter had divorced him. She was waiting with her baby for her father to come and bring her back to America. And the young minister on the deck was a Canadian who had been shell-shocked during the war. The war had deranged him. He was very nervous, and despite many attempts, he had been unable to take up his ministerial duties. His doctor was sending him to Europe as a last resort, hoping that if he visited the battlefields, he might again be shocked, and the shock would be sufficient to restore his mental balance. And there was that young Austrian with the snaky look who was making a fool out of that poor, sweet Flemish girl who looked so cute and so innocent in her peasant clothes. His wife had overheard that snaky Austrian when the fellow was making up to the girl. The Austrian filled the innocent thing with stories about what he'd done, the money he had spent, and she had sat drinking in all of it, believing his foolish stories. His wife had gone on telling of how the Austrian told the Flemish girl of the time he had crossed on the *Bremen*, changing clothes six times a day, and all that sort of bunk. And his wife said some of the women knew for a certainty that the snaky Austrian had already seduced the Flemish girl.

Maybe he shouldn't complain about his own life. There was the poor consumptive woman who ate at his table, and then, that minister. And some of the passengers were older than he was, and they probably didn't have as long to live as he had. And then there was the Canadian eye specialist. His wife had gotten some of the dope on him. Trust his wife to get all the dope on everybody. That Canadian eye specialist, now, he

looked to be in the pink of health and condition. And he was
going away because of a nervous breakdown. But he guessed
that it was true that the world was full of people, all right,
who had their own troubles and sorrows. He guessed that the
thing to do was to build something inside of yourself to prevent your being affected too much. And now he suddenly
felt that he could do that.

He turned from the deck rail and walked slowly along the
deck, passing the Canadian eye specialist and the Russian
woman who sat together in deck chairs. She was laughing over
something the fellow had said to her.

He went up again to watch the younger people playing deck
tennis.

v

Ocean travel after a couple of days didn't seem to be all it had
been cracked up to be. He felt cramped and restricted. He sat
in his deck chair, bored. He had looked at the ocean for what
had seemed to be interminable hours. He had walked around
and around the decks. He had watched games of deck tennis.
He had read the *Ocean Times* and had talked of its scanty
news with other passengers. He had fallen asleep at one of the
afternoon concerts and hadn't gone back to any others. He
had been somewhat excited on the previous night when he had
won five dollars in the mid-Atlantic Sweepstakes. But now he
was bored, and he wished the trip were over.

He had brought along several books to read. Again he
tried to interest himself in one of them, just as he had tried
almost daily. And again he fell asleep over his book. He awakened several minutes later, feeling stiff, tired, even weak. His
eyelids were heavy. Yawning, he looked at the print, but his
thoughts were vague, as if they were floating through fog.
Again he fell asleep, and he dreamed vividly that he was back
in his office. He was dictating a letter to his secretary, Miss
Snyder, and it had seemed an extraordinary pleasure. So representative and vivid did his dream become that it seemed exactly
as if he were back in his old routine. He awoke, heard the

engines purring, and saw before him the gray waste of water. He sat, tired and gloomy, lonesome. He walked about the ship to get the stiffness out of his legs and arms after his sleep. He passed trivial remarks with fellow passengers. He was lonesome, but somehow he got through the day.

And another day. Friday. Then, Saturday, and Sunday, and he'd be putting his feet on good solid land again. He would see different faces and no longer eat at the same table with untalkative people. But no, no, he didn't want to land. Then perhaps he would never again see the Russian woman. He had heard some passengers speak of her, of her vivacity, wit, and charm, and he had listened with greedy intensity. He never tired of thinking of her. He never saw her without experiencing a sense of wonder and an anguished lonesomeness and a pain of desire and frustration. But he didn't seem to see so much of her. And only once had she bowed to him. He had only once spoken to the Canadian eye specialist, and that had been about the weather one day when they had still been in the fog banks. It was peculiar, too, that he could never hold the image of her face clearly in his mind. Every time he tried to call up an image of her, he could not get the nose straight, or the forehead, or the lips, the eyes—something. But anyway it was the face of an intelligent person, a face revealing a woman of real character and poise. He was sure that she was a very remarkable, a very distinguished, kind of woman, nothing at all like most women, nothing at all like his own wife. Why, this Russian woman, mother of a girl of thirteen, seemed more beautiful, more desirable even now than his wife had years ago when he had first met her.

On Sunday the ship would reach Plymouth. If the Russian woman were debarking at Plymouth, she would be gone then, and perhaps he would never see her again. He sat in a deck chair thinking of this. The weather was balmy. He smoked a cigar. He tried to think of how, some place in Europe, Paris, Nice, Italy, Berlin, they would meet. They would come together like old-time friends. And then everything would move swiftly. He would leave his wife, giving her enough money to take care of herself, but freeing him to go with the Russian woman and build a life with her. Her husband? Well, he might die, and then he and the Russian woman might be able to get married. But formal marriage wouldn't matter. It was even better to think of both of them tearing off and living together in sin, he with a deserted wife somewhere, she with a jilted husband.

He dozed off and dreamed that she was leaving at Plymouth. He awoke, sad, convinced that his dream had told him the truth. He began to feel as if Sunday morning would be the saddest day of his life. He sought out his wife and suggested to her that they change their plans and get off at Plymouth rather than Cherbourg. They could cancel the hotel reservations they had made in Paris. His wife looked at him as if he were mad and dismissed the suggestion flatly. He tried tactfully to convince her, but she was firm in her refusal. He thought of getting off himself at Plymouth, and letting his wife go hang. If he did, perhaps he might be in the same compartment with the Russian woman on the trip to London, and who knows but what he might break the ice then.

The day became agonizing. In the afternoon he went to the top deck to watch the deck tennis tournament. And she wasn't there. Neither was the eye specialist. He went below and through the salons, but he did not see either of them. He became convinced that they were in her stateroom, and this thought clung to him like some idea fixed in one's mind during a nightmare. He wandered through the passageways, seeking to find out where her stateroom was. A steward eyed him suspiciously. He muttered that he had lost himself, and hastily went to his own stateroom. His wife lay in the lower berth complaining because she still had a touch of seasickness. He couldn't tolerate her. She was ugly. He went upstairs. He saw the Russian woman talking with the general's wife. The latter nodded to him, but not the Russian woman. Again he went to the top deck to watch the deck tennis tournament. He sat miserable, hoping that she would come up. But she did not appear.

He had made his little plans on the ship. They had all been futile. He had hoped, and his hopes had not been realized.

He had schemed to sit near her at afternoon tea and during the horse races at night. In vain. He had wistfully
daydreamed of their sitting out together in deck chairs, talking in the moonlight. Empty dreams! He had one last hope
now, the Captain's Ball on Saturday night. He'd ask her to
dance with him. It was going to be fancy dress, and everyone
would be gay. Everyone would be friendly. It would be just
the time for him to drive in a wedge.

All day Saturday he waited for the ball, acting and feeling
much like a very young man waiting to take out a girl he loved.
At the Captain's dinner, the people at every table but his
seemed to be having fun. The old general was walking about the
dining salon, throwing confetti, having the time of his life.
He tried to emulate the general. He got up and went to the
table where the Russian woman and the Canadian eye specialist sat. He threw confetti at the doctor. No one laughed.
Somehow he couldn't do certain things the way other people
did them. He returned to his table, chastened. His wife
frowned. Later he would hear from her. Well, let her! No matter what she said, it made no dent in him. Long ago he'd learned
how not to listen to her. Often at the end of a day he could
hardly remember five words she had said to him. Despite his
disappointment, there was still the ball, one last hope. But he
didn't have any costume to put on. He wanted to blacken his
face, put on old knickers and one of his wife's blouses. But he
lacked the courage. And she flatly refused him permission to
take one of her blouses. She said he must be out of his senses, a
man of his age. So he went upstairs in his tuxedo. It was still
too early. He was getting more nervous every minute and feeling like a boy. He knew he had no reason to hope for anything,
and yet there was this hope of his, stronger than his reason,
overriding the lessons of his whole experience. He sat in the bar,
drinking Scotch and soda, waiting. His last chance.

He drank two Scotch and sodas. He had intended to sip
them, but he'd been so nervous and restless that he'd drunk
them quickly. He walked outside and up to the deserted upper
deck. It was a clear night. He could see out, across black, bluish

stretches of water, with moonlight on them, the white caps breaking all the way across the visible ocean. The sea air had a tang to it, and he breathed deeply. A sense of the sea, the air, the sky with the new moon, the stars, all seemed to fill him, to enter his being. He was struck with wonder, and he was melancholy. He stood by the rail looking at the waves on the waters. His thoughts seemed almost to dissolve into the scene before him. Suddenly it seemed as if an ocean of mystery and wonder flowed through his being. He was sad. The pain of defeats in his life, the nostalgia for dreams unfulfilled, the impending loss of this Russian woman whom he had only seen, not known—all these filled him. He stood by the rail, looking, looking, looking over the waves, listening to them, a man brooding because he was lonesome and getting old and empty.

VI

The Captain's ball was dull, a tame affair. The dancers were not very gay, and the passengers were already divided into little cliques, and they did not break up and form larger and more sociable groups. He sat watching, trying to pump up a mood of gaiety, waiting for someone to be friendly and give him a cue to join in with them. No cues came. If he heard an attempt at a joke, he laughed no matter how pointless the joke happened to be. He sat with his wife. There was a fatuous, meaningless smile appearing and disappearing and reappearing on his face. He wanted to participate in good spirits. He wanted to let himself go, laugh and talk and joke, and, yes, dance, even if his dancing was quite old-fashioned. He wanted to act just like Benson, whom he watched with envy. He saw Benson dance with the Russian woman. He didn't know why he could not muster up the courage to approach her and ask for a dance. But he sat as if chained in his chair. After Benson, the Canadian eye specialist danced with her, and he observed her wonderful white teeth as she laughed, gliding by close to his table. Was there something between them? It was none of his business, but the question was a very important one to him. And he didn't know whether there was or not. And now there was Benson, dancing with the architect's wife. Damn it, he was going to dance. That was just what he was going to do. The next dance! But he couldn't do these modern steps and he might look like an old fool. The next dance came, and he didn't stir. He decided that he'd wait for a waltz. He could waltz as good as another. Only if he wanted to dance, it would have to be with his wife as a partner. Why dance with her?

Looking about him, seeing the faces, the dancing, hearing the music, glancing repeatedly at his wife, who would smile weakly when his eyes met hers, he pitied himself, and at times even pitied her. They had been married all these years, twenty-three to be exact. Why were they still together, except because of habit? He was hooked and could not break away; that was the truth of the matter. When he was young and first married, he'd never thought that it would all come to this. And here it was. He could remember, but not very clearly, the day they were married. She had been young and, yes, pretty, attractive, girlish and innocent then. When they had walked down the church aisle and the minister had pronounced the words, he had been a young man expecting a lot from life. And what had he gotten? For about two years he had been happy and in love with her, and from then on he'd been bored. Bored, that was just the word to describe how he'd felt about her ever since— for about twenty-one years now. And he was married for life. *Until death do us part!* Enviously watching the Russian woman dance again with the doctor, he repeated these words to himself over and over in irony. How many times had he slept with her just because he felt he had to, wanting it all finished, wanting just to sleep and forget her? And that had been before she had started to get old. And so now here he was, sitting beside her when all they had left, he might say, was a marriage certificate and a few habits in common. It was a terrible thing to wish that another person were dead, and how often hadn't he wished that she, his own wife, were dead? How often hadn't he thought of how he would be free then, and how he could find someone better suited to him! He had wished she would be killed just before the ship had left New York. Now he was terrified by the

audacity and the cruelty of his thought. And yet, this thought
had come to him often and stuck in his mind without his really
wishing it. Often, his mind would be on something else—business, a ball game at Comiskey Park that he was watching—and
it would suddenly pop up, stay fixed in his mind, as if it were
glued there. More music, and they were dancing. There his wife
was, smiling at them as if saying now that she was old and
settled, she could indulgently look at these young people having
their fun. There she was with that miserable smile on her face.
His wife, and she was actually a total stranger to him. Most of
the time he knew what she would do or say to him, and yet she
was a total stranger. She didn't know what went on in his mind.
He didn't know what went on in hers. She mustn't be happy.
She was always complaining of aches and pains, and he was sure
that most of the time she was imagining them. She had gone
to doctors and osteopaths, and she had fallen for spiritualism,
and for Christian Science, and for all kinds of crank lectures—
and all because he guessed she didn't know what to do with herself and found the going in their last years as hard as he sometimes did. Why hadn't he happened to marry a woman like the
Russian? Look at her! She didn't seem a day over thirty.

They sat, and the Captain's ball continued rather dully. Tomorrow he would be in Europe. He wished he were home and
still in business. Here on the ship, he had been nothing. When
he had still been active, he had gone to work in the morning,
and the elevator man said hello to him, his clerks and Miss
Snyder greeted him, he had business luncheons where he was
somebody. Here he was *nothing*. How he longed to be back in
the saddle. In business his name had meant something. It was
different when the elevator boy said Mr. Kent from when a
steward on the boat said it. Yes, to be back in the saddle. And
what would Europe have to offer him?

Perhaps it would have all been better if they could have had
children. But that was because of something wrong with her.
And even so, now the children would be growing up and getting away from them. He watched the Russian woman and

thought that tomorrow would be the last time he would ever
see her.

His wife yawned and said she was tired. He didn't want to
go down to bed, but out of habit he followed her, regretful,
disappointed. Lying in his berth, he began to think if only he
had stayed on up there, something might have happened to
bring him and the Russian woman together.

VII

He was up early after a restless night. His dreams seemed to
hang over him as he shaved, making him restless, disturbing
him. He could not remember them, except that he had awakened
when he was in the midst of a dream in which he was meeting
the Russian woman in Berlin. He was grateful that his wife was
not getting up for breakfast early. He went upstairs and into
the dining salon. A number of passengers were eating. He
looked toward her table. She was not down yet. It must mean
that she wasn't getting off at Plymouth. He relaxed. A few
more hours and still a last chance. He smiled and greeted his
waiter most cheerfully. He ate a big breakfast. Then he went
upstairs. He wandered about the ship. It was in the harbor, and
he looked out through the early morning fog, seeing the green
landscape and hills on either side, and ships in the harbor. He
hoped that the sun would come out so that he could get a better
view. The liner had stopped now to await the tender. Stewards
were bringing up baggage, and passengers were crowding about
the deck. He saw the eye specialist, and overheard him telling
another passenger that he was debarking. This was good news.
With the eye specialist gone, perhaps he would have a chance.
And there was the daughter. She didn't look as if she were
leaving. They were going to France. Perhaps he might meet
them in Paris. His chance wasn't gone.

He walked about among the passengers, stopping to light a
cigar, pausing to stand at the rail and glance over the harbor
and at the outlines of land surrounding it, now and then over-
hearing conversation. And again he was beginning to hope. He
tried to conceive of some plan whereby he might engage her or

her daughter in conversation. And he began to regret that the trip was almost over. Amidst all these good-byes, this miserable trip of his already began to take on the halo of something in the past to which one looks back regretfully, with nostalgia, with vague memories that blot out all boredom and erase all frustrations.

The delay at Plymouth was tedious. The tender came out, and there was the business of lowering the gangplank, getting rid of the baggage, freight, and mail, the good-byes and farewells, but finally it was all completed. The tender shoved off. The sun was now out, promising a fine day. The land on both sides was clear, and straight ahead could be seen the buildings toward which the tender moved. The ship pulled out and set across the English Channel to Cherbourg in a choppy sea. The trip was as good as over. Everyone waited for the next stop which would unload the major portion of the passengers. The Russian woman seemed to be busy packing or doing something and she was not to be seen on deck. He also had packing to do which he did slowly and reluctantly, not listening to odd bits of gossip and advice his wife imparted to him while she put her things into her trunk. He came on deck and walked about, seeing ahead the thin dark line of the coast of France. He felt that he was leaving something behind. He wished the trip were once again only commencing, and that he had all those days on the ocean to live over again. If he had, he might know now how to have made friends, how to have broken the ice with that Russian woman. Everyone was more friendly than before. But the talk was of landing, of plans for Europe, of how fine a trip it had been, of hotel reservations, the impending train trip to Paris, the tediousness of customs' inspection to which all debarking passengers would soon have to submit. Everyone seemed impatient.

In the early afternoon they pulled into the harbor of Cherbourg, and he saw the low lines of concrete on either side, with cranes looking almost like guns, and with people moving about, seeming like small dots in motion. All was soon the confusion of getting ready to leave. Finally, this, too, was finished. He was in the tender and then he was stepping on French soil. Blue-coated porters, rustling and shouting in a language he did not understand, surrounded them. The customs' inspection was quicker and simpler than he had expected, and he was led to his compartment in the waiting train. He overtipped his porter. Soon the train pulled out, and he was being carried through Normandy, en route to Paris, and he kept humming to himself the old song, *When It's Apple Blossom Time in Normandy*. The song called back to him his youth, and nostalgically he thought of how wonderful it would have been if he only could have come to France then, and on a honeymoon with someone other than the Mrs. Kent who sat across from him. She talked too much about the landscape, and he quit looking out the window because of her chatter. At supper, he failed to get a reservation at the same table as the Russian woman. And at the Gare Saint Lazare, he quickly lost sight of her in the bustle. He was hurried in a taxicab to a hotel, and his attention was caught by the funny noises the taxicab horns made. He was in Paris, and he would become another one of those American husbands, sore-footed, querulous, bored, dragged about Europe by a wife who, gasping and sighing at what hired guides tell her to admire, makes a pretense of drinking in all the culture of the old world.

1931-1939

Accident

I

"WHEN Louise and I march up that altar, we're going to feather our nest with dividends paid by those pumps out there," Syd said to his partner, Tommy Rourke.

They were attendants at Station No. 204 of the Nation Oil Company.

"You know, Syd, since those pumps are so good to you, I'd imagine that you'd have the kindness and the inspiration to treat them nice—you know, polish them up once in a while," Tommy said, pointing through the station window at the dirty red pumps which stood on a pump island in the center of the cement station driveway.

"Tommy, I'll be damned, but I was just thinking that you might have the same kind of a feeling toward them yourself. But then, I guess I was wrong as usual. It's a muggy day out, and liable to rain, so there wouldn't be much use in polishing and cleaning them today. If it's sunny out tomorrow, maybe you'll clean them then."

"I see that getting married is already making you kind and considerate," Tommy said, laughing.

"Oh, not so much as that."

"I guess it's a good thing I refused to take the promotion and become a supervisor. If I had, I might be your boss right now, and I might be driving in here in a company car and ordering you around. I guess if I had taken the promotion and become your boss, I'd have made you hum around here, clean-

ing up the joint until your fanny dragged all over the driveway."

"And I suppose you turned thumbs down on it just because
you wanted to avoid such unpleasant duties."

"Well, I figured, what the hell, with a supervisor's job all
that you get for your grief, besides a Ford to run around in,
is a hundred and sixty smackers a month. I thought I'd string
along pumping gas for my one hundred forty per month and
my commissions on oil."

"Your one hundred forty per month?" laughed Syd.

"Well, what I was driving at is that I don't care for the glory
of being a supervisor and bossing around dumb socks like
you."

"Sure!" Syd said ironically.

"Now, of course, if I was you, you'd have refused to take
that promotion because you can make more than it pays by
gypping the customers for all it's worth. But me, I got a conscience. I'm an honest sonofabitch."

"Sure!" Syd laughed.

"Me, now, I've been pumping gas for two years with this
company, and I'm the veteran of a thousand crank-case drains,
but I've never once been called in to the main office to answer
questions about any serious shortages at my station, and there's
never been any suspicion cast on my honesty. Why? Because
they know downtown that when a customer drives into a
station for service and Tommy Rourke takes care of him, the
customer gets what he pays for. If Cal Coolidge came in for
five gallons of gas, he'd get five gallons, and not four for five
like some of my partners would give him."

"You bastard, you know you're the kind of an attendant
who sits up all night doping out new and clever ways of cheat-
ing so that you can keep collecting your extra dividends."

"Well, I wouldn't say that it takes all night to figure such
things out," Tommy said jocularly, and they both smiled.

"Customer."

"I'll get him."

"I know you will. But give him a break. Give him at least

four for five," Syd said as Tommy went out to the old Hudson that had stopped at one of the pumps.

"Good morning, sir!" Tommy said to the driver, a middle-aged man in a khaki shirt.

"Five."

Unscrewing the cap from the gas tank in the rear of the car, Tommy observed that the gauge beside it registered half full. He inserted the hose nozzle and walked around the hose to the pump handle. He glanced quickly but covertly at the driver and saw that the man was looking straight ahead. Tommy turned the pump handle slowly with his left hand.

"Step on it!" the customer called curtly.

"Yes, sir!"

Seeing that the driver wasn't watching, Tommy stopped when he had pumped three and a half gallons. He drained the hose carefully and put it back on the hook. He swiftly screwed the cap back on the tank mouth, and went around to the left side of the car.

"Look at your oil today, sir?"

"Go ahead! But make it snappy!"

Tommy lifted the hood and looked at the oil gauge by the side of the greasy motor. It showed that the motor was nearly full.

"It can stand a quart . . . But have you had your crank case drained recently? You know, you ought to drain it every five hundred miles to get the best out of your motor and keep it in the best condition," he said, returning to the driver.

"It was drained last week. Throw in a quart of heavy oil," the customer said.

Tommy walked back to the station.

"Well, did you give the guy a break?" Syd asked, while Tommy stood at the barrel of medium oil, pumping out a quart.

"Sure. I pulled the pump at three and a half gallons."

"You're a bastard all right," Syd said.

"We need our dividends. How else am I gonna pay for that

roadster I'm plannin' to buy?" Tommy said, turning from the barrel and carrying out a quart measure full of oil.

He poured the oil into the motor and then reattached the hood.

"How much?" the customer asked when Tommy again approached him.

"Five gallons of gas is ninety-five, and the oil is a quarter. One-twenty, sir."

The customer handed Tommy a dollar and thirty cents and told him to keep the change.

"Need any air or water, sir?"

"No, thanks."

"Thank you, sir," Tommy said as the car drove away.

"I suppose the fellow didn't need any oil, either, and you sold it to him," Syd kidded when Tommy returned to the station.

"Boy, you're a wonderful guesser," Tommy said.

"I know you, that's all," Syd said.

"Well, what the hell is a lad to do? They ride our balls off to sell oil, don't they? There's only one way to keep in good with them down in the main office, and that's . . . sell oil. Well, then, sell it. This guy doesn't need it, and his car takes heavy oil. Well, I give him medium oil, because the gauge is up near the top. Heavy oil might smoke his car when he doesn't need any more. That's the way to do it, my boy. Use all your ingenuity in selling oil, if you want to stay in good with Prevost and the big moguls down town."

"The philosophy of salesmanship," Syd said ironically.

"Only, Syd, I feel like a heel for gypping that guy. He gave me a dime tip."

"You feel sorry? I'm laughing."

"Brother, I do say this. I'm not letting mine slip through my fingers while I get my chances. I've been pumpin' gas long enough to learn one thing. It's this! Get the dough while the gettin' is good. You'll never know when you'll be canned."

"Or promoted," Syd said.

"The minute I'm out, there's somebody else in who'll do the

same thing. I've never met a gas pumper, except that guy Peters who takes guns away from people, and a few other dummies, who didn't gyp," Tommy said.

II

"You know, Syd, I'm still learning at this game. I ain't a specialist at it like Gus Donaldson. Now, that boy is a marvel, the original pump-pulling wizard," Tommy said after he had given a woman in a Cadillac seven gallons for ten.

"I don't know him, but I've seen him at some of the pep meetings they call for the attendants on our own time."

"I used to be Gus's partner at 96."

"That must have been one station that nobody ever should have gone to to buy gasoline."

"Let me tell you! One day at 96, a guy drove in and told Gus to give him five. The guy went in the can. Gus, to make things look real, took the hose off the hook and put it in the tank, and even let some spillings fall on the outside. He didn't touch the pump. When the guy comes out, Gus pulls out the hose, hangs it up, screws on the cap, and takes out a dust rag, and says to the guy, 'I spilled a little.' He wiped the outside of the tank, and the guy pays for five gallons, and maybe all he got for his dough was a drop or two of drainings from the hose, and half of that went outside instead of inside the tank. Gus pulled that one, too, just as casual and as unconcerned as—"

"As you would," volunteered Syd.

"No, sir, I don't claim to being the gyp artist that Gus is," Tommy remarked.

III

"I knew that I smelled a big Swede," Syd remarked.

"Hello, boys," said Ole, a rangy tank-wagon driver in soiled overalls.

"What you got?" Syd asked.

"Center compartment is full up. According to the charts it holds 496, but when it's full up, it always has five or six gallons over."

"We won't complain on that account. Every gallon over is a neat little present of nineteen cents," Syd said.

"And listen, boys! I just made a big delivery to a privately owned station down the line, and I held out a hundred and fifty gallons on him. Can you boys take it?"

"Here's the story, Swede. We usually do seven to eight hundred gallons a day, but since Tommy and I came on our shift at three yesterday afternoon it's been awful slow. We've done, yesterday and today, about five hundred, I'd guess. That'd screw up our audit, and if the auditor should come snooping around on us and check up, well . . ."

"Hell with that, Syd. We'll take it, Ole. We can screw up our audit today, and the boys coming on at three can even things up tonight and tomorrow morning. We can divvy up with them on it," Tommy said.

"That's the idea. Then we'll all make a little extra on the side," Ole said.

Syd handed ten dollars to Ole.

"Ten bucks for a hundred and fifty gallons?" Ole asked. He calculated. "You'll sell this gas for twenty-eight bucks, fifty cents. I can go down the line and get more from some of the other boys in the stations."

"Hell, we got to split the proceeds four ways here," Tommy said.

"I'm giving you guys the break. What the hell!" Ole said.

"All right, we'll give you half. That's fourteen twenty-five," Tommy said, and Syd handed Ole an additional four dollars and twenty-five cents.

"Climb up on the trunk and look at the tank," Ole said, pointing to his tank truck parked on the drive way.

"Go ahead! It's all right. We know you're honest," said Tommy.

"Nope, boys, rules is rules, and it's a rule that we can't deliver any gas to the stations until the attendant signing for it climbs up on the truck and looks at the compartment and sees that he's gettin' as much as he signs for. My boss has been raising hell about this rule, and for all I know, a spotter is across the street now, watching to see if I make you fellows look at what you're signin' for."

Tommy walked out of the station with Swede. He gauged the station tanks with the measuring sticks and told Ole which ones to put the gas in. He climbed up on the truck and unscrewed the cap on the center compartment. It was up to the brim, and he nodded to Ole.

"Look in the last compartment," Ole said.

Tommy looked.

"That one holds 596. Want to gauge it to see if it's got one fifty in it now?"

"It looks all right," Tommy called, and he jumped down from the truck.

Ole, who had been attaching his hose to the spout in the back which ran from the center compartment, let the gasoline out. It could be heard gurgling down the pipe and into the tank. They returned to the station. Ole made out a receipt for 496 gallons of gasoline. Tommy signed it, and Ole placed the carbon of the receipt on the spindle which lay on the small desk which was placed over the safe.

"Smoke?" asked Syd, extending a package to Ole.

"Not nere. I tell you, it's dangerous smoking with all the gas around," Ole answered.

"Aw, come on, Calamity Jane," Tommy said.

"Kid me if you got to. But I won't be surprised if I come around here some day with a load of gas and find that you guys, with your cigarette smokin', have blown the station to hell and gone."

"Cut it," said Tommy.

Just as Ole left, the telephone rang. Syd answered it, and Tommy went out with Ole to look and see if the truck compartments were empty. Then Ole drove off.

"That was Norris at 46," Syd said when Tommy re-entered the station. "He was warning us that the city sealers are around this neighborhood today. They were just in on him."

"Catch anybody?"

"No. Norris spotted him, a fat little guy in a Ford sedan,

and he jammed the pump when it hit five to be sure that it gave a good measure."

"I never had one of those bastards. But I've had three partners they caught short measurin', and they got the boys fined and canned."

"I think I know the fat one who was just in 46. But, say, I told you you should have tested the pumps when we opened this morning to be sure they're throwing right."

"Hell, those pumps are always right."

"Come on, we better test 'em."

"All right," Tommy said reluctantly.

They took a five-gallon bucket outside and tested each of their six pumps to see if it were giving the correct measure. The pumps were all right, and two were even throwing a negligible fraction over five gallons.

"We'll have to watch our step. They might have several cars out today. I heard they were making a city-wide round-up. And now they don't only have dummy tanks in Fords. I hear that sometimes they have them planted in Dodges and Chevrolets. We better quit pullin' the pumps on all customers. That way, we're sure to be safe," Syd said after they returned to the station.

"Hell with 'em," Tommy said.

A Ford drove in, and he serviced it. He returned to the station, and said:

"If that guy was the city sealer, he got three for five."

"Goddamn it, Tommy, you better be careful."

IV

About noon they checked up to see how the station was running on their shift and to ascertain how much they were over. Their calculation showed that, irrespective of what they would make on the hundred and fifty gallons of gasoline they had bought from Ole, they were ten bucks over. Syd started working over the figures of their dummy audit to be sure that they had calculated correctly before they pocketed the extra money. A Ford sedan halted at one of the pumps. A short fat

man, wearing a derby, was at the wheel, and a tall thin fellow
sat beside him.

"Make it five," the driver told Tommy.

"Jake, the old man might be hopping on our tails for burning up so much gas," the thin fellow said.

"Well, we gotta have gas," said the one called Jake.

"Maybe three'll do us for the day," the thin one said.

"No, we better get five and play safe. Five, lad," Jake said.

He got out of the car, followed by the thin fellow. He lifted
the front seat. Tommy usually tried to be the one to insert
the hose in a Ford tank, in order to look at the tank and note
whether or not it was totally empty. That was his means of
protecting himself against spotters and city sealers. However,
he had his mind on other matters. He handed the hose to the
tall, thin fellow, who put it through the opened doorway of the
car and inserted the nozzle into the tank. The two of them
walked toward the station, entered it, and went into the lavatory. Tommy pumped. His mind was still not on what he was
doing and he gave four gallons for five.

He put the hose back on the hook, screwed the cap on the
tank, and was setting the seat back over it when they came
back.

"Fed her five, huh?" Jake asked.

Tommy nodded. The thin fellow got in front of him and
started handling the seat. The other one handed him a dollar
bill, and Tommy gave him five cents change. He asked if they
needed their oil tested, but Jake said it was all right. Jake
started to get into the car, and the thin fellow was in back of
him, as if to follow. Suddenly, as if acting on an after-thought,
he turned to Tommy and said:

"Say, kid, can you fix us up with a receipt? We better have
it to turn in with our expense account."

Tommy nodded. But he had a sudden and fearful doubt.
If they were the city sealers, he was cooked. He tried to chase
the doubt from his mind as he walked toward the station to
write out the receipt.

"They want a receipt," Tommy said to Syd as he searched through papers on the desk for the receipt pad.

"You didn't pull the pump on 'em, did you?" Syd asked nervously.

"Four for five."

"My God! It's the city sealers. I know the fat guy, I didn't notice him when he came in because I was still figuring on the dummy audit. Look, one of them is dragging a five-gallon bucket out of the car now, and the fat bastard is taking out the dummy tank with your four gallons in it. I told you to be careful. But, boy, you're caught by the nuts now," Syd said, half in panic.

Tommy quickly wrote out a receipt for five gallons.

The fat fellow began pouring the gas from the dummy tank into a five-gallon measure. They had the goods on him now. Tommy walked toward them a bit slowly, the receipt in his hand. He looked about dopily and absent-mindedly, letting his eyes fall on the signboard with the Nation Oil advertisement on it, which stood in front of the pumps.

"We got this guy cold, I think," he heard Jake say as he poured.

The tall one bullyingly told Tommy to hurry up. Still idly gazing at the board, but quickening his step, Tommy came closer to them. He took a quick step. He tripped and lurched forward, throwing his hands out as if to break the fall and simultaneously letting out a curse as if in anger over losing his balance. Tumbling forward, he knocked over the five-gallon measure into which Jake was pouring the gasoline. The fluid spilled out on the driveway, and Tommy was tangled over the bucket. The tall fellow had handled him roughly, trying to save the bucket from spilling, but he hadn't been quick enough. The evidence was spilled. They cursed him. He got to his feet, a sheepish expression on his face. He grimaced and held his left wrist. He tried to apologize, but stopped and groaned, bending over and still holding his wrist.

"We ought to turn you in, you wise punk," Jake said.

"I'm very sorry, sir, but it was an accident. You don't think

I go around trying to break my neck. Oh, Jesus, my wrist!"
Tommy said.

"Accident, you smart aleck! Think you're wise!" the tall
fellow snapped.

Syd rushed out to join the group and stood near Tommy.

"Listen, we had the goods on you, and that stunt you pulled
won't save your job. You're only makin' it worse for yourself.
Admit it and you'll save yourself trouble and dough on the fine
that's comin' to you. You were caught gyppin', caught red-
handed, weren't you? Weren't you?" Jake said sternly.

"Own up!" the thin fellow demanded.

"What's this? Hurt, Tommy?" Syd asked.

"To what? I gave you five gallons, and here's your receipt.
I'll give you five more for what I accidentally spilled. Oh, Jesus,
my wrist! I sprained the damned thing," Tommy said.

"Sink that line, wise guy!" Jake said.

"I tripped, and it was an accident. You got five gallons.
The pumps are throwin' right. Test 'em and see. You don't think
that I'm fallin' down and tryin' to break my wrist for fun,
do you? Look at it! It's swellin'. Oh, Christ, it hurts!" he said,
bending down and grabbing his wrist with his right hand as he
held it out from him.

"Listen, we got you!" Jake said.

"All right, go ahead and try turnin' me in. You got nothing
on me. You'd have seen that I gave you five if I hadn't tripped.
I'll give you five more to prove it. Test the pumps for yourself. But let me alone. My wrist is hurt."

"We tested the pumps this morning and they're throwing
a good measure," Syd said.

"Keep your two cents out of this, or we'll get you, too," the
thin fellow said.

"Your job isn't to come around here and frame and insult
attendants. We ain't workin' for you and takin' your orders.
It was an accident. I'm sorry. I damn near broke my neck, and
look at my wrist. We got work to do. Go ahead and test the
pumps if you want to, but quit tryin' to frame me. It won't
work," Tommy said.

"I'm the manager of this station. I'll talk to you. Go ahead and put some iodine from the first aid kit on your wrist, Tommy," Syd said.

"I ought to slap your snotty puss in!" Jake said.

"Go ahead!" Tommy said.

"Tommy, I'll call the union and let 'em know about this. They ain't going to frame you. I watched you pump and saw you hit the top and give five. I saw it," Syd said.

"Yeah!" sneered Jake.

The city sealers continued looking tough and bullying. But then they gave it up. Their evidence was gone. They finally tested all the pumps, found them working properly, collected their fees for testing, left receipts, and started to get in the Ford to leave.

"We'll get you yet, you wise sonofabitch," Jake said, turning to Tommy.

"Sure, come around early in the morning," Tommy said under his breath.

Seeing the car go out of the drive, both attendants laughed.

"You're goddamn lucky," Syd said.

"I got by."

"But you took one hell of a chance."

"They ain't catching this boy napping on the sacks. And let 'em try turning me in down at the main office. I got my drag there, and my record's as white as a lily. But, Jesus, my wrist. Look at the way it's popped up," Tommy said, extending his swollen wrist.

"Better let some cold water run on it," Syd said.

Tommy went into the lavatory and came out in about five minutes, after bathing his wrist.

"And the bastards forgot to take back the ninety-five cents they paid for the gas," said Tommy.

Both attendants laughed.

1931-1937

A Short Story

HE READ the newspapers in the reading room of the public library. He took a keen interest in the columns and columns of print, telling him of faro games, broads, millionaires, mergers, conferences, fires, dead generals, live generals photographed with a chest full of medals, accidents, deaths, and broads. There were many others in the crowded room reading newspapers for the same reason he was. Outside, it was beginning to get dark, and the room was warm and friendly with its humanity, its electric lights, and the forgetfulness in the dead columns of yesterday's and yesteryear's newsprint. He read on. An international conference, farmers going berserk and raiding stores for food, strikes, appeals for charity that made him laugh, mergers, broads getting married while other broads were getting divorced, broads in bathing suits snapped on the sands of California, murders, ministers, accidents, steamships, prize fighters, and broads, broads, broads.

Reading on, seeing the pictures of women in the paper, and scratching himself, feeling the dirt ingrained into his own body, he could not make himself believe that he actually belonged to the same species as these women whose pictures were in the papers. He had to force conviction on himself to believe that, yes, after all, these dames whose mugs and chassis were in the paper, they were only human too. He went on reading until he began imagining that he, himself, was a big shot and able to associate with broads just like these dames in the newspapers. He read on. Columns of print, columns that he read trance-

like until he couldn't read any more because of his hunger. Then
he concentrated on the food advertisements, trying to make
himself believe that he had been fed. Then, back again to the
society news to see what was going on in that realm. More
columns of print . . .

It was going to be pretty chilly walking all the way over to
the Munie for a free flop. Right now if he had sixty cents in
his jeans to spare, he could live like an aristocrat and take a
room for the night at the Mills Hotel at Thirty-sixth Street and
Seventh Avenue. But that was paradise. That was the flop house
where there was no delousing. And to think of the life of
some of these big shots whose names were in the papers. Press
one button for a meal. Two buttons for a drink. Three buttons
for a dame. The bastards, their life was almost that simple. Six
months ago, he'd got himself fixed up to look almost human,
and he'd gone to the Lonely Hearts Club and danced with a
dame. Jesus, what hadn't that done to him! And, Jesus, to be
with one when she was naked. Right now he'd rather think of
having a dame naked and willing in a room with him than of
anything else, even food. No, it was a toss-up between the
two pleasures. And since he could think of both of them, why
be stingy with his thoughts.

He was damned hungry. You'd think there was an ocean
storm in his guts. And if he only had a cigarette. Now that
would be kingdom come.

He got up and left the reading room, leaving the newspaper
file on the table. He went outside and walked around to the
Fifth Avenue steps. He stood there shivering, watching the
passing panorama. It was getting late in the afternoon of a gray
January day. There were noises, busses and automobiles, people, people who belonged to the human race. And there must
be a lot of rich dames in the crowd walking by on the sidewalk. He was seeing all kinds of fur coats. He tried to visualize
how some of these dames in the fur coats would look naked.
But he had business to attend to, some little conferences here
and there. He gazed about him with the shifty, beggary-eyed
expression of the stiff. He was looking for someone to hustle.

He turned up his coat collar, stuck his hands in his trouser pockets, and stood there, still shivering. He tried to hustle a well-dressed, sappy-looking young fellow who had an armful of books, but it was no soap. He descended the steps and picked out a clean-shaven bird with a pearl gray hat. He started to give the fellow a long hard-luck story about how he had just come in from Chicago where things were right fierce, and he was busted and wanted a flop, a chance to get a clean shirt out of the laundry, a good meal, a chance to spruce up and see if he couldn't rustle himself a job because he'd come all the way from the west coast since last fall and things were bad all over the country and he guessed it was best to try his luck in New York. He got a quarter and a half pack of Camels and, in offering obsequious thanks, he asked God to bless his benefactor. He hustled another dime, and then he walked around to Forty-second Street and over toward Broadway.

At Broadway he had more luck, unusual luck, and he stopped hustling for the day with the sum of one dollar in his pocket. Tonight he could sleep at the Mills Hotel in paradise. But first of all, he was going to stow away some grub. He ate in a Coffee Pot over on Ninth Avenue, and while he was putting away some hamburgers he thought back to his flight from home at seventeen, his wanderings back and forth across the face of America, warm nights in the jungles, cold nights in the cities, the time that he'd got a dose from a two-bit whore that he'd picked up on West Madison Street in Chicago, an idyllic summer that he'd spent on a farm. But he guessed that he was just one of those guys who was born to have it jammed up his can, and that was all. He kept remembering and remembering.

After eating, he went out and bought some cheap moonshine. The first drink warmed him, and he didn't mind its bitter taste. He'd drunk much worse. The second swig was even more warming. The third made his head a trifle light. He walked along the crowded streets of New York with a new-born confidence. He thought of movie actresses, society dames, chorus girls, rich broads, all of them parading before him. He held dialogues with himself, addressing obscene words to the images of motion picture actresses that he held in his mind.

Baby, there's many the broads better than you that I tossed out of bed. See! But just for the sake of sweet, sweet, sweet charity, and because I feel pretty good and at the top of my form tonight after cleanin' up on the street, and because I'm warm-hearted and soft and don't like to disappoint the gals, well, come on, kid! You can sleep with me this time.

He smiled. He disappeared in a dark entranceway for another drink. He reappeared on the sidewalk, smiling again with all his new-born drunken assurance.

He held more dialogues with the visions of naked women.

You, you're a bitch! I say you're a bitch! See! And there's only one way for a bitch like you to get tamed!

He saw himself with a naked movie star cowering before him while he advanced on her with a horsewhip. She shivered, drew back, screamed, crouched in a corner. He drove her from corner to corner, lashing her bare back and buttocks, horse-whipping her until her lovely back was welted and oozing blood.

He laughed raucously, and strangers stopped to look at him, all of them perplexed, some of them frightened.

He staggered on. The world became soft, friendly, and it made him so happy that he sang. He stopped several times for a drink, no longer bothering to go into corners or dark entranceways, but stopping in the center of the sidewalk, pulling out his bottle, and swigging. He walked on, singing drunkenly, happier than he had been since Christ knows when. The world became happier and happier, less and less hostile. He became one real guy all right. His belly was warm. He didn't feel any chill. He didn't need an overcoat now.

He zigzagged up and down streets and, reaching Third Avenue, he told the elevator girders that his name was Mr. Christ. In Tompkins Square, he kissed the bare trees and told them that they were lovely girls. He flopped down on a bench in the deserted square, pulled out his bottle, and had another drink. He felt the quarter in his pocket.

He got up and staggered on. A couple of trees seemed to punch him in the mouth. He called them dirty sons of bachelors and laughed. The world became full of blackness. It rocked, twirled, wheeled, spun, jigged under his feet. He swayed, and another tree seemed to punch him in the face, and then a white streak seemed to jab through a cosmic darkness. He fell down and whirled on the earth like one spun on a rapidly moving wheel. He labored to his feet and staggered along until he fell in a doorway on Third Avenue and lay there, as if dead. The wind whistled and snow started falling.

1930

The Only Son

I

It was Patrick McMurtrie's twenty-first birthday. He sat down to supper with his mother and father. Mrs. McMurtrie was a lean woman with tannish, rough skin. Her face seemed always drawn, her expression changelessly sad, her bony hands work-worn. The father was a gruff-looking little man with a weatherbeaten and wind-roughened face, the result of his years of work in the building trades. He was now employed as a foreman on a building under construction. Patrick was medium-sized, with a sensitive face, blue eyes, curly brown hair, and slightly hollowed cheeks.

All day his mother had been waiting for this moment. She had spent three times as long as usual in puttering about the kitchen and cooking the same kind of supper she prepared every evening. She blessed herself, bowed her head, and said grace, both father and son waiting in boredom while she performed this ritual. She always did the serving, and she served her son first, giving him a large cut of the thick steak and then filling his plate with potatoes and other vegetables. The father looked on silent and dour, watching her pass the plate to her son.

"Now you can serve the poor relation," he said as she reached for his plate.

Mrs. McMurtrie didn't answer him. Patrick frowned. They began to eat.

"Well, now that you're a man, with your schooling finished, and your fine college degree signed, sealed, and paid for, you can start paying back your old man the money he's spent making you so smart and highly educated," the father said, speaking slowly and with undue casualness as he ate.

Patrick said nothing. This was the old man's regular line.

"Joseph, why in the name of God would you be talking to your son like that, and this his birthday. You know that now the boy is working he'll be giving us back everything we've given him, and with interest," Mrs. McMurtrie said.

"Of course he will," the father said ironically. "I was just thinking out loud," he added.

They ate in silence. The mother looked as though she would cry, but no tears came. Patrick wanted the meal to be over with and to be out of the house and with Grace. The strained atmosphere at the dinner table was not unusual to him. It was a repetition of what happened almost every night. For years now he had known his father as a dour and bitter man, hating everything about his home, always making sarcastic remarks, constantly starting family squabbles. And for years now, also, he had known his mother as a sad and spiritless woman, fanatically religious, always seeming to suffer from the sharp gibes of her husband, sometimes fighting back, sometimes bearing herself with a painfully martyred expression on her face, as if she were going into a lion's den to die for her faith. He looked at her. That same expression. His mother embarrassed him. She loved him with such possessiveness.

Patrick's father always searched for something in the son's conduct that could be used against the mother. Patrick often looked upon himself as a kind of family No-Man's land. Patrick remembered how this had gone on ever since he was a boy, with fighting and the old man's drinking. But in those days he had been innocent and afraid of his father. Even so, he had quietly detested him. Now he did not detest his father. He was, at times, even sorry for the old man. Often he was contemptuous of him. And his mother was so damned religious, and she insisted that he be the same. Every Sunday he had to go to mass with her. His hypocrisy disgusted him. But he could not bring himself to tell his mother that he was an atheist. She was such a sad woman. She had so little in life to which she could cling. And then, it would give the old man a trump card to play against her.

Suddenly Mrs. McMurtrie began to cry. Her husband sarcastically asked why she was crying. She answered that it was because she was so happy.

"Joseph, remember when Patrick was a little gossoon, and you would be so often taking him to the park, and there he would be, chasing the squirrels. Patrick, my son, you always loved to chase the squirrels, and you couldn't say squirrel. You would always call them, 'quirrels.' You'd come home with your father and tell me of the great time you had, chasing the quirrels," she said.

"Yes, Mother," Patrick said, striving to hide his boredom.

"Ah, woman, will you forget that talk. That's all happened years ago, and what's the good in remembering it all of the time? Tell me, do I ever hear anything out of you but when he was a little gossoon?"

"And, son," she went on, ignoring her husband, "you were the good little fellow. On Sundays, often I would dress you up in your Sunday clothes and take you to mass with me, and sometimes I'd be taking you to see your Aunt Ellen, Lord have mercy on her soul. Yes, 'tis proud of you I'd be then. And now you're a fine young man, and it's prouder I am of you. And Lord have mercy on me, but how you would cry for ice cream when you were at your Aunt Ellen's. I wish she could be here with us now to see you as the fine young man that you are. But the Lord took her."

"Yes, and whenever you cried for ice cream, you'd get it, too," the father said.

"Why, Joseph!" she exclaimed, shocked.

"You always spoiled him by giving him everything he asked for. Is it any wonder he reads the books I see around here?" the father said.

"There's nothing wrong with the books I read," Patrick said.

"No, there's nothing wrong with Darwin, and men coming

from monkeys, and all that high-and-mighty nonsense. No, nothing wrong with heathen books," the father said.

"You don't know anything about the books I read."

"See, Mary! Did you hear what he said to me! Many's the time, woman, that I warned you you were spoiling him. Here's the fruit of your willfullness. Here we save all our life to educate him, and how does he repay us? He calls his father ignorant. So we're ignorant now?" the father said, and suddenly he turned from the mother and faced Patrick. "Well, my lad, it's not ignorant I'd be if I spent the money educating myself that I spent on you and your mis-education. Coming home now that you're a college graduate and acting as if you were somebody." He turned back to his wife, and with a melodramatic gesture of the right arm said, "Woman, I warned you!"

"Oh, quit putting on a show and acting as if I were still a two-year-old," Patrick told him.

"Son, you must not be saying such things to your father. If he provokes you or not, he's your father."

"Hell, I didn't ask him to be," Patrick replied, disgusted.

"Patrick, son!" the mother exclaimed in that injured, martyr-like tone of voice that she so frequently used.

"Mary McMurtrie, before he dies he'll disown his old father," Joseph McMurtrie declared solemnly, shaking his finger as he spoke.

"Well, from the way you go on, you'd think you were a section boss here at home, and that I was one of the hunkies working for you."

Patrick hadn't meant to reply to his father's provocation. The answer had come against his will and his determination, as it so often did.

"See, Mary McMurtrie! It's your doin'. See, he's twenty-one now and been to college, and right away he knows it all. Pretty soon he'll be too good to deign to live in the same flat with us. He'll be leaving us ignorant old greenhorns to go and marry that whore he runs around with," the father said, speaking with a bitterness that seemed to rise out of the depths of his being.

"Listen! Cut that out! You hear me!" Patrick shouted.

"Well, then, show a little respect for your father," Mc-Murtrie said, changing his tone of voice when he perceived the reaction he had produced in his son.

"People should do something in this world to earn respect," Patrick shot back at his father.

Patrick warned himself to exert more self-control. He understood more than his father did. He shouldn't let his old man get him so sore. With understanding, things should take on a different light. He knew that his father was jealous of him, bitter, unhappy, and that the old man had never loved his mother. Understanding all this, sensing causes underlying his father's conduct, he should take his father's words in his stride. But damn it, it was too thick. The old hypocritical fathead calling Grace a whore!

The father had been eying his son closely and observed a change, as if Patrick were softening while these reflections hastily passed through his mind.

"I'm boss in this house, and I want a little respect shown me! She's a whore anyway. What other kind of a girl could she be, sleeping with you," the father said.

The old man couldn't stand anybody else having any enjoyment or happiness in life, Patrick told himself, now determined to maintain his self-control.

"Saint Joseph, pray for me," the mother exclaimed in woe.

"Watch what you're saying," Patrick said to his father.

"As long as this is my house, don't ever bring that woman of yours into it," the father answered.

"Mother of God, protect my son from evil companions," the mother declaimed.

"How do you know she'd want to come here?" Patrick asked.

"Why should she? Why in the name of God should she be wanting to come into a decent household?" the father said.

"What the hell decency is there in this house?" Patrick asked, disgust rising above his efforts at self-control.

The father rose, trembling; he pointed an accusing finger
at Patrick.

"Out of my house, you young cur!" the father said.

"My son is not going to be put out of this house. Not while
I breathe the breath of life," the mother said.

Mrs. McMurtrie clasped her hands and silently prayed while
tears rolled down her cheeks.

"Goddamn you!" Patrick said to his father, flinging out each
syllable.

"I hope that God will never give you or that whore of yours
a decent day as long as you live!" McMurtrie said.

Patrick walked out of the room.

II

Patrick sat in his bedroom with the door closed so that he
could not hear his father and mother fighting. It was a small
room, with books scattered about, and holy pictures on the
walls. Right over the bed there was a framed picture of the
bleeding Sacred Heart. Yes, he didn't want to hear them. It
was often a puzzle to him—the fact that his old man never got
bored with the sound of his own voice uttering the same complaints against his mother that he had been uttering for years
and years in their endless squabbling. He never seemed able to
probe down to the real reason for his father's hatred and
jealousy. What had happened in the old man's life to cause
this? He knew that the old man had never been happy with
his mother. And he could understand that. Who would want
her for a wife? Who would want to sleep with her? As far
back as he could remember, she had always been the same.
The same religious fanaticism! The same air of sadness and
tiredness! She could give any man the creeps. She had always
made both him and his father feel that their home was redo-
lent of death. Always images of the same suffering Christ
on the cross plastered all around the house. He looked around
the room at the holy pictures. Christ was suffering over his
dresser. All the pictures were cheap and banal. Assuming
that there was a God, these pictures were a disservice to Him

and to His supposedly True Faith. They made Him out as no more of a character than his own father and mother, or than some ignorant Irish priest. He couldn't get to the bottom of his old man. Perhaps the old man hadn't wanted to marry her. Perhaps the old man hadn't wanted a kid. He didn't know. The old man was jealous of him now because he was young, had gotten a little education, and might have a different kind of life.

How many times hadn't his old man come rolling home drunk? But his father always had turned on respectability like a fountain to use in arguments with him. Yes, his father was a damned old hypocrite. Both his father and his mother were failures in life. They were mismated and they had botched their lives. Neither of them had ever seemed to be happy, except when his mother was smothering him with affection or praying, or when his old man was drunk with his cronies in a saloon or speakeasy. They were trying in their own way to drag him down to their own level. And he wouldn't be dragged down. He wouldn't! They were failures at living. They were going to make the same thing out of him if he let them. His mother wanted him to settle down into a successful nonentity. Well, he wouldn't. He didn't have much of a job, but he would do something, make something of his life. He didn't know what, but he would. Because he was out of college, he wasn't going to give up studying and trying to think. He was his mother's excuse for living. Somehow, he hated to hurt her. He didn't care about hurting his father. But she seemed so tragic a figure. Did she ever smile? Did she ever enjoy herself? Just looking at her suggested to him something of the cause of his father's bitterness.

He did things that he hated himself for doing, just because of his mother. Once a month, or once every two months, just to satisfy her, he said that he had gone to confession, and then, when she went to mass with him, he received Holy Communion. Sacrilege! It caused no fear, no terror in his soul. His nonexistent soul, he added with a smile. He asked himself were there many others in America doing the same thing as he was? Were there others with mothers and fathers such as his, and

were they compromising themselves and their dignity in their
own eyes by pretending to be Catholics, receiving the Sacraments of the Church sacrilegiously in order to preserve a little domestic peace and to nurture the illusions of older people?

Just now, his old man had gotten him damned sore when
he had slandered Grace. He loved Grace, and he would live
with her all his life. He wanted to marry her now, but she always counseled him to wait because neither of them had much
money, and because of his home situation. What the hell business did the old man have saying what he'd said about her?
Grace was unlike anyone he had ever known. And the old
bastard calling her a *whore!* It was only self-control that had
saved his father from getting something that he hadn't in the
least bargained for. And what was going to happen when he did
marry? He could see his father and mother alone in this house,
eating themselves away with unhappiness and mutual hatred
while they lived on, waiting only to die. There they would be,
each getting older, the old man getting more and more bitter,
the old lady growing more and more sad. She would throw anything she could in the way of his marrying Grace. She would
fight with all means to keep her son to herself. And it was
clearly a case of who should be the one that was to be sacrificed. He or his mother? He and Grace, rather, or else his
mother? Why was it this way? Why did life have to be this
way? Why did parents have to cling to their children like
drowning persons clutching a lifeline for dear life itself? It
was all more than he could make out. He stood up and told
himself that he was twenty-one and that, technically, he had
reached manhood's estate. He had to be a man. He had to walk
over his mother's unhappiness and misery, or else he couldn't
be a man.

To thine own self be true . . .

He quoted the line with seriousness and determination. He
wouldn't be just a dutiful son and a nonentity in an office all
his life. He vowed that he wouldn't.

He dropped back on his bed and reflected that the worst

feature of this whole situation was that there was no solution
to it. No matter how he thought it out, no matter how well he
understood his parents' motives, and his own motives, for that
matter, where did his understanding lead him? It could not
reduce one bit the pain and the agony and sorrow of his personal situation. He could not give up Grace without suffering
intensely. If he did that, he would have no heart to go on, to
go on and fight to make something decent of his life, to go
on and rise above the ranks of mediocrity. With her, he might
work, go to night school, study law, and make a career for
himself. That was a plan he had been thinking about. And if
he did not give up Grace, what about his mother? It was painful to think of his mother and father in this house alone, waiting to die after he had left them. And hell, what was it now
to live here? And where was it getting any of the three of them?
What was it getting them? Look at the scene at suppertime
tonight! And there they were, going at one another now in
the dining room.

He sat on the bed, glum. He heard his father slam the front
door. The old man would come home drunk and raise hell tonight.

III

Patrick was ready to leave when his mother entered the
room. She clutched him fiercely.

"You're all that I have. My son! My son! My baby boy that
I nursed. My baby!"

Held in an embrace by his mother, Patrick felt almost physically ill.

She kissed his forehead.

"I have to go, Mother. I got to meet a fellow and I'm late and
keeping him waiting on a street corner," he said.

Jealousy flashed in her eyes.

"Is it a lad you're meeting?"

"Why, of course, Mother."

"Patrick, you wouldn't lie to your mother?"

"You know I wouldn't, Mother. Why should I?"

And while he said this, he thought of how she forced him to lie to her; she had forced him to lie to her for years and years now. And she didn't know it, didn't know that it was impossible to tell her the truth about almost everything that he really felt or believed.

Wiping away a tear, she stood before him like a personification of desolation. That goddamn look of hers! Always that way! Always having to look at her standing there so silent, and so injured, and so sorrowful. He could understand a great deal about his father just by seeing her now, standing there before him.

Suddenly she drew a pair of rosary beads from her pocket. They were expensive ones, with a solid gold crucifix. She held them before him with great pride.

He waited for her to say something.

"For my son on this twenty-first birthday, from his Mother," she said, and her smile was a miserable effort.

"Gee, thanks, Mother! But you shouldn't have done that for me. They're expensive," he said.

"I had them blessed," she said.

She was so damned unfair and foolish. And the pity of her was that she didn't even know. And giving him rosary beads! His mother was a fool!

"Son, never lose your religion. God is good. Never lose your faith in Him," she said in a strained voice.

Again she wiped away a tear. Patrick was moved to pity his mother. But he was unable to express his emotion to her. And he dared not. If he did, then that would only serve to make the tie between her and himself the more intolerable. And so often, the ties which held flesh and blood together were so artificial. This realization made him hate all society, because it was society that kept firm these artificial ties. And just look at the hopeless mess it had made in his home.

He put on his straw hat and waited, anxious to get out, acutely uncomfortable here with his mother.

"Son, tell me the truth! Are you going to see that girl?"

"Why, Mother, I told you I was going to see a fellow and go to a movie with him."

"Son, she might be a nice girl, but she's not for you. I'm your mother and I know it."

Patrick did not answer her.

"Patrick, isn't there a nice Catholic girl you grew up with that you could take out now and again?"

"Mother, I'm late. And I'm going to be busy because I'm going to night school and study law in the fall. I won't be able to bother about girls," he said, feeling that he should blurt right out and tell her, force the issue to a showdown; but he was unable to make himself do that.

"Patrick, you do bother about that girl. I know you do. I can tell it. I'm your mother, and no one knows you better than your mother. I have been seeing how different you are since you've known that girl. I tell you this for your own good."

He asked himself why didn't he just tell her to mind her damned business.

"Son, you won't be having your mother with you always. You should stay in with me some nights, and that's little I'm asking of you."

"Mother, I've got to go."

Whether she did it purposefully or not, he wasn't sure, but she always succeeded in making him feel so damned guilty. And guilty of what? Just of trying to be himself and live his own life.

"I'll be home early," he said, unable to bear that look of hers.

She kissed him passionately, and he left. At the door he turned and said good-bye to her with what little sympathy he could force into his voice.

"Good-bye," she said again with all that sadness in her voice, saying it as if she were bidding him farewell for the last time in this world.

From the window she watched him disappear down the street. She sat alone, rocking in the darkened parlor, tears filling her eyes.

IV

Walking to the streetcar, Patrick thought gloomily that things would go on without any change just as long as the three of them lived together. If his mother died, what then? It would be better if she died first. If his father went first, he'd be left with her around his neck, depending on him, using every sentimentality offered to her by society to keep herself like a chain holding him at her level. Unless he wanted to continue going through such suppers and scenes as that of tonight, he had only one path to choose—to leave. And he couldn't do that while his mother lived. He knew that he couldn't. If she would only die. Death would be best for her. He thought of Grace. Suddenly he was fearful to the point of dread. He and Grace would get married, and one day they would be old, and one of them would die and leave the other behind. But that was years away. And they wouldn't grow old together as his mother and father had. They would build a free and beautiful life to-- gether. They would!

On the streetcar he accidentally put his hand into his coat pocket and felt the rosary beads that his mother had given him. He drew his hand out as if he had touched something disgusting. The beads brought him back to thoughts of his mother just when he had happily dismissed her from his mind. He thought of the meaning of her religion to her. It was all that she had. Her faith in him gave her nothing but misery, and earned from him nothing but annoyance and contempt and a kind of sympathy that would be insulting to any dignified human being. He hated her religion. Yet it did her good, saved her from utter misery and loneliness. He didn't care, he hated it! People had to learn to be brave and free, to face what life flung at them, and not weakly to ask the consolation of religion. But there she was. She came from a different world than he, and a different country, and she was a lone, forlorn woman in the present world. Yes, death would be gentle to her, a smooth, rippling, sleepy approach into darkness. And it would produce an irony that she would never experience. There was

no waking after death, and she would die, and she would not
wake up in any Heaven. She would die, and there would be no
more of her, and all her dreary life would have been in vain.
He wanted to revolt against it all. Life was a lousy business.
You had to stand up to the whole lousy business, he told himself with feeling and passion. Goddamn it, he would!

But he was going to Grace. And when he and Grace were
married and they had children, they would raise them intelligently, intelligently and free from all the superstition that he
had been taught. He vowed that he would. He had no God to
Whom he could vow. He vowed it to himself. Grace! She was
so lovely. And once with her, he would tell her all that happened, tell her all that he had been thinking.

The car stopped and he got off. He was going to Grace now,
and all of his home life would drop from his mind for a little
while, and he would find joy and love with her. He walked
briskly, a young man on his way to see his girl.

1930-1938

G. B. S. Interviews the Pope

AN IMAGINARY CONVERSATION

His Holiness Pope Pius XI is seated at his desk in his office where his private audiences are held. George Bernard Shaw enters jauntily, glances about quickly, approaches the desk stepping on the balls of his feet. He begins talking before he has reached the Pope.

G.B.S.: My dear fellow, you are even more difficult to see than I. *(Shaw pauses before the Pope's desk. Pius XI extends his left hand, on which is his large signet ring. Shaw gazes at the ring. He extends his own ringless left hand. The Pope stares at Shaw in astonishment.)* I say, let's dispense with formalities. *(Shaw sits down and comfortably crosses his legs. The Pope's perplexity increases.)* I trust that you are not dismayed because of my reputation. You know, it is delightful to meet you. You are the only man alive who has received as much dignified publicity as I have.

PIUS XI: In Rome we are accustomed to order, reverence, and the rendering of due respect to authority.

G.B.S. *(with a gesture of dismissal)*: I am fully acquainted with that subject. Clever fellow, Mussolini. He's done a fairish job of things, considering the bad human materials with which he has had to work. Before he became dictator Italy had not won a battle in centuries. Under him, you have succeeded in winning a few skirmishes with those fellows over in Africa, the Ethiopians. Before he is finished, Mussolini might even win a battle or two against a first-class military opponent.

Pius XI: We were oppressed by the tragic and unhappy spectacle of our countrymen at war in Africa. The re-establishment of peace brought great joy to our heart.

G.B.S.: I'll discuss that later. I have traveled a considerable distance in order to do you a favor.

Pius XI (with interest): Perhaps you have come to make a generous offering which will defray the expenses of constructing a floor in the new college we are building in Rome to educate the youth of Christendom for our struggle with the Bolshevik heresy.

G.B.S.: My dear man, I fear that you have mistaken me for one of those American Knights of Columbus. The youth of Christendom will be even better educated if it reads my books. And that will put money into my pocket instead of drawing it out. My purpose here is to save your organization from appearing ridiculous in the eyes of the civilized world. I have here a ten-thousand-word letter which I have just addressed to the London Times. It deals with the Americans. One of these days intelligent Europeans will face the task of civilizing the Americans.

Pius XI: We are gratified by the struggles our brothers in America are conducting against paganism.

G.B.S.: You are badly informed. The Americans are cutting up again.

Pius XI (as if uttering a mild malediction): Gloria in excelsis Deo! Anti-Christ walks the face of the earth, and we have courage only because of the promise of Divine protection which Our Master gave to Saint Peter.

G.B.S.: Saint Peter was neither a saint nor a clergyman; he was a boorish Syrian fisherman.

Pius XI (scandalized and in dismay): In nomine—

G.B.S. (interrupting with a flourish): Don't disturb yourself, my dear fellow. The Americans are not intelligent enough to understand socialism and bolshevism. The Americans are amusing themselves not with bolshevism but with censorship.

A group of amateur busybodies calling themselves Catholics and the Legion of Decency are meddling with art. They are disrupting the plans for the motion-picture production of my play, *Saint Joan*, which, as you know, has rescued Saint Joan from Protestant bigotry.

PIUS XI: We have been warmly encouraged by the good sense of the American people in their efforts to destroy the evil and satanic influence in motion pictures which are offensive to truth and poison the wellspring of Christian conscience.

G.B.S.: Stuff and nonsense! I am here to save you from being chagrined and disgraced by the Americans.

PIUS XI: There is no compromise with error.

G.B.S.: I agree with you. And have I not proved in my play, *Saint Joan*, that your organization is sufficiently flexible and intelligent to canonize a Protestant saint such as the Maid?

PIUS XI *(in alarm)*: You have described the great Saint Joan as a Protestant?

G.B.S.: I understand your confusion now. You have not read my play.

PIUS XI: Error is a cancer which must be destroyed, rooted out, and it is our duty to see that it is.

G.B.S.: I have stated that thought more clearly in my play. After you read it, you will be a better Pope, because you will learn how to express Catholic sentiments with greater force and clarity.

PIUS XI: The justice of the church is not a mockery, and we will not allow it to become such.

G.B.S.: I suspect that you are twiddling me. You *have* read my play, and you are giving me back the very lines which I have written. You really are a clever man, almost as clever as I. And do you remember the defense of the Dogma of Infallibility in my preface: "Perhaps I had better inform my Protestant readers that the famous Dogma of Infallibility is by far the most modest pretension of its kind in existence. Compared with our infallible democracies, our infallible medical councils, our infallible astronomers, our infallible judges, and our infallible parliaments, the Pope is on his knees in the dust confessing his ignorance before the throne of God. . . ."

Pius XI *(beginning to show signs of fatigue)*: We admonish that you pray for guidance. In our encyclical *"Divini illius Magistri,"* we have already deplored the possibilities for evil potent in the cinema and its misuses as an incentive to evil and passion.

G.B.S.: Do tell me! Do you approve of this Catholic Action, and this American Legion of Indecency?

Pius XI: We have imparted our affectionate and apostolic benediction to our bishops and pastors of souls who have organized, and who direct and guide, that great spiritual endeavor.

G.B.S.: Well, old chap, if you don't want to be made a fool of I advise you to read my play and restrain the zeal of those Americans.

Pius XI: We do not wilfully expose ourselves to heresy. And we again admonish you to pray for guidance and to repent the sin of pride while there is yet time. We instruct you to become one of the faithful, and we announce that Catholic authors must advance Christian doctrines in all their publications, and we forbid them to use the weapon of half-truth, however effective, against our adversaries. We further advise that you place yourself under the guidance of Saint Francis of Sales, whom we have proclaimed as the patron saint of journalism.

G.B.S.: I clearly perceive that I am a better Catholic than the Catholics.

Pius XI: We state that we bear no malice to heretics, and we bestow our benediction even upon our enemies, and upon our erring sons whose minds and Christian consciences have been blackened by the sin of pride and poisoned by the Protestant and Bolshevic heresies.

G.B.S.: My character Cauchon utters those sentiments much more clearly. You really must read my play. My dear chap, it has taken your outfit six centuries to canonize Saint Joan. But I have immortalized and understood her. It may take you six centuries to understand and appreciate my services. And when

you do, you'll canonize me. But I enjoyed my visit. I think that
now I'll drop in on Mussolini for a little chat. I'm anxious to
see how much he has learned in these last fifteen years. *(Shaw,
stepping lightly on the balls of his feet, goes out, and the Pope,
wearied, begins to nod his head.)*

1936

To Whom It May Concern

AND OTHER STORIES

". . . the trailing

Consequence of further days and hours."

T. S. ELIOT

Baby Mike

―――――――――――――――――――――

"WAKE UP, SHEEP! Baby sheep woke up."

It was still dark outside. Three-year-old Baby Mike lay in the crib in the chilled bedroom, his wide-open eyes peering into the darkness, talking to himself.

"Wake up, Dumbo!" he commanded. He searched for and found at his side a worn and faded Dumbo doll with whom he slept. He shook it energetically, laughing as he did so. "Wake up, Dumbo! Dumbo is a sweet little thing. He sweet. Little boy, blow your horn, sheep in the meadow, cow in corn, where is the little boy, look after the sheep?" He laughed again. "Where him is? Under the haystack, fast asleep. Wake up, Dumbo!" Once more he filled the bedroom with ringing peals of laughter. "Meadow, meadow, meadow. There's a Poppy Meadow, Mommy Meadow, and Baby Meadow. I have a birdie. My birdie name is Peter. He lives uptown-downtown on First Avenue. He went countwy in twain. He heard, oh so many noises. Cock a-doodle do. Bzzz-Bizz. Whip-poor will. Cats talk: 'Meow, meow.' Little babies pee in pants and cwy, 'Ya-ya-yan-yan.' My birdie Peter, he never cries any more."

Baby Mike screamed in laughter. He stood up, stumbled forward, leaned over the high panel at the foot of the crib, and began calling, at first plaintively and then commandingly:

"Mommy, come in! Come in, Mommy!"

Only half awake, Elizabeth crawled out of bed. It was a railroad apartment, and the bedroom was in the center, off the dining room.

"That little devil, why can't he sleep later?" she complained to herself, half aloud.

"Because if he did, then his father might get more rest," Andrew groaned sleepily from the inside of the bed.

"Oh, darling, I'm sorry I woke you up."

"The accomplishment is his—not yours."

"Go back to sleep."

"Do you hear your son going it? How can I?"

"Exasperating as he is—isn't it wonderful to hear him in the morning?"

"Yes, he comes trailing clouds of glory when his father wants to sleep."

She got into a warm house robe and went out to take care of Baby Mike. In the kitchen she switched on the light and put water on for coffee, acting mechanically, as she always did at this hour of the day.

"Mommy, come in," Baby Mike called on hearing her; he waved his hands and jumped up and down ecstatically.

"Why aren't you under the covers? Haven't I told you?" she exclaimed as she turned on the light in his room.

"I'm a sheep."

She looked at him momentarily with loving eyes. He had ringlets of golden hair, shining blue eyes, and a sensitive face.

"Oh, you lollypop," she exclaimed.

"No, I'm a sheep. I'm a sheep, Mommy Sheep," he answered her in a serious voice.

She picked him up and kissed and cuddled him and then carried him to the bathroom. He talked in a ceaseless stream. He emerged from the bathroom, wearing a scarlet robe and warm slippers. He walked erect and, as he passed through the dining room, he yelled a warning to his mother:

"Don't wake up Poppy Sheep!"

Baby Mike sat in a small chair at his little table near the kitchen window. Elizabeth squeezed oranges and strained the juice into a glass. Watching her closely, Baby Mike talked incessantly. When he saw steam rising from the water boiling for the coffee, he jumped up and down and hopped about.

"What are you doing, Mike?"

"That's steam dance. Like that, Mommy?"

"Yes, I do, you little angel."

"I'm a sheep," he corrected her, again sitting down.

His face grew pensive. He said nothing. There was a far-off look in his eyes. He carefully examined the peeling paint on the window sill. He stared, lost in his own thoughts.

"My birdie, there he is in a big boat. See him, Mommy?" Baby Mike exclaimed dreamily, pointing at the wall.

Elizabeth turned to gaze at him tenderly. Then she set a small glass of orange juice before him.

"Now, drink that!"

He remained transfixed. She took his bacon and egg from the icebox. His face lit up with excitement. He waved his hands.

"I want to touch bacon," he yelled.

She let him touch and smell the bacon. Then she put it on the stove.

"Want me tell you a stowy, Mommy?"

"No, not now. Drink your orange juice first."

He emitted a succession of strange sounds.

"Like that stowy?"

"Yes, and now you drink your orange juice."

"My birdie Peter," he said, paying no attention to her order, "his Poppy, Mommy never go out supper."

"Drink that orange juice," Elizabeth commanded with a stern voice.

Baby Mike took a sip.

"Mommy, what time it?"

"Five after seven."

"No, it's twenty after car comes in gawage." He laughed gaily, and his eyes shone with pleasure. "Mommy was wong."

"You like Mommy to be wrong, don't you?"

"Mommy was wong," he repeated, laughing.

After drinking his orange juice, he watched his mother preparing his bacon and egg. She lit a cigarette, made the coffee, watched the things on the stove, and poured herself a cup of coffee. When his next course was ready, she broke the bacon into the egg cup and set it before him. She sat beside him on a small chair and fed him the first spoonful. Then she urged him to feed himself.

"Tell me a stowy," he said.

She made up a very brief story about a giraffe that rode on a streetcar.

"Here's Poppy," he interrupted, hearing his father coming out to the kitchen.

Andrew came in, wearing a bathrobe.

"Hello, Mike."

"Have coffee, Poppy?"

Andrew lit a cigarette and poured himself a cup of coffee.

"I tell Mommy a stowy," he said.

"All right, if you'll feed yourself."

"Once upon a time there was a boy. His name Donald. He went to countwy in bus. It wained. He was a bad boy."

Baby Mike laughed at his mother.

Andrew went to the front door and returned with the morning newspaper. Elizabeth asked him what the weather report predicted, and he read to her that it would be cold and windy.

"No, it say wain, snow, sun, it does," Baby Mike corrected.

They looked at him with pride and love.

A struggle of wills developed between Baby Mike and his mother. She wanted to get breakfast over with. He was determined to take his time. He dallied and played, running his finger over the peeling paint, gazing about, twisting and turning in his chair, staring at the ceiling, gazing into the cup of partially eaten bacon and egg. Andrew read on, paying no attention to them. Elizabeth coaxed, urged, commanded, but Baby Mike took his own time in eating.

"These dolts! These stupid dolts!" Andrew exclaimed aloud in sudden anger.

"What's the matter?" Elizabeth asked.

"Dolts," he said, looking at her. "This book reviewer praises an utterly fatuous and ignorant novel about the French Revolution, written by some foolish woman. He writes that this stupid woman has contributed to our knowledge of history.

And this jackass even calls Hitler another Robespierre. The ignoramus!"

"Don't get so excited over it."

"Poppy Sheep 'cited. I like that."

"Such ignorance of history is inexcusable."

He expressed his anger by gulping the rest of his coffee. He poured himself another cup.

"You drink too much coffee, Andrew," she said.

Baby Mike took a long time with his egg.

After breakfast Andrew started dressing. Baby Mike assisted and impeded his efforts. He pulled at Andrew's shorts, discovered hair on his father's legs, and made a general nuisance of himself. When Andrew was dressed, Elizabeth put on Baby Mike's green snow suit. It had a cone-shaped helmet, and when he was dressed in it he looked like a little Dutch boy. Father and son left for their regular Saturday morning ride on the Fifty-ninth Street trolley car.

Elizabeth hung out the window, repeating final instructions and warnings to her husband.

"Now, watch him. Don't get into one of your fits of absent-mindedness and forget he's with you," she called.

Andrew impatiently assured her that the advice was unnecessary. He was sensitive about his absent-mindedness, because he knew it was a trait which couldn't be eradicated from his personality. On the way to the corner of Fifty-ninth and First Avenue, he had to play a game with his son. Mike would run into each successive doorway and stand there. Andrew then had to run and find him, poke him in the chest, and say "Boom." When he did this, Mike shook his mittened hands up and down with joy, laughed and squealed with pleasure, and ran to the next doorway for a repetition of the game.

Andrew enjoyed this little game with his son. At the same time, he was self-conscious. Though he wanted strangers to see that he was a devoted father and to notice his beautiful child, he was aware of himself as an assistant professor of history at Columbia University. And outside of the classroom or circle of his intimates, he was a very timid man, acutely conscious of strangers. He imagined that if one of his students were to see him playing such games with his son, he might appear slightly ridiculous.

It was raw and cold. They waited for the trolley car in the doorway of a restaurant on the corner. The prospect of the ride bored him. He wished it were over with. He wanted to get back home and begin working. Then a familiar thought recurred in his mind. Was not a live human being, in the process of development, innocent and unspoiled, much more interesting and instructive than books about life? He resolved to spend more time watching his son, playing with him, instructing him. He would even make notes about what the child said and did.

"Poppy, the car! The car, Poppy. Here it comes. See it come?" Baby Mike shouted, jumping up and down with joy.

A trolley car approached slowly.

"Look, Poppy," Baby Mike commanded.

Andrew obeyed. Baby Mike did his steam dance near the curb.

"What's that?" Andrew asked.

"That's streetcar dance."

Andrew smiled, picked him up, and they boarded the car. He sat on his father's lap, looking out the window.

"Poppy, why can't I see the wheels on car?"

"Because they are under the car."

"Why they under car?"

"Because if they weren't, the car wouldn't go."

"Why wouldn't car go?"

Passengers smiled, watched, and listened with amusement. Andrew became self-conscious. He had the same contradictory feelings he had had a few moments before playing the game of "Boom" with his son. Andrew finally distracted Mike by calling his attention to the streets. During these Saturday morning rides, he had taught Baby Mike the order of the streets on this route. The boy knew this order. But he started asking Andrew what street it was, and when Andrew would answer correctly, Mike would disagree and deliberately declare that the street they were passing was a different street. Then he would say:

"Papa was wong."

Habit overcame insight. Any incorrect statement about demonstrable fact always roused Andrew to state the truth. He knew that this was a kind of game for the child, but habit asserted itself. He would thus correct the boy, but with no avail. Then he would smile at himself with amusement and agree with the boy, and Baby Mike would say:

"I play tricks on Papa."

"But do you like Papa to play tricks on you?"

"No. I don't like that," Mike answered, going into a peal of laughter which delighted some of the passengers.

The car they had taken was making its last run. It was then to go into the barn. They got off. Mike wanted to see the barns and said:

"Barns is where cars go sleep."

He was frightened at the prospect of going inside. They looked through the entrance and boarded a car and rode back. After they had passed Madison Avenue, Mike became restless. He began pushing and poking his father. Knocking off Andrew's hat, he then got a firm grip on his hair. Andrew told him to let go, but the boy pulled until it hurt, and Andrew angrily forced his son to let go.

"Why Papa do that?"

"You were hurting me."

"I don't like you do that."

Andrew was glad when the car reached First Avenue. It had gotten colder. He wanted to hurry home. The child should not be kept out in such a strong wind. Baby Mike fell into another dreamy mood and stood on the corner, absorbed in his own thoughts. He took a few steps and gazed off at nothing. It took fifteen minutes to walk the block and a half home.

Elizabeth was rushing frantically to get some cleaning done and was disappointed because they had not stayed out longer. But noticing the weather, she agreed that the boy had to stay in. This meant that it was going to be a hard day.

Andrew had an unusually heavy schedule at school because of the War. He always looked forward to his weekends as the

time when he could get some work done. He was writing a
biography of Saint-Just and had taken on an extra chore, that
of translating some articles of Mathiez on the finances of Danton. He went to his office, hoping that during this week end
he would finish one of these translations. His office was in a small
room off the living room. It was neat and orderly. He sat down
to work. He paid no attention to the sounds of his wife cleaning
house, or of his son at play. But suddenly he became nervous.
Elizabeth was cleaning the living room and was speaking
sharply to Mike, who then started whining and yelling. He became impatient because of the distraction. He had reached a
pitch of concentration, and this noise had broken the spell. He
got up and walked into the living room.

"What's the matter now?" he asked in annoyance.

"This child is deliberately getting under my feet. I want to
get the carpet cleaned."

"Explain to him."

"I'm tired of explaining. He needs to be punished."

"Do you mean physical punishment?"

"I mean punishment," she answered with irritation.

"You know that I will never agree to the administering of
physical punishment on Mike," he told her with frowning determination.

Baby Mike yelled shrilly.

"I tell you it is wrong."

"Well, is it right for him to drive me crazy when I'm trying
to clean the house and I have no help?"

"Have a little patience."

"That's the trouble with him. He's been spoiled with too
much patience."

"Don't get so excited."

"I'm not excited. You're excited," she answered.

Baby Mike stopped shouting, distracted by the carpet
sweeper. While his father and mother argued as to who was
excited, he managed to get the handle out of it. He dragged it
around the living room, unnoticed by Andrew or Elizabeth.

"Don't you see?" Andrew said, striding back and forth,

"that if you use force, that means that all other methods of dealing with the child have failed?"

"Well, they have when he won't give me one moment's peace. He does this day after day. He gets under my feet in order to drive me crazy."

Gaily carrying the pole, Baby Mike narrowly missed breaking a lamp.

"If you punish a child with physical violence, you merely get yourself into a vicious circle. I'm surprised that you don't understand this."

"If you had the minute-by-minute care of him, you'd understand more and talk less," she answered.

"That's irrelevant."

"Yes, it isn't in a book."

"I'm merely talking common sense. When you punish a child, you then have to keep administering more severe doses of punishment. He is growing, becoming stronger all of the time, and thereby he is growing more able to receive punishment. To have an effect, you will have to keep hitting him harder. I tell you that you can't do that."

"Oh, for God's sake, I'm not talking about beating him. I'm merely saying that he needs a little slap now and then. Often a slap is the only means of shocking him into paying attention."

"You're making a grave mistake if you do," Andrew warned angrily.

Baby Mike carried the pole out to the dining room.

"Elizabeth, please sit down. I have something important I want to say."

"And I have a thousand things to do," she answered.

"We have to reach decisions about Mike's future."

She sat on the edge of a chair, painfully impatient.

"Recently I had to look back through the writings of Clausewitz," he began.

"Is that what you want to tell me? Can't you explain that to your students?"

"That's the trouble with you. You won't listen."

"Andrew, I went to college once. Now I have more mundane matters to attend to."

"I have some very practical suggestions to make."

"What are they?" she asked; even the way she breathed seemed sarcastic.

Baby Mike continued to play with the pole in the dining room, talking to himself and utterly unaware of his parents in the front of the apartment.

"All right, then, if you won't listen to me before I have even said what I wanted to say."

"I'm listening," she answered, glaring at him.

"Now, when I was rereading what Clausewitz wrote on strategy and tactics," he began.

It was with a great effort that Elizabeth maintained her self control.

"Now, this difference between strategy and tactics applies to the problems we meet raising a child. Each separate problem of behavior, that's a tactical one. It must be solved. But in solving these tactical problems we must have a perspective. We must have a longer view, that is, a strategical one. The way we use each solution, that is strategical. We must have what amounts to a strategy in raising Baby Mike. And we have to agree on it. We must—"

"For God's sake, go away," she screamed, interrupting him.

"See, you won't even be reasonable—"

"Last week," she cut in, "you told me I had to know Dewey, Freud, and Marx in order to raise my son. Now, this week, I must know Clausewitz. For God's sake, get out of here. Go back to your office before I go out of my mind!"

Andrew looked at her hopelessly.

There was a crash. They rushed out to the dining room. With the pole in his hands, Baby Mike cried as he gazed at the broken remains of six beautiful pieces of Mexican pottery which Andrew had given Elizabeth as a present.

"Look what he's done!" she exclaimed.

Baby Mike screamed mercilessly.

"And I walked miles to find those," Andrew lamented.

Elizabeth picked up Mike, kissed him, and told him not to cry and that he mustn't touch Mama's things ever again.

Mike broke into fresh tears.

"I want them all back. Put them back, Poppy."

"I'll get new ones," Andrew said, taking Mike from his mother and quieting him.

Mike squirmed out of his father's arms and ran into the front to look out the window at a coal truck being unloaded.

"Those were the only things we really cherished," she said sadly, looking at Andrew and then down at the mass of broken pottery at her feet.

"We can't do anything about it. And we can't blame Mike."

He put his arms around her and kissed her.

"Come, Poppy! Come in, Mommy! See coal truck," Mike called imperatively from the front.

They obeyed.

Then Andrew went to his office and Elizabeth swept up the pottery.

Baby Mike ran out to his mother and said earnestly:

"Mommy, let Poppy work."

"You let Poppy work."

"I will, Mommy."

He got his copy of *Mother Goose* off a shelf and took it into the living room. He sat down at the threshold of Andrew's office.

Andrew turned and said with annoyance:

"Now, I've asked you to let me work, Mike."

"Mike opened the book and gazed intently at the illustrations.

"I will wead to you, Poppy. . . . Ding, dong, pussy in the well—who put him there? Little Johnny Green. Who took him out? Little Johnny Stout. Where is little boy looks after sheep? Under haystack fast asleep. Meadow, meadow, meadow, bong, bong, bong. . . ."

"My God!" Andrew exclaimed.

"Like that, Poppy?" Mike asked.

He smiled cherubically at his father.

1943-44.

To Whom It May Concern

SINCE I had ulcers of the stomach six years ago, I've developed an extraordinary interest in my own skin. Or is it so extraordinary? What is more fascinating to any of us than our own skins? I am convinced that as one grows older, one develops this interest. It sometimes amazes me that I never become bored thinking of this skin of mine. What I put on it, what I put into it, what comes out of it—this all fascinates me. I have an abiding interest in my own digestive organs. I dwell upon the phenomenon of my own bowel movements more than I do on the beauties and glories of creation.

My hair is beginning to get gray. I look at myself in the mirror every morning. I examine these prophetic strands. At times, they frighten me. I tell myself, Ernest Kobat, your youth is gone.

When I was younger, I dreamed of writing. I wanted to be a free artist. My attitude was cynical, and I told myself I needed no faith. But I had faith, faith in art and in truth. I believed I would become a free man, a free artist. Now that I am forty, I have reached an age where one might be expected to be cynical and I need something to believe in. I have nothing. I came to New York to discover my old self—my true self. I took this room at the Brevoort because I used to live around the corner on Eighth Street. I'm searching for myself. Oh, rot!

I am here in New York on a vacation from Hollywood. Day after day since I arrived, I've sat down in my room here at the

Brevoort determined to write the Great Novel. I can't do it. There's no use kidding myself. How lonely this room is! How dreary! How frightened I am when I sit down to write! I am afraid concerning every word I put down. I tell myself that it is cheap—no good. If I publish something bad, I'll be laughed at. I am a perfectionist. I cannot write a perfect novel. So—I write pictures. Oh, crap! Why should I bother even to keep this diary? Why anything?

But I love to write. That is to say, I did love to write. I still do. Every time I do a picture on the coast, there is a lurking hope that this time I've clicked. I almost convince myself that, at last, I've done something terrific. I delude myself into believing that I've slipped something fine and first-rate into the picture. I tell myself that I've hit a peak. Then I go berserk. I begin to dwell on myself as a figure who will be remembered forever as the writer who wrote a truly great picture. But then I become ashamed of myself and go to the opposite extreme. I fume with hatred of everything I do. I feel contemptuous of most of the people I see. I think they really believe in all this make-believe. I become so lonely that I don't know what to do with myself. I grow antisocial. I sit by myself in a bar, brooding into a glass of Scotch. I am not supposed to drink because of those ulcers but I do. Nothing else solaces me in these moods.

You can count on your fingers the number of writers in America who pay a bigger income tax than yours truly. Why should I envy the novelists? They sweat out books that will sell a few piddling copies. If one of them is lucky, he'll make five thousand dollars out of a book he's taken a year or two to write. And I can make that much working two weeks in a studio. I am respected in pictures. Hell, I'm an important personage in this glamour industry—that is, as important as a mere writer can be. And I can write rings around the hacks out there. If I were more ambitious, I'd become a big person in the industry. I'd finagle myself a three-way contract to Hell and then would write, direct, produce my own pictures. I tell myself that I haven't the desire. I still feel that somehow I'm going to escape from Hollywood. That is why I don't save money. I fear that if I save money, I'll become rich and never do a decent piece of work. If I don't save, there's always the chance that I might. Does this make sense? But then, what man will really make sense if he honestly tells the truth about himself? I have all these contradictory feelings and desires and I do nothing about them. I go on, year after year, doing picture after picture, hoping that sometime I'll break away. Now I am forty. I've got to break away.

Another day gone. Time is rushing by me, and I am doing nothing. Now I write in this diary in order to escape from facing myself and from working. Perhaps I ought to give up. Why not reconcile myself to Hollywood? After all, it is easier to reconcile yourself when you can make big dough than it is when you're poor. Others have. Some of my fellow scribblers are happy. Why can't I be like them? Yes, Ernest, give it up. A man who nurses ambitions he can't attain is a jerk.

I am afraid I may be developing a kind of civilian neurosis. On the streets, when I see chaps in uniform, I feel guilty. Sometimes I can't look these men in the eye. I want to go up to them and tell them why I'm not in uniform. Often I explain my civilian clothes to some unseen fictitious judge of my imagination. I talk to myself as if I were a madman.

I've got to get over this. Isn't it bad enough to be a frustrated writer, without also becoming a frustrated hero? I become bitter. I feel bitter at this moment. You see, I am doing my part. I help build morale. I pay big taxes. I buy bonds. And I tried to serve. Rejected. Forty and 4F. But I wanted to get into this show. I wanted to be a hero. I am fed up writing stories about heroes. I want to be more fantastic than my own heroes. And yet I don't believe in the idea of dying for democracy. I'm not sure that this war is for democracy. I'm not sure about anything. I'm afraid I don't even believe in anything any more.

I wanted to get into this show because I hoped that in a battle I might find the guts I lack. I wanted to be a hero in order to prove to myself that I'm not a miserable coward. So here I am, forty and 4F, and all jazzed up with an incipient civilian neurosis.

Words! I am paid so much for every word I put on paper that I've lost faith in the meaning of words. To me, they are things that I sell, not symbols of faith and mirrors of truth. I've written and sold too many words I didn't believe in. I think most of us on the coast are the same. That's why I can't stomach those who believe in the racket. Oh, hell, and yet I sometimes hope, or try to hope.

I see many middle-aged men in restaurants. And old men, too. They are gay, talking, laughing, drinking, shining before the young girls they take out. The sight saddens me. Ah, we middle-age Don Juans! The war has given us social monkey glands. We're making dough, eating and living well. And then I think of this eternal skin of mine. I am no longer young. From now on, time will pass more quickly, more fruitlessly.

Lunch with my friend Phil yesterday. He's now an important literary critic. He is developing jowls. Phil and I were idealists when we were young. I couldn't tell him that I thought he wrote about books like a racetrack tout. But who am I to criticize? We both sold out. It was miserable when we tried to talk of the old days. As if by mutual agreement, we changed the subject and got on to the war. He's very encouraged about the way things are going, and I'm not. I got an awful jolt about Spain, and then, on top of it, came the pact between Russia and Germany. I guess I've never gotten over it. I don't know. But Phil was optimistic about the kind of world we'll have after the war. He can't be right. Nothing good can come out of this war. We'll win and be the big boss in the world. Pictures will boom. Perhaps I'll make thirty-five hundred a week instead of twenty-five hundred.

I glanced here and there, seeing so many gray heads, bald heads, pot bellies. There were a lot of businessmen near us. I reflected that I am really like them. They make and sell the goods of the nation and clean up on it. I sell the dreams of the nation and clean up on it. What is the use?

Is it my civilian neurosis? Look at the number of people who are starving. The American boys who are dying! Women and children smashed by bombs! And for me, personally, the net result might be a bigger salary. I tried to tell Phil how I felt. He doesn't feel that way. I was glad to leave him.

Why should I work myself into a dither because I can't write a novel? What difference does it make? The novel is outmoded. The motion picture has supplanted it. After working in pictures you sometimes begin to think that the novel is pathetically antiquated. Pictures are an infant art. In time, won't they be more free, more sophisticated and realistic? Then, look at what we'll be able to do. And, anyway, what novelists are there in America? None. The novel reached its highest development in the nineteenth century. Now it's horse and buggy. And sooner or later all of these uncomprising novelists go West. I don't believe them when they talk of their integrity. They're out for the big money, too. Haven't I seen them come out, one by one, and what's happened to them after they've come to Hollywood? We're all egotists. And the highest interest of the egotist is that skin of his. That is human nature. Idealists like to talk. They use those big words. The hell with this crap. I'm going out and get drunk. And the hell with my stomach.

Why did I get drunk last night? I have a hangover. My stomach can't take it. Not even the best Bourbon. If I keep on doing this, my ulcers will come back.

I've got a head!

Met Abner Gaylord, the new sensation who can recite the Lord's Prayer on the radio better than any man, woman, or child in these United States. Abner is just like his name.

Drinks last night to forget my hangover. Result: I feel rotten today.

Felt so rotten yesterday that I took in an old Berry Bryan-Natalie Jennings picture at a little Third Avenue movie house. Bum stuff. And yet I liked it. Natalie is forty-one and fighting like hell to hang on and preserve herself. I ran into her at a party before I left the coast and I could see the terror of old age in her eyes. It is a terrible look to see in the eyes of a woman who has to stay young.

I noticed the tenements on Third Avenue over the stores and wondered how people can live in them. How was I able to live when I was poor? I remember and I don't remember. Yesterday, I had the strangest feeling of being so removed from the realities of life; I felt different from the rest of humanity. This is what the celebrity world does to you. I thought how in pictures we have to soften these realities. I suppose I got sentimental. But I kept thinking that life must be so awful for so many people. I wanted to rush home and write a book, a true book. But I didn't.

Lonely and in the dumps last night. Didn't know what to do with myself. I got me a high-class whore. And after the details, I had her sit and listen while I talked about myself. She must have thought I was a lunatic. Everything about her was professional. What a banal business!

How bored I am getting! How boring my vacation is! Nothing to do, I walk the streets looking for something to do. I see people who don't interest me. I hope every day for something. And what can I hope for that I haven't already had? My God, how many bored people are there in New York who feel this way? The bars are crowded. The night clubs are jammed. The motion picture theaters thrive. Broadway is taking in dumb money. Are all these people trying to escape from being bored with themselves? I look for people, and as soon as I see them I wish I hadn't. I look for a woman, find her, and then I wonder why.

I ran into Catherine yesterday. The ex-number-one. I was embarrassed. After leaving her, I was melancholy. Catherine was a sweet girl. Once we were young and poor together, and we were in love. We had dreams together. We went to the Coast together and we were happy. The future was shining. Catherine wanted a beautiful home, and I was able to get it for her. My God, the story seems so commonplace. And it isn't. It was the best part of my life. The world was young to us. Now, the world is old. No, I can't lie to myself. We were both corrupted. We got bored with each other. I played around. She played around with D———, the director. She married him after we were divorced, and then she went to Reno again. Now she drinks like a fish. Catherine kept gazing at me with a sort of strange and knowing look in her eyes, as if to tell me that she saw right down to the bottom of my soul. We had a drink together and chatted. Catherine looks pretty good. Even though she drinks too much, she doesn't seem to show it. I was ashamed of my gray hairs. And when she asked me if I were completely cured of my ulcers, I felt as if ulcers were immoral. I was hurt when she asked me if I were writing my own stuff. She said it without any intonation, and yet I'm sure she meant it as sarcasm.

When she and I started to bust up, we had some awful scenes. I would get nasty to her. I'd blame her for everything. I'd tell her that she had made a literary whore out of me, and I'd turn the knife until she cried. When we agreed on the divorce, I hoped I would never see her again. I felt that now I would write. And yesterday after we parted I wished that we hadn't. Why did we? Why didn't I suggest that we go to her hotel room and try to recapture the past. Pitifully try to recapture it, because that is gone forever. I thought of Proust and wished I had had the patience to read all of him. I wanted to regain the past. I wanted to sleep with her again. This morning, I woke up determined to. I phoned her a little while ago and suggested seeing her for lunch. She was too busy. Didn't have time. Darling, I'm just rushed to death and I'm leaving town. I fear she guessed my intention.

I wonder what I'll do today?

I am moody. I feel that the past is not irretrievable. Somehow I am going to regain it, not in fragments, but all of the past with the full immediacy it once had. Somehow it is not gone. It is merely away somewhere waiting to be rediscovered. Yes, I will recapture it. That means I will get back the best years of my life. What am I thinking? Am I becoming an outright sentimentalist?

Since I saw Catherine the other day, I've thought of lots of things. I'm not the same person I used to be. But I changed without realizing I was changing. I recalled how I used to say that I wouldn't "go Hollywood" when I first went out. How did I go? At times it is difficult for me to recall any sense of what I was like before I went to the Coast. What was I really like? I used to have enthusiasms, passion. I used to be so full of what I was saying that when I argued, I'd forget about myself. Now I am always aware of myself. I always realize that it's *I* who am talking. And I've become conscious even of the way I talk. I speak differently to different people. If I'm talking to some poor writer who makes two-fifty or five hundred a week, I usually slur my words and speak in such low tones that he can hardly hear me. I sometimes talk like that to novelists. With my equals, I speak in a careless and well-modulated tone of voice. Sometimes, in restaurants, I talk loudly about pictures. Evidently I have an exhibitionist streak.

Why can't I just walk off, forget it, start all over again? If I did, where would I go?

Stork Club last night. B——, the columnist, was at our table for a while. I told a new Sam Goldwyn joke, and he's going to print it.

Ran into X—— at the Algonquin. X—— is on top of the wave now. And two years ago he was just a ham nobody paid any attention to. I don't like actors. They are all hams. X—— draws almost as well as Cagney. I knew him way back when. He cut me. It made me feel small. Often, when one is cut or insulted, one feels utterly alone in the universe. I felt that way. I still do. And yet I've cut people. In my world X—— has earned the right to cut a mere writer like me. X—— makes about two hundred thousand dollars a picture now.

I read a book last night. An accomplishment.

Berlin bombed.

Haven't written in my diary for six days. Too lazy. I sit down to write in it now. What's the use? Doing no work.

After all, I really am doing something useful, and so—what if I don't write this novel? I'm not ashamed of the pictures I write. They are generally recognized as among the best. I always inject something, some idea about democracy and the common man. A writer can't be too far ahead of his audience. In pictures you have problems that are different from those you have in writing a novel. The audience is so much larger.

I'm not going to let myself luxuriate in despair. And I'm going to prove that I can write a novel. I wrote my first chapter today. Even though I say it myself, it's pretty good. I was so excited that I couldn't contain myself. I walked the floor reading it aloud to myself. I wanted to kiss the manuscript. I've learned a lot working in pictures. I've made enormous gains in technical facility. I will finish this book!

When I left the hotel yesterday, I felt like a new man. It seemed as if years were lifted from me. I saw the streets as I used to see them when I was younger. I felt as if the very pulse of New York beat in my veins. I looked at everything—the people, the windows, the buildings, the sky—with fresh eyes. My head spun with words. I remembered the long, brooding walks I used to take in New York when I was young. I was regretful. So many years had gone out of my life, years during which I could have written as I wanted to. But still, it isn't too late. I am saved. One good book is sufficient to win immortality for a writer. I am only forty. I have years of work ahead of me. It isn't too late.

Johnny Parker is in town. I like Johnny. He's a big shot in pictures and he's a good egg. We talked shop for a long time. Who is more important, a writer, a director, or a producer? This is Johnny's favorite theme. He hates directors and producers. He likes Hollywood. The salary is good. He went over a hundred thousand last year. He likes the people. He likes the work. Everything is all right for him but the climate. He wishes Hollywood could be just as it is and yet be located in New York City. I wish I could be like Johnny. Is it because I'm superior? There I go again. I've always believed myself superior. But I like Johnny anyway. I thought of that climate out there. The monotony of that climate puts your soul to sleep. I am sure that if there be a Hell, it has a climate like that of Los Angeles. It is so enervating, so boring, the same day after day. The same abrupt end to each day. I hate it. When I am out there I long for slow and drawn-out dramatic sunsets. Last fall I was hungry to see the leaves turn.

But now, to work on my novel.

I reread my first chapter. It's hogwash. Why fool myself? Why waste my time and energy writing something that isn't worth the candle? It's no use. I wanted my cake, and I wanted to eat it. I have ulcers of the spirit as a consequence. And I might get my ulcers back also unless I stop drinking.

Last night I dreamed of Catherine. I woke up with a profound feeling of guilt and of melancholy. I remembered how sweet and fresh she once was, how lovely. This morning, after breakfast, I sat in Washington Square looking at the college girls. They are so young. I seemed so old to myself. I walked away from the Square, feeling like a rapist. I wanted one of these girls. I needed one. I need one now. I thought again of Catherine. She is in my mind now. When I first knew her, she was like one of those girls. Why didn't it turn out differently? I used to criticize her because she was so bourgeois. But I've outdone her. I must recognize that I've loved the life out in Hollywood. I've gone out of my way to be where famous people would be. I've sacrificed all pride in order to meet stars, directors, producers, columnists, even cheap gamblers and hangers-on who were pals of the big shots. I remember how self-satisfied I was when I attended my first opening. I was full of delight when I saw the crowd of gaping fools who came to watch the stars enter the theater. I wanted them to see me, envy me. Yes, I have found great pleasure in thinking of myself as being associated with the new royalty of America. I have done everything I criticized in Catherine. And now it is too late.

Revenge is sweet. Last night with some friends we were talking about X—— who cut me. I remarked: "The trouble with X—— is that he doesn't know the difference between himself and a great man." Good laugh line. I'll even use it sometime in a picture. I was in good form. Talking of Hollywood writers, I said of Dunwiddie: "He's one of the best. He steals only from the best books." It was a self-portrait.

Dinner with Randy last night. A fellow hack. He made only sixty thousand dollars last year. He wants to go to his farm in Bucks County and write a great play, but he has to go back to the coast and work. He hasn't the money to pay his taxes unless he does.

I think of Catherine, but not of Florence, my second. She was no good. Yes, my thoughts always go back to Catherine. I walk the streets filled with a painful nostalgia. We lived on Cornelia Street and couldn't even afford a phone or electricity. I used to think how I would one day be rich and famous. Of what I would do for her! How we would travel around the world! But, yes, even in those days I wanted money. We all do. Money poisons our life from the cradle to the grave.

I now read five, six, seven newspapers a day. I read the gossip and the Hollywood news first. Then I read the war news, and I even read the comics and the want ads. I read the papers in order to waste time. I forget everything I read. But this war is getting on my nerves. What's going to happen? I have to do something.

I wrote two pages of the second chapter of my novel. I re-read it. I fear it is just no dice. But I felt good. It shows that I at least have the will power.

What a jerk I am! Picked up a bored wife of a businessman. She slept with me because she seemed to think that anybody who had been inside a studio must have something that nobody else has. It was dreary.

Avilov wants me to do a picture for Grandiose. The idea is terrific. A boy meets a girl in Sicily. I turned it down. I felt good. It stimulated me to finish the second chapter.

21 last night. Drank enough to knock the hell out of my stomach. I feel too ill to work.

Is it singular that I now begin to have regrets over things that I didn't do years ago? Or is it my age? The other night someone remarked that men face a crisis at forty and said that the French call it *la crise de quarante*. That might be what's the matter with me. I feel worse than a woman having a change of life. At least, at times I do. More and more I keep turning to the past. Catherine, always Catherine. And there was a girl when I was twenty-one. I'd forgotten about her for years. I saw her only once at a party on Fourth Street. I can hardly re-member her. I recall that she had dark hair, was pretty, and that her name was Louise. She seemed to like me. She was with some young poet whose name escapes me. I planned to call her up. I am sure she would have slept with me. Now, what difference does it make whether or not she did? And yet it does. I think of what it might have been like. I went back to see that bored wife yesterday afternoon, and I imagined that I was in bed with this Louise. I spin daydreams about what might have been had I married her instead of Catherine. I've walked all around the Village hoping to find her.

What's the matter with me?

Should I go to a psychoanalyst? I'm afraid to. Why? Am I afraid that if I go I might free myself to write? I don't know. But suppose I lose my neuroses, what will I have left? One has very little real freedom in this world. My neuroses—now, that is something they can't take from me.

I worked on my novel some more. I don't dare read it. But it makes me feel so good that I'm going out to have a Scotch. But only one.

Got drunk last night. I forget what I did. I talked to all kinds of people.

I wrote yesterday with a headache. I felt that I had to do it for my self-respect, even if it might be no dice.

Met Randy last night. Saw a movie.

Reread my novel. Tore it up. I ask myself—what's the use.

Yesterday drifted away. Lunch at Sardi's with Charlie, my agent. He is here on a vacation. Wants to know when I'll be ready to go back. I was evasive. Saw a movie about the Russian war. Too gruesome. Dinner alone at the Brevoort here. Rang up Johnny Parker. Spent the evening discussing the relative values of a writer, a producer, and a director. Then we talked about the climate on the Coast.

I haven't made an entry in this diary for a week. Thank God, that bored wife is going to Washington with her husband. She had been troubling me for the last few days. And then this trip ended it.

At 21 last night various people discussed when the war would end. Nobody agreed.

Should I go back to the Coast? I don't feel like it. I don't feel like doing anything. Went to a dull party last night.

Saw a show last night. Didn't like it. Stayed out talking with people until three o'clock because I didn't want to go home.

I'm tired of keeping a diary. It even has a bad effect on me. It makes me gloomier. I think more about myself. I am having pains in the stomach. I'm sure the ulcers have come back. I'm afraid to see a doctor and find out.

My God, there are writers who would do anything to be in my spot. There are writers who would knife their best friends, lie, double-cross, plagiarize, do anything on God's earth to get where I am. And look at me!
What shall I do?
I want to know.
I wish I had something I could really believe in.

I'm going back to the Coast. I'm going to do the Sicilian picture for Avilov. Maybe I can make something good of it. I don't know.

1943.

Mr. Gremmer

MR. GREMMER is a nervous, bald-headed little man. He seems to be very mild, and he has a small mustache which is in keeping with his size. Of all the capacities a human being might theoretically possess, Mr. Gremmer possesses only one: he can make money on the stock market. Many of his friends, particularly his Broadway friends, have never been able to understand how he does it, but he is generally successful. He has made money on the market in good times; he has made money on the market in bad times. He has made money when it rained; he has made money when it snowed; he has made money when the sun was shining. In the twenties, he was vice-president of a concern making men's shoes and decided to retire. Wanting to start fresh on the market, he sold all his stock. Two days later, the crash came. Then his parents died, leaving him a huge country home that was heavily insured. He tried to sell it but couldn't find a buyer. But the house burned down, and he was paid the insurance. Thanks to his business success, he has developed a theory about the stock market. His theory is as follows: the stock market is the greatest romance in the world. However, one cannot expect to achieve romantic success unless one has the right temperament. The right temperament is the artistic one. He has this temperament. The stock market is, therefore, his art.

Mr. Gremmer is a jolly bachelor with a philosophy of life. As he has always explained, his philosophy is simple but sound. It asserts that life must be fun. He firmly believes in life and in

28

fun. It was this belief that led him into show business on Broadway.

About seven years ago, he rented an office near Times Square. It was located next door to the branch office of a downtown brokerage house. After considerable reflection and some bargaining, he made purchases for his office. He bought a carpet. He bought one desk and four chairs. He bought a cocktail shaker and a set of glasses. He bought a stand for these. He bought some coat hangers. He bought a metal filing cabinet. He bought paper and envelopes. He bought a typewriter. Thereby he became a theatrical producer. Then he managed to take out a young girl who had platinum hair and was an actress because she had had three jobs as an understudy—two walkons and one bit part. She gave him her autographed picture, and he placed it on his desk. He met an author whose wistful books are generally admired by literate businessmen. He had lunch with this author and received from him the original manuscript of a poem which had been printed in one of the quality magazines. He admired this poem. He had it framed and hung it on the wall behind his desk. He thought of it often because he felt that it expressed some of his own feelings about life. It stated that inasmuch as the rabbit has neither fear nor shame when it enters its warren, neither should man tremble nor hesitate when he does what he must do. When he explained why he had gone into show business, Mr. Gremmer sometimes referred to this poem.

Although Mr. Gremmer has become a producer, he has never produced a play. However, he has read scripts with an eye to their production. He has never been able to find exactly the right play to produce. And though he reads plays, he doesn't read too many of them. That would be a bore. Life is short, and if one is bored, how can one have fun? The scripts he does see usually bewilder him. In order to save time and spare himself bewilderment, he hired a play reader. This reader once enthusiastically recommended a play about an employment office. Mr. Gremmer read the first act and for a week thought about producing this play. Then he decided not to. He came to the conclusion the public would not want to see a play about an employment agency because that was bitter, and the public doesn't want bitterness. He is waiting to find just the right play. In fact, he haunts night clubs, restaurants, and shows, looking for an author who will write this play for him. He has met many people, but he has not found the right author. But even though his career as a producer has, as yet, led to nothing tangible, it has not been fruitless. It is fun. In fact, he has had more fun as a producer who never produced a play than he would have had if he had found the right play. For he has managed to enjoy all the benefits of the life of a producer and he has had none of the headaches. He takes actors and actresses to lunch. He hobnobs with those who are in the limelight and has become known, in the columns, as "Mr. Gremmer, the producer." He has found on Broadway what he has always lived for—fun and excitement. And his experiences as a producer have demonstrated that his ideas about life are sound. For he never tires of telling people that life *is* good. It has been good to him.

Once he became known around Broadway, Mr. Gremmer's personality expanded. He always has a smile on his face and a jolly word for whomever he meets. He has become, in fact, a rather voluble night-club philosopher. He drinks cautiously and always has his wits about him, and he likes to sit in the night clubs talking seriously. His favorite subject is life. And frequently, when he discourses on his favorite subject, he remarks that he believes in taking chances. Unless one takes chances, why, then, one cannot live the full life. He has taken chances, and not only on the market. Had he not, when practically unknown and inexperienced, plunged right into show business? And he has taken other chances. Why, once, he almost got married. Another time he slept on top of a mountain all by himself. Other men have tried to sleep alone on mountain tops, and some of them have become ill or have even died. But he once slept on top of a mountain and survived to tell the tale.

Another of Mr. Gremmer's favorite topics is art. He has ideas

on this subject. He knows what great art is. Great art is art
that is successful. As proof of this, he always cites the book
clubs. People read books recommended by these clubs, don't
they? Yes, they do. That proves that these books are art. One
night when he was expatiating on this subject, a bitter café
radical interrupted him to remark:

"I see, then, Mr. Gremmer, that you have faith in the masses."

Mr. Gremmer answered by affirming that he did have faith
in the masses, although he added that one should use the word
the "public." He pointed to the successful plays then running
on Broadway, proudly remarking on the fact that the public
supported these plays. His theory permits him to understand
things which puzzle others. He understands why art is art, and,
hence, why artists are artists. But he simply doesn't understand
why actors and actresses are out of work, nor why people complain that many of them, as well as many poets and playwrights,
are poor. If actors and actresses have ability, they'll find work.
If poets and playwrights are artists, they will be successful. This
is why he is glad the government no longer coddles failures
with W.P.A. theatrical and writers' projects. People who can't
make a go of it in the arts are either no good or else they have
the wrong philosophy of life. And that is why he can't understand their bitterness. And all people who say that current
artistic standards are wrong, or that society is to blame for
failures, are bitter.

No one has the right to be bitter. It is bad for the soul, and
even worse for digestion. The first thing that all such bitter
people should do is to change their philosophy of life. They
should learn that things are just the opposite of what they
think. They must learn that life consists of fun and excitement. And they must take chances. In brief, they should live
life up to the very hilt.

Mr. Gremmer is one of those enviable men who has solved
the major problems of living. This explains why he is so happy.
And now he is making more money than ever before. Every
new theatrical season finds him bursting with energy, and
with renewed hopes of finding the right play. But he hasn't

found that play—yet. However, he explains that he is not disillusioned with producing. He will not allow himself to become bitter or disappointed. He knows that he will find the right play sometime. He is not a man of little faith. And there is only one question that still bothers him. He doesn't know what is the matter with half-baked radicals. Why can't they have any fun? Why can't they laugh and have a sense of humor? Why do they criticize men who make profits? Why are they so bitter against bankers? If anyone can tell him the answer to these questions, he will take this person to lunch at one of the best restaurants in New York. But, he adds, they themselves must not be bitter. Because he insists that anyone who is bitter is half-baked. And he has absolutely no use for half-baked people. They don't understand life, and they never have any fun. They don't know how to live the full life right up to the hilt.

1936-43.

Patsy Gilbride

PATSY GILBRIDE STOOD in front of the Astoria Hotel in Hollywood. It was an enervating day, and the temperature was eighty-eight. Behind the parking lots across the street he saw buildings and the humps of mountains sheathed in California's heralded sunshine. Idle, contemplative, he posed on the sidewalk, while a giant-size, gawky uniformed hotel employee stood near by, ready to open the doors of automobiles and taxicabs that stopped in front of the hotel. Staring at nothing, silent, blank-faced Pacific Coast League baseball players sat on the veranda behind Patsy.

Patsy was a well-preserved man in his early fifties. He wore an oxford-gray business suit and a gray felt hat that slanted rakishly over his forehead. He might have been taken for one of the many businessmen who stopped at the Astoria. He swept the street with a majestic glance and fixed his eyes on a platinum blonde in pink slacks. He smiled after her with approval.

"Hi, Patsy," someone called from a passing automobile.

Patsy returned the greeting with a kingly smile and a magnificent wave of the hand, a gesture which had once been famous from one end of America to the other.

He concentrated on drawing a pack of cigarettes from his coat pocket and lighted one. Then he studiously regarded the burnt match which he held in his hand. He flipped it away gracefully.

"Hello, Mr. Gilbride," said the giant-size doorman.

"Hello, hello," Patsy replied democratically and with the easy assurance of a man accustomed to homage.

33

Precisely at twelve-thirty-five, Patsy stepped out of the California sunshine and entered the bar of the Astoria Hotel.

"Hey, Bud, who's that guy?" one of the baseball players asked the doorman.

"Don't you know him, sir? That's Patsy Gilbride, the famous star of the silent pictures."

"Who?" asked another ballplayer.

"Patsy Gilbride."

"I guess he's before my time," the ballplayer said, yawning.

II

The bar was modernistic and dimly lit. Patsy sat on a stool and stared into a glass of beer.

"Kind of quiet so far today," Patsy said to the bartender.

"Yes, it usually is, Mr. Gilbride, at this time of day," the bartender answered professionally.

"Yes, people are working out in the studios, working for the Jews," Patsy said bitterly.

The bartender didn't answer. He busied himself shining glasses.

"Christ, I forgot something," Patsy said as if he were referring to very important business. He slid off the stool and strutted out of the bar, his head held erect in dignity.

"Hello, Martha," he said cheerfully to the middle-aged woman at the newspaper counter off the lobby.

"Well, Patsy, how are you today?" Martha asked.

"I'm always in tiptop shape. But why should you ask me how I'm feeling, Martha?"

"Oh, you know, Mr. Gilbride, just to be passing the time of day."

"Well, I'm feeling in tiptop shape."

He laughed as if at a private joke and then lit another cigarette. He flung a nickel on the case as if it were a twenty-dollar gold piece, stepped over to the magazine rack, and picked up a Los Angeles paper. With a look of boredom he noticed glaring headlines announcing another Russian defeat at the hands of the Nazi *Wehrmacht*. He looked up and down the front-page items until he saw a little squib:

PATSY GILBRIDE RELEASED

Star of Silent Days Released on Charge of Drunken Driving

Patsy read the item three times with interest, but his face clouded in disappointment; his picture was not in the paper. He laughed to himself, folded up the paper, and stuck it in his coat pocket. He went to the desk.

"Hello, Mr. Gilbride," the clerk said respectfully.

"Hello, hello," Patsy answered with his air of democratic majesty.

The clerk looked through letters in a bin.

"Nothing today, Mr. Gilbride," the clerk announced.

"Thanks," Patsy said, turning aside in disappointment.

He strutted back to his stool at the bar.

III

"This town is getting dull. I don't know why I came here," Patsy remarked aloud, for the ear of a middle-aged, plump man who sat near him.

"Do you live here?" the man asked.

"I'm from everywhere."

"Well, my name's Bill," the man said.

"Mine's Patsy Gilbride."

"I'm a lawyer," Bill said as they shook hands.

"I'm Patsy Gilbride."

"Oh, I didn't recognize the name. You're in pictures, of course."

"Yes, I was in pictures. My friend, tell me, you're not a native of this devastated geographical area, are you?"

"Oh, yes, I've lived here all my life."

"And you don't know what goes on in this haunt of the Elders of Zion?" Patsy asked.

"Of course, I do," Bill answered knowingly. "This is the most degenerate town in the world. My friend, Hollywood is a word synonymous with degeneration."

"Yes, and de-Gentilization," Patsy said. "That's why I'm not in pictures any more."

"Of course, I don't know the inside story. But I know enough to know what kind of a place it is. Do you know what they do here? They pick other men's brains," Bill said in loud indignation.

"They cleaned me out, my brains, everything."

"They pick other men's brains. They steal from Shakespeare—"

"And Patsy Gilbride," Patsy interrupted.

"Is there a greater crime in the world, Mr. Gilbride?"

Patsy took a sip of beer.

"I write myself. I know whereof I speak. What is more degenerate than stealing the brains and the talents of other men?" Bill continued in a loud voice as he fixed his eye on the bartender.

"You say that you're a lawyer?" Patsy asked.

"Yes, I am. I've been in practice over ten years. I was in the army and I'm a reserve officer. I worked my way through college," Bill said in a self-justifying tone.

"So you're a lawyer? Well, I'm glad to meet you, Bill. I've got a little proposition. But first, here—drink up and have another," Patsy said, finishing his beer.

"Have one on me," Bill said.

"No, friend, have one on me, and then I'll have one on you, and we'll be even-Stephen."

Patsy ordered drinks with a fine flourish of his right arm.

"You say you're a lawyer. I'm glad to know that," Patsy said. "I've got a proposition I'd like to explain to you."

"Yes, I've earned my professional status. I worked my way through college, and I was over there, too, in the last war. This war is going to be different than the other. Well, let me say, Mr. Gilbride, this war is going to squeeze all of the degeneration out of Hollywood. You can bet your boots on that."

"You see, I have a partner. I have all the rights. We have a proposition," Patsy said.

The bartender served them drinks. Patsy slowly poured beer from the bottle into his glass. Several strangers drifted into the bar. Two couples talked in low voices at a corner table.

"You say you're in the army?" said a thin, dark boy who was slicing lemons behind the bar.

"Yes, I'm a reserve officer, a captain. I expect to be called soon. But do you know what war is? Stupidity! War is stupidity. There's war because man is stupid."

"I'll be in the army soon," the lad said, holding a lemon in one hand and a paring knife in the other.

"Drafted?" Bill asked.

"You see, Bill, I've got something good. Now, let me tell you about it," Patsy said.

"I'm going because I've got to," the lad announced bitterly. "I'll do my stint and then I'll get out."

"If you look at it that way, young fellow, then you'll never get anywhere in the army."

"You can talk. Yes, you can talk. You're an officer. But me, I'll just be peeling potatoes."

"You can advance. How do you think I got where I am?"

Patsy took a gulp and looked at the lawyer with disgust.

"How should I know?" the lad replied. "I know I won't get there. Why do you think I'm behind this bar? Because I've got to eat."

"Don't take that attitude. You should go into the army, obey, study, show your mettle, prove you've got brains. If you do, then you'll advance. You'll get somewhere."

Patsy looked from one to the other, bored.

"That's what you say," the lad answered.

"I say it on the basis of experience . . ."

"You should have had my experience," Patsy interrupted.

"Yes, experience," Bill continued. "How old do you think I am?"

Bill was talking so loudly that everyone in the bar kept looking at him, even the couples in the corner.

"I don't know," the lad answered.

"Now, with this war on, that proposition I want to tell you about . . ." Patsy said, unable to gain Bill's attention.

"I don't know about that," the boy said bitterly. "All I know is that I can't get anywhere. Don't feed me that stuff. Don't kid me. I know what's going to happen to me. I'm just going to be another sap, that's all."

"Boy, war is a colossal stupidity, but we've got to fight. We'll have to get in this war soon, very soon now."

"I agree with you there," the boy said.

"Who cares?" Patsy muttered in disgust, signaling for another beer.

"We're going to have a job to do, and boys like you will have to do it," Bill orated.

"But that doesn't mean I have to like it," the boy said.

"Why the hell do people talk so much?" Patsy asked the bartender, who tactfully refrained from answering him.

The boy pulled out his wallet and took a slip of paper from it.

"Here's my call," he said, handing the slip to Bill. "I report in four weeks. I'll report. I'll do my stint. But nobody in the world can tell me I got to like it."

Bill read the slip and handed it to Patsy.

"I only read checks," Patsy said, pushing the slip across the bar.

"Yes, it's my little present from Uncle Sam," the boy said, putting the notice back in his wallet.

"Listen, boy, I worked my way up from the ranks," Bill said.

"I worked up and down from the ranks," Patsy said with an ironical laugh.

"I've worked myself up from the ranks. And take the advice of one who's done that. Study! Learn! The army needs brains, and if you've got the brains, you'll get somewhere."

Patsy sighed with boredom.

Bill drank.

"Listen, Bill, do you want to make some money?" Patsy asked.

"Money means nothing to me, my friend," Bill answered

pompously. "I live. I get along. Money means nothing to me. Out here they make money by picking the brains of genius. I earn my money honestly."

"Money," Patsy said again, laughing ironically. "You'll never see as much money as Patsy Gilbride once had."

Bill mopped his brow with a clean handkerchief.

"But as I was saying, my friend, I've got a proposition to pick some pumice out of the earth. Now, that's a real proposition," Patsy said.

"I expect my call any day now," Bill told the bar.

"Maybe I'll be in your company," the boy said.

"Oh, no—I'll be in the Adjutant General's office."

"I can be your messenger boy and run around delivering papers for you," the lad said.

"Here, Bill, have another and let me explain this proposition to you," Patsy urged.

"Sorry, friend, but I've got to go. I work for my living. But have one on me," Bill said. He turned to the bartender. "Give my friend here, Mr. . . . ah . . . my friend here, another beer."

He paid his bill, leaving a ten-cent tip.

"What's your hurry?" Patsy asked as Bill slid off his chair.

"Business, my friend, business."

"But I've got some business to tell you about. This proposition is the slickest piece of business you'll ever fall into," Patsy said persuasively.

"Listen, son," Bill said, turning from Patsy to the bar boy. "You'll have to change your attitude or else you'll never get anywhere in this world."

"You can say that," the boy said. "You can talk that way because you're sitting pretty. They've got a desk all made out for you in the army, but not for me. I know better."

"Do you know where I got in this world?" Patsy asked. "But I'm going back up, not in this Jew industry out here, but with this proposition of mine. Anybody who knows me knows that whatever Patsy Gilbride touches turns to gold. Now, let me explain . . ."

Bill walked away.

"Who's that clown?" Patsy asked, looking after him.

"I've never seen him here before," the bartender answered.

"He should talk," the bar boy said.

"Yes, he should talk about pictures. He should talk about pictures to me, Patsy Gilbride, one of the men who made this goddamn town what it is today. Say, do you know how much money I lost on one of the pictures I produced myself? A half a million smackers—that's what I lost on one picture. Just like that, I lost a half million. Just like I throw a dime across the counter."

"Mr. Gilbride," the bar boy said.

"Call me Patsy."

"I'm Irish, just like you. My name's Dillon. You know, you can't get anywhere in this town because of the Jews."

"You're telling me," Patsy answered knowingly.

IV

Sweat oozed from Patsy's forehead. His shirt, under his coat, was wringing wet while he was in the telephone booth waiting to speak with Abe Blumenstock, a big executive at one of the large studios.

"Hello, hello," he called into the mouthpiece impatiently.

There was no answer. He opened the door of the booth to let in some air. He waited, cursing to himself.

"Hello, Patsy, how are you?"

"Hello, Abe. Hello, Abe. Just a minute."

Patsy closed the door.

"Abe?"

"Yes, it's me, Patsy. How are you?"

"I'm always tiptop, Abe," Patsy said confidently, but with his voice slightly thick from beer. "Always tiptop. How are you, Abe?"

"Pretty good, Patsy, pretty good, but busy. I've got a lot of rushes to see. What's on your mind?"

"I've got a little idea I want to explain to you, Abe."

"Listen, Patsy, I'd like to see you but I've got to see these rushes and clean things up here in my office. I've got to catch a plane out of here to New York tonight. I'll see you when I come back."

"When will you be back?"

"I'm not sure, Patsy, but my secretary will tell you. Call her up."

"I'll do that, and listen, Abe . . ."

"I'm listenin'."

"Abe, I'm inconveniently broke. Can you let me have a hundred for a week or so?"

"Of course, Patsy. Are you at the same address?"

"Yes, the same address."

"I'll send it to you by mail. Is tomorrow morning soon enough to be gettin' it?"

"That'll be O.K., Abe, and thanks. You know me, Abe, and you know you'll get it back."

"Don't worry, Patsy."

"And when you come back I'll buzz you. I have a little idea. Abe, we're old friends. We've known each other for years . . ."

"Yes, Patsy, I know. But I've got to hang up now and get some work done or I'll miss my plane. Take care of yourself, old man."

"I never felt better in my life."

"Fine. So long, Patsy, and thanks for thinking of me."

"Thanks, Abe, and happy landing. I'll tell you about this little idea when you get back. There's money in it."

"O.K., Patsy. Good luck," Abe said, hanging up.

Beaming, Patsy emerged from the booth. He returned to the bar, mopping his red, perspiring face.

"Do you know what happens when I call Abe Blumenstock at Grandiose?" he asked the bartender.

"What, Patsy?"

"I don't have to go through a rigamarole of talking with six secretaries. I get him like that. They tell Abe that Patsy Gilbride is on the wire, and he drops everything. And he better. That yid, why I knew him when he was nothing, nothing."

"He's a big man in pictures now. They say he's Avilov's right-hand man."

"Yes, and I knew them both when they were nothing— nothing at all in this town. You're damned right, Abe Blumenstock doesn't pull any tricks on me. He knows better. He knows who Patsy Gilbride is. Give me another beer."

v

The bar was crowded. Two girls stood at the far end. Patsy moved over to them. Despite all the beer he had drunk, he walked straight.

He stood behind the girls. They were platinum blondes who looked as if they had just come from a beauty parlor. He slanted his hat over his brow. They still didn't notice him. He reslanted his hat.

"Excuse me—that is, pardon me—that is, I beg your pardon," Patsy said insolently.

The two blondes turned and looked at him impassively.

"As I was just going to say, could I have the unbounded pleasure of buying you girls a drink?"

"We have drinks."

"Then I'll buy myself a bottle of beer," Patsy said, signaling to the bartender.

He edged in beside the girls, received his beer, poured it, and took a drink.

"I haven't seen you girls here before," he said.

"Oh, no, we haven't been here before."

"Where are you from?"

"Chicago."

"Chicago?" He feigned being quizzical. "Yes, Chicago. It seems to me that I once heard of Chicago. Oh, yes, I once produced a picture about Chicago. It cost me three hundred thousand dollars, net loss. Nothing much, just a little bit of change, three hundred thousand dollars. Yes, that's how I heard of Chicago." Patsy laughed. "But even after I tried to put it on the map, people elsewhere didn't seem to know anything about Chicago."

"Are you a producer?" one of the girls asked.

"No, I sell soap. Do you girls want to buy some soap?" He scrutinized them carefully. "No, I don't think either of you need any soap."

They laughed.

"Hello, Patsy," said an unprepossessing little man.

Patsy swung around and beamed.

"Oh, hello, hello, Weems. What are you doing?"

"Making B pictures now. What are you doing, Patsy?"

"Talking to these charming young ladies."

He took Weems' arm and led him a foot forward.

"This is Mr. Weems, and this is Miss Chicago One, and this is Miss Chicago Two."

The introductions were acknowledged.

"What—did these girls win some beauty contest?" Weems asked.

"They should have if they didn't," Patsy said, and the girls smiled with modest politeness.

"Tell me about yourself, Patsy," Weems asked, ignoring the girls.

"I was in New York—but here, have a drink," Patsy said.

"No, have one on me."

"All right, another beer," Patsy said, and Weems ordered. "But what about yourself—aren't you having one?"

"I just had one."

"You guys can't make as good pictures as I used to make, and you can't drink like me," Patsy bragged.

"Tell me about yourself, Patsy. Where have you been and what have you been doing?"

"I was back East in New York. There was nothing for me in that town full of ten-per-cent chiselers, so I went to Nevada, and then I went to Frisco, and here I am now on business. I have a little proposition in mind."

"Pictures?" Weems asked.

"Weems, you know what kind of a raw deal I got."

"No, I don't."

"The Jews came in and took things over. They cleaned me

out. They were supposed to distribute my pictures when I went in for producing myself, and they double-crossed me."

Weems, who had Semitic features, frowned, but said nothing.

"But now I have a proposition."

Weems nervously looked at his watch.

"Here, let me explain it to you."

"Gee, Patsy, I'd like to hear it, but I've got to dash. I'm late for an appointment already."

"It'll only take me a few minutes to explain it. Here, let me buy you a drink."

"Can't I telephone you, Patsy? I've got to dash."

"Listen, Weems, you've never been a goddamned fool, have you?"

"I've tried not to be, Patsy."

"That's why you've got to listen to me," Patsy said as Weems fidgeted away from him. "I'm going to do you a favor. I'm going to let you in on something where you can clean up money, big dough. Weems, you know me. You know I talk dough. When I was the pride of the nation, was I a piker?"

"No, Patsy, nobody ever called you a piker."

"You're damned right they didn't. You know me. Answer this—did I ever fool around with money for coffee and doughnuts?"

"No, you didn't, but let me give you a buzz about this, Patsy."

"Well, I'm not talking coffee and doughnuts now, either. I'm going to give you the opportunity to make money, plenty of it."

"But if I make it, I'll only have to pay it in taxes."

"Don't you believe in the government?"

The bar became more crowded and noisier. Patsy had to keep talking more loudly in order to be heard.

"Of course I do, but I pay plenty of taxes as it is."

"Come on, let's sit down at a table. We can settle this deal in a few minutes, and it's going to be the biggest thing in your life."

"I've really got to go, Patsy. I'll call you tomorrow," Weems said and, turning from Patsy, he paid his check and hurried off without asking for Patsy's telephone number.

Patsy sneered after him and then he gulped more beer.

"When I was in pictures, he was a little jerk," Patsy told the two blondes.

"A what?" one of them asked, bored.

"Coffee and doughnuts," Patsy said.

"You were in pictures?" the other girl asked.

"Oh, yes, yes, I had something to do with the industry in this town," he said, bored.

"Patsy, how are you?"

Patsy swung around again.

"Oh, Smith, hello, Smith, how are you?"

"I came for a little nip. You know how it is."

"This is Mr. Smith, Miss Chicago One and Miss Chicago Two."

They said how-do-you-do.

"Have a drink, Patsy."

Patsy did.

VI

By dinnertime Patsy had drunk so much beer that he was not hungry. Nevertheless he crossed the street and had a sandwich and a cup of coffee in an inexpensive restaurant and, while eating, told the blonde waitress that she'd make another Betty Grable. Soon he was back at the Astoria bar. He introduced himself to an elderly man who was smoking a cigar and sipping a Scotch and soda. The man's name was MacIntosh.

"So you're Scotch?" Patsy said.

"Yes, Scotch descent."

"I was in Scotland once," Patsy said.

He sang a few lines in imitation of Harry Lauder.

"When were you in Scotland?" MacIntosh asked.

"Years ago. I was in Glasgow about twelve years ago."

"How did you like it?"

"My friend, I don't remember. I was there, you see, under peculiar circumstances. I was running away from one dame and I was running after another. I spent all of my time in Scotland running."

"Did you run well?"

"I ran damned well," Patsy said with a leer, and MacIntosh laughed heartily. "But have a drink," Patsy said.

"I have one."

"Yes, I ran from Scotland to Ireland. And I didn't see Ireland, either, because I was running away from another dame."

"You must have been a popular buck," MacIntosh said.

"They clung to me like leeches."

"I was never able to do that, and now I'm too old," MacIntosh said, gazing into his drink.

"You're never too old. Why, man, you've just reached the prime of your life. You know, when experience makes up for the impetuosity of youth. How old do you think I am?"

"I don't know. How old are you?" MacIntosh asked.

"Fifty-three. And I don't feel the weight of my years, either."

"You mean your ears, don't you?" laughed MacIntosh.

"No, I don't remember Scotland or Ireland. When I went to Dublin I was met by the Lord Mayor with the keys of the city. I think his name was Finnegan."

"How was he with the dames?" asked MacIntosh.

"He feared for his immortal soul," laughed Patsy.

MacIntosh shook with laughter.

"Yes, the dames were like leeches. Once they get near you, they're leeches. And do you know who was the biggest leech of them all?"

"Who?"

"Cynthia Caldwell."

"Why, she used to be one of the biggest stars before talking pictures came in," MacIntosh said.

"Yes, but she wasn't much of a leading lady in bed. I spent two hundred thousand dollars on her, and I didn't get what I could have got for two bucks here in a Los Angeles hotel," Patsy said meanly.

MacIntosh looked at Patsy, astonished.

"What is your secret, man?" MacIntosh asked.

"Secret? The dames always fell for Patsy Gilbride and his bank roll. The pride of the nation," he said, laughing with bitter, inward irony.

"You were in motion pictures, I take it," MacIntosh said.

"I certainly was until the Jews got it into their noodles that I shouldn't be."

"I'm in the hardware business. I'm glad to meet you. Have a drink."

"When a Scotchman buys me a drink I never refuse," Patsy said, pouring his beer.

"Now I place you. Of course, I heard of you, saw you on the silent silver screen," MacIntosh said, drinking.

"Well, Mr. MacIntosh, I've also heard of the hardware business," Patsy said.

"Of course—everybody knows there's a hardware business," MacIntosh said.

"And, as I was just remarking—that is, telling my memoirs, *The Confessions of a Runner*—I've also heard of Scotland," Patsy said. "You should have seen the dame I was running away from in Scotland. She was damned all right for a weekend. But do you know what was the trouble with her, MacIntosh?"

"What?"

"She didn't know the difference between a weekend and eternity."

"I see what you mean," MacIntosh said, smiling.

"Yes, I was doing a hundred-yard sprint away from one weekend and forward to another," Patsy said, gesturing dramatically.

"Forward, that's a good one," MacIntosh said.

Patsy laughed in self-appreciation.

"Have another drink."

"On a Scotchman?"

"I say, friend, have a cigarette?" MacIntosh said, holding out a pack.

"Cigarette—I thought you wanted me to have a drink."

"Have them both—on the hardware business."

"Why not," Patsy said.

They drank and then they told dirty stories. Patsy acted out his with enjoyment, and then he told a Scottish joke, pulling up his pants to show his gaitered legs and wearing his coat like kilts. He marched around the bar, imitating Harry Lauder, and was followed by MacIntosh and three middle-aged men.

VII

Patsy staggered back and forth from one person to another, although he seemed to have himself under fairly good control, considering how much he had drunk.

"Why, you old sonofabitch," he said, suddenly spotting a stocky man with a broad and intelligent face.

"Patsy Gilbride," the man said.

"Johnny Flannagan, you no-good Irishman."

"You're looking swell, Patsy."

"I haven't seen you in three years, Johnny. You never looked me up," Patsy complained.

"How in hell was I to know where you were?"

"You couldn't find me, even if you were looking for me," Patsy said sarcastically.

"Have a drink, Patsy," Johnny smiled.

"I will. But have one on me."

"No, this is mine," Johnny insisted.

"All right. I have my beers in the afternoon, my Scotch and sodas in the evenings."

"What do you do in the morning?" Flannagan asked.

"I attend to items like sleep and other affairs," Patsy answered.

"The same old Patsy."

"What did you expect me to be?"

"Just that—the same old Patsy."

"Well, I am. And let me tell you this, Johnny, I'm coming back. I'm coming back."

"In pictures?"

"Hell, no—I couldn't—not with the sons of Zion in control."

"Patsy, you know damned well that that has nothing to do

with it. I was in on that Independent Films deal when you decided to produce, and I know, as well as you, that that isn't
what caused you to lose your shirt. Talk sense, Patsy. I'm sick
of this crap about races. From first to last it's lousy stuff, and it's
not true."

"I only lost the tail of my shirt producing my own pictures."

"When and where did you lose the rest?"

"Wall Street. You remember Tom Stack, my broker? Well,
Tom told me where to invest my shirt. I did, and I woke up
after the crash in my B.V.D'S," Patsy laughed. "But I haven't
any grudge against Tom."

"Did he lose his shirt, too?"

"He was too busy losing mine. Johnny, you're not in pictures
any more, are you?"

"Hell, no, I got out after the crash. Patsy, I want nothing
to do with pictures, nothing to do with them. Nothing at all."

"What the hell are you doing?"

"Airplane business. I came out here to straighten out a production jam, and I just got away from the plant. It was a headache. So I thought that I'd stop in here and have a drink or two,
and maybe meet five or six girls. That's the way I feel."

"Are you staying here?"

"No, I'm at the Beverly Wilshire."

"Did you think you might find me here?"

"Well, I had that in mind."

"You goddamn Irish bastard, I love you, and you haven't
seen me in three years. I've got a new wife, too."

"Yes?"

"Nice girl, young, healthy, twenty-four, and she's home now
—she stays home—keeps the home fires burning."

"Same old Patsy."

"Better than I ever was, Johnny."

"How?"

"Well, how do you think I could keep a young wife?"

"I don't doubt you. After all, I knew you, Patsy, in the old
days."

"Why did you get out of pictures?" Patsy asked.

"Why does any man with sense stay in pictures? It's a lot of make-believe crap. I lost forty-five thousand bucks, and the rest of my dough on the market."

"And how are you doing now?"

"All right."

They drank.

"Johnny, do you want to make a lot of money?"

"No, Patsy, I don't. I want to make just a little money."

"Listen, Johnny, I know you. You can't crap Patsy Gilbride. I'm asking you—-do you want to make a lot of money?"

"Patsy, I'm making as much as I want to make right now."

"Ah, you goddamn —— have another drink."

"I'm still drinking this one. Have one yourself."

"I will." Patsy signaled to the bartender. "Another." He turned to Johnny. "I talked to Abe today."

"Blumenstock?"

"Yes, Abe Blumenstock."

"How is he?"

"Oh, what the hell. Johnny, I got a proposition. Say, don't you want to make a lot of money?"

"Patsy, I've had headaches enough today. I don't want to make any more fortunes."

"Johnny, I never thought you were such a damned fool. All right, cut your Irish nose off for your folly."

Johnny finished his drink and got another.

"I have a partner who owns the mountain. We'll get soap out of pumice, and we'll sell it a nickel a bag, in little paper bags just as peanuts are sold. Christ, we'll coin money. All I need is five thousand bucks. Johnny, come in with me, and I'll make you a soap magnate, a baron. Johnny, you know how everything I touch turns to gold. Look at all the dough I made in the old days."

"Patsy, have a drink."

"Let me take ten bucks."

Johnny handed a ten-dollar bill to Patsy.

"Now I'll buy you a drink," Patsy said.

He did.

"I saw Mary Pickford a week ago," Patsy said.

"How is she?"

"What do I care? Johnny, do you remember me in *Beyond the Frontier?*"

"Which picture was that?"

"The one that lost most money."

"Oh, yes."

"I was good, damned good in it. Do you think any of these present-day glamour boys could act like Patsy Gilbride? Glamour boys! Glamour boys!" Patsy said, sneering.

"Well, Patsy, don't take it too hard."

Patsy drank.

"In that picture, Johnny, I made the nation think that Cynthia was hot stuff. I made her seem hot. And you should have slept with her."

"I'm glad I didn't."

"If you did, you'd have needed a hot-water bag to keep warm."

"Oh, Patsy, forget that. That's another day. Pictures have changed. Everything changes."

An expression of self-pity crossed Patsy's face. Johnny looked at him sympathetically.

A cigarette girl passed. Patsy bought a package of Camels and gave her a half-dollar tip.

"Same old Patsy," Johnny said.

"Johnny, five thousand and I'll make you a millionaire. The world needs soap, doesn't it? Soap in paper bags for a nickel. Johnny . . ."

Patsy leaned over the bar. Johnny got off his stool and said he had a headache. He told Patsy to call him up the next day. He paid and left. Patsy drooled.

VIII

About two o'clock, Johnny Flannagan returned to the Astoria Bar with a blonde. Patsy Gilbride staggered out, blind drunk. He didn't recognize Johnny.

"Who's that man?" the blonde asked.

"Patsy Gilbride. He used to make five thousand a week in the old silent days here."

"What happened to him?"

"That," Johnny said.

1941-1943.

A Teamster's Payday

AROUND NINE o'clock, Pat backed his single wagon into the stables. They smelled of manure. He jumped down off the wagon, unhitched his horse, talked to it gently, patted its forehead, rubbed its nose, and led it to a vacant stall. Finished with the horse, he drew out his time card and shuffled over to the timekeeper's window.

Pat was a tall, well-built man in his late thirties, and his face was lined and roughened by years of working outdoors in all kinds of weather.

"How was it tonight?" Charlie asked; he was a weazened man, with a bald head.

"Oh, it was pretty dead," Pat answered, pushing his time card through the opening to Charlie's booth.

Charlie lazily punched Pat's card and handed it back to him.

"Well, Pat, I always say there's no rest for the weary," Charlie said, yawning.

"That's the truth, Charlie. And the weary always have to work."

"Yeh, I guess that's the way it always was and always will be," Charlie philosophized, sitting down.

Pat spat out tobacco juice.

"Pat, I was thinking—now, if I was you, I'd hang around here a bit. It's payday, and some of the boys on the wagons will be gettin' in any minute; Dutch, Porky, Shifty Jacobson and some of the boys ought to be checking out of here soon. It'd be better, Pat, if you all went out together. Jerry Looney and some

of his bad boys have been hangin' around the express stables
all summer on paydays to knock the boys off and steal their pay
envelopes. A man like you, Pat, with a family, he needs his
money too much to be robbed that way by them goddamn hoodlums. If I was you, I'd just wait until some of the boys get in.
I got a hunch that Jerry and his boys might be around near
here. And them fellows is bad, plug-uglies. That's the way
they live, them hoods, too lazy to work and robbin' honest
workin'men. No, Pat, I wouldn't take a chance of gettin' my
head cracked and my pay frisked if I was you."

"Charlie, I know Looney. He comes from the same neighborhood I do. That dirty rat knows I ain't afraid of him. Remember
when he was on a wagon? I had it out with him then. He'll
never forget the pastin' I gave him. Jerry Looney'll always give
me a wide berth."

"I always say—there's no use bein' foolhardy."

"I've been takin' care of myself ever since I was thirteen, and
I'm still doin' it. Them hoodlums aren't going to want any
truck with me."

"They may be more than one against you, Pat."

"Charlie, I'm waitin' to get a chance at that punk, Looney,
again. The dirty rat, holdin' up honest workingmen who've
got families to support," Pat said angrily.

"Well, Pat, I still say—there ain't no use in bein' foolhardy."

"I know, Charlie, but I can take care of myself," Pat said.
"How's the old lady, these days?"

"Well, Pat, you know," Charlie began, making a wry face.
"We've both been kind of gettin' along in years, and she's
havin' her troubles. Rheumatism. You know how it is, Pat,
havin' an ailin' wife. I hate to admit it, but I got to—even when
you're gettin' along in years and feel dried up, you kind of wish
the wife would stay young and look like the girls you see on the
street every day. How's your old woman, Pat?"

"Not so good. She's havin' another kid, you know, and
sometimes that takes a lot out of a woman. The little visitor's
due to come any time now. It might be born and be squawlin'
and kickin' when I get home tonight. But, to tell you the truth,

it's not doin' my old girl any good. After the last one a year ago, she lost most of her teeth."

"How many you got now, Pat?"

"The new one will make five. All boys, too, so far."

"In a way, it's tough. But, still, it's a fine thing to have a family. Take me, me and the old woman, we always wanted 'em, but we couldn't have 'em. They'd be such a comfort to us in our old age. Yes, it might be hard now puttin' bread in their mouths, but time flies, Pat, time flies, and sooner than you think, they'll be growin' up like weeds, and you can send them out to work, and you'll have 'em to take care of you in your old age. Now, if I had some grown boys, I wouldn't be sittin' here in this place every night like I do."

"Still, it costs a lot of money takin' care of them."

"Some day they'll all be on the wagons, making their dough."

"Not if I can help it, Charlie. I want them to get some education and make something out of themselves."

"Sittin' here, Pat, I get to thinkin' sometimes—golly wouldn't it be something to be young again? Just think what the world's gonna be like when your little ones grow up. Automobiles and airplanes, and all kinds of inventions. You know, the day is comin' when they won't be havin' no horses at all here at the company. They'll only be usin' trucks. Think of it, Pat, the way times have changed since I was a boy. It's not so long ago that everybody was laughing at these horseless carriages. But they don't laugh at them any more."

"Yes, I thought they were damned foolishness myself," Pat said.

"And then take these here moving pictures, nickel shows. Do you ever see any of them?"

"Yes, I've seen a couple."

"Now, that's another invention. I tell you, Pat, before the kids of today cash in their chips, they'll see aplenty that we never dreamed we'd see."

"I don't doubt it," Pat said.

"Funny the boys aren't in," Charlie said.

"Maybe some of them got socked with loads by Gus Michaelson, the Dispatcher over at Atlantic."

"I hear he does that."

"Yeh, he grabs off every wagon he can."

"He's new. He was just taken off the wagons and put dispatchin' a little while ago. He's all right, only I can't understand him. He's a Republican, and says he's going to vote for Taft again next year."

"Well, I've got to be goin' along, Charlie."

"Pat, since you been hangin' around talkin' to me, why don't you wait a little longer. The boys will be in. Two weeks ago Jewy Moses was held up on pay night, and everybody thinks it was Looney and his gang. I tell you, Pat, they're mean customers."

"Don't worry about me. I can handle those rats," Pat said.

"I hope to God you're right."

"So long, Charlie, and don't do anything you'd be ashamed of," Pat said, leaving.

"I'm too old for that," Charlie called after him.

II

Pat was glad to escape from work, and from the old fellow. Charlie was a good scout, but he could talk your leg off. Tomorrow was Sunday, and he would go to church, rest, play with the kids. It was balmy out, a fine August night. He liked nights like this. He walked along a street lined with darkened factories, barns, and warehouses. The dark buildings seemed mysterious in the moonlight and the shadows. The street was lonely and melancholy, so different from what it was like in the daytime.

Yes, he liked the quiet now, this little walk from the stables on good nights. And then a drink in O'Connell's saloon, home, rest, and Sunday. He felt pretty good.

He turned the corner. Two blocks away he saw a lighted streetcar pass. Charlie had warned him of Looney. That rat! He had Jerry's number. Two years ago Patsy McLaughlin had caught Jerry with his pants down with a factory girl while on duty. Looney had never been any good, even as a kid. And now he was so low that he was shanghaing honest workingmen. He'd like to have it out with Looney again.

He walked on. From near by he heard the chugging and the bells of railroad engines. The engine bells sang in the night. When he had been a young buck, he'd wanted to travel on trains. But that was a while back, and now there was no use in his thinking of doing such things. But he always thought of traveling when he heard engine bells at night like this. He looked around to see if Looney was really in the neighborhood. The street was deserted. But he walked out toward the edge of the curb in order not to be surprised from a doorway.

When he got home, Nora might have given birth again. Another mouth to feed. But even so, he was glad. No matter how many you had, a new one was always exciting. It gave you a swell feeling. You looked at the red-faced little thing, held it, loved it, and thought of how it was yours. With all the grief they gave you, they were worth it. What would a man's life be without kids? Suddenly he was frightened. Suppose Nora should be called with this one? But no, she was healthy, and that wouldn't happen. But suppose it did happen? He felt helpless. For a moment he feared she would die, and a wave of bitterness came upon him. But then he realized that this hadn't happened, and that it need not. Nora had come through four such ordeals. His mother had had nine. There was no cause for worry on this score.

He glanced in several deserted doorways. Had to keep his eyes open. He edged over a little more closely to the curb and walked on. Ahead was the deep, dark doorway of the Caron Paper Box place; it was just the kind of spot for those rats to be lying in wait. He was tense. But he wouldn't be bothered, he thought with confidence. And if he was, he'd show them what he was made of once and for all. He and Looney had hated each other ever since they were in grammar school together.

Out of the corner of his eye he saw three fellows skulking in the doorway of the Caron Paper Box Company. Rats! Now, Pat, show what you're made of! He took a few steps forward as if he were unsuspecting, unseeing, unconcerned. If they didn't come at him, he'd cross the street. He wouldn't let them gang up on him from behind. He knew Looney's dirty tricks, all right.

He passed, alert, still watching them from the corner of his right eye.

"Hey," a voice called from the doorway.

Pat took a long step forward and in toward the building.

"Hey, fellow, know what time it is?" the voice repeated; Pat knew it was Looney.

"You can get an Ingersoll in a drugstore for a dollar, Jerry," Pat said, his anger mounting; as he spoke he took long strides toward the side of the building, diagonally away from Looney.

He kept on, moving catlike, his body keyed for action, his muscles tense.

Looney, a raw-boned stocky young hoodlum, approached him. Just behind Looney there was a medium-sized hoodlum with a peaked cap. The third one was short and stocky.

"You're a smart egg," said the hoodlum with the peaked cap.

"It's you, Jerry," Pat said.

"I suppose you think you're a tough teameo, Pat," Looney sneered.

"Can't you smell the horse apples on him?" the stocky hoodlum said.

"Yes, so here's Pat Kenny. We meet again," Looney said.

"That's my name, and I never did anything to be ashamed of it," Pat answered.

"I see!" Looney said, meditatively nodding his head from side to side.

"And, listen—if you're planning on pullin' one of your stunts, you've found the wrong man tonight. I licked better men than you and your snotnoses," Pat said.

"Why, Pat, what do you mean?" Looney asked with feigned innocence.

"Well, what do you want?" Pat asked.

"All right, boys," Jerry said.

They began closing in on Pat. The peaked fellow's hand went to his pocket, but Pat, catching the motion, stepped forward and swung. He caught the man off balance and sent him tumbling across the sidewalk. At the same instant Pat got a clip on the jaw from Looney. He reeled sidewise, blocked a punch from the stocky fellow, took one high on the cheek bone from Looney, and regained his balance. He hit the stocky fellow with a straight and well-timed right. The stocky hoodlum tumbled off his pins and into the gutter. Pat turned on Looney, caught his wrist, and twisted it until a billy fell to the ground, tripping him at the same time. As Looney got up, Pat drove into him with plunging lefts and rights, punching him across the sidewalk. Looney went down on his knees. The hoodlum in the peaked cap ran off. The stocky one came at Pat, and they traded punches, until Pat split the hoodlum's lip and put a welt under his eye. The other ran off, followed by Looney.

"Come on back and fight, you rats!" Pat yelled exultantly after them.

"You'll get yours, wise guy," Looney called back.

"If I ever catch you and your yellow rats around here again, Jerry Looney, I'll break every bone in your goddamn bodies!" Pat shouted.

He walked on. He thought over the incident of the fight, enjoying in retrospect the punches he had delivered. His anger turned into pride and self-justification.

III

O'Connell's saloon was noisy. Most of the men lined up at the bar or sitting at the tables wore work clothes. In the rear, a group of young fellows were harmonizing *Sweet Adeline*.

Pat was relaxed. He felt empty, almost dead after the excitement of the fight. His face stung from the blows he had received. His left cheek bone was bruised.

He liked it here. The saloon was a friendly place; its lights were a contrast to the dark and empty streets outside. It seemed like a second home, a second and better home where he could forget troubles and worries. It was a barricade of human warmth, a wall of forgetfulness, an oasis in a world of fighting, hard work, poverty, kids, sickness, dirty and overcrowded

rooms at home. It was a man's world, and, damn it, he knew
he was a man.

He listened with pleasure to the sentimental singing, remembering with an ache his own days as a youth when he had sung
that way in saloons, heedless of the future, confident in his
strength.

The bartender smiled at him, and he ordered a whisky
straight. From outside he heard the rumble of a streetcar and
the creak of wagon wheels. The group of singers took up *The
Last Rose of Summer.* He gulped down his whisky. It warmed
him. He felt new life and energy quickly flowing through his
body. He glanced down the line of faces at the bar, suddenly
becoming tense. Whenever he went into a saloon he felt this
way unless he knew everyone present. How many times hadn't
he gotten into fights or near-fights in saloons? Christ, the life
he had lived had been one of fights, and then more fights. But
he couldn't complain. Didn't he usually win? His blood was up
again. Hadn't he licked the crap out of three hoodlums? If anybody in here got tough, they'd better be ready. He had needed
a fight like this one. Goddamn it, a man needed something to
let things out of him, and what was better than a good hard
tussle? Only this one hadn't been so hard. If he were younger
now, he'd go in the ring. He could have gone far in the ring.
Often he had dreamed of it as a lad, but then he had met Nora.
They had gotten married, and he had had to keep hitting the
ball, with kids coming, expenses mounting, and wages not too
damned high. He wasn't sorry. There was something between
himself and Nora. She had given him the best that was in her.
Now she wasn't a spring chicken any more. She wasn't pretty
the way she had been. But he had to be loyal to her. And still,
damn it, if he hadn't met her, he might have gone in the ring,
and then life would have been so different. Why couldn't he
have become a champion, the White Hope who would lick Jack
Johnson? Often, on the wagons, or just before he fell asleep
at night, he thought of himself as a champion fighter. In his
mind he had fights with all of the top notchers, and he won these
fights. Funny about a man. Even at his age a man daydreamed

just the way he had when he had been a young buck, full of dreams and hopes of what he would do with himself in life.

Hell, if all life was just as easy as winning a scrap! If in every-thing you could just stand up and slug and the best man win. But it didn't go that way. It was the things you couldn't see that gave you the biggest belts in the puss. And you had your hands tied and had to take it. All you could do was get sore. That was why a man needed a good fight and a few drinks now and then. You got the soreness out of your system. You punched a rat who had it coming to him. It cleaned you up inside, made you feel you were really a man.

Pat had a second whisky.

It burned pleasantly in his stomach. He examined the knuck-les on his right hand. Bruised a little. Well, he had come out of some fights with plenty worse than this. Plenty worse. These fellows in here! They all looked like decent workingmen the same as himself. How many of them felt the things he felt? Some of them were young and they hadn't hardly had the milk wiped from behind their ears as yet. But they looked all right. They didn't know much. They didn't know what they had in store for them. Just as he hadn't known when he was a kid. Perhaps some of them thought that they might be fighters, might be something big in this world. They'd learn. Love, a decent girl, and then it all turned out so different from what a lad imagined it would. He felt sorry for these lads here drink-ing. And yet he would rather have Nora and his kids than anything else in the world. Damn it, he would! Only why couldn't things be a little bit better, a little bit easier?

The singers were singing *Auld Lang Syne*.

There was a catch in Pat's throat. He was flooded with memo-ries of the past, and he couldn't express to himself what he felt. He felt that he had lost something in life, something that could never be regained. He had lost his youth. He had lost hopes. All he could look forward to was more of this work, more of this never-ending fight with poverty until the kids grew up and could help out. But then he and Nora would be old. For *Auld Lang Syne*. Again he looked down the line of faces, some of them rough, some dirty after a day's work, some needing a shave. The faces of these men seemed friendly. He wanted to open up, talk, forget, be one of them. He was shy. He had always been this way. Sometimes too shy to speak. And then he would be tough, ready to fight at the drop of a hat. He was like these fellows, though. He minded his own business, took a few drinks, and he only fought if somebody else started it.

Nora was home, and he should get there soon with his pay envelope. He shouldn't even be spending this money for a few drinks. They needed so much at home, especially now with the new little visitor coming. When he got home, the visitor might have arrived, and he would hold him, look at the little fellow. Think of it, the little fellow would be *his*, too. His son. His kid. He never got over the mystery of how kids were born, how they grew up. He wouldn't get drunk. He wouldn't waste his pay. But, hell, he could give himself some relief. He could have one more. Nora was waiting for him. Well, he was coming soon. He needed a few drinks.

"Another," he told the bartender.

IV

"Hello, Pat."

"Ah, there's the fighting Irishman himself."

Pat was glad to see the boys from the wagons. He could tell them about his fight. No, this wasn't bragging. He would only say what he had done. They all knew that he was no braggart. He felt let down after the excitement of the fight, lonely, worried about Nora, and about how they would make ends meet. He wanted to talk a little, forget a little. They were decent fellows, too, even Porky Mulroy here who was a loud-mouth and always ready to give you bull. Heinie Mueller was with Porky; they were together on a double wagon. Heinie was a fine young lad, and Pat liked him.

"Say, Pat, Charlie, the timekeeper, was worried about you. He was afraid that Looney and his hoods were around and might have waylaid you. We waited to come together," Ambrose McGinty said.

"Charlie must be your brother, Pat. You're sure in good with him," said Porky Mulroy, a rolypoly red-faced young fellow.

"We was ready for 'em tonight," Heinie said. "We came out together and we was going to give them so damned much that they wouldn't be around again. Them yellow rats," Heinie said.

The boys ordered, and Pat had another whisky.

"We came out of the stables rarin' to get at that yellow punk, Looney," Porky said.

"Well, boys, it wasn't necessary," Pat said.

"Maybe they smelled the wind and wasn't around tonight because they knew we was waitin' for 'em," Ambrose Mc-Ginty said.

"No, Looney and his hoods aren't around here now," Pat said knowingly.

"I was wishin' he was. Boy, how I'd like to smack him just one between the eyes," Porky bragged; he gulped his whisky.

"Oh, they was around. I saw the rats all right," Pat said.

Pleased with the way he had introduced the subject, he swallowed his whisky. He felt so warm inside, so pleasant.

But he mustn't get drunk tonight and spend too much of his pay.

"Hell, Pat, did they get you? They must have. You got a bruise there on your cheek. Say, I'm sorry you didn't wait for us," McGinty said sympathetically.

"The low-down yellow rats!" Heinie said with rising indignation.

"I'm waitin' for the day I can clench these fingers around Looney's throat," Porky said.

"Maybe it won't be necessary. I saw them. I poked them around a couple of times, and the dirty skunks—there were three of 'em—they blew. They're still runnin', or else I miss my guess," Pat said.

They slapped Pat on the back. He smiled. He was glad he had dropped in here, and now he realized that he'd done it to wait for the boys, to tell them of the fight, talk and drink a little with them. Hell, he could have another. He'd go easy on the dough he'd spend next week to make up for this outlay.

"Pat, that's swell stuff," Porky said after Pat had gone into detail describing the fight.

He swallowed his whisky.

"That was a hot one, tellin' him that he could buy an Ingersoll for a buck when he asked you the time," McGinty said, laughing heartily.

"It sure was," Porky said, his stomach rolling as he laughed.

"Pat, how's the missus?" Heinie asked.

"She's bringing me another visitor," Pat said.

A sense of guilt came over him. He ought to go home. He shouldn't stay here, spending money. She might be worried about him. She might need him. Women could die in childbirth. He was a skunk if he stayed. He couldn't come floating home drunk tonight. He wouldn't. And he didn't want to go— right away, at least. It was jolly, and he wanted to talk, have another drink or two.

He ordered another whisky.

"Yes, we're expectin' the stork," Pat said.

"That calls for another," Ambrose said, pushing his glass of beer across the counter.

"Some day your kids'll all be workin' at the express company and they'll be calling the company after you," Heinie said.

"Nope, I want something better than that for them," Pat said, swallowing his whisky.

He was exhilarated now. But he thought of home. He wanted something better for the kids than he had had. He had to work to give it to them. He couldn't if he did this every payday. He didn't do it every payday, though. He shouldn't be doing it now.

"You won't raise your boys to be manure whalers, huh, Pat?" Porky asked.

"Dutch, you've just been married. When are you going to have the stork around for a little visit?" asked Ambrose.

"I'm doin' my duty all of the time," Heinie said, and they laughed.

Pat flushed slightly. He never engaged in dirty talk, and it made him feel self-conscious.

"When you gettin' hitched, Porky?" asked McGinty.

"I'm too young," Porky answered.

"Listen. Marge'll be grabbin' off someone else if you don't hurry up and pop the question," McGinty said.

"I can handle Marge now," Porky said.

"Yeh, but wait till she hooks you. She'll handle you then, Porker," McGinty said.

"I'll always wear the pants in my emporium," Porky bragged.

Pat laughed. Why didn't he go home?

He ordered another drink, but felt that he was no good for having it. This was beginning to run into money. Damn it, he was no good to do it. He was unfair to Nora, the kids, the new little visitor. He was going to name him Timothy. Suppose he should roll home drunk on the very night that Tim was born? A fine father he was. No, he would have this one and go. He wasn't drunk now, but was just feeling good.

"Porky, you'll be a man when you can have five like Pat here," Ambrose McGinty said.

The singers in the back started again, this time singing *The Old Mill Stream.*

They were all younger than Pat. Damned nice lads. They would soon be having families. He remembered the jokes he had listened to when he'd married Nora. He saw her in those days, young and in white, so shy, so pretty. How he had loved to stroke her silky hair. Now she was home swollen up, screaming. He had to go.

"Listen, Canaryville," Porky said to McGinty.

"Porky, when we ask you for your two-cents' worth, put it in the collection box then, and then only," McGinty said.

Pat smiled. He swallowed his whisky. He paid up, said so-long, and went, reluctant, but proud of himself for not staying.

He staggered slightly. The world was suddenly bright. Hell, he was going to get on better and better, and when he got home there would be a wonderful new little visitor waiting to see him.

Yes, he felt damned good. He was glad to be poor, to have to work hard, because when the kids grew up they'd know what an Old Man they had. Some day, think of it, he'd be telling them what happened tonight, the night that Timothy was born. Suppose it was a girl? She'd grow up to be a raving American beauty.

He walked toward the streetcar line. He wanted to get home and get the news. He hoped Nora wouldn't be worrying. He felt damned good, all right. He had had just enough to drink.

A small lad of about nineteen stepped out of a doorway and leveled a gun at Pat.

"All right, expressman, stick 'em up," the youth said nervously.

Pat was surprised. He stood still for a moment. He realized what was happening. He looked at the youth with contempt. He saw that the youth was nervous, too.

"Put that gun away, Sonny, before it goes off and hurts you," Pat said.

"Stick 'em up," the kid said, more nervous; his hand wavered.

"My boys play cowboy and Indian just like you do, Sonny," Pat said.

He was watching the lad closely, ready to close in on him. His head seemed to clear.

"Stick 'em up," the kid said, taking a step nearer.

Pat put up his hands, but at the same moment, he kicked out. The gun went off. Pat caught the boy in the groin with his foot just before a bullet punctured his abdomen. The boy groaned, clutched at his groin, and sank to the sidewalk in agony. Pat swung wildly, missed the falling boy, and tumbled on top of him. He felt an intense pain. He rolled off the boy, groped for the gun, and hit the boy over the head. The boy was knocked unconscious.

A crowd from the saloon heard the shot and rushed out. They found Pat dying on the sidewalk, with the unconscious boy beside him.

1936-43.

Street Scene

"SAY, DO I BELONG to the human race?" the old man asked himself aloud as he stood at the corner of Ninth Street and Michigan.

It was an Indian summer afternoon. Across the street, in Grant Park, there was a playograph recording the World Series baseball game between the St. Louis Cardinals and the New York Yankees. The old man wore shapeless clothes; his shirt was gray with dirt, and the toes stuck out of his army boots. He shuffled along and stopped in front of the gold and bronze entrance to the Nation Oil Building.

"Hell, I give up," he told himself.

He yawned. He stretched his arms like a sleepy man. He took off his coat, rolled it into a bundle, and laid it on the sidewalk. Heedless of those who stopped to gape at him, he slowly went through the gestures of undressing, putting on pajamas and getting ready for bed. He mumbled instructions to an imaginary valet, remarking that he wouldn't need a bath in the morning because he had decided to lie down and die.

He lay down on the sidewalk and carefully drew imaginary covers over himself. He made loud, snoring noises.

A small crowd immediately gathered about him.

"Nighty, night," he said.

Strangers gaped at him. He stared vacant-eyed at the sky. More pedestrians stopped to cluster curiously about him.

"Are you hurt, fellow?"

"Hell, he's just full of canned heat."

"What's the matter with you?"

67

"He was knocked down in a fight."

"Who is he?"

"You can see, he's coked up with wood alcohol."

"Somebody call a doctor."

"Where's the police? They're never around when they're needed."

"The man was knocked down by an automobile. Somebody call for an ambulance."

"Here's an officer."

"The law."

A burly, red-faced policeman pushed his way through the growing crowd. He looked at the old man, who met his gaze with innocent eyes.

"What's wrong?" the policeman asked.

"Hello, officer."

The policeman looked at him dubiously. He pushed his cap back on his head and scratched his head.

"What's the matter with you, huh? Come on, what's the matter?"

A woman tried to tell the policeman what had happened.

"I'm all right, officer. I've just laid down here because I feel kind of tired. I thought maybe I'd just like to lay down and die, that's all. I only want to be left alone so that I can lay down and die."

Some of the on-lookers laughed.

"What?" the cop asked, angry and bewildered.

"Can't you let me alone? Can't you let me alone to die in peace?"

"Come on, now, none of this wise stuff. Move on! Get up and move on! Do you hear me?"

"Can't I die in peace? I tell you, all I want is to die in peace."

"You heard me! Move on! I don't want any monkeyshines here. This is a public place."

He grabbed the old man's arm and tugged at it. The old man didn't resist when the policeman pulled him.

A portly police sergeant appeared on the scene.

"What's wrong, Mike?" the sergeant asked.

"There's nothin' wrong, sir. I'm only trying to die in peace."

The policeman let the man drop back on the sidewalk.

"Shut up, you!" The policeman turned to the sergeant.

"He's disturbin' the peace."

"What's the matter with you? You can't die there," the sergeant said angrily.

"Jesus Christ, can't a man die in peace, even in a free country?"

"Come on, quit blasphemin' and move on," the sergeant ordered.

"Move on!" the policeman commanded, prodding the old man with a club.

The old man didn't move.

The sergeant grabbed his sleeve and tried to lift him. Then both the sergeant and the policeman shoved him.

"I told you to be on your way," the sergeant shouted.

The old man rose. The crowd laughed hilariously. He limped on for about ten feet. He turned around and told the crowd:

"I only want to die quietly."

"Go on or I'll run you in," the cop bellowed as a number of spectators continued laughing.

The old man moved down a few more paces. He again stretched himself out on the sidewalk.

More people stopped to see what was happening.

"I'll run yuh all in," the sergeant said, turning to glare at the amused and voluble crowd.

The sergeant and the policeman stood over the old man, not knowing what to do.

"I only want to die in peace. That's all I want. You can't make me work. I'm too tired. This is a free country."

"Shut up, you!" the policeman snapped.

"I only want to say, work is too hard for me."

"Get up!" the policeman said, putting his foot against the old man's ribs. "Get up, I say! This is a public street and not a sanitarium. Get up and be quick about it! Do you hear me?" the policeman bellowed.

"I want to die in peace. Can't you leave me alone?"

"Are you going to get up?" the sergeant asked.

"No, I'm dying. Let me die in peace."

"Officer, that man's sick. Call an ambulance," an indignant lady cried out.

"Lady, move on and tend to your own business."

The sergeant turned to the policeman.

"Come on, let's get this bum out of here."

They bent down and tried to lift the old man. He stiffened his body. They dragged him along the sidewalk on his buttocks. Some of the on-lookers laughed. A few protested, but the police paid no attention to them. Still more pedestrians stopped to watch. The policeman and the sergeant continued to drag the old man along the sidewalk. His shirt was unbuttoned. Freeing himself from the police, he lost his shirt. He lay on the sidewalk, naked and dirty from the waist up. His ribs showed.

"Get a tow wagon," a wit from the crowd yelled.

"No, get Big Bill Thompson the Mayor over here," a second wit said.

The policeman and the sergeant puffed, tired from their exertion. The old man watched them with innocently twinkling blue eyes. He turned and winked at the crowd. The policemen again tried to lift him. He relaxed, refusing to cooperate. They let him drop back onto the sidewalk. He shivered. His feet dangled over the edge of the curb. Automobiles had stopped, tying up traffic. Automobile horns made an incessant racket. The crowd now filled the sidewalk.

"Dunning for that bum," someone in the crowd said loudly.

"I don't care what happens. Let a truck run over me. I don't care. I don't care. I give up. I wanna die," the old man said. His teeth chattered. "No, sir, you can't make me work. I'll die instead."

"Get an ambulance," someone called.

"Let him alone, officer," someone else demanded.

The sergeant talked to the policeman, and then the cops went off.

"Come on, button up, you! There's ladies passing."

Another policeman showed up.

"Get them people back," the sergeant ordered. The policeman began edging the crowd back. When he succeeded on one
side, they pressed forward on another.

"Just let me alone."

"Why don't you go to work, you bum?" a man yelled.

"It's too hard," the old man answered.

'Shut up, you!" the sergeant said.

A fat policeman joined the other cops and helped to push the
crowd back. The sergeant stood over the old man.

"You gonna get up?" he asked.

"Officer, please leave me die in peace."

"The wagon is on the way," the sergeant said.

Suddenly the old man stood up, picked up his clothes, and
put them on. He started walking away.

"Oh, no, you don't," the sergeant said, grabbing his arm.

The policemen escorted the old man southward. The crowd
followed. Near Roosevelt Road they allowed him to sit and wait
on the steps of an old building. He paid no attention to his
audience.

"I'll be dead soon," he soliloquized. "Then let the world go
to hell. It can die after me. It can die five minutes after me. I
don't care. I don't even belong to the human race anyway.
I don't care. I'm gonna die in five minutes. I won't work. All
I want is to die in a little peace. I'm goin' West. Go West, young
man. Ha! Ha! Everybody's goin' West, even cops. Ain't that
right, officer?"

He looked up at the fat policeman.

"Shut up!"

"Even cops die. Everybody's going to die."

He looked down at the sidewalk for a moment and then,
with a twinkle in his eyes, he looked up at the policemen.

"That's a good joke, isn't it? Everybody dies, even cops."

The patrol wagon arrived.

Two policemen lifted him roughly, while the others kept the
crowd back.

"Well, I must belong to the human race. They didn't send the
dog catcher's bus after me," the old man said.

They shoved him into the patrol wagon. It went off.

The crowd slowly broke up. A stranger asked one of the officers what had happened.

"Nothin' much. Another bum cooked on canned heat. He's gone coo-koo. The stuff makes 'em all that way. Well, he'll get thirty days in the Bridewell, but it won't do no good. Them bums is jus bums. They're just bums."

"You're right, officer."

The cop strolled back along Michigan Boulevard. There was a cheer from the crowd by the playograph, and it broke up. The Yankees had won the world series from the Cardinals in four straight games.

                                                    1930-43.

The Hyland Family

_____

"When virtue displays itself solely as the individual's simple conformity with the duties of the station to which he belongs, it is rectitude."—Hegel

I

IT WAS A radiant Sunday morning in July. Ten o'clock mass was just over at the Church of Mary Magdalen on the southeast side of Chicago. The crowd had begun to dwindle when Andrew J. Hyland, Sr. loomed in the center doorway with his two daughters and his son beside him. This was always a moment of quiet gratification for Andrew, Sr. He glowed inwardly with that sense of pleasure that only the good man can experience when he has done his duty. Andrew, Sr. knew that he was one of the leading members of the parish, and he accepted, as an obligation, the responsibility of fulfilling all his religious duties without laxity. He was one of the largest contributors to the annual church collections. He received the Sacraments regularly. He strove, in every possible way, to be a model Catholic layman. And for years he had required his family to remain kneeling for a few moments after mass, saying extra prayers, while others hastened and scuffled out of church. With the regularity of a clock, the Hyland family usually appeared in the church doorway at the same time every Sunday. They walked with dignity of bearing, conscious that they were the cynosure of many eyes. Even in their movements they seemed to reveal a sense of their own worth. But they did nothing to call attention to themselves. They dressed expensively and in fashion, but with good taste. If they stopped to talk with friends, they never raised their voices, nor did they laugh too loudly. They minded their own business. But their brief promenade out of church on Sunday mornings had become a parish event—in fact, an unmentioned but recognized family tradition.

Andrew, Sr. was a tall, thin man with a long, straight, almost hawklike nose and a tight, rather constricted, face. He was gray around the temples, but he looked well preserved and in the best of health. In every sense of the word, he appeared to be a solid and respectable citizen. Pleased as he was after Sunday mass, he also felt a twinge of pain. Five years before, his dearly beloved wife, Ellen, had passed away. All his memories of her were inextricably associated with the Church. She had been a pious woman. They had always received the Sacraments together, and it had been during her lifetime that he had begun the habit of kneeling to pray for a few moments at the end of mass. In church he missed her more than he did at home, and there were moments when he had to exert force of will to concentrate on the mass rather than lose himself in reveries of her. Sensing her beside him in spirit while he knelt in his pew, his sorrow was softened into resignation. No more than Job would he question the will of the Almighty. And yet the pain of her loss cast a somber hue over his emotions. Genuine as was his sense of gratification, it was nonetheless restrained. He remembered her and he missed her. And he drew from her death the lesson that even the happiest of lives, even the finest moments of joy are touched with sorrow.

Ruth Hyland was twenty-six; Helen was twenty-two; Andrew J., Jr. was twenty. The girls had attended the parish grammar school, Saint Paul's high school, and Saint Mary's of the Woods in Indiana. The son had been graduated from Notre Dame the previous June. The children were all fair of hair and skin, as their mother had been. Ruth was rather tall and thin, a bony, angular girl with high cheekbones and a pale complexion. Her face was drawn, but at times, and with the help of the clothes she wore, she looked attractive. Helen was plump and buttery, with rosy cheeks and vapid blue eyes; she still retained the virginal bloom of girlhood. Even when she was solemn it seemed as though her face would break into smiles. Andrew, Jr. was small of stature, bony like Ruth and his father, and prissy in his gestures. His lips were unusually thin, and he rarely smiled.

In public, the Hylands tended to act alike, as if by instinct. At times they even seemed to look alike. Promenading out of church, they walked in file. They knew they were on display and could not permit the slightest irregularity, even of gesture or expression. Ruth, haughtier than the other children, swept strangers with a gaze that verged on contempt. Helen, the most spontaneous of the Hylands, was tense with the necessity of being on good behavior. She was acting in imitation of her sister and in unconscious acceptance of the unmentioned family custom. Andrew, Jr. was dreamy, absorbed, and when he was in such a mood he appeared to be singularly pious, as if he carried outside of church the emotions, the feelings, the solemnity which were appropriate in the presence of God.

On this Sunday morning, Andrew, Jr.'s appearance was deceptive. It was his alertness which saved him from the embarrassment of having to speak to Marie Considine. She had had a crush on him ever since grammar school, and he had never reciprocated it. Because of her inability to hide her feelings, he had contempt for her. Although most people thought her pretty, she was a drab thing in his eyes. Her family didn't amount to anything, and her father had gone to a drunkard's grave. He saw her edging diagonally toward him and lifted his brows in annoyance. Years ago he had made it clear to her that he would have nothing to do with her. It was utterly preposterous of her to imagine he could admit her to his world. Withal, she was so lacking in character, so shameless, that she persisted in trying to attract his attention. And here she was, up to her old tricks. He saved himself from the discomfort of saying good morning to her by turning to Ruth and remarking in high seriousness that the morning was splendid. The weather was interesting to Ruth at the moment, because she was con-

cerned in not seeing a former high-school classmate who was
gauche. She spiritedly told her brother that the sun was shining.
Helen was flustered, because she saw Jimmy Norgrove, who
persisted in asking her to go out with him even though he knew
she was engaged to Jimmy Barry. She didn't even care a tiny
part of the fingernail of her little finger for him, but he always
pestered her in the most impertinent manner. Every time she
saw him she was confused and didn't know what to do. She
joined in conversation with her brother and sister, saying it was
a wonderful morning, wonderful. At the very same moment,
Andrew, Sr. noticed his poor relation, third cousin Ed Nolan,
gazing at him with searching, hurt eyes. Looking away from
Ed Nolan, he confirmed the judgment of his children concerning the weather. Having thus escaped those who would
intrude upon their dignity and self-respect, the Hylands
stopped by the curb to converse with Old Tom Gregory, the
millionaire chainstore man, and his wife. They inquired of the
health of the Gregorys, exchanged a few words, and concluded
by expressing perfect agreement with Old Tom when he said
that it was a fine morning. Then they marched off to their
Lincoln limousine and drove home to their nine-room apartment in a new building near South Shore Drive.

It was a comfortable home, spotlessly clean, and furnished
by Ruth in what she considered the best of taste. The furniture
was all new, and one could almost see the price tags on it. In the
parlor there was a large Baby Grand piano. There were oil
paintings on the wall, including a large one of the Holy
Family. Along one wall there was a large bookcase. On the
shelves were an odd assortment of novels, school books, the
works of G. K. Chesterton, and a complete set of Sir Walter
Scott in red morocco binding with gold stamping.

When the family returned home, Andrew, Jr. immediately
went to his room, changed to flannels, and left to play tennis.
Ruth brought slippers to her father, and he read the business
section, the news section, and the sports section of *The Sunday
Clarion*. Helen giggled over the comic section, Ruth curled up
on the sofa and pored dreamily over the society news.

II

"Ruth, you always see to it that everything is just jack-dandy for Sunday dinner," Andrew, Sr. said as he ate a hearty meal.

The table was attractively covered with a spotless heavy linen tablecloth, and the silverware gleamed.

"Somebody has to see to such things," Ruth answered with a slight neurotic tremor in her voice.

They all went on eating as if they had not observed this tremor in Ruth's voice. Ruth pecked at a small helping of food. She thought it was vulgar for a girl to eat too much, and everyone said she ate like a bird. In consequence, she was always hungry and munched candy and sweets constantly. No matter how many sweets she ate, she never gained weight. At times her slimness was a source of pride to her, but at other times she was troubled and wished she were a little more plump. She was often displeased because Helen had such a good appetite, and frequently warned her sister that if she were not careful she would become fat. Helen worried about her weight and she was continually going on diets and then breaking her fine resolutions.

"Did any of you notice Ed Nolan hanging around outside of church this morning like a dog without a bone?" Andrew, Sr. asked.

They shook their heads negatively.

"He was waiting to buttonhole me. I suppose he wanted to make another touch."

"I wish he'd move to another parish," Ruth said.

"Do you know, I think I'd pay the cost if he would. He's always parading himself as my cousin. He embarrasses me. I've told him many times that I can't afford to loan him money. He had many chances, and he's done nothing with them."

"He's common," Ruth said, as if this were the most damning judgment that could be made of her cousin.

"He's a darn fool. He had a little money saved up, and I advised him to buy a house. But do you think he took my advice? You remember how he invested his money in Imbray stock?"

"Yes, we all remember," Andrew, Jr. said.

"He's the kind of a fellow who courts bad luck. But who wants another helping?"

Helen passed her plate, and Ruth cast a disapproving eye on her.

Andrew, Sr. served Helen a second helping.

"Ruthie, you?" he asked.

"No, thank you, Father."

"Oh, a little more won't hurt you."

"I've had enough," she said decisively.

"Well, I haven't. This roast beef is jack-dandy. Ella sure knows how to cook."

He served Andrew, Jr. and then gave himself a second helping.

"Helen, did you notice Fran Sweeney's dress at church?" Ruth asked.

"Yes, I did. She wore brown shoes with a black dress."

"She's as common as Marie Considine."

There was a lapse in conversation.

"Father Kilbride preached a good sermon, didn't he?"

"Did you notice, Dad, that he mentioned G. K. Chesterton?" Andrew, Jr. asked.

"Yes. I'll have to read that fellow sometime."

"Dad, I wish you would. Read his book, *The New Jerusalem*," Andrew, Jr. advised.

"What's it about?"

"The Jews. He says the Jews are an Oriental people and that they should live and dress like Orientals instead of Occidentals."

"Say—that's not a bad idea," Andrew, Sr. exclaimed, the light of knowledge dawning in his eyes.

"Fran Sweeney is going steady with that bootlegger's son—Castano—think of that," Ruth cut in.

"I guess the old man wants her to marry him. Perhaps he smells the mazuma there. Old man Sweeney is in a bad fix these days. I heard the other night that he might lose some of his buildings," Andrew, Sr. said.

"Gosh, I wish I could understand why there has to be a depression," Helen said.

"Girls shouldn't trouble themselves about it," Andrew, Jr. told Helen.

"I wouldn't get anywhere if I did," Helen said.

"I was talking to Mr. Ames at the office the other day. He agreed with me that things would be a lot different if Al Smith was in the White House. But that's too much to expect. You see what they did to Smith here in Chicago last month?" Andrew, Sr. said.

"But, Dad, why are they all against us because we're Catholics?" Helen asked, a questioning look shadowing her face.

"Bigots," Andrew, Sr. answered with positiveness.

Noticing that they had finished, Ruth pressed the electric button for Ella, the colored servant. Ruth enjoyed this. She had had it installed after her mother died. Ella, a fat Negress, appeared, wearing a fancy organdy apron. She quietly removed the dishes and served the dessert and coffee.

Conversation became desultory. When they had finished, Andrew, Sr. bowed his head, and his children followed suit. They said grace aloud.

III

Ruth sat in her bedroom with the door closed. She was nervous. She wiped away a tear. She had just reread the letters of Joe Fontanna. Then she had put them back in the drawer where she kept her sacred mementos: Joe's letters, favors from parties, pictures, crushed flowers, dance programs, and other souvenirs.

She had a slight headache. Ever since Joe had died of a heart attack over two years ago, she had had headaches. She had strange aches and pains, too, and rarely felt well. She believed she was destined to die young, and yet she was not afraid. After what she had gone through, what terrors could there be in life, or in death?

As a girl in high school, Ruth had never been popular, and most of her friends had had more dates than she. For years she had lived for the night and the dance that would change her life. And while she was away at school, she had been invited to a Notre Dame homecoming victory dance by Tommy McGrew, a grammar-school classmate. He had lived in the same dormitory as Joe Fontanna, one of the ends on the Notre Dame football team. She had been introduced to Joe. Joe had exchanged dances with Tommy, and it had been love at first sight. Ruth, a frigid girl, had blossomed out. During the subsequent Christmas vacation, she had had several dates with Joe. After his graduation, they had become engaged, and three months before their expected marriage he had died suddenly of a heart attack.

Ruth knew there could never be anyone else in her life to take the place of Joe. He had been a tall, well-built, dark-haired, handsome Italian-American boy whose father was a wealthy wholesale grocer. Gruff and inarticulate, he had been a real diamond in the rough. She realized that she had had no real girlhood, no true happiness in life until she had met him. Most girls had not liked her. At Saint Paul's, she had usually been treated rather coldly. She had not been understood, and some of the girls had meanly thought her a snob. In her senior year, she had hoped to be on the Senior Prom Committee and thus get her name and her picture on the society pages of the newspapers. The girls had not voted for her, and her disappointment rankled even now, almost ten years afterward. It was only with Joe that she had truly been happy. Before that, she had wanted love but had been afraid of it, even disdainful of it. When boys had taken her to dances, she had been rather aloof, and when they had tried to kiss her, she had frozen up. But from the first moment she had set eyes on Joe she knew that he was different. She had melted. And then this tragedy had happened.

The way she had received the news had been a terrible shock. She had been expecting a telephone call from him. She had rushed to the telephone and had been told the news of his death. She had fainted. For a week she had been in hysterics. The doctor had kept her on sedatives for several months. Long after his death she would still burst into tears, even in public. She felt incomplete. She could not maintain her interest in anything. She rarely smiled. She brooded over him, going over and over again in memory the days of their courtship and engagement. She had so reconstructed her memories of their love that she could no longer distinguish what was fact and what was fantasy. She dreamed of him continually, and even events from her dreams became mixed with memories. At times, when she heard the name Joseph mentioned, or read it in print, tears would well up in her eyes. Although she knew it was sinful, she often regretted she had not given herself to him and, even taken the initiative in order that it might have happened. For now she could never know the fruits of love. Now she must go to her grave a virgin. And had she sacrificed herself, she could have confessed it, atoned for it, devoted her entire life to doing penance for that one sin. She consoled herself by visualizing herself as a tragic person. She saw her destiny as one of nobility and suffering. And yet she revolted against her destiny. The minute-by-minute reality of her life was hard to bear. Why, why had such a tragedy been hers? She wanted to live. She was only twenty-six. She could see nothing ahead of her but a barren future. She had nothing in life but memories of Joe.

She devoted herself to the care and management of the home. She did the shopping, attended to such matters as laundry, decided on what meals were to be served, strove to take the place of her mother. All this was not enough. She wanted her own home. She spun out every domestic chore, making it take as much time as possible. She complained that she had too much to do. She took needless time in shopping, in checking on prices, in finding bargains. She was continuously rearranging the furniture and looking for new things to buy. She read fashion magazines and bought dresses, coached Helen in what to wear, talked endlessly of style and clothes. She hunted for recipes for new dishes which she had Ella cook. She read romantic love stories and books about royalty with yearning sadness. All this was not enough to fill her life. She lived in her memories.

Now she heard Helen singing gaily in her room next door.

She had sung to herself that way when Joe had been alive. The mere presence of Helen, who was so much in love, made her memories more unbearable, exacerbated her nerves, and produced frightening feelings of envy and jealousy. Bitterly, she complained to herself of her fate, voicing over again the same laments she had voiced to herself ever since his death. She knew it was not fair of her to feel this way about her sister. She didn't want to be jealous of Helen or spiteful toward her. Such emotions rose within her without having been willed. What could she expect Helen to do? Helen was in love. And how well she could imagine Helen's feelings, her dreams and all the delights and hopes that filled her mind. When a girl was in love, when she had found the one and only person, every minute of the day was saturated with joy. Then she lived on wings of joy and expectation. Helen was feeling that way now as she sang in her bedroom. Ruth's sadness became overpowering. She wanted to cry. She struggled with herself not to. She sobbed softly.

Helen stopped singing. In a moment she knocked on Ruth's door.

"What do you want?" Ruth cried out impatiently.

"It's me. If you aren't doing anything, I just wanted to talk," Helen said.

"I was taking a nap. I have a headache. Can't you people let me alone," Ruth answered.

"Oh, all right. I'm sorry," Helen said in disappointment.

Ruth immediately regretted her impulsive action. She had spoken before thinking. But her eyes were red from crying, and she hadn't wanted Helen to see her. She should have talked with her sister. Perhaps the kid had something on her mind. Helen needed a mother. She had to be like a mother. Oh, she didn't want to. Why was this her fate?

Week ends were always the worst for her. This was the time when girls had their big dates. With Joe, Saturday and Sunday nights had been so divine. And Helen was a constant reminder of these. She had used to fuss on Sundays, just as Helen did now, in order to pass the time until Joe called for her.

That was the past!

A cold horror came over her. Nothing in life was more awful than the past. The very word was like ice laid on one's spine. She had to forget. She had to live in the present. She had to live.

She stared at the wall with tear-stained eyes. She imagined herself talking to Joe. She explained to him how she felt, poured out her heart to him in imagination. Her feelings dissolved into a soft melancholy. Her tears dried. She slipped into a mood of consoling sadness.

The telephone rang. She had a vague notion that it was for her. She heard Helen rush past her door to answer the telephone.

"It's for you," Helen called.

Ruth didn't answer. Helen knocked on the door.

"Who is it?" Ruth asked, annoyed.

An intense wave of anticipation gripped her. She suddenly believed this was a telephone call that would change her entire life.

"It's Teresa."

"All right. Tell her I'll be right there," she said sharply, her hopes collapsed.

IV

Andrew, Sr. awoke from a nap about three-thirty. The children were out. Opening his heavy-lidded eyes, he was momentarily disorientated. For a few seconds he didn't know where he was, what time it was, nor even what day it was. He was weary. Always, when he took an afternoon nap on Sunday, he would awaken in this way. And he would then be stricken with the horror of old age and of death. Now he was terrified. He felt a pain in his left armpit. It spread downward along his arm. It had come and gone all day, but he hadn't paid much attention to it. He guessed it was probably a touch of neuralgia and that a man of his age must expect a few such pains. However, you would expect neuralgia pains in winter rather than summer. Yawning, he sat up in bed and tried to reason away his fear. The pain seemed to disappear. It gave him a premonition of death. He laughed at himself. He knew that he was in good health and that there was no cause for worry. His feeling of weariness began to fade. He blinked his eyes. He sat rigid because he had a sudden heartburn. He reclined, sweating in fear, until this pain passed. A man of his age must watch his diet. He had eaten too much for Sunday dinner. He mustn't do that.

He sat up again. His pains were gone. He resolved to eat more cautiously and assured himself that he had no cause for worry. He'd been checked up by the doctor only a few months ago and he had been all right then. His acute fear changed into a state of vague depression. He went to the parlor, sat down in a comfortable chair, and tried to relax.

During the week, he always looked forward to Sunday. The idea of being away from his office at the drug company, of Sunday mass, of dinner with the kids, everything about Sunday appealed to him in anticipation. And then he would be disappointed when Sunday came. The day would be long, drawn-out. Time would creep by. He would keep wondering what to do with himself. He always expected something out of the way to happen on Sunday. But usually Sunday would crawl by, and he would be glad when it was over. But then, he got a rest. A man needed a rest. He was vice-president of a wholesale drug company and had many responsibilities, many things to attend to. They were doing a big business in warehouse receipts, and the responsibility and handling of these rested on his shoulders. He had to be very careful about them. This part of his work sometimes worried him. Yes, Sunday was refreshing, even though it was sometimes a little dull. A man needed to do nothing and to have no worries one day a week.

On Sunday he missed Ellen the most. If she were alive, they could do things on Sunday just as they used to. They could take drives about the city and into the country, go to a moving picture show, take a walk. How often he longed to stroll in the park with her, taking her arm, the two of them thinking of the past, of their youth. And this was all gone. Ellen was dead. At times it was still difficult for him to realize this, to realize the terrible meaning in the fact that Ellen was dead. He no longer had her to talk to. The girl he had loved, the girl who had so enthralled him in his young manhood, his lifelong partner and helpmate—she was dead. The mother of his grown children was no more on this earth. He was saddened by regret, a feeling of loss. Sunday without Ellen was so empty.

The afternoon was slowly passing. The minutes seemed long. It was as if time had such a feeble pulse. And yet time flew so quickly, rushing by until one was no longer young. He brooded over this thought as he lit a cigar and gazed out the window. An automobile passed. People walked by. It was warm and sunny. He turned away from the window and sat in a chair.

He was vigorous and in fine health, thank the Lord. That pain in his shoulder and the heartburn were nothing serious. But somehow he was getting so little out of life. The children had their own lives, their own thoughts, their own friends. Helen would be married soon. The others would, too. Ruth would get over Joe and she would meet some fine lad. His kids were sensible, and he took pride in them. He couldn't think of them not marrying. What young fellow wouldn't want his daughters? What decent girl wouldn't be more than proud to marry his boy? They would all marry, and then he would be alone. He didn't want to spend his last years alone. At times he wished the kids would marry and that he would meet a sensible and attractive woman with a good head, one who was neither too young nor too old. He'd marry her. It was no slur on Ellen's memory to want this. Lord have mercy on Ellen's soul! Looking down on him from Heaven, she would even approve, want him to marry again, if he found the right sort of woman. Would his children approve? But a man had his own life to live. He had vigorous years ahead. He was lonely. The kids could not fill up the emptiness of his life for him.

The past crowded back on Andrew, Sr. He thought of how Ruth resembled Ellen. That was why she was his favorite. Ah, yes, both of them, his dead wife, his daughter—they were thoroughbreds. If only she had been spared him! How often had he not thought in their happiest days, even in the rapturous days of their honeymoon, that some day one of them must go. How this thought had occasionally frightened him! And it had happened. Ellen had gone.

He picked up his newspaper and read it in order to forget. He wanted not to think. He was dreamy, and as he read he forgot everything he had just perused. He liked his Sunday paper. There was more to read in it than there was on weekdays.

v

Ever since he had been in grammar school, Andrew, Jr. had thought that some day he might write. At Mary Our Mother high school and in college he had always received excellent marks in his English courses, and his teachers had told him that he had talent and should go on writing. After his graduation from Notre Dame, Andrew, Jr. faced the problem of deciding what he was to do about his future. He had been voted the young man of his high-school class who seemed most likely to succeed, and he had never for one moment doubted that he would be very successful. In his moments of greatest self-confidence he imagined he would even be a famous man. Graduation had posed the problem of his future. He had no inclination for business, and with the depression ravaging the land, there were not many business opportunities for young men just out of college. Some of his classmates from Notre Dame had had great difficulty in finding work. Had he chosen to follow a business career, the only opening would have been in the wholesale drug company of which his father was vice-president. And since he believed he would be wasting his talents in the drug business, his choice of a future had narrowed down to law or literature. He had not made up his mind which of these alternatives he would take. Now he favored one, now the other; at times he thought he might follow both careers simultaneously. He was, however, faced with no need of arriving at a decision hastily. He could spend the entire summer thinking out the problem carefully. He had already discussed the question briefly with his father. Dad wanted him to return to Notre Dame and study law. This prospect was attractive. He had had a good time at Notre Dame and he had been a good student, graduating with an excellent average. Study was not a burden to him as it was to many young men. And to be able to answer questions in a classroom, proving that he had studied, was a pleasure. It enhanced his sense of his own worth and superiority. He was unable to make up his mind because he believed that writing was his first love, and he wanted to begin his literary career immediately. He hoped that he would become an overnight success and that his stories would be published as quickly as he wrote them. Were he to return to school and study law, he would have less time for literature. But when he would decide to devote himself to literature, he would begin to have doubts. Granting that he might succeed, how long would it take? If he had to wait too long for fame and money, how would he live? His father had educated him, and he could not expect his father to go on supporting him for years. A legal education would be very fine training in thinking, and it would be something to fall back on.

In the meantime, he did try to write. Since June he had been working on a story he considered a good exercise in style. Superficially, it seemed like many stories that were printed in *The Saturday Evening Post* and other magazines. It would recount how a young Catholic lawyer went to Havana on a vacation and there met a beautiful señorita who was the daughter of one of the best families of Cuba. He had never been to Cuba, but had read enough about it in the library to gain what he considered the necessary background material. He had chosen Cuba as his setting because it was a tropical island. The tropics were associated with romance. Romance would permit him to use and develop his style. But his main interest in this subject was that it gave him a chance to write beautiful descriptions. He was working on the story and had reached a point where he was describing the young lawyer alone in the moonlight, gazing out across the harbor after he had first met the heroine.

After dinner on this particular Sunday he had gone to his room to write, but he faced a snag. Rack his brain as he would,

he was unable to think up a new and original metaphor with
which to describe the moonlight glittering on the waters of
the bay.

After he had conceived and discarded about twenty figures
of speech, Andrew, Jr. began to feel sleepy. He went out for
some air. Strolling aimlessly and thinking of his story, he happened to pass the home of Jerry Davitt, a high-school and college classmate. He dropped in and saw Jerry and Mr. Davitt
for a few minutes and then he strolled back toward home. He
decided that he need not make up his mind about the future
immediately. The postponement of his decision affected him as
much as an actual resolution would have. He felt released. He
would drift along for a while, writing, reading, enjoying himself. And he would finish his story and might even sell it. It
might be printed in a Catholic magazine, and then he would
see his name in print. He prided himself, as if it were a personal
merit, because he need not go out and seek work. His thoughts
shifted from writing to friends of his who were struggling to
get ahead. He felt sorry for them. He revelled in a sense of his
own superiority. He was one person who need not worry about
grubbing in the market place. Despite the depression, Dad drew
a good salary from the drug company and he had not invested
money unwisely on the stock market. In fact, his father seemed
to be as well off now as he had been before the stock-market
crash.

He suddenly quickened his pace, wanting to get back to the
story.

The girls had gone out, and his father was alone in the parlor.

"You home?" Andrew, Sr. asked him, looking up from the
newspaper.

"I took a little walk and stopped in to see Jerry Davitt."

"How are they?"

"They're all right. Mr. Davitt told me to ask you if you can
help him get some of that Bourbon."

Andrew, Sr. looked worried for a moment.

"He understands, doesn't he, that I'm not in that kind of
business and do it for him only as a personal favor?"

"Yes, I think he does, Dad. I explained it to him."

"Well, then, I might. But, Andy, are you sure he doesn't talk about it to anyone?"

"I don't think he does. I told him not to, and I think he understands that you're doing it merely to oblige him."

"The girls have gone out. I wish Ruth went out more. I'm worried about her."

"She'll be all right."

"Yes, I think so. She's less nervous than she used to be."

Andrew, Jr. turned to leave the parlor, saying he was going to work.

"How's the writing?" Andrew, Sr. asked.

"Very good," Andrew, Jr. answered, leaving the parlor.

VI

Helen stood naked before the long mirror in her bedroom. She was proud and joyous at the sight of her body, and she was ashamed. She ought not to do this. If Ruth should catch her, Ruth would bawl her out, or even laugh at her. Ruth had always been an older sister and still wanted to treat her like a child. She was not a child. She was a pretty young woman who was engaged to be married to the one man in her life, the boy for whom she had been made. She thought of Jimmy Barry, but not in a sinful way. She was going to marry him. When she did, it would not be a sin. It was blessed, wasn't it, when you were married, and you did it to have children? She was afraid that it would hurt, awfully, to have children. She blushed, realizing that to have children you had to do that. Why was life the way it was? Why couldn't love be like it was now between Jimmy and her, dancing and kisses, and, oh, such wonderful, wonderful feelings? Why did there have to be this other thing? She was afraid of it. What was it like? How did it feel? This question popped up in her mind all the time, and there was no one she knew to whom she could go and find out.

Gosh, when she was married, what would she do? How could she find that out? She was really ashamed of herself because she had such thoughts. But she couldn't always help herself. These thoughts and questions would always come into her mind now. In a dream last night she had asked these questions of herself. She wanted to talk to someone. Today she had made up her mind to talk to Ruth, and she had knocked on Ruth's door. But Ruth had been cranky, probably crying about Joe. She was so sorry for Ruth, but she didn't know what she could do to help her. And even if she did ask Ruth, would Ruth know anything? She was sure Ruth had never done it.

She told herself that she was pretty, and not too fat. She felt good. She was bathed and warm, fragrant with perfume on her body. She posed naked in front of the mirror, holding her hands over her small upright breasts. Then she turned away and sat down on the silk coverlet over her bed. She wished she were dressed and that Jimmy had already called for her. Oh, she had such wonderful evenings with Jimmy. She was so happy. It made her feel sorry for poor Ruth.

But, gee, it was so wonderful to be a young girl in love. And just think, now that she had found the right person, her whole life would be like this. Oh, life was wonderful, wonderful, wonderful.

If there were only not *that* to make one so afraid, so ashamed of oneself. Why must she be so curious? Curiosity killed the cat.

Was it really sinful to think the way she did and to look at herself naked in the mirror? She couldn't help herself sometimes. Jimmy liked her figure. Whenever he had told her that he did, she blushed and was ashamed, but, oh, it was wonderful, wonderful, wonderful, hearing the words from his lips. It was like hearing music you loved. Jimmy had the most wonderful voice. She always used this word. Wonderful, wonderful, wonderful—it was a wonderful word.

She gazed at her image in the mirror again. Boys always liked to look at girls. Often when she walked down the street they would stare at her. Sometimes they'd have such a funny look in their eyes that she'd get all flustered and embarrassed. Was her brother that way, like some boys were? He went out with girls. Might Ruth possibly have ever done this when Joe was alive? Ruth had been so different then. Now she understood why. She'd like to tell Ruth that she understood, but she was afraid to, because Ruth was sometimes so peculiar, and Ruth didn't like to talk about Joe. Her figure was nicer than Ruth's. Ruth was too thin and bony. But, goodness, wasn't she mean to have such thoughts? She was sorry that she had thought this, this proud thought, and she wanted to erase it from her mind.

Erase it! Erase it! Erase it! she told herself silently, because that was what she always said when she wanted to get rid of a bad thought.

When she had been a little girl, she'd been jealous of Ruth going to parties. And now, just think, she went out with the one and only person in the whole world. Think of it, how for years she had wanted to be grown up and engaged, and now she was grown up and engaged.

In three months I'll be a married woman, she told herself, with uncontained joy, but immediately she shuddered with fear.

Oh, she wanted to be Mrs. James Barry so much, and she was so afraid of it.

She opened her mouth wide and her eyes popped in excitement. My goodness, it was almost time for Jimmy to call for her, and she wasn't even dressed. She started dressing in nervous haste.

VII

Jimmy Barry was talking with Andrew, Sr. while Helen finished dressing. He was a ruddy young man of twenty-eight, healthy, good-looking, and well-mannered.

"How are the plans coming along, Jimmy?" Andrew, Sr. asked.

"Fine, Mr. Hyland. That's what I want to tell you about. I thought of a great slogan today. It hits the nail on the head. I think it's going to assure us success. I cracked my brain for the right slogan for over a week, and I didn't have any luck. Then, just like that, I was walking home from church this morning, and it came to me out of a clear sky. I wonder if you'll like it."

"What is it?" Andrew, Sr. asked as Jimmy paused.

"A dime a dog," Jimmy said proudly.

Andrew, Sr. leaned back and looked at the ceiling and reflected. Jimmy sat on the edge of his chair, tensely waiting for Andrew, Sr.'s reaction.

"Sounds pretty good, Jimmy."

Jimmy relaxed. He smiled charmingly and with gratitude.

"Dad likes it. Now we're all set. Dad's signing the contracts this week, and we'll be in business next year. We're going to start with twenty-five hot-dog stands all over the South Side, and as things warrant it, we'll expand and cover the whole city with Barry's hot dog stands. We're going to have Neon lights, modernistic decorations, and we'll employ good-looking girls with high-school educations to serve."

"Fine, fine. I like your plans."

"After we get going, Dad wants me to run the business myself. Until then I'm going to do the promotion. A fraternity brother of mine from school is an advertising writer and he's working on a swell ad. We're going to take a big ad in the papers, announcing Barry's Hot Dog Stands. My picture is going to be at the head of it. We want to get the personal touch in it, you know."

"That sounds good. You ought to make a go of it."

"I know we will."

"I must say, Jimmy, I'm mighty proud to hear you tell me this. I always knew you had enterprise. If more businessmen did what you and your father are doing, we'd snap out of this depression in no time. Before we can get back to where we were, everybody has to get out of the rut they're in. They have the wrong psychology."

"We're starting, too, at just the right time. Costs and wages are at rock bottom, as you know. This thing's going to be done right. I think our slogan is enough to make this proposition a knockout. It's just right, the kind of a slogan that sticks in people's minds. You know, it's been running through my head all day."

"A dime a dog," Andrew, Sr. said.

"Gee, it does sound swell." Jimmy grinned. "A dime a dog."

At this moment Helen shyly entered the room. Jimmy jumped to his feet. Andrew, Sr. gazed at them benignly.

He talked with them a moment, and they left. Then he lit a cigar and puffed at it contentedly. He grew nostalgic, thinking of when he had courted Ellen. That pain in the inside of his arm returned. It radiated down to his little finger. He grew pale with fright. Men his age often had strokes. He bent his little finger and then dug his thumb into it. He felt the nail, and this gave him reassurance. It couldn't be a stroke. It must be neuralgia. Come to think of it, he'd had a touch of neuralgia last April. He sat still for a while, and his thoughts became vague. The pain went away. The best thing in the world for neuralgia was a nice medicinal drink of Bourbon. He got himself a drink. It was good stuff and warmed him.

He turned on the radio, but didn't listen. He turned it off. He heard Andy in the hall and asked where he was going. Andy said that he was going to see a movie. Andrew, Sr. decided that a good movie was just what he needed for relaxation. He said he'd go along.

At a movie he could forget all the troubles of the world, and then he thought that some pancakes would hit the spot. He had a sudden craving for pancakes.

He got his hat, while Andrew, Jr. waited. As they were leaving, Andrew, Sr. remarked that Ruth might want to go with them. They knocked on her door and asked her, but she answered that she'd rather stay home and read. She didn't mind being home alone.

They left.

VIII

Ruth was glad that everyone had gone out. She was sad and lonely in the large empty apartment. But she was by herself. She wasn't afraid. The door was locked. And whatever happened to her could be nothing compared with the tragedy she had already suffered. She curled up on the parlor sofa and munched chocolates while she read the memoirs of a Russian Grand Duchess. The book took her out of herself and her sorrows. Her mind was filled with magnificent court scenes. She saw herself moving amid the royalty of Europe. Reading on, she thought that perhaps it would have been better if there had never been an American Revolution. For if there hadn't been one, America might be part of England today. There would be royalty in America, and royalty always gave a better tone to society. She became bold. She imagined herself as the Princess Ruth, moving among kings, counts, dukes, barons, and princes. Princess Ruth, she repeated to herself as if this were a magic formula.

Her happy fantasies made her attractive, although there was no one to see her.

She gazed around the room, blushing as if she feared someone were watching her and knew her thoughts.

Oh, I am silly, she told herself.

She tried to laugh. The emptiness of the apartment seemed to frighten her. She turned pale. She imagined she heard noises and remained rigid for a moment. Then she ran to the front door. It was bolted, all right.

It was her nerves, that was all.

She returned to the book. But she grew sad and put down the book and stared gloomily about the parlor. Was she as tragic as these Russian princesses and grand duchesses who had suffered so because of the Russian Revolution?

Her thoughts returned to Joe. They seemed unbearable. She went to the piano and played "None but the Lonely Heart" over and over again.

IX

In the Tivoli Theater, Helen and Jimmy had held hands. When she came out of the theater, she scarcely remembered the picture she'd seen. Jimmy got a cab and as soon as they were inside took her in his arms. They went to the Neapolitan Room at the Westgate Hotel. They danced and had chicken sandwiches and coffee. They looked at each other with moon-struck faces, and there were periods when they scarcely talked. When they danced, Jimmy nestled his cheek against her hair. Helen pressed herself closely to him on the dance floor. She was too breathless to talk, and her heart palpitated.

"You look so pretty tonight," Jimmy said to her at the table after another dance.

"You think so?"

"You know I think so."

"What kind of furniture do we want?" she asked, changing the subject because she was afraid of her love, afraid of it as something sinful.

"The best we can get. That's going to be your job."

"Ruth wants to tell me what we ought to have. She always treats me like a big sister. Not that she doesn't want to be help-ful—but, gosh . . ."

Helen became inarticulate and couldn't go on speaking because she wasn't quite sure what she wanted to say.

"Never mind her. It's going to be your home—our home."

They danced again. Would he think her bad because she pressed so close to him? She couldn't help herself. And he seemed to want her to.

"Jimmy?" she murmured demurely.

"What?"

"Tell me you love me."

"You know I do."

"Tell me again."

"I love you."

Jimmy held up his head proudly, wanting to be seen, wanting strangers to know they were in love. When he held her in his arms, he wanted her, wanted her damned badly. He wished they were married already. She was so sweet, so pure, that at times he felt as if a fellow like him, who had had a little ex-perience, was lousy even thinking of wanting to marry her. And he always thought of what would happen on their first night. He had to control himself not to go too far as it was. He pressed her tightly to him.

They danced.

In the cab they kissed again, and they kissed in the hallway until Helen was disheveled. She didn't want to leave him. She had no control over herself. She clung to him and kissed him fiercely.

"I wish we were being married tomorrow," he said, suddenly leaning against a mailbox.

"I do, too," she said.

He looked at her tenderly.

"I suppose you think I'm terrible," she said.

"Why, sweetheart, I'm crazy about you."

"Just think, we'll always be together."

They kissed again, and finally they reluctantly parted.

Outside the door, Helen straightened her hair, smoothed out her dress, and then she went in quietly. There was not a sound in the house. Everyone was asleep. She hurried to her room and stood in the darkness.

Why am I so happy? she asked herself.

Poor little me, I don't deserve this, she told herself as she got ready for bed.

x

Andrew J. Hyland, Sr. discovered himself walking along a dim and narrow street toward a frame house with a red light over the doorway. Although he did not know how he had come to this street, he accepted it as if it were as familiar to him as his own home. He passed darkened houses; their strange, angular shapes jutted out of blackness. Without warning, he became troubled by the memory that he had committed some crime somewhere in some world. His mind clouded with guilt. His face grew grim and fearful. He lowered his head. He walked on, painfully sensing the imminence of an approaching horror. In vain he tried to recall a crime which he now knew he had committed in the desert of some unremembered world. He knew that he had to repent, and how could he repent what he did not even remember?

He came to the dismal wooden house with red light over the doorway.

His white-robed, twelve-year-old daughter, Ruth, rose up at his side, with the wings of an angel.

Don't do it, Father, she pleaded.

I am going in to denounce the iniquitous and to warn them of the Judgment Day, he answered.

Don't lie, Father, she said in tears.

I do what I must, he said, brushing past her.

She knelt in prayer, and her tears watered the ground.

He entered a dimly lit room where men, women, and devils were sinning on the floor in a wild debauch, while other devils laughed raucously and played tinkling music on phallic-shaped banjos.

He watched the sinning men, women, and devils with mounting excitement.

Shame, disgusting shame! he cried out feverishly.

A whore, with the horns of a devil, came to him, swayed her abdomen, and leered. He fixed his eyes intently on her navel. He must sin and he must not sin, and he wouldn't sin, and he took a step forward, wanting her, and he knew that he must not sin, and he told himself that he would not sin.

He fell on his face before her and, groveling, he told her in a weak, cracked voice:

Yes.

The men, women, and devils lined the wall and watched him grovel.

There is more joy in Hell for the ruin of one virtuous man, a devil said in a fiendish voice.

And Andrew J. Hyland, Sr. knew he had gone to Hell.

He rose. He took a step toward the door to flee, and he was where he had been before he took a step. The whore with horns rushed to him with opened arms.

No, he told her feebly, his eyes on her huge navel.

It's too late, she answered with a leer on her scrofulous face.

And there was a loud clamor. A huge rent appeared in the ceiling. The sinners shrank into corners and cowered. Andrew J. Hyland, Sr. looked up and saw the Sacred Heart of Jesus, its precious blood dripping onto the floor beside him.

I am saved, he exclaimed in exultation.

The sainted man has worked miracles, a girl cried out, trembling with fear as the sinners rubbed their faces in slime.

Get down in the slime! the voice of God thundered from the ceiling.

And Andrew J. Hyland, Sr. crawled through slime to join the men, women, and devils, and the whore with horns was beside him.

I was worth it, you old hypocrite, she sneered.

He groaned.

He knew that he was in Hell, damned forever, forever damned. He dare not even lift his head. Damned, damned for the crime he could not remember, damned forever and forever and forever and a day. He was dead, and he was damned, and he was alone in Hell and it was dark. A terrible sadness overcame him. There was nothing left. Only his regrets, regrets without end . . .

Andrew, Sr. woke up in his darkened bedroom. Momentarily remembering his terrible dreams, he was relieved. The dreams faded from memory, and he was troubled by vague regrets. He could not shake off a feeling of regret, and he did not know the reason why he felt this way. He sank back into his pillow and tried to sleep. He was unable to. He wished he hadn't eaten pancakes with Andy after the movie tonight. A man of his age shouldn't do that so late at night. He tossed in bed and began to worry about his health. He was over fifty. He didn't have too many years ahead of him. He had to be very careful. A cold sweat of terror broke out on his body. He became rigid. The very darkness frightened him. He felt a heartburn and he belched. Well, it was just a stomach upset. Nothing to worry about. In fact, he seemed to be feeling better already. He wouldn't worry. And if he were not all right by morning, he'd take a mild laxative. He closed his eyes. He would lie quietly until he fell asleep. He counted sheep and grew drowsy. He drifted into sleep, remaining vaguely conscious of himself lying in bed.

He awoke suddenly, gripped by a crushing pain in his chest. It tightened like a vice around his heart. It seemed as if there were some force within him crushing his lungs into the shape of pancakes. With mounting intensity the pain tore into his fluttering heart. His heart seemed to shrink and shrivel up within him. He sensed the pain as some powerful force, as strong as steel, closing its bands about his lungs to cut off the air from entering them. Then, in his agony, he imagined that a man of enormous weight was sitting on his chest. He grew weaker. He feebly tried to sit up. He lay back in bed. All his attention was focused on the pain, the constriction of heart and lungs within him. He did not cry out. He did nothing. He suffered in silence.

The pain slowly ebbed. He felt a burning sensation inside his chest and in his stomach. He sighed and breathed more easily as air seemed to be entering his lungs. He was taut from the shock of his pain. Another cold sweat of fear broke out on his forehead. He believed that he had almost died. He cowered. Without thought, he hid his head under the sheets. He pulled the sheets down. He lay still, gratified to feel the still ebbing pain. But it seemed to spread out from the region of his heart. He knew that he must lie perfectly still. Perhaps he ought to call his children. He decided not to. The attack had come and gone. He had survived it. The sense of survival in the imminency of death caused him to feel pleasure. He lay unmoving, enjoying even the dying pains within him. Yes, it had been a narrow escape. In the morning he'd see a doctor. God had spared him.

He must pray. Just as he formed the words of *The Act of Contrition* silently to himself, he was torn by another sharp and violent pain. He groped out of bed, switched on the light, and looked at himself in the mirror. He saw the image of a sick man who had, almost in the space of a night, seemed to grow old. Yes, that image was of him, and he had become, without warning, a sick old man. He was too weak to stand. He sat on a chair. Automatically, his head sank until his chin rested on his chest. The constricting fingers of pain were pressing on his heart like pincers controlled by an all-powerful and relentless force. He could not cry out. He could not move. There was no strength left in him. The beating of his heart was a weak and irregularly murmuring whisper, fading, fading into an awful quiet. His whole past life seemed to have been so short, and each second of this silent and tortured present seemed endless. The pain was now so intense that it seemed as if his lungs were crushed. His consciousness was a burning rhythm of pain. In one final instant of lucidity he tried to cry out to his children. Then his trembling thoughts broke up into small fragments. And with one final, violent spasm of pain, one last burning agony, he slumped forward. And Andrew J. Hyland, Sr. slid off the chair, crashing into eternity as his lifeless body hit the floor.

1933-43.

High-School Star

MEMBERS OF THE football squad of Our Lady were scattered over the park athletic field, waiting for the coach to show up. One group was punting back and forth. Another lackadaisically was passing a ball around. Captain Bob Stanton, the wiry quarterback, was flirting with two nursemaids. Big Pat Murphy, a line man, covertly smoked a cigarette and was gabbing away with two sheiks who wore bell-bottomed trousers. Coughlin, the husky tackle who had played the last three games with a broken nose, yelled wildly as he chased Goof McGovern with a switch; Goof was an underweight end whom almost everyone on the squad thought cracked. Tom Kennedy, an end, lay back near the shrubbery, patiently looking at the bulging gloom of the November sky. Two subs who had not gotten into a game all season leaned lethargically against a goal post and said nothing.

George, the coach, came along; he was a burly man. He gruffly ordered the squad to come together, though his kindly, wistful blue eyes belied his stern expression. He called the roll of those present and discovered that seven first- or second-string men were missing. He frowned.

"Do you fellows realize that you are playing one of the strongest prep teams in Cook County?" he snapped at them.

No one answered. He searched face after face before asking if anyone knew anything about the absent squad members. After a few moments of tense silence, various of the players began offering excuses for those who were not present. George turned aside, as if in boredom, and refused to listen.

"Well, Kennedy, how does it happen that you're out today? Couldn't you find anything else to do?" George asked sarcastically.

"I had my croquet lesson yesterday," Tom answered.

No one laughed.

"I hope it took some of the lead out of your feet," George said.

Picking out eleven men, he ordered them to run through signals.

"The rest of you follow along with Kennedy," he ordered.

Bob Stanton chased the eleven men up and down the field for some time in gruelling, boring practice. George followed, forcing them on, shagging their tails, demanding that they show more and more pep. He greeted every fumble, every forgotten signal, every slip with sarcasm.

"Now, Bob, try some passes," he ordered after a while.

The sweating eleven got into position, and Bob called pass signals. He threw a number of passes to Goof McGovern, but Goof missed every one. Goof was a regular end because he had guts and often didn't know when he was hurt. His was a brainless courage which kept him going, lunging, plunging, and wildly tackling no matter how much he was smashed up and battered. Whenever he tackled, he left his feet in a wild and untimed lunge; sometimes he got his man, sometimes he hurled himself in the air, hit the hard ground himself, and looked ridiculous. It was all a matter of chance. In one game he had been knocked silly but had gone on playing until Bob had observed that he didn't know what he was doing. He was defenseless against forward passes. He put up his hands to catch them stiffly, almost like a robot. Sometimes the ball would sail through his outstretched hands and hit him in the face. Now and then he sprained a finger because he didn't know how to catch a pass. For over a month, George patiently had tried to teach Goof how to catch passes, but to no avail.

It was too much to watch Goof miss any more passes, and George told Bob to throw some to the backs. They got butter fingers and began missing them, too. George's face reddened, and he waxed more sarcastic than ever. He kept telling them he'd have to get them all baskets to catch passes.

Tom trailed along with the subs, quietly kidding, making sarcastic remarks about the way Goof tried to catch passes. George kept turning to scowl at him, but said nothing.

George had Bob throw some more to Goof, and he missed four out of five. Tom told a sub that McGovern had better take out accident insurance. He spoke a little too loudly, and everyone heard his crack. Everyone but George laughed.

"Kennedy, take right end, and you can do ten laps around the field for every pass you miss," George said, snarling at Tom.

The team laughed at Kennedy now.

Tom laughed foolishly, slowly moving forward to take Goof's place in line.

"Snap into it!" George yelled at him.

Bob called the signal for a quick pass down the center with the right end running short and cutting in about five yards behind the line of scrimmage, while the left end ran down ten yards and cut in. Bob's pass went straight and high. Tom cut in, leaped into the air, and speared the ball with one hand.

"Pretty lucky," George said.

Tom slowly walked back into position. McGovern asked him how he did it, and he said he had a secret formula. George said there would be no more kidding. McGovern gaped at Tom, half-believing, half-quizzical.

George instructed Bob to keep throwing passes to Tom. He didn't miss a single one. He snared several long ones over his shoulder while on the run. He got another by a head-first dive. But George was relentlessly uncomplimentary and as a disciplinary measure kept Bob throwing passes to Tom until Tom was tired and perspiring.

George finally called off the signal practice and told them he had planned to have a scrimmage today, but that there weren't enough men out. Instead, they would have a blocking drill. He placed McGovern and Mike Hill in defensive end positions and told the rest of them to form two lines.

"You fellows," George said curtly, "should have learned all

of these fundamentals last September. I've drilled you in them thoroughly. But you've got lead in your heads as well as your pants. If you'd learned how to block, you would have shown me a stronger offense than you have this year."

Tom was first in the line, facing McGovern. He waited eagerly. George blew a whistle. Tom ran forward, low, lurched, turned his body into a horizontal fling in mid-air, smashed into McGovern's thighs, and clamped his right elbow around McGovern's right leg. McGovern was neatly smacked down.

"Now, let me see the rest of you do that. Good work, Tom," George said, smiling.

The line kept shifting as one man after another charged to cut down the ends. Tom liked it, leaving his feet, hurtling himself low through the air, knocking the ends off their pins. He tumbled Hill as easily as he had McGovern on his first try. As he left his feet and sailed at his man he forgot himself completely. He felt a keen thrill of power as he hit squarely and with good timing to take a man off his feet so cleanly. For him part of the fun of football was in tackling and cutting a man down. Leaving your feet to drag a runner down in the open field had anything else he could think of skinned all hollow. It was even more thrilling than necking or dancing with a girl.

Tom was ordered to take McGovern's place. This was his second and last season as end, and he knew how to play his position defensively and to fight off offensive players. He knew that an end had only to be a flash of a second quicker than the other fellow. He could take a quick step forward and catch the blocker before the latter had gotten momentum, or else he could side-step him and smack him down with his hands. By staying keyed up and alert, he could usually catch the blocker in that split second of hesitancy, of getting set before he turned to leave his feet, and then it was pie and he wouldn't be knocked out of the play. And he knew how to step in, use his hands, and give blockers some hard socks and slaps when he wanted to. It was all fun, because he knew how to do it, what to do, and because of the thrill of bodily contact, the sense of power gained from doing things right and mastering your opponent.

Tom put on a good show as a defensive end, and George complimented him for his skill.

It was pitch dark when George called off the practice session. He sent the squad through two laps around the long field and told them to turn in. Tom walked back to the showers at the school building. It was a couple of blocks away from the park. He felt good today. He'd had a good workout. Now, at last, he was in condition and clicking. The other players were ahead of him, and some of them were bragging what they would do to Augustine on Saturday. Some of the boys were like that, fond of proving their abilities and their courage with their mouths. Hell, they couldn't win on Saturday. Last year Augustine had beaten them twenty to seven. They'd be lucky if they could hold Augustine as well this year. He remembered the game last year. It had been one of the best games he'd played, and now he enjoyed in memory the praise he'd received. And he recalled Bob's ninety-yard-run for a touchdown. It had been a honey, coming on the second play of the game. Augustine had been caught flat-footed. This year they had all hoped to have a good season, but they hadn't, and now there was no spirit, no life in the squad. Their spirit was all in their faces and their words, and it melted like dripping snow in the sunshine.

"Tom, I'm thinking of keeping you on the side lines tomorrow," George said, suddenly dropping back to talk with him.

Tom didn't answer. He didn't know what to say, because he didn't know what he really thought. He wouldn't sit on the side lines like a dub, especially on a team that hadn't won a game and had scored only three touchdowns all season.

George stared at Tom, nonplused, bewildered. He didn't understand this kid. With deep conviction in his voice, George told Tom that his attitude wasn't right.

"I've got no yen for being a martyr and for becoming a sacrifice," Tom said.

"I can't understand a kid like you."

Tom grinned sheepishly. Did he understand himself? He said

he realized that players should work together and all that, but they should do their own thinking on the field, they should have some initiative. He said playing football was a matter of brains as well as of beef, and of following the coach's orders. George agreed with him, adding the proviso that to use their own judgment players had to have some experience, of course, and that high-school kids generally lacked the experience to play on their own.

Tom grinned. He didn't feel like arguing with George. He liked and respected the man. And he knew George liked him and that he could get away with murder if he wanted to.

"Yes, I think I'm beginning to understand you now," George said reflectively. "I had hopes that you'd have a great season this year, but you've disappointed me. And it's your attitude."

"What's wrong with my attitude?" Tom asked.

"You don't take the game seriously enough," George said, frowning.

They walked on for some yards without talking. Tom became a little embarrassed by the silence. But he said nothing.

"Tom, why do you fool around so much in practice?"

"I don't fool around so much."

"You know you do. Tonight is the first time this year you've shown any real pep and spirit in practice."

"Practice doesn't count."

"You're never going to get anywhere in the battle of life with that attitude. Why, no other coach would put up with a kid like you, not with the way you soldier in practice. I have because I had an intuition that you had good stuff in you . . . and because I like you."

"Hell, why should I break my neck in practice? I'll save that for the game. I like to tackle, block, and catch passes, but the rest of practice bores me."

"I know—you think you're good and think you can get away with a lot. But you don't see what you do to the rest of the team."

"Oh, I'm not so good," Tom said modestly.

"The trouble with you is that you know you are. You play

like a natural-born player. But what about the rest of my boys? You should be an inspiration to them, and you aren't. You don't help the team any."

Tom gazed aside at drab, gray buildings. Many windows were lighted. The autumn darkness made him melancholy. He smelled burning leaves from somewhere near by. A man and woman ambled under a lamplight and passed him. He felt like a louse. He was sorry, heartily sorry that he hadn't acted better toward George, hadn't shown more spirit. He had great respect for George, and George was decent. He treated them white. He wasn't a coach like French O'Brien, the old U. of C. player who was snotty, foul-mouthed, sarcastic. French kicked the tails of his players and slapped their faces all the time. George took care of his players when they were hurt. They could come to him with their problems, and he was sympathetic. He gave them all he could, as a labor of love, refusing to accept a salary from the school. And almost none of them had given George a break. Yes, Tom felt like a louse. George had a reputation to uphold, and here they were, not giving him their best. They played sloppily and haphazardly. They'd stalled through the whole season. They'd broken training, drunk and had parties on nights before games, and hadn't been really serious. He had cut practice at least once a week, and some weeks more than that. Practice was boring, and it was fun to cut it and get away with what you did, just as it was to bum from school and pull a fast one on the priests. If George had been a bull-dozer, then their attitude would be more understandable. But he wasn't. They hadn't been fair to him. He himself hadn't been fair. Yes, he felt mean and little.

"Tom, if you didn't know you were good, you'd have had a better season. You haven't developed the way I hoped you would. Tonight is just about the first time since last September that you've really shown what you can do. You had the makings of a great player in you and you've squandered your senior year fooling around. You could have been All-Catholic this year. Now you won't be. And you haven't made it easier for me,

either. You've let me down. Even though I like you, I'd tell
you to turn in your uniform if I didn't need you."

Tom had nothing to say. His feelings choked up inside him.
He glanced guiltily at his coach. He listened to the wind scraping trees across the street. He asked himself whether or not he
should get sore, at least simulate being angry, in defense of
himself. He wouldn't. He knew he was in the wrong. He said
nothing. He looked interestedly at a girl passing on the other
side of the street. She seemed cute.

"Tom, Saturday's game is your last game. I want to see you
play it the way you should have played for me all season."

Tom gazed after the girl. He wondered who she was.

George patted his shoulder, sent him on to the shower, and
walked off. Tom looked after him, disturbed. He went on to
get undressed and take a shower. The squad was noisy.

With lukewarm water flowing over his skin, Tom felt pretty
good. It was soothing. He stood under the shower for a long
time, forgetting what George had said. He was dreamy. He
liked this. He paid no attention to his noisy team mates, who
were having their usual fun kidding Goof McGovern.

Yes, he'd play a real game on Saturday, and do it for George.
It would be his last chance to leave a good record, a memory
behind him. If he starred, he would be remembered for this
game. He would graduate next June, an acknowledged athletic
hero of the school. The men who picked the All-Catholic team
would probably be watching the game Saturday because Augustine was so good. Maybe there would be college scouts in the
stands, and if he stood out he'd be offered a free ride to a college. Unless he were, he couldn't go, because the old man was
poor and dead set against his going to college. The old man said
he didn't want his son to be a football bum. He could be a
national hero, an All American. Then, wouldn't George be
proud of him? He wanted to play the best game of his career.
And he wanted to do it for George, too.

He knew he hadn't given all he could this year. But then, it
hadn't been entirely his fault. He'd had a succession of minor
injuries, scars and scabs on his knees and elbows, torn ligaments

in his shoulder, minor sprains of his right ankle, bad charley horses at the start of the season. He hadn't been in good shape. Now, he was. After the workout today he felt wonderful. No, it was more than that. He had become swell-headed, a grandstand player. He had seen that the team was no good and had played for the cheers of the spectators, and he hadn't played so well doing it. Yes, that was why he had felt like a louse talking to George. He had wasted the season, wasted his chances. To-morrow he had to redeem himself.

He thought of how he would play a brilliant game. Perhaps, with Bob and him carrying the burden of everything, they'd even beat Augustine.

He came out of the shower, dried himself, and said so-long. He walked home, brooding, moody.

II

The starting eleven for Our Lady ran through signals cursorily. On the other side of the field the heavier Augustine crew, wearing blue jerseys, went through signals with the snap and assurance of a well-trained, confident team. The game was to be played in a semi-pro baseball park, and four or five hundred spectators were present. Tom loafed through signal practice. He felt pretty good. But he didn't see the point of jumping and hopping all over the field now. Coughlin was full of pep and kept telling Tom to snap into it. Tom slouched along. Yes, he felt good today. He was right. And he knew the Augustine style of play. He was ready.

George ambled out on the field, called the boys together, and told them that they had to fight, that no member of the starting team would be taken out of the game unless he had to be carried off the field. These eleven men were going in there and they were going to show him what they were made of. He told Bob to open up and try all their plays, and to rely as much as he could on passing attack, because Augustine outweighed them, and they couldn't outcharge Augustine.

There was a cheer as the teams lined up. Our Lady spread out in a V-shape to receive the kickoff, with the backs ranged in box formation inside the V. Tom caught the kickoff on the ten-yard line near the side lines. He was brought down on the twenty-yard line by a vicious tackle. He shook himself, jumped up, hepped into position. Our Lady used an unbalanced line formation. When Tom hepped into position, he noticed that the tackle opposite him was Moylan, a husky All-Catholic selection from last year. The play was called. Tom tried to box in Moylan. Moylan easily pushed him to the ground and broke up the play. Bob called the signal for a cross buck on the other side of the line. Tom hepped into position a yard behind the line of scrimmage. The ball was snapped. Tom went through and cut down the Augustine right halfback, but it was meaningless. The play had been stopped cold. The next play was off the right side of the line. Tom squatted. With the pass, he leaped forward, turning half-sidewise as he did, clamped his elbow around Moylan's thigh, shoved, grabbed Moylan's heel, and tripped the big tackle with his left foot. The play went through for a five-yard gain. There was a cheer from the stands. Moylan, getting up, told Tom to cut out the holding. Tom looked at him impassively. George hadn't taught him that trick.

With fourth down and five yards to go, Bob signaled for a punt. Tom went out and squatted five yards away from Coughlin, who played beside him. He was down the field with the pass, running wide. He dodged past two backs, who tried to slice him down, and, hearing the thud of the punt, he looked over his left shoulder as he ran on. The ball was sailing high and straight to Cleary, the Augustine quarterback. Tom cut in, left his feet just as Cleary caught the ball, and hit Cleary, driving his right shoulder hard into Cleary's guts. Cleary didn't run the punt back one foot. He was jarred and got up slowly. Pleased with his work, Tom got up and walked away. A perfect tackle. He had left his feet at the right moment. He'd gotten Cleary just above the knees. And Cleary had gone down like a ton of bricks. He'd been really shaken up.

Nonchalant, Tom took his position as the teams lined up. He heard seven rahs, and then his name. He was about seven yards out from Coughlin. He waited. The ball was snapped. Connolly, the hundred-and-sixty-pound Augustine halfback, was carrying the ball, and the interference came at Tom. It was led by Cowell, the one-hundred-and-seventy-five-pound plunging fullback. Tom side-stepped Cowell, fought off the other backs, and turned the play in. Karzmanski, the Our Lady right half, spilled the ball-carrier. One yard gained. More cheers.

Cowell tore through the other side of the line with head up for a first down.

Block, Augustine left halfback, went through the left side of Our Lady's line for five yards. Connolly came around Tom's end and lost a yard. Cowell hit through the center of the line for twenty yards. On the next plunge he fumbled, and Pat Murphy recovered.

Our Lady lost in two off-tackle drives, and Bob punted on the third down. Tom went down the field, dodged Block, turned with the sound of the kick, and changed his direction. Cleary caught the ball sidewise on the run and lit out for the right side lines. Tom tore after him, left his feet, and caught Cleary in a flying tackle from behind, clutching the quarterback just above the ankles. Cleary had been nailed on his ten-yard line and was so shaken up that he had to call time out.

Tom lay on the field as if injured. He didn't know why he was doing this. He was being cheap, playing for the grandstand. He had done it without thinking. It wasn't necessary. But now he had to fake it through, so he stretched out and enjoyed the seven rahs given him by the rooters.

George came out and bent over him, concerned.

"I'm all right. Just shaken up," he said.

He was disgusted with himself. He got up slowly and went through the motions of recovering from being jarred in order not to give himself away.

"I'm all right," he said.

George patted him on the back, told him he was playing a fine game, and complimented him on the way he was covering Bob's punts. Still feeling like a skunk, he took his place in line.

Block started off toward the other end. Tom waited. He

guessed that the old army-end-around play was coming. Last year Augustine had used this play with Block starting it. He had guessed right. Kelly, Augustine's star end, came back toward Tom behind a two-man interference. Tom slipped in between the blockers and hit Kelly head-on, nailing him for a four-yard loss.

Working the other side of Our Lady's line, Augustine ran off a touchdown in six plays. They made another touchdown in a hurry, and at the end of the first quarter they led, fourteen to nothing.

The second quarter opened with Augustine kicking off. Bob ran the kick back thirty-three yards. He called for a quick pass over the center of the line. Tom cut in, leaped between Block and Cowell, speared the pass with one hand, and went on for a first down. He told himself that cheers were music to his ears. But he quickly forgot them and hepped into position. The blue Augustine line cracked Our Lady's offense. Tom couldn't handle Moylan and was smeared and out-charged. Bob punted. Tom went down again, but Block sideswiped him, knocked him down, and held. Cleary ran back the punt to mid-field. Tom got up, yelling to the referee that he had been held, but the referee hadn't seen it.

Augustine made a touchdown in three plays, the last one a pass to Kelly. Our Lady trailed by twenty points.

Bob kicked off to Cleary, who fumbled, recovered, and was downed on his ten-yard line. Connolly plunged off tackle and, as he crossed the scrimmage line, the ball dribbled out of his hands and off to the left. Tom and Coughlin went for it. Tom wanted to recover the fumble and score a touchdown himself. He saw that Coughlin was nearer, and in a flash turned and cut down Cleary who was racing for the ball. Coughlin recovered it and dashed over the goal line for a touchdown. Tom's play was unnoticed. He got up, pleased with what he had done, feeling he had somewhat redeemed himself in his own mind for having feigned injury in order to get easy acclaim. And yet he was disappointed that he hadn't been the one making the touchdown.

Bob booted the goal, and the score stood AUGUSTINE 20, OUR LADY 7.

The Our Lady rooters awoke to cheer with enthusiasm, as if their team had a chance of winning.

Augustine elected to kick.

While the cheers resounded, Cleary kicked off. The ball sailed straight to Tom on the right side lines. Momentarily, he was befuddled and nervous. He caught the ball on the five-yard line and ran inward at a right angle. He was acting as if he were an automaton. Far away there were dimmed cheers that echoed in his ears. He saw red- and blue-jerseyed players like figures in a dream. A flying V of Augustine players converged toward him. Automatically, he reversed his field and went down the side lines oblivious of the cheers. He was in the clear, and only Cleary was ahead of him, standing between Tom and the goal line. His head cleared. He had no fear of Cleary and could get by him. He tore on, ahead of Augustine tacklers. Cleary was slow. He came to meet Tom. Tom feinted to the left and neatly side-stepped Cleary one inch inside of the side lines. But he lost his balance in the action, and before he could regain it and pick up speed again, Cleary lurched at him, slowed him up, and two other tacklers came up to down him from behind. He was tackled on the Augustine forty-yard line, a fifty-five-yard run back.

He got up, slowly, gloomily. He wasn't injured. It had been a soft tackle. But just after he had seemed to be in the clear, he had lost his chance to have taken a kickoff and gone through the whole Augustine team for a touchdown without interference. The chance was gone. He had muffed it. With that one play he might have won himself an All-Catholic selection. A free ride to college. Why, a Rockne scout might even be in the stands. Fame gone! Gone in a fraction of a second when he was off balance.

Time-out was called, and his teammates congratulated him, patted him on the back. He didn't respond.

Play was resumed. He hepped into position. Moylan broke up an off-tackle buck by shoving Tom into the play and spilling the ball-carrier. Two passes were grounded. Bob punted. Tom, covering the punt, missed Cleary, and Cleary ran it back forty yards. Augustine put over another touchdown and led twenty-six to seven.

Our Lady received the kickoff and gained nothing on three plays. Then Stanton punted to Connolly, who was tackled on his own thirty-five-yard line.

Tom snapped out of his gloom. The game had to go on. He decided to change his style and play a smashing end game. He was forgetful of the stands, of everything but the immediate details of the game. He played as if he were a will-less mechanism. He no longer thought of what to do. He acted, but he acted correctly. He charged in and broke up plays before they started, and sensed other plays and waited to turn the ball-carrier in or break them up. He guessed right on passes and dropped back intercepting two and knocking down another one. He liked the game now. He was right today. Our Lady couldn't win. But he was in his element. He found himself wanting Augustine to have the ball so that he could tackle. He wanted more of the thrill of open-field tackling when he left his feet, hurtled in the air, knocked down a man hard and cleanly, tumbling ball-carriers heavier than he as if they were chopped and felled logs. No more glances at the stands, no thoughts—just the game, the game going on play by play, with Tom reacting to each one according to each situation as it unfolded. He was playing the only really good game of football he had ever played. His mind cleared. He was confident and conscious of what he was doing. He was poised. And he had found himself. Yes, at last he had become a football player.

But again, his mind seemed to be clouded. But he played on as before, doing things correctly.

The bark of the gun ending the first half seemed to awaken him as if from a dream. Head down, he trotted slowly off the gridiron, becoming conscious of the crowd again and glowing inwardly as his name was cheered. His features were expressionless, as they always were when he walked off the field. But he couldn't resist making spectacular gestures, and on the side lines he picked up a bucket of water and doused himself for the crowd to see. He sat down, disgusted with himself again. He sat off a little by himself. Slowly, he became conscious of his surroundings. The day was muggy, the sky sunless. There was an echo of talk from the stands. Subs patted him on the back. George squatted and talked to the squad, pointing out mistakes, encouraging, praising, and criticizing. His manner was gentle. He was not sarcastic. He turned toward Tom.

"If it weren't for you and Bob, Tom, I don't know where we'd be," he said.

George went on. Now he tried to fire his squad with fresh enthusiasm. He told Bob to use more passes, and also to run with the ball more himself. He told the linemen to charge harder, to try and get the jump on the Augustine line. Then he told Tom to play right halfback on defense instead of end, and to watch for passes. Tom was glad of these instructions. He would get more chance to tackle. Today he wanted above all else to tackle. Yes, above everything else you did on a football field, he liked to tackle. A defensive halfback got more chance to tackle than an end. Big Cowell was running through their line as if it were paper. He wanted to get Cowell, and he would. Cowell was easy to nail in an open field. If there were scouts in the stands, if there were journalists picking an All-Catholic team for the year, they'd see something. Watch him get Cowell. Cowell got through because of his weight. He ran badly and could be sideswiped easily. And then he wanted to have an open chance at Connolly. Connolly was faster, ran better, and could shift. Well, he'd get him. Watch him go. And, yes, they could just about order the stretcher for big Cowell.

Our Lady trotted back for the second half. Their supporters cheered them. Each player was given seven rahs. The cheers for Bob and Tom were most enthusiastic. They were bearing the brunt of the game for Our Lady.

Bob kicked off, and Connolly was stopped on his thirty-yard line. The team lined up. Tom stood, hands on hip in the defensive right half-back spot, five yards behind the line of scrimmage. Cowell went off the other side of the line for twenty yards. Tom couldn't get near the play.

The teams lined up. Connolly came through tackle. Tom dove through the interference and nailed Connolly, just as he had planned to. There was a pile-on. Someone fell on Tom's right knee.

Coughlin had been knocked dizzy and lay stretched out at mid-field. Time out was called. George hurried onto the field.

Tom stood off by himself. He felt a strange sensation in his left knee. It felt funny. He sat down, pulled up his pants, let down his stocking. His knee didn't exactly hurt, but it felt soft, yes, it felt funny. It was swelling up like a balloon, a soft, spongy swelling. He made a dent in it, and then the skin slowly rose. He stood up. His knee was getting stiff. He pulled up his stocking and fixed his pants. He tried to kick the funny feeling out of his knee, but it seemed to lock on him. He limped around in a circle. He tried to kick. His knee was definitely stiffening on him. Something was wrong. Again he moved about in a circle, trying to exercise the soreness out of it. He wouldn't leave the game. He was having too good a time. He wanted this game to go on and on, and he wanted to go on tackling and intercepting passes. He'd intercept one and make a touchdown. Bob noticed him limping and called attention to it.

"Hurt, Tom?" George asked.

"No."

A look of apprehension crossed his face. George might take him out.

"You're limping."

"Just a bump."

"Let me see it!"

"It's all right," Tom said.

"Sit down and let me see it!"

"There's nothing wrong with me."

"Come on, sit down and let me look at it."

Tom obeyed. George examined his knee.

"You'll have to come out, Tom," George said gently.

"Hell, no! I won't! I'm all right. I tell you, I'm not hurt."

"Better come out. But you played a fine game, Tom."

George walked off the field. Tom limped around the field, holding his helmet in his right hand. His knee was stiff now. He couldn't bend it. He stayed on the field. He wouldn't leave.

McGovern ran out, reported to the referee, and the referee waved to Tom to leave. He stood still a moment, cursing. He tried once again to bend his knee. He felt a sharp pain in it and was frightened. He was angry, deeply disappointed. He limped off the field with his head down. Tears almost came to his eyes. He didn't hear his name being cheered.

"You played a fine game. I knew you had it in you," George said, meeting him at the side lines and patting him on the back.

George then told him to go to the showers and soak his knee in hot water until the game was over. After the game, George would look at it and strap it up.

Tom slowly limped to the showers, his eyes on the ground. A cheer went up. Tom turned and watched Bob, who had just intercepted a pass, race eighty yards for a touchdown. He was thrilled. But he was disappointed. Yes, he was even envious. He limped on slowly. Someone yelled something to him from the stands. He didn't hear it. As he limped into the clubhouse, there was another cheer. It was getting dark.

Alone, he slowly undressed and got under a shower. He winced from the pain in his knee, but the hot water was soothing.

It was all over. His football career was ended. If he had had the chance to play out the game, it might have been different. He had just gotten going. He tried to remember the sensations he had had during the game. He couldn't recall them clearly. He tried to imagine himself still on the field, making miraculous plays. But he was too disheartened even to daydream. But how had he felt during the game? No, he couldn't remember. These things were to be experienced, not remembered. Now they were gone. He was afraid he had played his last game. He had had this tough break just when he was making something

of his ability. And he feared his knee might be so badly injured that, no matter what happened, his career was ended.

He couldn't stand the hot water any longer. He took a quick
cold shower, limped out, dried himself, and sat on a bench in
front of his locker, gloomily looking at his swollen knee and
waiting for George to come in and attend to it. It hurt him. He
winced with pain.

He choked up and almost cried.

1933.

Omar James

I

NATHANIEL JAMES, nicknamed Omar, was a medium-sized, nervous man. His head was oval-shaped, and he had small blue eyes, an aquiline nose, and a thin, wide mouth. His voice was deep, and when he was angry he snarled and roared. At the age of twenty-one, he had gone to work for an express company driving a single wagon. Almost from the beginning he was unpopular with the other wagon men. They considered him a boss's man who spoiled it for everyone else and, because he used many big words, they thought he had a swelled head and was trying to put on the dog. During the War he was promoted to the supervision as a Wagon Dispatcher in one of the Depots. And shortly thereafter he became Chief Wagon Dispatcher in the Wagon Call Department. His new position carried no increase in his pay, nor any change in his status, but nevertheless he prided himself in the honorific title of Chief. He was in charge of the special gas-car service and had authority over the department clerks who answered telephones and kept the wagon record sheets. He considered his new work a great opportunity to prove himself as an express man.

Omar was broken in by Bryan, an old-timer in the business. Bryan worked on the outside in collaboration with the Chief Dispatcher, acting as a sort of trouble shooter. As soon as Omar was left on his own, he began wielding his authority like a relentless taskmaster. He drove the chauffeurs on his special trucks until they began to hate him. He rode the clerks in the office, treated them with unnecessary harshness, and often bawled them out for even the most trivial reasons. He quarreled incessantly with the Route Inspectors, who were his equal in status. His gospel was one of efficiency, and he tried to implement it in the most rigid manner. It became almost impossible for the men working with him to preserve their equilibrium. After watching the clerks answer the telephone calls with hawk-eyes, he became convinced that they were too slow. He ordered the buzzers connected with the call boards to be put in working order. These made such a disturbing racket, he reasoned, that even the laziest of clerks would prefer to answer the phones promptly rather than hear the annoying sound of the buzzers. Even without the buzzers, the Wagon Call Department was so noisy that expressmen called it the Madhouse. No one ever talked in this office; everyone shouted. The buzzers produced an unbearable racket, and even the most experienced clerks, whose ears were trained to hear over the telephone despite the noise, began making mistakes. Nerves were exacerbated. And with things going wrong, Omar met these new difficulties by bawling out the clerks with increasing anger and violence of language. Lambert, the Chief Dispatcher on the night force, kept silencing the buzzers every night. He and Omar had bitter words over this. The dispute was finally taken to Patsy McLaughlin, Superintendent of the Wagon Department, and the Old Man ordered James to abandon use of the buzzers. Omar swallowed this defeat, but was convinced he was misunderstood. And when he became even more harsh with the clerks and chauffeurs he was cursed and disliked on all sides.

Omar wouldn't take a lunch hour unless Bryan were able to relieve him, and this wasn't possible every day. Casey, the most experienced clerk in the office, kept Omar's record sheets and was of invaluable aid to him in dispatching; he could easily have substituted for Omar during the lunch hour. But Omar didn't believe so. However, when Bryan could get into the office, Omar would go out to eat a light lunch, determined that he would relax. On such days, he liked to walk around the streets of the Loop, gazing at the legs of the young girls and thinking of the future. He would daydream of how he would one day retire and claim a homestead in Utah. Then, he would live simply. He would raise cattle, grow his own vegetables, and devote long nights to communion with himself, nature, his books, and God. He was never able to sustain these daydreams, because in the midst of them he would fear that Bryan would slip up on some call that was supposed to be made promptly. Then, if a complaint went to the Old Man, it would be on his record. He wanted responsibility and knew that unless a man accepted it, he could not climb up the ladder. And yet he sympathized with himself because of the penalties he must pay for his position of responsibility. He could never relax properly when he must see to it that big shipments, some of them from the most important business concerns in the country, were waiting on platforms to be picked up by his gascars. If anything went wrong, and the shipments were delayed, they would fail to make the scheduled trains. Such delays cost money. It was his duty to be certain that they didn't happen. Business couldn't come to a standstill because he wanted to take an hour off for lunch. Usually he rushed back to the office in a nervous sweat, only to discover that everything had gone smoothly during his absence.

Omar prided himself on his anxieties, accepting these as proofs that he was a better expressman than most of his colleagues. And he believed, with unshakable faith, that he would one day be rewarded for all he did. He looked ahead to the time when he would become an Assistant Superintendent, and after that, perhaps Superintendent. Sometimes he even saw himself in the role of a big express executive. Spurred on by his ambitions, Omar finally abandoned taking a lunch hour out. Instead, he sent a clerk for sandwiches and coffee and gobbled these down while he worked. He became pasty-faced and developed a chronic condition of spastic colitis. With the passing months, he became more nervous. When he had served as Chief Dispatcher for a year, he was the most unpopular man in the entire wagon supervisions.

II

Omar lived in a frame house on Parnell Avenue near Thirty-fifth Street. It was a cheerless home, but the rent was cheap, and he was economical, saving his money for his old age which he hoped to spend in Utah. Sarah, his wife, was a plain and rather beefy woman, who wanted a nicer home than he would allow. She had long since given up trying to make their home more attractive and satisfied herself with keeping it clean and orderly. She always had his supper ready for him when he came home from work. Unfailingly, he complained to her about how hard a day he had put in. She was troubled because ever since he had become Chief Wagon Dispatcher, he hadn't been looking well. But he paid almost no attention to what she said. He believed that most people wasted too much time eating and was almost scornful of her when she cautioned him about the way he gobbled his food. Concealing his attacks of colitis from her whenever he could, he explained that when an automobile was driven into a gasoline station for fuel, it was serviced quickly. The table was man's filling station. The function of food was that of fueling up the human system. A busy man like himself had no time to waste on fueling. One evening, his wife told him that if he would only eat differently, he would not sleep as restlessly as he did. He answered her by saying that Napoleon Bonaparte had never slept much and that Napoleon was one of the greatest men who had ever lived. She was bewildered. At times she feared he might be a little mad. Unable to change him, she generally resigned herself to silence.

But Omar was often anxious about his health. He took all kinds of pills, and he would have gone to see a doctor but for the fear that he would be ordered to change his habits even at the expense of his ambitions. During his restless hours of sleep, he often had terrifying dreams of death. In his waking hours he was recurrently assailed by the fear that he might have a nervous breakdown. He even tried to change. But he couldn't. He drove himself without let-up, and he exerted all the force of his will to appease his own fears.

Omar devoted most evenings to what he called study. Sarah, having nothing to do, was bored. She became a prey to bitter reflections. She had few friends, and almost no life with her husband. She merely serviced him. She didn't understand why he couldn't be satisfied with what he had already attained at the express company. Often she wished he were back on the wagons, doing a hard day's work each day without having to carry any responsibilities on his shoulders. She had been happier then. But as she now realized, he had even been a little bit peculiar in those days. He had always talked strangely. At first, she had believed this was because he was so brainy. Now, she wasn't sure of that. She no longer loved him. She loved the memory of her feelings during their courting days and when they had gone to Niagara Falls on a honeymoon. Alone, she often took out her souvenirs of those days, postcards, a faded rose, a hotel menu, and other little mementos, and cried over these. She wondered if there were many other wives of her own age who had thoughts and experiences similar to her own. Was hers the lot of many women? She wished for friends with whom she could talk about this. She had none. If all hopes of young love died as hers had, then what was the use of living? If all marriages ended this way, then marriage was awful. But such questions and reflections frightened her. She was ashamed because of them. A person shouldn't think that way. And yet what was a woman to do? She felt guilty. She brooded about herself, fearing there were inadequacies in her own nature. But she had tried to be a good wife. She had done all she could.

She believed that if they had had children, then their lives would have been different. Did Nathaniel want children? She wasn't sure. They had both wanted them when they were first married. Now the subject was never mentioned. She couldn't help it that she was incapable of having children, but she considered this a personal failing on her part. And when she saw other women on the street with their babies, she would be sad. Out of her sadness would come anger, jealousy. Sometimes she would stop little children on the street and speak baby talk with them. Other times she would pause to scold little boys who were noisy or too boisterous. Her moods always oscillated in this fashion. After periods when she blamed herself, she would silently condemn Nathaniel for having been the ruin of her life. But she was too much afraid of him to express what she really thought and felt. A deep resentment slowly grew within her. Bitterly, she even told herself that she was merely her husband's second-hand automobile. She had no other importance in his life. She was of little use to anyone. She felt trapped.

Heedless, in the main unaware of his wife's feelings, Omar worked away, night after night. He pored over maps of Chicago, studying the streets so he would know them by heart. He calculated distances in order to figure out a table of the average driving times of gascars between various locations in Chicago. If he knew these figures, he could often catch chauffeurs who were stalling and soldiering. It was his duty to see that the men working for him gave the company every minute of the time they were paid for, and he was determined to do this. And if he worked out such tables, he might eventually be able to save the company money on gasoline, tires, and the depreciation on trucks. He would be recognized for such a service. He knew that Gas-House McGinty used to do the same thing, but he was scornful of all McGinty's efforts. To him, McGinty was a fat slob with no brains. Omar also read the dictionary, memorizing the definitions of words because he considered good diction and a large vocabulary the mark of a superior man. If he used good diction and displayed a large vocabulary, he would gain the respect of his superiors and of the public. His reputation would grow. It would become easier to advance. And then, he had to read. His favorite author was Dr. Frank Crane, to whose views he subscribed. He also admired newspaper articles written by H. G. Wells and George Bernard Shaw.

Sarah went to see many movies. For a while she had urged him to go with her, but finally she had given this up. She left home troubled and lonely, but eager for the solace she would gain at the neighborhood theater. Once there, she fell into swooning reveries and, associating herself with the heroines, she imagined herself loved frantically by such heroes as Wallace

Reid, Charles Ray, and Patsy Gilbride. She always wished for the pictures never to end. And she left the theaters more saddened than when she had come. She was walking from a world of her dreams back to one of cold and empty reality. When she got home she would find Omar still at the table, working away. Then they went to bed. And they had little sex life. More and more she felt there was nothing left for her to expect from life.

Omar usually woke up tired. On some mornings he vainly tried to bring back to mind the troubled dreams he had experienced. But he was generally unable to remember his dreams. His body would be heavy and his muscles stiff. Lying awake, he would not want to rise. Fears of ill health would even cut him like a razor. Then he would exert his will power. After waking Sarah, he would rush to the bathroom, take his setting-up exercises, shave and wash, and sit down to breakfast. With food, his optimistic spirits would grow. He would become restless, nervous, anxious to get out of the house and on down to the day's work. Every day he hoped that something would happen which would prove his merits and aid him to gain advancement.

He rode to work on crowded streetcars. And one morning, when he shoved his way in from the platform, he found himself wedged face to face with a pretty girl who had dark hair and dark eyes. They were pressed against one another, abdomen to abdomen. He tried to read his newspaper. The car rocked and swayed. Omar was roused. The continuing pressure of the girl's body thrilled and tantalized him. He was grateful for the crowd, and his mind filled with images of lust. He made a show of seeming stolid, as if he were unaware of the girl. Suddenly he was stricken with dread. Unless he were careful, he could be mobbed by other passengers as a moron who molested women. He reasoned with himself as if he were explaining to a stern judge or an angry mob that he was guiltless, that he had done nothing to disturb this girl. He had no intention to annoy her. But he was only human. She was so warm against him. She was young and pretty. And it was years since he had had a girl like this. He could hardly remember what it was like. Sarah, after all, was different. He was afraid he was even beginning to hate her, and that sleeping with her was merely disgusting.

The car stopped. More passengers crowded into it. Now he couldn't edge away from her, even if he wanted to. And she didn't seem to mind either. He began to sense that there might be a friendly and knowing glance in her eyes. He wanted to talk to her, perhaps make a date with her, but he lacked the courage to try. He said nothing. In a few moments the ride would end for him. Possibly he might never see her again. Now was the time to dare. He did not dare. And she was still warm against him.

They both got off the car at Harrison Street. He had still another opportunity. He remained tongue-tied, and consoled himself by proudly thinking how he had acted toward her like a gentleman. He had a pain in his groin. He lagged behind her, and as she turned the corner ahead, he realized that she must work in the telephone exchange on the same street with the Wagon Department. He had acted wisely, for he would see her again. This morning had only been a beginning. The fact that he hadn't been brash, hadn't acted like a masher, would weigh in his favor the next time he saw her. He quickened his gait and saw her enter the telephone building. He felt a fresh sense of himself as a man. After all, he was only thirty-eight. He was in the prime of life.

He entered the office, smiling almost like a cherub. He peeled off his coat, put on his black arm bands, and set to work. He spoke over the telephone with especial dignity and authority, as if she were listening in.

At noon he went out to lunch, turning his work over to Casey. Outside, he found Francis McGillicuddy, the clerk who flirted and talked so much about girls that he was nicknamed Coose, leaning dreamy-eyed against a wall. It was three minutes after twelve, and Francis was due back in the office at twelve. Omar lit into him, warning him that if he knew what was best for him, he'd think less about the skirts. Then Omar had a hasty lunch, and haunted the neighborhood, hoping to see the dark-haired girl.

III

The girl became a part of Omar's life. He was stirred by a new sense of himself. Every morning he left home hoping to see her again. He was eager to be on the streets, and when he was, he ravished young girls with his eyes. If an uncrowded streetcar came along in the morning, he let it pass and waited for the next one. He built endless fantasies about her image. He pondered about her. He wondered what her name was, what she was like, where she lived. In fits of jealousy, he asked himself if she went out often with young fellows. He lived in the expectation of seeing and knowing her. At work, his mind often wandered from business. He went out to lunch every day, leaving Casey to take over if Bryan couldn't relieve him. He dreaded the passage of his lunch hour as much as did any of his clerks. He felt guilty in Sarah's presence. As a consequence, he nagged her, was sharp with her, and even cruelly suggested to her that she should try to take care of her appearance. When she did, he didn't notice it. Lost in his daydreams, he wouldn't even hear her talking to him, and then he'd dismiss her troubled questions with impatience. Couldn't she even let a man think? He found it difficult to read and study. He warred with himself. His resolutions not to think of the girl were all made in vain. He even practiced exercises in concentration in order to make these resolutions effective, but without any success. He woke up with her troubling his mind. He left the house determined to abide by a fresh resolution. But he waited for the streetcar, tense and anxious, inevitably feeling disappointed because morning after morning he didn't see her.

It became apparent to all at the office, and especially to Casey, that Omar was troubled about something. He had difficulty in making decisions when he had to give orders to his chauffeurs. Alternately he worried and fretted, or seemed to be far away from what he was doing. His irritability became more marked. He gave vent to inexplicable angers. And then, after these fits had cooled, he would adroitly get Casey, Francis McGillicuddy, and the others to talk about girls. At such moments he was even genial. He made mistakes himself, even giving addresses of shippers to drivers incorrectly, and then he bawled them out mercilessly, denying that the mistakes had been his. He quarreled more than ever with the Route Inspectors. Every day his character seemed to become more contradictory. When he was out of the office, everyone wondered what was happening to him.

Omar knew what was happening. He couldn't forget the girl. He couldn't abandon his hope of meeting her. What he was unable to understand was why such a chance contact had so unsettled him, had, in fact, practically made a different man of him. At times he was overcome with sorrow for himself and, deep in self-pity, felt as if he were standing by as an impotent spectator watching a man named Nathaniel James lose all control of his will. He feared he was being watched with suspicion. In consequence, he became secretive. And at the same time he talked more and more of his colitis. Finally he was forced to stay home from work for two days because of a particularly severe attack. He went to see a doctor in a mood of terror, fearful that he might even be dying. The doctor diagnosed his case properly, put him on a diet, and cautioned him against overwork. He made new resolutions, but these availed as little as the old ones. He began to believe that others were looking into his mind and even guessing what was troubling him. At times on the streets he would suspect that strangers knew what he was thinking. Then, if his eyes met those of a stranger, he would cast them down and slink off guiltily. He kept telling himself that he had to snap out of it. And he convinced himself that he would if he could only meet her. If he could only sleep with her, he would become his old self once again.

He went to work day after day, a harassed man because he did not see her.

IV

One morning during a sudden lull in the telephone calls, Francis McGillicuddy began flirting with an outside operator with whom he happened to be speaking. Calling her Twinkle Toes, he said he'd bet that she was a raving beauty. After a few moments of conversation, he asked for her name. She told him it was Violet Smith. He told her that he was Mr. McGillicuddy, and suggested meeting her for lunch. The other clerks disregarded the phones in order to listen in on Francis. Omar took it all in, and gave Francis a furious tongue-lashing. While in a rage, it occurred to him that this Violet Smith might be his streetcar girl. He dismissed the idea. Such coincidences only happened in story books. And his girl was too superior to be wasting time on cheap clerks like McGillicuddy. But he swelled with anger, and within five minutes he again raved at McGillicuddy. Turning back to work, he reflected that his clerks were all lazy and irresponsible kids who took nothing but skirts seriously. He warned them all that the next one who flirted over the phones could go into the front office and get his time. A far-off look came into his eyes. He became sad. These kids were in the full flush of youth and he was thirty-eight. His own youth had rushed by him. Now, he was hungering for it. He felt very old.

Violet became a topic of bawdy conversation in the office. Francis returned from lunch with her, beaming and giggling. Omar even joined in with the others and razzed Francis. Fresh nostalgia for his youth softened him. Francis proudly announced that he had Violet dated up for the evening. Omar again thought that Violet might be the girl. He casually queried Francis about her looks. Francis raved about her beauty, but his description was vague in details. Omar was fearfully uncertain. It might be the same girl. He tried to forget her in a rush of work. Around five o'clock, she came back to his mind. He realized that he was reverting to the moods of his adolescence. He was becoming more foolish than these punk clerks. Fortunately, no one knew his secret. But, still, he was not acting like a man. He tried to justify himself. After all, this sort of thing could happen to any man. And nothing irreparable had happened. If Violet were the girl, and she had a crush on Francis, let it be. He confidently believed that he had suddenly become cured of his need for the girl. It was all over now. And since it was, he could smile at himself. When Francis had left at five o'clock, Omar spoke of him with contempt.

That night he slept badly. He left home the next morning in a state of excitement. She wasn't on his car. He rushed into the office, anxious to hear what Francis had to say about his date. But Francis had not come down. He got angry when Francis still had not showed up at ten after eight. He said it was nobody's business what the clerks did at night, but if they had dates which prevented them from getting to work on time, they could get new jobs. Just then Francis phoned in to say that he couldn't come to work because he had a sprained ankle. Omar was surly to him on the telephone. When Omar told everyone why Francis was off, they all laughed. Here was a new office joke. Casey said he'd heard of fellows getting into all kinds of trouble over it, but that this was the first time he had ever heard of a fellow spraining his ankle in the well-known position. All morning someone kept referring to Francis and Violet, and it was generally agreed that she must be *some* dame all right, or else she couldn't have sprained Francis' ankle. Omar spoke of the affair with blunt obscenity. And the creeping suspicion that Violet was really the girl came over him. He was almost convinced now.

Suddenly he realized that he had been foolish. All this time he had gone looking for her at twelve o'clock. She probably went out to lunch at eleven. If he changed his own lunch hour, he'd see her. Francis' sprained ankle was a stroke of good fortune. He might see her today. He was restless all morning, and he left Casey in charge at eleven o'clock, saying that he had some errands to attend to. He hastened out of the office and, as he got downstairs, she passed him on the street. He gazed at her with eyes of recognition. She didn't notice him. He followed her into a drugstore on South Dearborn Street and sat at the fountain while she was near him at a table, chatting with several girls. The place was noisy, and he strained his ears to overhear what she said. He caught some references to a fellow, but was unable to hear what the fellow's name was. Then he heard her giggle. Disillusioned, he thought her conversation was all chatter. She was a silly girl. But he kept looking around at her until their eyes met. Hers were cold. This proved there was no use in his considering her any more. He had been a fool. Now he would learn his lesson and forget the whole episode. With this determination fixed in his mind, he left the drugstore. He walked around the Loop, trying to assure himself that this business was settled once and for all. Yes, he was certain he was cured of her.

He returned to the office poised and self-assured.

v

Omar's confidence had been false. He could not give up the idea of the girl; he was as distracted as ever. He saw her once again on the street and looked at her with pleading eyes. She passed him by. He brooded over his hesitancy in speaking to her.

Francis was off for a week. Then he limped into the office at eight o'clock, and was immediately prodded with questions about Violet. He said that after leaving her on his date, he had slipped on a banana peel. Everyone thought this was a hot one, and they kidded him without let-up. He refused to answer point blank as to whether or not he had been successful with Violet. Instead, he replied with giggling evasions and insinuations. Omar watched him all day, filled with hatred. He decided to fire Francis at the first opportunity. But he was immediately ashamed of himself for even thinking of such action. It would be grossly unfair. He had to be fair and honorable. That was his code. All was fair in love and war, wasn't it? He knew that if he acted on this principle, he would feel guilty about it for the rest of his life. But if he did find a good excuse for firing Francis, that would be different. When Francis tried to get Violet on the telephone, Omar told him that if he bar-

bered any more with girls, he would be fired. He said that this
was a final warning.

That night, Omar made a decision. He determined that the
next day he would leave the office at five o'clock and meet her
outside the telephone exchange. He would speak to her; in fact,
he would try to date her for the evening then and there. This
plan seemed wild to him. He changed his mind and decided to
abandon it. He sent Sarah to the movies and paced back and
forth in the dining room, restless, distraught. He determined
that whether or not his plan were wild, he would carry it out.
He couldn't go on as he had any longer. When Sarah came home
from the movies, he told her he wouldn't be home for supper
tomorrow evening. He had to attend a dinner of the Expressmen's Club. She expressed surprise that he hadn't mentioned
this before. He told her curtly that he'd forgotten about it.

The next morning he woke up full of confidence that his
plan would succeed. Stranger things than this had happened
in life. In all ventures one had to be bold and daring, and he
would be. He shaved carefully and put on his Sunday blue suit.
He left home at his usual time, but didn't go to the office. He
phoned that he would be late. He waited until the bank in which
he deposited his money was open, and he drew out twenty-five
dollars, getting it in brand-new single dollar bills. He stuffed
these in his wallet and then looked at them. The very feel of the
wallet gave him tremendous confidence. When he reported for
work Casey asked him if he were seeing a cutie on the side. Omar
said that he had business. Francis also had come to work dressed
up. This made Omar acutely apprehensive. But Francis said
that he had to attend a Holy Name affair.

All day Omar alternated between hope and despair. But he
continued to feel confident that he would catch her in front
of the telephone building and that they'd go to dinner together. If he wasn't able to go the full distance tonight, he'd
lay out the ground so that he could in the very near future.
Sexual fantasies ran through his mind all day. Several times he
went to the lavatory merely in order to look at the money in his
wallet. About two o'clock he had a fit of utter despondency.

He realized that he was a fool. He decided to give up his plan. He would meet her on the street, talk to her, and then gradually get to know her before he suggested taking her out. And, above all else, he ought to make certain whether or not she were Violet Smith. But he knew that he was going to try and carry out his plan. He was determined. And it was a daring thing to do. In a small way it was Napoleonic.

Time passed very slowly for Omar. Casey eyed him quizzically. He wasn't acting normally. He was dreamy, inattentive to work. He couldn't conceal that he had something on his mind.

Four-thirty finally arrived. He cleaned up carefully in the lavatory and at a few minutes before five he departed, leaving the office in charge of Heinie Mueller. He hurried to the corner of Harrison Street and waited there nervously for about a minute. It seemed much longer than merely sixty seconds Then he planted himself in front of the telephone building. Some of his clerks might pass him any minute now, and he was anxious about this possibility. But he calculated that it would take them a few minutes to wash up, leave, get their time cards punched, and pass this spot. At all events, he'd take the chance—he would now take any chance to win this girl. If he succeeded, if Casey or someone else from the company saw him walking off with her, he would gain the reputation of being a romantic person. Then they would all know that there were no flies on Omar James.

Girls poured out of the telephone building, many of them chattering and laughing. He became tense. He watched them sharply. And there she was. He had forgotten how beautiful she was. Tears came to his eyes. He took a step toward her. His vision became blurred. Losing all self-control, he approached her like a man in a dream. In a husky, frantic tone of voice, he asked her if she didn't remember him. She stared at him blankly. Then an expression of annoyance crossed her face. He asked her if she didn't remember that morning on the streetcar. She snapped at him that he had the wrong number. With a note of lustful insinuation in his words, he asked her what she was doing for the evening. She laughed in his face, repeating that he had the wrong number. She glanced off impatiently. He was sure now that she was Violet Smith. She was probably waiting for Francis. And that dirty liar had said that he didn't have a date tonight and was going to some Holy Name affair. He was a lying, dishonest little bastard. Omar was desperate. He clutched her arm awkwardly and suggested that they go to a nice swell restaurant for dinner. She jerked away from him with a look of horror. At that moment he turned and saw Francis approaching. Francis waved to her. She called back. Omar slunk off, hanging his head. But he couldn't resist the impulse to turn around. He saw the girl talking to Francis and pointing at him. Utterly confused, he ran to Harrison Street. He turned the corner and stopped, out of breath. He peeked around the corner, but they were gone. He felt very tired.

Why had he done this? Why had he been such a fool?

VI

Omar James was a forlorn spectacle as he paced the streets of the Loop. His feet carried him on aimlessly. His mind and his senses were confused as crowds of people passed him. Jarring traffic noises and the strident cries of newsboys bombarded his unhearing ears. He brooded over the fact that he did not have a friend. He had humiliated himself, turned himself into a ridiculous figure. He walked on and on, dwelling on what he had done. He wanted Violet more than ever. He could not ever have her. And he was doomed to spend the rest of his life working where he would be jeered at because of the way he had tried to get her. He walked and walked, feeling he was an old man. Suddenly he thought of Utah. If he could only go there.

He walked on. It was after six, and the crowds were still flooding the sidewalk. The mere pressure of so many hurrying people caused him to feel more acutely alone. These strangers didn't have to face the humiliation that was his. He envied them. He wished he were one of them. What were Francis and Violet doing? What were they saying? Were they talking about him? Were they laughing at him? Perhaps he could catch

Francis in the morning and fix it up with him not to say anything. Yes, that was what he would do. He was Francis' boss. He
could frighten him. Or else he could make it easy for Francis in
the office. This idea was repugnant to him. Where was his honor?
Was this the kind of a man he had become? He could deny
everything that Francis said. But if he did, would his word be
taken against Francis'? Would it when so many of the dumb
bastards in the company hated him for his superiority and
wanted to get the goods on him? His superiority? God, a man
didn't understand himself. There was so much more in a man's
nature than he ever realized. When a man was on the threshold
of his forties, he thought that his life was settled, organized.
But it wasn't. What would he do? How would he face this
humiliation?

He resolved to face it and let them say what they wanted to.
He would be strong in the face of their ridicule. He would now
prove that he was a man of firm character. He would meet them
with quiet courage. It was the hardest way, but, also, it was the
noblest. He had the mettle to stand up to the cheap ridicule of
cheap people. What if he would be a lonely figure in the company? He could do that with pride and dignity. He would not
let this passing folly ruin his life. Nathaniel James was not that
kind of a man.

He looked longingly and impulsively after a doll-faced girl
who walked with swaying hips. He had an impulse to follow
her. Deliberately, he turned in the other direction. From now
on, in his life mind would be master of matter.

Buoyed by his resolution, he ate a meal in an inexpensive
restaurant on Randolph near State Street.

VII

After eating, Omar didn't know what to do with himself.
He couldn't go home because of the excuse he had given his
wife. He stood in front of the restaurant picking his teeth. He
watched three young lads stride by and gazed after them with
wistful eyes. Yes, they were lucky they were still young and
without responsibilities. The public library was near by, and

he could go there and spend the evening reading for the improvement of his mind. He didn't want to. He thought of finding a whore, and decided that he didn't want that, either. He walked about the Loop until he was footsore, and he thought and brooded until he was emotionally and morally exhausted. Then he queued up in a moving line of men who were purchasing tickets to a burlesque show on South State Street. There were two pimply-faced youths immediately in front of him. He gazed at them with contempt. They were afraid to get it directly and so they came here instead. But who was he to be throwing stones from a glass house? Ashamed of himself, he bought a ticket and hurried inside.

He sat in the front of the old theater, munching chocolates and anxiously waiting for the show to begin. He suddenly became terrified lest someone from the express company might be in the theater and see him. Expressmen often went to burlesque shows. He slid down further in his seat. A sweat broke out on his forehead. After hearing about his effort to pick up Violet, it would be too much if they knew he had then come here. That would be more than he could bear. He wished he hadn't come here to waste time and money. He felt like leaving. But then, suppose as he walked out an expressman in the audience spotted him. He was better off sitting where he was. And this was where he had come after all the fine resolutions he'd just made. He lost all of his confidence. He determined that, after seeing the show, he'd go home and in the morning face the music with absolute calm.

The orchestra played a jingling, suggestive tune. The lights went out. The curtain went up. The audience applauded as scantily clad girls trotted on the stage. Then a painted leading lady appeared and led the girls in an abdominal dance. Men cheered and clapped as she rolled her stomach orgiastically. Omar tried to feel aloof. He was filled with self-disgust, but he watched intently. He began to perspire. He knew that he was the same as most of the other men present. Like them, he was frustrated. They were yelling for the girls to take everything off. He shared their desires. He felt that something would happen to him if these girls would only remove their strips of loin cloth and the little bands which covered their breasts. When the ensemble act ended, a roar went up for the girls to take off everything. Omar clapped vigorously; his mouth was parched. The girls trotted off stage, but the applause was so deafening that they returned for an encore. When it was finished, the leading lady followed the chorus girls to the wings. She stood there, shaking her buttocks. She faced about, grimaced, and removed her breast strap. She shook her flabby breasts at the audience for about ten seconds and then disappeared. Omar heard wild yells all around him.

An act followed with burlesqued Jewish comedians. Omar enjoyed it, laughing heartily. He forgot everything that had been on his mind, leaned slightly forward, and hung on each of the jokes. Then the curtain rose on a darkened stage. Suggestive groans were heard. Floodlights gradually revealed a man and woman in bed. An enraged man rushed through a door. Finding the couple in bed, his hand went to his heart in a gesture of despair. The man in bed suddenly jumped out. He wore no trousers. He grabbed a pair of trousers and ran toward the door. The other man pulled out a gun and shot. The philanderer clutched his buttocks, turned around, and died melodramatically by the footlights. The enraged husband dragged the woman out of bed. As he pulled her hand, a third male crawled from under the bed and plopped the visitor over the head with a mallet. The curtain fell to applause and laughter. Omar guffawed.

The girls then reappeared and did some hootchie-kootchie dances. The audience reacted as it had to the opening act.

Following the girls, there was an act with a baggy-eyed vaudevillian in white duck trousers and his stooge named Algernon. The act ended with jokes about homosexuals.

The show continued. There were more acts and jokes, and between these the girls returned to dance. After the last ensemble act, the leading lady appeared for a final encore. She was cheered when she threw away her breast strap. Clad only in a purple loin cloth, she dropped down onto the piano in the pit. She danced, rolled, twisted, wriggled and squirmed until the audience raved like madmen. She ran into the wings. Suddenly her purple loin cloth was thrown on stage. The curtain descended slowly. The cries of the audience were ear-splitting.

Omar felt limp. He rose slowly and pushed his way outside. South State Street seemed garish. He was depressed. Now he must again face a dull and humiliating reality. And this show was all he had gotten out of the evening on which he risked all hopes, even his very dignity. He thought of Francis and Violet. What were they doing? What should he do now? He didn't want to go home. He had wasted the evening, and he was excited. He thought of the dancing girls and wished he knew one of them. What should he do with himself? What would he do tomorrow morning? How could he face everyone at the office?

He watched people pass. The lights of the marquee were out. An express truck rumbled by, and he turned his head to avoid being recognized by the driver. He tried to think. His mind seemed blank. He felt as if there were bubbles of air in his mind.

Slowly, he walked away. A pimp approached him. He followed the man a few yards and then up the wooden stairway of a cheap and grimy hotel. He didn't care what happened. His shoulders sagged as he entered a noisy room on the second floor.

Omar didn't go to work the next day. He stayed home for three days, and that was when he had a nervous breakdown and was sent to a sanitarium.

1931-43.

Autumn Afternoon

THE SHRIVELING PARK proclaimed November. There was no
sun, only a rough wind that was scattering the dead leaves.
It rolled them down a small incline, so that they resembled a
drove of scurrying, frightened animals. The boy, Tim Kenny,
waded through stiffened leaves, crunching them underfoot.
Stopping at a spot where the ground was a gray-black circle of
dirt, he picked up stray leaves, examined their structures,
cracked and tore them. He crushed them into little wads and
threw them. They scattered and floated to the ground. He sat
down in the leaves and gazed at the friendless park horizon.
Before him, the dead grass slowly descended to the steely lagoon; across the water was the knob of a small hill with trees on
it. The steady wind rattled in the trees. Listening to the
monotonous wind, Tim felt shivery and afraid, as if he were
a small child instead of a boy of twelve. He was filled with as
much dread as if he were sleeping alone in the dark for the first
time and were horrified, stricken dumb with terror by the
noises and sounds which the night made strange. If only he
could see the signs or a figure of a human being! But the park
was forlorn. And the sky curved down in the distance like the
arch of some enormous, mysterious, and awe-inspiring structure.

Getting up, he walked down to the edge of the small lagoon,
where the chilled water was whipped into small waves that
slapped against the narrow line of pebbles on the shore. He
gazed across at the small hills of the wooded island, observing

the trees, the desolation which the season had wrought upon nature. The hills seemed to him like faces of the dead. He picked up a twig and walked on, swinging it and enjoying the swishing sound it made. A brood of sparrows suddenly descended on the island, and they clucked and fought like housewives, transforming the scene before him, bringing life to it. He watched them; an old wish came back to him, the wish that he might talk with birds.

He strolled on, falling into hurt, boyish retrospection. Billy Malone had started it. Billy was a goop, and he hated him. Billy was always saying things against him. He had to wear old hand-me-down clothes from his brothers, and Billy always laughed at him about them. Many of his classmates did. They had fathers to buy them clothes. Billy's mother didn't work. His mother took in washing. All day long in school, Billy had been doing things. He had beat his pen on the desk, imitating a band; he had made clucking noises with his mouth; he had giddapped like a pack of galloping horses. Billy always said things that made everyone around him laugh, even when you didn't want to. In class Billy was always poking him in the back. All day today Billy had kept going, and Sister Teresa had got sore because of the disturbances Billy had caused. This afternoon she had lost her head and blamed him for what Billy had been doing. He had denied it, and she had told him he ought to be ashamed of himself to lie like that when his mother worked so hard. The whole class knew he was poor, and she didn't have to say that. Probably everyone in class knew his mother couldn't afford to pay his tuition and that she had had to go to Father Kiley, the parish priest, and ask him to let her children in school free. Maybe if his father hadn't been killed, they wouldn't be so poor and he wouldn't be treated the way he was. He had never seen his father. His father had been held up and shot on the day he was born. He was proud of his father, even if Papa was dead. Mama told him what a fighter his father had been. On the night he had been killed, he had beaten up three burglars who had tried to take his pay from him. And then he had been held up by someone else, and his father had gone after the burglar who had a gun. Even though he had been shot, his father had knocked the robber out, and then the police had caught him. The robber had been hung. He wanted to be like his father. But he couldn't go on fighting so many kids all the time. He didn't like to fight and had to make himself do it. Sister Teresa hadn't been fair to him. He was the poorest boy in class, and nobody was ever fair to him. She had bawled him out in front of the class, said all sorts of things to him, and Mary Latham had heard it all. He had refused to admit that he was sorry for things he hadn't done. So she had made him come up to her in the front of the room and she had beaten him over the knuckles with the edge of her ruler. His knuckles were still red and bruised. He had cried, not because of the pain, but because it was so unfair, and in his tears he had tried to tell her that he had done nothing. The whole class had seen him cry. Mary Latham had. And then Sister had lost her temper again, just like water boiling over a kettle, and she had screamed at him:

"Timothy Kenny, you're a perfectly worthless boy. You're good for nothing. All you ever do is start fights and make trouble. You're a worthless roughneck, and if you don't mend your ways, you will break your poor mother's heart and die on the gallows."

She had screamed at him, and then she had made him go into the dressing room and stay there for the rest of the afternoon. She had promised to punish him properly after classes.

He had spent a long time in the dressing room, thinking, and afraid. He'd wished he didn't have to go to school but could work like his brothers. His mother wouldn't let him quit until he graduated. And only last week he had lost his job at the flower store, and it hadn't been his fault. It had seemed that this afternoon would never end. He had looked at the hats and coats of everyone in the class. He had sulked, and walked up and down the narrow room, thinking of how he would get even. He had hated Sister Teresa, even though she was a nun, and it was a sin to hate a nun. And then he had touched blonde Mary Latham's red sweater. He had kissed it as if it were sacred, like the relic of a saint. It was like something holy on the altar of the church next door to the school. His feeling for her was religious, the same as it was for the saints and the martyrs.

And when school was over they had all come in for their hats and coats. The boys had come in first, and they had laughed at him and called him names. And then the girls had come. Some of them had not spoken. Others had made faces at him. Mary Latham had looked at him as if he were dirt under her feet. She had said:

"Look at roughneck Timmy Kenny."

When she said that he'd felt as if his heart had dropped out of him. He hadn't cared what happened to him. They all left, and Sister Teresa went with them, to see that they marched out of school in line. It was then that he had made up his mind he wouldn't stay after school and let her beat him up for something he hadn't done. No, he hadn't cared what happened to him and he had sneaked down the back stairs.

He had caught up with some of the kids at Garfield Boulevard and Wells Street. Billy had started on him, and he had lost his head, walked up to him, and smashed him in the nose. That was what his father would have done, wasn't it? All of them had gotten sore and told him to pick on someone who could fight. He had challenged them all. Then he had challenged Pug Foley. His father was a Doctor with a lot of money. Whenever anyone at home was sick, they had to see Dr. Foley, and he never charged them a cent. Walter Foley knew this, and one day he had told Mary Latham all about it. Everybody said that Walter Foley could fight. But Walter had refused to fight him fair and square. Foley had said he wouldn't soil his hands on a roughneck that everyone looked down on. And then they had laughed at him and said that he was crazy about Mary Latham, and that she liked Walter Foley and didn't care one-two-three for him. They had said things to him he could never forgive or forget. They had laughed at him because he was so poor. They said they were going to play football in Walter Foley's yard and that he couldn't play with them. And just before they ran off, they had said his father had been killed in a drunken fight. He had picked up stones and thrown them after the guys. He had cried.

He had stood on the corner, feeling so all-alone. His all-alone feeling had made him feel cut off from everyone in the world. He had wiped his eyes and started walking, not thinking where he was going, walking like someone in his sleep. He had thought of his father. He had imagined he was talking to his father in Heaven, explaining to Papa how he felt. He had walked by the front of the school. Sister Teresa was on the steps, and she called to him, ordering him to come to her. He had looked at her for a moment, stopped in his tracks. And then he had run off before he had had time to think of what he was doing. She must have called to him more than once. His conscience told him he shouldn't have disobeyed her, and yet he had done it. He had had to do what he had done. Maybe his bad angel had made him run away. When he was out of her sight, he had stopped. Then he had thought of how he was now in more trouble than he had even been in before. He had stood looking at the bakery across the street. Mama sometimes sent him there to buy stale bread. Everyone in his class knew this and taunted him because his mother tried to save money by buying stale bread. He used to hang around the bakery and dream of how he would drive a bakery wagon when he was bigger, instead of working for the express company the way his two oldest brothers did.

Then he had walked on. He had thought about what had happened, telling himself he hadn't been in the wrong. Sister Teresa had been. She had made a mistake. She would never admit she made mistakes. Wasn't that wrong, even if she was a nun?

He had walked all the way over here to Washington Park. He had forgotten his troubles. He had wandered on and on, sleepy-minded, wishing for things to happen to him so he could just do something like flying away. He had wished the War had never ended back in 1918 when he was small. He had wished it had gone on and on until he would be old enough to be a soldier and go over there and be the American hero who captured Kaiser Bill.

Tim drifted on along the edge of the lagoon and came to the squat stone bridge that connected the south end of Washington Park with the wooded island. He leaned over the iron railing on the bridge, looking at the water below him. He saw his image distorted on its surface. Then he saw a school of minnows, looking like silver arrows darting in the water. He noticed the shadows from the bridges and the shadows of the trees and shrubbery on both banks digging their reflection in the lagoon. The shadow images on the water made the lagoon seem deeper than it was. Some leaves floated by on the back of the current. He liked to watch leaves floating like that. He imagined the lagoon was a river in the jungle, and that its king was a river giant who was always capturing people and making them his slaves. He had captured Mary Latham, and he was going to . . . rape . . . her. It was terrible. But then Tim Kenny, braver even than Eddie Polo or William S. Hart, arrived on the scene and rescued her. He and the river giant fought a great battle in the water, with splashing as if it might be a fight to the death between a shark and a whale. And so Tim Kenny saved blonde Mary Latham, and he sent her back to civilization, while he walked proudly on, scornful of her, ready for new adventures in the jungle. He gazed on at the lagoon, brooding over a boy's troubles.

As he moved onto the wooded island, dusk was building barriers against the paling day. Walking slowly along the cindery dirt-black bridle path that was flanked by wind-twisted trees and shrubbery, he was suddenly frightened, terrified. He would be expelled from school. He wouldn't be allowed back at school until his mother or his older brother went to see Sister Teresa. They might even have to go to Father Kiley, and he was more afraid of Father Kiley than he was even of Sister Teresa. And what wouldn't there be to pay? His oldest brother would beat the living hell out of him. Yes, his older brother, Pat, would beat him up and yell at him. Pat would talk of how he worked so hard and let a punk little brother become a tramp at school. He listened to the wind, and its ominous whistle seemed like the snarl of the Devil on the hunt for souls. He took his top out of his pocket and practiced letting it down the string. That stopped him from thinking and worrying. He broke all his records, and this gave him a feeling of triumph. He made fifteen letting-the-top-down-the-string frontward, and forty-nine backward; then he did fourteen letting-it-down in a combination of both frontward and backward. A man with a shaggy airedale on leash passed. He put his top back in his pocket and watched the man and the dog. The man unleashed the airedale, and the dog bounded and ran about joyfully. He wished he had a dog like that.

He walked on, and things kept making him sad: the wind, the bent, bare trees, the dead grass, the loneliness of the park. Yes, he wanted to talk to someone, something, birds, that dog, the lagoon, the sky, a tree, something. He wanted to feel that they were understanding, that he could take them and own them as some boys owned dogs. He wanted to make them a part of himself, the way his religious feeling for Mary Latham was a part of himself. There was nothing to talk to. He heard no human sounds, and saw only a surface of things and colors, of blackish-purples, grays, shriveled greens, dry yellows, and the cracking tan of the leaves. All these colors were fading in the dusk and, like everything else in the park, they seemed to be part of some great sorrow, a sorrow greater than his. He told himself that the park was sad. He told himself that the park was very sad. He sat down on a couch of leaves under a large and twisted oak tree, and he leaned his head against the gray, rough-surfaced bark. It hurt his head a little, but he didn't care. He listened to park noises, and then, far away, he heard dim echoes of kids playing somewhere. He wished he had someone to play with. He observed small details of the scene about him. The horse path was on his left. Straight in front of him was the small, black mass of autumn-killed shrubbery. Before this there was a gray patch of dirt, surrounded by the yellow corpse of the grass. He looked up at the sky; it seemed like a black coffin lid that was closing down over the earth.

Sitting there, he planned revenges. A squirrel, shying forward, distracted his attention. He watched it hopping hesitantly in his direction, but when he stirred, the animal fled and disappeared up a tree. He sat back in the leaves. The wind swirled them around him, and their noises deepened his sense of melancholy; these noises grew and beat into a terrible monotony. He imagined that the Park was Purgatory and that the wind was the voice of God, speaking in Wrath and Justice. All the cracking leaves were souls tossed about in punishment for their sins on earth. There they were, all helpless. They waited for winter to freeze over them because, after all of the suffering and snow, spring would come, and then its winds would be the voice of God speaking in Mercy, and the souls of the dead would be all green again, happy in the trees with the sun of Heaven warm and shining on them. Every dead leaf was a soul. He picked up the dead souls and crunched them, flung their torn pieces into the wind. The first dead soul was that of Walter Foley. . . . The last was that of Mary Latham. He tore her dead soul into fragments and dropped them, one by one. He kissed the last fragment of the leaf.

Chilled, Tim arose and walked on, thinking, dreaming as he slouched along. He paused at the low wooden bridge which led off from the northern end of the wooded island. Its logs seemed old and even a little rotted. He had heard that it was dangerous and about to be condemned. What if it collapsed with him on it? Leaning over the log rail, he imagined the bridge falling apart with him and Mary Latham on it, he somehow managing to save her life, even though he would be killed. On a picnic he had stood on this bridge and talked to her. That day, she had been friendly. He walked on, crossed the stepping stones below the log bridge, and followed the little stream, which ran like an avenue through shrubbery from the small spring which was the source of the lagoon. The spring was clear, pure as the soul of Mary Latham. It gurgled up, causing small bubbles. A semicircular mound of boulders surrounded it. Leaning over, he drank. The water was too cold, and his stomach began to ache. Still, he drank more, feeling that he was cleansing himself in some symbolical manner. He felt as if he were drawing power and courage from a blessed and magic spring, and that with

this power he would control his future. He was drawing into
himself a power that would make Mary Latham like him, love
him.

Exalted, his dirty face shining with a new happiness, he
skipped on. He crossed the driveway which divided the park.
He came to the ball field, vast and blurred in the twilight. The
wind crossed it in an onslaught. He didn't care about anything.
He was happy and walked with his face to the wind. Suddenly
he was conscious of shouting boys playing football. He looked
toward the gridiron, its goal posts vividly white against the
accumulating darkness of evening. He saw dim, moving figures
of boys forming into small masses and then dissolving with
each play. Maybe he could play with them. Maybe he could get
into the game and play like a star, running for a touchdown.
Maybe they had a team and would want him to be their quarterback, and then they would play the team from Saint Rose's,
and he would help beat Walter Foley and the gang. The game
broke up just as he reached the gridiron. The boys who had been
playing left to go home, none of them noticing him. He watched
them, thinking that they were going to happy homes where
there was enough to eat, and where they wouldn't be bawled
out and even hit. When he got home, he would be late for
supper. If his mother hadn't heard yet from Sister Teresa, she
would. He would have to tell her sooner or later, and until it all
came out into the open, he would be in misery. And once he
told, or once it was found out, he would never hear the end of
it. His mother and Pat would believe Sister Teresa. Yes, Pat
would beat hell out of him.

He walked back toward the drive. He was alone now, and
the park seemed so vast. And the sky was as big as Heaven must
be. All of the world was so big, and he was just a little kid of
twelve. With tears welling in his eyes, he shook his fist at
all of this vastness and determined that he would get even with
it. The wind beat, shrilled, moaned until it became almost too
terrible for him to bear. He imagined the wind and the park
to be filled with imaginary demons. He shuddered in fear of
the people of his own imaginings. He wished Mary Latham

would care for him. If she would, he'd have no fear of these demons. He wished he were on better terms with his class-mates. But he wasn't. And he swore that he'd get even with them, pay them back. He wished the trouble at school were settled. He wished he were a grown-up man, free and rich, and able to tell everyone where to go. He wished he could fly away like a bird or be in an airplane and just go away in it. He wished his father were alive. He continued wishing for every-thing he desired.

He left the park and passed the large home for old people at Garfield Boulevard and South Park Avenue. Wells Street seemed a long way off. He walked on.

An expression of reckless calm settled on his face. He felt doomed, and he tried to convince himself that it didn't matter and that he didn't care. He was going home to face the music. Maybe it wouldn't be so bad. Anyone could stand a licking and a bawling out. These didn't touch what was inside you. No one could touch what was inside of him, his wishes, his thoughts. He stuck his hands in his pockets and continued on his way, half afraid. He thought of the image of Mary Latham, and his mind filled with new wishes and fresh daydreams.

1929-43.

A Sunday in April

THE TWO CHILDREN were fed, and Red and his wife had their breakfast. He shaved and washed, snorting and splashing as he doused his face in cold water. He went to his bedroom and put on a freshly laundered white shirt and the trousers of his new blue suit. He carefully combed his curly hair. He stood before his tie-rack, selecting a brown cravat with diagonal white stripes. Facing the dresser mirror, he knotted it tightly and evenly. He put on his vest and double-breasted coat and placed a handkerchief in the breast pocket. He stood back and surveyed himself. The new suit was a real humdinger. It had class. Made to order, a neat job, and it didn't make him look so fat. God, though, he had developed quite a corporation these last few years. Well, since he had gone on the wagon, he hadn't taken on any more gut. A man couldn't have everything in life. And, anyway, his belly wasn't a sign of starvation.

"Ready, dear?" his wife called to him.

"Just about," he answered casually.

She entered the room, wearing a new blue dress.

"Gee, Toots, you look like a knockout," he said with pride.

"I have to walk to church alongside of that handsome husband of mine. Stand back and let me see your new suit." He stepped back. "You look handsome, and it's a wonderful fit. But, here, let me fix that handkerchief better." Approaching him, she rearranged the handkerchief in his breast pocket.

"You're kidding the old man, Toots," he smiled.

"Don't you call yourself an old man," she chided.

She kissed him.

He put on his gray topcoat and his pearl-gray fedora. She wore a new hat. They left for church. It was a warm and sunny morning, and they strolled along slowly, walking west on Fifty-fifth Street, past the hotels facing the northern extremity of Jackson Park.

"Lovely day, dear," she said, her arm snuggled under his crooked elbow.

"You bet it is, Toots," Red said profoundly, walking along with his shoulders flung back, the erectness of his posture giving him the appearance of greater height than he possessed. His shiny, well-fed, ruddy face beamed. People passed them, strolling. Ahead, they saw an Illinois Central electric shoot across the viaduct.

"I was just thinking, Toots," he said reflectively.

"What?" she asked.

"I used to be a damn fool all right."

"Now! Now! Now!"

"I was. I'm serious. I used to be a plain damn fool."

"You never were. You always were a darling."

"No, I was. I was just thinking of how much nicer it is to be up and going to Mass this way instead of having a hangover and a headache, feeling so damn jittery that you didn't know if you were coming or going, kind of ashamed of yourself for some damn-fool clown stunt you had pulled the night before when you were barreled and didn't know what you were doing."

"You used to be cute when you were drunk," she said as they passed under the viaduct.

"Cute, my eye! I was a damn fool. I tell you, I'm damn glad that I went on the water wagon. And I think it's pretty good. I've been on it for a whole year now," he said proudly.

"But, dear, don't you ever want a drink any more?"

"Never!" he said with finality.

"Not even a glass of beer?"

"You couldn't even tempt me. The boys at the Hall often try to, but they don't get to first base."

"I'm so proud of you," she said.

He beamed.

II

Red and the missus came out of church with the crowd and stood on the curb. Red looked around to see if he could spot any friends. Several fellows and two couples nodded to them, and near by a raggedy fellow barked loudly in an attempt to sell the weekly paper, *Christian Justice,* edited by Father Moylan, the radio priest. Red refused to buy one.

"Hello, how are you?" Jim said, approaching him, his tall, bony wife at his side.

"Hello, Jim! Hello, Jim! How are you?" Red said cordially, his hand shooting out.

The two wives talked. Jim made a face, looked at his wife, made another face, pointed at his head.

"Better lay off the stuff, Jim. It never does you any good. I feel a thousand times better since I went on the wagon," Red said.

"I guess you're right, Red," Jim said.

"Well, how are things going, Jim?"

"Oh, Red, I have no complaints," Jim said.

"They working you hard?"

"I'm not dying of overwork," Jim said.

The two wives talked about curtains. Red bowed and nodded to several who greeted him.

"I'm glad the primary is over, though. I damn near wore my knuckles out rapping on doors. I'm sure glad that it's over," Jim said.

"Well, my can was worked, too. Out every night. You fellows made a good showing in your precinct, didn't you?" Red asked.

"Yes, we carried it. We did all right."

"So did I."

"But we had to wear out plenty of shoe leather."

"It was down state that turned the trick for Kline. But, anyway, even if Anderson did lose, things were still sewn up pretty tight in the county as far as local things go for the organizations."

"Yes, and that's what counts, that and Roosevelt."

"They can't beat the President no matter who they put up next fall. A great man. He done a lot for the people, and he's our friend. That's why I wouldn't buy the paper put out by Father Moylan that this guy here tried to sell me. A priest should stay out of politics and he shouldn't attack Roosevelt," said Red.

"Yes," Jim said, grinning.

They both acknowledged other greetings.

"Well, I'm glad you held your end up, Jim. You know, Jim, I kind of feel like I got you under my wing since I put you on your first job in the Hall," Red said.

"Yes, Red, you've been damn decent to me," Jim said.

"And, Jim, you've proved yourself regular. There was a time back around Fifty-eighth Street when you were at the University and we thought you were going to lose your faith," Red said, and Jim grinned fatuously.

Phil and his wife approached. Loretta was stout and broad-hipped, and her face had filled out and taken on a bovine expression. She spoke with the other wives, and Phil shook hands with Red and Jim.

"You boys still in the political game?" asked Phil.

The two of them nodded.

"How's it go by you, Phil?" Red asked.

"Oh, Red, not so good. You know I tried my hand at several business ventures, and then I went into the laundry business. If this thing doesn't go, I'm going back to the books. A respectable business has its points but, after all, my lads, money talks. There seems to be more money keeping the books than there is in the laundry business. I'm learning that," Phil said.

"Things are better than they were a couple of years ago," Red said.

"Sure they are. I ain't got any kicks. It's just that I didn't get a handle. It's hard meeting stiff competition. Maybe the laundry business will pan out. I'm going to give it a little more of a go. But then, if it don't, I'll start back again as a bookie," said Phil.

"I hope it works out for you, my boy," Red said.

"How are things going by you, Red?" asked Phil.

"I can't complain, Phil. I can't complain," Red said.

"Good! Glad to hear it. I see some of the old boys, and they aren't getting on so well. I saw Tubby not so long ago. He isn't doing any too well as a glazier. He only gets three days' work a week," Phil said.

"Well, I tell you, Phil, there are plenty of fellows in this man's town who are making less dough than a glazier gets for working three days a week," Red said.

"You're right there," Phil said.

The three wives continued chattering.

"But tell me, Red, hitting the bottle these days?" asked Phil.

"Been on the wagon a year now. I don't touch a drop any more," Red boasted.

"Good! Neither do I. It's the only sensible thing to do," Phil said.

"I feel a hundred times better, too, Phil, since I went on the wagon," Red boasted.

"Oh, sure, there's nothing in that stuff," Phil said.

"It never gets you anywhere," Red said.

"It sure doesn't," said Phil.

They parted. Red and his wife walked home, Red walking proudly, his shoulders flung back, his face firm, almost set in a frown, his alderman sticking out.

"Say, Phil turned out much better than I ever thought he would," he said.

"His wife is such a lucky girl. Only she's stout," said Mrs. Kelly.

"You know, she is. She's going to look like a barrel soon if she doesn't reduce. I tell you, darling, I'm always so proud of you when I see you alongside of other women. You are so thin beside her, and so much better-looking than Jim's wife," he said.

"That's just because you like me," she said, smiling.

"You're damn right, I do. You're the best little wife in all this man's town," he said affirmatively.

She snuggled her arm in his elbow.

"But, as I was saying, Phil certainly turned out to be a decent fellow. Why, you couldn't have imagined a Jew coming over to our side of the fence and becoming as good a Catholic as Phil. But he did."

"He's nice," she said.

"He turned out better than a lot of them that was Catholics and should have been something and didn't. He's a decent member of the community," Red said.

"When I go to church with you, I'm so proud of my husband," she said.

They walked on home.

III

After playing with the children, Red took off his shoes, put on a pair of comfortable slippers, sat down in a parlor rocker, and read the Sunday edition of *The Chicago Clarion*. He always enjoyed this moment of the day. He went through the funnies, smiling and laughing, thinking of how he had always liked the funnies as a kid, and how it was nice to read them and let your mind go and imagine all kinds of things. And soon he would be reading them to his own kids. Ah, life was a strange thing! A fellow never knew what it meant to have kids until he had them. And then it was a great thing to watch them grow the way his own were starting to. Any fellow who said he didn't want kids was nuts. He didn't know what he was missing. He took the front section and began reading the news of the day. Politics had died down since the election. But here was a piece predicting that the local machine would make peace with Governor Kline, who had licked the organization in last Tuesday's primary election. He swore, thinking of the Governor's victory. Of course, it hadn't jeopardized his job, and the organization was sitting pretty in the county. And it looked good for the fall elections. Roosevelt had polled more votes unopposed than both Borah and Knox had together in a hot fight. Yep, it looked good. But, what the hell, he had plenty of politics these last weeks. He wasn't going to act like a cab driver on a holiday and read the

political news now. And most of the politics you read in the
newspapers was just paper-talk anyway.

He read about the rape and murder of a woman in New
York City. The fellow who committed the crime was lower
than a snake. He remembered the rape pulled off by Weary
Reilley. Weary was still in the can. Well, that was where he
belonged. Suppose some moron had done that to his wife, like
it was done to this poor woman. Some moron had got into her
house in the morning and raped her and then murdered her.
These morons running around loose could get into anybody's
house and do that to any man's wife. Suppose some moron
should do it in his home while the little woman was at home!
An overpowering fear gripped him. Goddamn it, something
ought to be done to the morons in the world—put them away
or something.

He read on. In France, it was said that the Reds were getting
too much power and threatening to kick up a lot of rows. Something ought to be done about them. But it was good that we
didn't have many of them over here. He didn't put much stock
in all this talk about there being so many Reds over here. There
weren't. And it was baloney what the *Questioner* said about
Roosevelt having anything to do with them. That was why he
stopped buying *The Questioner*. But *The Clarion* was just
about as bad when it came to the President.

He read on. Some shine was arrested for cutting up another
shine with a razor. Well, so long as the shines only cut each
other up, that wasn't so bad. And then something about this
fellow Hitler. He didn't go much for Hitler. Hitler was always
fighting with the Church. Mussolini, now, he guessed was all
right for the wops in Italy. And he didn't fight the Catholics
the way Hitler did. But if you asked him to write his own
ticket, the name he was going to write down on it was FRANK-
LIN DELANO ROOSEVELT.

He picked up the sports section and turned to an article on
Joe Louis, the sensational Brown Bomber who seemed on the
way to the title and looked like the best heavyweight since
Dempsey.

IV

Red, in his shirtsleeves, cut the roast beef, and they had their Sunday dinner. The year-and-a-half-old child sat on the high-chair next to the mother, who fed her, wiped her chin, and watched her as she struggled to eat. The other child was able to eat by himself now.

"I hope you like the dinner," the wife said.

"Like it! Say!" Red said enthusiastically.

"Well, I tried to make you a nice Sunday dinner," she said. The oldest child ate and chattered.

"And you didn't fail none," he said, his mouth full of food.

"The little fellow here likes it," she said, nodding at the boy.

"A chip off the old block," Red said, smiling at the lad.

"You should have let me get you some beer to have with your dinner," she said.

"Hell, no! When I say I'm off, I'm off, and that even means beer," he said.

She blew him a kiss across the table. He blew one back. The baby started blowing kisses. They both laughed, and she doted over the youngster. They ate.

"This is the first peaceful Sunday I've had in over a month," he said.

"You had to work so hard in the campaign," she said sympathetically.

"Well, that's what happens when you're in the political game. But I'd rather be in that than doin' lots of things. Now, take when I was sellin' refrigerators. Why, I didn't have the prospects that I got now. You know, baby, if I work along and slowly build up a following and keep my nose clean, who knows, I might get myself fixed up later and become the ward committeeman some day, and if I get that far, why, maybe I can become an alderman, even if I don't have any education to speak of. I might not know law, but I know politics. I'm in a game with a future. And in this town we broke the Republicans. We'll have this town by the . . . neck, just like Tammany Hall has New York."

"Wouldn't it be fun sometime to go to New York?" she said.

"We will. If things go right, we might even go to Europe some day. We could see the Pope at Rome," he said.

"Wouldn't that be grand!" she said.

"Yes, things are going sweet and pretty for us. As I always say, I think that we have given them the real knockout drops, and from now on, honey, this city belongs to the Democratic Party. And that's good news for your breadwinner," he said.

"I always had faith in my darling. That's why I married him," she said.

v

"I'm so glad we got a carriage like this. We can put both the children in it, and it makes it so much easier for us. Junior's just over his cold, and I don't want to let him walk. He'd want to run on the grass, and often the grass is damp at this time of the year," she said.

"You know, I never thought I'd be doing this on a Sunday afternoon," Red said, wheeling the carriage.

"What do you mean?" she asked.

"Pushing a babycart," he said.

"If you don't want to . . ." she said rather huffily.

"Of course I want to. Say, I love it and I'm proud of my kids," he said, drawing a smile out of her.

"Well, there's nothing wrong in a man doing that, no more than it's wrong for a man to dry dishes," she said.

"I didn't say there was. I was thinking of myself ten or twelve years ago, when I was a tough punk and I thought my spit bounced," he said.

"That's awful language," she said.

They crossed Fifty-fifth Street and entered Jackson Park. He slowly pushed the carriage along a gravel path, and the two children squirmed and cooed. He and his wife constantly looked at their offspring with fond parental eyes. It was still too early for the green to be out, but the earth was soft, moist, with a few beginning peeps of grass. The trees were bare. There was a warm and invigorating sun shining upon them. Many automobiles hummed by. People, all types, were strolling along, their manner relaxed, their gaits slow and easy, almost dream-like and drooping. A lazy Sunday atmosphere seemed to pervade the park.

"Ah, this is the life, taking it easy and just strolling along with you and the kids on a warm Sunday afternoon," he said.

"You poor dear, you were so worn out by the campaign," she said.

"Yes, but that's over. I don't have so much to do down at the Hall now, and I can take it easy most of the summer. But in the fall, with the election, things will hum plenty," he said.

"Are you sure Roosevelt will win again?" she asked.

"Sure! The people won't forget what he's done for them," he said.

"It would be awful if he didn't," she said.

"Not a chance of him losing. Watch the way we get out the vote for him in November. And even if he does, the other side hasn't got the chance of a snowball in hell of whipping us locally," he said.

"It would be awful if they did," she said.

"Not a chance. But let's drop politics. I had enough of them for a while . . . plenty, in fact," he said.

"When do you get your vacation, darling?" she asked.

"Any time I want it," he answered proudly, holding the carriage at a drive while automobiles zoomed by.

Waiting beside him, she bent down and rearranged the children, showered loving words upon them, kissed them, told them in an affectionate voice to be quiet and not to get themselves tangled up. Red crossed hurriedly with the carriage. She skipped hastily by his side.

"Whenever you want me to take my vacation, I will," he said.

"August might be nicest, and then we'll go to the beach in Michigan. It was so much fun up there last year," she said.

"I had a swell time. And it was a pretty decent gang of people there. Say, remember the swell time we all had sitting on the porch that night and singing old-time songs, with the moonlight on the lake just below the cottage?" he asked.

"It was all so ducky. We'll have just as good a time this year, too, won't we?" she said.

"You said it, Toots," he said.

"And, darling, you know we never dance any more. We'll dance, too, won't we, right on the pavilion by the lake. It'll be so wonderful," she said.

"Yeah," he said.

They walked on and then turned toward home. They talked little on the way home, and he began to yawn. When they got back she put the children to bed for a nap. Yawning, he went to lie down and sleep himself.

VI

They had cold meat for supper, and a woman came in to watch the children. They walked along Fifty-fifth Street to the Illinois Central to go downtown to see a movie.

"Well, it's been a swell day, hasn't it, Toots?" he said.

"I like Sunday because you're home all day, and, well, I always liked Sunday. You feel a letdown from the week," she said.

"Yeah," he said profoundly.

"Sundays are going to be nice, too, from now on. I like it when winter is over," he said, biting on a cigar.

"We can do so many things now," she said.

"We'll have our new car next week and we'll have to start taking drives on Sunday again," he said.

"With the new Fords, I don't feel ashamed of owning one. They're so pretty," she said.

"Even if we had more dough in the bank, I'd still stick to the Ford. It's a honey, that car of ours is," he said.

"I must learn to drive," she said.

"Nix! Nix on that," he said.

"But, darling, there's nothing wrong in my driving. Look at all the women who drive nowadays. Times have changed. There's nothing wrong with a girl driving," she said.

"I didn't say there was anything wrong with it, did I?"

"Well, then, why don't you want me to drive?"

"I'd be too worried. I don't want my Toots getting banged up," he said.

"Oh, darling, don't be so ridiculous," she said.

"I mean it. I don't want you getting banged up," he said.

"But I won't," she said.

They entered the station, went upstairs to the long wooden platform, and waited for their train.

"You men, you're so silly sometimes," she said with tolerant kindness.

"I meant what I said. I don't want my Toots getting her pretty face cracked by glass in an accident," he said.

"Well, I could say the same for you," she said.

"Listen, you can't find anybody in this man's town who drives more carefully than I do," he said as their train stopped.

They rode downtown and saw *The Prisoner of Shark Island*. They liked it, but she would have liked other pictures better. It was kind of sad until the end. Afterward they had waffles and coffee in a good restaurant and came home yawning, weary and tired but feeling that they had spent a wonderful Sunday together.

1937.

Clifford and William

SCENE:

Bench in a park, placed downstage center. A small hedge to the right, upstage.

As curtain rises CLIFFORD *is discovered lying flat on his back on bench. His knees are bent, and his hands are shielding his eyes.*

WILLIAM *strolls onto the stage with a clay pipe and a bowl, blowing soap bubbles. He sees a place to sit on the very edge of the bench where* CLIFFORD *is reclining.*

WILLIAM (*sitting as though in great comfort*): Forgive me. I'm very happy. (*He blows a bubble.*) As I always say, the way to be alive is to. . . . (*He blows another bubble.*) Do you care to join me and find the way to be alive.

CLIFFORD (*he looks at* WILLIAM *askance. He runs his hands through his hair and speaks to himself*): Am I living? Am I alive? The earth is flat. How do I know? I'm being pushed over the edge. (*He rises nervously and starts to walk off.*)

WILLIAM (*about to blow another bubble*): Stay! We're just getting to know each other. Where are you going?

CLIFFORD: I'm stifled. I can't breathe. I need air.

WILLIAM (*as though he were handing something to* CLIFFORD): Here, take some. There's A LOT OF AIR. Just breathe it into your lungs like this. (*He inhales deeply.*) And then let it go out like that. (*He exhales noisily.*)

CLIFFORD (*with a gesture of despair, as he starts to walk off again*): Aw, nuts!

WILLIAM: What's your hurry?

CLIFFORD (*Stopping suddenly in his tracks*): I think I'll do something fantastic. I'm going to the end of that path. (*He points and* WILLIAM *looks rather bored.*) Then I'll turn the corner, walk three-eighths of a mile—and buy me a bag of popcorn. (*He turns and looks at* WILLIAM.) Do you know what popcorn means, my anonymous friend?

WILLIAM: Anonymous friend? (*He laughs patronizingly.*) You don't know who I am?

CLIFFORD: I should know who you are, when I don't know who I am! Who was your mother? Who was your father? My father always rolled his own. He lost his dream. He never knew that he lost his dream. I kept mine. (*He beats his breast.*) It's here, see! It's locked up in my heart and crying for sunshine.

WILLIAM: How many pounds do you weigh? You're a shrimp. The trouble with you is that you don't eat with gusto. Do everything that you do with gusto. Live, my boy, live! That's the great lost secret of the universe. (CLIFFORD *starts to walk off.*) Wait a minute, popcorn! Forget those kernels! Sit down, my boy! You remind me of an uncle of mine. He must be an old man now. A Syrian. Not too smart. Not too dumb. Just a Syrian.

CLIFFORD (*sitting down and looking quizzically at his companion*): You wouldn't fool me, would you? Listen, are you just a cheap cluck like me? Trying to sing a song and look the world in the face?

WILLIAM: Forget your harmonica a minute. Look over there. (*He points.*) See those people? Those wonderful people lolling on the grass? In three years, some of them will be dead. In fifty years maybe I'll be dead. Do you think I'm likely to be remembered as someone who went out to the park, joined that vast multitude of swarming human life to loll on the grass? Do you think that's what I'm going to be remembered for?

CLIFFORD: What do you do?

WILLIAM: Do? I am! I'm the walking and sitting symbol of myself—I'm the talking, gesticulating, outgoing, ingoing personification of ME—I—MYSELF. (*As he takes a pack of ciga-*

rettes from his pocket.) Here, have a smoke. They say nicotine is a poison, but my Syrian uncle has smoked all his life, still smokes, and promises to outlive the next three generations.

CLIFFORD (*taking a cigarette*): Do you know what you are? You're me, upside down.

WILLIAM: I'll tell you who I am. First of all, I belong to the living. When I laugh, I laugh with the mirth that you and your ilk lost long ages ago. Listen to me laugh. (*He laughs energetically.*) And when I get angry, I get plenty angry. Angry with the indignation of 89,000 Syrians. I function. That's what I do. Without shame. And I love humanity. (*He makes a gesture as though to embrace the world.*) That's why I'm so profoundly interested in life, in everything. (*He looks at* CLIFFORD.) In you, too. My interest does not exclude you. Tell me, who are you?

CLIFFORD: Me? I'm just a toy balloon trying to be the Yankee Clipper.

WILLIAM: What seems to stop you?

CLIFFORD: I'm a penny whistle pretending to be a siren in a blackout.

WILLIAM (*he gets up and walks around the bench, studying* CLIFFORD *carefully*): You lack confidence, my boy. Confidence. You haven't as yet, like myself, gotten rid of original shame.

CLIFFORD (*he strikes a histrionic pose with his chin protruding*): Are you trying to hint that you're better than me?

WILLIAM: Hint? I'm telling you that I am.

CLIFFORD (*slapping his brow*): Did I die, I keep asking myself? Or am I alive? Yes, I, too, want to live. (*He rises as if in a trance.* WILLIAM *watches him very closely.*) Listen! Do you hear? (WILLIAM *tilts his hat, takes a pear out of his pocket and begins to eat it.*)

CLIFFORD: Listen to the hum, the music of the city. The million heartbeats of the metropolis. If I were a poet—and I'm not, I'm just a poor cluck—I would capture that heartbeat—and then—

WILLIAM: That reminds me, I once knew a Japanese boy in

San Francisco—he had four cousins, a stepfather, and three uncles. One day he said to me—

CLIFFORD: Do you know what I would do? (*He remains in his trance, looking out.*) I'd tell them all what to do with their stifled heartbeats—they don't know it's this civilization—

WILLIAM: When I was fifteen years old, I picked olives in my uncle's vineyard.

CLIFFORD: I'd tell them— (*He stops a moment and combs his hair with his hands, desperately.*)

WILLIAM: That's where I first met the Japanese boy. His name was Yoshio Katsumi Sujimoto—the one with four cousins, a stepfather, and three uncles— (CLIFFORD *looks off in the distance and motions for* WILLIAM *to keep still.*)

WILLIAM (*continuing, and ignoring* CLIFFORD'S *motions*): He, too, picked olives in my uncle's vineyard. That's how I learned the few words of Japanese. I can say, HOW ARE YOU—IS IT NOT A FINE DAY?—and—HOW IS YOUR GRANDFATHER?

CLIFFORD (*he turns to William*): Look! She walks! Look! Her young lithe limbs sway like an Italian fugue on a Venetian harmonica. (*He raises his eyes skyward.*) The hum has died out. Birds are chirping. And only Man is vile.

WILLIAM (*looking off and noticing a girl*): I say. (*He takes out a mirror and comb and starts primping.*)

CLIFFORD (*looks annoyed at* WILLIAM): Please! Can I help it if I got here first? And that this park bench is my only home? Am I J. P. Morgan?

WILLIAM (*his tone very generous*): Can I help it if I'm the most generous, the most gallant? I'll go behind the hedge. Forget me, boy. Forget you're a penny whistle. (WILLIAM *goes behind hedge. A rather ordinary, very pretty, and slightly hard-boiled girl strolls onto the stage, walking as though she were going nowhere in particular.*)

CLIFFORD: How do you do? (*The girl sees him but ignores him.*)

CLIFFORD: Are you looking for someone? I'm a shy young man—with millions of words—but no voice—

GIRL (*looking contemptuously at him*): I take a stroll in the park and look what I meet.

CLIFFORD (*undaunted, he moves toward her*): See! I'm not rat poison. The past was a dream. But this is real. You are real. I'm a shy young man—searching—confused—and now the search is ended. (*He points yonder.*) Three-eighths of a mile in that direction. Popcorn. I was waiting for you.

GIRL: Oh, yeah? Do you know what I'm doing? I'm taking a walk. I got a charley horse and want to get rid of it. (*She exits.*)

CLIFFORD (*clutching the air*): I'm the boy who slept out in the open under the stars—got my best blue serge pants wrinkled trying to talk to the moon through a keyhole in the sky. (WILLIAM *comes from behind the hedge and joins* CLIFFORD. *He leads him back to bench.*)

WILLIAM: I'm sorry, boy. MAN is MAN, and WOMAN is WOMAN. I once fell in love with the most beautiful girl in the world. She was an Armenian. Did you ever stop to think that an Armenian girl could be the most beautiful? But that isn't the point. I'm not going to tell you about the Armenian girl. I don't suppose you ever had to eat a bunch of bananas so that you'd stop from thinking? Or ice cream sodas when what you really wanted was watermelon.

CLIFFORD: I'm just a new penny thinking I was a ten-dollar gold piece.

WILLIAM: The trouble with me was that I never wanted to do without. The whole thing came to me suddenly—

CLIFFORD: She had shadows under her eyes. She couldn't find the door to her cage. (WILLIAM *rises abruptly.*)

WILLIAM: Look! She's coming back. Walking more quickly. Watch me. I'll show you something. (*He motions for* CLIFFORD *to go behind hedge this time.*) Clipper! Listen and learn something. (CLIFFORD *rises and goes behind the hedge. Girl walks on stage.*)

WILLIAM (*he makes a sweeping bow with his hat*): If you're not the one I'm looking for, you should be. Are you she?

GIRL (*very haughtily*): I beg your pardon.

WILLIAM: I grant you your request. Are you sure you're not looking for someone who looks something like me?

GIRL: Who do you think you are?

WILLIAM (*coming very close to her*): Would you like to know who I am? I'm the greatest guy in the world—I'm the wittiest, the most original, the staggering Kid of the 1940's— I am a genius.

GIRL (*intimidated*): Where do you live?

WILLIAM (*taking her arm as they walk off. The girl acquiesces thoroughly*): The universe is my home, My Heart's in the Highlands, and I'm Having the Time of My Life. (*They exit.*)

CLIFFORD (*he emerges from the hedge in a most melancholy state and beats his breast*): I thought I was dying. No. I was sawing wood. I was dead—but now, I'm born. I'm two minutes old, and I want the whole city to hear! I'm on my way to being the Clipper! (BLACKOUT.)

Tommy Gallagher's Crusade

The dog-star razes! nay, 'tis past a doubt,
All Bedlam, or Parnassus, is let out:
Fire in each eye, and papers in each hand,
They rave, recite, and madden round the land.
— ALEXANDER POPE
Epistle to Dr. Arbuthnot

I

"READ *Christian Justice!* Father Moylan's *Christian Justice,*
ten cents a copy! See page three of this issue and learn what
Father Moylan says of the Red menace. Get your *Christian
Justice,* ten cents a copy!"

Tommy Gallagher stood on the curb in front of his parish
church in Brooklyn, selling his magazines as the last Sunday
mass let out. Tommy was a lad of twenty-five, husky, broad-
shouldered, with a large round face, sensuous lips, and dark
brows which contributed to the ferocity of his expression when
he frowned. The parishioners poured out of the church. Small
knots of people gathered on the sidewalk to talk for a moment
or two, while many others moved away.

Young fellows whom Tommy knew, some of them grammar-
school classmates of his, grinned at him. Now and then older
people nodded, parishioners he had known for many years,
friends of his mother and father. Most of the people were not
interested in his magazine and passed him by. Several men faced
him with unmistakable hostility but said nothing. A man of

167

middle age in shabby clothes came up to him and bought a copy. The man said that Father Moylan was the real one for the common fellow. Tommy said sure he was. The man said that he had been out of work for two years, had been on relief, W.P.A., had looked for odd jobs, and he was fed up and felt that the only one who had spoken out for the poor devils like himself was Father Moylan. Tommy agreed. The man folded his copy of *Christian Justice* under his arm and walked on, a seedy, broken-looking figure.

"Read Father Moylan's *Christian Justice*! Ten cents a copy! Read *Christian Justice* and kick the Reds out of America!"

The crowd was almost gone now. Tommy stood there, hoping to make a last sale. He held up a copy of the magazine. It was printed in bold type, looked something like a newspaper, had large headlines and a picture on the front page. But he guessed that he'd have to call it quits. Jimmy Powers, a thin, overdressed lad of Tommy's age, came over to him, smiling as he approached.

"What the hell, Tommy, when did you become a Red?" Jimmy asked.

"What's that?" Tommy answered, taken by surprise.

"Ain't you a Red, selling magazines on the street?"

"Father Moylan's magazine! Read it and see what the Reds and the eagle-beaks are doin'," Tommy replied, holding up a copy.

"Oh! I thought it was only Reds and newsboys who sold magazines and papers on the streets."

"Here, Jimmy, buy one, it's only a dime."

"What'll I do with it?" Jimmy asked.

"Read it!"

"Sounds too much like work."

"Jimmy, it'll open your eyes. Come on, buy one," Tommy said, trying to thrust a copy into Jimmy's hand.

"Hell, Gallagher, *The Brooklyn Eagle* gives me enough readin' matter."

They were alone now in front of the church. Jimmy lit a

cigarette. He offered Tommy one and held up a lighted match while Tommy lit his.

"Jimmy, you're a Christian and an American, ain't you?" Tommy asked.

"I guess so. And I'm a Dodger fan, too."

"Well, you ought to buy this magazine."

"Workin', Tommy?"

"I'm sellin'. Sellin' this," Tommy answered, and again he held up a copy.

"Hell, that ain't work," Jimmy said.

"I ain't ashamed of selling *Christian Justice*. You don't understand, Jimmy. Let me explain it to you."

"Explain what?"

"Oh, about Father Moylan and what he's doin'."

"I got to trot along. I got to get out to Ebbets Field early today if I want a seat. They're gonna pitch Van Lingle Mungo and I want to see the big boy come back. Tell me another time. Good luck, and hope you make a few pennies with your work there," Jimmy said, and he walked off.

Tommy looked after him, dour. He guessed he never liked that guy. He stuck his hands in his pockets and fingered his change. He'd only sold ten copies this morning. Hadn't made much dough. Well, he had about five bucks of his own. Maybe he'd have better luck next week. Carrying his bundle of magazines, he started toward home.

II

The Gallagher family sat down to their Sunday dinner. The father was a lean man in his fifties with graying hair; for years he had worked for the telephone company as a repairman. A mild-mannered and genial man, he had never manifested much interest in politics. He had always voted the Democratic ticket and let it go at that. Mrs. Gallagher was a plump woman with lovely black hair that was beginning to be streaked with gray. The oldest boy, Joe, was tall and lean like his father. He had a pretty good job working in the pay roll department of the telephone company. Bill was twenty-one, heavier and more burly than Tommy, with a jolly face and light hair. He was a clerk in an office in Manhattan and earned thirty dollars a week. All during the depression, Bill, Joe, and the father had been fortunate in retaining their jobs, and the family was able to satify its normal wants.

The father and Joe had been talking about the telephone company and the dinner was progressing when Mrs. Gallagher suddenly looked at Tommy and said:

"I saw Mrs. Malone at early mass today. She was nice as pie, and told me that her son had a good job, and then she says she sees you in front of church every Sunday selling newspapers."

"He works for kikes. Catch me workin' for one of them eagle-beaks," Tommy blurted out.

"Why don't you say catch you working, and stop there?" Bill said, looking across the table at Tommy.

"Say, you punk, when you was still in school I had a job," Tommy countered.

"And you sure overworked yourself getting out of jobs and losing 'em ever since."

"Why don't you cut it out?" Mr. Gallagher asked.

"It seems to me that you ought to show a little consideration for the rest of us. You ought to be able to get something better to do with that outfit you run around with besides selling newspapers," Joe said.

"I don't sell newspapers. I sell a magazine and I do it because it's my duty," Tommy answered.

Bill burst into hearty laughter.

"You talking about duty. You're gettin' so funny they ought to put you on the radio," Bill said.

Tommy glared at Bill. There was a dense expression on his face. He was trying to think of a quick comeback.

"That's what you say," Tommy finally said.

"Tommy, I don't know what's happening to you. You're gettin' touchy and always go around with a chip on your shoulder," Mr. Gallagher observed.

"I got my eyes opened," Tommy answered.

"And I'm gettin' mine open, too. Here Joe and I are saving

our dough to get married, and he won't even look for a job,"
Bill said.

"How you gonna get a job when the Jewrocracy runs the
country? Maybe if I had a name like Rosenstein I'd have a
good job."

"Well, why don't you change your name to Rosenstein then
and get a good job?"

No one spoke for a few moments, and they went on eating.
Tommy was smouldering. He hadn't been able to think up anything to say to Bill's last crack.

"Tommy, the last time I went to a Holy Name Communion
breakfast, I was talking to a young priest, Father Smith. He's
a damned bright priest and well educated. I asked him about
Father Moylan, and he said he couldn't go along with Father
Moylan on this Jewish business, and it was going to give the
Church a bad name. A priest shouldn't be mixing in politics
like he does. If he does, what are the fellows on the other side
of the fence gonna think?" Mr. Gallagher said.

"You don't understand," Tommy answered.

"Well, I'm tryin' to find out. Now, I used to think Father
Moylan was all right, but when he turned against Roosevelt
in the last election, that wasn't right. President Roosevelt is
doin' the best he can, and if we pull along with him, he's goin'
to get us out of all this mess."

"Rosenfeld," Tommy sneered.

"What's that?" Joe asked.

"I told you, Rosenfeld. And Mrs. Rosenfeld is a Red."

"Why, Mrs. Roosevelt is a lovely woman. I read her column
every day in the newspaper, and it's wonderful," Mrs. Gallagher
said.

"Tommy, that's no way to talk about the President of the
United States and his wife," Mr. Gallagher reproached him.

"Hitler kicks the Jews out, and we make them governors of
our states and let 'em walk all over us," Tommy said.

"Joe, what do you think he'll do when he takes over Roosevelt's job?" Bill asked sarcastically, nodding his head toward
Tommy.

"Listen, you, I'm fed up with your insults!"

"Well, what you gonna do about it?" Bill asked, looking straight at Tommy.

"No fighting! Not in this family. This is a home, not a street corner," the father interposed.

"That'll be news to him. He doesn't act like it was," Bill said.

"I told you, you punk!"

Bill jumped to his feet in anger and challenged:

"Try tellin' me with something besides that tongue of yours!"

Joe and the father were on their feet. Joe grabbed Bill and told him not to be doing anything rash. The father gazed from one to the other, disturbed.

Mrs. Gallagher banged on the table. They sat down and were quiet. Tommy ate hastily now. He pouted.

"There's going to be no more fighting at this table. Not while I'm alive," Mrs. Gallagher declared with determination.

"I didn't start it. Don't look at me," Tommy said.

Bill looked at Tommy critically, smiled sardonically, said nothing.

"I don't know, but it seems to me we all ought to live and let live. That's my philosophy, and it's always been that. It's the same for the Jews as for everybody else. There's good and bad in all kinds. We have too much fighting and hating in the world as it is, and the world is never going to get any better until it stops all this hating and fighting. We all got to make up our minds that we're gonna live and let live," Mr. Gallagher said.

Tommy looked arrogantly at his father. He was silent.

III

Tommy Gallagher marched in the picket line carrying a sign which read:

FREE CHRISTIAN AMERICA FROM JEWRY

The line was moving back and forth in front of the entrance to a large building in the Fifties in which were located the offices of a radio station that had refused to sell Father Moylan

time because of the priest's provocative addresses and because
he had been widely charged with having made false statements.

There were about three hundred people in the picket line. It
had been organized by the Association for Christian Freedom
to which Tommy belonged. He and many others in the line
wore buttons on their coat lapels testifying to their member-
ship in this organization. The main body of the demonstration
consisted of young men, many of them unemployed. A number
of them were dressed poorly; frayed collars and cuffs and an
occasional shiny seat to a pair of trousers could be noticed in the
moving line. The remainder of the crowd was mixed, including
older men, girls, and corpulent women. Back and forth the
line moved, going on the outside of the sidewalk by the curb,
turning some distance down from the entrance to come back
on the inside. In the crowd one could see fanatical faces, harried
expressions, surly and sneering stares, sudden smiles. But the
dominant mood of the demonstration was one of pugnacity.
The crowd was spoiling for a fight. Policemen were lining the
curb and were grouped at either end of the sidewalk area which
the pickets covered. Passers-by and bystanders were hurried
along; crowds and groups were forbidden to congregate. No
magazine venders were permitted except those selling magazines to which the demonstrators were not hostile. Every now
and then a few persons would join the demonstration and a loud
cheer of approval would sweep down the marching line. In
single file, they paraded back and forth in front of the building
entrance.

Tommy was thrilling with pride as he marched. In front of
him there was a little fellow with one elbow almost out of his
coat. He carried a sign which read:

FOR A CHRISTIAN AMERICA

What this little fellow lacked in size he made up in voice,
and at times even drowned out Tommy's yells. The lad behind
him was shorter than Tommy. He was snappily dressed in a
stylish suit with pleated trousers. He had a pin-point mustache,
and as he marched he constantly fingered it and smoothed

down his greasy black hair. He wore a button and carried a sign bearing the slogan:

BREAK THE RULE OF THE ATHEISTIC JEWS

Tommy kept looking at those passing in line on the opposite side of the sidewalk. He nodded frequently as he recognized faces of people he had met at meetings of the Association. Spotting Al O'Reilley, he smiled and read the sign Al was carrying.

SMASH COMMUNISM

He walked in line, feeling a sense of unity with all these people. He felt that he was one with them and that they were one with him, all ready to fight together. He thought what a fine sight it was to see this picket line of Christian Americans who had all come out like this in defense of Father Moylan.

A trim little girl of about eighteen, with blonde hair, passed on the opposite side and let out a screeching yell.

Twenty million Christians murdered in Russia!

Exercising all his strong lung power, Tommy repeated her shout and was pleased when he got a smile from her. The yell spread up and down the line of marchers and it reverberated with increasing volume and swelling hatred. Again and again it was taken up and shrieked out.

Twenty million Christians murdered in Russia!

The slogan was dropped as suddenly as it had been picked up. A sudden roar demanding free speech for Father Moylan arose and died down. Tommy saw a man with a red nose and gray hair swagger by, carrying a picket sign which demanded:

KEEP AMERICA OUT OF WAR

He started thinking that if there were any attempt to break this line he would haul off and go swinging into the center of the melee, and more than one dirty Red disrupter and hook-nose would know he'd been hit.

The marchers began singsonging another slogan:

Free speech for Father Moylan!

Tommy reiterated the slogan without thinking of what he

was saying. Flashes of himself in the role of a heroic street war-
rior, slugging the Reds and Jews, kept coming and going in his
mind. His arms tired because of the sign he carried and he
wished he were not lugging it in the demonstration. Al
O'Reilley went by again, and he noticed that Al had gotten rid
of his sign.

Tommy trudged along, and he thought how this demonstration was bringing people together. This sense of unity
thrilled him. And at the same time he wanted to stand out from
these people and be noticed. He joined in a new cry, seeking to
send his voice soaring above all the others.

Defend Catholic Mexico!

He walked self-consciously erect and flung back his head as
he again exploded the new slogan. He ought to stand out from
the shrimps ahead of and behind him. He threw back his shoulders and put on his fiercest frown. He walked now with his
shoulders held so tensely that the muscles of his back hurt,
and his arm was tired from the weight of the sign. He watched
out of the corner of his eye to see whether or not those passing
him would look. He read a sign carried by a red-haired woman:

NO MORE CHRISTIAN MARTYRS TO
RED ATHEISM

He frowned, grimaced, made faces. He had to relax his posture a little because he was fagging himself by holding himself too tensely. No use wearing himself out this way because
he'd need what it took if there was a fight. He marched on.

A swarthy girl in summery clothes that brought out her
figure passed, and her sign read:

FREE SPEECH FOR FATHER MOYLAN AND
ALL CHRISTIAN AMERICANS

He'd like to know her.

Suddenly he noticed that there were newspaper photographers around taking pictures. Nearing two photographers, he
contorted his features and let out a roaring demand for free
speech for Father Moylan. He had hoped that they would snap

him in action and that his picture would be in the newspapers tomorrow. But no pictures were taken when he passed
the cameramen. He shuffled along, scraping his feet on the sidewalk. He looked at those opposite him, dragging along as if they
were starting to get pooped out. It seemed as if many were now
becoming weary of shouting. They walked more slowly, they
yelled more sporadically, and they just drooped on. He hoped
the photographers would not go away before he passed them
again.

"Snap it up. This ain't no way to walk," he said to the fellow
in front of him.

"You tell 'em that. I can't go any faster than the one ahead
of me."

He tramped along. A yell arose and spread up and down the
line.

We demand free speech for Father Moylan!

But it soon faded out. The demonstration was losing its unity
and its energy now. The slogans were being shouted out with
only a momentary display of spirit.

Tommy again walked toward the photographers. He threw
back his shoulders and held himself erect. But suppose he
were snapped and his picture did appear in the papers tomorrow
morning, and the Reds saw it and recognized him, and then
some day he might be alone some place, walking along, minding
his business, and they would remember him from the picture
and pile on him? But, no, that wasn't likely to happen. And he
could take care of himself. He could handle plenty of 'em.
Everybody knew they were worms.

We demand free speech for Father Moylan!

The cry died out spiritlessly.

Like a speaker had said at one of the Association meetings,
the Reds were all yellow. And yet it made him kind of afraid.
Suppose five or ten of them jumped him? Just as he was thinking of this, he came in camera range, and the photographers
were taking pictures. He averted his gaze without even exercising any volition; it was like a reflex action. He walked on,

dragging his feet, and he began thinking how he hated the Jews and the Communists.

Buy Christian!

It was a girl who started this cry, and they took it up like a college crowd shouting a cheer.

Buy Christian! Buy Christian! Buy Christian!

The spirit of the marchers suddenly lifted as they chanted the slogan. They marched now, and many tried to keep step. And they kept up their chant.

Buy Christian! Buy Christian! Buy Christian!

But again they dropped their cry and straggled. Tommy was now passing the cameras. He conquered his inclination to look away and looked bravely into the lenses, clenching his lips and holding the muscles of his face taut to seem tough. He walked on.

We demand free speech for Father Moylan!

The demonstration began to break up. Many were leaving it. There were gaps in the lines. Tommy remained in line until the crowd dispersed.

IV

After the demonstration had broken up, Al O'Reilley asked Tommy to come along with a couple of the fellows and have a drink. Tommy was introduced to them. Pete Sullivan was a burly young man wearing a shiny blue suit. Then he met Eddie Slavin, a skinny lad of about twenty-one with a pimply face, small and suspicious black eyes, and buck teeth. Tommy noticed that he had on a neat suit. He was glad his own gray suit was still in good condition.

A fellow belonging to the Association was going to a parish house where they often met, and took the signs in his automobile, and that relieved them. They went over to a bar on Ninth Avenue, and sat together at a table having beer and sandwiches while a radio was blaring swing music, and several fellows lined up at the bar were talking knowingly about prize fighters. They were enthusiastic and excited because of the demonstration and talked about it for a while, and then they got to talking about jobs.

"I'm in slavery," Eddie Slavin exclaimed.

"You're lucky," Pete Sullivan said.

"You wouldn't think so if you had my job. I'm a doorman in an apartment hotel down near Washington Square. The bastards make me work ten hours a day, and with the little dough I get, one of the guys there is trying to steam me up to join a goddamn union and pay 'em dues," Eddie said.

"Is the guy a Red?"

"I guess so. I see him comin' to work and goin' home with books under his arm, and he acts like a screwball," Eddie said.

"If you need any help, just say the word, boy," Al remarked.

"Boy, am I fed up! Some of the people livin' in the place are fine people, but then, others aren't. Christ, there's one damned bitch who's always bellyaching about me. And most of the people who come to see her got noses that make me suspicious. And, goddamn it, I don't see why I, a freeborn white American, have to be a flunky for Jews, open doors and elevators for 'em, say yes sir and yes ma'm to 'em, run their goddamn errands, take crap from sheenies. I tell you, I'm fed up," Eddie Slavin went on. With a resolute gesture he lifted his glass of beer and took a drink.

"You're a lucky bastard, Al, with your old man doing good," Pete said.

"Me and Father Moylan are O.K. with my old man. He likes what I do and says it's for the good of the country," Al explained.

"You know, my old man just can't get anything into his head. He thinks I'm a screwball," Tommy complained.

"Well, I'm fed up, boys, and so is the old man. He had a hat store out in Flushing and he was doin' good, and then with bad times it went kerflooie, and he's on his ear now. He works for the W.P.A. and he's always down in the mouth," Pete said.

"You want to explain to him what's wrong, tell him it's the Jews," Al told Pete.

"I got it figured out that if there weren't so many dames working, why, guys like us would be better off," Eddie Slavin said.

"That's why Hitler told the dames to stay home where they belong and have babies, and let the men work," Al declared.

"Say, Slavin, any chance of my gettin' a job where you are?" Pete asked.

"Gee, I don't know. They're full up, but guys are always comin' and goin'. If there's any chance, I'll tip you off."

"Do, will yuh," Pete urged.

"Sure I will. Only it's one goddamn lousy job, if you want to know."

"I don't care. I'm fed up," Pete said.

Tommy thought to himself that they could just catch him being a doorman and wearing a flunky's uniform. Catch him!

They had another round of beers.

Pete told a story he'd heard about the Reds and their girl friends, and they discussed girls. When they finished their beer, they paid their checks. Pete Sullivan said he was lucky he could pay his share. He'd had a pretty good week selling *Christian Justice*. They left and walked four abreast over to Eighth Avenue.

Tommy wanted something exciting to happen. He felt a kind of letdown after the afternoon's activity. He wanted girls, drinking, fun, action. He remembered how often he had felt just like this, having nothing to do, and wanting a little fun and excitement, and how he'd cruised around with guys he knew, looking for something to happen, and nothing had, and he'd gone home feeling that another night had gone down the sewer. He was kind of afraid that tonight might be the same. All his life he'd had a feeling that something big was going to happen to him, and it never had. Since he'd gotten interested in Father Moylan and joined the Association for Christian Freedom, this feeling had gotten stronger in him. And, damn it, life had gotten more exciting. He had things to do that gave him a feeling of his own place in the world that he'd never had before. Yes, he had the feeling now more than ever that something big was going to come to him that he'd never had before and that he'd always wanted and waited for.

They turned onto Eighth Avenue and heard the rumbling of the subway underneath the sidewalk. A few feet ahead, Tommy saw a couple strolling toward him, and both were clearly Semitic. The fellow was smaller than Tommy, and the girl was good-looking and had a neat figure.

"Close ranks, boys!" Tommy said quickly and under his breath.

They linked arms. The couple came face to face with them, surprised to find their path blocked by four sneering, tough-looking young men. The Jewish fellow was taken aback. The girl clung to his arm and her lips trembled.

"Lots of sidewalk out there," Tommy said curtly, pointing beyond the curb.

The fellow and girl tried to go around Tommy on the right, and a few pedestrians paused to watch what was happening. Tommy and his companions moved over.

"Get out on the street and make it fast!" Eddie Slavin yelled.

The Jewish lad blanched. He moved over to the curb, stepped off, walked with the girl on the street for a few feet, and then regained the sidewalk. The four boys laughed heartily, and spectators didn't know what was happening. The Jewish lad and his girl were lost in the crowd. Tommy and the boys walked on, laughing.

"Before we finish, boys, there won't be a Jew in New York," Tommy boasted.

They walked on. Pete Sullivan remarked that the two Hebes were lucky they didn't get worse. Tommy looked dour. He wanted excitement. Maybe a fight! With the others along, it wouldn't be too dangerous. No, he wanted it to be dangerous. But he knew he didn't want this. And knowing it himself, it filled him with hate and envy.

"How about another beer, boys?" Al suggested.

V

Feeling low, Tommy woke up and saw that it was already eleven o'clock. He got out of bed but felt dizzy. He went back to bed and turned his eyes away from the light. Lying down, he felt all right. He tried to remember last night. They'd gone to several bars, and he recalled how he'd almost gotten into a fight in one of them. But he couldn't remember clearly just what had happened.

He was going over to New York to sell the magazine on the street, but he could stay in bed a little while longer and go down in the afternoon. He had to sell, too, because he was broke. He'd spent all his dough last night. He dozed off and awakened a half hour later. He lay in bed, attracted by his own imaginings of his fighting ability, and he imagined himself knocking out Jews and Reds. He dozed off again in the midst of his fantasy and got up at twelve-thirty, feeling a little better for the extra sleep.

He got dressed and went out into the kitchen for breakfast. His mother didn't say a word to him. He was hoping she wouldn't be sore because he didn't want to be quarreling with her.

"Hello, Mom," he said with forced cordiality.

"Up late, Tommy," she answered.

"I know, Mom. I didn't get in early last night."

"Neither did your brother Bill, but he was up bright and early this morning and over to work at his office."

"He's lucky. He's got a decent job."

"You'll never find a decent job if you go out looking for it at this time of day."

"I've been looking for jobs so long, I'm fed up."

"Whenever you had jobs, you lost them."

"It wasn't my fault. I ain't responsible for conditions. And then, at most of my jobs they never liked me. The last place, the boss was against me. How can you have a job when the boss is against you for no good reason?"

"Sit down and have your breakfast," she said.

He dropped into a chair at the kitchen table. He remembered that he didn't have a red cent. He'd have to ask her for money again. He'd been a damned fool for not getting up early, because then it'd have been easier to get something off her. But he couldn't have done it, feeling like he did. He was still low and nervous and breaking out with sudden fits of sweating. But he'd get over it. A bigger problem was how he was going to ask her for money.

"Gee, Mom, you don't have to act so sore at me," he complained in a whining, injured voice when his mother set coffee and toast before him.

"I'm not angry with you," she replied curtly.

"Well, gee, what's the matter then?"

"Eat your breakfast. I've got lots to do. We can't afford servants in this house," she said, leaving the kitchen.

He sat munching toast and drinking coffee. He lit a cigarette. He only had a few left, and didn't even have the price of another pack. He felt sorry for himself. He was getting a raw deal. He had never had a decent job in his life. Most of the jobs he'd had were lousy and he'd had to go to work and ride in the subways in dirty old work clothes while others went to work and came home dressed up. They were all against him. Mom was treating him like a stepson. They were all against him, and they didn't understand.

Sulking, he finished his cup of coffee, went to the stove and poured another, and came back to the table and sat down with it. He still sulked.

He broke out in another sweat. He felt weak. Gee, how was he going to get through the day? And how was he going to get any money from Mom when she seemed so sore at him?

His coffee was lukewarm. He dumped it in the sink.

VI

It was a sunny afternoon in the middle of the week. Tommy stood on the corner opposite the New York Public Library at Forty-second Street and Fifth Avenue selling *Christian Justice*. He had a good position, but near by were three girls selling a magazine hostile to Father Moylan. Four cops stood around to prevent trouble. There had been a small riot on the same corner only two days before, but Tommy hadn't been there that day. Today it was quiet. The presence of the cops made Tommy feel more at ease. Several of the boys were supposed to have come around to protect him in case there was any trouble. But they hadn't shown up, and he'd given up hope now that they would come. But, anyway, they wouldn't be needed when there were only girls around selling that magazine.

"Anti-Semitism is un-American!" the girl selling the magazine cried to the passers-by, while her companions stood at her side.

Tommy called out his magazine, holding up a copy. He tried to watch the girls out of the corner of his eye, but people kept getting in his way. He wanted to see if they were selling more than he was. The girls didn't look Jewish, and the one with the magazines in her hand was pretty, with dark hair, a slim figure, and nice legs. She looked as if she might even be Irish. He couldn't seem to keep his eyes off her. She was more than good-looking enough to date up.

"Read Father Moylan's *Christian Justice!* Read it and see who are un-American and un-Christian! Read *Christian Justice!* Father Moylan's *Christian Justice*, ten cents a copy. Get *Christian Justice* and kick the Reds out of America!" he cried out.

"Yes, and kick Father Moylan out with them," a middle-aged woman screamed at him as she walked by. A cop frowned but said nothing.

Tommy scowled after the woman.

There was a steady flow of people along the sidewalk. A number hastened or drifted by without paying attention to any of the venders. Others strolling along paused to look at the girls and at Tommy, stood gaping for a few moments, and then passed on. Whenever too many people collected and remained too long to watch, the cops told them curtly to break it up and move on. Now and then pedestrians stopped to talk to the cops, to ask questions, and to protest about one or another of the magazine sellers.

"Go on back to Russia," a well-dressed man with a sleek shiny face said to Tommy.

"Read Father Moylan and kick the Reds out of America," Tommy yelled quickly.

A man halted and stood gazing at Tommy. He was powerfully built and looked as if he were a Swede. He said nothing. He placed his hands on his hips and stared. Tommy was so disconcerted that he could not meet this stranger's cold blue eyes.

"*Christian Justice*, ten cents a copy," Tommy cried out rather weakly, so disturbed by the man that he toned down his sales cry.

Tommy tried to appear busy and unaware of him. Suddenly he was drawn to look directly at him. The man sneered. He spat on the sidewalk. He walked on. Tommy looked after him.

"Another Red sonofabitch!" he muttered to himself.

He scowled ferociously.

"Hitler kicks 'em out. Read what we do for 'em in *Christian Justice!*" he bawled out, holding a copy aloft.

A passing girl gave him a smile. He smiled after her and wished she'd said something, or he'd had something on the tip of his tongue to say to attract her. Maybe standing here, a swell-looking girl would pick him up. He wandered off in his thoughts and forgot to call out his magazine. Suddenly he looked down and saw the black-haired girl selling a copy.

"Twenty million Christians murdered in Spain, Russia, and Mexico. Read *Christian Justice!*" he barked.

A little fellow came up to him.

"Why do you do this?" the little fellow asked in a sad voice.

"Huh?"

"Why do you spread the fires of race hatred like this, young fellow?" the man asked.

"Scram!" Tommy said.

The man walked off, shaking his head. Tommy stood there, scowling, grimacing, barking out his cries, feeling that if he looked tough as hell, perhaps it would make them afraid, and that was half the battle won. But he wasn't making many sales. He'd only sold about nine copies. He glanced down at the girls. They seemed to be selling some, but he didn't know how many.

The endless crowd filed past Forty-second Street and Fifth Avenue, and the steady stream of traffic poured by. He was getting fed up. His arm was beginning to tire from holding up the magazine. He shifted his bundle to his right arm and held a copy before his chest with his left hand. It seemed as if at least a half hour went by without a sale. One person after another passed, either not seeing him or else looking at him with a hasty, apathetic glance. Out of the corner of his eye he saw the girl sell another copy. He clenched his teeth. Someone ought to tear the damned rag out of her hand and slap her face.

"Why don't you get a job, you bum?" a passing woman yelled at him.

"I will when you Jews are thrown out of America," he yelled after her.

"I'm a better American than you are," she retorted.

"Read *Christian Justice* and save America," he barked.

"Bum!" the woman said before passing on.

A well-dressed man gave Tommy a dime. Tommy handed him the magazine and said thanks. The man casually moved off, tearing the magazine up and tossing the scraps in a large wire basket used as a public trash receptacle. Tommy cursed and grimaced.

And the crowd flowed by. No more sales.

"Here you are, Father Moylan's *Christian Justice,* only magazine in America telling the truth about international bankers. Read *Christian Justice* and smash the Reds! Ten cents a copy!"

And suddenly he was finding out that he could not check himself from looking down at the black-haired girl.

"Read it! Read it! Here you are, read it, a defense of American morality, *Christian Justice!*"

She was taking all his business away, and for what? To sell a filthy Communist rag!

The crowd passed on. Few people now showed any interest

in either magazine vender. Neither Tommy nor the girl was making any sales. And the crowd passed them in an endless stream.

"Read *Christian Justice!*"

"Anti-Semitism is un-American!"

VII

"Joe, here's the newsboy," Bill remarked when Tommy got home.

Tommy didn't answer. He went to his room, left his magazines in the closet, and then came to the living room.

"Extry paper! Read it and save the world! Read it and weep!"

"Sell any papers today, Tom?" Bill asked.

"What's it to you?"

"From newsboy to dictator," Joe said.

"You guys mind your own business," Tommy said curtly. He walked across the room and stood looking out of the window, his eyes fastened vacantly on the red brick two-story building across the street. Once a sweet girl named Mary Cecilia Connor had lived there, and he had used to sit here and watch for her to come out and had thought of her a lot and of how he would like to take her out and be in love with her, and he had never gotten beyond a nodding acquaintance with her. Her family had moved out to Jackson Heights, and he'd never heard anything about her again. She had been a nice girl, and he was suddenly nostalgic, nostalgic for the days when he would sometimes see her come out of that building, and sometimes pass her on the street and say hello. He finally turned from the window and glared at his brothers.

"Aw, let him alone," Bill said, winking at Joe.

"You guys mind your own goddamn business," Tommy snapped.

"Didn't I tell you to let him alone?" Bill said.

"And you, too, shut your mouth!"

Scowling, he stamped out of the room. Both brothers laughed.

VIII

"They didn't build America! The Christian built America!" the lean baldish speaker said in his deep bass voice, drawing a roar of applause from the one hundred and fifty-odd persons attending the meeting in the little hall on Third Avenue in the Sixties.

He paused and looked dramatically at his audience, which consisted mainly of young fellows like Tommy and middle-aged women. Just as the shouts died down, an elevated train rumbled by outside, drowning out the voices within. Behind the speaker there was a banner of the Christian American Party, a small political organization under whose auspices the meeting was being held. It was part of the Association for Christian Freedom. Around the hall there were signs and banners calling for the destruction of the Red Menace and for the freedom and prosperity of Christian America. The speaker was the last one on the evening's program, a man from out of town. The preceding speakers had worked up the audience for him, so that when he had begun, he had them in a frenzied mood, ready to yell and applaud almost his every sentence. And he had played upon them and was now going along full steam, with the audience having become almost a unit in its cheering, roaring, hissing, catcalling, and yelling as the appropriate stimuli were released.

Tommy sat near the exit in a row of camp chairs, and beside him were young men, all wearing the Association button. Tommy was slouched a bit in his chair, and there was a faraway look on his face.

"*They* didn't do the pick and shovel work to make America what it is today. Oh, no, not *they!*" the speaker said, emphasizing his words with a heavy and obviously sarcastic tone of voice.

Again he paused while he heard sarcastic laughter. Tommy's face seemed to light up with sudden interest, and he sat erect and attentive.

"It was the Christian who did the pick and shovel work to

build America!" the speaker yelled, accompanying his words with flourishing gestures.

The audience roared in agreement. Tommy thought this was true, and told himself that since it was, why should Christians, Christians like himself, have to do the pick and shovel work today? Why should he have to take a laborer's job and ride in the subway in dirty clothes and let everybody see he couldn't be any better than a common workman? Let *them* do that!

As the applause died down, a stout woman with a pudgy face yelled in a loud voice:

"Name them!"

"My fellow Christians, I don't have to name *them*," the speaker replied, smiling unctuously.

A lean woman, whose face was beginning to crack with wrinkles, jumped to her feet.

"I'll name them!" she cried in a shrill, high-pitched voice. "I'll name them! The dirty *Jews!*"

"Hear! Hear!" a red-faced little Irishman shouted.

There were many boos and catcalls.

"Down with the Jews!" Tommy boomed.

"Up the Gentile!" the red-faced little Irishman shouted.

"Down with the kikes!" Tommy boomed, but an elevated train drowned out his cry.

The speaker stood poised, and when he could proceed he smiled knowingly.

"Far be it from me, my fellow Christians, to be an anti-Semite," he said suavely, and many of the audience laughed good-naturedly. He continued. "Anti-Semite is now the gutter phrase which the Reds use to cast scorn on those who would do their Christian and patriotic duty."

More boos and catcalls.

"I am not afraid of the word when aliens, Reds, hook-nosed parasites hurl it at me," he cried out in a rising voice. "No, when I am called that by such ilk, it is a badge of honor. When they call me that, they prove that I am not veering from the right course."

He paused to receive an outburst of cheers.

"Down with the Reds!" Tommy shouted with all his lung power, and his cry was taken up.

"I am not here to talk against this race or that," the speaker continued. "I am here to talk about American conditions, about the problems which are facing Christian America in its gravest and darkest hour of peril."

More cheers.

"My fellow Christians, what has America come to when a man of God, a clergyman, a great American, a great Christian, a champion of the common people, is barred from speaking over the radio in the name of justice because he tells the truth?" He waited for the catcalls, hisses, and boos. "Why is he barred from the radio?"

"Ask the Jews!" a woman screamed.

"Why is he barred? Because he tells the truth."

The audience cheered hysterically, rising to its feet, climbing on the chairs, drowning out the rumble of another passing elevated train. Tommy was on his chair, yelling until he was hoarse and out of breath.

"He tells the truth, and certain gentlemen, so-called, do not like to hear the truth. And, my Christian friends, I might add that these gentlemen are not named Murphy, or Gallagher, or O'Reilley. No, they aren't named Smith or Jones, either."

He paused for another reverberating catcall.

"But what of it? Do these gentlemen, so-called, care for the truth? Ask me another. Do the rulers of Red Russia care for the truth?"

"Save America from the Jews!" a red-haired woman screamed, and many took up her cry, shouting it in unison.

"Save America! Yes, my Christian compatriots, save America! Save America from all the enemies within her gates!" he shouted with the practiced inflection of one who knew how to mold his audience. And then he waited for the proper response of assent. Another elevated train interfered with this assent, and then he was able to continue.

"But America will be saved!"

Roars.

"And America will be Christian!"

Hysterical roars.

"Last week," the speaker continued, "I spoke in Philadelphia, and six hundred people joined our party, six hundred Christian Americans."

The audience once more was on its feet, screaming enthusiastically. Tommy, once more on his chair, was shouting and thinking of how things were moving, and he was thrilling with the sense of belonging to something that was growing in power and numbers.

"Two weeks ago, I spoke in Chicago. Two thousand joined us." The speaker produced another wave of cheers. "Two thousand Christian Americans who see eye to eye with us."

From without came the sirens of fire engines, and the hall seemed like a bedlam.

"Tremble, Judea!" a tall, emaciated woman cried, standing on a chair and waving bony arms.

She was cheered. The fire-engine sirens were heard again. The tall woman was waving her arms and lost her balance, but as she fell from the chair, two men caught her. Tommy and some of the other young men laughed.

"My friends, our movement is greater than the Crusades. It is the New Crusade."

More noise.

Poised and waiting, his face beaming with smiles, the speaker watched the audience seethe. He casually poured water from the pitcher on the table beside him, took up a glass, drank.

"And that reminds me," he went on, smiling disingenuously, his voice in a low key. "That reminds me." They knew something was coming, and waited. "Where did the Crusaders go in the Crusades of the Middle Ages?"

"Jewrusalem," a women yelled, and many parroted her, and there was much laughter.

"And the new crusaders are coming to Jew York," the red-haired woman yelled.

"Down with the Jews of Jew York!" Tommy boomed.

"That reminds me of something funny that happened to me when I came to this town to make my speech here. You know, when I came in, the customs inspector stopped me, and I had trouble smuggling in my Bible with the New Testament. And I had forgotten my passport. You know, coming here, I forgot that I was coming into a foreign country."

There was more laughter; then hisses, boos, and more cat-calls.

He went on. Tommy felt that he wanted to be in with every-body here, to yell with them, boo with them, shout out cries which would make them laugh and yell, and make them turn and look at him, see that he'd made them laugh and yell, feel that they liked it and respected him and thought he was all right and regular. The speaker continued. Tommy suddenly wasn't listening. He remembered how when he'd been a kid in school he would often find himself unable to listen to what was said, and sometimes now he found he still couldn't listen for a long time. He leaned forward in his chair and told himself that he would listen. He kept thinking and telling him-self now what could his family say if they knew all this, heard and saw this here tonight, came here? And how could the Reds answer this man? What would people say who insulted him, gave him dirty looks, made dirty cracks at him when he stood on the street selling the magazine? What would they say if they were here tonight?

"If *they* did not control the press, the radio, Hollywood, even some of the highest offices in the land, then, then the Christians of this country would know of the danger facing them. But they *do* control so much that they pull the wool over the eyes of the descent Christians of America. And it is the old, old story. *They* have climbed on the backs of others, and it is to *their* interest that the truth be strangled and treated with con-tempt, that the truth be denied to the Christians of this coun-try."

Tommy was still leaning forward, attentive, straining and forcing himself to listen to every word. And he reminded himself that he would have to remember some of the things this man said and use them when he was out selling *Christian Justice*.

The speaker went on, describing plots and revolutionary schemes to drench America in blood and turn it into a Soviet state. These plots were being hatched in Mexico, and a Red Army was being organized to march into America and to turn it into another Spain, another Russia, another Mexico. He said that, in fact, these other countries had only provided the dress rehearsals for the terror now being planned for America.

"If *they* have *their* way, *they* will get more than Shylock's pound of flesh!" he shouted.

"Kill *them*. Kill the Jews! Kill the Reds!" a hysterical woman shouted, and her cry was taken up fanatically.

By the time the speaker had finished, there was a unified mood of hostility and fanaticism pervading those present. Tommy was stirred. He wanted to strike a blow immediately for the cause. But he was afraid, too. At times during the evening he and many others had trembled when the speaker had described what the Reds would do if their revolution succeeded. He had even imagined himself being tortured, torn limb from limb by Reds. He wanted to see them stopped before they got too powerful, and perhaps it was too late already.

With the meeting over, women were crowded around the speaker. A neat well-dressed man with a mustache was signing up seven recruits to the party, and literature was being sold at a table by the exit door. Tommy stood indecisive. He wanted to go up and tell the speaker he was with him, give him his name, bring himself to the attention of the speaker. Just as he started up, Al O'Reilley came up to him.

"Doin' anything, Gallagher?"

"Why?"

"Give him some of the stickers, Frank," Al said.

A dark-browed fellow handed Tommy stickers on which was printed the slogan BUY CHRISTIAN. Tommy took them.

"We're goin' out to past these around," Al said.

"Can you wait a minute?" Tommy asked.

"Why? What for?"

"I wanted to go up and say a word to the speaker," Tommy answered.

"Come on, do it another time. We got to get busy. It's gettin' late," Al snapped at him.

Disappointed that he was missing the chance to make himself known to the speaker, Tommy left with Al and six others.

They went along Third Avenue, pasting their signs on darkened store windows and elevated posts. They bumped into a lone fellow with a large nose and Semitic features. Tommy and Al clouted him in the face, and the fellow was knocked groggy and unable to defend himself. They surrounded him, jeered him as a Jew, and punched him some more. Al laughed while Tommy pasted a sticker on his coat. Then Al gave him a kick and told him to beat it. The man staggered away. One of the fellows found an old tomato and whizzed it after him but missed. They hooted until the man was out of sight, and went on pasting up their stickers.

When they reached Fourteenth Street, they had used up all they had. They walked over to Union Square, making dirty cracks as they walked. At Union Square there was a small group on a street corner discussing politics. The boys busted into the group and began arguing. The group was dispersed by cops. One of the fellows, with a Yiddish accent, demanded that the cops arrest Tommy and his pals, and the cop told him that he had better blow, and blow quickly. The cop then told Tommy and the boys to watch their step in this neighborhood with all the Reds around. Al said that he knew of a school run by the Socialist Party, more Reds, near by, that they ought to do a job on. They made their way to an old loft building on a dark street off Union Square.

IX

Tommy, Al O'Reilley, and a number of the boys had been going around, starting street fights with persons whose features were clearly Semitic, and breaking up street meetings. They had usually been successful in these tactics. They had had fun and had escaped serious injuries. Al and Pete Sullivan had been arrested and in court. The judge had warned them to stop and count fifty before they got into any more fights, and then let them go. This had made them heroes, and Tommy had envied them their honors. When they broke up street meetings, they used a regular technique. They would saunter up to a meeting in twos and threes and place themselves strategically in the crowd, with a number of them up in front to be in a good position to rush the speaker and beat him up. Before they would get down to the serious business of bruising and punching, they would first try to disrupt the meeting, frighten the speaker and listeners, and make their work easier by a preliminary process of demoralization. They would mill about, push and shove, step on toes, heckle, interrupt, and boo.

On a pleasant Saturday evening, a number of them took a subway up to the Bronx, planning to break up a street meeting. They had broken up one at the same corner two weeks before, manhandling a number of the listeners and slugging the speaker. Tommy had carried off honors in that fray. He had moved about during the fracas doling out rabbit punches in the back of the neck that had had telling effects. They had learned that, despite their work, meetings were still being held in the same place, and they decided to drive them off that corner for good.

It was a corner by a vacant lot in a workers' district, and there were small brick buildings along both sides of the street. The speaker stood on a stand from which an American flag drooped. This evening the speaker was a gray-haired man with a rich, full voice. The crowd was larger than it had been on the night the boys had broken up the meeting. A number of the crowd appeared to be workingmen, but a still larger proportion were youths, radical lads and girls, many of whom were students. There was also a good sprinkling of the inquisitive, those people who look at building construction going on, watch fires, listen to harangues from soap boxes just in order to pass the time. Some of the youths looked pretty burly and they were to be found in the crowd in groups, one group of ten or twelve standing directly before the speaker's stand. Only ten fellows had come along to break up the meeting: Al O'Reilley, Tommy, Pete Sullivan, Eddie Slavin, a little fellow named Johnny Brown, and five bruisers whom Tommy didn't know. Coming up on the subway, they had had a lot of fun kidding with Pete and Al about counting fifty before they hauled off on a Red or crashed their fists into a mockie. They sauntered up to the meeting in the usual fashion, but since there were fewer of them than they had expected and the crowd was a little large, they stuck close together on the right wing of the crowd. Before they had come, there had been some bitter heckling of the meeting coming from a group of Communists. The speaker had countered the hecklers, and finally they had marched off in dudgeon after calling on all workers assembled to shun this Trotskyite meeting like a plague. After they left, the meeting proceeded in an orderly fashion. Gradually, people out strolling had stopped to listen. When Tommy arrived, he gazed about with an apprehensive look, because there was a bigger crowd than he had counted on. The first words he heard were:

"When the Fascists rear their heads here, only the revolutionary working class can smash them and liberate all mankind from fascism and capitalism. Comrades, fellow workers, friends, this is the lesson of revolutionary defeats suffered in Europe, and this is the lesson we must learn in America before it is too late."

Tommy grinned. The usual boushwah of the Reds, he reflected. He thought how he might be arrested, and get out scot free, and that would be something to raise his stock. He smiled to himself, wondering what the family would think if he got pinched.

"That is why we have issued calls for a Workers Defense Guard to be prepared to smash the Fascist gangs when they raise their heads in America as they have begun to do," the speaker went on.

Tommy frowned. What did this bastard mean? Well, in a couple of minutes he'd eat his words, and maybe he'd eat them along with a couple of his own teeth that would be knocked down his throat. He looked around. The crowd was growing, and some of those around liked what this Red louse was saying. He noticed, too, that a number of Jews were listening. And some of the Jews, he reflected, said that the Jews weren't Red. Well, they were. And still, there were some big guys around here. Well, maybe it was just as he had heard speakers say at meetings, the Reds had no guts. And again he glanced around. Some of the guys here were pretty husky.

"Let's get going," Al whispered to Tommy.

"They ain't worth smacking down, these bums," Tommy said quietly to Al.

"What's the matter, gettin' yellow?" Al answered in a low voice, and all the while the speaker was continuing his harangue, launching into an attack on Father Moylan.

"Who's yellow?"

"Well, why did you make that crack?" Al said.

"They're punks," Tommy said.

"Punks or not, we're gonna get 'em! Now, let's start grinding the organ," Al said.

Neither of them observed that they were being closely watched, and that a group of youths and men edged through the crowd and stood near them.

"Comrades, you know the Moylanites broke up our last meeting. Comrades . . ."

"Litvinov's name is Bronstein and Trotsky's is Finklestein," Tommy yelled.

He had blurted it out before he knew exactly what he was saying. He trembled now, and he was nervous. But this would show that he wasn't yellow.

"Get down off there, Finklestein!" a husky yelled.

"Quit hidin' behind the flag, Finklestein!" Al O'Reilley yelled.

There was movement in the crowd. Some started edging away. Others, mainly youths, began going over toward the hecklers.

"Do not let yourself be provoked, comrades! Defend yourselves and your meeting if attacked," the speaker yelled.

People around Al, Tommy, and the others were telling them

to shut up. Near Tommy, an argument about Americanism broke out. A tall Slav with a foreign accent told the Moylanite boys to shut up and leave the meeting.

"This is a free country, and we're Americans," Eddie Slavin replied to him.

There was a tension pervading the meeting now, but suddenly the audience was quiet, and the speaker was going on.

"Who is this sanctimonious hypocrite who bellows Fascism over the radio?" the speaker said, raising his voice.

"Don't say that again, you!" Tommy bellowed.

"Quit hidin' behind the flag!" Al yelled.

The tall Slav told them that they should shut up or leave the meeting. Arguments were breaking out in the crowd, and the speaker couldn't be heard.

"Quit hidin' behind the flag!" Al O'Reilley yelled again.

All his companions started shouting this cry in unison. Somebody was pushed. Somebody had his toe stepped on. A girl yelled. There were scuffles. Pete Sullivan suddenly rushed a youth and they traded blows. Tommy saw Al O'Reilley slip on brass knuckles and cut the jaw of a fellow in a blue shirt. Tommy caught the fellow off balance and clipped him on the other jaw. The fellow's knees sagged. The fighting was general. The crowd opened up, and there was slugging on all sides, curses, screams, yells. Many who had stopped to listen hurried away, while others stepped aside and watched. The youths near the stand closed in on Tommy and his companions.

Tommy moved to polish off a little Jew in front of him. Just as he took a step forward with fists cocked, he was smashed in the left eye. He seemed to see streaks of irregular light. He felt a sharp pain in his eye. He had a sick thudding headache. His whole body seemed to grow weak and powerless. He bent forward, holding his eye. He was pounded on the face until he dropped. He moaned.

Everything now was like a nightmare to him. Curses, cries, angry taunts, screams, groans, swinging fists, clashing bodies were all about him. His head cleared a little. He noticed there was blood on his hands. He tried to rise and he was knocked down. Groggy, he staggered off to one side.

Al O'Reilley was backing away with a welt on his cheek. Pressing him was a broad-shouldered worker whose face was streaming blood, but who came at him pumping his hands like dynamos. Al swung out but not so swiftly as his opponent, and the broad-shouldered laborer sent him spinning backward. Eddie Slavin, his shirt ripped half off, suddenly bolted out of the crowd and ran lickety-split down the street.

Women were screaming and spectators were yelling for the police to come. People came running down the street from the near-by houses.

"Kill the Fascists!" many began to cry.

"Inhuman, barbarous," a man watching was saying.

"Is this democracy, heh?" a Jewish man with gray hair said on the side lines.

All those who had come with Al and Tommy to disrupt the meeting were backing off. Tommy's head had cleared a little. He was like a sick animal. He could feel his eye swelling. He saw the brawling and slugging with his good eye. It looked bad for the boys. He slunk away from the fighting.

Al and the other boys continued to retreat, taking severe punishment. They were now outnumbered, and the defenders of the meeting fought with fury. A young Jewish boy yelled: "Down with Fascism," and rushed headlong at Pete Sullivan. Pete caught him coming in, square on the jaw with an uppercut. The boy half turned from the force of the blow, and his knees gave way. He dropped on the street, unconscious. Pete was smashed in the nose. He turned and ran off. Police sirens were heard. Al and all the others beat it down the street, followed by taunts, angry cries, and a few flying bricks.

x

"Boy, your face looks like a slow-motion sunset," Bill said.
Tommy frowned. He looked grotesque. There was a yellowish, purplish-black spot around his left eye, covering the swollen lid and circling down under the eye. The eye was blood-

shot and watered constantly so that while he ate he had to keep dabbing at it with a handkerchief. He found also that he could not chew on the left side without his jaw hurting.

"Let him alone," Mr. Gallagher said.

"He's got it coming to him. He goes around telling us we don't understand, as if he knew something. He had it coming to him, the hoodlum," Joe spoke up.

"It wasn't a hoodlum fight," Tommy said.

Mr. Gallagher looked pained.

"All I want to say is I'm fed up with him. Why doesn't he get a job and not expect others to feed him?" Bill said.

"Tommy, I hope you learned your lesson. You might get killed going out this way," Mr. Gallagher added.

"I swear I don't know what the world's coming to, with this fighting. And when I saw him Sunday morning, I thought I was seeing a ghost," Mrs. Gallagher exclaimed.

"Or a cartoon of Ripley's," Bill said.

Tommy glared at Bill. His eye watered. He dabbed it with his handkerchief. He felt humiliated.

"Well, he wasn't only afraid to be the newsboy yesterday morning in front of church. He was afraid to go to mass for fear somebody would see that interior decorating on his face," Bill said.

"I can take it, don't worry about me. And let me tell you, the kikes will pay for this."

"Tommy, why don't you cut this stuff out and try and get a job? You know there's no good in all this fighting, no good is ever going to come of it. I don't care what you say you're fighting for, it's no good. You got to learn to live and let live, and if you do, the other fellow'd be the same to you," Mr. Gallagher said.

"Maybe you want to have 'em walk all over you. Well, I don't," Tommy answered.

Joe and Bill burst into laughter.

"You sure look like you got stepped on and tramped over," Bill said.

Tommy jumped from his chair and stalked out of the room.

His mother followed him, while Joe and Bill told each other that nobody should give him sympathy now, because he'd gotten what was coming to him. Mrs. Gallagher found him sitting on his bed with his chin sunk in his cupped hands.

"Thomas, you come and eat your supper," she said.

"I don't want any," he answered.

"Please, for my sake."

"Can't you let me alone? You're all against me," he whined.

"I'm your mother!"

"Please, leave me alone. You don't understand."

"Now, Thomas . . ." she began.

He walked past her and went into the bathroom. He locked the door. He looked at his eye in the mirror. It was watering, and he touched his handkerchief to it. Pains, coming and going in that region, stabbed him repeatedly. He had never had a shiner like this in all his life. He kept examining it carefully, thinking that the bastards had made his face look like a rainbow. He went back to his room, closed the door, and lay on his bed with a handkerchief over his eyes. Immediately he began to think how it might have been different. They'd been outnumbered. Some of the guys who said they were coming hadn't shown up. Suddenly he was arguing with himself against his brothers. They could let him alone, couldn't they? It wasn't their business.

Maybe he shouldn't have gone Saturday night. He wished he hadn't. He tried to console himself by thinking that he was a martyr, but he couldn't find any consolation in this thought, not with a badge of shame pounded on his face. He was afraid even to go out of the house and let people see it.

He felt another pain in the eye. He was afraid that he might be permanently disabled.

After his brothers left, he went out to the kitchen and finished his supper. His father came out and sat with him.

"Tommy, tell me what this business is all about. It looks bad to me," Mr. Gallagher said.

"You don't understand."

"Tom, I saw Joe Cannon today. His brother owns a three-

story building, and Joe thinks his brother needs a superintendent, and I spoke to him about you getting the job. It's
not so much of a job, but after all it's work, and will you
take it as soon as you're . . . feeling better?"

Tommy didn't answer. He was fed up with everything
here at home. He ate with a surly look on his face, chewing
carefully because of his jaw.

"Will you take it?"

Tommy nodded. He and his father sat in the kitchen, saying nothing.

When the swelling had almost gone, Tommy went to work
as the superintendent of the building owned by Joe Cannon's
brother. He hated the work, and told himself over and over
again that superintendent was a high-toned word for janitor.
He had to empty garbage wearing dirty clothes, and this
he hated more than any other thing he had to do. And two
of the tenants were Jewish. He could scarcely be civil to them.
And he kept thinking how in the winter it would be damned
cold in the mornings and he'd have to be up early, before
dawn, to tend to the furnace. After a week he gave up the
work. He decided to go back selling the magazine. After all,
it was a cause and it would pay him in the end. Why should
he be a dope?

The family was angry and disappointed when they learned
he had given up his new job. He resumed selling *Christian
Justice*. He came home one Sunday morning after selling in
front of the parish church, feeling glum because he'd had
few sales. During the first part of the meal no one talked to
him. But Bill and Joe kept glancing at him accusingly. He got
sore.

"Cut it out!" he snapped.

"Nobody's saying anything to you," Bill replied.

"I ain't doin' nothin' to you," Tommy said.

"Goddamn you! I'm fed up!" Bill yelled, and he jumped
to his feet and rushed around the table.

Tommy started to get out of his chair, but as he was doing
so, Bill caught him on the jaw and tumbled him over the

chair. Tommy gazed up at Bill, bewildered, holding his jaw. Mrs. Gallagher was on her feet and in tears. Joe and Mr. Gallagher got between Tommy and Bill.

"Fine guy you are, hitting me before I had a chance," Tommy said.

"Shut up, you bum! I'll give you worse than you got!" Bill cried.

Again Joe and the father tried to pacify Bill. They led him back to his chair, and he sat down. Mrs. Gallagher sobbed.

"You wouldn't do that to me outside," Tommy said.

Bill had calmed down. He looked at Tommy scornfully.

"Tommy, your brother lost his temper, but he's right. You got to turn over a new leaf. You made me look like a monkey running out on the job I got you," Mr. Gallagher said.

"I didn't ask you to do it," Tommy answered.

"Who the hell's going to feed you?" Mr. Gallagher asked, suddenly losing his temper.

"Jesus Christ, but ain't you a nervy sonofabitch," Joe said.

Bill was pushing back his chair. Mrs. Gallagher screamed and yelled out that she would not stand for this. Her tears stopped Bill. While she shook with sobs, Tommy got to his feet.

"All right, if that's the way you feel about it," he said, leaving the room.

Her head bent, Mrs. Gallagher wiped her eyes. The front door was heard to slam.

"He'll come back. That guy likes a meal ticket," Bill said.

"Come now, Mother," the father said as he put his hand tenderly on her shoulder.

"I'm damned glad I socked him," Bill remarked.

XI

Tommy was bitter. He walked alone in the milling Sunday night crowd on Broadway, past the lighted theaters where crowds waited in line to be admitted. The brightness of the street, the many people, the atmosphere of pleasure-seeking, all emphasized his aloneness. He looked at fellows with girls. He saw a number of foreign or Semitic faces, and every time he saw one, hatred flared in his soul. They were the kind whom he blamed for his plight. He smoked his last cigarette and walked with hands stuck in his pockets. Then he wanted another smoke. He thought of bumming the price of a pack off someone, and he didn't have the nerve to. He told himself again and again that he couldn't go home, he wouldn't. They didn't understand him. He was never going home. They all thought they had him down, did they! Well, they had another guess coming.

Aimless, he wandered along, going over to Fifth Avenue. Many people strolled by, walking slowly, looking in windows, drifting on. A bus stopped beside him, and from the top came the laughter and joshing of two young couples. He looked at them with envy. He strolled along, titillated by shapes of the women who passed. He turned at Forty-second Street and wandered back over to Broadway. He paused in front of a motion picture theater that presented Russian movies, and he cursed Russia and the Reds. He told himself that somebody ought to throw a stink bomb in the place. He wandered on. He picked a cigarette butt off the curb and smoked it. He wandered back to mill along with the slow-moving crowds on Broadway and to watch the people.

He wandered about Broadway, Seventh Avenue, and Fifth Avenue until around midnight. Dismally, he spent his last nickel on subway fare and slumped in a seat in a partially filled subway car. Across from him were several couples on a date, now homeward bound. Seeing fellows with girls like this made him feel more alone. Directly across from him was a tired couple, and the girl rested her blonde head on the fellow's shoulder, while he had his arm around her. A little way down was a good-looking, red-haired girl with a greasy-looking fellow who had a small mustache. They held hands, rubbed knees, and talked low and intently. And he had no girl. And he wanted one. Hell, even if he did have one, he wouldn't have any dough to spend on her. He'd always been a football to be kicked around. He was fed up. His goddamn brother, too, the punk, cracking him when he was sitting down and didn't have a chance to defend himself.

He looked around the car at the couples. His mood changed. He was filled with contempt for those he saw. He wanted to stand up in the car and curse them all with the most obscene words he knew. He dozed off, fell asleep. But luckily he awakened at his station.

He sneaked quietly into the apartment. Bill, who was in the living room reading the baseball scores in the Monday morning edition of the *News,* heard him come in. Tommy went quietly to his room, quickly took off his clothes, and got into bed. When Bill came into the room to go to bed, Tommy lay with his face to the wall, feigning sleep. Bill looked at him with contempt.

"You haven't even got the guts to sleep in the park," Bill said, beginning to undress.

Tommy pretended not to hear. Making a little noise, Bill finally got undressed, turned off the light, and went to bed. Tommy lay there unable to sleep. He lay awake, pitying himself, telling himself that he was brave, thinking of his hatreds, vowing over and over again that his day was coming, and assuring himself that when it did come, it would be a day of bitter vengeance. Look at Hitler in Germany! Hitler had known days like this, too!

1939.

The Life Adventurous

AND OTHER STORIES

The Life Adventurous

"I COULD BE A SUCCESSFUL BABBITT if I wanted to," Lewis Gordon boasted.

"I know you could," Powers Norton answered.

They were smoking cigarettes. The difference in their characters was observable in the way each of them smoked. Lewis, a prepossessing young man in his twenties, was sitting on the park bench, relaxed, smoking casually, holding the cigarette between the index and the third finger of his left hand and now and then taking a puff. Powers was a ruddy-faced man with touches of gray around the temples. He was in his late thirties, and there was a harassed look in his brown eyes. He was medium-sized, with light hair. He seemed physically soft. He puffed nervously, taking a few puffs on a cigarette, and then throwing it away and lighting a new one.

Lewis and Powers had met at the Sour Apple, a Bohemian forum on the near North Side, and they had quickly become friends. Now they sat talking on a bench in Lincoln Park, near a path where people passed, and they could see before them a broad sweep of well-kept grass.

"It's easier and it's safer to be a success in business than to live as you do," Powers said.

"And duller. The curse of life is dullness."

Powers didn't answer. He seemed to be reflecting, and Lewis watched him closely.

"Would we have met at the Sour Apple, and would we be

friends, if both of us didn't want to free ourselves from dullness, the dullness of the bourgeoisie?" Lewis asked.

"Well, I suppose not. I never could quite understand myself," Powers said.

"Powers, the trouble with you is that you want to blame yourself for the faults of the world. I don't. I blame the world. Come on, old fellow, snap out of it. Be an extrovert. The introvert never has any fun."

"I suppose you're right, Lewis."

"The whole world is run on a series of fictions. It is all as if this were so and that were so. It is as if a man's property were his own. It's his own just as long as I admit that it is. When I no longer admit it, the fiction vanishes like smoke, like a will-o-the-wisp."

"Yes, there's something in what you say, but, then, a policeman and a jail aren't mere fictions," Powers answered.

"Hell, that's the least of my worries, and it should be the least of yours. Nothing can go wrong with my plan. I've worked it out carefully. There's no chance of a slip-up, not unless we lose our heads. And we're not going to lose them. Our heads weren't given to us to be lost. But, there, I'm getting metaphysical. If I say our heads weren't given to us, I recognize that there is a Giver of heads in the universe. If there is a Giver of heads, that Giver is supreme over us. It is in His hands, or Its hands, to control us. And that is impossible. Because we are supreme in ourselves and unto ourselves. Ego is King, if king there need be in the world," Lewis explained.

"You've built up a whole philosophy to justify your kind of life, haven't you?"

"It's merely a recognition of the facts. The facts about ourselves and our nature. And I don't believe in drawing conclusions merely for the sake of drawing them and talking about them. I'm not a Bughouse Square or Sour Apple soapboxer. I want to draw conclusions in order to act on them."

"I have no philosophy. I have nothing."

"You have yourself, your ego. You and I have formed our own League of Egotists."

Powers nervously lit another cigarette. He looked off, troubled.

"Sometimes I can't believe I'm where I am and what I am," he said moodily.

"You taught sociology, didn't you?"

"Yes. I was going along. I was in a rut. I know that. If I hadn't been in a rut I wouldn't have acted the way I did. I have no regrets."

"One of the cardinal principles of conscious egotism is to have no regrets. Regret is folly."

"You know, Kitty was wonderful. I still think of her. My God, I think of her naked body on the bed. I guess I was bored with my wife. After I slept with Kitty I felt like a new man."

"She must have been necessary for your ego."

"We spent a summer at the sand dunes. I came into town for the second half of the summer quarter. And Kitty was a school teacher from the country. But there was nothing school-teacherish about her. She seemed like the sweetest, prettiest thing. She looked so innocent. And she was crazy with lust. No, it wasn't love. It was lust."

"Lust is one of the fine fruits of egotism."

"Anyway, I was bored with teaching and I was even bored with myself. I was seedy and rusty. The first day I took over the class, I noticed her. I couldn't help looking at her. And she didn't seem to mind it. Do you know, within a week I was sleeping with her."

"You had a good time."

"But I ruined my life."

"What's ruined about it?"

"Look at me."

"Your life isn't ruined. You've escaped into freedom."

"I acted like a kid."

"Listen, Powers, I want to act like a kid, in that sense, all of my life. I never want to grow old and smug."

"If you're married, and you have two kids, and you're living quietly, and then suddenly you let go the way I did, you get unhinged. I was. Christ, kid, I couldn't think of anything but

Kitty. I wanted to be in bed with her forever. I'd go to class every day exhausted."

"What better can you want from a woman? Young, beautiful, without shame."

"I used to wish I were twenty-one."

Lewis laughed heartily.

"Where's Kitty now?"

"I guess she's back in Iowa. It's funny you never heard of the mess. The papers carried the story on the front page. University Professor In Love Nest With Student."

"You should have been discreet."

"But what I can't understand is the way I felt toward my wife. When this mess was in the papers, I found out that she had been having little affairs of her own. I was so damned jealous. I knew I had no right to be jealous. Hadn't I done the same? And yet I was."

"What did she do?"

"She took the kids and ran off with a tap dancer. I don't know how she met him, but she did. It broke me up. And Kitty was dismissed from school. I lost my job. Her father came to Chicago to shoot me, and, when he found her, she was in bed with some kid."

"Did the father shoot?"

"No, he didn't. Hell, it was a disgusting mess. My colleagues avoided me like the plague."

"I'll bet they envied you," Lewis said. He continued: "Are you still brooding over it?"

"No, I really am not. I'll tell you, I'm still bewildered. It's almost a year since it happened."

"You never hear from Kitty?"

"No. Nor from my wife and kids. I keep wondering where they are, what the kids are like."

"Hell, you're free. You and I have no responsibilities. You stick with me, and we'll go places."

"I really don't care what I do or what happens to me. What difference does it make?"

"It makes no difference except for your ego."

"Let's get a drink."

"All right. We'll get a bottle of gin."

They got up and left.

II

"Instead of looking so gloomy, why not be glad we have enough dough to eat breakfast with?" Lewis said.

"My gloom is purely physical. I'm not as young as you are. At my age, a man can't drink the way you can and not feel the effects," Powers said.

They sat eating ham and eggs at a marble-topped table in a restaurant on North Clark Street. It was noon, and the restaurant was crowded and noisy.

"I have a headache," Powers said.

"It was an amusing evening, and the two dames weren't so bad either, were they?"

"No, they weren't," Powers said, but he agreed with Lewis because he didn't want to disagree. It would have been too much effort. He had a wretched hangover, and he didn't even want to talk. It was too much of an exertion even to utter the words.

There was no sensible reason in the world why he should be disgusted with himself for getting drunk and sleeping with the girl he'd picked up. In fact, he could feel proud of himself in a way. Here he was, a man who had had little youth, who had worked his way through college, become a sociologist. He had been Puritanical, repressed, timid. And now, look at the way he lived. Why should he seem ridiculous in his own eyes?

"Oh!" he exclaimed, half aloud, without realizing it.

"Come on, snap out of it. Eat. You're going to feel better. We'll sit in the sun in Lincoln Park and philosophize."

Powers looked blankly at his ham and eggs. He ate slowly, with weary motions.

"I always did have a preference for telephone operators. I don't know why, but I do. All of the telephone operators I've known have been dumb. But I don't mind a Dumb Dora if she has looks and knows the tricks."

—What the hell does it all mean? Powers asked himself.

He wanted to get out of this damned rut he was in, and he didn't know how. Every time he resolved to do something about himself, he broke his good resolutions. His self-confidence was gone. He didn't have the will power necessary to get out of his rut. He wanted to be a respectable married man. A smug professor. And he couldn't be. He was afraid he wouldn't even be able to get references, and what else could he do?

"Mine's name was Dora. Well, Dora gave us what we needed to change our luck. I suppose by now she's discovered that I pinched a five from her pocketbook. Poor Dumb Dora."

Powers was disturbed.

"I don't see why I shouldn't have done it," Lewis said.

Powers didn't answer. Yes, arguing was too much of a form of violent exercise for him this morning. It wasn't right to do such things. He was as responsible as Lewis. Wasn't he eating out of the five? God, he was disgusted with himself. But nothing mattered. Nothing mattered. If he only didn't have this hangover.

"In fact, I gave her something. I gave her some of my manhood," Lewis said, enjoying his own witticism.

Yes, he had been a promising professor with a promising and secure academic future ahead of him. Now he was a bum. What was so attractive, so pleasurable in a fly-by-night success with a stupid telephone operator? The lack of consequences and responsibility? But he didn't mind that—that is, he hadn't when he was first married. He had to realize that the past was irrevocable.

"Hell, sex is half a fraud unless you decorate it with logical 'as ifs.'"

"It wouldn't have mattered in my life one way or the other whether I'd met this girl and slept with her, or not," Powers said.

"Now you're showing some healthy cynicism," Lewis said.

Powers smothered his resentment. Think of it—allowing this kid to patronize him.

"Well, Dumb Dora loved it, and that's no boast. But do you know what occurred to me, Powers?"

"What?" Powers asked, wiping up his plate with a piece of bread.

"She wanted to talk about everything we did. And she didn't know who she was with, because suddenly she blushed and asked me if I thought she was awful because of the words she used. The actions didn't seem to give her any qualms of conscience, but the words did. And she wanted to keep using them. Do you know why?"

Powers didn't say anything. He stirred his coffee.

"People have to build ideas and emotions around sex. She had to fill in the gap between desire and fulfillment with talk because she wanted more than she got. Ah, the pitiful damned fools who belong to what is called humanity."

"I kind of felt sorry for them, poor kids."

"They got what they wanted. Weren't they itching for it? But my observation is very good—even if I admit it. I always admit I'm bright, though, when I am. My Dumb Dora wishes that you could have some rousing bedroom sport every minute of your life."

"She was a nymphomaniac."

"They're the best kind of Dumb Dora to get. You know, they generally can't become pregnant either. I like 'em. Give me a bitch every time."

Powers was uneasy because of an acute sense of loss. He wanted to be back with his wife and children. And yet he hadn't really wanted his wife and children. If he had wanted them, would he be here now? Hell, there was no free will. He had not been a free agent. He had done what he couldn't have prevented himself from doing with all the will power, self-restraint, moral sense, and decorum in the whole world.

"I suppose I'd feel the hollowness of it if I weren't an egotist. I have my way of enhancing such mundane details of life. To me, a female is a delectable piece of warm, living, panting property that I can own. And when I do, I score up another triumph for my ego. I look on a woman's body as a violin, and I'm touching all of the strings. I begin with great delicacy, and I like to end in lust, with a few smacks and some bites to finish it off. And my Dumb Doras like it. But, then, they're generally bitches. As I said, give me a bitch every time in the week. It's not merely their experience that I appreciate. They aren't encumbrances. In a way, I guess they have something of the real old ego in them, too."

Powers drank his coffee.

"Have some more. It'll fix you up."

He signaled to the waitress, and she brought him more coffee. He drank it black and without sugar.

"What are we going to do?" he asked.

"Contemplate a blade of grass like Walt Whitman."

"I don't mean immediately. This five isn't going to last forever."

"It's too early in the day to discuss that. We'll see."

Powers gulped his coffee. He didn't seem to feel any better. And, besides his physical condition, there was his deep depression. He was ashamed of himself, filled with self-disgust.

He wanted to get out of the restaurant. He had nothing to do to make him want to hurry anywhere, but he wanted to get out and go to Lincoln Park.

"Let's hurry," he said.

"I want more coffee. And then we'll restore our souls in the sunshine," Lewis answered.

He lit a cigarette and sipped coffee. Powers tried to think of nothing. He imagined a tennis game in his mind, a trick he always used on himself when he had a hangover. He would play tennis games by himself for hours because he found this a means of not having to face himself, to assimilate his sense of shame. He shouldn't be ashamed. What difference did it make? His reputation was ruined anyway. What he did mattered to no one. Why should he be ashamed? He played mental tennis with himself.

"Dumb Dora asked me what I did, and I told her I was the president of the Junior Chamber of Commerce."

Powers nodded.

"Listen, I've got it. We've stalled enough. Let's carry out our plan now. I'm fed up with this burg anyway," Lewis said.

"But . . ." Powers began.

He stopped, shrugged his shoulders, and said: "All right."

III

They waited for the bus at Sixty-third and South Park Avenue. Lewis gazed across the street at White City. He had gone dancing there a week ago, picked up a dame, shot her a line, and she had come across.

"Well, the bus will be in any minute now," he said, turning to Powers.

Powers nodded. He fingered his Masonic pin nervously. Lewis questioned himself about Powers. Would he turn yellow on him? He liked the guy, but he wasn't sure of him. Oh, hell, everything was going to work out all right. It had to. Everything always had to work out all right for L. Gordon. He'd been born under a lucky star. He was destined to get all the luck that was supposed to come to anyone who found a four-leaf clover. He had found one in Lincoln Park this afternoon. For a while, as a boy, he'd even had the nickname of the Four-Leaf-Clover Kid.

A blue bus stopped in front of the curb. Each of them carried two suitcases. They followed others into the bus, put their luggage on the rack overhead, took seats, and lit cigarettes. The day was ending. The sun had gone down, and it was slowly getting dark. Lewis watched a Whiting, Indiana car pull out. Their suitcases were overhead, and they puffed on cigarettes, saying nothing. Lewis watched a girl pass. She wasn't bad. No, she wasn't bad. Just the build he liked, slender but with enough flesh on her so that she wasn't skinny. He would find more girls like that, plenty of them. Hell, he was leaving to get everything in the world that he wanted, everything in the world that the little heart of L. Gordon desired.

Yes, this was a sucker country, and a smart lad like himself could live in clover. There was justice and reason to his boyhood nickname, the Four-Leaf-Clover Kid. He had been born smarter than was good for the world. He smiled, proud of himself and of his mind.

"Well, it'll be off soon. And it's not a bad ride we're going to take, either," Lewis said.

Powers nodded.

"I'll never hear from my wife again," Powers said, almost to himself.

"Listen, Powers, when a dame acts that way, there's only one thing to do—forget her."

Lewis squashed his cigarette and, for want of something to do, lit another one. He glanced about the bus. A few salesmen, a few Hunky workmen, a fat middle-aged woman—a typical conglomeration of dumb human dopes.

"Say, suppose someone asks us what we do—what do we say?" Powers nervously asked in a whisper.

They talked in low voices.

"Salesmen. Hell, the country's full of 'em."

"What do we sell?"

"Anything. Peanuts."

"I'm serious," Powers said, getting more nervous.

Again Lewis had his doubts about Powers.

"I'm worried. I wish the bus would get going."

"Listen, Powers, forget it. Nobody's following you. Hell, the checks are finished, past. What did you say about forgetting? Well, forget the check. Forget the dumb manager of the Warwick Hotel. He won't know where the hell to look for us."

"Strange things happen. Did you ever read Thomas Hardy?"

"It's all right to believe in evil fates in a book, Powers, but that doesn't mean that one is going to pursue you. Listen, we're not dopes. How can we be caught up with? Not if we're smart and clever, and not if we play our cards right. Relax. Take it easy. Worry's bad for the blood pressure."

"Lewis, look at my face."

"It's all right. Nobody would take you for an ex-professor, if that's what you're worrying about."

"No—don't you see any little clusters of red veins around my nose?"

"I never noticed."

"Well, they're there. I've had high blood pressure for six years now. I can't do anything about myself, and so, what can I do about it?"

"Stick with me, and you won't be sorry. We're going to have a good time, Powers. Listen, don't you want to have a good time? Christ, wait until you see what New York's like."

"I wish the bus would get going," Powers said.

He eyed the door nervously. Finally they pulled out, the bus slowly moving off.

They sat back in their seats. Powers relaxed.

"Well, that's finished. I don't think they had anybody watching us at the bus station there, do you?" he asked, very gently.

"Listen, Powers, you're not getting yellow on me, are you?"

"Lewis, what have I got to live for? What do I care what happens to me?" Powers answered, looking sincerely at the young man. His hands twitched.

The bus sped along South Chicago Avenue, past factories, garages, gas stations, shacks, near the steel mills.

"I always pity the poor saps who work in steel mills. You know, I think they're saps, but I sympathize with them."

"I'm glad I'm getting out of Chicago. I never did like it. I never was happy there. You know, once we get to New York, I'm going to pull myself together and do something."

"Now you're talking, Powers. Of course you are. Hell, you're still young yet, aren't you?"

"I'm thirty-eight."

"You don't look it."

"Oh, I think I do."

They lapsed into silence. Lewis stared out of the window, thoughtful, planning the first stage in their journey to New York.

IV

They got off at the bus station in Carmody, Indiana, lugging their suitcases. Powers again looked around nervously, eyeing strangers with apprehension. Lewis noticed him but said nothing. Perhaps he'd have to shake the tail off this fellow. If he did, he'd have to get someone else. It was easier to pull this racket with two than it was with one.

"Let's go to the railroad station to check our luggage."

Powers followed him. He glanced behind him.

"Powers, for once and for all, no federal marshals are on your tail," Lewis said.

"I guess you're right. But there's no use in taking any chances."

Lewis didn't answer. He led the way to the station. He took the grips in which he and Powers had put their belongings and checked them, while Powers waited outside with the other suitcases.

"Well, let's register," Lewis said, handing Powers a baggage check, pocketing one himself, and picking up his grip.

Lewis led the way to the Hotel Metropole, the best hotel in town. A doorman took their grips. Lewis sauntered to the desk, and Powers followed. He was calmer now. They took a double room with bath and registered as John Keen and Thomas Allen. The bell boy led them up to a comfortable room, typical of hotels all over America. Lewis tipped him, and, when they were alone in the room, Powers sighed with relief.

"We'll have to remember the names we used," Powers said.

"That's easy. Listen, Powers, don't think you're palling around with a dope."

Powers sat down on the bed. Over and over again he silently told himself the name under which he had registered and the false one Lewis had signed. Lewis smoked a cigarette and watched Powers with a twinkle in his eye. He enjoyed Powers' nervousness, the man's fears and apprehensions, because these proved how superior he was to the older man.

"I'll remember now," Powers said, relieved, ending his practices in memory.

"Good, I knew you would."

Powers lit a cigarette and asked: "What'll we do now?"

"Wash up and eat. I'm hungry."

"I'm hungry myself."

They washed, went out, and found a restaurant.

"I wouldn't do this if I didn't think it was a sure thing, Powers," Lewis said as they ate.

"I know it. I'm not worried. I was a little nervous, but it's not because of the bad checks I forged at the Warwick. It's my condition. I've really been in bad shape since I was fired from the University."

"Well, you're going to do better with me than you did as an instructor in sociology," Lewis smiled in appreciation of the remark he was going to make. "You're going to practice economics and sociology."

Powers ate rapidly.

"Not bad food for a hick town, is it?"

"No, no it isn't."

"Well, we'll have better grub than this. Don't you worry."

Finishing their meal, they had coffee and smoked. Powers lit one cigarette after another.

"Let's find a place and get a shot," Powers said.

"Oh, hell, forget it. That's bad medicine for us now."

"Yes, I guess you're right," Powers said sheepishly.

v

They had strolled around the town and then come back to their room. At the desk when they'd got their room key, and in the elevator, Powers had made a point of addressing Lewis as Jack. Now they were sprawled out in their B.V.D.'s on different ends of the bed, talking.

"When I get to New York, I'm going to get myself in shape. I've got to. I've been a damned fool these last few years."

Lewis looked up at the ceiling, watching the smoke he blew after inhaling.

"Yes, I've been a damned fool," Powers said.

"I've learned that the best thing in the world to do when you've been a damned fool is to forget it. That's pragmatic; it works. When I was eighteen, I was a damned fool over a dame, and I learned then and there—if you've been a horse's ass there's nothing you can do about it except forget it. So I forgot it," Lewis said.

"If I were eighteen, I'd say the same thing. But I'm not. I'm old enough to know better."

"Powers, you worry too much," Lewis said.

"Maybe I do, I don't know. Lewis, you're a young fellow. You haven't gone through what I have," Powers said.

"My aim in life is to go through only one thing—the other fellow."

"You're different from me. You're an extrovert. I'm an introvert."

"You take life too hard, Powers. Hell, you're busted up with your wife. Forget it."

"I'm forgetting her. It's hard, but I rarely think of her now. But it's hard. Perhaps it is my vanity. But sometimes a sudden bolt out of the blue can hit you, hit you very hard. I was getting along, working on my book, teaching, and I didn't even know that she was betraying me."

"You ought to see that it's an experience that teaches a lesson and then learn the lesson. *Be hard*. Hell, you've got to be hard in this world. It's gyp or be gypped, right from the moment the bell rings until the end of the last round."

"No, I was hit hard. I couldn't understand why it happened. I was happy, but I didn't know what she was doing. She fooled me. She was lying to me all of the time, lying. I'd worked hard for a number of years, and this blow was too much. Well, I won't go to hell. I won't let myself. You know, Lewis, I've thought a lot about what happened to me, what happens to men. I've decided that there's one reason above all others which should lead us to keep ourselves in check, save us from ourselves even when we want to let go and allow ourselves to disintegrate, and that's pride. Pride. It's a matter of pride, isn't it, to keep a firm grip on yourself?"

Lewis nodded philosophically.

"Well, I'm going to get a good start, a new start."

"Of course you are. Now let's get our plans straight. To-morrow morning we ask for mail at the desk. Then, before we do—or, better still, just after we do—as we're going away from the desk, remark about the check, but do it casually."

Powers nodded.

"Then you take the bus back to Chicago and mail the letter. We'll get it the day after, in the morning, and I'll have the letter as proof. I'll do the rest, and we'll get the hick manager of this place to okay it. Then we get our stuff at the railroad station, and we blow."

"But do you think it'll work?" Powers asked skeptically.

"Why won't it?"

"Don't you think that hotel managers come up against such tricks regularly?"

"But they get taken into camp regularly, too. Did we have any trouble at the Warwick?"

Powers shook his head, a dubious expression on his face.

"I tell you, it's easy."

"It makes no difference to me. What makes any difference?" Powers exclaimed, suddenly filled with self-pity.

"Listen, the letter I wrote is damned clever," Lewis bragged.

Powers didn't answer. He brooded.

VI

Powers took a long time shaving and diddled as he dressed.

"Christ sake, let's step on it," Lewis said.

"We haven't got anything to do, why hurry?"

"Hell, you're still worried."

Powers didn't answer. He was still nervous. They finally left. Lewis sauntered up to the desk. Powers came behind him,

walking slowly and gazing about as if absorbed in the atmosphere of the hotel lobby.

"Any mail for me?" Lewis asked casually.

"No, Mr. Keen."

They left and walked off to a cheap restaurant. They had
ham and eggs and coffee for breakfast. They sat eating.

"I'm going to eat this slowly. I don't know when I'll get as
good again," Powers said.

"You can take the bus to Chicago, and mail the letter and
get back here this afternoon. Tomorrow we'll have our important documents, and we'll cash the checks and clear out of
this hick town. We'll go to South Bend, and I'll write a letter
ahead to us care of the hotel there. We'll change our names,
though. I'm not so dumb as to use the same name twice running," Lewis said.

"You know, a chap like you could go a long way in life,
and without taking chances the way you are," Powers said.

"I am going a long way. Don't worry about that."

"You could, without taking risks."

"It wouldn't be as much fun. The risks add spice, and, hell,
I'd have to work. I want my pickings fast and easy, and I'll get
them, damned fast, and as easy as water rolls off the proverbial
duck's back."

"You know what you want."

"When you go to Chicago, can you raise any jack?"

"I don't know where."

"I was just thinking—we need some dough for our dinner
tonight. I don't fancy the prospect of going hungry."

"I don't know where I could raise a cent."

"I'll tell you—I think that I better go, then. I can always
grab off a five in Chicago. With a fin, we'll have a good meal
tonight and take in a movie to pass the time."

"You'll come back, won't you?"

"Of course I will."

"I meant right away. I don't want to stay here alone, with
no money. You know, I don't like to be alone under any circumstances."

They finished eating and, smoking cigarettes, sauntered out-side. Powers walked with Lewis to the bus station and waited with him. They talked a little, and Powers kept looking around unobtrusively, as though he were being spied on, followed by detectives. He was relieved when Lewis pulled off, and he turned to go away. He had been fearful of returning to Chicago. He knew that his fears were probably irrational, and that there was no reason why the hotel manager in Chicago should know that he was registered in Carmody, Indiana, under the name of Allen. But despite his explanations to himself he had been fearful.

He didn't know what to do with himself. He returned to the hotel, and was almost shaking as he approached the desk. There were three guests there, and this was a relief for him. The clerk casually pushed his room key across the counter to him. He slunk off and entered the elevator, standing in a corner, avoid-ing meeting the gaze of the colored elevator boy. He got out of the elevator, unlocked the door of their room, locked it from the inside, sighed, and slumped onto the bed.

He felt suddenly safe. Here, in the room, he did not have to look anyone in the eye. There was no danger that he would give himself away by a nervous gesture, a fearful glance, a mishap.

Safe here. Suppose the management should come up with a detective and ask him his name and address? Suppose he had been followed, and they were merely playing cat-and-mouse with him, waiting for him to try to cash a forged check?

He sat on the bed, pale and perspiring as his fears became intense. He looked out of the window at a dreary inner court-yard. He heard footsteps in the corridor and stood rigid with shock and fear. The footsteps passed. He heard a door closing, a man's voice. With envy, he thought of the sleek, well-dressed men he'd passed in the lobby. They were not worried about jails and detectives. They earned money, spent it, had no fears of any kind. They were within the law.

Why had he let himself in for this wild venture? It couldn't succeed. This boy was young and wild, foolish. Anyone as cocky as Lewis was riding to a fall. There was a Nemesis in this world. Each man was the pawn of Nemesis, and he was coming to his day of reckoning.

He dropped down onto the bed. He brooded a while, and fell asleep.

He awoke perspiring in about half an hour. His heart was pounding violently. His horrible dream had already escaped from his memory. He looked around, and his sense of the present returned. Sun came in the hotel window. The curtains waved slightly. He stiffened as he heard footsteps in the hall. They passed.

He sat up, mopping his brow. He waited in terror for someone to come and get him. No one came. He waited. If a detective or a city policeman came, what would he say?

He got up and pulled the suitcases from under the bed. They were filled with stolen telephone books and newspapers. They had not been opened. At least they didn't seem to have been. But who could tell? He pushed them back under the bed.

He heard the hotel elevator. He waited.

The sound died.

Nervously, he went to the bathroom and drank a glass of water.

What could he say? How could he get out of it?

Would the judge let him go as a first offender? He was older than the kid. He would be blamed. Lewis might get off. Not he.

Suddenly he decided to leave. He washed his hands and face, tied his tie, and combed his hair. He left the room. He walked to the elevator, his head down, even though no one was in the corridor. He waited for the elevator, perspiring with his growing anxiety. His armpits were wet. His lips were tense. He felt his heart palpitating.

The uniformed elevator boy casually opened the door.

"Hot today," he said.

"Yes," mumbled Powers.

He looked down. The elevator seemed to take a long time to get to the first floor.

Emerging from the elevator, he paused, and took his time

lighting a cigarette. When he saw several guests approach the desk, he hurried out without leaving the key. Once outside, he turned to the right and moved rapidly along the main street. He turned a corner and then he walked on, turning several corners and taking a roundabout way back to the railroad station. He entered it, perspiring, fearful that he would be picked up. He got his suitcase with no trouble and left.

He lugged his suitcase out of town and stood on the main highway, flagging automobiles to get a lift to Indianapolis.

VII

Confident, satisfied with himself, Lewis strode into the hotel. He was smoking a cigarette and whistling a tune. The letter had been mailed, and everything was set. In the morning they'd get the letter at the desk, and he'd give the manager a spiel, and after they got the dough they'd be off. Life was sweet, and he was proud of his cleverness.

An attractive girl passed him, and he turned and looked after her.

In time, he would have many such girls.

He walked up to the desk.

"Good evening," he said in a tone of naiveté and graciousness.

"Oh, good evening, Mr. Keen."

"Is Mr. Allen in?"

The clerk looked into the box and didn't see the key.

"Yes, he is."

The clerk turned and nodded his head, and at that moment the house detective stepped up and grabbed Lewis.

"Don't make any trouble," the house detective said.

"Take your hands off me," Lewis said.

"Don't make any trouble. Come along with me, Bud. I want to ask you some questions."

"All right, but take your hands off me. Who are you?"

The house detective relaxed his grip. Lewis swung with his right at him and started to run. The house detective, a burly man, was rocked, but quickly recovered and ran after Lewis, and, making a flying tackle, caught him before he got outside. Lewis went down, his face hitting the floor. He was pulled to his feet with a bleeding face and dragged to a room by the house detective, while surprised guests looked on.

The police were called, and he was taken to jail.

VIII

The sun was hot. Powers trudged along the side of the concrete road, lugging his suitcase. He set it down and waited. He put out his hand, but the cars whizzed by. He picked up his suitcase and trudged on. He didn't know where he was going, nor why.

The Philosopher

I

DR. EMERSON DWIGHT quietly bid good night to Peter, the elevator man in the main library building, and walked northward across the campus. The scene was tranquil. The grass was neat and trim. The Gothic buildings, arranged in quadrangles, were gray against the blue sky.

He was a tall, sturdily built man. His face was sharp and distinctive; his hair and beard were gray; he had lively gray-green eyes and a prominent forehead. But he was beginning to walk with a tired gait, and his shoulders were beginning to stoop. He was sixty-nine years old.

He had spent two hours in his office, reading Whitehead's *Process and Reality* and making notes. When he had finished reading, he had been disappointed in his notes and had torn them up. One of his major disagreements with Whitehead concerned Whitehead's "ingression of eternal objects" into the process of nature. Here was, in reality, the old, old philosophical problem of the One and the Many. Whitehead's "eternal objects" were the One.

Now, walking across the campus, slowly and like an old man, he reflected that Whitehead, with all his brilliance, with all his wealth of speculation and fluidity of thought, was still a traditionalist, a rationalizing myth-maker. And perhaps one key to the understanding of Whitehead was the fact that the man had come late to philosophy. He had begun with mathematics and logic, and then, at a relatively late date, he had turned to philosophy. He revealed the deficiencies of a late starter. He

had had to gobble up large slices of philosophy in haste. He
was weak in his historical sense, in his interpretations of the
development of ideas from one thinker to another, from one
age to the next. He was a mathematician turned philosopher,
and this was inherent in the weak side of his thought. And it
suggested one reason, probably, why Whitehead had to invent
his own language and why he was a traditionalist using the
screen of a new language for this traditionalism. He was an
interesting figure in the history of modern thought, a genius
who was fertile, brilliant, stimulating. A great and original
thinker who mingled the most original of modern ideas with
a re-expression of traditional ones. Often, his thinking was
striking in its lucidity. His respect for Whitehead was enormous. But he could clearly perceive all the holes in Whitehead's system. The man was a victim of his own over-crystalli-
zation. He, himself, had been fighting this danger during his
entire intellectual career. He wanted a system of explanations of
the world as process without eternal objects. But he often feared
he might stamp too much finality upon expression. It was always
too easy to defend one's verbalizations. One's ideas hardened.
One fell unsuspectingly into the traps which had caught the sys-
tem-makers. He smiled wistfully. Did it all mean anything? Did
it mean anything if Whitehead was, or was not, subtly spiritualizing the universe? Did it mean anything if he himself did not
complete his life's work?

Whitehead was subtly spiritualizing the universe, and the
universe was not spiritual. The effort of philosophers to spiritu-
alize the universe was unscientific—it was myth-making. And
in the end, did it matter?

An overpowering rush of feeling came on him. It did matter.
It mattered to the man himself. Intellectual adventure was art.
All life was. And life gave to man—consummations. It mattered as consummations. Life was joyful. Through consummations man lived fully for himself and for his fellow man. It
did matter.

He glanced idly about the familiar campus, the familiar campus where he had spent thirty years studying and teaching.

Familiar and yet ever so new. It was a little miniature of life, full of novelty, ever changing. Always there was some new value, some new impression to be gained. Even the grass seemed never quite the same. The sun would always strike it in some new way. There would always be something fresh, as well as something seemingly eternal, in it. Now the sun, dropping in the west, colored the grass with a kind of opulence. The grass, the sunlight on the buildings, the University towers, the long windows, the sounds of birds in the spring, the presence of young men and women, these formed a pattern, became parts of the ever-freshness, the eternal newness of life. The world seemed to be recreating itself anew every minute. The world, nature, was the great improviser. And it was the effort to handle this element of novelty in the world that paralyzed his writing. It cut the nerve of action in him. This explained why he had written so much less than so many of his colleagues. This campus, the rows of small blades of grass before and behind him, these were full of worlds, and they became a focus for the central problem on his mind.

He walked slowly northward across the campus where he would probably eat supper alone. Again his tiring eyes wandered over the grass; it was so refulgent in the sunlight. When he looked at a field of grass, he systematized it, isolated it. He drew upon past impressions. If he looked away and then looked back, the grass did not seem quite the same. Within him, as within every human being, there was a laziness—Proust had written of it beautifully and perceptively in one of his books when he described a railroad journey. And out of this laziness and inertia one tended to rely upon routine, upon systematized impressions. The mind and the spirit of man were hampered by this inertia. The thinker had constantly to struggle against it in himself. Habit, inertia, was always destroying the wonder of the world. He walked on slowly, his shoulders still bent.

He was lonely, and this pervasive loneliness cast its shadows upon his mind. He had given long and patient years to his study, his thought, his teaching, but required many more years to complete his task. And he would not have these years. He was sixty-nine years old, and his life paradoxically seemed to him to be both long and short. He had the premonition that he would die with his work uncompleted. All men die in a world that moves, and in a world of movement nothing is ever completed. His loneliness seemed to run in an ever-deepening current within him.

His wife was dead. For two months of the academic year now ending, he had gone to the university every day, teaching, working, while she lay dying. He had taught by habit, read by habit, studied by habit, formulated the ideas for his papers and articles by habit. There he had been, alone in his office, writing, tearing up the sheets of paper on which he had written, writing again, again destroying what he had written, struggling intently, sometimes struggling for a whole day or week to express one idea, one formulation, one thought clearly and lucidly, and finding at the end of his effort that there were qualifications he had neglected, so that he had to begin all over again, and still discover that his formulations were not sufficiently precise, not expressed in the proper phraseology. And all that time she had been at home, dying. Each day she had had less strength, less life in her. The process of her dying had gone on before his eyes. The woman he loved, the woman with whom he had lived all the best years of his life, had suffered day after day in a protracted agony of death. And this, too, was a process. For a moment, he thought bitterly of his own philosophical views. Agony, declining strength, death, these, also, were novelties in the process of emergent events. He had seen her die, he had heard the death rattle in her throat, and he had felt her forehead, her hands, after she had died. Something of courage, of scholarly ambition, of interest in life had seemed to leave him, never to return. Before her illness and death he had been much haler, better preserved. He had prided himself in the small and rather excusable vanity that he was something of a marvel on campus, that colleagues younger in years than he were stooped and falling into crochety old age while he remained straight and limber, his beard and hair still partially red. Until her illness and death, he had ridden his bicycle to campus daily, astounding many colleagues with his vigor. After her fatal illness had developed, he had never done this again. Something had gone out of him. He had turned completely gray. He had begun to stoop. He walked less briskly. Perhaps he, also, was now a dying man. Every day there was less strength in him, less energy. His mind alone seemed to resist this process, to function as well as always.

Because of his loneliness, a cynicism, foreign to his spirit and nature, seemed to be growing in him. A severe break in his life had come on this very day. He had written out the formal statement of his resignation as Chairman of the Department of Philosophy, and he had accepted the professorship offered him by a large eastern university. His younger colleagues had resigned with him, almost in a body. Their loyalty had touched him deeply. He had felt tears welling up in his eyes. He had spoken to them, telling them that he had accepted this new post, and his voice had broken, the suggestion of a throb coming into it.

He was leaving the University now after his long dedication and service to it. He would not walk across this campus to an empty home for many more days. When he left the campus, it would be as though he were leaving his life behind him. And yet his life would go on. New classrooms, new students, a new office, a new city, and still that unceasing mental strain and effort to formulate his thought clearly and to put it into lasting shape.

He no longer cared to control his bitterness against the new young president of the University. He had worked for years with and through the thought of many men, great and small. He had traversed and absorbed more fields of knowledge than perhaps any other man in America. He had devoted his life to a study of the basic works of literature and of civilization. He had studiously traced out the history of philosophy and of science. He was at home in the contemplation of the civilizations of Greece and Rome, the middle ages, England, France, Germany, America, and of much of the art and literature of

continental Europe. He was aware of how intellectual and philosophical systems were built, of the patient and humble labor of
many thinkers, scientists, and artists that was necessary to con-
struct a philosophy, a philosophy which would then be expressed
and developed as one of the peaks of human achievement by
some great thinker. This awareness of his had checked in
him any undue pride of achievement, any irrelevantly magni-
fied conception of himself. But still, he was proud. Now he
was a very proud man whose pride had been wounded. His lips
curled ironically as he walked past the campus tennis courts.
He remembered the fanfare and publicity that had greeted the
arrival of the miracle-making young president just a year ago.
The newspapers had been full of this vain and empty publicity concerning "the boy president."

Here he was, a man who had always emphasized newness,
freshness, fluidity in thinking, and he was an old man. But this
fluidity of thought he struggled to achieve was a characteristic
of youth. And he was actually being pushed out of the University by youth. Fresh blood! He sneered again, and with
contempt—a contempt usually foreign to his nature. He was
full of contempt for many of his colleagues, professors in other
departments of the University, men younger than himself. He
was convinced there was a genuine issue involved in the fight
he had just lost. The almost wholesale retirement of his department was not merely a personal tribute; it was not mere
loyalty to him. This struggle had been a test case concerning
who would retain control of the appointments of new members
to the faculty—the boy president or the separate departments
and their various chairmen. Yes, there had been a clear-cut
issue involved. Would those who teach have any voice in university affairs, or would control be completely centered in
administrative hands? He and many of the other men, living
and dead, had not worked at this University in order to make
it the kind of institution the new administration wanted. For
if the boy president gained complete control of appointments,
the results could be foretold easily. The boy president had al-

ready forced through some appointments, and these appointments were a prophecy. The caliber of the new men, yes, the
young men, was low; they were a laughing stock. Perhaps in
time they would turn the University into a laughing stock. He
recalled having recently heard a graduate student remark:

"All the University needs to do now is to appoint Will
Durant to its Philosophy Department to make the president's
work complete."

The boy president had a sophomore's view of traditional
philosophy, and, on the basis of this view, he was going to reform an educational system and revise an established educational theory. And his reform was what? An abandonment of
the democratic theory of education for one based on the idea
of authority. His struggle with the boy president involved an
intellectual issue as much as it involved University politics.
And yet many of his colleagues had hedged at the meeting of
the faculty senate. They had strangled the issue in compro-
mises and had protested against the new administrative policy
only in the weakest and most cowardly way. Men whom he
had known for years, men whom he had respected—they all
had revealed a lack of backbone.

As he crossed the street to enter the faculty club, he could
not resist a rising tide of anger and contempt.

II

He sat alone in the club restaurant. He ate slowly, without
interest. There was a steady hum of conversation about him.
At the next table a colleague in the History Department sat
with his wife and children. The girl had recently graduated
from the University and was leaving for the Sorbonne. The boy
was getting an appointment in the fall as an instructor in history
at a Southern university. He directed his contempt at this historian. He recalled the war, for his attitude on the war had been
one of his own major and regrettable mistakes. For years now

he had regretted his conduct, even at times stigmatizing himself for it. And this man, this historian, was still preserving the attitudes and even the prejudices of 1918. He had written a book on Woodrow Wilson in which he had shoveled up all ·the wartime myths. Thanks to his own bitterness, his contempt for the historian was intensified. He smiled a greeting, however, when his eyes met those of the other man. Respect —all, almost all of them, were respectful toward him. Empty respect when they had to face an issue. He did not want that kind of respect. He was, he felt, being driven from this University where he had spent his life. On the other side of the dining room he saw the man who was director of publicity for the University. It would be this man's task to minimize the struggle with the president and to prevent the University from receiving any unfavorable publicity because of it. Here he was, a man who all his life had retained a persistent faith in the principles of democracy and had argued for their application, not only in the broad affairs of government but also in other domains, in university life. He had made contributions to the life, the work, the prestige of the University. And now he was being undemocratically shelved. His bitterness stung him profoundly. Listlessly, he ate a light supper. After eating, he left, and in the hallway he met a colleague from the Department of Sociology.

"Is that new book of yours ready yet?" he asked the colleague, to make conversation.

"No," the colleague answered. "But when it is, Doctor, I'll send you a copy. I'm anxious to know what you'll think of it. You know, Dr. Dwight, I'm profoundly indebted to you for your papers. They've been a great stimulation to me, and they've had a permanent influence on my thinking."

"Bill, I'm indebted to you for your books on statistical method in sociology. They've been very valuable to me."

"Your generosity flatters me. But, say, I was very sorry I couldn't get to that meeting of the faculty senate. I had to go downtown that day. I couldn't get out of an errand. But I want you to understand that my sympathies are with you. I tell you that he is going to ruin the entire University if he has his way."

"Thanks," Dr. Dwight said curtly to his colleague; the man was a coward. He did not want to hear him talk about the matter now, when it was too late for his voice to have any influence.

"Dr. Dwight, how about a game of pool?"

"No, thanks, Bill. I've got to go home to get some work done."

They parted. Dr. Emerson Dwight, the philosopher, felt the smugness of Bill Randolph. Smugness and hypocrisy, he told himself. He walked home. It was a lovely spring night. A fresh breeze was coming off the lake. There was something invigorating in the very air. And here he was, a stooped old man. Well, he had one consolation. With such a man as the new president of the University, it was better that he was leaving. Far better not to have any further association with him. Far better that way than to have constant fights and disputes. This trouble was distracting him too much from his work. With his resignation, and the new post, the greater part of this time-wasting distraction was ended. At sixty-nine, he couldn't expect to live indefinitely, and he was anxious to leave behind him a finished structure of work. His students had come to him with the collected papers he had written, and with stenographic notes of classroom lectures, and had proposed that these be published. But he had put them aside on his desk because he had not had the time to work over them and would not have them published in book form without carefully revising and checking them.

The spring night stimulated a sense of his youth in him, of his early days of intellectual struggle, particularly his struggle with and against God and the Absolute. He remembered his student days in Germany and his undergraduate years at the University of Michigan. He remembered that far-off exciting night when he had first opened a book of the great Hegel.

He had traveled a long road intellectually since those days, and
yet Hegel's influence on him had been permanent. He was nostalgic, wishful that he could recapture the feeling he had had in
those days. He wished he could once again read the works of
Hegel for the first time. He had been a clergyman's son, and
before Hegel his nonconformity had never amounted to much
more than a few Emersonian platitudes. Yes, he had traveled
since those days, and the chilly God of his heritage had been left
at the wayside long since. And the transcendentalism he had
avowed, the dualism he had espoused, these two also had been
dropped along the route. At the same time, a major part of his
life had been devoted to the preservation of his heritage. He
had tried to develop a body of thought where value, ethics, was
set inside the framework of nature as intrinsic factors. This
ethics was at the core of his thought. And it was his heritage,
also.

But on this spring evening he felt like a stranger in the world.
Other men, younger men, had come up. Even though he was
resigning because of his principles, he was, withal, resigning.
And it was because of the new president—*the boy president*.
The boy president believed there must be new blood in the Phi
losophy Department. And so *the boy president* had brought
from the East a slick, smart chap named Milgram, who was to be
one of the fresh infusions of blood. This chap prated and lisped
Aquinas and had only a nervous and superficial intellect. All
he really had was a snappy and clever manner of expressing
himself which would, of course, appeal to the intelligence of
the boy president. Milgram represented new blood. New blood
in the Department of Philosophy was not a question of age.
It was a question of ideas. Still, he was considered an old fogy,
and a lad who came forward with stale, pretentious, and regressive ideas, a lad expressing a new medievalism and a debased
conception of Hegelian dialectics, was youth, was the infuser
of new and fresh blood in the faculty. He who had all his life
struggled within himself in order not to harden and rigidify
his ideas, he who had published so little because of his sense
of the dangers of overcrystallization—he was now an old fogy.

III

She was gone. She was a decaying corpse now, and he would never see her again, and she would never see him, not in this or in any other world. He had no hope, no consolation, no belief in any after-life. All that remained of their relationship was its effects in this world. Their children, now grown and living their own lives. The memories he treasured. He had written often on the question of the past. Here, the past affected him in the most intimate sense. And, when he died, the memories he treasured would all be destroyed. When the cerebral cortex in his organism decayed, then all these beloved and precious memories would vanish from this world forever. It was as if worms, maggots would eat these very memories. Worms, maggots would eat the structures and patterns which the associations of these memories had formed in his brain, just as the worms and maggots had eaten the body of the wife he had loved. Nothing else would remain. He quoted the word from Poe's poem . . . *Nevermore.*

Often when he returned home, slowly climbing the stairs to his second-floor apartment, he had the feeling, the illusion, that she would be waiting for him. He had the illusion that when he entered the apartment she would be there and would come to him, kiss him affectionately, and that he would talk with her for a while before he pitched into work for the evening. He had such an illusion now. He felt strongly that he would see her. He found his key, put it in the lock, turned it, opened the door, entered the darkened and lonely apartment. He realized, like a man opening his eyes after having been knocked unconscious by an unexpected blow, that he was entering an empty apartment. He pushed the button to light the entrance. He hung up his hat and topcoat in the closet next to the front door. He went into his large, neat bedroom and study and turned on the light. He stood in the center of the room. He went to the dresser and picked up her picture, a picture taken in her youth. Her hair piled high on her head, her face fresh and lovely; she stood in a long, lacy white dress. A smile was on her lips, a smile he so well remembered. He set down the picture. He hung up his suit coat, put on a pair of slippers, and went to his desk. Although it was piled with papers and books, it was orderly. He carefully sharpened a pencil. He commenced to write slowly. He wrote several long and carefully phrased sentences. He scratched them out, rewrote them. He became absorbed, lost in work. All the rest of life was closed out, as if a door had been closed in his consciousness. He worked steadily until eleven o'clock, producing four neatly and carefully written pages on the character of scientific and perceptual objects. He was satisfied with what he had written. But he still felt that it would be just as it had been so often before. In the morning when he'd wake up these pages would seem utterly inadequate. Tomorrow evening he would work over them again. Writing was this kind of misery for him. He put the papers into the desk and went to bed, falling asleep quickly.

IV

The next day he continued on his usual daily routine. On his way to a morning class he met the vice-president of the University, a sly, corpulent man with shiny jowls. Dr. Dwight nodded coldly.

"How are you feeling this morning, Dr. Dwight?" the vice-president asked with unctuous cordiality, his manner that of a man trying to make pleasant conversation.

"Very well, thank you. How are you?" he replied, wondering at this unctuousness and preparing himself for what was to come.

"What's this I've been hearing, ah . . . about the little difficulty you've been having?"

"You must know about it fully."

"Well, Dr. Dwight, I've never heard your side of the story. And . . . ah . . . I'd like to. I'm very anxious to see that this difficulty, this misunderstanding is, ah . . . patched up. I've been hoping I'd meet you so I could arrange for us to have a talk. I was planning to send you a note, but, now that we've met, let's arrange it directly."

"There's little for me to say, sir."

"Come, come, now, Dr. Dwight. We're old friends, colleagues, and we've been here at the University together for years, two decades. We can discuss this matter like friends. I'm sure that you and Al, that is, President Johnson, can come to some understanding. You know, we all have the good of the University at heart, and we have to settle this difficulty in the best interests of the University, for the future that awaits it. After all, Dr. Dwight, this University is your life's work and mine. We're getting on in years. It developed under us, and no man has contributed more to its development than you have. We all know that and pay you great honor for your work. We want to look ahead. Now, what do you say, Dr. Dwight, about our having lunch some day this week? We can have a long talk and go into this matter properly, and in a friendly spirit. I'm free any day this week."

"I am sorry, sir, but I have nothing more to discuss, and I have other engagements for lunch."

"But, Dr. Dwight, you know this is a very unfortunate occurrence. You know what we in the administrative end of the University think of your work, your distinguished career. We hate to be losing a man like you, and we hate to have an unpleasant end even if you are going to a more remunerative post. We hate to allow unfortunate difficulties and disagreements to intrude in our official relationships with you now, after you have had such a brilliant and distinguished career in our midst. And I can assure you, Dr. Dwight, that there's nothing personal in Al's, ah, President Johnson's, feeling toward you. He is acting in terms of what he considers to be best. You know, Dr. Dwight, we all have to see things in a broad light, in terms of the University as a whole instead of one department or one science. He, President Johnson, has to take into consideration policies and plans for the best effect on the University and its future as a whole, whereas you have only to consider the af-

fairs of your own department. Now, Dr. Dwight, I earnestly
believe that if you and I can sit down and thrash over this
entire problem calmly, I can clarify certain points on the other
side of the argument and act as a go-between to straighten out
these unnecessary hard feelings between you and the President.
You know, he'll be mortally aggrieved if this difficulty is not
straightened out."

"I shall be proud that, following this quarter here, I shall
never again have to meet . . . him," Dr. Dwight said heatedly.

"But—"

"Good day, sir."

He walked on toward the library building, where his first
class was scheduled, striving to check and control his anger.
A passing student nodded a respectful good morning. He
nodded. He took the elevator up to his office before going to
the class. There was some correspondence on his desk, and he
looked through it hastily. One letter was a formal and curt
acceptance of his resignation, signed by President Johnson.

It was finished. His affiliation with the University was formally ended. His anger and hatred turned to weariness. He
suddenly became a man sapped of purpose. He sat at his desk,
listless. This was like a death. There were many deaths in a
man's life, and this was one of the deaths in his life. He envisaged the University under this new guiding hand. He saw
new streams of thought introduced, regressive streams of
thought. He remembered the University in its early days, re-
calling the program, the ideas, the early idealism of that period.
All this was now eliminated. The entire educational theory on
which the University was built would be abandoned. A spirit
of failure clogged him. He looked vaguely at the papers in his
office. He was sixty-nine years old. That was a long time to
have lived, long enough to have taught a man to meet failure
with equanimity. Whenever you are distressed and likely to
lose your temper, look at the stars: Bertrand Russell speaking.
Look at the stars, old fogy! Look at the sky, look at the sun,
look at the grass! Look at the world! The world which ever
creates itself anew, the world which is a thousand, is a million,

is an infinitesimal number of acts of recreation and emergence at every second. Look at it! Keep your eyes fixed on it, and not on yourself, not on your sudden inclination to develop a sickness of soul. Look out of yourself, and at the emergent novelty and beauty and ever-recurrent wonder of the world. Value is in process, value is in nature, value is in your own acts, your own doing, and you must go on, you must be and remain a part of the process, you must go on to new scenes, to gain new values. Apply your philosophy, old fogy, apply it!

There was a duality in him, in his formal teaching and thinking, on one hand, and his personal life, on the other. There was now no composure, but neither was there a spirit of adventure in him. He had no adventurous desire to go forth to his new work, the new university, the new surroundings. He wanted to stay here, to go along as he had. While here, he constantly found himself holding the comforting illusion that she was not dead, but just away. As with the character in Proust, dipping the *madeleine* in a cup of tea, so, with him, many scenes revealed a spread in experience, a spread going back into the past and forming into the future—sights, sounds, scenes touched with memories, and these led him to newness in his memories; they preserved in him an ever more keen and poignant sense of his wife and the life he had lived with her. She often seemed to him not to be dead, only half dead at the most. And to go away, that meant to break off these scenes, these lines of reverie and internal discovery; it meant that all the normal familiar sights, sounds, and stimulations to memory and recollection would be gone from his everyday environment. He would be forced to do abruptly what he had been doing slowly and less sadly—to assimilate the irrevocability of her death.

He was proud of himself for not having surrendered one inch to the new president. And yet, deeper than his pride, there was a biting regret. He felt that henceforth he would go on in life an unhappy man. Henceforth he would go on struggling against time and disappointment in order to finish a life's work and to leave behind him a little of worth, of stimulation, a contribution to the continuing process of understanding the world and of organizing experience. His personal life was largely over. His ambitions were all centered in his work, his race against time. And his life, which he felt to have had so much richness and fullness, would be a meager and poor thing. The pleasures of intellectual discovery, the joys of intellectual struggle, the anticipation of completion and consummation of this work—these seemed to be but poor and miserable goods.

Other strains in life ran deeper. He was an old man. His beloved wife, companion of decades, was dead. His habits of working in this city and at this institution were to be broken. He had begun his work here, and here he wanted to finish it. The Department of Philosophy in which he had worked, which he had helped to make renowned and famous, was now being ruined, reduced to a kind of degradation by mediocrities. This was a further disappointment, and it had a forceful impact on him. He whose philosophy emphasized notes of hope and was a call to doing was now himself miserably pessimistic. He whose work was perhaps even open to criticism because of its excessive generosity now felt hopeless as well as bitter. He felt almost as if he were beginning to disintegrate within himself. His discipline was relaxing. He was alone now. Was he falling apart?

v

For the remaining days of the term, Dr. Dwight went his way, struggling harder than ever to retain a hold and a discipline on himself, and adding a page here and there to his work. He spoke to almost no one. He remained within himself. He finished off the work which he had to do as retiring Chairman of the Department of Philosophy. He planned a summer of work in the country, and then a journey east to take up his new post.

Three days after the quarter ended, he was stricken with pneumonia. He lived a week in the hospital, fighting for his life, wanting desperately to live. He died with his life work incomplete.

Young Artist

BOB WHIPPLE WISHED HE HAD FOREGONE EATING. Because he hadn't, he now had to walk to rehearsal in the snow. Every time a streetcar passed, he thought of how comfortable it would be to ride. He moved rapidly, his thin body bent, his eyes blinded by the flurrying snow, his face stung by the icy wind, his toes numbed.

As he hurried along, with four more blocks to go, he tried to think. It was extremely difficult. His feeling of misery, his physical suffering, contributed to the sense of futility that was conquering him. He was afraid of contracting another cold; a cold would incapacitate him again; he would be forced to abandon his singing temporarily . . . and he couldn't afford that.

He recalled how, as a boy, he would sometimes escape from the books his parents said he should read and wander through the snow. He would allow his mind to entertain endless fantasies, glorying in them and in the silence of a world covered with whiteness. He remembered his father, a tall, silent, dignified Methodist clergyman. He thought back over the man's tragic life. How he had struggled in one parish after another, through Arizona, Kansas, and Oklahoma. His father had died penniless, of a ruptured appendix; he'd become a crushed man whose severe physical agonies had been accompanied by the realization that he was leaving a faithful wife almost in poverty. Once his father had been a rising young clergyman. But he had defied the authorities by accepting a parish in Arizona, against their advice and wishes. The Methodist Board never forgot or forgave him. And the years had rolled over the man; he had aged; his family had grown up into a new world full of ideas hostile to his faith. The years had rolled over him, cancelling what had been dear to his heart. His life, his struggle, his faith! Futility! Bob believed his father had been heroic. As he walked on, he suffered for his father. The man had held firmly and nobly to his principles and ideals; he had striven to live by them, to raise his family according to his lights. He had gone on like a patient hero. At fifty, he had looked old. To Bob it had been very sad, terrible to watch. And he suspected that his father had died without hope.

Bob was worried about his family. He had always been their hope. From earliest childhood he had been impressed with a sense of his personal worth and talent. He had been isolated from other children, kept to himself, to his music and his books. He had suffered many a bitter day because other kids had sneered at him, the minister's son, the bookworm, the sissy who sang in church. His father and his mother had always drilled into him a sense of his great future. In their well-intentioned way they had hammered into him the fact of his supposed superiority to others. Again and again they had spoken of the distinguished life he had before him. Now, walking along the cold, drab, snow-covered streets of New York, he saw a hard irony in all this; and he felt a resentment that seemed to sting more than the wind chafing his face and blowing through his thin coat.

And he hurried along to another rehearsal.

Back home they had felt that he was a coming singer. His brothers and sisters, now scattered over the country, believed in him. His sweet mother, running a boarding house for students in Oklahoma, lived in the expectation that some day his fame would bring the family together, lift it to the realization of those early dreams she and her husband had entertained. The comedowns he had met in the city, where he was an unknown, the lonely bitterness of the experiences he had had to meet, had led him to curse his whole past, his education, his very existence. When the trio with which he now sung had gone on the radio for the first time, the station had been flooded with letters,

letters from his brothers, his mother, from old family friends, from forgotten parishioners of his father scattered through Kansas, Arizona, Arkansas, Iowa. They had brought back pathetic recollections of these people, their uneventful, unsung small-town lives, their slow journey on to the degradation of senility. He probably represented a justification of their lives; he was one of their number sent out into the larger world to conquer. Could that radio concert be called conquering? He had sung trashy, popular songs, used his talents for the sale of health-giving sausage. His voice had helped to lull people into a state of enfeebled sales resistance.

He now walked on, sad with the recollections of the life he had lived and known in these distant American small towns. He thought of the good, simple people he had known there. He still had faith in people. He knew that their lives were meager, brutal, and crude; that their cherished religion was barbaric. Yet he recalled them by their generosities, their attempts to live by their lights; deliberately he forgot their meanness, narrowness, smallness, savagery.

Two weeks ago he had talked with an elderly lady, the wife of a famous historian, who had made a difficult fight to sing and who had won a small measure of success, a crumb of compensation for the efforts she had made. She had described it as a "ghastly struggle," and those words had had a significant meaning to both of them. The words were fixed in his mind, as if they had been nailed there. They represented the grim fight, the relentless pace, the worry, the long, intense effort of practice, the merciless going on from day to eventless day, from week to fruitless week, from month to empty month, from year to unsuccessful year, all demanding the sacrifice of pleasures and comforts. This struggle required a terrific concentration, a grueling preparation, an intense straining of one's entire self, and then, when one's chance came, one slip, one false note could damage one's performance, stamp the seal of failure on all that one had done, convince one of one's incapacity, drop one down into the deep and defeated doldrums. Time after time this had happened to him, as it had when he'd sung a solo so badly at the Good Friday services out at the University chapel; this experience had given him an almost abiding sense of incompetency and failure. Now, sensing, convincing himself of his own ineffectuality, he gave way to anger and, requiring an object upon which to vent it, he cursed all those who had told him that he would one day be famous. He had seen singers, writers, other artists, some of them with more, some of them with less, talent than himself, who had grimly gone on into painful and silent defeat; and he felt that their fates were but a forecast of his own. Often he had even hoped and yearned for the insensitivity of a pig, for anything that would erase the black uncertainty of the future and that would endow him with even a slender measure of security. He had reason to hope, because he had talent. Or had he? He had known many persons whose faith in their talents had been illusory, and who had gone through poverty, disease, sorrow, humiliation, nursing hopes that were unfounded, and who, for their straining sacrifices, had earned only ignominious defeat.

He walked on, trying to convince himself that he had more talent than others, that his struggle would not be in vain, that his present failures and defeats were but the necessary preliminaries to success, prestige, power, power over himself and his voice. He tried to convince himself that he was marked for success, a child of destiny; but this seemed to be nothing but a mere acquiescence to his own wishes and dreams. He hastened on, and he drew out his struggles with melodramatic coloring, intensifying the drama, as if it were more vital and important than it seemed, as if his battle meant something in the large, noisy city, as if his fate had some meaning to the millions of strangers who daily struggled for food, clothing, and shelter. It was a battle, he told himself, a battle in which he would have all or nothing, in which he would become an artist or else ruin himself in the effort. Again he envisioned a tomorrow in which all his self-discipline, his sacrifices and stinting, his crushing of impulse, his failures, his hours of miserable practice and even more miserable brooding, would be justified, would be, in fact, a crown of personal glory. And then he thought of fame, and of women. He wanted women; a wife. Others whom he knew had wives, or at least mistresses. But he was still romantic, perhaps foolishly so. For him, sex borrowed all the trappings and conceits of romantic poetry, and he yearned for a soul-mate, a Shelleyan abstraction of a woman. A gust of wind, rustling under his overcoat, restored to him some sense of balance.

He laughed at himself ironically, and with that twisted sentimentality so characteristic of many romantic and oversensitive young men. A streetcar rumbled by. He wished he were in it. But now he had only a block and a half to go. He tried to move more quickly. His feet were numb; his face was red and raw; his ears burned; his eyes watered. He was now almost terror-stricken by the fear of catching cold.

His thoughts rolled on. Fame was, after all, only an abstraction. It was something other than fame which he sought; some balance and harmony within himself, some organization of impulses. Again he damned his parents and his early teachers for befogging him with false words, for confusing his ends with a lot of rotten rhetoric. Music gave him something else, something other than a doorway to money, noteworthiness . . . fame. Without it, he couldn't live. He had learned this when he had sold insurance in Arizona, when he had worked in a department store, when he tried to make himself over into a student of philosophy and anthropology. These had all been periods of restless misery. He crossed a corner. It was his last block. He hastened on, condemning himself for being so much like the moody young men in nineteenth-century Russian novels. Growing melodramatic, he thought of suicide, briefly debating with himself whether it should be by gas, by gun, or by jumping into the river. He knew it would be none of these. He loved life; he feared death. His was an organism attuned not to less, but to more, living. And his singing was what gave him the power to achieve this. It resolved, harmonized, bestowed benedictions on the chaos of his impulses. Repressed, limited as he was in the present, he needed music now even more than he would in the future. It was not a curse, it was a blessing. All his vague aches and confusions, all his sensitive responses to the life around him, to the city whose ugliness was itself a form of beauty, all the mystery of the universe, that sense of similarity and union which he felt when he perceived sunshine falling over the lake, the delicious joy he experienced when spring winds touched his hair, the mystery of budding girls, of life and death—all could be pressed into one song and could leap from one song in an expression of wild joyousness. To be the instrument expressing such joy—this was given only to the artist. It was enough! It justified him. It was a gift for which he was thankful. Now, with the last few steps of his walk before him, he no longer envied the cart horses of humanity who were doomed to live in a squalor like his own; he no longer envied them the compensations and releases they derived from gin, sexual excess, and street brawls. He no longer envied them their insensitivity. Feeling a joy within him, he still shrank from completely envisaging what his future might hold for him, the skimping, suffering, saving, sacrificing, the long hours of practice, the cold, cramped rooms, the frequently unnourishing meals.

He told himself that he was committed to this life whether he liked it or not, whether fortune would smile or frown upon him. It gave its own rewards. Even if it didn't provide one crumb of ulterior compensation, even if it offered him nothing, he was committed. There was nothing else he could do. The thought of his many failures returned to him. He had worked himself up to a certain pitch, time after time, and . . . then he'd failed. Perhaps his ability was limited. Perhaps he was a mediocrity. Perhaps he would never get beyond singing in churches or occasionally over the radio, where standards of accomplishment were dubious. Perhaps . . . but he was committed. He had no alternative. Even though it meant starvation, sickness, tribulation, he had no other choice.

He entered the cold, dreary hall, and the trio practiced. It was a good rehearsal. And their director informed them that he expected something to break at a radio station—perhaps three or four commercial programs that might net fifty dollars for each participating artist. Bob felt good, buoyantly hopeful. If the thing went through, he could save to take lessons from the famous Camelli. And he thought of finding some girl to marry. He left the hall in good spirits. He had borrowed carfare and money for his meals. A decent dinner helped to change the complexion of his spirits.

The Triumph of Willie Collins

AFTER SUPPER, Willie Collins rode downtown, nervously expectant. What a great and historic day in American history! How wonderful it was merely to be alive on this day! Coolidge's victory was already conceded! There would be a Republican landslide. Why, Coolidge might even win by a greater majority than any other president in history, even greater than that of Harding, the dead Chief. Yes, it was a great day, a day for rejoicing, and there would be great doings in the Loop tonight. There'd be a hot time in the old town tonight—a hot time in the old town tonight, and now let McGinty from the office talk! Why, the bastard was such a damn good Democrat that he hadn't even taken the trouble to vote.

He looked around the car. The other passengers seemed so calm, so casual. He wanted to talk to someone, to tell them that he was a good Republican, and a friend of Eddie Chance, one of the Republican muckety-mucks in Cicero. He wanted to talk. But there these people were, sitting in the car, just as if it was any night in the week. Well, it wasn't. And this showed why Willie Collins was different from most people.

Downtown, something was going to happen to him, too, something damned swell. He hesitated to admit to himself openly what he expected this wonderful event to be and even assured himself that, no, he was a mature man, a responsible one, and not like the punk clerks in the office who ran after tail like stray dogs. No, that wasn't what he was going downtown for. He was going downtown because tonight was a night of history. Still, that expectancy spurred him on, and the hope of a romantic adventure, which still he dared not clearly acknowledge to himself, remained with him, contributed to his hopeful feeling of being really on the verge of some wonderful and joyful experience. He was impatient to get to the Loop. The car didn't go fast enough.

He read his newspaper, which already headlined the Coolidge victory. He studied the picture of the cold New Englander, wondering to what extent his own face showed as much character as Calvin Coolidge's. He shook his head in an inexpressible thrill of admiration. Yes, Coolidge was a great man, a great President, a great Chief, a man with a mighty brain.

He got off the car at State and Van Buren. The Loop was crowded. The electric lights shed a warming glow over State Street. But there wasn't as much cheering as there ought to be. People milled back and forth and up and down, while a few blew horns. But Willie had expected that there would be a big celebration, as great as or even greater than there had been on Armistice Day.

"Hurray for Coolish," a drunk yelled, standing at State and Madison, spitting as he talked and blowing an alcohol breath into Willie's face.

Willie bought himself a ten-cent cigar in honor of the occasion. He walked down State Street like a strutting little peacock.

People surged past him. Someone tooted a horn. A fat, homely woman yelled in a cracked voice:

"Coolidge! Coolidge!"

Willie thought how wonderful it must be to be a man like Coolidge. Look at how many of his countrymen had voted for him. His name was talked about all over the country. His picture was on the front page of every paper. Think of all the people who were speaking his name tonight, at this very moment.

How close he felt to Coolidge. Of course, compared with the Chief, the President, he was not very important. And, yet, wasn't it true that the whole country was able to get on with its business and be such a wonderful country because of its Chiefs. And he was a Chief. Yes, Chief Wagon Dispatcher at the Express Company. And Calvin Coolidge was the Chief of all the Chiefs. He stared at passing strangers and wondered how many of them were, like himself, one of the Chiefs who helped make the wheels go round. Tonight was the night when the Chiefs like himself could feel mighty proud because of the election of the Big Chief.

His cigar was mellow and mighty fine. He walked along with a feeling of his place and importance in the world, and he was right in thinking just this. If he ever met Coolidge, Coolidge would like and understand him. A Chief could always understand another Chief. Yes, he was a little Chief, and Coolidge the big one.

Fine cigar. He felt mighty fine, yes, sir, mighty fine.

And now them Europeans don't need to think we'll join their League of Nations and go over there and fight any more of their wars for them, Willie reflected.

He strutted on. People stopped to look at him. He continued on, wondering where to go, what to do.

A drunk stumbled up to him and said:

"What's happened?"

—The goddamn drunken slob! Willie told himself, filled with contempt and indignation as he strutted on.

He turned to gaze after a flapper. He forgot Coolidge for the moment and thought about her full young body. He wondered what to do, and he strutted along with his big cigar in his mouth. He joined the swirling, shouting crowd in front of the Republican campaign headquarters.

"Well, I'm glad Coolidge is in, stranger. He's a strong, silent man. That's what this country needs," a fellow said to him.

"You said it, brother. I'm a Republican myself, a member of the Cicero Republican Club," Willie boasted.

All around him, men and women, mostly men, however, yelled loudly and senselessly. The shouting sounded good to his ears. These shouts were the noises men made in recognition of the fact that tonight was a night of history. And, yes, standing here, smoking his cigar, listening, looking, he was a part of history. One of the little Chiefs who made the wheels turn.

Why, damn it, where would the country be if the wheels of the express vehicles stopped turning? And didn't he help make them turn? No one in the Wagon Call Department had ever made them turn better than he did. Damned tooting, no one ever did.

He beamed. His ruddy face glowed with pride and good nature as he listened to the senseless yells swelling into one mighty roar of human gibberish.

"Well, friend, I said it was a-gonna happen," declaimed a mustached man in a ten-gallon hat, as he leaned on a cane behind Willie.

"Say, I'll bet those boys up there ain't drunk a-tall now," a little fellow on Willie's left commented knowingly.

Down the street a band was heard pounding out *There'll Be A Hot Time in the Old Town Tonight.*

"Swept the country," a man said in accents of profundity.

"The people are goddamn fools, votin' for the Republicans," beefed a tall, thin-faced man. Willie stared at him angrily.

"Yeah, boy!" a man yelled.

Willie wanted to join in this yelling but restrained himself. It was not quite in keeping with his dignity, responsibility, and position to yell. Yet he approved of it.

"Coolidge ain't nobody's fool," someone said.

"You said it," someone replied.

Again the senseless yells resounded through the Loop and rose over Randolph Street.

Willie squirmed and strutted in and out among the crowd, first standing to look up at the bannered windows of the Republican campaign headquarters and then crossing the street to join the crowd at the entrance to watch men of importance enter and leave the hotel. He wondered how many of them were men of political influence. Someday he would be able to enter as they did, he dreamed.

"I was in Boston," a man said wisely, "the time Coolidge ended that police strike, an' that's what won him my vote.

Coolidge is a strong man, the kind that don't say much, but when he does he talks with a punch and a wallop."

Willie wanted someone to talk with, and he looked hungrily from face to face as he edged about continuously. Once again he looked up at the bannered windows. What was going on behind them? What words of jubilation and victory were being spoken? Were drinks being passed around? Yes, what was being said? Who was there? How was everyone acting? Were they making as much of a joyful rumpus as the people down here on the streets?

He imagined himself upstairs, moving about among the high muckety-mucks, getting slapped on the back by them, slapping them on the back. But the continuous shouting drowned out his dream; he gazed about in a daze.

He wanted to shout, but he could not break down his barriers of dignity. He again stood dreamily staring up at the bannered windows. With lonesome eyes, he read the sign:

REPUBLICAN CAMPAIGN HEADQUARTERS
VOTE FOR COOLIDGE AND DAWES

He was the kind of man who belonged up there instead of down here with the ordinary mob. And, think of it, there was singing and dancing and a good time all over America tonight, and he stood outside the Republican campaign headquarters, thinking. Gee!

"Got a match, fellah," asked a middle-aged man.

Willie fished out a match and stood there while the fellow cupped his hands and lit his cigarette. Willie observed how carelessly dressed the stranger was. No, he wasn't one of the Chiefs. Out of a need to speak with someone, Willie said in a voice of condescension:

"Some celebration!"

The man puffed at his cigarette, drew it out of his mouth, and emphatically nodded his head in agreement.

"It's a good thing for the country," Willie said. "We know what kind of a leader Coolidge will be and we don't know what Davis would do. You know, we know Coolidge has the stuff."

"He'll give us a cautious business administration," observed the stranger.

Behind them a fellow shouted the name of Davis. He was drowned out with raspberries. Willie turned and looked at the Davis booster as if the latter were a lunatic.

"Well, I gave him my vote," Willie told a stranger.

"Me, too. I believe in lettin' well enough alone. I think this country is going along all right now under a Republican Administration, and I say this— Let well enough alone."

The senseless shouting and milling continued.

The stranger passed on, and Willie thought of what he'd tell McGinty and the rest of them Continental Express Company Democrats tomorrow morning at work.

"EXTRA PIPEE—LANDSLIDE FOR COOLIDGE," a newsboy bawled.

Willie suddenly saw a well-dressed man entering with a slight stagger. He looked pop-eyed; it was Eddie Chance. Willie squirmed forward a little and yelled:

"Eddie."

But Chance did not hear him and immediately disappeared inside the hotel.

"That's Eddie Chance, a friend of mine," Collins told a stranger who paid no attention to him.

Knowing Eddie Chance, who could go up to headquarters, Willie was now bathed in the reflected feeling and pride of influence. He was not just a rank outsider. If Eddie had seen him, he might even have invited him inside. Other well-dressed men entered the hotel, and the noisy mob eyed them closely, half with admiration, half with envy.

Disappointed to have missed catching Eddie Chance's attention, Willie finally crossed the street. He elbowed about, looking at faces, hoping he would find someone he knew, someone in whose eyes there would shine the light of recognition, hoping to find one face he could single out, speak to understandingly— the face of one comrade, one kindred spirit.

He stood behind a group of young fellows who carried books and who were probably students.

He heard one say:

"The triumph of democracy."

He missed the sneer in the voice and shook his head in a gesture of agreement and acknowledgment. It was just that, and watch him spring it on all the Democrats at work.

—The Triumph of Democracy!

He elbowed and moved about the Loop until eleven o'clock, eager to celebrate but not really knowing how to do it. Still anxious to shout and whoop, he couldn't bring himself to let out a yell.

He thought of what he had read in the papers about President Coolidge being a strong, silent man.

—Still waters run deep, he told himself.

Yes, and the still waters of his own soul ran deep. He resolved that from now on in his work, he, too, would be a strong, silent man. He wouldn't barber and gas with the Route Inspectors. He would be quiet, dignified, strongly silent, and he would impress them all, impress Wade Norris, the chief clerk, the assistant superintendents, and Patsy McLaughlin, the superintendent. He walked wearily down to Van Buren Street to get a streetcar home. He nursed his resolution, nursed it as a consolation for the gnawing sense of disappointment within him. Just think—he had almost met Eddie Chance, had almost been taken up to headquarters where he would have met the muckety-mucks. But, then, a strong, silent man in whose soul the still waters ran deep could bear such disappointments. And he would!

Father Timothy Joyce

I

Mrs. Joyce's commonplace and full-cheeked ruddy face broke into a significant expression of inordinate pride when she opened the door of her married daughter's flat and saw her oldest son, Father Timothy Joyce, standing before her. Her maternal exclamations, her almost fierce maternal kisses, embarrassed the tall, boyishly handsome, curly-haired young priest. Smiling defensively, he entered the flat.

"Hello, Tim," exclaimed Bill, his younger brother, as Father Timothy entered the parlor.

"William, you know you shouldn't call your brother that. He is Father Timothy. You should show respect for the cloth he wears," the mother scolded in her characteristic brogue.

With a gentle tone of deprecation in his voice, Father Timothy remarked that, at least in his own family, formalities might be dropped. He sank into a soft chair in the parlor, and his mother plumped down onto the overstuffed couch to face him, her eyes fixed on him devouringly, her face happy with an almost overweening pride. Aware of the way his mother stared at him, Father Timothy flushed in some embarrassment.

The flat was on the first floor of a three-story, brown brick apartment building at Seventy-fourth and Luella Avenue. The deceased father, a police sergeant, had left this building to his wife. The family had lived in a two-story brick building over near Grand Crossing, but when the daughter, Katherine, had married, she and her husband, Jeremiah Duffy, who, like Bill,

53

worked at City Hall, had come to occupy this flat and look after the building.

The mother and two sons sat in the parlor, and the daughter called from the kitchen that she would be right in.

"Well, Tim, how's everything going?" the brother asked.

Both of them noticed the frown Mrs. Joyce flung at her younger son.

"Now, Mother, we needn't carry on such formality. Gee, I even let the kids at school I know well call me Tim and don't make them call me Father," Father Timothy said.

"Your brother, he has no respect for your station in life," Mrs. Joyce said self-righteously.

"Hello, Sis," Father Timothy said, rising and kissing his sister as she entered. She was rather tall and very thin, with a drawn, tight face, circles under her dark, pretty eyes, curly black hair, and a delicate mouth.

"How are my nephews today?" the young priest asked.

"Oh, Tim, they're healthy and happy, and thank the Lord they're taking their nap. They have me done in," Katherine said. "They're simply gorgeous nuisances," she added, with a white-toothed smile.

The mother quickly cast a disappointed glance at her daughter, but she said nothing.

"How is Jerry?" Father Timothy asked.

"Oh, Jerry's all right. A father enjoys his children. A mother takes care of them," the sister said.

"You children were no trouble at all to raise. My son, Father Tim, he had the sweetest disposition of any boy," Mrs. Joyce said.

"Not when he punched me in the nose under the viaduct at Seventy-fifth that summer," Bill cut in.

"You didn't throw a rock at me, of course," joshed Father Timothy.

"Ah, you were just boys, and boys you still are," Mrs. Joyce said.

"The way my two keep me going, Mother, I don't know how you stood it," Katherine said.

"Your father, Lord have mercy on him, how proud he would be to see you in that cloth," exclaimed Mrs. Joyce.

"He does. I am sure, Mother, that he looks down on us from heaven," Father Timothy said, his voice and manner changing from that of the son and brother to the more formal one of the priest.

"He was a good man, and now he has a son to pray for him."

"I say at least one mass a week for Pop," Father Timothy said.

"The Lord be praised that I should live to see this day," the mother exclaimed.

"Well, how's tricks with you, Bill?"

"I'm having my vacation, that is, the vacation I don't enjoy, working in the City Comptroller's office," Bill boasted.

"You don't work hard?" laughed the priest.

"I have to keep my job, don't I?"

"You should have my work, correcting English composition themes of freshmen. And the penmanship!" Father Timothy exclaimed.

"Is is hard, son?"

"Not really, Mother. It's just boring sometimes."

"Bill, are you going to play basketball in the Order of Christopher League this year?" asked the priest, a trifle wistfully.

"Don't know, Tim, I'm getting old," Bill smiled.

"Hey, listen. I still play around the school with the kids, and I'm in condition and find I can still make myself go the limit. Come on, come on," the priest said.

"Well, maybe I'd be the same, Tim, if I was around a gym regularly," Bill said.

"Come on, kid, you're getting lazy, getting lazy," the priest said.

Bill took out a package of cigarettes and offered one to his brother. The mother frowned again and then leaned back with a smile when Father Tim refused. Bill lit his cigarette and took a long, contented puff.

"Well, lazy or not, I can still go with you. Someday we'll have to put on the gloves."

"You certainly are rash about the affairs of the City of Chicago," Father Tim said drily.

"How come?" asked Bill.

"You want to mess up the affairs of state by causing one important cog in the City Comptroller's office to spend two weeks in Mercy Hospital," Father Tim said.

"No, you mean I want to get those kids of yours out of writing those themes while you recover from what I'll do to you," Bill said.

"Bill, have you no respect . . ." the mother started to remark, and the daughter interrupted her with a gesture of annoyance.

"Mother, just because I'm a priest, that's no reason why I must put myself in a glass case. Sure, some day, I'll come around, and Bill and I'll go out in the back yard and put on the gloves."

"That's a go," the younger brother promised.

The two brothers smiled at each other self-confidently. There was a pause in the conversation, and then the priest asked his mother how she was feeling. Beaming, she remarked that she had no complaints and no ailments. He smiled, expressed his pleasure, and added that he offered up daily prayers for her specially, and also prayers for the whole family. Her proud, motherly smile expanded. The sister rose and said that she would make tea. Mrs. Joyce got up, too, and with a bustle of activity waddled out, insisting that she would make tea for her sons. The sister protested, and the mother loudly dismissed her protests as she and her daughter walked out to the kitchen together.

"What kind of a football team you going to have at Mary Our Mother this season?" Bill asked.

"I think we're going to cop again, and I wouldn't be surprised if our kids took the public-high-school champs, too, if they'll play us. As far as the Catholic title goes, Bill, it's in the bag," Father Tim said.

"Well, I hope so, since you're athletic director," Bill said.

"You want to come to the games. Our first game is in two weeks with the Christian Brothers from Joliet," the priest said.

They were still interestedly talking about athletics when the mother returned with a tray of tea and cookies. Her daughter, smiling in a tolerantly apologetic manner, followed her and offered to help, but the mother shook her head and shooed her off, insisting she was going to serve her own sons. She brought the tray to Father Timothy and coaxingly asked if he was taking enough cookies, and then, with less attention, took the tray to her younger son. Sipping tea, they continued a desultory discussion of athletics, and the two women sat, the daughter relaxed and tired, the mother leaning forward with intent and adoring interest.

Suddenly Mrs. Joyce interrupted her sons to remark in a hearty and energetic manner:

"Sure, Tim's boys will beat the Jesuits' boys from your school, Bill. It hasn't a lick against Father Tim's boys."

They smiled with filial indulgence.

"When I was playing, Mother used to come to basketball games and root for us," Bill exclaimed.

"Yes, because you are my son. But now I know that Father Tim's boys, with that fine coach they have, and with Father Timothy as athletic director, they can't be licked, can they, son?" Finishing her remarks, she looked at her priest son.

"Mother's a real fan!" exclaimed the priest.

"And, Father Tim, how is Father Michael? Sure, isn't he the saint of God like yourself!" Mrs. Joyce remarked.

"Yes, he is a fine priest, a fine man, and he's in perfect health yet."

The daughter collected the teacups and, after Father Timothy replied negatively three times to his mother's insistence that he have another cup of tea, she carried them back to the kitchen, and running water from the sink could be heard.

"Timothy, sure, if your father was only alive to see you now!" Mrs. Joyce exclaimed.

"Mother, that reminds me, I'm saying another mass for dad tomorrow," Father Timothy said.

"And won't he be proud! Looking down from heaven on his

son, a priest, a priest remembering him and saying masses for
his soul," she said, an exultant note in her voice.

Father Timothy smiled, pleased because his mother seemed
happy.

"Dad, Lord have mercy on his soul, many's the time he said to
me, 'Ma, I want one of my boys to be a priest,' " she said.

"Well, he knows now that his wish came true," Father
Timothy said, just making conversation.

"And if he could see the bouncing grandchildren he has,"
Mrs. Joyce continued.

Just then there was a baby's cry. The daughter took them out
to the cribs, and they looked down at two babies. The daughter
exclaimed that they were wet, and Father Timothy flushed, almost imperceptibly. He and Bill went back to the parlor, while
the sister and mother each changed the diapers on one of the
babies, and they could hear singing and cooing. Bill and Timothy
talked of old times when they were boys, of their exploits,
stunts, baseball and basketball games. In due time, the babies
were brought in. Father Timothy seemed uncomfortable when
he was given one of his nephews to hold, and he sat there, holding the baby as if it were a rare and fragile vase, while his mother
and sister both smiled at him benignly. They talked some more,
and then the priest announced that he had to be leaving. He
kissed his mother and sister good-by on the cheeks and shook
hands with his brother. He walked out.

II

He walked slowly back toward Seventy-first Street, trying
to make up his mind whether he should walk or take the I. C. to
Sixty-third Street. Suddenly, and inexplicably, he felt uncertain and gloomy. He was shaken by doubts, not of his faith,
which was deeply entrenched in him, not of his faith in God,
but of his faith in himself. The balminess of the day, the
lazy, casual charm in the quiet street, only caused him to become
sadder. Life would be empty if he lost his faith. He was aware,

vaguely aware, of fear in himself, fear of even daring to articulate his own thoughts fully in his own mind. And yet, he knew, knew without having ever dared to articulate them, what these thoughts were. Sleeping not too soundly in his consciousness was the conviction that somehow life, the world, even his own mother had done him an injustice. He recalled how, sitting at home there, with his mother so lovingly proud, sitting there for that brief and harmonious period with his own family, that old pride in the cloth he wore and the priestly powers that were given him unto death had stirred up within him, and he had experienced a lulling sense of happiness. And now where was it? How quickly it had been dissipated and shoved into retreat by forces of doubt and wonder, by this lack of faith in himself. He asked himself, had he or had he not a vocation? Had he been pushed into the priesthood by his mother's eagerness? He looked around him at a street mellow and domestic in the afternoon September sunshine, with a sense of impending autumn in the warm and beneficent air, with women out going to the stores, women with their babies, kids coming home from school playing along the street. Several of them, seeing him, became quieter and more orderly, tipped their hats to him, and chanted:

"Good afternoon, Father."

He endeavored to return to them a kindly and warm smile.

He slowed down his pace further, not wanting to reach Seventy-first Street, where the necessity of deciding whether he should ride or walk home would face him as a problem. He became weak with his doubts of himself.

He thought of how his mother took such pride in him, and of how he so frequently felt himself unworthy of that pride and respect. After all, he was only a man, only a human being, and not a saint. Her naturally saintly religious feeling and her love for him, her son, caused her to look at him as if he were—inhumanly holy. The very phrase made him feel as if he had committed a sin.

He thought of the kids at the high school, kids that he taught, knew, saw every day for one, two, three, four years. Then they went out into the world, and he did not and really could not

ever know them and their lives except as an outsider. He saw
them go out to work, to business, and to marriage. Saw them
with girls, pretty young girls, at alumni dances, proms, athletic
games. He was the victim of the old temptation, that temptation
to think of committing the one sin of the flesh he dare not
commit. It came upon him with a surging force, and he compared the force of this temptation to that of winds and waves
pounding a frail shore. As always in these moods, he prayed to
Mary for strength to resist temptation. He flushed, and walked
more rapidly, his eyes cast on another world, the words of the
Hail Mary running through his mind. Crossing Seventy-second
Street, he was calmer, and he slowed down his gait. A thrill
surged in him, the thrill of having been able, with the help of
God and Mary, to conquer temptation. With grace, yes, the
weak sands of his soul could withstand the battering waves of
sin and doubt.

A girl emerged from a building. She was young, bursting
with beauty and life, the life he had forever renounced, the
life he had vowed never to know. She was a seed blooming into
a summer flower, and his eyes, against his will, could not resist
looking at her, at her legs, and at the motion of her body as she
walked with so much ease and girlish grace. And she looked at
him in a peculiar way. Many girls did. He flushed, and gazed
across the street. But without willing his thoughts, he saw himself going out alone into the woods with such a girl in the
springtime, and he saw himself and her . . . committing a sin
of the flesh. Shame filled his mind and he feared that his feelings
were like words printed legibly on his face. He turned his eyes
to the other side of the street again and watched a boy of about
twelve rolling a hoop.

An old lady blessed herself and muttered a Jesus Mary and
Joseph, Good day, Father, and he smiled and told her God bless
her. Pride again welled up in him. He was proud of his office,
of the distinction it gave him, and of the way it marked him
off for respect among simple people.

He dallied along, so that the girl would get way ahead of him.
When she had disappeared on Seventy-first Street, he walked

more rapidly. He had sinned. He strove to convince himself that it had been merely a temptation, a wile of the Devil, a snare cast at him in an unguarded moment. But, no, it had been a sin, a mortal sin. For he had consented to this temptation, enjoyed the vivid images of sin which Satan had flung into his mind. But, then, he was sorry and he had thrust the sin out of his thoughts. He had looked off. He had prayed for grace. He had not given in, given in wholly. But yet. Girls. Girls so young, so fresh, so supple. Their laughter. God had made them not merely to tempt man. No, God had made them to be loved purely, to bring joy into the world, joy that he would never know. He was almost sorry for himself. He would go to his grave never knowing the mystery of girls, girls so lovely to look at. But, no, he must not think this. He was winning salvation for himself, for others. Yet, his doubts returned. His faith in himself once again was shaky. His young, handsome, almost girlish face was torn with suffering. He walked on toward Seventy-first Street, wishing he were old, an old man, an old priest no longer torn by these desires of the flesh.

He was very hungry and, thinking that it would be some time yet until supper, he stopped in at a drugstore fountain on Seventy-first Street and had a chocolate malted milk and a ham sandwich. He ate almost greedily, aware that now and then people in the store stared at him. At times, these stares made him acutely self-conscious. At other times, he was proud, proud to be a priest set off from others, a shepherd who guided poor sinners. But then, was he a good shepherd? These doubts. Oh, God help him, help him in the face of doubts and desires. Terrible Doubt, terrible Desire! Oh God, oh Mary, pour the strength of grace into his frail soul so that it would not be destroyed by these pounding waves of life. He finished eating and paid the pretty girl at the desk, his face frozen. He looked away and caught her smile only out of the corner of his eye.

He left the drugstore and walked hurriedly to the station at Seventy-first and Jeffery and sat waiting for his train. An old man tipped his hat, and Father Timothy acknowledged the salutation. His train came along, and he entered, sat by himself, and read his office, concentrating literally on the words he silently mumbled. Alighting from the train at Sixty-third Street, he realized that he was still hungry and that he had to wait for over an hour before he would eat. He decided to go to the school gymnasium, shoot baskets, perhaps find enough kids around to get up a game. If he played vigorously, he knew he would work all these uneasy feelings out of his system.

Joe Eliot

I

"WELL, MY BOY, how's it today?" Willie Collins asked Joe Eliot, a route inspector.

Collins fell into step alongside of Joe, walking toward the car line after the day's work.

Joe was tall and loosely built, and looked ruffled and unkempt. Little Collins, with his fire-sale gray broadcloth shirt, his dotted jazzbo, and his brown hat which seemed to float on top of his oversized head, looked neat but bizarre.

Joe shrugged his shoulders and stole a glance of contempt at Collins.

"Well, my boy, it's fine out now," Collins said.

"Yeah," snapped Joe in a withering manner.

A chubby, gum-chewing girl emerged from the entrance of the telephone exchange. She had black hair with bangs, her thick legs were encased in dirty stockings with runs on both insteps, and she wore high-heeled pumps. She had on too much powder and rouge.

"Hmm!" exclaimed Collins. "I'll bet that broad don't wear no pants."

"Maybe not," Eliot said without interest.

"Yeah, you know, the broads are getting worse every day. It seems as if they don't even need no invitation nowadays. It's a little bit different from when we were young, huh, Joe?"

Instead of answering, Joe lit a cigarette.

"I see you smoke a lot of cigarettes, Joe," said Collins.

"Yeah," Joe answered, bored.

63

"I don't like to smoke too many. I enjoy a cigarette after breakfast, and a good cigar after supper, and I like a chew now and then. I like my tobacco, but I always like to keep fit and give my heart a chance. So I see to it that I don't smoke too much," Collins said.

They walked along.

"It's starting to pick up, and things are getting harder up on the board," Collins continued. "You know, everybody is on my tail for trucks."

Joe Eliot didn't comment.

"Hm!" from Willie, as he shook his head at the sight of a passing flapper. "What do you think of these flappers, Joe?"

"Oh, they're all right. Some of them have more guts than their mothers and grandmothers had."

"Well, my opinion is that they don't come up to snuff in the womanly way their mothers did. You know?" said Collins.

Joe didn't say anything.

"Going home?" asked Collins.

Joe had intended taking a car, but he didn't want to ride with Willie. He decided he might as well stay downtown. It didn't make much difference whether he went home to a rooming house or stayed downtown.

"No, I guess not," he said.

"Well, here's where I get my car," said Collins.

"So long," Joe exclaimed, unable to repress the sudden rise of surly feeling.

"Say, Joe, that tonight's paper?"

"Yeh."

"Finished with it?"

"Here, take it."

"Thanks. Well, so long, Joe," said Collins.

Joe walked off.

II

Joe stopped at a paper stand and bought another newspaper. He went into a cheap restaurant and took a table in a corner,

near an electric fan. He waited while a peroxide blonde, with
powder packed on a middle-aged face, set a glass of water, a
little butter plate, a napkin, knife, fork, and spoon before him.
He ordered liver and bacon and spread his newspaper before
him.

"Liver an' bacon," she yelled in a harsh, grating voice.

He looked at his paper. Another murder! He read a few lines
about it. A pastor had murdered his wife because he loved a
choir singer with whom he'd been intimate. He read a little
about Mussolini and the black shirts and a headline about the
French in the Ruhr. When he had gone into Germany after the
Armistice, he had liked the Germans. He read an account of
how a rich American boy had drowned himself in the Seine.

He recalled the Seine in the Paris mist and moonlight back
in 1918. The mist had hung over the dark waters, and over
Notre Dame, so magnificent, standing on the island, half lost
in darkness. He remembered walking along the almost deserted
quays in an early autumn evening in 1918, when he had been
on leave, and he had seen soldiers there with girls, kissing. He
recalled tender nights hanging over the Seine, into which the
rich young American had thrown himself. He had forgotten the
war on those few nights. Then he'd gone back to the front, and
the war had soon ended. They had advanced into Germany,
and he'd received a letter saying she had died, but without giving the circumstances. The letter had just mentioned an op-
eration, and then a later one had stated that she had died of
appendicitis.

He had given up a lot for that woman.

—The goddamn dirty, filthy bitch!

He had given up a lot for her, a career. He thought of the
word career and laughed nervously and neurotically. Hell, he
had a Harvard degree, and had been all-American halfback
on Walter Camp's eleven, first team, too. He could have had
something. He could have been a bond salesman. He could have
been a business executive. Maybe a sports writer. Sure, he could;
perhaps he could even have been something big. Instead he'd

come out here to Chicago, started driving an express wagon, and here he was, a route inspector.

He had taken her out of a restaurant, the dirty bitch.

He ate.

He remembered one of those nights, close to dawn, when he had walked along the quays looking at the dark waters of the Seine and he had heard an American doughboy singing:

There's a silver lining through each dark cloud shining,
Turn the dark clouds inside out till the boys come home.

Plenty of doughboys had sung such songs. He remembered some of them singing one night in a Y hut in France. He was drunk another time in Amiens, and he had sung it with several lads who were kicking up the daisies now. Smitty, a boy from Princeton; Bates, a farm kid from Iowa who wanted to be a baseball player. Murphy had been a streetcar conductor and was always talking about his Lithuanian sweetheart.

Turn the dark clouds inside out till the boys come home.

That blonde bitch, too. He had tossed his goddamn old bastard of a father's fortune away, and he'd landed a laborer's job in the express company. He hadn't cared. He'd been young, and he had loved her, and God, Jesus Christ almighty, she'd been beautiful. When he came back he should have killed the bastard. His old man, too! The dirty, old, filthy, bald-headed bastard. And he'd made plenty during the war and was still making it, but Joe wouldn't talk to him. No, and he could keep his money, too. He had had a letter two months ago: Let bygones be bygones. We are all getting along now, and we all know we have made mistakes. It is for God to decide which of us has sinned the most and which of us should be punished. Let him keep his money, and his tin Jesus, too.

Joe glanced back at his newspaper. He read a well-authenticated rumor that Trotsky had been hanged and quartered and that fierce Red barbarism would break loose in Russia. What did he care? He didn't care about it. He hadn't fitted into the world, and he didn't give a good goddamn. The world had been saved for Democracy. Let Democracy have it.

He finished his coffee and pie, lit a fresh cigarette, left a fifteen-cent tip, paid his bill at the cash case, and walked out. The summer sky was deepening, and now the city was quiet. The falling twilight seemed a delicate thing, a thing of peace, softness, and beauty.

A fellow in bell bottoms snapped by him, humming a jazz tune. A blind man tapped his cane and half staggered along. Two sleek businessmen passed.

"And I told him. I told him, hands off! Hands off!"

He smoked, and decided to take a walk.

III

Joe Eliot's mood of sarcasm and cynicism vanished as he walked about, smoking one cigarette after another.

A slattern dragged her creaking bones past him.

Two girls walked from behind him, moved alongside him for an instant, and then forged ahead.

It was about eight o'clock, and the twilight seemed like a thin veil waving and fluttering between night and day. The redness that had burst full-blooded in the western fringe of the sky was now dying.

A boy and a girl walked by, hand-in-hand, engrossed in chatter.

"Tell me! Tell me! Tell me, Harry, because I wanna know."

Joe walked on, lighting another cigarette. He thought of his life, with all the unfulfilled possibilities that lay strewn across its path. He thought of it as a scattered thing now, a shambles. All those dreams and hopes of his youth on which he had drawn expectantly for the future had come back to him—bad checks. He nervously puffed a cigarette and thought inconsolably that he was a failure. He was a failure in more than a merely financial sense. It might have been because his father had been rich that he had never thought much

of money, and it might have been a temperamental inclination
or propensity. Withal, it was a fact. He was a failure in achieving things, in achieving something valuable—love, knowledge,
something that would be significant and personal and worth-
while. He was a mere collection of habits that functioned like
an electric system on an automatic telephone. He was a failure.
He walked with slow aimlessness about the Chicago Loop,
which was popping into life with the coming of night and the
theater crowds.

An aging, conservatively dressed couple passed him; their
faces were lost in an apparent dreamlessness, a stupefying con-
tentment that was an expressive abnegation of all feeling.

Joe felt that he had grown akin to such people; or to the
men at the Continental like Porky Mulroy, Collins, and the
Gashouse.

He happened to glance upward, and he saw, as if it were
a discovery, a sky streaming with stars that were radiant on
the surface of a deep blue. There was a seeming lavishness about
them. He felt humble and weak, and like a child lost in the
darkness. He fixed his eyes on a nameless blue star and was
inwardly inarticulate. Vague impulses, without names or tags in
his consciousness, awoke as from a long sleep within him and
stirred like an unborn child in a mother's womb.

He walked on. A man couldn't stand on a corner of Dearborn
Street and look up at the sky like a country jay-walker who
came to town and gawked at tall buildings. But he walked with
the happy feeling that he just sucked a flashing moment of
significance from the weltering insignificance of human life.

Three lads passed, one of them with a pimply face and a
loud voice; he wore a green shirt and a purple tie.

"Yeah, and I told the bastard, fight with yer fists, not yer
mouth."

He reflected that the lives of all men were miserable things,
and that all men were failures who accomplished only a minimum of the things they dreamed of accomplishing in their
youth. Yes, nearly all men failed, failed even to become human

beings. Yes, there was almost no love, no honor, no justice, no decency among them. Life was a shambles, and it toppled over, smothering sentiments like love and friendship.

A gaudy young woman passed, wriggling her buttocks as if they were a billboard display.

Life was a promise of anything and everything in youth; it narrowed and was squeezed down to one man's mortal and miserable little life. He thought of this, and he was acutely aware of his loneliness.

"Hell, that nigger Wills never could take Dempsey, not in a thousand years," a passing man exclaimed.

A blind beggar, led by a thin, miserable-looking woman with a shawl over her head, passed. They were like a slow procession of death.

His wife. Again he snarled the word *bitch* to himself, but he knew he didn't mean it. He did not hate her. No, and he hated no man or woman. And even if he did hate her, it made no difference. She was dead. She was nonexistent. She lived only in the effect she had on the lives of other people, on his life—and that was an evil effect. She was dead, and her bones were rotted in a cemetery. She who had blushed with such sly, maidenly innocence, or apparent innocence, in those premarital days, she who had come to his bed, naked, in that sly and innocent way, she was dead. He had loved her then, and he still loved her. He tried to summon up memories of her, but they were thin and tired memories. But thin and insubstantial as they were, they gripped him. He loved her yet, and he painfully recalled her silly but beautiful blonde face, the face for which he had turned his life into such a shambles.

Now everything was too late. Life gave a man no quarter. Mistakes could not be rectified. Once they were made, it was too late. Too late, and nothing else need be said.

He looked about him. He was on Randolph Street, with all the lighted theaters. It was an ugly scene. Big electric advertisements, announcing cheap, sentimental shows and movies, glared at him. Heaped and tumbled store windows ran along the sidewalk. People passed him, crowds of them. They, too, seemed cheap and ugly. They were America, and this street, with its blazing lights and its stupid shows, was America.

He felt that not only he was going to hell but also Chicago and the country were going to hell. And it was not a merry journey, either, but merely a stupid one.

Suddenly he thought of his little girl, Marie. If she had lived, maybe she would have helped him find some purpose in life. Then living would have acquired some meaning. He thought of her blonde hair, of her face so like her mother's, when she had played before him with such serious and concerned childlike naiveté.

He lit a fresh cigarette and thought that she, too, was a rotting corpse.

He recalled how he had been so delighted to watch her growing. And then her death caused by a speeding automobile—it seemed doubly malignant and uncalled-for. In his mind the concept of death took on a loathsome ugliness. He realized how death reduced all men to a rotting and stinking vileness of equality. It was a messy conclusion to a mess.

Holding hands, smiling with absorbed silliness, a brightly dressed lad and a lass in organdy walked by him.

IV

He walked through Grant Park and over by the lake, where the waves came piling in, smashing against the breakwater. The skyline of the city rose behind him. A few lights glittered on the dense stone hulks. The noise of automobiles was audible but echoed as though from far away, and as if they had no meaning. They bore no relationship with the noises of the waves slashing against the breakwater piles.

He sat down and gazed out across the lake. It seemed coldly and inhumanly beautiful, streaked with lines and avenues of moonlight, waving and wrinkling beneath mists. The very air was a delicate breath, shimmering and flashing above the waters. Rolling wave after rolling wave crashed relentlessly

against the wooden piles. He was pleased and calmed by the wind
and waves. He sat there, looking far out over the waters which
seemed so monotonous but held his attention none the less,
while his eye sought out small changes in their patterns:
shifts of moonlight and starlight, rolling waves, patches of
darkness, where the waters were a dense blackness. He listened
to the monotonous slapping of the waves. It seemed to echo
something important inside himself. He was appalled and
soothed alternately by the insensateness of the waters and the
inhuman power they displayed in their continuous drive against
the piles.

He wanted to make some contact with the waters. He wanted
to hold them and feel them, manipulate and control them, put
them inside of himself and hold them there as caged and beautiful things. He dipped his hands into the water. A wave broke
and splashed over his shirt.

He sat back and glanced out toward the misty horizon. He
saw a world of waste, heedless and removed from man and
man's destiny, alien, totally unrelated to his human aches and
sufferings and maladjustments. Behind him was man's created
world. He had come from it bored and frustrated. Here he
sat, as if hung between that created world and this mindless
world. He listened to the noises of the water and the strain
on the soggy piles, caused by the pitiless pressure of the waves.
It was beauty. Why, he did not know. He sat there choking
for this alien world, feeling that it furnished the objects he
needed; again he looked out over a black waste. He wanted
to own that waste, possess it in some inarticulate fashion.

The noises of the water changed from a monotony to a
terror beating upon his senses. He sat. Waves and more waves
came in, and the undertow dragged them out again. He was
torn by his own incoherent emotions. He lit a cigarette and
scratched his arm where he had been bitten by a mosquito. A
sense of time encircled him, and he thought of how this was a
century-long process, and he tried to gain some sense of how
the waters had come in and gone out, century after century

after century. And they would go on, century after century after century, until all life had vanished and there was no memento left of man, or of the life from which he had evolved. This lake preceded human history. It would outlive man. The stones behind him on Michigan Boulevard would one day tumble in a heap, while the waves of Lake Michigan came slapping in monotonously, unconsciously, heedless and insensate.

He was struck with terror, and sentimentally he wondered why men went on, why generation after generation lived and suffered and died creating what would end in dust. Life became a horror of monotony. Men stood before his vision as so many creatures registering impressions, registering endless impressions, trying to build and order them, suffering and aching and agonizing, blundering, killing one another. He wondered why the race did not blot itself out. But he knew why. They loved life. He loved it, empty as it was to him, and he did not want to die. He feared death, feared and dreaded the day when he could not come to the water's edge and sit there, listening to its noises and looking out over its shifting surfaces.

A young man and a girl passed him. She giggled and then said:

"Help me. I'm afraid. Oh, don't let me fall. . . . *Henry.*"

Henry helped her over the rocks.

"Oh!" she muttered with admiration, and they moved out of audible range, so that their voices became mere fading sounds.

Joe saw them sit down on the rocks and embrace one another.

He lit a fresh cigarette. Some spray brushed his face. He took his coat and, carefully folding it, set it beneath his head. He lay back and gazed vacantly upward, his hands crossed under the lower part of his head. He was calm now, and his mood became one of speechless melancholy. He watched a floating cloud and then saw a star shoot across the heavens and vanish. He drew a deep breath. All he could do sitting there was to try and translate his feelings and sensations into words, and this was an almost hopeless effort.

He recalled how, when he had been a young man, he had lost his faith in God. All the world had then been tied together in a unity, and now it was a chaos; it was a chaos spread inhumanly about man, and there was nothing to explain or to give reason to his efforts and his humiliations. He had walked about on many evenings, contemplating suicide. Now he never thought of suicide. He fumed, and cursed, and drank himself almost into insensibility. But he never thought of suicide. He had lost things more substantial than God, and yet he sometimes felt that the reason for his despair was his loss of a Presbyterian God.

Once, about two years ago, he had gone into a Catholic Church, and he had been tempted and seduced. The singing, the candles, the incense, the Latin had all been suggestively mysterious. But he had quickly departed, thinking that it was sheer barbarism, and that the priest, in gold-cloth vestments, was like a medicine man incanting among a cannibal tribe. And it seemed to him the Catholics were cannibalistic. Swallowing their God, as they claimed to!

Behind him the automobiles purred, and in front of his prone body the waves piled in.

He almost ached for the past. Trivial things that had been long forgotten arose in his mind, odd words he had spoken in France and at college, ball games he had played in as a boy, meals he had grabbed hastily at forgotten restaurants, people he would never again see. He found himself wanting them all back. He sank into a revery, and its course wandered aimlessly. The sky stretched widely above him, and the lake was wide, and the wind that brushed over him and through his hair came from these wide places. Earthly terrors, broken loves, betrayals, death, disease, treachery, failure, these were now all inconsequential and irrelevant. He was at peace. He lay there. Cigarette ashes fell on his shirt, and he carelessly brushed them off. He was at peace, in a womb of calm. He recalled that he had read somewhere the statement of a scientist who declared that man was happiest as an embryo in the mother's womb, and he felt as if he were in a womb. He lay under the wide sky, by the edge of the wide waters, and the wind brushed through his hair. The fierce earth on which he lay,

and on which his race had built and would build its many
Chicagos, now seemed to him to be that womb. He lay there,
opening and closing his eyes, listening and not listening to the
waves.

Finally he rose and put on his damp and crumpled coat. He
glanced down to his right, and a flash of moonlight exposed
the boy lying and moving upon the girl. He started back across
Grant Park.

v

Joe Eliot crossed Michigan Boulevard and walked along
Madison to Wabash. The Loop was pretty well emptied. An
automobile roared down the street, and its noise heightened his
loneliness, which he transposed to the objects about him. An
elevated train rumbled overhead.

He paused, indecisive, on the corner of Madison and Wabash,
wondering what to do. He did not want to go home. He knew
what he wanted to do—go to a whorehouse. He lit a cigarette
and glanced around him. A kid passed, shouting the newspaper,
and he bought a morning paper.

He walked on, glancing at the headlines, and, coming
upon a Thompson restaurant, entered it. The place looked
dreary and forlorn, and as he took his check the man at the
cashier's stand opened his mouth in a wide, toothless yawn. A
white-aproned, red-faced fellow casually mopped the floor.
At the counter he ordered coffee and pie. Then he sat in a one-
armed chair and read the newspaper, not knowing what he
read. He was merely wasting time. He drank some coffee and
found that he had not put any sugar in it. He took his coffee
to the stand and put two spoonfuls of sugar into it. He stirred
it overlong. He returned and ate his pie and coffee, and then
read more of his newspaper. He read a column written daily
by a University of Chicago English professor, Paul Morris
Saxon. But he thought it boring.

He glanced around him. A thin-faced, lonesome-looking
man to his right vacantly stared about and sipped coffee. In a

corner on the other side, two men about forty-five or fifty and dressed in cheap suits were arguing, but Joe could not hear the subject of their argument. A bum was huddled over a cup of coffee in the rear. The aproned employee mopped the floor, swinging his mop back and forth unenthusiastically.

He did not want to go home. He did not want to leave the restaurant. He envied the men working, not knowing why, and wished he might sit here indefinitely. He turned back to his paper. Then he rose and left.

He walked aimlessly about. The night now was very soft and tender, and he, too, felt very soft and tender. The street was a scene of deserted life, with dark buildings whose emptiness seemed to yawn. They seemed to be waiting for the morrow, when their rooms and offices would be full, and the slow midnight tempo of life would give way to a daytime fierceness. He wondered about the people who worked in them—about their tragedies and hopes and plans and dreams. He thought how each office reflected a world that was almost closed within itself, just as the Wagon Department at the Continental was a world almost closed within itself.

He walked around, reflecting on how he was a stranger to all these little worlds of the city, and on how he only touched the edges of a few of them. He had no common bonds with anything, it seemed. It was almost as if he were a member of another species, rather than a man. Perhaps that was why the city appealed to him more now than in the daytime. Its desertion meant that its many little worlds and private universes were only reflected things, and that their life did not unroll before his eyes.

He walked around, and his thoughts welled around and around, tearing over familiar and much-ploughed emotional ground. Finally he clenched his fists and, summoning forth all the disgust and loathing he could command, muttered through his teeth:

"JESUS CHRIST!"

He boarded a streetcar and rode dully home to his rooming house. He felt very tired.

Scrambled Eggs and Toast

THE RAW AIR bit and cut to the marrow. A morning mist hung over the Boulevard Montparnasse, and, while it was slowly receding, the sun was still obscure. Tram cars jangled by. Crowded autobusses clattered along. A few taxicabs cruised by. On the sidewalks, merchants were dragging forth their displays of merchandise for the day, and the *garçons* were sweeping the café verandas, moving and stacking and replacing the chairs and tables, restoring them to their regular order after the night and the sweeping. From below, the metro trams could be heard thundering into and out of the station at the Rue Vavin. Pedestrians walked by—workingmen in rough, unpressed clothing; slovenly and poorly dressed lower-class French women of middle age; a Turk wearing a red fez; a trim officer with a small waxed mustache; schoolboys; several lads in blue army uniforms; a sprinkling of Americans, one of them dazed, sleepy-eyed, and showing the effects of drinking as he stumbled along; blue-caped *flics*; a tall, handsome, and seedily genteel blond Russian; a few ragged beggars, soiled half-creatures who seemed to belong to a subsidiary species between man and animal.

The chairs and tables had been rearranged on the veranda of the Café du Dome, and a few customers began to sit down at the tables, breakfasting or having drinks. In one corner, a well-known pro-Soviet Russian writer sat reading a French morning newspaper, occasionally looking up from his paper to glance at the people sitting at the tables or passing along the sidewalk. Over toward the tables near the center aisle leading to the interior of the café, a thin American with baggy eyes, dissipated features, and a sodden expression sat like one in a half-sleep. On the right side, in a corner toward the front, there was a young Frenchman with a mustache and blue beret who sat over coffee and croissants. Several tables behind him, a young American, presumably a student, sipped at a glass of coffee and interrupted a reverie to stare at several plump midinettes who passed.

The morning was starting to run its normal course along this Paris street. A stout American woman walked along the center aisle, carrying a poodle in her arms and attracting attention by her appearance. She was a peroxide blonde, her face was caked with powder. She was obviously over forty, and she wore an expensively tailored black suit with a fluffy white shirtwaist, and a black Princess Eugénie hat tilted over her left eye. As she took a table toward the rear and just off the right side of the aisle, some of the other customers stared at her and then turned away. She made a fuss about getting seated, and she talked to the dog in cooing baby talk as she placed it on a chair beside her. Several times she admonished it to be good, pronouncing the word as "dood."

"*Bonjour, Madame!*" muttered a corpulent *garçon* with a waxy face and a mustache, bowing obsequiously at the same time.

She turned rudely away from him and stared out at a tram bound for the Porte d'Orléans which had momentarily halted at the corner. Then she ordered in a loud voice:

"*Café au lait pour moi,* and scrambled eggs and toast for Ruffles." She smiled up at the *garçon* and added, "*Parlez-vous anglais?*"

"Yes, madame," he said slowly, his manner still ingratiating.

He turned from her and disappeared into the interior of the café.

"Little Ruffles, oo is hungry, isn't oo? Well, oo is going to det a nice big man's breakfast, oo is," the woman cooed, and several of the customers gave her brief, questioning glances.

The dog jittered nervously, its tail wagging, its fluffy ears cocked, its hairy, grayish-white body tense. It raised its head toward her with asking black eyes and then, setting its paws against her, attempted to lick her face. She held the dog off, smiled, pointed a warning finger at it, and said maternally,

"Now, Ruffles, oo must have manners and show the French that oo is a polite American dog. Ruffles must be patriotic and act like an American with breeding." She drew the dog against her, and in a lower tone said, "Ruffles, oo is a darling!"

Then the dog laid its front paws in her lap and looked at her, its dark eyes pathetically expressive. She took it in her arms and permitted it briefly to lick her face, smiled at it, and then placed it back on the chair beside her and warned it to be a good dog. She stroked its head and patted it. It sank its wet snout into her lap, and she again waved an index finger at it and mumbled, "Ruffles mustn't!"

More customers had entered, and the stream of pedestrians had grown bigger. The mist had receded rapidly. The sun was bright over the street. A *flic* drew a taxicab to the corner around on the Rue Delambre and began to argue loudly and with gesticulations with the driver, who had violated a traffic regulation.

The American woman looked out onto the street and superciliously regarded this small drama between the policeman and the taxi driver. She was distracted from this scene by the reappearance of the waxy-faced and corpulent *garçon*, who had brought her order on a tray. He set on the table the plate of yellowish and liquid scrambled eggs and beside it a plate of buttered toast. He set a glass of coffee before the woman and from an adjacent table corralled for her a basket of croissants.

"*Garçon!*" she said with sudden officiousness, and the waiter bowed. "*Serviette* for Ruffles, *s'il vous plaît.*"

The dog laid its paws on the table and thrust its nose forward. The woman shoved the plate of eggs out of its reach, and with her index-finger gesture she warned it:

"Ruffles must wait for his little napkin, and he must not show boarding-house manners. Dogs that are bad and eat too fast get indigestion, and then they have to take nasty-tasting castor oil. Does Ruffles want castor oil?"

The dog looked up at her, its eyes beseeching food. She smiled and failed to notice that one of the Americans from a near-by table turned to laugh at her.

The waiter reappeared with a white napkin. The woman almost tortured the dog by tying it around the animal's neck. She broke bits of toast and dropped them on top of the egg. Then she held the dog while it greedily devoured the food. She watched the dog eat, smiled, coaxed it with baby talk, and, when others turned to stare at her, she haughtily elevated her nose. Outside on the sidewalk the policeman had finished lecturing the taxi driver and was writing in a little book. The taxi driver watched him, forlornly answering questions.

Two old French beggars shambled along the sidewalk. The man, in rags, carried a large burlap sack on his shoulders and dragged his run-down shoes over the paving. He had gray hair and a soiled, sloppy mustache. His face was creased and lined, and dirt was ingrained in the wrinkles. His eyes were shifty, beady, and they contributed to the dejected expression of his face. The woman was taller and gaunt, similarly wrinkled, and her gray hair was unkempt. She wore a spotted black dress with an uneven hem, and a rip along the side revealed underwear so dirty that it was the color of a sidewalk. She had a shawl thrown over her head.

Looking dully at the people around the tables, they spotted the American woman who was holding the dog while it consumed scrambled eggs and toast. The man laid down his burlap bag, and both of them stared at her meekly. They held out greasy palms.

They stood, statuesque for a moment, the almost subhuman products of poverty. The American woman, cooing over her dog, did not see them, and she dotingly watched her dog lapping over the plate.

Failing to attract her attention, the two beggars commenced.

to sing in cracked, tuneless voices, the street noises intermittently drowning their song.

> *Sous les toits de Paris*
> *Dans ma chambre ma Nini . . .*

A small, wiry *garçon*, serving a table toward the front, curtly pointed a finger at them, indicating that they should move along. Ignoring him, they sang on. The woman held her palm outward. The man hunched his shoulders more pronouncedly. Both of them eyed the American woman, their begging gestures and expressions as craven as had been her dog's before she had started to feed it.

Finishing the plate, the dog turned and twisted to look again at its mistress, its melancholy eyes asking for more food. She removed the napkin from its neck. Its ears were cocked. The woman squeezed the dog against her and in baby talk told it that it was a hungry rascal with a hole in its stomach. Stimulated by the cooing voice of its mistress, the dog became more lively and strained in her arms.

> *Oui l'amour . . .*

The American woman noticed the beggars. At the sight of their silent, accusing glances, her middle-aged face, with powder caked in its wrinkles, toughened into an annoyed frown. The waxy, corpulent *garçon* emerged from the interior of the café. He spotted the beggars; his lips curled. She looked up at him petulantly and said, in heavily accented and ungrammatical French, that she was being annoyed. She pointed a disdainful finger at the beggars. Their song completed, they groveled, and the man held out his crumpled gray cap, its lining sweat-stained.

Her waiter moved quickly and asthmatically down the café aisle. After he had curtly told the beggars to move, they looked at him and said nothing, but pointed at the American woman, and seemed to annoy and distress her with their glances. With the dog down against her bosom and her head elevated in self-righteousness, she met their stare and then turned away. The *garçon* spoke volubly to the beggars and pointed down the street. A policeman appeared as the man, with calculated slowness, commenced to lift his bulky burlap sack. The conversation became loud and operatic, and the policeman shoved the two beggars. They turned from the café and started to drag themselves slowly along. Unperturbed by the sneers she received from other tables, the American woman watched the scene with pleasure, and in a half whisper she was heard to exclaim:

"*Merde!*"

The beggars crossed the street to proceed on along the Boulevard Montparnasse in the direction of Saint Michel. The *garçon* returned to the American woman and offered bowing apologies. She set her poodle in the chair beside her and, since her coffee was cold, ordered more. The *garçon* returned with a hot glass of coffee. She daintily dipped pieces of croissant into it and ate them, occasionally feeding her dog with fragments.

The tables began to fill up. The sun was now warm and soothing, and its rays turned the streetcar rails into gleaming and dazzling bars. The sidewalks were crowded with pedestrians. The traffic was heavier, and the policeman regulating it barked and gestured almost like a character in a comic opera. Another policeman halted a German in front of the café and, after conversation, the German extracted papers from his jacket pocket and handed them to the policeman. The policeman read the papers and returned them, and the German rejoined the procession of people. The American woman slowly finished her small breakfast. She signaled the *garçon* for the bill, paid him, and handed him a one-franc tip. He scornfully bounced the franc piece on the table, and it rolled off. He breathed rapidly in insulted protest.

"Why, the idea," the American woman exclaimed, tossing back her head, looking about the café for sympathy from those who watched, enjoying the scene.

The *garçon* pointed to his left palm with his index finger and shouted at the woman.

"Je ne vous comprends pas," she kept repeating loudly, quickly shaking her head from right to left.

While the waiter persisted, she gathered up her poodle and stalked away from him, her head tossing in flushed indignation, her crumbling, lifted face taut and angry.

Watching her enter a taxicab, the *garçon* exclaimed, *"Américaine! Vache! Merde!"*

After she had departed, he searched for the one-franc piece, pocketed it, shrugged his shoulders, sneered, and waited for new customers.

The sun was now hot and strong. Traffic swept along in increased volume. Pedestrians strolled by. The *garçon* stood looking out onto the street with folded arms. A lone, wizened beggar paused and stared at the customers with extended palm. The *garçon* caught his eye. He turned and moved away rapidly at a shuffling gait.

Saturday Night

DOPEY slouched into the dining room and sat down carelessly at the foot of the table. Listlessly, he laid a nicotine-stained hand, with its bony protuberance of wrist, on the white table-cloth and smiled when his sisters, Kate and Beatrice, greeted him. Kate glanced at Aunt Anna, a large woman with a full, milk-fed face and a mass of light auburn hair. Aunt Anna glowered at Dopey. She filled their plates with steak, carrots, and peas. Kate, noticing the expression on her aunt's face, fidgeted and remarked that it had been thrilling to listen to the radio broadcast of the Notre Dame football game this afternoon. Uncle Mike, seated opposite his nieces, plunged into his supper.

Dopey sat slumped inertly. He was a tubercular-looking young man in his mid-twenties, with thick, sensuous lips, sunken cheeks, and a bony face. His hair was dark brown and curly, like that of his two sisters. His dark eyes were sunken.

With an irritated expression on her face, Aunt Anna handed the plate to Kate, who in turn passed it on to her brother. The family ate in an atmosphere of tension and constraint. Aunt Anna frowned constantly. Kate suddenly laughed at some un-expressed thought. Beatrice glanced at her, slightly annoyed. Dopey looked at the older of his sisters, his lips curling. Kate was plump, with a round, fat face, dark eyes, and black curly hair, and she looked like a school girl in her blue serge dress. Dopey cynically reflected that Kate giggled nervously, like a virgin.

Kate explained why she had just laughed. At the school where she was now teaching, they had received eight dozen potato peelers. Uncle Mike asked what they were for. Kate answered that no one at the school knew. Mike screwed up his lips and ponderously explained that in a large city you had to expect graft and that, anyway, graft meant sales, and sales meant more production, and that lessened unemployment. Kate said it was awfully funny, but all the teachers were angry because of the difficulties they had in getting necessary supplies and because the city was behind in paying them their salaries. Aunt Anna proclaimed it an outrage. Dopey said that everything was a racket anyway, so what difference did it make. Aunt Anna forked a piece of steak, but, seeing her nephew bolt his food, she held it in midair, glared at him, and said angrily:

"You eat like a pig!"

Dopey twisted in his chair, bored; he hoped she wouldn't start all over again, at the beginning.

Kate hurriedly intervened to remark that she hoped she would be transferred to a school in a better neighborhood, because now she had to teach dirty Polacks who would never be any good for anything except possibly to become thugs and bolsheviks and go on causing trouble all their lives, just as they did now in the classroom. Beatrice, after a nudge from Kate, joined in to say she was tired of having to work in the office at Carter School and that she only got a chance to teach when a substitute was needed. And the regular teachers were disgustingly healthy, so she didn't get much chance. She was fed up. And the pupils at her school were worse than Polacks; they were niggers. UGH! Uncle Mike said it was only because he had known Barney McCormack, the politician, and had some pull that Beatrice had gotten any kind of job in the schools, for there were still girls who had finished Normal a year ahead of her who were waiting for appointments. She should be glad she had an appointment instead of complaining.

"You might at least show some manners when you eat," Aunt Anna said to her nephew in a loud, rasping voice. "You'll have no stomach left, and if you get ulcers of the stomach, who's going to pay your doctor bill?"

"Uncle Mike, do you think business will improve soon?" Kate hastily asked to make conversation.

Before Uncle Mike could answer, Aunt Anna burst out at Dopey:

"You have the habits of a ditch digger. To see you eat one would imagine you didn't even know what the inside of a decent, refined home looked like!"

"Aunt Anna, please!" Kate pleaded, while Dopey grinned weakly.

"Katherine, don't interrupt me! Those who live in my house without even making the effort to pay one cent of board are going to listen to what I say. It's just about time somebody spoke seriously to you, young man, yes, *it's just about time.*"

She glanced toward Mike.

"I'm disgusted with him," she went on. "He's nothing but a bum, despite all we've done for him. I'd like to know what he thinks we all are—morons? If he does, he's mighty mistaken. He shan't continue living under my roof and go on as he has been. We've all gotten him job after job, but he's quit them. All he's interested in is horse races and getting drunk. Tell me who your friends are, and I'll tell you what you are. His friends are all bums, and birds of a feather flock together. Well, I won't tolerate him any longer."

"But Joseph is going back to his new job on Monday, aren't you, Joseph?" Kate said conciliatingly, turning to her aunt, whose face was flushed.

Dopey wasn't even listening. Instead, he thought how he would have gotten the gravy, rich and thick and brown, this afternoon, if he'd only had two bucks to lay on Red Pepper after Len had come around the corner with that hot tip. But it was always his lousy luck to be stony when he got a real tip. . . . Red Pepper had paid forty to one. Two bucks would have paid him eighty; five, two hundred; and he could have blown town for New Orleans, and then maybe he could have shipped out to Europe or Asia, or at least for the West Coast through the Canal Zone. But it was just his horse luck to be stony when he got a tip right out of the feed bag. . . . And, Jesus Christ, his aunt became a bigger and broader pain in the rump to him all the time. She'd been teaching sixth-grade Polacks and Hunkies so long that she thought she could treat everybody as if they were one of her sixth-grade pupils. And all that old crap about work and save, and grow old to be like Aunt Anna or Mike. Become a carbon copy of Michael J. McGuire, have a few bucks salted away in a bank that was liable to go bust any day, and be an old fox with your hair turning gray, telling your nieces and nephews how to be a Puritan while you had your bonded liquor and your women on the side. That crap had never gone with him. He remembered the one time he had shipped out of New Orleans and gone to Liverpool, and he wished he'd stuck it instead of coming back home because his Aunt Mary wrote him those letters. They could jam their work and save and pray just where it all damn well belonged.

He watched Aunt Anna eat with a vengeance; he hoped she was all talked out now.

"Joe, don't you think you could find some kind of work to stick at and make a future for yourself?" Mike said to him.

Dopey sighed. Mike got a self-righteous kick out of talking this way. Let him talk!

"Yes, you're starting to get old now; soon you'll be sloping down the years quicker than you imagine. Yes, sir, the slope down the years is a little quicker than we'd all like it to be, and before a young fellow knows it, he wakes up one morning and finds out he isn't as young as he wishes he was. You ought to have some thoughts of settling down, some plans for a future. Pretty soon you're going to have to take care of yourself. Your father is married again and he has other children beside you and your sisters. He has a baby. And his business is going very badly at present. And your Aunt Anna and I aren't so young any more, and what with taxes and the mortgage on this building, we can't go on taking care of you, much as we wish to help you. Yes, Joe, speaking straight from the shoulder, don't you think it's time you started thinking seriously about your future?"

Mike hadn't noticed Aunt Anna's frown when he said she was not so young any more. Finishing his steak, he went on to remark that a young fellow should have enough pride and ambition to want to win himself a place in the world, and that anyway he had to or else he'd be scratched, because the race for success wasn't for the slow or the shiftless, and every man in this world sooner or later had to take care of himself.

"Yes, Joseph, you really ought to listen to Uncle Mike and think of the advice he gives you," Kate said in the manner of a school-teacher.

"Mike, you're only wasting words on him," Aunt Anna said, and as she talked on her voice assumed a tone of exaggerated despair. "In all my livelong days, I never saw a boy as worthless as he is. He's always been the same. He wouldn't study and finish high school so he could go to college and study law or engineering, like his father wanted him to. His father said only the other night, after getting him this last job, that he couldn't do any more. It's no use. We've helped him, fed him, clothed him, waited on him, coddled him, tried to point the right way out to him, but it's just not in his bones. If it was, he'd have amounted to something by now."

"Every good job I ever had, I got myself," Dopey said.

"Joseph! Please!" Kate pleaded.

"You see, Mike! He hasn't even the decency to appreciate what was done to help him. After all his shiftlessness, his father last week got him another job, and this is what he says. And he works at it for only three days and then goes out drinking with his bum friends and can't get up in the morning to go to work. And he didn't even have the sense of fairness to telephone his employer and say he wasn't coming to work."

"But what kind of a job was it?" Dopey asked.

"Yes, I know what you want. A banker's job from twelve to one, with an hour for lunch," Aunt Anna said.

"Since your friend Pete Flanagan's bank failed, I don't think I'd care to be a banker."

"Joseph, you know that Pete was honest, and his failure was an honest one. That indictment against him is the work of soreheads and politicians who want scapegoats so they can make demagogic appeals," Mike said.

"Sure!" Dopey said ironically.

"He even slanders a friend who has been so good to him all his life," Aunt Anna said.

"Oh, Auntie, please!" Beatrice said.

"Well, I said my last word. He wouldn't go to work today. I wash my hands of him," Aunt Anna said.

"What kind of a job was it?" Dopey asked again. "If I'm to be treated like a high-school pupil, I want more than seventeen bucks a week. That wasn't a job. It was a slave factory for dopes. You had to get there at eight-thirty before a bell rang, and if you were a minute late you went to the chief clerk with an excuse, just as if you were in high school. He wrote you out a note permitting you to go to work. And if you had to go to the bathroom, you had to raise your hand, just as in school. And a bell rang for lunch, and after lunch another bell rang, and at five-thirty, a bell rang, and your work was checked, and you were given an average. The average was posted on a bulletin board with grades and letters and colors. If I stuck at the job, I'd be given homework to do next week. I'm no slave."

"Well, all I say is this. I'd never have the patience with you that your father and your Uncle Mike and your Uncle Pete have shown. I'd let you roll in the gutter where you belong."

Beatrice took out the soiled dishes, and Kate served coffee and pie.

"He hasn't one iota of manhood in him, and I shan't go on feeding him. I'm no fool. He worried my sister Mary while she was alive, but he won't worry me!" Aunt Anna said, pouring cream into her coffee.

Dopey did not answer. He drank his coffee and thought of his deceased Aunt Mary. He saw her, gray-haired, sweet, gentle, worrying. She seemed to walk into the room and take her accustomed place next to Mike. She seemed to sit there, quietly and unobtrusively. She seemed to smile at him in anxiety and

sadness. She had been like a saint, and even though she had
worried about him, she had been understanding. She had known
that her nieces and her nephew had their own lives to lead.
He remembered the first time he had thrown up a job and
bummed to New Orleans. How she had worried and prayed
for him and sent him money. And the way she had slipped him
a ten-dollar bill the morning he had left. She had raised him and
Kate and Beatrice, given her life for them, taking the place of
their dead mother. And then she had quietly died. She had been
the only one in his family that he gave a good goddamn for,
and when she had died he had felt sorry. He remembered her,
a nun-like, thin woman, who, now that she was gone, seemed
holy. She was his one sentiment, his one cherished memory,
the one memory that made him feel, made him sad. She was
dead, but he imagined he saw her sitting there at the table.
Things had been entirely different in the goddamn menage
ever since she had died. He imagined her sitting at Mike's left,
and he wished she were alive. He even wished he had caused her
less worry during her lifetime.

"I've had enough of him," Aunt Anna said, rising at the
end of the meal. "He can go out tonight with those bums, but
when he returns the burglar's lock will be on the door. His
father and stepmother won't have him. Well, neither will I!"

II

Mike called Dopey into the bedroom they shared. Dopey sat
on his own unmade bed and wondered if he would be able to
stem his uncle for a loan. His uncle did everything he did, only
in a bigger way. He played the ponies, got his tail, smoked cigarettes incessantly, despite his bad lungs, drank, sat up at all-
night poker games. Now he was going to sound off like a
Y.M.C.A. secretary.

Mike held out a box of cork-tip Egyptian cigarettes. Dopey
took one, and they lit up. Mike fingered his black knit necktie
and looked his nephew in the eye. He ran his soft hand through

his thinning hair. He crossed and uncrossed his legs, puffing at his cigarette meditatively. Dopey slumped back on the bed and waited.

"Joe, I want to speak to you," Mike said dramatically.

Suppressing a smile, Dopey also checked an impulse to exclaim:

—Oop, you're telling me something!

That was the way he and Al Herbert always razzed anybody who told them dumb stories. Mike inhaled and let the smoke out his nose. He cleared his throat.

"Yes, Joe, I've been wanting to speak with you for a long time," Mike said. He paused. "Joe, you see, I feel that somebody should have a man-to-man talk with you. Now, your Aunt Anna, she loves you very much, and she wants you to do right and amount to something. But, after all, she's a woman. She has your best interests at heart, but there are things a woman can't naturally understand. So I decided I better speak with you, and I want you to understand that I'm going to talk with you straight from the shoulder."

Dopey spilled ashes on the rug, and Mike asked him to be careful. If Aunt Anna saw him doing that, she would go up like a kite. Mike lit a fresh cigarette with his old one.

"Joe, all the young fellows you pal with are getting somewhere. Take Ike Dugan. He's with the Mid City Utilities making good money, and he has a future there. And Marty has a good job selling for the Nation Oil Company. And you were telling me that Al Herbert has gotten himself a good job in a bond house, and that his employer thinks well of him. And Phil Garrity is on La Salle Street. Pardon me for saying it, Joe, but they all seem to be a little bit wiser than you. They have their fun. They're not goody-goody Willies, but they stick to their jobs, and they all seem to be getting somewhere. They use a little bit of common, ordinary, everyday horse sense and don't let their fun and amusements interfere with their work and their future. Joe, you're just as intelligent as they are. In fact, I think you're a damn sight smarter. I remember when you were in high school. You were smart as a whip in mathematics. If you'd only applied yourself more you would have been a shark in that line. There is no godly reason in this world why you shouldn't go miles farther than they, except that you're lazy. A little bit of get-up to you, Joe, and they couldn't see you for dust. That's straight, the God's truth, because, Joe, I've got faith in you. I'm talking frank, and I don't want you to feel hurt when I say you're a little lazy, because, Joe, I'm only trying to give you constructive criticism, and I believe that we all got to recognize the truth when it is told to us. Joe, I have faith in you, and that's why I'm bothering to tell you that you need a little more get-up to you. Maybe these are hard words to say to your face, but, Joe . . . the truth is always a little bit harder than we'd like it to be."

Dopey, who had been simpering while Mike talked, nodded and exclaimed that he'd never found an interesting job.

"Joe, you always put the cart before the horse. . . . But, here, have another cigarette. . . . Got a light? . . . All right, Joe, you got to realize that you can't go through life waiting for an interesting job to come along. People don't work because they find it interesting. They work because they want to make money, because with money they can be somebody and not be ashamed of themselves. They can do things with money, show the community that they are somebody. Work is a curse, the curse of Adam. Do you think I like to work? Do you think I enjoy the insurance business? Not on your life, not on your life! Nobody likes their work. People work because they've got to, because they want *money*, esteem, the independence that only money can buy. When Shakespeare said that your pocketbook is your best friend, he said one of the truest things any man ever said."

Mike paused. Dopey slouched, wondering how long Mike would go on this time.

"Joe, I've been wondering for a long time why you don't stick to a job. Now I know. You've gone along looking for a job that's interesting. Well, you won't find interesting work, except by a rare piece of good luck. You've got to make yourself like whatever work you get. You got to stick to it, and keep your nose on the grindstone, and say to yourself with determination, 'I won't quit, and no one can make me quit, because I've got courage and brains and faith in myself!' If you want to be somebody, you've got to grit your teeth and stick to your job no matter if it kills you."

"I've had plenty of jobs all over this country," Dopey said in a toneless voice. "I don't go for that stuff. It's the bunk. A lad's fun and his life are worth more than a measly twenty or thirty bucks a week. And nowadays you can't start in as the office boy and work yourself up and become a big shot. Those days are over. There's no one starting on a shoestring and making a wad like John D. Rockefeller did. Now you've got to accept being a clerk and a flunkey for some big corporation. The only way you get rich now is in a racket, or by having a lot to start with, or having some luck on the races, or something like that."

"Joe, that's pessimism. If everybody thought like you, we'd all be communists and anarchists, and then how would the world's work get done?"

"There's plenty of suckers to do the world's work, and, anyway, if the world didn't have so much work for itself, we'd all have a better time. Most of the jobs I've ever had were useless ones. I'd add up figures on a comptometer machine, make out useless reports and forms, and prepare records that would be filed and never looked at. Then they'd be tied up, put in a storeroom or basement. And when there were enough records stored up, they'd be burned. And I'd go on filling up new cabinets all over again."

"Joe, you're damn near talking like a bolshevik. Here's one idea you have to get straight. There isn't any work in a good office that's useless, unless it's in politics. I run an office and I know. I know business and businessmen. They aren't dumb. The fellows who have risen to be heads of corporations have their jobs for one reason only—they're smart as whips. If they weren't, they wouldn't be at the top of the ladder. They know economics because that's their business. And they know that according to economic law everything that isn't useful and profitable is naturally eliminated, because it has to be by the law of supply and demand."

"In most of my jobs, there's always been plenty of demand."

"Joe, I'm talking serious, and it will profit you not to be . . . facetious. You're twenty-five now, and you can't afford to fool any more time away. If you do, what's going to become of you? Did you ever stop to think of where you'll be in five, ten, or fifteen years?"

"Yes."

"Well?" asked Mike as they lit fresh cigarettes.

"I may be in Shanghai."

"That's not a serious way to look at it. You know there isn't anything in a life like that for a fellow as smart as you. That's a life for bums and dumbbells. Don't be a fool! Such a life would mean nothing but hardships, drifting, disgrace, vice, poverty. You'll have no decent friends, no home, nothing that the ordinary civilized person has. You'll be a drifter without a cent in the bank, with no place in the community, nothing. If you work hard and keep straight, you'll have something, and be somebody, and be able to walk out of the house every morning with pride and with the feeling of the honest blacksmith in the great poem who owed no man a penny. You'll be somebody that way. You won't be a failure, a disgrace to yourself and your family, and, yes, to your country, because being a failure is being a disgrace to your country, too."

Dopey drew on his cigarette and let the words drum meaninglessly on his ears.

"Joe, what do you think you'd like to be?"

"I'd like to go back to sea or else be a bookie."

"Joe, can't you see that that will never get you anywhere?" Mike asked emphatically, gazing nonplussed at his nephew. "If you were still nineteen, your attitude would be all right, because at nineteen a young fellow still has a few years to waste. But you've wasted enough of your life. You've had your adventures. You've seen more of America than I have. And you

never made a go of that kind of life, either. You've gone away
on your own more than once, and you had to telegraph for your
fare back to Chicago. You had a good job in a Wall Street
brokerage house paying you seventy-five dollars a week, and
you were a fool for throwing it up. Joe, you better give up some
of your ideas before they land you in a mess, with your life
and your health wasted. Get yourself a good job, stick to it, invest a little of your money soundly. Then you can have your
good times in the right way. I have my good times, and I always
had 'em. But I never was foolish. If you're not foolish, you
won't have to sacrifice your fun. If you take my advice, you'll
get somewhere, and then you'll have money for good times in
the right way. I don't say you shouldn't play around a little
with girls, take a drink now and then, or even put a little
money on the horses. That's all right in its place, and if it's
done with moderation. But you've got to harmonize those
things with your work so you'll not be a failure. And if you
let yourself become a failure, every friend you have will turn
his back on you, and you'll be like an outlaw."

Dopey could see that Mike was enjoying himself.

"Joe, I want you to think about these things, and to remember that life isn't so long, and that time crawls up on you
just like death does. Time, as well as death, is a thief in the
night."

"Well, I don't see much enticement in success if it's very
hard to get."

"Joe, I wish you wouldn't joke, because this is a matter that
requires serious thought," Mike said as they again lit cigarettes.

Dopey refrained from smiling. He suddenly decided that
he'd better agree with his uncle and hurry up with a good gag
to get a loan. Mike had talked himself into a swell mood. They
sat smoking, and Dopey said in an insincere but serious voice:

"Maybe I had better start considering things in a new light."

Mike beamed. Dopey told him that Phil Garrity had said
something about there being a possible opening where he
worked soon, and, since Phil was in good with his boss, Phil

might get him the job. Anyway, it sounded like a good proposition.

"If you get that job, I'll guarantee to get you good references, and we'll turn over a new leaf, forgetting the past and its errors. And, Joe, go to work determined to stick at it until hell freezes over, and after it freezes go get ice skates and stick some more. If you do, I'll bet that you'll become a new man. You'll find yourself feeling better, free and independent. You'll buck up and be more chipper and know that you've found your place in the scheme of things."

"Yeah, I guess I better get some sort of a racket where the bucks come in regular."

"Snap up this opportunity if it knocks on your door."

"I think I will."

Mike talked more of inspiration, and Dopey nodded in agreement. Mike took out a bottle of bonded whisky and they had a drink. Dopey told Mike that he owed Phil Garrity three bucks, and that Phil needed it, and that since Phil might help him land that job, he'd like to be able to repay Phil. Mike frowned.

"Do you have to pay him tonight?" Mike asked, scratching his poll.

"I don't exactly have to, but I'd like to because I know he has a heavy date and needs it."

"Well!" Mike exclaimed, screwing up his lips. "Well . . . all right . . . I'll take this last chance on you."

He handed Dopey a five-dollar bill, and Dopey thanked him several times. He asked for another cigarette, and Mike gave him a box half full of cork-tips. Mike patted Dopey's shoulder and said that he had to get dressed to go out. But he was mighty glad to see that his nephew was turning over a new leaf.

Walking into the parlor, Dopey heard Mike telling Aunt Anna that all Joseph needed was a good talking to. He'd given it to him, and Joseph was going to straighten himself out. Dopey felt that Mike wasn't a bad guy. And he was proud of his chiseling. He felt the crisp five-dollar bill in his pocket.

III

Kate and Beatrice sat in the parlor listening to the Gold Dust
Twins on the radio. Dopey came in. Kate asked for a cigarette,
and he handed her a Lucky Strike. She listened by the hallway.
She came back and asked what Aunt Anna was doing, and
Dopey said Aunt Anna was talking with Mike in the dining
room. Kate lit the cigarette. Noticing the cork-tip in her
brother's mouth, she accused him of holding out on her. He
said he'd gotten it from Mike and didn't have any more. She
listened by the hallway again, returned to the couch, sat down.
She got her throat filled with smoke and coughed.

Dopey glanced at Beatrice. She was twenty-one years old,
and, he decided, had sex appeal; he sometimes wished to hell
she wasn't his own sister. She was a nice touch for some guy,
no use kidding himself. Was she or wasn't she a virgin like Kate?
She had gone with Al Peppler from around the corner of Sixty-
third and Stony, and Al had had the reputation of making
every girl he took out. Beatrice had gone heavy with him for
a while, and he was dubious about there being any exception
to Al's rule. But he didn't know. And when Al had run away
with funds from the bank he was clerking in, Beatrice had
damned near bawled her eyes out. Al had gotten out of the jam,
though. Dopey didn't know what had happened between Beatrice and Al, but he believed Al had given her the air. She hadn't
gone out on many dates for a long while after she and Al had
stopped seeing each other. Fellows ought to like her, though,
because she was a nice enough job. He looked at her trim legs.
Well, why not? Maybe this brother-and-sister stuff was just
hooey, just like everything else.

He studied Beatrice. She was a little pigeon-toed, and had bad
lips, just as Kate did, and her teeth were crooked, too. But, even
so, she was still pretty neat, and before she had gone with Al,
particularly, she had been paged plenty. She didn't seem to go
out on many dates, and he couldn't figure out why she was on

the shelf. But even if she was, she wouldn't be on it for long unless she wanted to be.

"I thought you were going out tonight?" Kate said to Beatrice, fidgeting on the couch while she spoke.

"I'd just as soon not," Beatrice answered.

"Well, I thought you were," Kate said archly.

Dopey looked at Kate with annoyance.

"Joseph," Kate said suddenly, "I do wish you would take better care of yourself. You know, we all worry about you."

Yawning, he told her to shut up. She acted hurt and shocked.

"You're mean. When someone tries to tell you something, only because they like you and know it will be for your own good, you won't even listen to them. You get mean and insulting. You're vile, and I hate you!"

"Save it," he said.

Beatrice hummed the tune of a popular song.

"You're horrid!" Kate said to him, wiping away a tear.

Dopey laughed. Beatrice yawned.

"Joseph, I really do wish you wouldn't act like that. People say things to you only because they're interested in your welfare. And, Joseph, you really don't look so well, and you're much thinner than you should be. You really ought to take care of yourself. You look awfully pale and you smoke too many cigarettes, and they're not good for your lungs. I wouldn't be surprised at all if there was something wrong with you. And you don't even go to Mass any more, either."

"Jesus Christ!"

"I don't care! Go ahead, insult me and curse me all you want to. I don't care. I do think that Aunt Anna was perfectly right in bawling you out. You ought to listen to her, or to . . . somebody."

"It seems like I have to, even when I'd rather listen to the radio."

"You needn't get so sarcastic."

"Every minute I'm home I hear it. Some of you ought to try sending your tongues away for a vacation."

"But, then, you're not home so much that you hear very much," Beatrice laughed.

"If I was, they'd drive me into the booby hatch."

"You're just incorrigible. Go ahead and have your own way then. Someday you'll be sorry when it's too late. . . . You're just perfectly incorrigible."

Dopey laughed at her. She pouted.

"But, Joseph, won't you *please* try to take a little better care of yourself . . . for your own good?"

He sneered. The doorbell rang. Kate hastened to answer it. Dopey rose and went over to a corner to turn off the radio.

IV

"Hello, Big Shot!" Kate said, greeting Phil Garrity with affected naiveté, as she let him in.

He returned a silly smile, shot out his hand stiffly from the hip, and pumped hers in a collegiate handshake.

"Put it there, Kid from the Limberlost. I ain't seen you in steen million years. How you was?"

"My, but you're strong," she said, and he manfully patted his chest with his left hand. "Why, Phil, you're all togged out like Joe College. New suit, topcoat, scarf, say, you'll look like a collar ad if you're not careful. I'll bet you're scheduled to sing some place tonight. Or maybe you have a new girl on the string. Do tell, Phil, are you *in love?*"

Phil blushed and faked a cough. He shoved his left foot forward, leaned his weight back on his right foot, placed his left hand inside his double-breasted blue suit coat, and smiled insipidly. Kate looked at him with innocent eyes.

"Say, kid, I get 'em in droves," he hurriedly said, gesturing clumsily to emphasize what he was saying.

Taking his beige topcoat and gray felt hat to hang in the closet, she giggled. Phil walked flat-footedly into the parlor, and Kate followed him, squealing as she glanced at his new tan brogans. He smiled insipidly as his hand shot out to Dopey, who shook hands limply.

"Phil is dressed up like a circus," Kate giggled.

Phil squinted sidewise at her through his gold-rimmed glasses.

"You must have played Red Pepper today," Dopey said.

"Nope. Never play the races. Guess again."

Sitting down, Phil carefully pulled his trousers up at his knees in order to preserve their press.

"Who died and named you in the will, Garrity?" Dopey asked, grinning.

"Wrong again," Phil replied.

"Phil looks like he had a heavy date scheduled," Beatrice said.

"I'm stepping out, high, wide, and fancy with something better than Clara Bow," Phil said.

"He's so cute," Kate tittered, and Phil blushed. She added, "Gee, don't you think he ought to wear a flower in his button-hole?"

"Kate, don't make him blush so," Beatrice said.

"Come on, Phil, what's the lowdown?" Dopey asked.

"Well, kid, I knocked 'em dead," Phil said, sliding his right hand out sidewise in an emphatic slicker gesture.

Dopey scratched his head, puzzled.

"Phil, the girl lucky enough to be dated with you tonight should be proud, and, when she steps out with you in that new outfit, she'll certainly have pride and lovelight in her eyes,' Kate said.

Phil quickly sneezed. He blew his nose.

"I knocked 'em dead, Joseph, and it was on the legit. It was on the legit," Phil said.

"Phil uses such quaint language," Kate said with assumed innocence.

"Razzing doesn't phase me, Kate," Phil said, grinning fool-ishly.

"Cut it, Kate!" Dopey said.

"Phil, do me a favor?" Kate said.

"Katherine, anything to oblige, anything to oblige," Phil said, rising awkwardly to bow before her with mock chivalry.

"Well, keep standing and turn around so we can see how perfect a fit you got," Kate said.

"Teasing him like that will spoil the poor boy's evening, Kate," Beatrice said, winking at her sister.

Phil sat down, grinning foolishly.

"Well, it fits," he said like a sap.

"And it's good goods, too," Kate said.

"For Christ sake, Garrity, spill the dope. What kind of a windfall did you have? You got me going," Dopey said.

"I knocked 'em dead this week. And it was on the legit," Phil said equivocally.

"I'm gaga with curiosity. Tell us," Kate said.

Phil pulled up his trousers at the knee again. He crossed his left leg over his right and fingered his bright blue tie. Kate commented on the clocks on his socks. Phil seemed uncomfortable because of the sudden lapse in the conversation. He mopped his face with his blue-bordered handkerchief.

"Dopey, my ship came in," he said.

"But really, Phil, I mean it. You have a good-looking suit on," Beatrice said.

"Thanks, Bea."

"It's the berries, Phil," Dopey said.

"Quite nobby, I should say," Kate said.

"And it was cash, no budget plan," Phil said.

"It makes you look like the answer to a flapper's prayer," Kate said.

"Here's the answer to a flapper's prayer," Phil said, showing them a wallet fat with money.

"How much?" Dopey eagerly asked.

"Plenty. . . . *Plenty!*"

"How did you make the haul?" Dopey asked.

"That's the secret. But get me straight. It was on the legit."

Laughing, Kate told Phil that he just couldn't do anything that wasn't above-board, and he flushed.

"Come on, Garrity, flash the tale. This ain't a detective story," Dopey said.

"I knocked 'em for a row. And you ain't seen all, either."

"I'll faint if you say you bought the ring," Kate said.

"She's a beauty, a genuine bargain," Phil said, palming his hands outward in a gesture of emphasis.

"You talk as if you bought her at a bargain counter," Kate said, giggling.

Phil went to the window, and they stared at a long, impressive, polished second-hand Lincoln, parked at the curb.

"I'm going buggy riding," Phil said.

"Did the old man break down and blow himself to that tin? Or did you rent it for the night?" Dopey asked.

"I told you I knocked 'em dead. I just peeled three hundred bucks spot cash off the roll. And you should hear that Lincoln motor purr. Smooth as they come, runs just like new. It's a beaut," Phil said.

"Jesus Christ!" Dopey said, amazed, and the two girls laughed.

When they left the window and again asked how he got the money, he preserved his air of mystery.

"Phil, you won't make your girls walk home, will you?" asked Kate.

"Listen, little Nell of the Limberlost, I'll knock 'em for a row now. When I get 'em out in this chassis of mine and step on the gas, their hearts will pop right out of their mouths— they'll cry for more like babies cry for Castoria," Phil said.

"Ooh!" sighed Kate.

"Kate, you ain't cute. Lay down and die," Dopey said.

Kate ignored her brother and asked Phil where he had such luck.

"Well, I sure get 'em off on this. You coming around in new togs and a Lincoln. You must be a magician," Dopey said.

Phil beamed.

"Phil is a real slicker. He's been holding out on us all these years," Beatrice said.

"Phil, did you meet an heiress?" Kate asked.

"Well, me lads and lassies," Phil said, beaming, and he paused.

"Hurry up or I'll faint with suspense," Kate giggled.

"With a mean boat like the one you got, you'll be a menace to public safety. When you get snozzled, it'll be even worse. Instead of being nearsighted, you'll be double-sighted. But, boy, you'll have some buggy rides," Dopey said.

"Oh, do tell, Phil. I'm agog," Kate said.

Phil started to brag of the rides he'd have.

"I'll bet that Phil will start thinking that lampposts are Christmas trees and his car and his friends are ornaments to be hung on them," Kate said, interrupting.

Phil glowed. He and Dopey lit cigarettes, smiling at each other with mutual understanding.

"Will you take me for a ride sometime?" Kate coyly asked.

"If you can take speed. Speed's going to be my middle name."

"Phil will put just a wee bit of zip in the car," Dopey said, and they laughed.

"Phil is so *cute*," Kate said.

"Kate, you always razz me. But just to show you that my heart's bigger than an apple, I'll take you for a ride," Phil said.

"I'd just love it," Kate said.

"Let's barge out of here," Dopey said suddenly.

He put on his hat and coat and walked out without saying good-by. Kate helped Phil on with his coat.

"How about a date next week?" he asked.

"Please tell me how you got the car?" she asked.

"Why not have a date tomorrow night?"

"I won't answer you until you tell me how you got the car."

"I got a hot tip in the office and cleaned up on the market," he said.

"That's grand! Why, someday I'll bet you'll be a real financier," she said laughing.

"How about the date next week?" he asked hoarsely.

"I'm not usually asked that way," she said.

"But, Kate, I would like to come over for you and let you see how the boat runs, and we could do something," he said.

"Well," she said evasively.

"How'd you like me to teach you to drive it?" he asked.

"That would be adorable."

"Let's make it definite," he said.

"Hey, Garrity, shake those flat feet of yours," Dopey impatiently called from the landing below.

"What night?"

"Call me up," she said.

"I'll call, but I suppose it's no use. I don't count anyway. I'm nothing but a chump. It won't be any use to call you up, but I'll do it because I'm a chump," he said.

"Now you're getting sarcastic again."

He slowly went down the stairs.

"Have a good time," Kate called sweetly after him.

v

Dopey asked how Phil had gotten the rake-in, and Phil told him. They got in the car, and Phil started it. He drove silently, brooding, thinking that, after all, he was just No-Soap Garrity and that he'd never be anything else. He had had so many plans and dreams about tonight, he had anticipated so much, he had looked forward to his appearance at the Carberrys and the way he would impress Kate. And he had counted on the date he would make with her. She'd put him off, and he guessed that she wouldn't date him. She hadn't given him a date in six months now, and he believed she laughed at him behind his back. There was a wrong twist in his make-up, and there had been even back in his high-school days. He had been one of the best students in his classes, and from his sophomore year on he had done most of the covers for the school magazine and the annuals. But that hadn't made him a regular fellow with the guys. He hadn't even been able to make any of the teams as a sub. He'd never been a good fighter. When the time came for dances and dates, he couldn't learn to dance decently, and he'd always had poor luck in getting dates. He just had a wrong twist in his make-up somewhere. He knew it. He knew he had always been something of a clown. When Dopey and the fellows had had their frat back in their high-school days, they had never bid him for it, even though he had hung around to get bid. He didn't have the social graces lots of other lads had. He just didn't click.

"For Christ sake! Watch your driving," Dopey said excitedly and angrily, as Phil, nearing Sixty-fourth Street, barely managed to swerve away from a collision with a Dodge.

"It's all right, pal. We won't hit anything, and if we do, it'll be the other mug's fault, and some poor bastard's tough titty. This car is built like a dreadnaught, and I mean *built.* Nothing is going to smash into it."

"Be careful. I'm going on a bender not a funeral," Dopey said.

Still brooding, Phil turned onto Sixty-fourth Street.

"Watch that driving," Dopey said, as a car cut in ahead of them.

"I am. I know how to drive."

"You're so goddamned nearsighted you couldn't see the blind sight of a barn," Dopey said.

Phil winced. Always having to take it. Just a misfit. Couldn't even see to drive. Chump Garrity. Like a fathead, he'd thought his clean-up on the market, his new suit, and his car would give him a new personality. And he was still a misfit. He wasn't a regular fellow like other guys were. He couldn't talk their lingo and make it sound like the real stuff, couldn't get girls, couldn't really feel his oats the way Dopey seemed to. He shouldn't be going around the corner. He hadn't in the old days of Nolan's dance hall, because he'd known he didn't belong. Misfit! Maybe he should have been an artist. In high school he had planned to be one, but most guys thought that artists were goofy, and he couldn't stand being laughed at as an artist. So he gave it up, didn't go to art school, and got himself a job in a brokerage house. He made dough now, too, and he was envied for his salary and the extra dividends he made playing the market on his own. But that didn't make him regular either. Yes, maybe he shouldn't have given up art. The priests in high school had told him he was promising. And he knew he had been. Sometimes now he felt that he was, and he went to the Art Institute with materials, and he looked at pictures, taking a hill from Cézanne, mist from Monet, a few trees from Corot, a sky from Inness, and making it a picture of his own. Doing that, he'd think of Kate. And down at the office he'd think of her, think of her as *Mrs. Katherine Garrity . . . Mrs. Philip Garrity . . .* He had enough money to marry on, and with her teaching, too, they could get on jake, save, have a little apartment, and they ought to be happy. If she only would realize that he loved her and would give him a chance to make her love him. He'd like that better than bouncing around and drinking with the fellows as he did, not having any fun. And they always wanted to go whoring, and he still had his cherry, even though he pretended that he'd lost it. If they knew, they'd give him the horse laugh and a nickname like *Cherry Garrity.* Maybe tonight they'd go to Twenty-second Street. But he didn't have the guts. It was sin. God might punish him with an automobile accident, death, a dose. Most of the fellows hadn't taken their doses seriously, but he was afraid of getting one. He didn't want to be going out to get drunk either, but he had to when he was feeling the way he did tonight. He couldn't have a good time with the guys when he was sober. Sober, he was a clown, not knowing what to say, a dunce before girls. Well, he'd get drunk, goddamn them all, he'd get polluted, maggoty drunk. He didn't like the taste of the stuff, but he'd down it like water. He'd even take pure alcohol. He'd show 'em! If he couldn't do anything else better than other lads, he would put on a better drunk than they did. And let Kate hear about it, let her know that they all went to a whore house, let her know everything! Let her see he could go on living without giving a good goddamn. He could be wild, carefree, dashing, romantic, brave, a guy who didn't care two hoots in hell for anything in the world.

Somehow, he'd go romantically, carelessly to hell . . . But, no, he didn't want to. He wanted Kate. If he could only call her *his Kate,* marry her, build a beautiful life, the two of them together, a life better than he now lived . . . *I'm all alone . . . so alone . . . with no one else but you . . . I'm all alone . . . dancing with tears in my eyes . . . With someone like you, a pal so good and true. . . . I'd like to leave it all behind. . . . And go and find . . . Some place that's known to God alone. . . . Just a little spot to call our own . . . We'll find perfect peace . . .*

VI

The corner of Sixty-third and Stony Island was bustling with Saturday-night activity, crowded with people, noisy with the traffic of automobiles and streetcars. The elevated trains kept rumbling into and out of the station overhead. Fellows, most of them young, were lined in front of the drugstore on the southwest corner by the elevated steps, the bus station near it, and the restaurant, modernistically decorated, which was a few doors farther down. Dopey and Phil entered the drugstore. Phil bought four packages of cigarettes and handed two to Dopey.

"Hello, boys," Slag Stone said, smiling at them.

Dopey asked him how he felt, and he said pretty good, considering.

"Considering what?" Phil asked.

He said that he had been pie-eyed last night and thrown some sugar bowls at people whose faces he didn't like in Sally Carns's restaurant. And, feeling rotten, he had to start to work tonight as bouncer in a new cabaret down on Cottage Grove Avenue. He ambled away, a tall, broad-shouldered, powerful fellow of about thirty.

At the door they met seventeen-year-old Young Evers, who had already been kicked out of three high schools. His forehead was breaking out in a rash, and his face was surly.

"Got a jit? I need a couple more jits to get a bottle," he said.

"You still mooching around here?" Dopey said sarcastically.

"You ain't got a monopoly on the business," Evers snapped back in good humor.

"I don't like competition from amateur chiselers," Dopey said, while Phil handed him a quarter. Dopey added, "Why don't you try working for a change?"

"It doesn't agree with my drinking."

"How they coming, lads?" Eggs Mahoney asked, as they lined up outside by the drugstore window.

"O.K.," Phil said insinuatingly.

"Well, if I'd had the dough to play on Red Pepper this afternoon, I'd be swimming in good nature," Dopey said.

"Me, too. I was flat. Jesus, what a break," Eggs lamented.

They lit cigarettes and moved down the line to say hello to Buddy. His face was battered up, and they asked him what had happened.

"Say, got a drink? I feel scrawny," Buddy said.

"We ain't started yet," Dopey said.

"Well, I got to hustle one. I feel snaky," Buddy said.

"But what's the matter with the lamps?" Phil asked.

"I just got let out of the station. Was there since three this morning," Buddy said.

"Another fight?" asked Dopey.

"Yeah. Say, got a fag?" asked Buddy.

"Here's a coffin nail," Phil said, talking out of the side of his mouth and extending a pack to Buddy.

"Thanks," Buddy said, taking one.

"Keep 'em," Phil said.

"Thanks," Buddy said, pocketing the cigarettes. He lit up and added, "I got snaky last night on Whaley's bum gin, and some big foulball of a dick came along. You boys know how I like dicks, so I hung one on the elephant, getting him square in his goddamn loud Irish mouth. He hauled off on me, and we tangled. I might have handled the bastard, but the bastard got reinforcements, and they hauled me off to the station and beat my pants off. The bastards! I'm laying for that big dick, and, when I get him alone, I got a bill to pay."

"They're plenty tough. But, say, your brother was looking for you this afternoon. He had a tip on Red Pepper, and it paid forty to one," Dopey said.

"That's always my goddamn luck," Buddy said.

"Playing football this year, Buddy?" asked Phil.

"Too old for that now. I'm thirty now, and I already played quarterback for four colleges. Saint Vincent's wanted me back again this year. I was told that all the guys I played against when I was with them six years ago would be through now, or should be, and that I wasn't likely to be recognized. But I'm married with a wife bringing in the dough, and I'm getting too old for that stuff. Let younger lads collect the dough in that racket, and if they can't hire any players, the hell, let them use their regular students," Buddy said.

"I see," Phil exclaimed knowingly.

"I'm crawling along to mooch a drink from Whaley," Buddy said, moving on.

Wils Gillen approached and shook hands all around.

"Say, boys," he said, "I got a date tonight with a really *mean mamma*. I tell you, she's *mean*. All class, and what she hasn't got just ain't worth having. And that includes her papa's Cadillac. The old man's a big shot. He sells things here to the schools."

"Maybe he's the guy who sold potato peelers to my sister Kate's school," Dopey said.

"You boys should see the château they live in out on South Shore Drive. It's as grand as a church, and the parlor's so big you got to megaphone to be heard from one end to the other. She's red hot. I'll tell you who her old man is. Connolly, he's big stuff, a ward committeeman who's somebody in the Democratic organization in this country."

"Gettin' up in the world, huh, Gillen?" Phil said, hiding his envy with a smile.

"And, boys, I'm not seeing Maureen Connolly for nix," Wils said proudly, strutting off.

Jean Fournier and his wife came up to them, and Dopey asked Jean what he was doing these days.

"I'm in one of Al Capone's rackets," Jean said.

"Bootlegging or gambling, Jean?" asked Dopey.

"It's another of the Scarface's rackets. I'm driving a wagon for a cleaning and dyein' outfit. It's a pretty good job, considering hard times, and I ain't complaining," Jean said.

Joey White joined them and said he'd lost his job, but that he had a little dough set aside and was going to a school to study aviation, and Jean's wife stood smiling as they talked.

"Well, look who the hell is here!" said Phil, laughing, pointing to a smiling, puffy young man who approached.

"Careful, there's ladies around," Joey whispered to Phil.

Dressed in expensive clothes, and weighing close to two hundred pounds, Marty shook hands with everyone. They kidded Marty about his weight, saying he was guzzling too much beer.

"What's the matter with Lillian tonight?" asked Dopey.

"I had a row with her, and she gave me the ring back," Marty said with a good-natured smile.

"You've been going with her for six or seven years, and you've frozen away all competition. You ought to marry her, at least for charity if for no other reason," Joey White said.

"What the hell, she gave me the ring back," said Marty.

"You'll be back with her," Dopey said knowingly.

"Nope, I'm free, and I got a date tonight with the niftiest polack. She's . . ." he noticed Mrs. Fournier and seemed embarrassed. He added flatly, "She's plenty on looks."

The Fourniers walked on, and Marty told them how, a few years ago, Jean had been the idol of every bum and pig in Woodlawn. It was damn funny that he should have ended up marrying such a sweet and nice girl, like he did.

"Say, changing the subject, I seen a picture down at the show the other day, and do you know who was in one of the mob scenes . . . Slicker Morrie," Joey White said.

"He'll make the grade in Hollywood. He was one guy with a line. He could sell snowballs in hell with his lingo. His tongue was nothing but pure oil," Phil said, to be horning into the conversation.

"If you want my opinion," Joey White said, "I say that not even the Hollywood stars can resist Slicker Morrie. In the old days when Nolan's dance hall was here on the corner, every decent-looking jane who came to the Sunday-afternoon dances was gone on him. Slicker Morrie made more dames and copped more cherries than any lad in the history of Louisa Nolan's dance hall."

They reminisced about Louisa Nolan's dance hall, which had burned down five years previously, about the girls made and not made, the crap games in the can, the fights, the drunken parties, the days that were gone forever. They talked about the lads from those days who had drifted on, and about the girls. There had been Marjorie, broken in by Slicker Morrie, and after his pioneering effort she had laid for every guy in the place. But she hadn't been so dumb, even if she was a pushover. She was married to a guy who had so much dough that he could light his cigars with dollar bills if he felt like it. And there had been sixteen-year-old Myrtle. She'd been well laid before she was out of grammar school, and by the time she was fifteen she had been plain lousy with clap and syph, and she had had gonorrheal rheumatism, and one day she had just jumped into the Jackson Park lagoon and polluted the drinking water for the gold fish. And Esther, poor Esther, the dancing fool, a goddamn swell and decent kid even if she had been a teaser. In those days she used to dance every night in the week, and twice on Sundays, and not even a broad as husky as she was could stand the dancing pace she set. She danced herself right into consumption and the grave, poor Esther, and some of the lads had even bawled at her funeral. Poor Esther. And some of the boys, Al Tolan, for instance, who had been in the army with Pershing in Mexico and could drink like a fish without showing it. And where was Al? And Susie, the fag who used to give out bum checks, the dirty fairy. And Three-Star Hennessey, the lousy little cake-eater who used to rob girls' pocketbooks while he danced with them. Ah, those old days, 1920, '21, '22, '23, '24, and '25. Gone forever. And Phil, who had not known them, stood listening, aching with nostalgia for all this vanished splendor.

VII

Phil, Dopey, and Marty went down the street to a speakeasy. Phil ordered a pint of gin. Dopey said he had better make it two. He bought two pints and gave Dopey one, and Marty also bought a pint. They put their liquor in their pockets and left to go and see Jack Kennedy. Phil parked the car in front of a gaudy apartment hotel and followed them to the entrance-way under a garishly striped canvas awning. The front showed polished brass, and they passed through a lobby which contained much red plush. They got off the self-service elevator at the fourth floor and walked along a narrow hallway, hearing sounds from behind closed doors, a radio singer crooning *Just A Gigolo*, a woman laughing, a baby bawling. They knocked on the door of Jack's apartment.

"What ho!" they heard Jack shout after they had loudly rapped on the door.

"Open up, chappie!" Dopey said.

"I say, open up, chappie," Phil parroted.

"Jack, I got two bums here," Marty boomed.

Jack opened the door and faced them, a medium-sized, dark-haired fellow wearing a shirt with a soft collar open at the neck. They entered noisily. The apartment consisted of a large room and small kitchen. Most of the space was taken up by a wide in-a-door bed, which was unmade. Glasses, bottles, playing cards, and books were scattered about, and articles of male clothing lay on chairs and the wine-red rug. Jack looked carefully and emphatically at Phil's new clothes, and expressed surprise. Phil smiled at him self-consciously.

"What, ho, the chappie is all togged out and looks like a blighter of ripe intellect," Jack said, drawing back a pace and continuing to eye Phil.

"Yes, Mr. Wodehouse," Dopey cut in.

Carefully taking off his top coat, Phil hung it in the closet.

placing his scarf, hat, and gloves on a corner of the disordered
shelf.

"Races, Phil?" asked Jack.

"Nope. I made a killing, and it was strictly on the legit," Phil
said, emphasizing his words with a slicker gesture.

Dopey crabbed Phil's effect by saying that Garrity had
cleaned up some jack playing the market. Phil and Marty
handed their bottles to Jack. He went to the kitchen and returned with filled glasses on a tray. Dopey and Marty sat on
the bed, and Phil dropped into a cloth-covered chair beside
a table where there was a row of books. He looked at the titles—
a collection of essays by Emerson, *The Indiscretions of Archie*
by P. G. Wodehouse, *Kept Woman* by Vina Delmar, *The Great
Gatsby* by F. Scott Fitzgerald, a book of short stories by Irvin
Cobb. Phil carefully pulled his trousers up at the knees, and he
smiled with gratification while Dopey spoke of his car.

"Better times, friend!" Jack said, holding his glass aloft, and
they drank. "What's on the program?" Jack asked then.

"Count me out. I've got a date," Marty said.

"A bender and Twenty-two," Dopey said.

"We're going to get drunk," Phil boasted.

"Sweet words, those, chappies. Your schedule magnetizes me.
Let's have more drinks to inaugurate it," Jack said.

He took their glasses, returned with the drinks, and asked
if there was anything new.

"My aunt told me that when I come home tonight, the
burglar's lock will be on the door. And my uncle had a heart-to-
heart talk with me. He nearly wept on my shoulder trying to
turn me into a Babbitt," Dopey said.

"Did you chisel anything out of him?" Jack asked.

"All the bastard gave me was one cork-tip cigarette," Dopey
said.

"Then you can't pay me the buck you owe me," said Jack.

"Say, if Dopey ever paid his debts, the world would come
to an end," Marty said.

"Boys, I'm holding heavy, and tonight's my treat," Phil
said.

"Well, Joseph, if you're homeless, you can stay here if you want to, but, of course, if the landlord rudely disturbs your slumbers and unceremoniously shunts you into the street, don't accuse me of a lack of hospitality," Jack said.

"I see you still haven't paid your rent," Dopey said.

"How long have you been living here gratis?" asked Phil.

Jack led them into the kitchen and pointed at the cabinet. It was chuck full of empty liquor bottles. He pointed to additional bottles lined up on the floor.

"I've been here that long," he said, and they laughed. Still pointing at the bottles, he continued, "Gentlemen, a necessity of every modern home."

They drank a toast to the landlord and returned to the other room.

"Listen, Jack, will you do me a favor?" Dopey said.

"Anything if it isn't a request for lucre," Jack answered.

"Would you fix my aunt up for me?" said Dopey, and they laughed.

"Sir, she's over forty, and my age limit is fifteen. I'll have to call on one of my assistants. Marty, you take care of that job for me. If, as a consequence, you are driven to the booby hatch, we'll pray for your soul," Jack said.

Jack changed the subject, razzing Marty because he had put so much of his pay into Nation Oil Company stock and the stock had fallen about seventy-five per cent. Phil started telling them how to play the market with real pleasure. Marty said he wasn't playing the market. He bought the stock because he was selling oil for the company. Phil began again on the stock market, but Dopey interrupted him to say that all he was hoping was that he got a decent broad when they went to a whore house.

"Same old Dopey with his mind in the gutter," Jack said, clucking in mock disgust.

"With my mind in heaven, you mean," Dopey said.

Phil thought of the can house, and of the chance of getting a dose. He thought of going around the corner and casually bragging about it, talking about his condition and his treatments as he had heard so many of the lads talk. He shuddered.

Kate, he said to himself yearningly.

He went to the kitchen and tossed down a drink so quickly that he gagged on it. He heard them greeting Al Herbert. He went back and extravagantly shook hands with Al, a thin and pallid young man whose face seemed unduly flushed.

"Say, Jack, maybe I'll double up with you," Al said, after parking his coat and hat.

"The more the merrier. Only I make a strict rule which absolutely forbids anyone to pay rent," Jack said.

"What happened, Al?" Dopey asked.

"I had another scrap with the old man. He's getting more like an old woman every day. I got sick of hearing him shoot his trap off. I can't help it if he's my old man. He talked too damn much, and so I lost my head and socked him in the mouth. I pay my board, and he has no strings on me, and I'm fed up with his canned advice. Every day since he lost his job he's gotten more crabby. But that ain't my fault."

"So you socked him, huh, Al?" said Phil in a tone of camaraderie.

"That's what my aunt needs, a poke in the kisser," Dopey said.

They had another drink. Al told about how his kid brother was in love with Eloise Flannery, a nice girl who had gone to Saint Paul's. Phil, silent, thought of Kate and wished he could even be kidded about her. Al Jones, a baby-faced, collegiately dressed fellow with wavy hair, came around. He smiled superciliously during the greetings.

"How's the high-school boy?" asked Marty.

"You are in high school again, aren't you, Al?" said Jack.

"And he started at Mary Our Mother just after it was changed from St. Stanislaus, following my own graduation. He played football with Pat McGee. And when he got out he played freshman football at Loyola, and now he's a high-school student playing basketball for Park High," Marty said, and they all laughed.

"Jones is a young Ponce de Leon, the fountain of time," Jack said.

"You fellows can rub it in if it gives you any fun. I'm having my fun. I date the best-looking bims in Sigma at school, and I'm a Kappa, the best frat there, and I'm going to play on the heavyweight basketball team, and we're going to win the city championship," Al said.

"And what a different guy he is from the nice, quiet kid who used to be an altar boy when I was in high school. In those days he wouldn't look twice at a broad. But these young lads, they feel their oats," Marty said in good-natured razzing.

"I was only a kid then," Al protested.

"And now the malted milks you drink put hair on your chest," Jack said.

"Not only malted milks," Al said, his remark a signal for more drinks.

"But what I want to know is how you get away with it? Don't they know you played three years with M.O.M., that you starred there, and then played freshman football in college?" Marty said, a glass in his hand.

"No, and I haven't changed my name, either. A week ago we played a practice game with M.O.M., and I wasn't recognized. We won, twenty to eight," Al said.

"How many baskets you make, Al?" asked Phil.

"Oh, five," Al said nonchalantly.

"You must be the school hero," Marty said.

"We got a good team," Al said modestly.

"With your experience, you ought to have a crack team. But I still don't understand how you get away with it," Marty said.

"Aren't you a bit light for heavyweight basketball?" Phil asked.

"I get by," Al said.

They drank again, and Marty talked about when he was in school with Danny O'Neill. Al said he had heard that Danny had become something cracked, a socialist, and that he was supposed to be trying to write books and stories that were cracked.

"That reminds me. The day after the millennium the socialists will all break their harps," Jack said.

"I heard Father Houlihan talking about socialists in church.

They want to destroy religion. They're chickenshit," Marty said.

"Yeh, the day after the millennium they'll all break their harps in the ensuing riot, and it'll be tough on the Russians because of their beards. Trotsky will be running around yelling, 'My kingdom, my kingdom for a barber shop'" Jack said, and Phil laughed, wishing he could be as witty as Jack.

"Well, I'd hate to be as overworked as a Russian barber must be," Marty said, laughing.

"Al, want to get laid with us tonight?" asked Dopey.

"He's the hero of Park High. Think he has to pay for it?" said Marty.

"I'm getting mine. Tonight I got a date with a Sigma, a keen babe, for a hop at the Shoreland Hotel. I'm hoping pretty strong too, boys," Al said.

"In the old days when Fanny was a girl's name, there used to be plenty of it at Park. Pierre Richard used to go there, and he used to tell me how, after football practice, the football team would get broads up in empty classrooms," Marty said.

"We're not missing anything now," Al said.

"Times have changed a little, Marty. Now they start in grammar school, and the streets are full of jail bait," Jack said.

"I'm gettin' enough, and the only thing I wish is that I could stay at Park for about three more years. I'm having a swell time, better than I had at M.O.M." Al said.

"You were innocent then," Marty said.

Al Herbert drew Dopey aside and asked how about that ten bucks Dopey owed him. Dopey complained that he was stony.

"Al, Dopey's chicken. He doesn't borrow money. He just thinks every day is Christmas and asks for his presents in cash," Marty said.

"He's chicken, all right," Al said.

Dopey smiled in good-humored helplessness.

Phil looked around, slightly bleary already, and Dopey said: "Garrity's drunk already."

They looked at Phil, sweating and nervous in his chair.

"Can't take it like a man," Marty commented.

"All right, go ahead, pick on me, I know I'm a chump," Phil said, his eyes watering.

"He's on a crying jag, boys," Marty laughed.

Hurt by their remarks, Phil thought of Kate. He wouldn't be so affected by them if he could count on her. But, no, she didn't care. He vowed again to show them, to show Kate, to show the world, by getting drunk. Phil took another drink and talked of his new car.

"Born of the moment, built for years," Jack said. He pointed at Phil. "See, men! The Newest Smartest Styled Alden-A Shirts and Shorts for the well-dressed man. Phil, take off your pants to show us your shorts. And look at his hair. He's training for a permanent with Vaseline Hair Tonic."

Al interrupted to brag about the babe he had dated. Marty and he left.

Dopey told Phil to drive back and get more gin, and Phil said they could all go. Dopey dictatorially told Phil to do it. Phil left, sore, but then rapped on the door and asked if one bottle would be enough. Dopey said two would be better, and Jack said Dopey should also bring back some ginger ale.

"And, chappie, now for a facial cocktail," Jack said, going to the bathroom to shave.

Dopey waited until Jack was out of sight. He pulled out his bottle, gulped, and put it back in his pocket. Phil returned, gay and smiling. Jack finished shaving, and they mixed drinks, wondering what to do next.

"I got a bright idea," Jack said.

He explained it was to be a joke on his friend, Al King, but added that he didn't receive credit on his phone calls. Phil was sent down to the desk to pay twenty cents for two calls. Jack called a near-by drugstore and ordered it to send two rolls of toilet paper and a bottle of Pluto Water to Mr. Jones, care of Ellen Thomas, 6191 Woodlawn Avenue. They laughed and drank while waiting for the delivery. Jack telephoned Ellen Thomas and shot her a snappy line of talk. He asked for Al, and both Phil and Dopey could hear her giggling from the other end of the connection. Hearing Al speak at the other end, Jack said:

"Few people realize the seriousness of toilet tissue until it is too late. Tissue that is of a crinkly, sharp-edged texture is apt to . . ."

Al interrupted him in a loud, complaining voice. Jack slammed the receiver on him. They laughed, and drank.

VIII

Red Murphy staggered up to them as they were getting into Phil's car. He sat in the back with Jack and Dopey.

"Boys, I'm drunk, drunk! I'm looking for trouble. Did any of you fellows see any trouble? If you did, where was it? Let me know if you see any of it, because tonight that's what I'm looking for, trouble, and plenty of it," Red Murphy said, as the car went along.

"All that I want to do tonight is get laid," Dopey said.

"Ever want to do anything else?" asked Jack.

"I wouldn't mind that, either, but I'm not holding. And, anyway, I want to find some trouble first," Red Murphy said.

"Phil's holding big," said Dopey.

"Red, I'm with you on finding trouble," Phil called back, talking out of the side of his mouth.

"My old pal, Garrity," Red said.

"Garrity, you goddamn fool! Watch where you're going or it'll be our funeral," Jack said in nervous irritation after Phil had quickly swerved the car to avoid a collision.

"Maybe he put alky in the radiator and the chassis is snozzled," Red Murphy said, laughing in appreciation of his own wit.

It was a fine autumn evening with a gray mist in the air. They drove north to the Midway.

"Say, have you boys any fluid? Another drink, and I'll be just rarin' to go, and any mother's sonofabitch can just try and get tough with me," Red Murphy said.

Jack handed Red a bottle. Red drank. Handing the bottle back, he swung lustily at the air and almost tumbled out of the automobile.

"That proves that nobody better get tough with me tonight," Red said.

Jack drank. He leaned back in his seat and began to recite *Casey at the Bat*. Phil was driving slowly. Red Murphy asked for more speed. Jack said "no" to that because the street was dark, and Phil was nearsighted. Phil said he could drive well, but he did not increase the speed. A chorus of protests and complaints greeted him when he barely missed a safety island. Jack resumed his recitation. Dopey asked for something else. Jack sang:

> *My mother sells hops to the snowbirds,*
> *My father sells barber shop gin,*
> *My sister sells love on the sidewalks,*
> *My God how the money rolls in.*

"Garrity, do me a favor like a pal, will you? Just drive right head on into trouble," Red Murphy said.

Dopey took a drink and told Phil to turn around and go back to Sixty-third. They might find some pickups.

"We're liable to get pinched for mashing on Sixty-third. I heard the Law is watching that pretty close," Phil said, as he laboriously turned the car around.

"Quit singing 'em," Dopey sneered.

They cruised along, up and down Sixty-third Street. Finally they spotted three females in front of a bank building, and Phil was told to pull up. He obeyed, trying to talk and act with foolhardy desperation in order to quiet his fear.

"Get in, girls," he said tremulously.

"Don't wear your shoes out, babies," Dopey called.

"It looks bad, three girls like you there, alone at this time of night," Jack called.

The three girls came toward the car and, as they approached, the fellows within could see that they were not so young. They looked into the car, closely scrutinizing the occupants.

"Boys, better grow up! And you, sonny!" one of them said, finally fastening her gaze on Phil, "you, sonny, you better wipe that milk from behind your funny flap ears."

Laughing hoarsely, the women walked on. All the fellows but Phil laughed. He silently condemned himself and blushed. He drove back to the Midway, turning onto it.

"See them!" Jack said, pointing at the Gothic line of University buildings, "Well, there is many a co-ed around those august halls of learning who learned about life from Jack Kennedy."

"Bull," Dopey said.

"And I suppose you even taught Queen Marie, you liar," laughed Red Murphy.

"I charitably volunteered to, but all she would promise to do in return was make me prime minister. I wanted more than that, so we got no connections," said Jack.

"You mean prime mover, don't you?" Dopey said, and they laughed.

A Ford, with two young lads in it, cut in ahead of them.

"Sonofabitches! Think they own the boulevard," Phil said, in anger.

"Get 'em Phil!" Dopey said.

"They're just the wise bastards I'm lookin' for. Step on it, Garrity, pal!" Red Murphy said.

Protesting that it was no use to go after them, Phil stepped on the gas.

"Catch 'em, Phil! We're behind you, Phil boy. Red Murphy wants trouble, and this is where he finds it. Step on it, Phil boy!" Red encouraged, as Phil stepped on the gas.

The lights at Cottage Grove Avenue held them up. When the lights changed, he shot forward into Washington Park and hummed along through the deserted park. He stopped alongside of the Ford at the exit to Washington Park at Sixtieth and South Park Avenue. Red Murphy was first out of the car, followed by Jack. Dopey watched them.

"You lads want trouble?" Red Murphy asked, jerking open the door of the Ford.

"No," the lad driving it said in a voice of fear and surprise.

"Are you tough?" Red asked.

"We're minding our own business, lad," the other occupant of the Ford said.

"Well, what's the idea of hogging the boulevard then?" Phil said snottily, having joined Red and Jack.

"Are they tough?" Dopey called while the two lads apologized.

"You're getting away lucky this time, but don't try gettin' wise again, or you both might be going home with your teeth left behind to ornament the boulevard," Red said.

"And watch the way you drive, too!" Jack said, slamming the Ford door shut.

They got back into the car and turned around to drive north inside of the park. Under a lamppost along the park driveway, Phil saw many glittering pieces and chunks of broken glass. He stopped and clambered out, followed by his companions. They looked about, curious.

"There's blood on it," Dopey said, holding up a broken chip.

"Must have been a nifty job," Phil said.

"Good business for the mortician," Jack said.

"Too bad we missed seeing it," Dopey said.

"Carberry, you always were morbid," Jack said.

"It must have been a damn neat accident. Look, fellows, there's blood all over the driveway," Red Murphy said.

"And just our luck to miss seeing such a gory show," Jack said.

"It would have been a handsome sight," Phil said huskily.

"Seeing all this blood and glass, my guess is that someone must have been ticketed straight to the morgue," Red said, kicking glass.

"Must have been a drunken driver," Jack said.

"Why?" Phil anxiously asked.

"The remains suggest a thorough accident. A sober driver would not have been in the proper mood to perfect such an accident as this one. Only a drunken driver could have done that," Jack said.

"Drunken drivers don't have accidents. They have a drunk-ard's luck," Red said, while Phil, swaying near them, wondered if this were really true.

"The best way to stay out of trouble is get drunk. Then nothing happens to you," Phil said with bravado.

"Please take that back, Phil. Please. For Red Murphy is drunk, and he's looking for trouble," Red said.

"Drunk or sober, the guys who sprung this accident were artists. Look at the way they spread around the gore and glass," Jack said lightly.

"Look at this chunk!" Jack said, picking up a hunk of glass over a foot wide. He flung it away, and it shattered on the driveway.

"And here's some rich red gore," Phil said, almost retching at the sight of it.

He staggered to the edge of the grass and gazed off to the east, where the darkness was intercepted by moonlight. In the distance he saw the quiet waters of the lagoon, glassy with the rays of the moon. A feeling of peace entered him. He sud-denly wanted to paint, to paint this scene in sombre colors so that he would always have it to look at, so that he could put into it the feelings within him, the feelings of peace, quiet, yearning.

"We're getting bigger and better accidents all the time. Progress!" Jack said, and his words destroyed Phil's mood.

"It's always our damn luck to miss seeing them," Phil said, turning, swaying back toward his companions.

"Don't worry, Garrity. With your new boat and your near-sightedness, you won't miss all the fun," Jack said.

"I know how to drive," Phil said, wincing.

"What the hell, I saw one last week that would have made this one look like a piker," Red said, reeling around. "I was going home about midnight, walking down Stony Island Avenue on the west side of the street, no, the east side. Well, a crazy car crashes through the gates of the I.C. tracks at Seventy-first, misses getting knocked into smithereens by a train, smashes through the gates on the other side of the tracks, shoots down the street for hell and gone, the motor sounding like it was a zeppelin dropping bombs. I said my prayers and nearly pissed in my pants. I knew the guy driving was going to smash over the curb like Joe Savoldi going through the line, and I was ready to fold up and dive. When he passes me, I blesses myself, and down further he jumps the curb like a hurdler, slides off a lamppost like Red Grange evading a tackler, and hits a buildin' that's standin' inconveniently in his way. He was halfway through the windshield, and you should have seen the car. They took the pieces of that poor bastard to Jackson Park Hospital, but they could have saved themselves the trouble and the gas and carted him to the morgue."

"Murphy, that wasn't as good as this accident," Jack said, while Phil was weak with fear, wondering would such be his end.

"How come? You seen neither accidents," Red argued.

"Look at the remains. I deduce that this one must have sent three upstairs to play harps, with others turned in for serious repairs. Why, I'll bet that there wasn't enough left of these cars to interest Warshawsky, the junk dealer," Jack said.

"There's a lot of blood in one person. This blood might mean just one poor sonofabitch killed. And he couldn't have been any more killed than the poor bastard I saw last week," Red said.

"Anyway, it was rummy luck for the bastards in this accident. Maybe they had broads with them and were looking forward to tail, too," Jack said.

They returned to the car. Phil laboriously backed up, skirted the drive, went carefully northward. He was afraid. He had a premonition that something would happen to him tonight. He wished he were sober and out alone on a decent date with Kate.

The fellows in the back seat drank, and Jack began reciting *The Face on the Barroom Floor.*

"Hey, you goddamn fool! Watch your driving!" Dopey yelled after Phil just missed bumping into a car at Forty-seventh Street.

"The boy well nigh filled a mortician's that time," Jack said.

"Phil, I know better ways of dying," Dopey said.

They all insisted that Jack drive. Phil was shaken, but refused to give up the wheel.

IX

They decided to take in the Sour Apple on the near North
Side, hoping to find some pickups. Phil parked the car on North
Dearborn Street, and they clambered out. Phil was keyed up,
excited. There might be girls. And artists were supposed to hang
out at the Sour Apple. He asked if they had enough gin. Dopey
said he better buy another bottle. He suddenly remembered
that back at Whaley's he had given Dopey a bottle. Reminded
of this, Dopey slowly remembered that he did have a bottle
in his pocket.

"You're not a heel. You wouldn't hold out on your pals,"
Jack said, masking his irritation with a smile.

Phil defended Dopey as they turned into a narrow and dingy
dead-end alley. Halfway down, there was a dim green light, and
beneath it the entrance door to the Sour Apple, painted in
orange. Beside the door they noticed the bulletin board, with
an announcement.

WEDNESDAY FAREWELL PARTY TO MENDEL MARKOWITZ

"Know that guy, Jack?" asked Phil, pointing to the sign.

"He's a crazy Bohemian who gives lectures here sometimes.
I heard him speak, but nobody understands him," Jack said.

They read the sign painted in black on the door.

He who enters here leaves his dignity without.

"That means virtue, too, Phil," Red said.

Phil looked at Red, blushing.

"Go ahead, kid me! I'm only a chump," Phil said.

"I was only kidding, pal, and I'll fight the man that says
you ain't my buddy," Red said, putting his arm around Phil's
shoulder.

They entered, Phil last. Neglecting to duck in the low passageway leading to the ticket window, Phil bumped his fore-

head. At the end of the narrow passageway, which was walled
in between the forum and the tearoom, was the ticket window.
Phil shouted that it was his treat. He faced a tall, slatternly,
poorly dressed woman at the ticket window and fumbled in
his pocket for money. He heard the sounds of many voices
within. The anticipation of excitement, a good time, surprises
to come, stirred him up with hope. He paid three dollars and
was given four tickets, which he handed to an unwashed
middle-aged woman who pulled a bar aside and admitted them
to the tearoom.

"Who's the hag takin' tickets?" Phil whispered to Jack when
they were inside the crowded, noisy, smoke-filled, rectangular
tearoom.

"Atmosphere," said Jack.

The crowd, the steady talk, the strangeness of the sight all
confused Phil. The walls of the tearoom were plastered with
badly drawn murals, the colors largely a combination of weak
blues, pale pinks, eye-straining and raucous greens, violets, and
oranges. In most of the murals there were graceless, overweight
nudes done in bad imitation of Picasso, and Bohemians drawn
to look like Apaches. Along both sides of the room there were
booths painted in black and Chinese red, with black-topped
tables. At the far end there was a small counter. People shuffled
from group to group. The jazz band in the adjoining dance hall
blared. There was a crush through the narrow entranceway to
the hall. The music roused Phil. He told himself that he was
raring to go. To the left, there was a wooden stairway leading
to the second floor, and they trooped up it to the checkroom,
which was tended by a woman with bobbed hair and a wrinkled
face.

"Jesus, I hope the floor doesn't cave in on us," Dopey said
after they had checked their wraps and were standing indecisively near the stairway, glancing around at the disordered
slivery upstairs of a barn.

They pushed into the unswept men's room. The washbowl
was filthy, and a gurgling running sound came from the bowl.
They drank from their bottle and came out again.

"Hello," said a chubby little fellow in corduroy pants who stood near the stairway. "I remember you. Your name is Kennedy. Mine's Wolcroft."

Jack introduced the others to Wolcroft.

"I'm still on my summer vacation," Jack said.

"When does it end?" asked Wolcroft, smiling.

"Next summer," said Jack.

"Will you get a job then?" asked Phil.

"Well, the golf season will be going full blast then, and after the golf season it will be time for next year's vacation," Jack said, and they laughed.

Wolcroft asked for a drink, and Jack handed him the bottle. Wolcroft thanked them. He turned to Phil and Murphy and asked them how they liked the Sour Apple.

"It doesn't impress me as much as a can house," said Dopey.

"There's girls here, but you got to make the grade with them," said Wolcroft.

"You an artist?" said Phil.

"Yes, I write poetry. I'm reading some of it here at the party next Wednesday. One of the Sour Applers here, a fellow named Markowitz, is going to New York with his wife on his way to Europe. The lucky bastard married a girl at the University, and he's being sent to Paris with her. But we're glad he's going. He talks a lot," Wolcroft said.

"Say, I studied art. I can draw. I can. Sure. I was going to study art some more, but I went into a brokerage house instead. But I know something about art and drew for the school magazine in high school," Phil said.

"Well, come around. We have artists here. I'm a poet," Wolcroft said patronizingly.

"I will," said Phil.

"The hell with art. Biology is our topic tonight, boys," said Jack, and they smiled.

"There isn't a place in Chicago like the Sour Apple. It's unique. It was once the artistic center of Chicago, and all the great writers came around here, Ben Hecht, all of them. And artists, too, like Szukalski," Wolcroft said.

"Ben Hecht? I read his books. Say, he's a radical, isn't he? He doesn't believe in God, does he?" Phil said.

"He writes realism. That's old-fashioned. My poetry, now, it's superrealist. I'm hoping to get some of it published in Paris," said Wolcroft.

"Say, can you spare another drink?" asked Wolcroft.

They went back to the lavatory, and the bottle was passed around.

"As I was saying, there isn't another place in Chicago like the Sour Apple. It's unique. Now, you take Bill Bridges, who runs it, he's unique, too. He's a showman. Here, come along, and I'll show you something," Wolcroft said.

"Who's he?" asked Phil, as they followed Wolcroft toward rafters spun with cobwebs.

"You'll see him downstairs. He's got bobbed hair and needs a bath," said Jack.

"See these?" said Wolcroft, pointing at some loose boards.

"If I had a hammer I could nail them up in a minute," Phil said.

"They show just where Bill Bridges' genius lies," Wolcroft said, and they stared at him, dumbfounded.

"Anyone else would fix them. But not Bill Bridges. He leaves 'em loose. He hasn't touched them for five years. Do you know why? Because it gives atmosphere to the place. It's just that little touch, that little something, which stamps Bill as such an excellent showman. It's just what I'd do, too, if I was Bill," Wolcroft said.

"If you ask me, I'd say that he ought to have an atmosphere around here that includes a little air," Phil said.

Wolcroft looked pityingly at Phil. He smiled.

"Say, one of you fellows got a cigarette?" he asked, and Phil handed him one; he lit it.

"They do have air here, Phil, at their Sunday-night speeches. It's all hot air," said Jack.

"No, we have some good talks here. Markowitz talks on art, and he knows a lot. I'm speaking here on pure poetry and sex three weeks from tomorrow night, and I'll read some of my poetry. Come around," Wolcroft said.

"Let's go downstairs and see what broads they got," Dopey said.

"Well, I hope you like the Apple," said Wolcroft.

"That depends on the fems you got here," said Phil.

"We have intelligent ones, and some of them are poets," said Wolcroft, leading the way.

"Yes, boys, you'll meet the higher brand of hash slingers here," Jack said.

"A lot of sex-suppressed people from Iowa and the colleges come here, particularly on Saturday nights for the dances. The regular Applers come here more on Sunday and Wednesday," said Wolcroft.

They trooped downstairs. Wolcroft walked off toward a group of odd-looking males who were leaning against the wall and smiling superciliously. The others stood indecisively at the foot of the stairway. The air was heavy, almost fetid, thick with cigarette smoke, heavy with alcohol breaths. The orchestra was playing nerve-stimulating jazz. Then it stopped. The dancers emptied into the tearoom, and there was loud conversation and much moving about. Bohemians, many with long hair, leaned wearily against the walls, smiling at the crowd. A tall, handsome man entered, followed by three nondescripts who had the manner and air of sycophants, and the group around Wolcroft greeted him obsequiously. Phil asked who the bloke was.

"John Connolly, King of the Soap Boxers," Jack said.

"Another nut?" asked Phil.

"He's no nut. He's a smart fellow and a goddamn good talker. Don't let him hear you calling him a nut. He's really tough," Jack said.

Phil looked at the man, envied him for his apparent strength and magnificent physique.

"Is he radical?" asked Phil.

"Yes," said Jack.

"Then he doesn't believe in God. Anybody who says there is no God is crack-brained," said Phil.

"Don't argue with him. He knows more than you, and he's tough, too," said Jack.

Phil's sense of humiliation deepened. He regarded the big man with awe and envy. Here, he thought, was a man who could think and fight, who wasn't afraid of anything in the world. He became sensitive about himself. He was afraid his own personality was small. He wished he were an artist, and that he could come here and feel as though he belonged, feel at ease and at home in this place. He glanced around the walls at the murals, thinking that he could do better. Jack pulled at his sleeve, and the group moved over toward the dance hall to wait for the next dance. A stupid-faced, drunken young fellow in a blue suit wavered by them, stopped before a scraggly girl in a stained gray dress, pointed his finger at her, held it under her nose, and proudly said:

"You know, you look just like my suppressed desire."

The girl smiled at the drunk. They moved off, and Phil watched them enviously. Could he get started as easily with one of the broads here? Suddenly there was a commotion and loud talk around the group. The drunk who had moved off with the girl was shouting that he would fight any goddamn Bohemian. Bill Bridges suddenly appeared, wielding a club. He was a rough-looking, wrinkled man, wearing brown corduroy pants and a blue corduroy coat. He crushed through the noisy crowd. The fellows followed him, but could not get close enough to see what was happening. They heard Bill yelling that he would brain anyone for starting a fight. Finally the crowd parted. Bill led the drunk to the exit. The drunk left, protesting. Two fellows followed him outside. Bill walked back, growling.

"What's the matter, Bill?" Phil asked knowingly, ranging himself alongside of Bridges.

"Trying to ruin my business. I'm taking that little bitch off my free list. I got my back to the wall with taxes, and they start fights to ruin my business," Bill said gloomily, and then he walked off grouchily.

The orchestra started to play again. Phil crowded through the narrow entranceway with his companions. The dance hall was a large converted barn, dimly lit; the stone walls were painted with murals similar to those in the tearoom. The floor was of stone and there were many posts spaced around it, supporting the ceiling. Wolcroft danced by with a skinny girl, both of them seeming bored as they danced by like sticks. Then Phil saw Dopey, shimmying. He swayed. He was lonely and felt vacant inside. He wanted a girl. His inferiority clung to him like an inescapable shame, or like something as disfiguring and as permanent as a birthmark. He tried to strike a nonchalant and disinterested pose, as if to tell everyone present that he was not dancing because he didn't feel like it. He covertly glanced about, fixing his eyes on isolated girls he might ask for a dance. An attractive blonde in purple stood to his left. He watched her out of the corner of his eye. He casually, slowly lit a cigarette. He wiped the perspiration from his face. He continued to eye the blonde. He calmly puffed at his cigarette. Passing him, Jack winked. He smiled at Jack. He stepped sidewise, closer to the blonde. He mustn't appear overanxious. He was confused because of his fear that she'd turn down his request for a dance. He was a misfit, and she would know it. He hoped she wouldn't. He must appear calm, interesting. He must have her feel he was accustomed to dancing with pretty girls, taking them out; he must have the air of a lad who knew his way about. He moved closer. He perceived that she had noticed him and knew he was going to ask her for a dance. His foot was in the bucket now. He stood before her, timid, blushing, and choked out his request. She acted as if she had not heard him. He repeated it, humiliation eating inside of him. She thanked him, but said she was sorry because she was not dancing this dance.

He moved away in chagrin. He told himself she was nothing but a goddamn polack anyway, so what the hell? He watched the dancers, aware that he was blushing. Others must be watching. His humiliation must be plain to them. And that dirty

blonde polack was quietly, cruelly laughing at him. Girls were
that way. They were sadists. She, just a lousy little polack,
even she had pierced through him, read the thoughts in his
head, saw his inside as if it were a naked body ugly with sores
and dirt. His head seemed to be getting more giddy. The dancers
seemed to be on a floor turning and whirling by him as if on a
rickety wheel. He tried to act normal, nonchalant, as if he were
thinking none of the thoughts that were actually burning in
his head. He wanted them to see him as someone superior to
everything going on about him. He saw Bill Bridges dance by
with a girl. He decided that Bill Bridges was as graceful in his
movements as an overladen camel, with his body bobbing and
jerking, his left arm woodenly extended like a traffic signal.
Even a louse like Bridges could get a dance. And he couldn't.

He wandered along the edge of the dancing space, assuming
various postures and positions, contorting his face in his effort
to appear unconcerned. Two more girls refused to dance with
him. He went upstairs for a drink and came down, expecting
to be more successful. Another girl refused him. He stood in
a corner, murmuring to hell with them. To hell with the world.
To hell with them, with Kate . . . *Kate, you go plumb to
hell . . . Kate, Kate, I love you . . . be mine . . . my wife
. . . Kate, I'm getting goddamn drunk . . . Kate, you go jam
bananas up your old tomato* . . . He went back upstairs and
poured more gin into himself, fighting to keep it down. He
sweated and was uncomfortable under the armpits. His head
throbbed. It seemed terribly weighted. He staggered back
downstairs, holding onto the rail as he descended.

The dance had ended, and he rejoined his companions. He
clung awkwardly to Dopey.

"Dopey, my pal, my old buddy! Stick with me, pal! Carberry, you know me, know me, known me for ages, since
Hector was kittens. You know I'm all right, okay, doncha,
Dopey? Joe, boy, you know I'm regular, just like other guys,
doncha? Ain't I right, regular? Tell me, Dopey, my best, best
pal," he said, emitting a foul gin breath, slobbering saliva on
Dopey's cheeks as he spoke.

"You're drunk, you bastard!" Dopey said, laughing as he freed himself from Phil.

"All my pals ditch me," Phil sighed, tears coming.

Dopey said sure he was Garrity's friend. Phil wobbled, and his companions seemed vague before his eyes. He frowned. He sneezed. The orchestra started again. He asked a pock-faced girl for a dance, and she nodded. He reeled after her to the dance floor. Taking her in his arms, he tripped. They collided with another couple. They danced, and he stepped on her toes. He talked incoherently and roughly pulled her tightly against him. They hit head on into a twirling, twisting couple. She walked off the floor. He stood bewildered amid the dancing couples. He made his way to the edge of the floor, cursing her. Dopey came up to him.

"What was the matter with the dance you had?" Dopey asked.

"Couldn't stand the pig," Phil said, almost falling on his friend.

He stood there, and crude images of naked girls mobbed his brain. He tried to make himself feel desires, and he could not rouse them, despite the images dancing in his brain. He thought of Kate and silently muttered to himself that he wanted to lay his head in her lap and go to sleep. He staggered aimlessly away from Dopey.

The place was getting noisier, more raucous. Drunks were staggering back and forth. The talk was loud. Couples began to neck publicly. The orchestra played more blatantly. The air was stifling. The cigarette smoke was like a fog. Body odors became so heavy that they seemed almost to possess substance. To Phil, everything was noise and vagueness. He danced with a drunken girl and tried to tell her that he was a student of Notre Dame and a pal of Carideo's and Joe Savoldi, who were stars on this year's Notre Dame's undefeated team. He tried to make her understand that next year he hoped to play on the varsity for Knute Rockne. She didn't understand him and seemed annoyed because he was continually stepping on her toes. As the dance ended, he asked her to go riding with him. She reeled away from him without replying.

"I'm sick of this goddamn joint," he told Dopey back in the tearoom.

The next dance started, and he was alone again. He pushed through the crowd to the dance hall, trying to imagine himself a Notre Dame halfback hitting the line. He asked girls to dance, and they laughed in his face. He tottered back to the wall and stood there in a slumped position. He saw faces dimly, indistinctly, and he imagined himself going through the place like a comet, punching and smashing faces to right and to left, cleaning up this whole damn bunch singlehanded. When the dance ended, he again staggered to his companions.

"Thish is a lousy place," he said.

He staggered away and, passing Bill Bridges, he said hello to him, receiving no answer. The orchestra was now playing a series of college songs: it burst into the Notre Dame *Victory March.* Phil tried to sing:

> *Cheer, cheer for old Notre Dame*
> *Ring out the echoes . . .*

He saw a noisy group, hopping in unison, their ankles twisting and bending, their legs turning into rubber, their buttocks wriggling, their torsos twirling, whirling. It seemed funny to him. The *Victory March* and that dancing. Couldn't dance to it. It wasn't dance music. He staggered toward the group, laughing. He tried to tell them they were trying to dance to the Notre Dame *Victory March* when it wasn't dance music.

"Say, pal, you can't dance to this," he said, tapping a husky redhead on the shoulder.

"What?" the redhead bawled, looking closely at Phil, while his friends, three husky lads, crowded behind him.

The friends asked the redhead what the guy had said.

"He said we can't dance to the Notre Dame *Victory March.*"

"We can't, huh?"

"No," Phil said, and he seemed to gag and be unable to utter any additional words.

"We can't, huh?"

"Smack him again, Pat!"

Phil went down from a stiff punch in the jaw. The blow
cleared his drunken brain. He was rudely jerked to his feet and
punched again. He felt his glasses twist and fly off. Unable to
see clearly, he caught another punch in the face, and his head
throbbed. A noisy crowd collected about them. Red Murphy
piled into the fight, and with a straight right sent one of Phil's
attackers stumbling back into the wall. Red was smashed
simultaneously from two sides, and the fight quickly became a
free-for-all, with many punching and scarcely anyone knowing
whom he was punching or why he was fighting. Women and
girls began to scream. The milling crowd became larger. The
shouts rose.

Jack advanced toward the fight. Dopey disappeared. Bill
Bridges went into action with a club, pushing into the center
and managing to halt the slugging. Phil and Red were dragged
away, Jack following them. The other group was pinioned also.
Bill Bridges began to deliver a lecture on his taxes and on how
fights ruined his business. Red yelled that he wanted trouble,
broke away from the fellows holding him, rushed back toward
the other group. He was caught and dragged away more
forcibly. Phil loudly declared that he had been hit and had lost
his glasses, so that he couldn't see. A girl went to him with the
glasses and said that they had caught on her dress. He yelled
that he had been hit. Phil and Red were brought to the tearoom
and joined by Jack and Dopey. A crowd collected. Phil sat on
the lower step of the stairway leading upstairs.

"Look what the bastards did to me," he kept repeating,
proudly pointing to his black eye.

"Carberry, they wouldn't let me sock the skunks," Red said.

"I'll get 'em," Phil said, grimacing.

But Bridges passed by and, seeing Wolcroft, asked him if he
knew what had started the fight.

"Four drunken Irishmen with liquor, four sober Irishmen
with girls," Wolcroft said dryly.

"The goddamn fools, trying to ruin my business," Bill said, walking off in a funk.

The confusion was cleared up, the orchestra started, and most of the customers resumed dancing. The other group, pacified, came to the tearoom and approached Phil and Red.

"What's your name?" Jack said to the redhead.

"O'Connell," he answered.

"Mine's Kennedy."

"We're both Irish."

"And here's Garrity, Murphy, and Carberry."

"Glad to meet you. Sorry we had the rumpus."

"Garrity, my name's Flannagan. We're both turkeys. Shake."

"It's funny, micks like us fighting each other."

The causes of the fight were explained, and they all laughed.

"Micks should battle side by side," O'Connell said.

"All of us lads is Irish, and so's all of you. The fight was wrong, Murphy."

"Yeah, kid, the Irish should be scrapping side by side together, just like the lads from N.D. on the football field," Phil said.

"Say, didn't they win today though!"

"And there's plenty of Polacks and fairies around here that we might have socked instead of turkeys with the name of Murphy and Garrity. But no hard feelin's because it was just a mistake. Sorry I blacked the lamps, Garrity," O'Connell said.

They trooped upstairs and drank gin and sang songs.

X

They could get no pickups at the Sour Apple, and they left for a brothel on Twenty-second Street. But unexpected police raids had closed the brothels. Cursing, they sped on south. They picked up four girls at Sixty-second and Cottage Grove who were leaving the Bourbon Palace dance hall. The girls giggled and said they would like a party. Phil bought gin and drunkenly drove out south to Jeffery Avenue, and then on to Jeffery Road.

They passed houses along the road with cutout open and roared on past country fields. Phil drove one-armed, and the couples crushed in the back pawed one another, breathed heavily, drank. Large shadows raked the road, and the car whipped on. Occasional houses seemed unreal, almost like dream structures. The moon blunted through a heavy mist which lay thickly over the quiet, heavy earth. They roared on. The car smashed head on into a Cadillac which was going as swiftly as Phil's Lincoln. There was a thunderous crash, screams, the sounds of broken glass, and the two cars hooked together and toppled by the roadside. There were more screams, moans, sobs. Drunk and dazed, Phil squirmed out of the wreckage with his newly found girl friend. She was speechless with fear, and neither of them realized what had happened. He staggered into the fields, dragging her with him, heedless of her maniacal sobs, talking deliriously.

A motorcycle policeman found them and said gruffly:

"Come on, you, pull up your britches. And you, too, bitch!" He dragged her to her feet, and she babbled. He looked at Phil's scratched face, flashing a light in Phil's eyes as he socked him. Phil fell. The cop pulled him to his feet and pulled them back to the road, where there was noise and talk as people struggled in the wreckage to get the passengers free.

"You ought to swing for this, you sonofabitch," the cop told Phil.

Automobiles were lined up along both sides of the road. Men and women were crowding around. Injured passengers moaned pitifully. The girl with Phil and the cop screamed, and then she fainted. Two men carried her away. Just as Phil stepped back to the road, whimpering, the dead bodies of Jack and Dopey were pulled out of the wreckage. Phil talked deliriously. He didn't know where he was or what had happened.

A Love Story of Our Time

PETER, a serious and sensitive young poet, came to New York, the mecca, from the Middle West. During his high school days, the depression had blighted his youth and influenced him to become vaguely opposed to the entire capitalist system. He wanted to live in a better world. And he wanted to feel secure. He was a poor boy, and he knew how one can be gnawed into doubt and paralysis of will by a feeling of economic insecurity. He was unsure of himself. He felt that if he did not become a poet—a great poet—his life would be useless. And the social system was against him.

He worked hard in New York, trying to make a living by writing. He wrote book reviews and, in order to add to his income, sold the review copies of the books. He made scenario reports for motion picture companies. He did some ghost-writing. By dint of various kinds of such literary hack work, he eked out a living. He managed now and then to get some of his poems published. They were genuine and sincere, if minor, and they expressed his own doubts and fears. His major theme was doubt, insecurity, anxiety. Now and then he would write a poem of hope, but it would be hollow, inflated; one such was published and heralded in *Mass Action,* but it was his worst poem, an optimistic poem in which the conceit of history was pressed into every line and image. He made friends and came to know some literary people. His doubts infected his rather loosely accepted political attitudes, and many of his friends used to tell him he was a confused liberal. He had a few affairs with girls, but none of these was lasting, and, when they were over, there was no serious heartache on either side.

Then he met Ruth at a party run to raise funds for a new radical literary magazine. This was in the fall of 1936. Many of his friends and acquaintances were excited in those days by the first Moscow trial, but it merely bewildered him. He found it hard to believe that the trial was on the level and not a frame-up, but he avoided making up his mind or taking any stand. At the party there was discussion and argument, and he wearied of it. Bored by the argument, confused, weakly indecisive, he sat looking off vacantly while two Party supporters were telling a writer that opposition to the trial was a way of committing intellectual suicide. It was at such a moment that he saw her. He was drawn to her immediately. She was a pretty chestnut-haired girl, sleek and slender, her girlish figure nicely revealed by a brown dress. She had blue eyes and a very friendly face. He smiled at her. She smiled back. They sat side by side on a couch, sipping drinks.

"This is all over my poor head," she said with a note of irony in her voice.

"I don't know enough about it," he said.

"What importance has it for us over here?"

They talked about poetry and discovered that they shared the same tastes. She told him that she liked those of his poems she had read. He beamed when he heard her praise. They left the party together and walked through the Village and then had coffee in a cafeteria. A quick sympathy seemed to grow between them. Peter found himself able to talk to her without strain or self-consciousness. He told her how he felt about life, what he wanted to do, how he had to be a poet, and how he believed that a poet, too, could help make the world better than it was.

"Of course he can. It's much better to write poetry than to waste time arguing and arguing about that trial in Moscow. Who cares?"

"Of course, I want socialism," he said.

"So do I. But we have to fight fascism now," she said, rather pensively, looking more beautiful to him than any other girl he had ever met.

His delight in her, his admiration for her beauty, caused him to think that anything she said was true. Facing her across the corner table of the small cafeteria, he found himself wanting to think of things to say with which she would agree. He tried to present himself to her in a sympathetic light. He wanted her to fall in love with him. And he suddenly became shy. He desired her, but he feared to do more than gaze, gaze and talk. But she did seem interested in him. She called him by his first name, smiled when he smiled, and by little innuendoes seemed to suggest that she was one with him in spirit. Their knees touched under the table, and she didn't withdraw hers. This slight contact with her flesh made her seem all the more wonderful to him. He felt toward her all the emotions he tried to express in his poems. As he talked, lines of poetry for her and and about her traced themselves out in his mind. With her, he would know love as only a poet could know it. He talked with her for more than an hour, trying to prolong their conversation because he feared he would blunder when he took her home. Finally she yawned.

"Gee, it's late," she said.

He picked up her check.

"Please, let me take it."

"Oh, it's nothing."

"But, after all, I think women and men are equal. They should be comrades and equals," she said.

"They should. That's one of the evils of the system," he said rather pompously.

Outside, she took his arm crossing a street. She kept hold of it as they walked on. He gazed, moonstruck, at the sky. Having nothing else to say, he remarked on the beauty of the night.

"Autumn is my favorite season," she said.

"Mine, too. I love nights like this," he said.

"Isn't it heavenly?"

"I'll have to write a poem about it, and dedicate it to you. Would you mind?"

"I'd love it. I'd feel flattered," she answered, laughing merrily and squeezing his arm.

She lived alone in a small Village apartment. He stood at the entrance way, not knowing what to do. She looked at him with shining eyes and pursed lips. Her face seemed to melt before him. He knew that he should kiss her. But he was still too shy.

"Peter," she said, paused, and then continued, "Peter, I don't believe in beating around the bush. I can't stand this bourgeois sparring between men and women. Kiss me."

He did. She held him in her arms a long time.

"Come upstairs with me," she said.

They went upstairs. Her apartment was neat and charming.

"I like it with the lights on," she said, immediately beginning to undress.

A vague sense of disappointment troubled him. She was so casual about it. The mystery he had felt sitting with her, touching her knees under the table—this was in danger of being destroyed. But he desired her intensely and forgot everything but his immediate excitement.

"Yes, so do I," he said, confused.

She was quickly undressed and stood before him, smiling.

"Do I pass muster?" she asked gaily.

He nodded his head, almost swooning with desire and confusion.

"Well, you haven't even started to take your clothes off."

He began undressing, still shy. She helped him.

In bed with her, he felt inexperienced and feared he would seem to her like a lout. Then she sank her head onto his moist shoulder without saying anything. He lay back, feeling a consoling fatigue. His mind was blank. He was very happy. She was a wonderful girl.

"Don't go home tonight," she said finally.

She jumped out of bed, turned out the light, and crawled back beside him.

"You're wonderful to sleep with. I'm glad I met you," she said.

"I love you."

"I'm simple, Peter, and I like to call things by their simple names. I don't like bourgeois words like love."

"Whatever words you want to use, you know what I mean," he said.

In the morning they talked about their night together. Ruth said she liked to talk about it, using the four-letter words. These were good words and they weren't dirty, she argued. He agreed with her, but was inwardly disturbed. But she took him back to bed with her, and he lost his disquieting feelings.

He felt as if he had become a different man. A beautiful girl loved him, slept with him. His personality expanded. He had needed a girl like Ruth, a girl who would really stimulate him. Love was the real basis of poetry.

He saw her almost every night and spent many nights at her apartment. At her suggestion they called each other "Comrade" instead of the names lovers usually give to one another. She seemed to him to be frank, direct, realistic. He quickly adapted himself to her tastes and adjusted his ideas to fit hers. He learned that she was a Party member and he respected her, gazed at her in awe. He had, he decided, never had the courage to be a Party member. He began seeing her friends, mostly her comrades, rather than his own.

Although she had said, that night they had first met, that such questions as that of the Moscow trial didn't interest her, he found that she was always talking about politics, about the Popular Front, the war in Spain, the Soviet Union.

Now and then something she said or did seemed mysterious or puzzling to him, but he quickly forgot these little mysteries about her, these little moments of puzzlement that bordered on suspicion. She did not work and said that she lived on an income from her bourgeois family. But, when he asked her about them, she was vague, or didn't want to talk. In general, she didn't like to talk about her past. And on some nights she couldn't see him but said she was at Party meetings.

And now and then he was curious and suspicious of friends of hers, but he reasoned that this was only jealousy.

Gradually she began to talk more and more about Spain.

Peter, disquieted, insecure, was afraid that Franco would win in Spain. Whenever he expressed his fears and doubts, she would tell him that he would have to rise above such petty bourgeois defeatism, and that Franco wouldn't, and couldn't, win. Her confidence and enthusiasm heartened him. She talked often about friends of hers who were going to Spain to fight.

At the same time, she seemed to lose interest in his poetry. When he wanted to talk about poetry, she would change the subject to Spain and politics, and this disturbed Peter. But he was in love with her, and she had made him the slave of her body. The fact that she allowed him to sleep with her seemed to him a privilege of which he was unworthy. He didn't understand how such joy could have come to him.

One night, after their affair had gone on for about a month and a half, he came to see her. When he entered, he embraced her, wanting to kiss her passionately. She was lackadaisical.

She didn't want to go to bed with him, she said, but instead she wanted him to meet some friends. She took him to an apartment on Twelfth Street, where he met a number of couples. It was a party. He was no longer disappointed. She would sleep with him after the party. He compared her with the other girls. None was so beautiful, so intelligent as she. Most of those present were young. But they seemed to be serious young people. Instead of dancing, talking lightly, and holding hands, they discussed Spain.

"Fascism has to be stopped in Spain," Ruth said with an intensity that surprised him.

"The Soviet Union won't let Franco win," another girl said.

"Franco couldn't win if there were enough men in the world with guts. Look at Peter, here!" she said.

He was bewildered. Her voice was hard and cold.

"Peter, here, loves to sleep with me, to eat well, and write poetry while the world is burning up. But will he fight?"

"But I try to fight fascism with my pen," he said in self-defense.

"The world is burning up. The pen isn't enough. While you

are here laying me and writing poems, what's happening in Spain? Aren't you man enough to fight?"

He was shocked. She had so taken him by surprise that he didn't know what to say, what to think. Meekly, he gazed at her. Everyone present was staring at him accusingly. He couldn't meet their eyes. He looked off, troubled.

"But I don't understand you."

"Yes, you do, Peter. You say you are a comrade. Do you know what that means?"

"Why, I think I do."

"It's a sacred word," a young fellow said.

"But what—what should I say?"

"This is no time for words," she said.

"Yes, Ruth, too many fellows love to talk. And write. I love poetry, but the world is burning up," another young man said.

"If I were a man I wouldn't be here," Ruth said.

Peter blushed, ashamed of himself.

"But I don't understand."

"There's no time now for confusion. When the fascist beasts are in New York, what price will you pay for confusion? No, history doesn't allow you to be confused. If you are confused, you aid the common enemy."

"But what should I do?"

"Fight Franco!"

Other girls began to say the same thing to some of the other young men present. Peter was glad now to find he wasn't alone.

But Ruth was persistent. He suggested that they leave and have a talk.

"There's no time for talk. Will you fight?"

Confused, fearful, apologetic, he shook his head affirmatively.

"I knew you were a comrade," she said and, interrupting the others, she shouted:

"Peter is going to Spain."

He gazed blankly about the room as he was congratulated, patted on the back, kissed by the girls. And yet, he wished he hadn't said yes. He didn't know how to fight. He might be killed. He had not had time to think. This was all a surprise.

He didn't really believe he would go to Spain to fight. He remained bewildered. Ruth went home with him and all the way to her apartment she clung to him, praised him.

"I love you. I'm proud of you, comrade," she said, kissing him passionately in her apartment.

In her arms, he forgot all about his predicament. He awoke the next morning, ashamed of himself. Even though he didn't want to go to Spain, he had let himself be pushed into it. But Ruth dominated him. She was very loving to him during the succeeding weeks. And then he left for France with a false passport. He had a heavy heart, but he was proud of himself. His feeling of insecurity had vanished. He was doing something. The ideals with which he had come to New York had crystallized now. He was going to do something greater than writing poetry. He was going to fight, fight for a better world. What could be more poetic than this?

He was smuggled across the Pyrenees. But fighting in Spain was not what he had expected. He was able to withstand the shocks of battle, to conquer fears. But gradually, against his will, he saw many things that disillusioned him. When he expressed doubts or asked questions, he was looked at askance. Unwittingly, he betrayed a comrade who had doubts. He never saw that comrade again. Guilty, disillusioned, feeling betrayed, he wanted to get out, not because of cowardice, but because of his disturbed moral conscience. He didn't know what to do. He considered a bullet that almost caused his death a kindly intervention of Providence. But, after he had recuperated enough to travel and return home, he was kept in Spain for a long time, interrogated, cross-examined, spied on. Finally he was allowed to leave. His health shattered, he returned to New York and was received by the comrades as a hero. He said little. A mass meeting was held in his honor. He got out of making a speech by pleading bad health, but he had to sit on the rostrum and listen to himself described as a hero. He heard speeches about Spain which he knew to be lies. He went home alone, disgusted, ill at heart.

Ruth had been out of New York. He wrote to her. Her letters were breezy, but a little cold. He longed for her. And yet he knew now that she had been an agent of his disaster. Finally he decided that he could not live with himself unless he talked. He wrote two articles trying to tell the truth about what he had seen in Spain. He was denounced as a fascist spy and a coward.

It was then that Ruth came to New York. He heard she was in town. But he didn't see her. His health had waned. He was in a charity ward in a hospital for a while. He got out on a day in spring, pale and thin and penniless. He saw Ruth on the street as he was walking about wondering where to go, what to do.

He stopped as she came toward him. She was as beautiful as ever. He was stirred by memories of his old love for her.

Then he smiled rather ironically.

She called him a fascist dog and walked on. He walked on in the opposite direction, a worn-out, broken young man. He walked the streets until he was almost exhausted, dispirited, sick, and afraid. And he knew that, despite all that had happened, he still loved her. Late at night, he returned to his room in a cheap rooming house on the East Side. He could not sleep. He tossed about in bed and thought of Ruth. He wanted to cry. He told himself that he had lived his life and could only go on now as though he were a human shell.

—Why did this happen to me? he asked himself plaintively as he saw the dawn coming through his bedroom window.

Olsen

WHEN I FIRST heard the stories about Olsen, the crazy Swede, I didn't really believe them. They seemed too exaggerated. But I repeated these stories anyway, because when you tell a story you want it to be a good one so you can get a laugh. Everybody shoots a little bull when he tells a story anyway. Like when my pals talk about the old days when we were nineteen and twenty, we always exaggerate the way we drank, and the fun we had, and everybody gives everybody else something to feel good about when we talk of the old days. Well, I thought these stories were exaggerated and I told them to make them seem funnier and better and I always talked about Olsen as if I knew him. I liked to say:

"Now, Olsen, that crazy Swede."

It made it seem I knew him, was a buddy of his. As if I had some share in what he did and I was like him. Because I wouldn't have the guts, or maybe because I ain't crazy enough, I couldn't be like the crazy Swede. But I wanted to. And damn near every other gas pumper I know did. The big crazy Swede was the most popular supervisor there ever was working for Nation, and all the lads liked him, even those that didn't know him just like I didn't know him for a long time.

All the lads who talked about him always called him crazy, but they said what a regular guy he was, the best one to work under in Nation, and that if all the bosses were like him, pumping gas would be a job no one could beat. But, then, if all the bosses were like the Swede, there wouldn't be no Nation either.

He was a crazy Swede all right, but he was regular. He never came around snooping or sniffing, and didn't give a damn about all the rules, regulations, instructions, and the whole damned rigmarole. Now and then he'd get sore and bawl a lad out, but he never turned you in downtown at the main office. He knew every trick to be known in the stations, and many that nobody else knew, and more than one lad tells of how, when he was short, the Swede would help him make up shortages on the pumps and would pull the pumps more than most gas pumpers. They tell all kinds of stories like these, and, as I say, I always repeated the ones I heard, but I never quite believed them. I always looked forward to meeting the crazy Swede and having him for my boss, too. Hell, you could sit on your can in the station, for all he cared, read the papers or a good adventure story, open up late, close up early, do pretty nearly any damn thing you wanted. He didn't care. He didn't only let you get by with murder. He helped you out on it now and then. The Swede didn't give a damn for anything, most certainly not for Nation. The closest he ever came to giving a damn was about a dame and a bottle. He liked the dames, and he had a cast-iron gut.

One of the stories they always told about Olsen was how there was a lad in one of the stations over near South Shore Drive, and this lad was taking a crack at some tramp that was passing by and that he'd coralled into the station. The lad had her in the little supply room inside of the station and he was taking his crack at her, and it must have been a damn good crack at that, because outside customers were lined up honking at the pumps. Olsen was the lad's supervisor, and he happened to drive into the station, and so he took care of the customers and soft-soaped them, said he was the boss, and the lad was in the can or something, and then he caught the lad taking his crack. So Olsen told him to finish up and, when he did, Olsen took a crack at her himself. That was the kind of a guy he was.

I always used to think of him, long before I worked for him, when it would be dull and slow in the station, and I'd wish a dame would come by, some tramp I could take a crack at, and I'd think, now if I was working for the crazy Swede, maybe he'd just be like a magnet and attract the dames to my station and take care of the trade while I got my crack. When you hang around a station, and it's dull and slow, and there's nothing to do but stand and wait, you think of all kinds of things, and, more than anything else, you think how you'd like to pass the time by taking a crack at a dame. And you can tell a nice story about yourself, how the dame came in, and how you talked her into it, and you took your crack at her.

And of course all the lads talked about how Olsen had been a great gypper when he was pumping gas, and all sorts of things like that. And about how he always warned the lads when spotters were around, or about the City Sealers being out. I felt like I knew him and he was my best friend long before I worked for him. But I always had a hunch I was going to work for him, and then there was some change downtown in the main office, where they ain't got anything else to do but think up changes, and so I drew the Swede. I thought that now I'd begin to like my job. I'd been getting so fed up with it that I was beginning to think I'd let Nation stick its job up the old you-know, although I knew I wouldn't, because where could I get as easy a job as gas pumping, all things considered. Anyway, I liked to think of myself kissing the job good-by. And, anyway, I was glad to get Olsen for my boss.

And I learned he was a crazy Swede all right. He took a liking to me and used to come around often. It was a funny feeling I had, myself actually wanting and hoping the boss would come around. I used to laugh thinking of it, and tell myself I'd like the boss to be coming around to do some of my work for me, because the Swede seemed to like to get at the pumps. It was a damn funny thing. Think of it, your boss likes to come around and wait on the trade for you, and sometimes he'd pull the pumps on a customer and come in and tell you he'd made your lunch money and carfare. I never could dope him out. Maybe it was because he was a Swede. Anyway, he was a nice guy, a swell guy, but the marbles in his head weren't placed the way they are in anybody else's. He didn't give a damn for nothing,

nothing in this damned world, and he gave less of a damn for Nation than he did for anything else on Christ's well-known green earth.

The first time he came around he comes in stern and frowning and says to me:

"Small?"

"Yes, sir," says I.

I guessed it was Olsen, because he came in a Nation Ford coupé, but the picture didn't fit, him coming this way, frowning.

"Isn't there anything you can do, standing around here, doing nothing?" he went on.

I started giving him a line, but he was only kidding and he tells me he's Olsen, my new supervisor.

"Small, we got to get efficient," he says. "Know what efficiency is?"

"Yes, sir," I says, thinking that these stories about him was all crap.

"Well, the Company wants efficiency. Did you ever stop to think what efficiency means to Nation?" he goes on.

So I started saying yes, of course, and so on, and he laughs, and goes on to say something about Nation not making enough money, and it had to make some more, so we had to be efficient, and he sits in the chair, and lights a cigarette.

"You're not allowed to smoke on the premises, are you?" he says.

"No, sir," I says.

"Well, we have to be efficient but, then, what's a cigarette between friends? Here, have one?"

He was always like that, always wanting to help you break the rules, laughing at them. He was the craziest boss I ever had. He was wild, too, let me tell you. He took a liking to me, and used to call me Smallsy, and it wasn't long after he was made supervisor for our district, that he and I was running around, and never before nor since did I ever drink so much beer and home brew, or do so much whoring. He loved to go to beer flats, and he liked the broads, and liked can houses the best, although

I don't know why. Broads always went for him. I guess they always like a lad to be a little bit crazy or screwy.

He used to come around and tell me to close up early and come on out with him.

"But I got orders not to close up early," I'd kid.

"Smallsy, who the hell is your boss?"

"You, sir," I'd go on kidding.

"All right, close the goddamned place. How long have you been earning a living by the sweat of that stupid brow of yours?"

"A long time, sir," I'd kid.

"And not long enough to know you should do what your boss tells you do. Listen, you insubordinate sonofabitch, close the goddamned station up! I know you'll break your arm doing it, because you hate the very idea, but I'm supervisor here. And you—you're just a goddamned gas-pumper. Now do what you're told."

So he'd light a cigarette and sit on his fanny and watch me closing up, and he'd say:

"Shake your goddamned ass. I never saw a lazier attendant. Shake your tail, boy."

"I'm doin' the best I can, sir," I'd say, kidding, you see.

That's the way we'd talk. And then, off we'd go. Of course, he was only supposed to use the coupé the company let him have for work, but he used it all he wanted, and we'd go to some beer flat, or can house, or to pick up some janes he knew in it, and it was like my having my own private car and chauffeur. And the way he drove. The only trouble with going out with him was that he drove so recklessly he always had you with your heart in your mouth. He drove like hell on wheels, and I don't know how he and I are alive as it is. But then he never worried about nothing, and least of all about his job. And he had a drag, after all, so that Prevost and none of the bosses like that in the main office could do anything to him. Boy, it was good to hear him talk about Prevost and the rest of them in the main office, good to my ears. He talked about them like they was just a bunch of punks, that's all.

He was a crazy Swede, and we had one hell of a time for six months. More dames than I can count. I tell you, one way and other, I got mine traveling with the Swede. He never seemed to get enough of it, and yet, it was funny. He really didn't seem to get so much of a kick out of it and he never talked like a guy that loved it, loved all of it he could get. I never really could dope him out. But he was a guy that didn't care. He raised hell because he didn't care, like a guy wanting to forget something. Now most lads get cockeyed in order to make themselves seem like a hell of a lot more than they are, because when you get some shots into you you feel mighty goddamn good and you feel you're hot stuff all right. And the same, when you lay a dame, now, no matter what kind of a tramp she is, still you keep thinking now I laid her, and she wanted me to, and that's one more I laid, and, besides the feeling itself, there's the way it makes you feel about yourself. If the dames want you to lay 'em, why you feel you're hot stuff. But not the Swede. He wanted to forget something.

"Smallsy, I don't give a good goddamn about anything," he always liked to say to me, and I believed him.

I know he came from a rich family, and he hated his old man who lived in Cleveland. He used to talk about his old man.

"Smallsy," he'd say to me, "my old man is a sanctimonious old hypocritical bastard. He did every goddamn thing he wanted to and he probably left kids of his from one end of America to another, and now he's old, and there he is, getting religion. He's no good. Not one of the Olsens in this classification of Olsens called my family—not one of them is any good."

And there was a dame, but he didn't say much about her, a dame that gave him the go-by and, in some way or other, just about left him there in the church. He went to Princeton and got thrown out, and he used to brag about it, and brag about having been thrown out of more places than anybody he knew. You see, he just didn't give a good goddamn. And that was one reason why a lad liked him. Because a lad just doesn't want to give a good goddamn, but he's got to because he has to get one job or another, or do something, and, after all, you liked to think you don't give a good goddamn but put the chips down, and you do. But not Olsen. He didn't, and meant it.

It was a lot of fun traveling with him and being able to kid your own boss and call him a bastard in kidding and be familiar with him, but, at the same time, you were always on tenterhooks and worried. You got nervous running with him. After all, he had friends on top in Nation, but then I didn't, and I didn't want to be no goat. And, still, I never had such a time as I did traveling with him. He was always good company and, as I said, reckless as they come.

Well, I'm going on and on about the Swede, and I better come to an end about him, and all of what I said was merely what they call the prelude to my wanting to tell about that last night.

It was a slow night, and in he comes, staggering, and he was smiling kind of queerly. He planks himself down on a barrel, and he looks at me, and he says, kidding like he always did:

"Come on, Small, shake your tail. Look at that air compressor. The damned thing has two inches, six inches of dust on it."

So I gets out a dust rag and hands it to him, and he laughs. But his eyes were funny, and he looked really drunk, looked really like the crazy Swede he was. I hands him the rag, and he hands it back to me, and he says:

"Throw the godamn rag in the refuse bin."

"I always obey orders, sir," says I, throwing the rag in the bin.

So he lights a cigarette and he says:

"Light up, or I'll turn you in, you insubordinate bastard."

So I lights a cigarette, but I'm kind of nervous. He's really drunk this time, and he doesn't give a good goddamn, but then, after all, I can't afford to lose my job and I'm nervous.

"Smallsy, I'm drunk. Drunk," he says.

"Yeah, I see that," says I.

"Smallsy, I never said this, but I am now. You know, this job I got is a goddamned stool pigeon's job, that's all it is."

I liked that, because, after all, it shows what a regular guy he was, even if his marbles were different from everybody else's.

"You gotta be drunk all the time, or else you won't have no self respec'. Not on this job," he said.

"Yeah, it must be pretty bum to have the job you got, almost as tough as having mine," says I.

"I got to be a rat. Rat Olsen. See. You gotta be a goddamn rat to keep my job. See! See! Say, you know what I wish. Wish the bolsheviks would blow up the goddamn works. Blow it sky high, jus'—blow it—wheesh," says he, throwing his hands up in the air.

"Wait a minute, I got a customer!" says I.

"Tell him to pound cue balls up . . ." says he as I rush out and service a customer.

When I come back, Olsen, he asks:

"Pull the pumps? Huh? Get four for five? But I don't care. Let the bolsheviks come and blow the works up sky high— wheesh!"

"You're drunk," says I.

"Down in the office, Prevost, that sonofabitch, wants to tie the can to me. Ha! Wants to kick me out on my tail in the cruel col' col' world. Can't. Ha! Can't, because I gotta drag. I gotta drag, see, kid, that goes up to the board of directors, you know them sonofabitches. I gotta drag, and Prevost can't give me the gate even if I won't be a sonofabitch and turn you guys in for doing the same goddamn things them guys upstairs do. See! Well, hell with them. See! Let the bolsheviks come, blow 'em to smithereens. Wheesh!"

Then he almost fell over the bowl, and I knew he was drunker than I even thought he was.

"I'm sick of being their stool-pigeon, their goddamn gumshoe rat. Get drunk. Drunk, and save your self-respec'. See!" he goes on.

Then he pulls out a bottle and says:

"Have a drink."

So we drink, but I'm feeling really leary, so he goes on jabbering and then, Holy Christ, he whips out a gat and starts

waving it around. I asks him for it, but he won't give it to me.
I plead, and even try to snatch it from him, but I can't.

"Let the bolsh. . . . Say, I'm gonna start things for the
bolsheviks," he yells.

I don't know what the hell to do. I'm scared, and I mean it.
Because he really don't give a good goddamn. And then he aims
the gun at a five-gallon can of motor oil on the top shelf. He
fires and hits inside the top part of the first N in the Nation
lettering. Oil pours out in a little stream. I plead and try again
to get the gun from him. He shoots at a second can. People in
cars stop and people look in the station, and then they run.
And he shoots a third can, another can of oil hit.

"Let the bolsheviks come around and finish the works.
Wheesh!" he yells and he shoots again.

So there I am, and the Swede is really out of his head, and
he's shooting up the station. I'm shaking at the knees, and I
don't know if I'm coming or going, and you can see by his
eyes that he don't know what he's doing, and don't care, and,
why, how do I know but what he's going to shoot me? And he
has the bullets bouncing about, and people are watching across
the street, and some are running away, and I don't know what
the hell to do, and I run into the supply room, and I think,
Holy Christ, he might shoot me. He's nuts, and so nuts he
really don't give a good goddamn, and my ears seems numb or
something with the shots and the noise they make, and he's out
there shooting up the oil cans, and the oil is coming out of them.
It was a sight, I tell you, because soon I'm outside again, with
cops around, talking, and he doesn't seem to cause them any
trouble, and the oil is pouring down off the shelves, and the
station is one holy mess. Like what I always wanted to do to
the station myself, shoot it up, just like he did, only, after all,
enough is enough. Well, the cops, they got him, and they're
tough, and he tells them who he is, and I confirm it.

So they don't know what to do, and there's a crowd outside,
and it's exciting, and I'm rushing out to wait on customers, and
having to tell them what's happened, and more cops come, keeping back the crowd, and they don't know what to do with him.

"Yes," I tells another cop, for I don't know how many times it was, "he's my boss, and he's got a drag with the board of directors. He's just drunk."

And so Prevost comes around, and asks me what's up, after he talks with the cops, and what can I say?

"He just comes around this way, a little drunk, and he shoots at the cans," I say.

And so there it is, and there he is, sitting very calm, and he keeps saying, he says:

"Let the bolsheviks, let Lenin and Trotsky come and shoot the rest of it up."

So they pow-wow, and I'm outside, and I'm still scared, and I keep wondering, will I get canned now, and what can I say or do? So finally the cops and Prevost get him into the paddy wagon, and he waves and yells:

"Small, let the bolsheviks finish it up now."

And Prevost comes back, and he says to me:

"Small, he's just broken down. Now, you don't tell anyone about this and clean the station up. Dump all the oil you can in the barrels and make an audit. I'll have the auditor here as soon as he can come, and you clean up."

So I got to clean the station up, and that's all that happens to me. The crazy Swede shoots the station up because he's drunk and don't give a good goddamn, and I got to clean the shooting mess up, and people come around to ask me what happens, and the auditor comes, but I jockey the figures and the oil a bit before he comes, and make some dough of the shooting, enough for a good date, anyway. And so Olsen, well, he merely gets put in a sanitarium for a while, and they say he had a breakdown, and I don't know what happens after that. I never heard. But I'm still pumping gas.

But I often think of the Swede, and there's more stories about him told by the lads in the station. And if you want to know the truth, every damned one of us in our hearts would like just once in our lives to say we don't care, either, wheesh, and shoot things up that way, if we only could get away with it. Yes, I liked the crazy Swede, only he was a really reckless guy. But then, he could be, and nothing really happened to him that counted because he didn't care if he lost his jobber, and he didn't get put in jail or anything like that, and I'll bet that he's just the same as he ever was, wherever he is. The lads all talk about him, and every one of them talks as if he was their buddy and they did the same things he did. But I was really his buddy. And, nervous as I was running around with him, we sure had a time of it while it lasted. Yes, Olsen sure was a crazy Swede, all right.

A Lesson in History

SCENE: *The large classroom of the second-year class at Saint Stanislaus High School in Chicago. It is a spring after-noon in 1921. The stage is cut into two sections; the large classroom is the dominating one, and on the right is a small portion of the corridor outside. In the classroom, back, left, is a wall with windows, and the back is a long blackboard. The teacher's desk is against the wall, right, set on a dais in the center of the room. To the right of the desk is a wastepaper basket and a map that is rolled up like a shade, and to the left of the desk, lower right front, a swinging door that leads into the corridor. Facing the teacher's desk are the rows of seats, almost all filled except for a few in the back, and except for Danny O'Neill's seat, the fourth from the front in the center aisle.*

FATHER KRANZ (*seated at desk and finishing the roll call*): Zivic?

ZIVIC (*student in rear far row*): Here.

FATHER KRANZ (*as he talks there is a dragging quality in his voice*): Well, now, we'll begin the lesson. Of course, I know you've all recuperated from the effects of Friday. (*They laugh. Various students turn to look at Bart Daly, sitting in the second seat third row, and Marty Mulligan in first seat, fourth row.*) I know that you've all studied and come here prepared, perhaps even prepared to teach me a little history. (*Students all over are noticed trying furtively to steal quick*

157

looks into their textbooks.) I can see Mulligan there suffering the throes of anxiety. Aren't you, Mulligan? (*Laughs.*)

MARTY: No, Father. (*More laughter.*)

FATHER KRANZ: What do you mean, *no*, Father?

MARTY (*smiling*): I mean, yes, Father.

SHEEHAN: Father, he means that he would rather have you ask somebody else.

FATHER KRANZ: All right, Sheehan. Since you're so quick with your tongue, I'll let you answer. (*The class laughs.*)

SHEEHAN: Father, I'd as soon remain silent.

MARTY MULLIGAN: Father, he's already got a charley horse in his tongue from talking.

FATHER KRANZ: Well, we'll exercise the charley horse out of your tongue. (*As Father Kranz says this, Danny O'Neill is first heard, then seen running to the door admitting to the classroom.*) Now, Sheehan. . . .

DANNY O'NEILL (*bursting breathlessly into the classroom*): I see that the cohorts are all here.

FATHER KRANZ: Yes, and the jackass has arrived.

TIM DOOLAN (*as the class laughs*): He's not a jackass, Father. He's a *jumentum.*

FATHER KRANZ: No, he's a jackass in both English and Latin. (*Again the class laughs.*) I think we've had enough humor, and now we'll go on with the lesson. (*Again there are attempts to sneak quick looks into the textbooks.*) And don't do your studying now. You should have done it over the week end.

DANNY: Father, I'm in perfect agreement with you.

FATHER KRANZ: That's such a good start, O'Neill, that I'll give you more opportunity to show how much you agree with me. Don't get too anxious.

DANNY: There's no danger, Father.

FATHER KRANZ: Sheehan, what is the lesson for today?

SHEEHAN: History. (*Laughter.*)

FATHER KRANZ: Sheehan, how did you think up such an answer? Did you listen to me here last Friday?

SHEEHAN: Yes, Father.

FATHER KRANZ: And so you answer my question by saying that the lesson of the day is history.

SHEEHAN: Well, it is, only I was going to go on from there but. . . .

FATHER KRANZ: But what?

SHEEHAN: Well, all this horseplay (*he points around the room*) made me forget. (*Laughter.*)

AD LIB: Yeah!

Try again, that ain't so good.

You talking horseplay.

FATHER KRANZ: Quiet. Now, everybody will be so quiet for thirty seconds that we can hear a pin drop. Quiet. (*A strained quiet of from fifteen to thirty seconds.*) Now, Sheehan, has your memory been restored to you?

SHEEHAN: Well, Father, the lesson is. . . .

FATHER KRANZ (*marking on card before him*): Sheehan, if I could give you a mark lower than zero for your brilliant recitation, I'd do so. You'll have to be satisfied with zero. But to make up for the fact that that is the best mark I can give you, why, you can stay after school at two-thirty and copy the lesson out of the book. Maybe that will help you to remember tomorrow.

SHEEHAN: Gee, Father, I tell you, I did study. I had it all right at the fingertips of my mind, but these distractions made me forget.

FATHER KRANZ: All I'm doing, Sheehan, is giving you something to do that will be an aid to your memory in the future.

SHEEHAN: Aw, gee, Father, I tell you, I did study.

FATHER KRANZ: And I'm going to help you to study more effectively.

SHEEHAN: But, Father. . . .

FATHER KRANZ: You'd better sit down now, Sheehan, before you begin to abuse my patience.

SHEEHAN: But, gee, Father, that's an awful penance to give me.

FATHER KRANZ: Come on, sit down now. (*He looks around the room.*) Mulligan, you look bright today.

MARTY: Looks are often deceiving, Father.

FATHER KRANZ: Well, we'll find out.

MARTY: No, Father.

FATHER KRANZ: What do you mean? No, Father, what?

MARTY: I mean no, Father, I don't feel bright.

FATHER KRANZ: You tell Sheehan and the rest of the class here what is the history lesson for the day.

MARTY: But if I do, Father, they'll know as much as I do.

DANNY O'NEILL: That won't be very much.

MARTY (*turning toward Danny as many laugh*): Wise guy!

FATHER KRANZ: Sit down, Mulligan. You can stay in the jug with Sheehan.

MARTY: But, Father, I got basketball practice this afternoon.

FATHER KRANZ: The team won't miss you. And writing out your lesson might make your hands more limber.

MARTY: I don't think so. And, Father, I don't know what I did to get a penance.

FATHER KRANZ: I'm telling you what you're going to do.

MARTY: But that's not fair, Father.

FATHER KRANZ: Don't talk any more!

MARTY: But listen, Father. . . .

FATHER KRANZ: I told you, Mulligan, to keep still. Now do it, or I'll have to make you! (*He flushes with sudden anger.*) All right, O'Neill, you like to talk. Stand up!

DANNY (*rising*): Yes, Father.

FATHER KRANZ: What is the lesson today?

VOICE (*whispering*): Adrian the Fourth.

FATHER KRANZ: Hurry up!

DANNY: Adrian the Fourth.

FATHER KRANZ: Who was he?

DANNY (*there are whispering voices telling him, but he can't catch what they say*): King.

FATHER KRANZ: King of what?

DANNY: England.

FATHER KRANZ: Tell me, O'Neill, who told you that?

DANNY: The book.

FATHER KRANZ: I heard prompting all the way up here, so tell me who told you that?

DANNY: A lot of them.

FATHER KRANZ: Well, a lot of them are wrong. I think I'll let you keep company with Mulligan and Sheehan after school.

SHEEHAN: Couldn't you let somebody else take his place, Father?

DANNY: Yes, Father, I don't think I should stay with them if they don't want me.

FATHER KRANZ (*as he talks, a student in back seat, far row, is shooting spitballs around the room with the aid of a rubber band*): It's not what they want but what I'm telling you to do when the bell rings at two-thirty and good students like Daly, Shanley, Dawson, and Doylan can all go out.

DANNY: Well, of course, Father, if you insist, then I'll stay. (*Laughter.*)

FATHER KRANZ: I thought you would O'Neill, you are very obliging. (*Laughter.*) Now, let's see. (*He looks around the room.*) We have such a bright bunch here. Doolan, you look as if you were awake this afternoon. Stand up.

MARTY (*as Doolan arises and Danny sits down*): Father, that's a mistake about him being awake.

FATHER KRANZ (*curtly*): Mulligan, if that penance I gave you isn't enough, there are other things I can give you. From now on, you can speak when I speak to you first.

CARRIGAN: I wouldn't let him speak either, Father. He hasn't got a nice voice.

FATHER KRANZ: Carrigan, how are your knees?

CARRIGAN: Well, Father, we had a retreat last week.

FATHER KRANZ: Good, that gave you a chance to practice them. Now we'll test them. For the rest of the class hour, kneel in the hallway outside the doorway. I'm getting tired of some of you fellows. (*Carrigan slowly, sulkily walks to the door.*) All right, Doolan.

TIM DOOLAN: Father, you know, I've been puzzled by a question I wanted to ask you.

FATHER KRANZ: Yes? (*Interrupted by laughter caused by*

Carrigan, who made a face as he went through the door to kneel in the hallway in view of the audience.)

TIM DOOLAN: Yes, Father, I wanted to ask you the derivation of the name Adrian.

FATHER KRANZ: Are you interested in etymology, Doolan?

DOOLAN: Of course. (*Laughter.*) You see, Father, I was reading the lesson, and I got to wondering and asking myself, now where did this name come from?

FATHER KRANZ: You did? Good. Now, I want to ask you a question.

TIM DOOLAN: Honest, I did, Father.

FATHER KRANZ: I know. And, of course, Doolan, I appreciate such curiosity because I know how well most of my students here have studied the day's assignment. So I appreciate the curiosity you have shown. However, before I answer your question, I want to ask you something. Now, Doolan, will you tell the class what you read about Adrian the Fourth?

DOOLAN: Sure I will, Father. But first, could you tell me where the name came from?

FATHER KRANZ: Did the assignment you read for today say anything about the derivation of the name?

DOOLAN: No. It said. . . . (*He pauses.*) It said. . . .

DANNY: Father, I know what it was. He was so concerned worrying over etymology that he forgot everything else.

DOOLAN: Hey, Goof!

FATHER KRANZ: Did it say that too? Hey, Goof! What historical character said that, Doolan?

DOOLAN (*as there is laughter*): Well, Father.

FATHER KRANZ: You told me that about Well, Father. Now, what else? (*Doolan stands in long and nervous silence; students around him furtively look in books; others shoot spitballs; and outside Carrigan gets off his knees and stands against door listening.*) Doolan, you'd better keep your friends company after school. (*Looks around classroom.*) Close your books, everybody!

SHANLEY (*raising his hand*): Father, I know.

FATHER KRANZ (*to Shanley as Marty directs a contemptu-*

ous look at him.) I know you do, Shanley. I want to try to find out if some of the others know. Now, I wonder who else is as interested in etymology as Doolan. (*Catching Marty furtively starting to begin his penance.*) Mulligan, put that pencil and paper away, close your book, and do your penance after school.

SHEEHAN: He can't tell time, Father.

FATHER KRANZ: If you don't like the atmosphere of the room, Sheehan, you can join Carrigan outside.

SHEEHAN: Oh, I do, Father.

FATHER KRANZ: I'm glad you do, Sheehan. Thank you.

SHEEHAN: You're welcome, Father.

FATHER KRANZ: Smilga. (*He rises from his desk on dais.*)

SMILGA (*Rising as Father Kranz stands over Sheehan.*): Yes, Fadder.

FATHER KRANZ (*taking off the black belt he wears around his middle over the brown habit of his order*): What was the Bull Laudabilitor? (*Hands go up and fingers snap from students who know the answer.*)

SHEEHAN: Father, that might hurt.

FATHER KRANZ (*hitting Sheehan several blows on the back as he speaks*): Did you hear the question? (*At this moment Danny O'Neill is hit by a spitball and turns and shakes his fist toward the rear of the room.*)

SMILGA: Yes, Fadder.

FATHER KRANZ: Well, do you know the answer?

SMILGA: Yes, Fadder.

FATHER KRANZ: Why don't you give it to me then?

SMILGA: Is dat what you wanted, Fadder? (*Laughter.*)

FATHER KRANZ: You don't think I wanted you to tell me who won the basketball game last Friday, do you? (*More laughter.*)

SMILGA (*speaking rapidly, and with an accent, and pronouncing his "th's" as "de"*): Well, de Bull Laudabilitor is supposed to have been a bull issued by de Pope, Adrian de Fourth, to de King of England to give the King of England right over Ireland.

FATHER KRANZ: The first one in the class I have called on

who could answer a question. Thank you, Smilga. Now, Doolan, tell Sheehan whether or not this particular bull was really issued by the Pope.

SHEEHAN: Father, the bull was only bull anyway.

FATHER KRANZ: Shut up, Sheehan, unless you want some more wallops. If I didn't give you enough, I'll oblige you more satisfactorily a second time.

DANNY: Father, Sheehan ought to be able to talk all about bull. That's all he knows.

FATHER KRANZ: And O'Neill has spoken his last word of this class hour. (*He aimlessly wanders toward door, and Carrigan slips back to his knees.*) Tell us, Shanley. (*Faces class.*)

SHANLEY: It was a forgery, Father, composed after the death of Pope Adrian the Fourth.

FATHER KRANZ: Suppose it were not a forgery? What was the argument behind the theory that this bull was a true document, and what is the justification for this alleged grant on the part of Pope Adrian the Fourth?

SHANLEY: The Pope, as a feudal overlord over all of Christendom, would have had such a right to grant a fief, like Ireland, to the King of England as his vassal.

FATHER KRANZ: O'Neill, are you listening?

DANNY (*points to his closed lips*): Can I talk, Father? You said I should be silent for the rest of the hour. (*Laughter.*)

FATHER KRANZ: Stop the nonsense and answer my question.

DANNY: Yes, Father.

FATHER KRANZ: Well, thank you for your attention. Now, Daly, tell Mulligan who was the Holy Roman Emperor during the papacy of Pope Adrian the Fourth.

DALY (*rising*): Frederick Barbarossa.

FATHER KRANZ: Can you tell me anything about the relationships between the Pope and the Emperor?

DALY: Yes, Father.

MARTY (*turning to Sheehan and yelling loudly*): Cut it out.

SHEEHAN: Get me a pocket knife and I will.

FATHER KRANZ: What's ailing you scholars? (*Laughter.*)

SHEEHAN (*to Mulligan*) : I want to cut it out for you since you asked me to. (*Laughter.*)

FATHER KRANZ: Mulligan, haven't you been assigned a sufficient penance?

MARTY: I didn't do anything. Sheehan was shooting spitballs at me.

SHEEHAN: Father, I wasn't, and he's maligning me.

FATHER KRANZ: Someday, you kids are going to abuse my patience beyond the limits of endurance.

SHEEHAN: And, Father, he's abusing mine. (*Points at Marty.*)

MARTY: Yes, and I'll abuse more than your patience.

FATHER KRANZ: Shut up, both of you! If you're looking for a fight, come and fight me.

DANNY: But, Father, why don't you pick on someone your own size. (*Laughter.*)

FATHER KRANZ: O'Neill, come up here and kneel in the front of the room. (*More laughter.*)

DANNY (*rising and walking forward*) : Gee, I don't want to wear my pants out.

FATHER KRANZ (*meeting Danny before his own desk*): You talk too much. (*Slaps Danny's face. Danny tries to cover up and gets a second slap on the side of the face.*) Enough is enough from you kids. (*Turns to Daly, and Danny goes to kneel in a corner.*) All right, Daly.

DALY: Father, Frederick Barbarossa wanted to be coronated by the Pope as the Holy Roman Emperor. When he and the Pope met. . . .

FATHER KRANZ: That's enough, Daly. I see that you know your lesson. I think I shall find out some more from some of my other really bright boys and interested students. Rychewski.

STEVE RYCHEWSKI: Yes, Fadder.

FATHER KRANZ: Tell Mulligan what Daly was trying to say.

STEVE RYCHEWSKI: He was talking about de meeting of de Pope and Frederick Barbarossa.

FATHER KRANZ: Well, what about the meeting?

STEVE RYCHEWSKI (*after a long pause*): Why, Fadder, they met.

FATHER KRANZ: Are you sure they met?

STEVE RYCHEWSKI: Yes, Fadder.

FATHER KRANZ: How do you know? Why are you so sure they met?

STEVE RYCHEWSKI: Because I know dey did.

FATHER KRANZ: How do you know?

STEVE RYCHEWSKI (*after another long pause*): Daly said so, didn't he? (*Laughter.*)

FATHER KRANZ: Did you study your history assignment over the week end?

STEVE RYCHEWSKI: I always study.

FATHER KRANZ: How do you study?

STEVE RYCHEWSKI: I read de lesson you tell us to.

FATHER KRANZ: And what do you learn?

STEVE RYCHEWSKI: Whatever de book says.

FATHER KRANZ: What book? Buffalo Bill, Nick Carter, what book? (*Laughter.*)

STEVE RYCHEWSKI: De history book.

FATHER KRANZ: What history book?

TIM DOOLAN: He doesn't know that one, Father.

FATHER KRANZ: Then he's as bright as you, isn't he?

TIM DOOLAN: He comes from my home town.

DANNY (*turning back toward class*): Father, where they come from, West Pullman, the sidewalks are taken in at nine o'clock.

FATHER KRANZ: Do I hear noises from monkeys or what?

MARTY: No, Father, that's only O'Neill.

FATHER KRANZ: I wonder now, Rychewski, do you really know what a history book is?

STEVE RYCHEWSKI: Yes, Fadder, de textbook.

FATHER KRANZ (*returning to desk and holding before the class the thick, green-bound history textbook*): Tell me honestly, Rychewski, did you ever see this book before?

STEVE RYCHEWSKI: Yes, Fadder.

FATHER KRANZ: Do you know what's inside of it?

SCHAEFFER: Father, it has big words inside of it.

MARTY: And pictures.

FATHER KRANZ: Now, don't you fellows tell him. Rychewski, what is inside this book?

STEVE RYCHEWSKI: History.

FATHER KRANZ: And what is history?

STEVE RYCHEWSKI: Well, Fadder, history is. . . .

FATHER KRANZ: Mulligan, see if you can redeem yourself by telling Rychewski what history is.

MARTY: History is the thing that keeps me in the jug and gives me writer's cramp.

FATHER KRANZ (*glares at Marty and then looks woefully at Steve Rychewski*): I'll tell you, Rychewski, and I'll tell the whole class what history is. Now, listen closely. History is something that I cannot under any circumstances, and no matter what methods I use, manage to teach to you numskulls.

STEVE RYCHEWSKI: Yes, Fadder.

FATHER KRANZ (*irritated*): Sit down and take a load off your brains. You can keep your comrades company after two-thirty.

STEVE RYCHEWSKI (*sitting down, smiling meekly and in a friendly way*): Yes, Fadder.

FATHER KRANZ: How many here studied today's lesson? (*All hands go up.*) How many of you here know the Ten Commandments? (*All hands again go up.*) How many of you know that one of the Ten Commandments forbids lying? (*All hands go up.*) Well, I'll find out. Now, McDonald, answer me, at the risk of your immortal soul.

MCDONALD (*reluctantly rising*): That's a big order, Father.

SCHAEFFER: Father, he spent the week end studying how to comb his hair with vaseline.

FATHER KRANZ: You never studied, did you, Schaeffer?

MCDONALD: Father, he's defaming me. (*Points to Schaeffer.*)

FATHER KRANZ: Well, now, don't you, in turn, go and defame the memory of Pope Adrian the Fourth.

MCDONALD: Father, you can prevent me from doing that.

FATHER KRANZ: How?

MCDONALD: By not asking me any questions.

FATHER KRANZ: Good. Sit down, and stay after school, and do the same penance as the others.

MARTY: We don't want him in our jug, Father.

FATHER KRANZ: What can I do about that?

MARTY: You can let me go, and keep him.

FATHER KRANZ: That would be unfair.

MARTY: But, Father. (*He is laughing and grinning and he looks up at the priest.*) . . .

FATHER KRANZ (*interrupting Mulligan*): Shut up, I'm being too lenient with you kids as it is.

SHEEHAN: Lenient?

FATHER KRANZ: Sheehan, you can speak when you're spoken to.

MARTY: Yeh, Sheehan, freeze your trap.

FATHER KRANZ: Mulligan, you're talking too much. Why didn't you talk when I asked you to recite?

MARTY: I would have, but I didn't want to show the rest of the class up.

DANNY (*turning around from his kneeling position*): Mulligan doesn't think much of himself, does he?

MARTY: Shut up, Dope!

FATHER KRANZ: Mulligan, are you the teacher?

TIM DOOLAN: Thank Caesar's ghost that he isn't.

MARTY: If I was, Father, I wouldn't be so hard on a guy.

FATHER KRANZ: Mulligan, I'm tired of you.

MARTY: Father, you aren't any more tired than my hand will be this afternoon.

FATHER KRANZ (*rising and walking toward Marty's desk*): Do you talk to hear your own voice, or what?

DANNY (*again turning*): To reveal his ignorance.

MARTY: That's enough from you, O'Neill. You're only a goof.

FATHER KRANZ: Shut up, O'Neill. (*Moving more rapidly toward Marty.*) Mulligan, was your opinion of O'Neill asked?

MARTY: You don't expect me to listen to him making cracks like that at me, do you?

FATHER KRANZ: Mulligan, who do you think you're talking to? (*The class, seeing that this time the priest has actually lost his temper, becomes suddenly tense. Marty looks up at the priest, his friendly grin suddenly turning into an expression of surprise.*) Answer me. (*Mulligan's expression becomes one of fear.*)

MARTY: What do you mean, Father? (*Father Kranz punches Marty's face. Marty covers up as the second blow lands.*)

FATHER KRANZ (*punching angrily*): Answer me (*He continues punching as the curtain falls.*)

The Dialectic

I KNEW JAKE AND EDDIE IN COLLEGE, back in the early 1920's. They seemed brilliant then, but my standards were different from what they are now. I have often reflected on what I thought of them in those days, and I am aware that I over-estimated their characters and capacities. However, they were two of the best students of the time at Columbia, and they were unquestionably superior to most of their contemporaries; they were more disinterested, had more intellectual ambition—as contrasted with ambition for success—than the great majority of students. Those of us who knew them expected that they would develop, that they would achieve something, something more humanly important than any mere bank account. Like others in our group, Jake and Eddie were idealistic, and, when they dreamed of careers, they thought of some type of work which would, in some way or another, contribute toward the betterment of mankind. They had both been YPSLs, Eddie in New York, Jake in Brooklyn, while they were still kids in high school. When they began at Columbia, they were outstanding in their class. They were better read and more aware of what the world was like than most of their class. But, combined with their idealism and intelligence, there was also a vein of the cynicism and aggressiveness of the streets. They became intimate friends early in their freshman year. Those of us who knew them fairly well, who often talked with them in bull sessions and went out together to cat houses, who lived the same kind of life as they—we always thought of them together.

They were close friends, and they shared their hopes, their dreams, their feelings about girls with each other. It was a Damon and Pythias friendship.

Jake wanted to be a poet; Eddie planned to become a philosopher. In those days Jake was thin, handsome, charming. He was very witty and had a genuine flair for impromptu characterizations. How often in the dormitory—for two years they roomed together—Jake would have us all rolling off the bed and on the floor at his take-offs of some of our professors. Eddie was quieter, a short and stocky fellow with a moon face. He was outwardly more serious, but he had a quiet and cutting irony. They were both leaders of our group, and they were usually able to dominate the rest of us intellectually. We admired them, looked up to them, found them stimulating as well as buoyant and full of fun. I, at all events, often envied them. They could be so serious and yet so gay. They seemed to know so much and to learn so easily. Yes, they seemed to be so gifted and so promising.

After graduation, Eddie had to find work. He came from a poor family and had to do something. Instead of going on to be a philosopher, he managed to get a job as a newspaper reporter. Jake's father had money; he owned a large hardware store and several buildings. Immediately after his graduation, Jake made a trip to Europe. He used to write wonderful letters, and I've always regretted that somehow or other I lost them. He wrote most often to Eddie, but I saw Eddie fairly often in those days and he'd show me Jake's letters. They were delightful, so full of Jake's charming and ebullient personality. Everything he described seemed to have been felt with such a fresh, such an open, personality. He wrote about the girls he met; his impressions of cities, especially of Paris; amusing little incidents about American tourists; accounts of political news in the French and German papers; and, at times, passages in which he expressed his indignation about the lot of the workers. He was, or seemed to be, growing, gaining new impressions, deepening and widening his sensibilities and experiences, all in preparation to becoming a poet. Eddie believed that Jake would develop into

a great American poet. And Eddie wrote frequently to Jake and
told of his experiences as a cub reporter. Their friendship was
neither sundered nor weakened by distance.

When Jake returned after having spent seven or eight months
in Europe, they picked up just where they had left off and once
again were inseparable. After graduating, they held to the
same views and values they had had in college. At times Jake
seemed to throb with idealism. Their expectations concerning
their own careers were inseparable from their belief in socialism,
their desire to do something for the betterment of mankind.

In those days many of us were stirred by the Russian Revolution and the ability of the Bolsheviks to resist the counter-
revolution and the imperialist invasion. We were inspired
without having any real practical sense of politics. We were,
considering our ages, well read in socialist literature, and most of
us had tackled *Das Kapital*. But at the same time our revolutionary enthusiasm and our socialist faith were matters of intellectual ardor; in terms of practical experience we were naive. Our
socialist activities in college had been intellectual; in the main
we were student and debating socialists. We had no real experience or contact with the working class. But we had great hopes,
and because of our hopes we felt superior to other students and
different from them. Our feeling of superiority, however, encouraged us to read, to study, to dream more. It helped us to
learn from the books we read. We looked to the Soviet Union.
We idolized the leaders, and especially the dying Lenin and
Trotsky. Jake, I know, identified himself with Trotsky and
always talked of him. When he was in Europe, shortly after
his graduation, he was able to obtain some of Trotsky's work
that was unavailable in America. He attempted to model himself after Trotsky, and for a time—since Trotsky was Soviet
War Commissar—he read many military books, and his talk
would be a mélange of military words and poetic metaphors.
I believe—although this is something he would never have said
to me, and I doubt even to Eddie—that Jake dreamed of himself as becoming the American Trotsky, of being a military

revolutionist leading the workers in America to the day of final victory.

There was nothing truly preposterous in such dreams. The Bolsheviks had been victorious in Russia. Lenin and Trotsky, unknown a few years before except in revolutionary circles— had risen to shake the foundations of history. We knew that the course of history had been irreversibly altered by the Russian Revolution.

When Jake returned to America, he was bursting with energy, and full of tales of love and life. Eddie had a little room in the Village, Jake one near by. I used to go to one or the other room often. We talked half the night through, as we had done as undergraduates. The future was still before us, and we were confident about it. Eddie and Jake continued to dream the same dreams. Eddie tried to write stories, but none was published. He read them aloud to Jake, who admired them. And Jake—who was now and then getting a romantic poem published—read his poems to Eddie. They admired each other's work. Eddie was getting along better in the newspaper world; he had completely abandoned his plans for a career in philosophy, but he continued to read avidly. He was growing; in fact growing more than Jake. He had not lost his interest in socialism, although his socialism, in the practical sense, was—like Jake's—bohemian. At the same time he hoped to work himself up to the position where he could become a Moscow correspondent, and he believed that in this way he would serve the revolution. John Reed was an idol of his, and, in fact, Eddie had once heard Reed speak. Jake suddenly was able to publish more poems, mainly in radical and liberal magazines. His name began to appear regularly in many places as a book reviewer, and he started to gain a small reputation. He was a promising literary man and poet.

At this time we were receiving fragmentary news of the factional struggle in Russia. This was disturbing. It confused us, and we didn't know what to think. But both Eddie and Jake hoped—especially Jake—that Trotsky would win; they were sure he would. With Lenin gone, he seemed to us in New York to be the greatest and most brilliant man in the world.

Eddie continued slowly to advance as a journalist; Jake proceeded successfully in his career as a poet and critic, and he drifted closer to the Communist Party, finally becoming a member. However, he didn't seem to change his way of life, and he didn't seem to do much Party work. In his middle twenties, he was handsome, charming, witty, slender, and unusually attractive to girls. He had endless love affairs.

But after Jake joined the Party, he and Eddie began to see less of one another even though they retained the same respect and mutual affection of college days. Eddie married a girl from the Midwest, and Jake was his best man in the ceremony, if such it could be called, at City Hall. Then he was out of New York on newspaper work, but I forget where he was. When he returned, I think he and Jake saw each other occasionally. At any rate, I gained that impression whenever I ran into them. In 1927, Trotsky was expelled from the Communist Party of the Soviet Union. Jake was bitter, almost broken-hearted. He and Eddie met me shortly after this, and I sat with them drinking dago red in a Village speakeasy, and they were glum, disconsolate. Jake expressed himself rather violently, condemning, cursing, loathing, denouncing those who had expelled Trotsky. But at the same time he remained in the Party.

As we left that night, Jake was a little drunk. He staggered between Eddie and me toward Washington Square, and I remember him saying:

"They'll have to take him back. He's the Sword of the Revolution, and they need him." Then he seemed to glow with inspiration and he repeated feelingly: "The Sword of the Revolution."

I didn't see them much after this for a while. But I heard that Eddie finally realized his ambition. He was sent to the Soviet Union as a Moscow correspondent. I didn't see him before he left, but Jake told me about it. He went in high hopes, with great enthusiasm. He—and Jake to some extent—had forgotten about Trotsky. He had gone, bound for home, bound for Utopia. Jake envied him, and yet was delighted for Eddie. Eddie wrote Jake for a while, and sent me one boundlessly enthusiastic letter. Then his old friends didn't hear from him. I ran into Jake occasionally. He was the same, except that there was no marked progress in his writing. In his cups, he would speak of Trotsky, and he was convinced that the day would come when Trotsky—already in exile—would come back, or be called back. In all, Eddie spent almost three years in Russia. He then returned to the United States, but disillusioned. I met Jake shortly after Eddie returned. I asked him how Eddie was, and he was curiously aloof, and finally said:

"Eddie's been a capitalist journalist too long. He doesn't understand revolutionary politics."

But from Eddie I learned that Jake had listened to him, avid, enthusiastic, and glum by turn, when Eddie had described his experiences, impressions, and his change of mind as a result of his having spent so much time as a correspondent in the Soviet Union. Shortly after this Jake went to Russia for six months. I didn't hear from him, but when I saw Eddie once or twice on the street I asked if he'd had any news from Jake. Eddie answered negatively, but once he said:

"Jake will learn, too."

Jake sent back a few glowing articles on conditions in Russia, and these were published in the Party press. I showed one to Eddie, but he merely smiled ironically.

On Jake's return I saw him, and he went into a long account of how socialism was triumphing in Russia. He was then writing a series of six articles on conditions in Russia. He had not one criticism to make, and in one of his articles he stated that even the air was different, purer, as one crossed the border from capitalism into the Socialist Soviet Fatherland of the workers.

When he was asked about Eddie, he would answer that Eddie was a bourgeois journalist, but he'd say this in such a way as to suggest that Eddie was much worse than this, and that if he, Jake, wanted to, he could give information to show that Eddie was.

By this time Jake had abandoned writing poetry or, at least, none of it was published. For a while he worked for Soviet agencies in America, and he didn't seem to write anything for publication. He lectured now and then on culture for Party or front groups. And he did a variety of different kinds of contact work for the Party in bourgeois intellectual circles, employing all his charm for such purposes and usually managing to explain away anything that needed to be explained away. And, of course, he had more love affairs, married, and was divorced.

After Eddie's return to America, it seems that the word had come to Jake from higher-ups in the Party that Eddie wasn't to be trusted. In time, I am told, when they met they acted almost like strangers or mere casual acquaintances. Jake seemed uninterested in what Eddie had to say or wanted to say about the Soviet Union, and once Jake flatly told me that Eddie had sold out to bourgeois journalism and was, in the objective sense, a dangerous enemy of the Revolution. Eddie had lost his faith. It was a troubled period for him. He was nervous, bitter, hurt. But once, when they were together and Jake was a little drunk, he was entirely different. He spoke of Trotsky, telling Eddie and me that, of course, Trotsky was a bad politician, but that he was a brilliant writer, a brilliant orator, a brilliant man, and, of course, Jake didn't really think that he was a counter-revolutionist. However, politics was politics, and you had to be realistic in politics, and, of course, that demanded a bitter war against Trotsky because Trotsky was wrong. And then he wistfully lamented on how so brilliant a man could have been so wrong.

Jake's face was a trifle flushed when he talked this way. His eyes were vaguely watery. He leaned drunkenly over the table, pounded it with his fist, and said in a thick voice:

"You've got to have Bolshevik hardness."

I wanted to laugh, but didn't, and Eddie with quiet irony said:

"Someday you'll know something about that hardness."

"If I become like Trotsky, I'll deserve it," he said.

Eddie grinned, but with a touch of bitterness. Eddie was really hurt at this time.

But Jake, drunk and more ebullient than ever, continued to

speak of Trotsky, and suddenly, in genuine and deeply felt and intoxicated admiration, he exclaimed:

"But Trotsky, even wrong—what a man!"

Eddie went back to Europe as a correspondent, but not to Russia. I read his dispatches occasionally, and although they were competent, they usually were merely factual. They revealed that although he had managed now to get a good and a responsible job, he was not realizing any of his dreams of college days. In a sense this proved that Jake was right about Eddie. Eddie had become just another bourgeois journalist. He was recalled to America by his paper and given a desk job as a foreign editor, with a raise in salary. He became their expert on European affairs. The effects of his long journalistic career were more than apparent. All of his early idealism was gone. He was cynical—bitter; his comments on international politics were usually superficial. He took great pride in the fact that he had met, seen, and interviewed many of the statesmen of Western Europe. He looked at events purely from the standpoint of a spectator. In fact, in my random and irregular meetings with him—meetings which were generally accidental and unplanned —I could perceive that he was almost of the opinion that world events happened so that he as a journalist could write about them.

But it was clear that Jake had fared no better. He was getting fat and had become lazy. He was merely a Party writer, and his pieces were no different from most others appearing in the Party press, regardless of the subject. His work showed the same rigidity, the same adherence to formula, the same reliance on character assassination as did that of the other Party hacks. One could frequently take the beginning of an article by someone else, cut it in half, paste it to the conclusion of an article by Jake, and scarcely tell the difference between the two parts of the article. And then he wrote for *Mass Action,* which, while not officially a Party organ, was really Party controlled. In fact, Jake was the Party man on it, for a while, giving Party directions and responsible to the Party for what appeared in *Mass Action.*

At this time, I met him once on the street, accidentally, and he suggested that we have a cup of coffee. We sat in a cafeteria, and I asked Jake if he couldn't write better than he did.

"These dopes won't let me. But don't worry, I will," he said, and he launched into diatribes against many of his comrades.

"Have you seen Eddie, Jake?" I asked.

"There's a tragedy," Jake said, with a glint in his eye.

I waited for him to go on, and he did. Eddie had lost faith. He had sold out. He'd married a bourgeois wife, and she had helped ruin him. Because of her Eddie had bought on the Russian black market, practically taking commodities away from the Russian workers, who were building socialism. And then he hinted, but only hinted, that Eddie was really an agent for foreign governments which were hostile to the Soviet Union and even planning to invade it. When I asked him for proof of this, he said that he couldn't divulge his proof now, and then he let the cat out of the bag. He said that when I read Eddie's forthcoming book on the Soviet Union I would see in it the objective proof showing that Eddie had become an anti-Soviet agent.

From others I met from time to time, I learned that Jake was continually denouncing Eddie, and that he did him considerable harm; in fact, Jake really helped to stigmatize him. Eddie, though he was now merely a journalist, occasionally signed a petition and, as if in expiation of guilt, now and then gave a small contribution to some left-wing but non-Party or anti-Party group. And then Eddie's book came out, an account of his observations and experience in Russia, journalistic in tone, but containing facts we have since learned to know as definitely confirmable. Jake wrote a long and vicious attack on it, in which he went back to their old days as friends, distorted and garbled remembered remarks, even misquoting passages from the book. After this I learned that they didn't talk to one another.

Time passed. I saw neither of them. I occasionally heard about them or saw something one or the other had written. Jake—I could assume from his writings—had become merely a Party wheel horse. He became a kind of cultural godfather of the young writers the Party was attracting to itself. And yet when he was in his cups he spoke of Trotsky in the same old way, or so I was told. When the Moscow trials surprised the world, Eddie wrote analyses of them, denouncing them, and calling them frame-ups; in these articles there were flashing nostalgic traces of his lost idealism, his buried faith in socialist ideas. Jake answered these articles with a counter series in which he denounced Eddie as a Trotskyist, and even a fascist; and he couldn't find words strong enough to denounce his hero, Leon Trotsky.

Eddie was now a truly prominent journalist. He again went to Europe and became more personalized in his reporting, and at the same time wrote collective security, antifascist articles, even though he was bitterly anti-Stalinist. He returned to America for profitable lecture tours, preaching antifascism to ladies' clubs at high stipends. He had abandoned all traces of his college socialism. But now and then he did attack the Party.

Jake's position in the Party never seemed to change one way or the other. But, thanks to his many indiscretions when drinking, he was under suspicion. In due time, and to the general surprise of those aware of these matters, Jake was expelled from the Party and denounced in its press. Among the things that were said about him, the least insulting characterized him as a hack. He was also called a concealed Trotskyist, a concealed bourgeois, an enemy of the people. He wrote no defense of himself, nor did he make any other kind of statement. He began his career writing pretentious novels about the American past. Eddie likewise had taken to writing books regularly, and was a best-seller journalist with an international reputation, one of those of the new crop of journalists alleged to possess inside information about history. Just on the eve of the war, they were both on best-seller lists with current books.

Eddie, recognized as one of the journalistic prophets who had predicted everything, who had called for the antifascist war against Hitler and who had attacked the Munich agreement, was hired as a radio commentator. In no time he became one of the most popular, influential, and highly paid of the commentators. And then, following the German invasion of the Soviet Union, he changed his views, began to speak differently of the Soviet Union, and, I heard, was seen with Stalinists and fellow travelers in night clubs and elsewhere. His name suddenly appeared on the lists of "front" organizations, especially in connection with sponsored and Party-organized swanky dinners. More and more, in his comments and writings, he explained events in terms of the most favorable light he could cast on the Soviet Union. And then, suddenly, and without the slightest reference to past writings, he came out on the radio and made a statement which in effect amounted to an acceptance of the official version of the Moscow trials. The Party press exploited this, and Eddie then flatly defended the official version of the trials, again, of course, without explaining why he had previously denounced them. Known as a journalist with inside information, his defense of these trials influenced many people.

Jake wrote another novel which was well received, and he spoke in bond-selling campaigns. He tried to convince people— I learned—that he had never really been a Communist, or, rather, a Stalinist.

They were both now in their late thirties, and they had changed. Each was married for the second time. Each was fat and successful. Jake was getting bald. Eddie's hair was turning gray. He also had stomach ulcers. With the progress of the war, they both came more and more into the public eye. They had become rich and famous. They owned country houses in Connecticut. Jake—it was announced in the papers—was hired to work in Hollywood at a very good salary and went out there; in time his name appeared on pretentiously empty films which were interpreted as revealing the new social consciousness supposed to be developing in Hollywood. Eddie flew back and forth to war capitals, to the war fronts, and in the midst of all this he managed to write an autobiographical book which ended with an account of himself as a war correspondent and which became an immediate best seller. The movie columns announced that it had been bought by a studio at a reported price of one hundred thousand dollars. And soon after this I saw in some column that Jake had been assigned to work on the treatment of Eddie's book. And then a note that Eddie was in Hollywood giving advice on the way the book should be made. In the book, of course, Eddie more or less apologetically explained away his college radicalism. And Jake was to take this and to make a film out of it, when Jake knew all about Eddie's views and attitudes in the old days. And then—a note in a gossip column that the two of them were seen together in the Brown Derby in Beverly Hills and elsewhere. And a publicity story about their being old friends.

The gossip columns announced that they were both present at the grand world premiere of the film in New York. The film, too, was a smash hit.

What did they say to each other? How did they sit down together and work out the film? I don't know. But eventually I saw the film, and it was a lie from beginning to end; it so glamorized Eddie that I felt almost ill as I saw it. And Jake's name was signed to it. Jake had written this. There was a touch of Eddie's earlier anti-Stalinism in the film, but it was presented by showing Eddie as the passing victim of a beautiful international spy, a girl vaguely supposed to have something to do with Trotskyism, also.

One day I ran into them. I was walking along Fifth Avenue, when I saw Eddie, and he said:

"Hello."

"Hello," I said.

He was nervous when I said I had seen the picture.

"We were damned fools in the old days," he said, and this was all he said.

And then Jake happened along. He was fat and bald. He and Eddie seemed embarrassed.

"Hello," Jake said.

"Hello," Eddie said.

"Where have you been of late?" asked Jake.

"I've been busy," Eddie replied.

"So have I," Jake said.

They stood there. They both seemed embarrassed. It was an

unpleasant scene. They were uncomfortable in each other's presence. They both knew they had co-operated in a money-making
lie, and they were silent and awkward in their guilt. They shook
hands, and each went his separate way, after they had vaguely
agreed to get together sometime. I walked on. I doubt that they
ever see each other. Eddie is still on the radio, and the book
columns announce that Jake is writing another historical novel
about America's democratic past. I often wonder, however,
what really goes on in their minds when they are alone with
themselves.

Young Convicts

THEY WERE THE CHILDREN of Slavic immigrants and lived in the manufacturing district around Thirty-fifth and Morgan. Their fathers worked in the factories located in the area. Their sisters, even before they started to bloom and lose their gawky pre-puberty figures, also joined the ranks of those who trooped to the factories at six and seven in the morning. At six, seven, eight o'clock, rain or shine, morning after morning, their fathers, mothers, older brothers, sisters, all became part of the long line plodding to work.

There were six kids in this gang. Tony, the eldest, was a boy of twelve, and Stanley, the youngest, was eight. They all liked candy. They liked to go to the movies, especially on Saturday afternoons, when the serial was shown. They liked serials and movies of that type best because there was danger and adventure, shooting, robbing, train wrecks, bandits, outlaws, Indians, Mexicans, battles. And they scarcely ever had money for candy or for movies.

But they liked candy and they liked movies. And they liked to do dangerous, brave things, to pull off stunts like those pulled off by the older fellows in the neighborhood. They wanted to fight and steal, and then brag about it, just as they heard their older brothers bragging. They could be heroes just like the older boys. And when they could steal, they could have money for candy and the movies.

Home to each of the kids in the gang was much the same. A wooden shack, one or two stories high, with an outside privy that smelled you out every time you wanted to take a leak. Three, four, five rooms, generally dirty, full of rags, papers, the smell of kerosene lamps. Dark bedrooms, old beds, dirty sheets, two, three, four, and five sleeping together in the same bed, and on cold nights there was always a fight for the blankets. A mother and a father who were generally over-tired from work, and from raising a family. And the mother and father didn't speak English. They were greenhorns. And once every week, two weeks, three weeks, the mother and father would get drunk. They would curse and fight, throwing things at one another, shouting, even brandishing knives and cutting one another up, until the police came with a paddy wagon. These kids' homes were alike.

They didn't like school very much. They didn't like their studies, and in the classroom they groaned, twisted, squirmed, itched, dreamed of high deeds like those of the movie heroes and villains in the Saturday-afternoon serials, like those of the older fellows, like those of Al Capone. In school, they waited for the end of class. They were afraid of their teachers, and they neither liked nor trusted them. The teachers, some of them young girls from good families who were waiting until they found a husband, did not like the bad boys much either. Sometimes, in the hallways, the kids would hear one teacher tell another that she wished she would be transferred to another school where there was a better class of pupils than these incorrigible Polacks and Bohemians.

Often, they didn't learn their lessons. They bummed from school regularly, and went scavenging through vacant lots and streets, keeping their eyes peeled for the overworked truant officers. Or they went to the railroad yards with sacks and wagons for coal that was needed at home. In fact, they learned to steal in the railroad yards. The parents would send them out at night to get coal, and they'd go down to the yards and get it, one kid getting up in a car and throwing chunks down to the others. From the railroad yards they went to the stockyards, going over the fences and leaving with anything removable that could perhaps be sold. They stole everything they could, and finally stealing got to be a nightly occupation.

They knew about hold-ups. They knew that some of the older guys in the district had pulled off hold-ups, and that made them heroes. So they determined that they too would be heroes and pull hold-ups. That would get money for candy and movies. And they would be living like the heroes they saw in the movies. One night, Tony, the gang leader, picked out the Nation Oil filling station on Thirty-fifth Street. They played across the street from the station for two nights. They goofed about, ran, played tag by a closed factory, getting a line on what time the station closed and what time the cop on the beat passed by after it had closed. When they were sure of their time and their layout, they went to work. Young Stanley tossed a house brick through a side window. Tony then stood on a box, put his hand through the broken glass, and unlatched the window. He went in, followed by the others. The money was in the safe, and that could not be touched. So they tore the telephone box from the wall and scooted with it. They broke it open in a vacant lot and divided the nickels that were in it. The loot was three dollars, and, although it was to be divided evenly, Stanley was cheated out of a quarter.

Successful in their raid on the filling station, they made other raids. They robbed every filling station in the district, always running off with the telephone box, and they enjoyed the fruits of their robbery in candy, cigarettes, and movies. Tony liked it. He bossed his gang with an iron hand. Night after night he drove them in raid after raid. If they complained, he kicked them in the pants and slapped their faces. If they talked back to him, he cracked them. He saw himself as a young Al Capone. He dreamed of shootings, gang fights, submachine guns, robberies, money, automobiles, everything the gangsters had in the movies, everything Al Capone had in real life. And he always planned out the raids, instructing each kid in what he should do, going to the place in advance to get the lay of the land. He always had money and gave some of it away to younger kids, to girls whom he would try to bribe in order to get them alone with him in basements. He hung around the corners and the poolrooms late at night, watching the older fellows. He imitated them in walking, talking, gestures, held his cigarettes as they did, borrowed all their remarks. He pushed and pressed his gang constantly, always discovering new places to rob. One night they robbed a chain restaurant. Stanley threw a brick through the back window, and they entered and ran off with the cash in the till. Two nights later, they returned to the Nation Oil Company's filling station and again ran off with the telephone box full of nickels. This time they noticed that the attendant had gone home, leaving his safe open. In it, they saw bills, many of them, dollars and dollars, more money than they had ever seen before. They were so surprised by the sight of the money, so afraid, that they did not take it, satisfying themselves with only the small change in the safe. And on the night after this robbery they returned to the chain restaurant. They were caught by a watchman and a city policeman.

They were brought before Judge Katherine Henderson in the Juvenile Court; she was a woman jurist who was known beyond the city for her good work. The court was crowded with its usual array of young culprits and harassed, shamed parents. The boys had to wait their turn, and they sat with other boys, cowed and meek, and with their shabbily dressed immigrant parents. Nearly all those waiting to be tried were the children of working people, most of them of immigrants. Some were released, some placed on probation, some sentenced to the Juvenile Detention Home. Judge Henderson spoke crisply, hastily, perfunctorily, often in a scolding tone. She hurried through case after case, disposed of it, making instant decisions, bawling out parents, often telling immigrant fathers and mothers that they were responsible for the delinquent conduct of their children.

Judge Henderson just didn't have the time. The cases had to be disposed of. Tomorrow there would be the same number. The juvenile problem was insoluble. There was no settlement of it. The same boys were warned, but they were brought back.

Parents were warned, but they were helpless. There was nothing to do but rush through from case to case, let so many off, put so many on probation, send so many to the Detention Home. Day after day, this must go on. The law must be upheld. There was no time for her to delay, study, probe into the causes of these delinquencies. All she could do was reach out and try, and hope that a few boys would be rescued from crime, and a few girls from the life of a prostitute. That was what she did. Lectures, warnings, scoldings, questions, sentences. Next. Next. Next. All morning. Next. All afternoon. Next. Tomorrow. More. Next.

Tony and the gang were called up. The bailiff rounded them up and prodded them in the back, his language curt and sharp. He shoved them up to the bar of justice. Judge Henderson read the papers on the case, closed her lips as she read, nodded her gray head. She raised her brows. Her benign face showed worry. She seemed to be wondering and thinking. She looked down sharply at the six boys before her. Their heads dropped. They were afraid to look her in the eye, just as they feared looking teachers, or policemen, in the eye. Her gaze shifted. She stared at their parents, who stood silently behind the boys. She asked each of the boys what his name was. The first answered that he was Clement Comorosky. Where was his mother? He shook his head. Again she asked where his mother was. Again he shook his head. More stridently, she asked where his father and mother were. He said that both were working and could not come down. Stanley's mother then spoke in Polish. An interpreter was called, and she spoke to him. He told the judge that the woman had said that the father and mother of the Comorosky boy worked in a factory and were afraid to stay out because they were too poor, and needed the day's wages, and they were afraid that if they didn't report for work they might be laid off. Please, she would take their place.

"All right. Now, do you boys know what you did?" the judge asked.

None of them answered. They stood with averted eyes.

"Can any of you talk? Can you talk?" she asked, sweeping

her eyes from one to another, fixing them on Clement, who was ten years old.

He nodded his head affirmatively.

"Do you know that it's a crime to break into other peoples' homes and stores and to take things that don't belong to you?"

"I'm sorry . . . ma'am," Clement said.

"How long have you been doing this?"

"Just this time," Clement said.

She looked through the papers before her and called out Stanley's name.

"You were here before, and I told you that I didn't want to see you brought back. And why don't you go to school?"

He looked at her with large-eyed awe.

"Are your parents here?"

A small Slavic woman said that she was his mother; her face was lined, and an old black shawl covered her head. The judge asked her if she ever tried to keep her boy in at night. She shook her head, and said that she tried, but that he went out anyway. The judge looked down at Stanley, glowering.

"And what did you do?"

"Me? I thrun the brick through de window."

Many who heard him smiled. The judge continued to question them in a brusque manner which inspired fear. Their answers came slowly. They were evasive. They did not understand all of her questions. She became more brusque. She seemed annoyed. She listened, with increasing irritation, while the watchman who caught the boys gave his testimony. Then the gas station attendant testified that twice the station had been broken into, and the telephone box had been ripped off the wall on each occasion. The restaurant manager gave testimony also.

"You boys have to learn that you can't go on breaking into places and stealing money. That is not right, and it is not permitted. Do you hear me?"

Six heads nodded.

"Well, why did you do it?"

Her additional questions brought out the fact that Tony was

the leader and inspiration of the gang, that Stevie Lozminski was his lieutenant, and that the raids and burglaries had been committed under their direction. Both had been in the court before for truancy and burglary, and the truant officer testified that all her efforts to do anything that would keep them in the classroom, where they belonged, were fruitless. Their teachers and the principal of the school had turned in written reports describing them as incorrigible. The judge continued her brusque questioning, directing some of it at the parents, who stood in silent awe and fear. She lectured the parents about taking care of their offspring and insisted that the interpreter translate her remarks so that they would surely be understood. Tony, Stevie, and Clement were all sentenced to six months in the Juvenile Detention Home, and the others were put on probation. The mothers cried. They looked with bewildered grief at the judge, their pleading eyes almost like those of sick animals. The boys were pulled from their parents' arms and taken off. Two of the mothers cried.

The next case, that of a colored boy caught stealing, was called.

The mill of the court continued.

Pat McGee

I

IT WAS TOO EARLY FOR PAT TO LEAVE. He sat down in the parlor and opened an early edition of an afternoon paper. He was in a state of restless inner excitement. The old days were gone forever, and yet he wanted to bring them back. It was hard to accept what he knew, to accept the fact that he had passed his athletic prime. The time that had already passed somehow hurt him. He was still too young to be looking backward instead of forward. And these days he was always looking backward, wishing that he had the chance to relive the time of his life that was already gone. Sometimes, for a moment or so, he would believe that he was still living in the old days. He would believe this with ardor, and then he would remind himself that this wasn't so, and he would become gloomy. Yes, the fact that the old days were gone really hurt him.

This afternoon, when he'd made up his mind to go out to Jackson Park, he'd had this feeling about the past. But now it was lost again. He looked moodily at the paper, his mind vague. Turning to the sports pages, he read the football news. He wished that he'd gone to a big university instead of a small college. He might have been an all-American, just as he had been an all-Catholic-High-School football star. That was the biggest mistake of his life. Why had he been afraid of stiff competition, and why had he not thought more about his decision after graduating from high school? It was too late. The best years of his life were gone, and he was only twenty-five. Yes, only twenty-five, and yet he feared that his dreams were over. Now, reading the sports page, he winced.

He read news of the Catholic High School League, but it bored him. He couldn't really work up an interest in the names of kids he didn't know. Of course, he always wanted Mary Our Mother to win, because it was his alma mater. He wanted to see the name of Pat McGee on the sports page. Pat McGee was really a might-have-been, he sadly thought.

He put his paper down and nervously looked at his watch. It was only one-thirty. He wished it were time to go out to Jackson Park; he wondered what he'd do with himself until it was. He could go out, of course, and take a little drive in the park, but he didn't feel like it. Sometimes he liked to drive, merely to drive, to feel his hands on the wheel, to feel himself in control of the car and know that the car was moving because he was in control. Then all thoughts and worries left him. He'd drive aimlessly, looking straight ahead, knowing what he was doing, drawing power from the wheel of the moving automobile. Pleasant, dreamy thoughts would float through his mind, sweetly pleasing thoughts which he'd forget almost as soon as they came into his mind. And he had time to go to the agency and see if Chuck, the Sales Manager, had a prospect for him. But his heart wasn't in selling cars. He'd just sit around here and wait, and let the time pass.

He picked up the newspaper again and read the comics, his mind in a swoon. He wished each strip were longer. He finished with the comics, wishing it were already tomorrow, so he could read new comics. He put his paper down for the second time, rose, and turned on the radio. He listened to jazz music, his face softened by his sentimental thought.

Pat looked like an athlete. He was a clean-cut young man. He weighed one hundred and eighty-two pounds; he was solidly built, muscular, and hard as nails. His calves were thick; his shoulders were broad. His frame was powerful. His light hair was cropped short. His face was broad and genial. His eyes were light blue, eager, and friendly. His skin was fair, reddish. His hands were big, and several fingers on either hand were crooked. He seemed boyish and could have passed for a lad of twenty-one.

At five minutes to two Pat jumped up. He shook his head and blinked his eyes. After listening to the jazz music, he felt just as he often did when waking up after a nap. He got his hat and topcoat, called to his mother in the kitchen that he was leaving, and went out of the apartment. He got into the model Studebaker which belonged to the agency. He stepped on the starter and the car moved away from the curb. That feeling of power came back to him, a feeling of power that was second only to the old thrills he had known in athletics. He drove across the Illinois Central tracks at Seventy-first Street and then on toward Jackson Park. He remembered how, when he was in high school, he'd ridden to school on the Sixty-third Street car, with his lunch and books under his arm. Usually he'd daydream about the next baseball or basketball or football game in which he'd play. And how often hadn't he imagined himself in later life going back around the school just as he was doing today? Yes, today he was doing exactly what he had dreamed of doing back in his high-school days. But his life had not turned out the way he had thought it would.

Next year he'd come back. He tried to convince himself that he would come back, but he had no real confidence in himself. Still, when the kids now at M. O. M. saw him, knew who he was and what he'd done, they'd look at him with respect. He might give Jim McBride a hand with the coaching. Jim was a fine man, and had made him what he was. No, he was a born athlete. But Jim had helped him, taken him in hand as a freshman and taught him. Jim had seen what his possibilities were. He'd developed into an all-Catholic fullback under Jim, and they'd almost won the championship in his senior year.

That seemed to be only yesterday. But it was now seven years ago.

The thought of time having passed this way saddened him. It was, damn it, it was hard to believe that all this had happened seven years ago.

Gosh, he'd be glad to see Jim and to see the kids practicing. Maybe he'd see one of the lads from the old days who might just be coming around as he was. Perhaps he'd see Tom Moss.

Good old Tom. He and Tom had been thick in school. They'd
been the two stars. Tom was a regular fellow. Even though his
folks were rich, he'd never acted like a snob. He'd been decent
and quiet, and damned handsome with his wavy hair. But Tom
hadn't ever futzed around like Marty Mulligan, Tim Doolan,
O'Neill, and that crowd when they were in school and the star
athletes. His crowd had gone farther in sports than they had.
His crowd had been much better than their crowd. Think of it,
O'Neill used to get the call on him at end. But O'Neill and Tim
and Marty had been good. They'd started the pigskin rolling
at school, and they could have made the team the year
he and Tom and the rest of the boys had almost brought the
title to M. O. M. The team in his senior year had been the first
of the many really crack teams the school had started turning
out. When these new kids saw him, they'd think of this
and look at him with awe. He'd feel good. And it would be good
to see old Tom or some of his other comrades of those days.
It would be great, all right. It would make him feel swell.

His mood became buoyant. He decided that Pat McGee was
no mere might-have-been. Yes, he would come back. He was
going to lower a bucket into the past, and it was the past that
was the best part of his life. High school—high school with Pat
McGee a reigning star in Chicago high-school circles. He had
been able to do everything in sports, and the future had been
bright while the present had been fun. It had been great, wonderful fun to play—to pitch, play basketball, trot out there
on the gridiron—to do all this and feel as sure of yourself as he
used to feel. He was going back to all this, going back to a
day in the past.

He swung the car into Jackson Park at Sixty-seventh and
Stony Island.

II

Pat parked his car near the football field in Jackson Park,
got out, and walked to the gridiron. It was located on a rec-

tangular strip of ground, running parallel to Stony Island, from
which it was separated by bushes and a picket fence. Seeing
the old field once again, it was just as familiar as it used to be.
It hadn't been changed. He thrilled for a moment, and in ela-
tion told himself that he couldn't change, either. But he had
changed. Still, it was mighty good to come out here and see the
good old field. He knew every spot on it. He gazed lovingly
at the bushes across the field. A sense of the old days over-
whelmed him. He remembered himself in odd moments of the
past, looking up at the sky, the bushes, and he recalled how
sometimes the laps around the field would be so long that he'd
think them endless, and, jogging along with tired muscles, with
a charley horse, he'd try to think of something that would take
his mind off the distance still to be run. But he had never been
able to sidetrack his thoughts, and he would jog slowly and
dully, wishing it were the last lap. Those days couldn't be gone.
One couldn't lose them. And yet they were lost.

He looked at his watch. It was twenty to three. The squad
was not out yet. He stood by himself, gazing about. He was
alone with the old days. The field became vaguely peopled with
Tom and the other boys of those days.

—It's the same old field, he told himself, moved.

Noticing some park loafers shooting craps, he strolled over
to watch them. He was bored, and he turned back and again
stood at the edge of the field. He wanted to go out and run the
length of it, from goal post to goal post. He imagined himself as he used to run, going like a power house, knees hitting
high, head low, his full hard body crashing and smashing forward. Running with the ball, smashing through a hole in the
line and breaking out into the open, that had been his biggest
football thrill. And he'd gone sixty-five yards like that for a
touchdown against St. Rose's in his junior year.

A fellow didn't know how wonderful, how valuable those
days were to him until they were all over. He shook his head
from side to side, sadly and wistfully. There was a far-off look
in his light blue eyes.

III

Pat watched the squad come out. They arrived in groups. Soon there were about thirty-five kids on the field, passing and kicking and running about. They didn't know that one of their alma mater's greatest of the great was watching them. The kids seemed so young. It was hard for him to think of himself as having been as they now were. He could remember the feelings, but not how he might have looked as a high-school freshman, raw and green and young, weighing only one hundred and thirty-five pounds. He watched a lean, tall kid show off by catching passes spectacularly. He had never shown off. But then, he hadn't needed to. Even when he had had a rotten season in his second year, he had always had that confidence in himself. He'd known that he didn't have to show off. He was a natural-born athlete. In football, in baseball, it had been the same. He had always got the hang of things quickly.

He turned and looked at the playground next to the field. On the path running around it, Jim would be appearing any minute, striding along with that burly walk of his. Good old Jim. Gosh, he'd be glad to see Jim. Good old Jim. He owed a lot to Jim. Jim had taught him a lot.

He moved closer to the practicing kids. A skinny lad muffed a ball thrown to him, and a husky redheaded kid razzed him. In his day, it had been just like that.

The skinny kid missed a second pass.

"Better put a catcher's mask on," the redhead yelled at him.

"Skinny, if you sell yourself to a farmer, you'll make dough with all the butter you got in your mitts," another player called, and Pat smiled.

"This is only practice," the skinny player retorted.

"Practice in muffing makes perfect," the redhead shot back.

Yes, just like the old days. These kids were the same as he and his comrades had been. These kids didn't know how lucky they were to be living through the best days of their lives at this very moment.

And there was Jim, rolling like a barrel toward his squad, good old Jim. He was heavier, must weigh about two twenty-five now. The same red, smiling face. Pat drew back a few feet and waited. He wanted to surprise Jim.

"All right, hep into it, everybody," Jim called in the same old barking voice that masked his kindness.

The squad quickly ringed around Jim. Pat watched but he couldn't hear what was said. But he could guess. Jim must be telling them to line up for scrimmage, giving the names of each squad, telling them to shake the lead out of their tails.

He saw a lone football left in midfield.

Several squads lined up. Jim barked at them in the same old way. Pat watched, waited, a sheepish smile on his face. He saw that Jim used the same unbalanced line formation, a variation on the Minnesota shift, that he had in the old days. He approached Jim. A little quarterback barked signals, and the boys ran off an old, familiar play. Jim snapped at them to pep it up.

Pat was deeply excited, but said nothing and went closer to Jim. Jim's face lit up.

"Why, hello, Pat, how are you?"

They shook hands. Jim's hand was bigger than his, and he still had a grip in it.

"You look in shape, Pat," Jim said, giving Pat the once over.

"Oh, I am," Pat said, smiling sheepishly. "You look swell, Jim."

"I feel good, but I'm gettin' old now, Pat," Jim said.

"All right, hep it up, you fellows," he barked.

"Same old Jim," Pat said.

Jim smiled that embarrassed smile he had always shown when one of the kids spoke this way to him. He was watching his squad out of the corner of his eye.

"Lead out of the tail, Sheehan," he bawled. He turned and asked, "What are you doing with yourself, Pat?"

"Oh, I'm selling automobiles."

He noticed the surprise on Jim's face.

"Last month I pitched a few semi-pro games for twenty bucks a game. I think my arm's coming back," Pat said.

"Why—what happened?" asked Jim, a look of surprise on his rough face.

"Didn't you know? I threw my arm out in mid-season at Terre Haute and had to give up. But I'm coming back."

"Say, I'm sorry to hear that. I didn't know it. I'm sorry. What happened? Bursitis?"

"I'm not sure. My arm just went dead on me. One day I just found out that I had a dead arm. But it's coming back. I'll be all right next year," Pat said, trying to sound both casual and convincing.

"You won't be back at Terre Haute?"

Pat shook his head.

"I got my unconditional release. But I think I might manage a tryout with one of the big league teams."

"I hope you do. I always had faith in your ability. Pat, you're a natural-born athlete," Jim said.

The words were soothing to Pat, yet at the same time they didn't really convince him.

He was worried about his dead arm, and, at this moment, a feeling of utter depression came over him. He looked off at the squad running through signals up and down the field, feigning interest. He didn't want accidentally to reveal his depressed spirits to Jim.

"I'm glad I saw you. I had you in mind, Pat. Would you like to play some Sunday games, or aren't you playing any more football?"

"I haven't lined anything up, but I'm in good condition. I'd like to. I'd like the feel of hitting the line again. You know, Jim, once you get it in your blood, you don't lose it," Pat said, while thinking that he could use the money because he wasn't so hot as an automobile salesman, and, with the depression on, how could you be a hot-shot salesman?

Jim's face softened with sympathy and nostalgia. He nodded his head understandingly. Pat sensed how Jim felt. Jim loved the game, too, and had played pro football. But he was too old now. He had never gone as far as Jim, never reached the National Professional Football League. Jim had been a halfback and had played with Paddy Driscoll and against Thorpe, Fritz Pollard, and Red Grange. How he would have liked to have done that, and have brought Thorpe, Pollard, or Grange down in the open field.

"Yes, Pat, I know how it is. Tell me, do you still live at the same place?" asked Jim.

"Yes."

"I'll have this Pullman team get in touch with you. I'm glad I saw you, because I was thinking of you, Pat." Jim smiled wistfully, a smile almost too soft with emotion and friendliness for a man as powerfully built as Jim was. "I miss playing," Jim shyly added.

Then he turned and barked through his hands:

"Hep into it, you fellows. Where's all your ginger?"

Pat tagged along, watching the first strong team snap through signal practice. He recalled that game in fourth year when Loyola had beaten them 7 to 0 and won the title. In the fourth quarter they'd carried the ball to Loyola's eight-yard line. Goal to go, four downs, with a tie for the title at stake. And Morrissey at quarter had called his signal. He'd plunged for about three yards. He'd lined up, confident. His signal was called again, and he'd been so confident that he'd turn the trick. He'd bent down, hands on knees, and decided to dive over the line. But they'd knocked him back a yard. And still he'd been confident. He could do everything in football, and he had determined to do this, but he'd failed. He'd cried after the game, and now he recalled this failure, regretted it, recalled his four plunges to the two-yard line, now imagining himself having made that touchdown. He was sad. He daydreamed that he had made that touchdown by diving over the Loyola line and over the goal line for the touchdown.

IV

Kavanaugh didn't look much changed. But he seemed to be down on his luck. Pat sensed that Al Kavanaugh somehow felt

as he did. Things weren't going right for Al. He had been a
good end, but hadn't made Notre Dame.

"I thought I'd come out and look at the team. Remember
how we used to come out just like these kids every day?" Pat
said.

"I wish we were still doing it, Pat."

"I'd give anything if we were," Pat said.

"Cigarette?" Al asked, extending a pack.

Pat shook his head.

"I tried smoking for a while but I gave it up. I can keep in
condition easier if I don't smoke. And I'm gonna get myself
in good condition this winter. I'm coming back next year. I'm
getting back in the game. I'm ready to go up to the big leagues
after I get a few games under my belt."

"I'm sure you are. Pat, you're still the greatest athlete
M. O. M. ever turned out."

Pat was gratified but thought that while this was possibly
true, look where he was! A dead arm. Only able to play semi-
pro football.

"What happened to you last year?" Al asked sympathetically.

"I had a bad year. My arm just went back on me. The soup
went out of it, and I couldn't pitch. I had to come home. But
my arm's getting stronger every day," Pat said.

Longing to be pitching, he went through a pitching motion.
As he did, he was gripped with a sudden fear and, instead of the
loose, easy motion he intended to make, it was a stiff and un-
natural motion, the one he had developed when the pains had
first hit him last summer. He winced, thinking that his lame arm
had snapped his self-confidence,. and he asked himself could he
really come back? He looked off at the leafless trees and then up
at the gray sky. He watched the kids scrimmaging on the field.
They had dreams like his. They didn't know, didn't know what
could happen to you.

"Yes, I'm coming back. I pitched a couple of semi-pro games
last month and won them."

"Swell, swell. You got what it takes, Pat. We always knew

you had, and so did Jim," Al said, but Pat remembered how he had merely lobbed the ball up in those semi-pro games and had won because of the inexperienced players against whom he was pitching.

"Two years ago I had a good year. And last summer I won sixteen and lost fifteen with a sixth place team, and then, the souper went dead."

"Keep a stiff upper lip, Pat. The good old M. O. M. spirit, and you'll be up there," Al said.

They stood there.

"Seen Tom?" asked Pat.

"I don't see him much. I don't know. I just don't see him," Al said meaningfully.

"Did anything happen between you?" Pat asked, curious about Al's tone of voice.

"No, not at all," Al said, but Pat sensed that something had happened between Tom and Al: they'd been such good friends.

Out on the field, Jim was barking out instructions to two scrimmaging squads.

v

"Hello, Pat," Tom Moss said blandly.

Pat saw that Tom was as handsome as ever. But he was a bit heavy and looked a little soft. He had jowls and, because of his added weight, he wasn't the same good-looking lad he used to be. Moreover, there was an aloofness in the way Tom had said hello.

They stood there facing each other. Pat had been so glad when he'd seen Tom coming along, and now Tom was standing there not saying much. And they had had so much in common in the old days. Was it that Tom looked down on him because Tom had gone to N. D. and been a star in some games and a brilliant second-string man on one of Rockne's undefeated teams?

Tom stood there, looking around with a smirk on his face and an air of condescension. Pat was afraid that it wasn't the same old Tom. His desire for the return of the old days became so painful emotionally that he looked off, unable to control the hurt expression on his face.

"What are you doing?" Pat finally asked him.

Tom acted as if he hadn't heard. After about a minute of silence, he said:

"I'm representing Stebbins and McCreary."

Tom handed Pat an engraved card with his name in the corner and the words *Sales Representative* after it.

"Are you selling bonds?" asked Pat.

The thud of a football being punted echoed across the field.

"Paint materials," Tom said.

Pat realized that it wasn't the same old Tom, and in his present mood this distressed him. He was ill at ease.

Tom said nothing for a moment, and then, with that same note of condescension in his voice, he asked:

"Are you doing anything, Pat?"

"Oh, I'm selling cars, but I'll be back in baseball next year. I'm going to do some semi-pro playing with an eleven out in Pullman, too. I love the old game same as ever, Tom," Pat said, hoping this would restore their bond of high-school days.

"Oh," said Tom.

"Are you going to play any more football, Tom?" asked Pat, regretting now that he hadn't been able to go to N. D. as Tom had.

"No, I wouldn't be a professional athlete. It makes a bum of you," Tom said cuttingly.

He turned, offered a limp hand to Pat, and said:

"Well, old man, it was good seeing you."

He pumped Pat's hand and slouched off. Pat was so bewildered that he didn't get angry until Tom was almost out of sight. But even then he wasn't really angry. He shook his head sadly. He couldn't understand how Tom could have changed so. Tom had practically said that he was a bum and had cut him. He shook a bewildered head, and there was a stupefied expression on his face.

VI

It was dark out. He was driving home through the park. He didn't have that feeling of power with his hands on the wheel. This darkness—he used to return to the showers in such darkness. And all that was gone. Tom was so changed. Tom thought he was a bum, had cut him, insulted him. And the kids hadn't known him. Jim had been friendly but busy. Good old Jim. He had not got the joy and thrill that he'd hoped to get out of this afternoon. They forget you. He, the greatest athlete ever turned out by M. O. M., was forgotten. He was forgotten in the Three Eye League, too.

He drove on, bewildered. He tried to tell himself that he was coming back, but he had no confidence. He was Forgotten Dead-Arm Pat McGee. He sensed that at twenty-five the best years of his life were over, gone with those days that he couldn't bring back by visiting the old scene in Jackson Park.

He drove out of the Park at Sixty-seventh Street. The lights of the street seemed warm and friendly. He drove on.

He shook his head, still bewildered. He didn't know why he had such tough luck. He had never done anything to merit the bad breaks. Again he shook his head in bewilderment. He drove on home for his dinner.

Lunch Hour: 1923

MY SWEETIE *went away, but she didn't say where, she didn't
say when, didn't say why,*
  Or bid me good-by . . .

Tom Finnegan and Al Bates rushed into the song shop on
West Monroe Street. It was a large store. The floor was of tile,
and silver dollars were embedded in it in a regular pattern. On
the right of the entrance there were counters, and on the left-
hand side, directly down from the doorway, there was a glass
case. In the back, there were several glassed-in booths with
victrolas and chairs inside them.
  "Rain'n', all right," Al Bates said.
  Tom nodded.
  The female song plugger, a blonde with a slightly bloated
face, sang to the crowd in a cracked falsetto.

*I know she loves another, but she didn't say who, she didn't
say which, she didn't say what her papa has got—that took
my sweetie from me.*

  "Keen, all right," Al said.
  Tom nodded. He looked around at the crowd of youths like
himself, and at the girls, cake-eaters and flappers who came
here almost every lunch hour to listen to the new songs. They
were all about the store, singly and in groups, and some of them
swayed and kept time to the songs by swinging their shoulders
or tapping their feet in fast rhythms.

"I'd like to have all of them on the floor," Al said, pointing at one of the silver dollars.

I know that I'll die—Why don't she hurry back home . . .

Al mumbled the first lines of the song, *My Sweetie Went Away,* and then he said:

"Keen."

Tom, medium-sized, blond, good-looking, gazed around to see if he might spot anyone he knew, or else try and catch the eye of a girl.

"Nice mamas come here," Al said.

"Uh yeah," Tom answered. "If I had dough, though, I wouldn't be coming here."

"That's why I said I wish I had the dollars in the floor, and more of the same," Al said.

The proprietor sang in a broken-voiced tenor.

> *You're the kind of a girl that men forget,*
> *Just a toy to enjoy for a while . . .*

"Sad song," Al said.

His eyes roved here and there and fastened on a thin blonde girl in a raccoon coat. She stood by herself, her face betraying a sentimental absorption in the singer.

"You'd get a lot of mamas if you owned a shop like this," Al said.

> *And you'll soon realize you're not so wise . . .*

"I like the blonde mama in the raccoon coat," Al said.

"Me, too," Tom said.

When they play Here Comes the Bride, you'll stand outside
Just a girl that men forget . . .

Young people came and left continually, and there was a constant noise of shuffling feet. Three cake-eaters lounged by the glass case a foot or so away from Tom and Al and sur-

veyed the scene with an air of sophisticated superiority. Al and
Tom looked at them. They were better dressed than Al and
Tom, taller, and better built.

"Those cakes are dressed collegiate. Keen. Hot," Al said.

"Uh huh!" Tom exclaimed.

They wore long, loose, beltless coats, and their black hats
slanted devilishly over their foreheads. Their shirts looked brand
new, and they had on colorful ties. They wore new tan
brogans, also.

Tom looked outside. He was not so well dressed. It was raining out, and his clothes were damp and had lost their press. He
looked back a bit enviously at the three cakes.

No, no, Nora, nobody but you, dear . . .

Many in the crowd shuffled their feet. Patent-leather toes
wiggled, slid on the floor. Bell bottoms flounced, and hips and
shoulders swung and swayed.

And would I trade you for kisses?

"Ah, boy. Keen," Al said.

A blond youth began moving and dancing back and forth
in a radius of about two square feet, doing what seemed like
a combination of the 'frisco and a cake walk, sticking out plump
buttocks now and then, shaking and wiggling them, holding
his chest erect, his face clouding with an expression of intense
absorption in himself and his movements. He snapped his fingers, bent, squatted, rose, swayed, and toe-danced, while others
clapped and cheered, and swayed their shoulders in rhythm
with him.

"Ummm," exclaimed Al.

No, no, Nora, no, no!

Then there was a bustle of conversation in the store. A girl's
giggle rose above the talk. Al and Tom looked outside. It was
still raining.

A lad of about seventeen with full, round, red cheeks was

flirting with the girl who had giggled. He wore a blue herring-bone suit with wide bell bottoms, a belted overcoat, and a brown felt hat with its crown squared. The girl who had giggled was talking with him and smiled. He noticed Al and Tom.

"Hi!" he exclaimed.

"Hi!" exclaimed Al.

"Hi!" exclaimed Tom.

"Like it?" he asked.

"Nice," Al said.

"Yeh," Tom said.

"Nice mamas here," he said.

"I'll say they are!" Al said.

"The cat's," Tom said.

Tom watched a baby-doll blonde with avid eyes.

"Like her?" asked Al.

"Yeh."

"I'd like to make her on the back porch," Al said.

"I'd like to make her any place, back porch, front porch, park, on a raft, any place."

"Nice," Al said.

Yes, we have no bananas . . .

Al looked around greedily. Tom rubbed his hand over the down on his upper lip. He gazed down at the frayed cuff on his bell-bottom trousers.

"I know that one," he said, nodding in the direction of a brunette.

"Yeh?"

"Her name is Peggy," Tom said.

"Nice. Peg of my heart," Al said.

"I'd let her be the peg of my heart," Tom said.

> *Monday night, I sat alone,*
> *Tuesday night, you didn't phone,*
> *Wednesday night, you didn't call . . .*

A tall lad, of athletic build, wearing a yellow slicker, was talking to the girl named Peggy. Tom frowned at him. The lad took off his gray fedora and held it ostentatiously, exposing his blond, wavy hair.

"Handsome brute," Al said.

"Vain. He gets his hair curled," Tom said.

"Maybe she's the peg of his heart?" Al said.

"He looks like a bum halfback to me," Tom said.

"More like a parlor athlete to me," Al said.

But you brought three girls for companee . . .

Al swung into the rhythm of the song, snapped his fingers, twirled his feet, shook his shoulders. Others did likewise, and soon the store was full of shuffling, swaying, dancing, 'friscoing boys and girls, while an infant-faced songplugger sang with a whine in her voice, and the piano jingled. Eyes met eyes, and smiles were exchanged. With ecstasy and desire shining in his eyes and on his face, Al tapped on the floor and shook. Tom was caught up in the rhythm, and he imitated Al. As he did so, his eyes met those of the girl named Peggy. She smiled at him. He smiled back.

The music stopped. Peggy left the lad in the slicker and came toward Tom and Al. She smiled.

"You don't remember me," she said.

"Peggy, of course I do."

"Do you come here often?" she asked.

"No, I came today because of the rain."

"So did I."

"Yes, it's rainin' out," Al said.

"Say, I'm glad I saw you. How about a date on Saturday night? Saves me the nickel for phoning," Tom said.

"Use a slug," Al said.

"Why, all right, I'm not doing anything," she said.

"Suppose I call at eight-thirty?"

"Okay."

"Oh, excuse me. Peggy Shanahan, this is Al Bates. He works in my office."

"How do you do," she said.

"I do do do doodle de do." Al said.

"I have to dash, but I'll see you Saturday night then, Tom?"

"Be ready 'bout half-past eight," Al sing-songed.

"All right. We'll go dancing," Tom said.

"I'd like that. And I'm glad to have met you, Mr. Bates," she said, and she walked out.

They looked after her, eyeing her slender, young figure.

"Keen. A neat mama you copped off."

"Yes, she'll pass in a crowd."

"Ever take her out before?"

"No, but I've been thinking of trying to date her. She's a decent girl, but a good dancer, and she's good fun."

"Neat, neat and a hot mama."

"She's pretty," Tom said.

"Yeh. Keen."

"She graduated last June from Saint Paul's," Tom bragged.

"Does she rate?"

"Yes, she rates. That's why I dated her."

"So, she rates?" asked Al.

"Yes, she rates," Tom said proudly.

A look of weariness came over the round face of a girl near them, and she exclaimed to another girl:

"If I dance tonight, I'll die-e."

"But, dearie, Jack and Pete are going to be at the Gardens tonight, and you know they're simply divine."

"So are we," Al said.

"What?"

"Divine," Al said.

"What an old line you got," the first girl said.

"Da-dad-dad-da-da deedee da da . . ." Al sang at the girl.

"You sing worse," the second girl said.

"But you don't know what I can do," Al said.

"I don't want to," the first girl said, turning her back on him.

"Tramps," Al said.

"Polacks," Tom said.

"Smarties," Al said.

"You know, Peggy, now—she's different," Tom said.

They heard thunder outside, and some of the lads and girls hurried in, laughing.

"I'm going dancing tonight. Keen. Come along," Al said.

"No, I'll have to save my pennies for Saturday night's date. She rates. I'll have to take her in cabs," Tom said.

"Too bad. It's going to be keen," Al said.

"I'll get enough dancing Saturday night," Tom said boastfully.

"Is that all?"

"She's decent and rates."

"Can't she kiss?"

"Well, I'm not sayin'," Tom said.

"Let's go in and play some records," Al suggested.

They went into an empty booth. Al put a hot jazz piece on the victrola. Tom sat on the couch. His face was thoughtful.

"Thinking of Peggy?" asked Al.

"I'm not sayin'," Tom said.

"She looks worth thinkin' about," Al said.

The music was very fast, and they tapped their feet on the floor.

"Makes you wish you had a piece on the back porch," Al said.

"Or any place," Tom said.

"Hot," Al exclaimed enthusiastically, as a cornet wah-wahed.

Al got up and danced, shaking his abdomen and making eyes at the glass.

"Daddadada," he sing-songed.

He paused, looked at Tom, and said:

"Whoops, Finnegan, where's your pep?"

"I'll save it for Peggy."

"I think you're gone on her already," Al said.

"She rates," Tom said.

Al danced, shook his buttocks, and mumbled to the wild, burning jazz.

"Ummmmmm," he exclaimed as the cornet again wah-wahed.

He stuck his tongue out, slobbered it across his lower lip, and made slobbering noises with his tongue by forcing saliva against the membranes of his mouth. Tom swayed his shoulders and tapped his feet to the music.

The record ended.

"Say, we got to dash or we'll be late," Al said.

"Yeh," Tom said.

They left the booth. The store was still crowded.

My wonderful one . . .

"She's singing about your Peggy," Al said.

"I wish she was mine," Tom said, moodily.

"Maybe she will be. Don't give up the ship," Al said.

"I wish it was Saturday night," Tom said.

"We'll have to run," Al said.

"The damned rain, too," Tom said.

They lit out east on Monroe Street, running in and out among people with umbrellas.

Winded, they entered the building where they worked.

"Well, you achieved something on your lunch hour," Al said.

My wonderful one, whenever I'm dreaming love's love-light, I'm dreaming of you.

"Yes, you're singing about her already," Al said.

"You'd sing, too, if you had a date with her. She rates," Tom said.

They entered the elevator and were whisked up to their office.

Called on the Carpet

I

WADE NORRIS, Patsy McLaughlin's chief clerk, left a letter before Collins, at Willie's end of the call board. Willie read it eagerly, while Wade went down to chat with Heinie Mueller at the other end of the board. There was a lull in the office.

"Hey, Wade what's this?" Willie called anxiously.

"Why it's a committee appointed by Mr. Minton, the new vice-president of the Chicago district, to investigate overtime. The company has appointed a new efficiency expert, and he's studying the whole works. He's going through every department. He is chairman of this committee, and they're going to be working on overtime very soon. Every man in the wagon supervision will be called on to explain why his men are drawing overtime."

"When my men draw overtime," Willie said loudly, pompously, and at the same time defensively, "it's because it's necessary. I watch the overtime like a hawk, you know. You can ask Casey here or look at my records. If any of my chauffeurs get overtime, it's something that's necessary, absolutely."

"I know that, Willie," Wade said reassuringly. "This is something they got cooked up over at main office, and we just got to comply with it. That's all." Wade shrugged his shoulders. "Willie, I don't think anything will come of it."

"Well, I ain't afraid. My expressmanship and record stand for themselves," said Willie.

"I don't believe that anything will come of it," Wade repeated, leaving the office.

"Listen O'Neill," Willie said, "I want you to watch them overtime sheets and let me see the sheet of every driver who gets more than an hour's overtime. There's a big rumpus about it, and I'm getting called on the carpet. Now you watch them."

Danny O'Neill nodded.

"Efficiency expert. Huh. What does a bastard like that know about the express game, huh? Tell me," Collins said to Casey, across from him.

"You know the way it is. Them guys over there have to cook up something to keep themselves busy," Casey said.

"They'll get you, Willie. You won't sound so much like the Chief when they get through with you," McGinty called over from his tractor board.

"Yeah. You think you're wise. Well, they ain't got nothing on me, and they won't. I'll just show them my record, and it will shine for itself," shouted Willie.

"Mr. Collins, here's Pick, regular man for Michelson. He's got a call he can't handle," yelled Stratton, the clerk from the other end of the tables.

"What's he got?"

"Six cases."

"Why can't he handle six cases?"

"He says they're too heavy, and he has regular calls to make."

"Tell him he's got to make it."

"He says he can't."

"Well, I can't either."

"Well, what about it?"

"Tell him to go ahead and make it."

"I did, and he said he can't."

"All right, take the call and give it to Michelson. Mark down on it what he says, and let Michelson handle it. I can't. I'm not going to get called on the carpet to answer for them route inspectors." Willie turned to Casey. "If they think I'm going to be their goat, they got another guess comin' to them."

After a rush of calls, Willie sat back in his chair and bandied back and forth in order to seem calm and unruffled. He shouted,

"Jesus Christ, them wise guys over there. Calling me on the carpet. Well, let 'em. I'll answer for my expressmanship."

He leaned back in his chair. He puffed on his cigarette, trying to calm his attack of worry.

Goddamn it, this was a wise idea! An efficiency expert! Efficiency expert! Yeah, efficiency expert! How did they expect the calls to be made? The company wanted business, all it could get. Well, how did the efficiency expert expect to get it? If the calls came in, they had to be made. If they weren't made, he'd damn soon be hearing from the main office. Goddamn soon. But then, when you did get the calls, you had to go over to the main office to answer damn fool questions about overtime.

He was the best man that Patsy McLaughlin had ever had dispatching up on the board. They couldn't take the ace out of there. If they did, they wouldn't have to take long to find out that they were up the creek. He had done his work to the very best of his ability. You could not ask a man to do more. He could not have done one thing better than he had done it. What did they want him to do? Go out on a truck and see that the men didn't stall? He couldn't watch them all even that way. He couldn't be every place at the same time. What did they expect of him?

The world was always against a good man. When you were too good, they were just jealous bastards, because they knew they weren't as good as you were. Take those route inspectors, all trying to keep piling their work on him. He shook his head and tightened his fists with stern determination. He would go over there. He would go on the carpet and lay his cards right down on the table, flush up, every one of them. He would go with his records and show them!

But suppose they didn't understand him? What did the efficiency experts and the damned muckety-mucks know about expressmanship?

He was so nervous and anxious that he rose and went out to the lavatory to calm himself.

II

Willie sat at home, thinking.

"You look tired," his huge wife said.

"I am. What do you think I do all day, play? I have a job with responsibilities."

"Maybe you'd like to go to a show with me."

"No," he snapped.

"See here now. Don't you talk like that to me. I shan't have none of it. Not a word more out of you," she said like a Brunhilde.

He looked at her like a spoiled and saddened little boy. He complained, "Well, gee whizz, gee! I work hard all day. Can't I have a little peace? You don't know how hard I work or what responsibilities I have, with no one to give me a helping hand. I got to fight all day with the public, and with all them route inspectors and dispatchers. It's fierce."

"I know it is. I know you work, and I only suggested you going to a movie to calm yourself and to forget," she said, patting his head maternally.

He slumped in his chair, nervously restless.

III

Willie knelt upright in the front of St. Peter's Church for the noonday Lenten Mass. He prayed with his hands posed solemnly. Now and then, as he prayed, he was filled with pride and self-righteousness. Anybody seeing him pray would know that here was a man who knew how to pray. He looked at the priest on the altar, clad in purple vestments. He lifted his head to the high ceiling. God was above there, and God was looking down with pleasure at Willie Collins, because Willie Collins

served God. It wasn't everbody who would come to the noonday Lenten services.

Willie prayed to God to help him get out of this overtime
mess, to give him strength and fortitude to pull through it with
colors flying as he deserved. He prayed that God would give
him justice. He wanted that, no more. He wanted justice because his record was clean, as his life was. He did his work well,
and he supported his family, and contributed to the support of
his pastor, and performed all his religious obligations. He was
making the nine first Fridays and attending Mass every day in
Lent. He was acting as a good man should. He knew that God
would not forget or forsake him, and that He would see that
justice was given unto him, and that he would not lose his job
or be transferred because of this new efficiency expert.

Willie lowered his head and stroked his breast in a *mea culpa*
to the sound of the *Sanctus* bell. . . .

He liked the quiet, too, in the church, the hush, which was
pleasingly interrupted by the priest's prayers. Outside the
church was the rattle of traffic, noises that now seemed part of
another world.

When the collection was taken up, Willie magnificently put
a quarter on the plate. He hoped the fellow would remember
him. He even felt that he'd like to help by taking up the collection during the Mass. But he guessed parish men did that.

He looked piously at the altar of God who would not, no,
never, forsake Willie Collins, and he went on praying. His
thoughts twisted and squirmed back to the overtime investiga-
tion. He imagined himself before the committee, and thought of
what he would say to the committee members and this new
efficiency expert. He made a dazzling impression on them all.
He knocked them dead with his figures. He showed them he
was a businessman. He showed them his record was clean. He
showed them he was an ace. He showed them he knew his business. He showed that he was their equal and even their superior.
They had no comeback.

Willie looked at the altar and prayed.

IV

After supper, Willie sat in the dining room, with his papers before him, studying the figures on overtime and the record of calls that Danny O'Neill had prepared for him. He was going to have everything down in black and white.

His ten-year-old son started to sing.

"Get out of here," Willie snarled.

"Tommy, your father is busy," Mrs. Collins said, looking up from darning her husband's socks.

"Keep them out of here. This is important. I got to know everything and have it in black and white tomorrow for them wise men and efficiency experts."

He looked at his papers. Suddenly, he glanced up and remarked, "You better go in and light the kerosene lamps. There's no use in wasting electricity. It costs money. They're young and got good eyesight. Let them study under the lamps. It won't hurt them none. And tell them to watch out so they don't start any fires."

Mrs. Collins did this and went into the parlor. Willie was attracted by the rows of figures showing the number of calls he had made from day to day, showing the rise of from eighty in June on up to two hundred and seventy-five and three hundred during the Christmas holiday rush. All that was business he had taken care of and had brought to the company. And it meant plenty of dollars and cents. And, think of it, some damn efficiency expert was coming along to tell him he didn't know his business.

His wife returned to the dining room and resumed darning his socks.

"They're jealous of me down at that office," he complained.

"Don't let them blacken you to your superiors. Don't let them," she said in an embattled manner.

Lighting a cigar, Willie said, "They can't do that. The old man knows I deliver the goods. They can't do that. I'm the old man, Mr. McLaughlin's, ace. He knows I deliver. If they try to blacken me, you know, they'll only blacken themselves. Nobody else could hold down the job as well as I do. It takes brains. That's why Mr. McLaughlin made me the Chief!"

Mrs. Collins nodded her head, continuing her darning.

"That's why they're all jealous of me. But a lot of good it will do them!"

"Small penny it will do them," Mrs. Collins said.

"Well, efficiency expert or no efficiency expert, I'll be staying right up there on the board. They ain't got anybody to take my place and do the thing to perfection like I do it," Willie said, again puffing on his cigar. "When I go out of there it will be to something better, and I don't think I need worry, because I'm delivering the goods, and, when they need somebody to show the stuff at a better job, they'll know where to look for him. Of course some of them other fellows in the supervision, they got more seniority than I got, but they'll find out who's got the stuff up here." Willie proudly pointed at his large head.

"You don't want to let them blacken you in Mr. McLaughlin's eyes. And, Willie, wear your new suit tomorrow for this meeting. I have that new white shirt of yours washed and ironed. And I'll put your new shoes out, and you can wear your new hat. And don't forget that new watch that you got for giving such fine service to those watch people."

"I won't," said Willie, irritated.

"And you just don't let them bluff you."

"My record stands for itself, and I got it all here for them."

Willie again studied the figures, but his mind quickly wandered. He saw himself astounding the committee. Then he was afraid he might not astound them and he feared for his job. He wondered if he could get a job through Eddie Chance if he was fired. He imagined himself getting fired and getting into politics through Eddie Chance and rising to be some kind of Chief . . . COLLINS ELECTED ALDERMAN. . . . Suppose that happened. Then the Express Company and all them bastards would be lumping plenty. But suppose he didn't? Suppose he was taken out of the department. But he wouldn't be. He couldn't be. He wouldn't be. He was a good and an honest man. And tomorrow he was going to go to confession before six o'clock Mass and offer up Holy Communion and a blessed candle or two so that he wouldn't.

"I haven't nothin' to worry about tomorrow. Nothin'. Them fellows won't show me up," he said.

"But, now, don't be insulting. You must be careful and not rouse their anger. You be polite and listen to them, but don't let them accuse you of anything."

"Me! What can they accuse me of? Nothin'. Nothin'. And if they are going to start changing men around and firing, well, there's a lot to go before me, a lot, yes a lot of 'em."

"Now don't you go being a fool for them men—them route inspectors. Don't you do it."

"They should try it. They couldn't with Mr. McLaughlin, and if they try, if they do, I'll just bust their damn jaws in for them."

"Now, Willie, don't you be fighting like a roughneck."

"I won't, but I can see myself letting them put something over on me."

Tomorrow who could tell but he might be out of a job, and he had three mouths to feed, and a wife and two kids to clothe, and he had to keep a roof over their heads. And it would all be because of some damned efficiency expert who wouldn't know what the hell to do if he was put up on the board or in a depot to dispatch.

"I ain't afraid," Willie said.

v

Weary, as much from worry as from his efforts to go over his figures and records, Willie put his papers into a paper folder and yawned. He looked glumly about the small dining room. It was neat and clean. No man had a neater wife than he, no sir.

He looked at her, a huge blonde woman, tenderly. He said, "I wouldn't have it so hard, only them drivers all play for overtime. They are all stallers. They won't play the game right. None of them will. I'm the only expressman in the company. There's not another expressman like me."

He looked out of the window. It was black and lonely outside. He didn't like the blackness and loneliness. Death. He recalled the tremors and fears he had had at the office before leaving, when Lumbert, the night chief, had happened to mention poor Jim O'Neill, Lord have mercy on his soul. Jim was lonely now, too, out in the cemetery. He didn't like to look out of the window. He looked at his hefty wife. Yes, he liked her, and she was a good mother of his kids and a fine wife and manager of his household. But now, well, he had nothing to talk of, he was weary and tired and overworked, and he felt— he didn't know what he felt. It was dark out and pretty cold. He was a man thirty-three, with the hair thinning away in the center of his head, and some day he had to die. There were many things in life he wanted to do. He didn't think of these things specifically. There was just something that had to happen, and, after it did happen, life would be different, and then he would do these many things. He relit his cigar butt. He tried to sink back comfortably in his chair and smoke it. No, he'd come out all right tomorrow.

He rose and paced the room.

"Willie, now you just sit right down here and don't be fretting yourself with worry."

He sat down. She knelt and took off his shoes and brought him a pair of slippers. She put a pillow to his back. She gave him his newspaper.

"Now, you forget all about that. You know the Lord will help you tomorrow," she consoled.

Willie shook his head and read his newspaper.

"Say, here's something. The husband of Sallie Morris, the Hollywood star, has committed suicide. It looks funny. You know them movie actors is fast," Willie idly commented.

"Wicked," his wife said.

"Look what that Arbuckle did. And because he has influence, he got out of it. Well, I'd never go to see a picture of his."

"And I wouldn't let little Willie or Tommy go, either."

"There's something funny about this. The paper says that it's a love triangle."

"Wicked," his wife said.

"And here's an old lady who's willed three hundred thousand dollars for a home for pigeons. Pretty nice for the pigeons. Only seems to me she might have left it for the poor."

"I'll see that the children get to bed now," she said, rising.

Willie rose, went to the parlor door, and barked with authority.

"All right, you kids, get to bed now, and good night."

They said they would, and Mrs. Collins left the room. He sat down and picked up his newspaper, but his thoughts drifted, and he worried again about tomorrow. He stared again at the darkness outside.

It was only five after nine. It was a bit early to go to bed. But he felt tired tonight. He wanted to go straight to sleep when he got in bed. She was a big woman, and she could stand a lot. Sometimes she tired him out, and he had to be in the pink for the meeting. He hoped she'd let him sleep. But he could tell by the look in her face tonight that she probably wouldn't. Well, he'd just roll away from her. Goddamn it, why didn't a woman realize that a fellow sometimes got tired, and that there was a limit to certain things, and that a fellow had to keep in the pink to earn a living. Well, tonight he was just going to roll over and go right to sleep.

He was confused. He paced the room. She returned and sat down. He went to her like a timid little boy, sat on her lap, and laid his head against her large breasts. She stroked his head. He felt cozy, warm, protected in her arms this way, against her huge warmth.

"Take me up to bed," he said.

"Yes, my last boy must be put to bed," she said tenderly, and she led him upstairs to their bedroom.

With her, he couldn't lose out, and he wouldn't.

VI

Willie had been on edge all morning, waiting till Mike Mulroney and Porky Mulroy came in. They were the first route inspectors who had been called over to the committee on the overtime. He would go after lunch. He wished this ordeal were over. When they came in, he turned and asked them about it.

"Hell, it's just like I thought. Nothing," said Mike after entering the department.

"Hell, them bastards didn't put nothin' over on us," Porky boasted.

"What did they say?" Willie asked eagerly.

"They didn't put nothin' over on this boy," Porky bragged.

"Huh, Mike?" asked Willie.

"They just ask some questions," said Mike.

"What questions?" Willie asked, leaning forward in his high swivel chair.

"Oh, do you watch your men and check their overtime sheets?"

"Yeah, well I do that . . . Hey, O'Neill, are you watching them overtime sheets?"

O'Neill nodded.

"Listen, every day from now on, you bring me in every over-time sheet on which there is any overtime drawn," said Collins.

O'Neill nodded.

"What else?" asked Willie.

"Oh, they asked us if we watched our men about stalling," Mike said.

"Well, I do that. Say, Casey, you're watching them sheets and keeping tab on all those guys and watching their driving time, aren't you?"

"You know me, Willie," said Casey.

"Well, they haven't anything on me," Willie asserted.

"Hell with them," Mike said.

McGinty winked at Porky Mulroy and Porky waddled over to him. They talked in low voices. Porky rolled back over to

Willie and began speaking with him in low and serious tones.

"Listen, Willie," he said, "I don't want to worry you, but they're tough. They put you through a grill. Jesus Christ, it's awful. They bawl you out for every minute of overtime and they talk to you like you was a dog or a flunkey. Christ, watch yourself and have all the dope you can on hand. The more figures the better. Jesus, they got me worried about my job. I don't like to say this to everyone because you know the way these bastards kid you. But Jesus Christ, Willie."

Fear crossed Willie Collins' face, and he looked suddenly like a very little and scared man.

"Goddamn them, they ain't got nothin' on me. I'll tell them," he said, almost trembling.

VII

Willie sat with a blushing red face. He hoped his new blue suit would impress these muckety-mucks. It fitted him well, but then all suits fit to a T.

Five men faced him across a table in a large office. A girl sat at one end, taking a stenographic report of the proceedings. In the center was Mr. Veltman, the new efficiency expert. He was a thin, tall man with a sharp nose, and although he was scarcely thirty, he was beginning to grow bald. On Veltman's right was the gray-haired new vice-president of the district, Mr. Minton. The three other officials were elderly.

Willie fidgeted, unable to control himself.

"There's all the records of my work," he said, nervously.

"Just a minute, please," said Veltman in a voice of cold and confident authority.

"Yes, sir," said Willie, while he silently cursed the sharp-nosed efficiency expert.

"Mr. Collins, is that it?"

"Yes, sir."

"You're the dispatcher in the Wagon Call Department?"

"Yes, sir, I'm the chief dispatcher in charge of special gas-car service. I pick up the whole city, taking care of all calls that the regular pickup men can't handle."

"Just a minute, please," interrupted Veltman.

"Yes, sir."

God would not desert him after he had received Holy Communion this morning, lit five blessed candles, and remained after Mass to say a decade of the rosary.

"You see, Mr. Collins, there is, we feel, more overtime than there should be. Now, how many men do you have working under your supervision?"

"That all depends. Sometimes I have eighty-six, and then on Mondays I have five extra gas-cars, and some Mondays I have six. Around Christmas and Thanksgiving, when there is a rush, I have ten or twelve extra gas-cars, and on Mondays, that is on Mondays during the Christmas and Thanksgiving rush, I have maybe fifteen extra gas-cars."

"But on the average, how many?"

"Eighty-five."

"Is that eighty-five men, or trucks?"

"Trucks."

"And how many men?"

"Well, there's a driver and a helper on every car."

"I see. Then, on the average, you have one hundred and seventy men."

"Yes, and I have the overtime records here."

"Is there any way you could reduce that overtime?" Mr. Veltman interrupted.

"Well, it's pretty low already, you know. I keep my overtime down as much as I can. It's impossible, you know, to work without some overtime, because I got the whole city to pick up. Some nights at a quarter to five, you know, I'll get calls from the regular man on some route for something he can't handle. Sometimes it will be at a firm that's payin' its men overtime, you know, to wait till we get a man there, and if I don't get a truck there soon, they burn up the wires and write letters in complaining to Mr. McLaughlin. You know, well, on such calls I got to send in the first truck that comes up, regardless of what time the driver is out, because the calls have to be made. Every night at a quarter to five, and five, and even after, I get calls that got to be made. Then, too, you know, I can't move my trucks around perfect-like. There are always things happening that you don't know about until they've happened, and then it's too late for you to do anything about them. Sometimes I'll count on a car for a call and the car will break down or something else will happen and delay me. I got all kinds of things like that to contend with, you know . . ."

"I understand, Mr. Collins, that there are many practical difficulties to contend with in the course of your daily work, and I sympathize with you. But what we want to do is get together and see if we can't overcome some of these difficulties," Veltman, the efficiency expert, said in a crisp voice.

"Of course, but I can't stop a truck from breaking down and I can't make the public stop giving me calls at a quarter to five."

"We understand that, Mr. Collins," Mr. Veltman said.

"We are going to spend a lot of money in advertising on a campaign to educate the public and to impress the shipper with the advisability of getting his shipments prepared at a regular time, preferably at a stated hour in the early afternoon," Mr. Minton said in a cultivated voice.

"Well, I think that would help us a lot. Now, out at Sloan's Deerfield, they never have their shipments ready at the time they say they will, and, when I send cars out there, over half the time the drivers have to wait. It's things like that that causes overtime."

"I know, Mr. Collins," Mr. Veltman said. "Now what I want to get at is this. We've all got a part to play in the Company and we've got to weld our parts together. We've got to make a synthesis of them. Understand? Now, the reason we are calling you wagon supervisors over here is so that we can effect this synthesis of parts. We know that some of the overtime drawn by wagon men is both justifiable and necessary. But our problem is to keep our necessary overtime down to the minimum without in the least lessening the efficiency of our service and the speed with which we answer all the calls and demands the public makes upon us. Now, do you think it can be done?"

Willie looked lost-eyed at his inquisitor.

"Do you?"

"Do I what?" he asked.

"Do you—Mr. Collins was it?"

"Yes, sir," Collins volunteered.

"Now, do you, Mr. Collins, believe that we can keep our necessary overtime down to as absolute a minimum as possible?"

"Do I? Why, yes."

"Well, have you any suggestions to offer?"

"Well . . ."

"Mr. Collins, that is, do you or do you not think there are any mistakes being made, or that we have any bad express habits, or that carelessness permits the increase of our overtime," asked one of the other members of the committee.

"No, sir. Not in my department. I got my records all up to snuff to show how I run my department."

"Well, do you think you can do anything to lower the overtime drawn by wagonmen in your supervision? Or do you believe that we or anyone could?" Mr. Veltman asked.

"Well, if the route inspectors would watch their men so that I would only get calls to pick up that their route men absolutely cannot handle, and if the shippers would have their goods ready earlier in the afternoon, you know, and if I would get co-operation from checkers at places like Sloan's Deerfield, I might."

"I see," said Veltman.

Willie waited, still fidgeting.

"Well, Mr. Collins," Mr. Veltman said, "it has been a pleasure to have had you over here so that we might mutually gain and educate ourselves in the express business. Now we trust that you will expend your very best efforts to see that the overtime is kept at the absolute minimum for this year."

"Yes, sir," Willie mumbled, nodding his head.

"That's all," Veltman said curtly, and he turned to show Mr. Minton something on a paper he held.

Willie rose and waited.

Veltman, noticing him, paused in his conversation with the vice-president and said in dismissal:

"That's all, Mr. Collins."

"But, pardon me. Didn't you want these records of what I do?" he asked.

"Why, no. We have overtime records from the payroll department."

Willie felt suddenly small. He paused there a moment, picked up his records, and said: "Good-by, Mr. Veltman."

Veltman said good-by and shook hands with him. The other four men shook hands.

Willie left, dazed, with his folder of records under his arm. In the long corridor outside, he was confused. But, then, the vice-president and other muckety-mucks had shaken hands with him. And he had got a clean bill of health. He smiled and strutted to the elevator.

But outside on the street, walking back, he once more felt small and unimportant. He cursed the damned efficiency expert.

—They didn't put nothing over on me, he boasted to himself, but not with great confidence.

VIII

Puffing on a fat ten-cent cigar the next day at noon, Willie boasted to a crowd of route inspectors:

"It was nothing, you know, just formality. They gave me a clean bill of health and said this department was all right, up to snuff, up to snuff. And they're gonna advise the route inspectors, checkers at places like Sloan's Deerfield, and guys like them, to co-operate more with me. You know."

He got the horse laugh and then, flustered, he hurriedly went on in a loud and boastful voice:

"And listen, Mr. Minton, Mr. Minton himself shook hands

with me and asked me to give him suggestions on how to make the service better and cut down the overtime."

Again he got the horse laugh, and the inspectors all talked at once, kidding him insultingly.

Gashouse McGinty, over at his tractor board, immediately called up one of the depot wagon dispatchers, and his booming voice could be heard above those of all the others:

"Say, did you get it? Mr. Minton invited Collins and his old lady to dinner. Yes, they're putting him on the board of directors. Yeh, now it's Collins and Minton."

McGinty heaved with laughter.

"Go ahead, you bums, say what you want. Mr. Minton shook hands with me, and asked my advice. Now stick that wherever you please," Willie shouted in an even louder and more boastful fashion.

They laughed again. Willie rose and, standing on his tip-toes, his five-feet-five of flesh taut, he screamed:

"When Mr. Minton shakes hands with you. . . ."

They laughed so uproariously that he was drowned out.

Comrade Stanley

I

STANLEY GRADEK was a tall, thin man of thirty-nine, slowly
growing bald. He sat in his small, dimly lit apartment, clad in
his long, brown monk's robe, the hood thrown back on his
shoulders. His hollowed face wore a brooding, reflective expression. His fingers were long, thin, and sensitive, and his well-
cared-for hands were soft. The narrow rooms of the apartment
were filled with chairs, bric-a-brac, exotic objects, a studio
couch, oil paintings by Chicago artists, and a few books.

Stanley suddenly twinged with guilt. The mood casting a
spell over him, like his monk's robe, was a residuum of the past.
Those days! He remembered how he used to sit in this apartment, wearing this same costume, with the candles, stolen from
a Greek Catholic church by friends, flickering just as they
were flickering now. Then, he had fancied himself mysterious,
exotic, and his fancy had even helped him to become reconciled
to growing bald. Baldness went with monkishness. Ah, yes, the
pathos of distance! Even though Nietzsche had been a petit-
bourgeois aristocrat, he had sometimes happened upon excellent
phrases. And what phrase of Nietzsche was better than . . .
the pathos of distance.

He mixed himself a drink and, sipping it, grew wistful. Holding the glass in his right hand, he glanced about and thought
about the days when he had tried to write, aspiring to become
the American Huysmans. He stared at the wall. He sipped his
drink again, held the glass, and continued to let his eyes rove
about his place.

228

Tonight he was lonely. He reflected on what he called the dialectic of age. From one point of view, thirty-nine was old. From another, it was young. Until a year ago he had been tortured by a pervasive sadness about the weight of his years. But in the last year, since he had joined the Party, he no longer had that pathetic, yes, pinched, petit-bourgeois fear about growing old. Time, the fact of death which lay behind the fact and the fear of time—these no longer seemed so melancholy. At least they didn't very often. Now and then, however, he did have bad moments when hangovers from his petit-bourgeois past troubled him. But he assured himself he was irrevocably done with all that. He cast a thin, sardonic smile at the objects in his apartment. Now, he shouldn't truly blame himself for any pretensions of his past. For even Bohemianism was a premature, primitive, and personalized expression of negative revolt. But why couldn't he have been the son of a South Chicago Polish steel worker? Yes, all that in his past had been a form of groping. And first, before you lost your personality and your individuality in the masses, you had to discover it. There was a pattern and a logic to his past—a dialectic.

Stanley took another drink.

The election was two months off. He flushed with pride. Think of it, here was Stanley Gradek, the standard bearer of the Party in this district. Suppose he should really be elected alderman. It was impossible. The Party was still weak and had to meet the full force of the class enemy. But still, suppose Stanley Gradek should become the first Communist alderman in the city of Chicago. On its face, this supposition seemed ridiculous. But was it so ridiculous? No, it wasn't. Someday he might well be the first Communist alderman in Chicago, or even, when the sleeping giant of the proletariat began to break its chains, the first Communist mayor.

He imagined himself in the City Council, rising to make a speech. How he would flay the other aldermen, the City Administration. Roosevelt would probably defeat Hoover in the election. He'd flay Roosevelt, too. From the President down, he

would consign all these bourgeois politicians to the garbage can
of history, where they belonged.

Stanley's face grew stern. His lips were drawn tight. He
clenched his soft fists. He sat with his torso hunched forward,
alert, eager, tense. The speech he dreamed of giving in the
City Council swept him along into a mood of emotional exaltation.

But it was getting late, and he ought to be turning in. Tonight he had relaxed and had a few people in. Someone had
brought a girl from the University, Charlotte Brand. She was
so young, so fresh. Her body was such an invitation. Just at the
best period of a female's life, the period of first virginal bloom.
When he'd seen her to the door, he had invited her to come
again, and she'd seemed pleased and jolly when she'd answered
that she would like to. Now, take a girl like Charlotte, alive,
healthy, with such a fine young body, take a girl like that and
save her from the horrible bourgeois world, win her over to
the movement, and you would have achieved something. As for
the rest, she had a body, and he had a body, and, despite all the
maledictions, curses, horrors, and outworn and outmoded
prejudices expressed in bourgeois morality, what was a body for?
He would like to make a girl like her his comrade, his co-worker,
and his mistress. The two of them would work together, fight
together, and after long days devoted to Party service they
would come home, tired. Love, sex in all its natural, normal,
physical nobility would refresh them, and then, side by side,
they would fall asleep.

Stanley began to perspire. He paced the floor nervously.

II

"Got a drink, Stan?" Al asked.

"Gee, Al, I'm sorry. I haven't a thing in the studio," Stanley
said.

Fatigued, Stanley sat relaxed in his most comfortable chair. It had been another hard day of conferences. An important New York comrade, Comrade Mortimer, had talked endlessly at the meeting. Stanley was all in. He felt like a drink. But Al never bought his own. He was always bumming drinks from somebody.

"Well, it's too bad you haven't a drink."

"Well, I'm sorry, Al. Are you working?"

"No. I went over to the Employment Bureau at the U again, but they can't give me any help. I went to school there but what good does it do me? I can't get a job."

"Al, I explained why you can't get a job. You're declassed. You're being driven down into the ranks of the proletariat."

"Well, whatever is happening to me, Stan, it's nothing that a drink couldn't remedy."

"Gee, I'm sorry I haven't anything."

"Listen, I got half a dollar. If you chip in, that's a buck. I'll see if Garfield is around. He's always ready to chip in to buy a bottle of booze."

"All right, I'll go in with you," Stanley said.

He handed Al half a dollar.

Al put on his hat and left. Stanley smoked a cigarette and made himself a drink and drank it hastily before Al could get back. Why should he waste bonded whisky on such people?

III

"Look at me. I've never been a plutocrat, have I?" Al asked.

"I didn't say you were a plutocrat. I explained, Al, that you need understanding. With understanding—the understanding of Marx, Engels, Lenin, and Stalin—and the discipline of our Party, we will conquer."

"Garfield, will you have some more of this understanding?" Al asked.

Garfield, a middle-aged, bald-headed man who had once been an architect, nodded. He handed Al his glass. Al made three drinks.

"Al, I don't like your making fun of serious things. I'm with Stanley a hundred per cent," Garfield said.

"I didn't mean it seriously. I'm with you, too."

"Well, you have to understand, Al, that the Party isn't something to joke about in your drinks."

"I wouldn't joke about it. Of course it's serious. Damned serious. I ain't got nothing to lose by being for it. Nothing to lose."

"Nothing to lose but your chains," Garfield said.

"Garfield, got a cigarette?" Al asked.

"Gee, no. Stan, have you got any cigarettes?"

Stanley reluctantly handed Garfield his package of Camels. Garfield and Al each took a cigarette. They lit up and drank.

"How does it feel to be running for office?" Al asked.

"I'm merely running for office as a duty," Stanley said with modesty. "My Party has chosen me. It is my duty. You know, fellows, the great feature of Party life is its discipline."

"That's why I can't join. I'm an individualist," Al said, taking another drink.

"I'm not good enough for the Party. If I were good enough, I'd join," Garfield said, also taking another drink.

"We're not the Kingdom of Heaven. And, fellows, the Party will change your entire life, your entire mental horizon."

"That's what I'm afraid of," Garfield said.

"Why be afraid? I wasn't. I couldn't begin to tell you what the Party has done for me personally. I'm a different man now, a totally different man," Stanley said.

"Maybe you're not like us. You're stronger. I'm too selfish and individualistic. That's why I can only be a fellow traveler, a camp follower," Al said.

"How much Party literature have you read?" Stanley asked.

"Oh, I've read enough. I know what it's all about," Al said.

Stanley got up to get some pamphlets for them. Garfield and Al each mixed another drink for himself.

IV

"Perhaps you ought to go to bed," Charlotte Brand said.

"Oh, no, not at all. We Communists have a sense of life," Stanley said, observing how plump and rosy she was.

He was tired, damned tired. For the last three days he had worked himself until he was ready to collapse. Meetings, conferences, speeches, and then, more meetings, more conferences, more speeches. A meeting about a rent strike at Fifty-fourth and Lake Park Avenue. A meeting with Negro comrades. Another meeting with Mortimer on the West Side for a thorough exploration of the problems of the election, and then a meeting which lasted until five in the morning while Mortimer had explained dialectical materialism. Yes, he was dead tired.

"We Communists have a sense of life," Stanley repeated.

"Yes, it must be so thrilling," she answered.

"Oh, hello," Al said, staggering up to Stanley and Charlotte, glass in hand.

Stanley frowned.

"How are you?" Al asked.

"I'm well. How are you?" Charlotte responded.

"Me? I? Myself? How am I, me, myself?" Again Stanley frowned at Al. "I'm all right, too. Have a drink," Al added.

"Al, we're speaking seriously," Stanley said, irritated.

Al slunk away.

"That's what society does to people. It's one more reason why there is a Party like ours," Stanley said, looking after Al, who was over at a table now, fixing himself another drink.

"I'd be afraid to join the Party," she said.

"Why? We won't eat you," Stanley said.

"Oh, but the work you do, it's so self-sacrificing, so noble."

"Oh, not at all. It's merely in the line of duty," Stanley said.

"Comrade Stanley."

Stanley looked up, disappointed. Comrade Jake Jackson from *The Fist* stood leering at Stanley and Charlotte.

"Miss Brand, this is my comrade, Jake Jackson," Stanley said.

Jackson took a drink, sat down on the couch beside Stanley, and said, eyeing Stanley enigmatically:

"Well, Stanley, this is a nice little party you're having!"

"Yes, but I'm pretty tired from work," Stanley said, disliking the way Jake looked at him, but saying nothing about this.

"Have a drink to the Party," Al said drunkenly, holding up a glass.

V

"I wouldn't even think of saying a word against real proletarian leaders of the workers' advance guard like Eldridge and Johnson. They are great men, and they have in them the making of the American Lenin," Stanley said to his comrade, Abe Goldstein.

Abe Goldstein nodded.

"But I do think there is something about New York that can easily turn even a good comrade into a bureaucrat," Stanley said.

Abe didn't answer. Stanley watched him closely but unobtrusively, cautiously seeking to note any changes in Abe's expression that would signify whether Abe agreed or not.

Stanley held out a package of cigarettes. Abe took one, then Stanley. They lit up.

"Yes," Stanley went on reflectively. "Yes, you see New York is a kind of island removed from America. It's part of America, but, then again, it isn't part of America."

"I know what you mean," Abe said thoughtfully, puffing away on his cigarette.

"Yes, New York does something to people, even to some of our comrades," Stanley said.

"I noticed that. You know, the local comrades are so much more simple than the ones who come from New York."

"That's just what I mean; New York spoils them. It does something to them."

"Stanley, I've been thinking. New York isn't the best place in the world for Party headquarters. Chicago is an industrial town. New York is full of chiselers and litterateurs. Chicago is different. It's the center of America. Someday, Stanley, Chicago is going to be the heart of proletarian America."

Their eyes shone. Stanley got out a bottle of good liquor and fixed drinks. They tipped glasses and drank.

"I was in New York for a few days about five months ago, and I must confess that I left with some bad impressions. Yes, very bad impressions. I wouldn't say this to anyone but a Party comrade. But, I tell you, I didn't like some of the things I saw at all."

"The Party wanted me to go to New York, but I managed to convince them I was needed here."

"I'm glad to know that. We need you here. You're in the streetcar men's union now, aren't you?"

"Yes, I was sent into it."

"That's good. We Communists must stay close to the workers. The hell with these Bohemians, these litterateurs, men who scribble poems, paint pictures, and drink themselves into cirrhosis of the liver."

"Of course, I've never worked on the cars, but then I can give guidance. I'd rather do that than work in an office in New York because—I hate to say it, but damn it, it's true—there are a lot of bureaucrats in the Party in New York."

"Yes, I observed that when I was there."

"I tell you, Stanley, the sight of many of those who call themselves comrades would disillusion me if I didn't realize so fully that the Party is bigger than this or that bureaucrat who worms his way into its ranks."

"Some of them use the Party for all sorts of personal adventures. Why, they even act like petit-bourgeois libertines," Stanley said.

"Yes, they come out here and act like big shots. They give us orders, pose all over the place, and what do they do out here?

They spend their time trying to explain dialectical materialism while they're in bed with a girl. And it doesn't matter if
the girl is some local comrade's sweetheart or wife, either."

"If Eldridge and the Ninth Floor only knew what some of
these walking delegates from Greenwich Village do in Chicago
and other places where we are busy leading and organizing the
workers."

"Yes, if Eldridge only knew."

They had another drink.

VI

It was Saturday night. Stanley was having a little party to
raise funds for the election campaign. Drinks were being sold,
and there was a table at which three girls from the University
were serving them. People were gathered in little groups and
milling about in the small apartment. The air was heavy and
smoke filled.

"Comrade Al, I want you to meet Comrade Gumowski.
Comrade Gumowski is a worker," Clem said, introducing Al
to a tall, blond, horny-handed Pole.

They shook hands, and Al winced at Comrade Gumowski's
grip.

"Comrade Gumowski works in the steel mills. He's a worker."

"I'm glad to meet you. Of course, I'm not technically a comrade, but I'm with you, Comrade Gumowski," Al said.

Comrade Gumowski grinned.

"I won't be on the other side of the barricades. Come on, let's
have a drink," Al said.

He took Comrade Gumowski by the arm and led him to the
table where the drinks were being sold.

"Violet, Irene, Jane, this is Comrade Gumowski. He's a
worker," Al said.

The girls smiled at Comrade Gumowski. He blushed.

"Fix Comrade Gumowski and me up with drinks."

Blonde Irene mixed them a drink, and Al laid half a dollar on the table.

"Comrade Gumowski, to the Revolution," Al said.

They tipped glasses. Comrade Gumowski downed his drink in one gulp.

Al looked at Comrade Gumowski, amazed.

Garfield staggered up to them.

"Comrade Garfield, this Comrade Gumowski. Comrade Gumowski is a worker," Al said.

Garfield and Comrade Gumowski shook hands, and Garfield, too, winced at the husky Pole's clasp.

"Have a drink," Garfield said.

He bought them three drinks.

VII

"Look at him, Charlotte," Stanley said. "He's so simple. You know, it's heartening, inspiring, to talk to a real worker. A real worker is so different from the intellectuals who come over to the movement. Lenin, you know, never trusted most of the intellectuals."

Stanley sat beside Charlotte on a corner of his studio couch, slyly looking down at her dress falling over her thighs, and at her silken legs.

"Yes, one honest worker like Comrade Gumowski is worth a lot of intellectuals from New York, intellectuals who come over to the movement. You know, when I returned from New York, I went out to South Chicago and had a few beers with Comrade Gumowski. I tell you, Charlotte, it was a heartening experience."

Charlotte watched Jake Jackson out of the corner of her eye. She didn't answer Stanley. She tried to catch Jake Jackson's eye. At the other end of the room, Jake was talking with a colored girl. Charlotte bit her lip. Stanley frowned.

VIII

"Stanley, do you know Goldstein very well?" Jake Jackson asked him.

The two were alone in a restaurant near Fifty-seventh Street and Harper Avenue.

Stanley stirred his coffee, took a sip, set his cup down.

"If you mean is he a close friend of mine, no."

"I'm glad to hear that," Jake said. "He's unreliable."

"Well, of course, I always suspected that," Stanley said promptly.

"What do you know about him?" Jake asked.

Stanley didn't like the way Jake was fixing his eyes on him, but he met Jake's gaze without flinching. Stanley knew he must not give Jake any opening. He didn't trust Jake. He didn't want Jake going back to New York and saying anything to the comrades on the Ninth Floor.

"Oh, Jake, nothing in particular. It's just his manner. There's something about his manner," Stanley said.

"Isn't there anything more specific?"

"No, nothing that comes to mind. Except that I have always been guarded and cautious in his presence. I've never conveyed more to him about inner Party affairs than was strictly necessary, and whenever I've had anything to say about such matters I've always kept him off important committees and out of any confidential work."

"Good. I'm glad to hear that, Stanley. You showed real Party instinct. I've always been convinced you are a reliable comrade and have good Bolshevik instincts."

"Well, I'll tell you," Stanley said. "You know my background. You know that I come from Polish nobility. But I was brought up as a little boy in a working-class district out in South Chicago. I think that unconsciously I learned more in those days than I realized."

"That often happens. But, Stanley, I'm not the only comrade who suspects Goldstein of Trotskyism."

Neither of them spoke for a moment.

"Is it that serious?" Stanley asked gravely.

"He's a disrupter, sowing the seeds of discontent in the ranks. He doesn't trust the leadership. I think he has organized a secret faction here. I was supposed to go back to New York but, when I heard that, I got in touch with the comrades back east. I'm staying on to look around here. I think there's an unhealthy condition, a cancer in the party ranks, here in Chicago. Now, Stan, I want you to help me."

Stanley kept his face expressionless.

"Yes, I want you to keep mum on this. It's confidential. I'm telling you because you're reliable, and with your help I'm sure I can cut the cancer out."

"You know, Jake, the Party comes above everything with me."

"Let's have some more coffee."

"George," Stanley called to the Greek waiter in a stiff tone of voice.

George, the Greek, came over.

"Two more coffees," Stanley ordered with authority.

Jake took Stanley's pack of cigarettes, which lay on the table, and lit one. Stanley noticed this, but said nothing. Jake never seemed to smoke his own cigarettes or to pay a check.

"The Ninth Floor's worried about conditions in the Party here," Jake said.

"What's the matter, Jake? You know we're doing some very good work here. My campaign is bringing in good results."

"The recruiting drive seems to have slowed down. Not enough copies of *The Fist* are being sold. And there is this dissension, this crabbing, backbiting, and discontent in some of the units. But I think it's mostly due to the Goldstein faction."

"Are you sure it's that serious?"

"That remains to be seen."

The waiter brought them their coffee. They put in sugar and cream, stirred the coffee, and puffed on their cigarettes.

"Keep your eye on Goldstein and keep your ears open," Jake said.

"Of course, I will."

When they finished their coffee, Jake let Stanley pick up the check. They stood outside the restaurant a moment. Jake then shook hands with Stanley and walked off west, in the direction of the University.

Was he going to meet Charlotte? Stanley was tempted to follow him, but he didn't dare. It would look too suspicious. And what Jake had told him was enough cause for worry. Suppose Goldstein should repeat remarks he'd made about Jake? He stood in his tracks, frightened. He envisaged expulsion from the Party, denunciation. Well, no, he could prevent that. But Charlotte? He went into the drugstore at the corner to telephone her.

IX

"Stanley, you ought to rest more. You do so much, so much for the Party," Barbara Morgan said.

She was a plain-looking, serious comrade who had once been Stanley's mistress.

"Barbara, what am I alongside the workers?"

"What are any of us, Stanley, compared to the workers?"

"Have a drink before we go to dinner," Stanley said.

"All right."

"The drinks are in the cabinet. Mix us two," Stanley said.

He sat and waited while she mixed drinks. He thought of her. She seemed to be such damaged goods, so drab, so ordinary alongside of Charlotte. Charlotte had been home when he'd phoned her this afternoon, but she said she couldn't see him for tea or for dinner. He had asked why. Busy. An engagement. She wouldn't say what it was or whom she was seeing. He knew. And so he had to be content to dine with Barbara. Barbara, good comrade that she was, was something of a bore. He heard her fixing the drinks.

"I'm seeing Abe Goldstein tomorrow night," Barbara said, returning with the drinks.

Stanley frowned.

"What's the matter?" she asked.

"Oh, nothing."

"Abe's a very loyal comrade and a good friend of yours, isn't he, Stanley?"

"Not particularly."

"Stanley, I know you well enough to know there is something on your mind when you act this way."

"I don't think you should see much of Abe."

"Why?"

"Barbara, I don't think Abe can really be trusted."

"Why? Has he done anything? What has he said?"

"He likes to be a general. If he can't be one, he's discontented. And you know, Barbara, that's very bad orientation for any comrade in our Party."

"But, Stanley, are you sure? Why, I always thought Abe was a very loyal and devoted comrade."

Stanley looked at her, annoyed, impatient.

"Stanley, you look at me as if I were a fool not to understand you. But I don't understand. Tell me what Abe has said or done to provoke your suspicion."

He continued to look at her, annoyed and impatient. He took up his glass and slowly took a drink.

"Barbara, you know you are a very good comrade. But you lack a certain kind of political insight."

Barbara watched him, bewildered.

"Yes, you don't see the political meaning in a great many little things. But, you know, in our rotten world of capitalist decay, Barbara, everything, everything has a political meaning."

"Yes, you're right, Stanley. You know, Stanley, I have never seen such development in a man as I have in you during this last year," she said.

Stanley glanced at her, displeased.

"Stanley, don't look at me like that because of what I said.

After all, we all had to come to the movement through various
channels."

"I know that. But, Barbara, you know me, and you know
me well enough to know that I was always, instinctively, a
revolutionist."

Barbara said nothing. She squashed her cigarette and took
another sip from her glass.

"But all this is irrelevant. I want to warn you, Barbara, you
have to be careful of a man like Abe. He's dissatisfied with the
Party. I can tell it from the way he talks. He is always griping,
always complaining of comrades, always attacking the leadership in a snide way."

Barbara seemed puzzled. She looked at Stanley, bewildered.

"But, Stanley, I thought Abe had the same views as you,"
she asked, interrupting him.

"Barbara, devoted comrade that you are, loyal and able Party
member that you are, you still lack political insight. There is a
distinct difference between my attitude on this question and
Abe's. Abe is always griping. He doesn't practice Bolshevik self-
criticism. All he does is snipe, snipe, and snipe away subtly in
order to sow confusion in the ranks."

"But, Stanley!" Barbara exclaimed.

"Don't say I didn't warn you," Stanley went on, ignoring
her exclamation. "Barbara, I know more than I can say. And
what little I can reveal is strictly confidential. But listen to me.
Abe's days are not long in the Party. Why, I even think he is
trying to start a Trotskyite faction here in Chicago in our very
ranks."

"Stanley, are you certain of it?"

"Absolutely."

"You mean Abe is really a dirty hypocritical social fascist?"

"Yes, I do. But, of course, I don't want you to quote me."

"You know I wouldn't. But, Stanley, maybe I had better not
see him tomorrow night."

"I wouldn't if I were you." Stanley finished his drink and
rose. "But, come on, Barbara, finish up your drink, and we'll
go out to dinner."

x

Stanley sat with Charlotte in the Coffee Shop at the University. It was only half full. He glanced around. He liked to be in the presence of youth. He noticed that there were a number of fresh-looking girls at the tables. Attractive girl students, wearing trim aprons and caps, were moving back and forth with orders. There was a pleasant feeling to the place, he reflected.

"I don't get a chance to do this often," he said fingering a teacup.

"To do what?"

"Sit and drink tea with you. Sit and act as if I were a *rentier*."

"What's a *rentier*?"

"Charlotte, you should pay more attention to economics. Instead of spending so much time reading dead poets, you must read economics."

"Yes, Stanley, aren't I dumb?"

"Charlotte, you're a very intelligent girl."

"Don't flatter me, Stanley."

"Not at all. I mean what I say. You're an extraordinarily intelligent girl."

"Stanley, please tell that to my professors, won't you?"

"Professors, what do they know?"

"They want to know what I know."

"Say, what's that book you're reading?" he suddenly asked, noticing a red-covered book under her pocketbook on the table.

He reached toward it.

"May I look at it?"

"Of course. You know more about that subject than I do," she answered, still speaking in a casual and disinterested tone of voice.

Stanley reached for the book. It looked familiar. He saw that it was Engels' *Anti-Dühring*, and his eyes lit up as he turned the pages.

"This is a great book," he said.

"Jake asked me to read it. He's going to explain it to me. But, Stanley, I'm not smart enough to understand it all."

"Of course, you are. You're a brilliant girl."

"I only wish I were."

Jake was using Engels as a means of seducing Charlotte. That a Communist would use one of the great books of a founder of Marxism for such ends! What could he do to Jake? He had to watch his step. Had Jake been giving him a subtle and indirect warning the other day when Jake had spoken about Abe Goldstein?

"Tell me, Charlotte, what do you do with yourself all day?" he asked.

She smiled, revealing beautiful white teeth.

"Stanley, I don't know. You know, time just passes, and I don't get anything done. It's the middle of October already, and I don't seem to have gotten anything done yet."

"Time flies for all of us," Stanley said wistfully.

Charlotte toyed with her teacup. She seemed to be complacent, almost bovine, and was prepared to sit and wait and let Stanley talk if he wanted to. If he didn't she seemed to be prepared merely to sit.

"But it is wonderful to be young enough still to feel that you will live to see the great transformation of society under socialism," Stanley said pompously.

Charlotte seemed bored. Stanley wondered what he could say to arouse her interest in him.

"Have you been seeing much of Jake of late?"

"I saw him a couple of times," she answered casually.

He was sure of it. Jake had slept with her already.

"I've been wanting to see him. I was hoping he would come around and see me," Stanley said.

"Why, we can do it tonight. I'm meeting him for supper, and we haven't any plans for after supper," Charlotte said.

The way she had pronounced *we* was suspicious. Flustered, he didn't speak for a moment. He felt that Charlotte saw he was flustered, too.

"Of course, by all means come and see me," he said.

"I'll ask Jake. I'm sure he'll want to."

Yes, from the way she was talking, he could tell.

XI

"Stanley, something I can't understand has been happening to me," Abe said, alone with Stanley in his apartment.

"What's the matter?" Stanley said guardedly, wondering how he could get rid of Abe, hoping Jake wouldn't drop in or any of his other comrades.

"It's strange. Comrades are acting in a peculiar way toward me."

"What do you mean?" Stanley asked. The name Abe had been on the tip of his tongue, but he had checked himself and didn't call his comrade by name.

"Even Barbara acts distant, cold. They act as if they didn't trust me."

"I don't know anything about it," Stanley said.

Stanley wondered—was he being unfair to Abe? Should he stand up for Abe and make a fight against Jake? Should he tell Abe that this was Jake's doing? But if he did, and Jake maneuvered against both of them, then where would he be? If he were expelled from the Party now, or even put on probation, could he stand the blow? He had burned all his bridges behind him. What would life mean to him now, at the age of thirty-nine, if he were expelled from the Party? Go back to trying to write? He had no confidence in himself as a writer. He knew in his own mind that he was glad of his political life because it gave him a reason for not trying to write. Before he had joined the Party, he had really stopped writing. He hadn't written since he left Paris in 1929, and he had done damned little work when he had lived on the Left Bank.

But he had to say something to Abe, and he wasn't sure just what he ought to say.

"Stanley, you're my friend, aren't you?"

"That's a strange question to ask me."

"You've been busy with campaign speeches. Maybe you haven't come in contact with what I mean."

"No, I haven't."

"You seem cold, Stanley. Are you against me, too?"

"What do you mean? Don't get a persecution complex."

"I'm not getting any persecution complex. I know what I'm talking about. Why, the comrades will hardly speak to me. Why? What have I done? What have I said?"

Stanley saw how excited Abe was. He wished Abe would go. He wondered what excuse he could give to get Abe out of his apartment.

"Stanley, I gave up everything for the Party. I left home. My old man and I don't even speak. I sacrificed my education. I broke with all my friends, with my whole past," Abe said.

Stanley waited, embarrassed.

"I was living on fifteen dollars a week I got from the Party. Jake told me today that I'm not going to get that any more. What have I done?"

"Abe, I don't know why you ask me that question. I don't know anything about it. You know, I don't play any role in intra-party disputes. And Jake is here from the Ninth Floor."

"Stanley, as a friend and as a comrade, tell me, have you heard anything about me? Do you know anything about this business?"

Stanley looked at Abe, trying to seem bewildered.

He hadn't heard that Abe had lost his Party job. He knew that he had to get Abe out of the apartment, and do it quickly. If Jake should drop in, Jake would have something to use on him later. Jake was unscrupulous. He wanted to help Abe defend himself, but he didn't dare do it. Party considerations were above all personal matters, all personal feelings.

"Abe, I don't know. I haven't heard a word. I've been campaigning. Yesterday I made four speeches. Today I made another speech. I have to leave now to attend another meeting."

"Will Jake be there? Can I go with you?"

"I'm sorry. It's special Party work. I have to meet some University people, innocents."

"Can't I come?"

"No. It's special Party work. And, besides, these people are Nordics. A comrade named Goldstein wouldn't be the best one to come along with me."

"You're with them. You're against me, too," Abe said heatedly.

"I? Abe, don't get a persecution complex. You know the Party. If the Party disciplines you, it has its reasons. You have to take its orders. We're soldiers in the army of the Revolution, Abe. Our duty is to do what the Party directs. The Party knows better than we. We can't set ourselves up against the Party."

"But what did I do? I was doing good work. I was getting results."

"What orders did you get?"

"I don't know yet."

"Well, go see Jake and have a heart-to-heart talk."

"He won't see me."

"I don't know what to say, Abe. And I'm sorry, but I really have to go."

Abe picked up his hat and glumly left the apartment. He turned at the door.

"So long."

"So long," Stanley said, his voice formal.

He was relieved that Abe was gone. But now he had to go out. Otherwise Abe might be in the neighborhood and see the light on in his apartment. He wondered what to do. He put on his hat and coat and left. He walked about aimlessly, ashamed of himself for not defending Abe. But he was helpless. The Party was bigger than he. And the Party was his life.

XII

Stanley was encouraged by reports of the campaign. Election day was drawing near, and he was hopeful of polling a good vote. The campaign was an avenue of propaganda to reach the workers, and the size of his vote would reveal the success of his work. Of course, there weren't very many real workers in the ward. There were a lot of workers of brain, but, of course, intellectuals were petit bourgeois, too. Still, they had to be won over and used. He was reaching them, reaching key people at the University. If he could poll a relatively big vote, it would be good for him in the Party and show that he was popular and had a following. If he built up a good following, he would be safe from comrades like Jake in a way that Abe wasn't safe. But, more important, yes, more important by far, a good vote would show that the Party was growing, was gaining in influence.

Barbara was busy these days canvassing from house to house, selling copies of *The Fist* and soliciting votes for the Party, and she had reported surprisingly good results. Many families had been cordial to her, had invited her in and talked with her, and Barbara had explained the Party's program for the election. He had tried to line Charlotte up to campaign. She was pretty, young, and came from a good family. A girl like Charlotte would be a wonderful campaigner. She would make a good impression in the homes of University people. But he couldn't convince her, and, also, Jake had vetoed his proposal. Here was an instance of how Jake worked against the best interests of the Party. He had originally interested Charlotte in Marxism. And now, with Jake as her lover, she was not going to join the Party. Jake had said she would be of more use outside the Party. He didn't see it that way, but Charlotte, naive girl that she was, had gone simply gaga on Jake.

But he had to forget all this now and work. He got out paper and pencil and began jotting down notes for a speech he had to deliver tonight.

XIII

Stanley left the meeting hall with Jake, and they went to a restaurant on Fifty-fifth Street. He was disappointed that Charlotte hadn't come to hear him speak. He had been hoping that she would come and see him at his best. Comrades told him he was a fine speaker, and once, after he'd delivered a speech, Abe had said he was the young Lenin of Chicago. Abe was on the way out of the Party. He avoided Abe now.

Stanley wanted to ask Jake why Charlotte hadn't come to the meeting, but he didn't.

"Do you really think my speech went off all right?" Stanley asked.

"Sure. A good speech. But there were a couple of points about it I want to take up."

"Yes?" Stanley asked anxiously.

The waiter brought them the coffee and sandwiches.

"What points?" Stanley asked when the waiter had gone off.

"First of all, you didn't mention how absolutely necessary it is to read *The Fist.*"

"I know. I thought about it and decided I wouldn't because of the class composition of the audience."

"That's a mistake. It's not the right tactic," Jake said.

"I don't agree with you there, Jake. I know my audiences in this district, Jake, and I know how to handle them. I've made five converts at the University already."

"Just a minute," Jake interrupted.

Stanley controlled his feelings of resentment.

"I can see that Goldsteinism has had its bad influence through all the South Side cadres of the Party, among all of them except, of course, the Negroes, where all the members in the units are real workers, real stalwart proletarians."

"Goldsteinism?"

"Don't interrupt. I want to tell you about your speech."

"But Goldsteinism?"

"Goldsteinism and Trotskyism are synonymous. But you

made a great mistake. You are talking to a petit-bourgeois audience. What is the political character of a petit-bourgeois audience?" Stanley opened his mouth to speak. Jake raised his hand. "Just a minute, now, and listen. What is the political character of a petit-bourgeois audience? The political character of a petit-bourgeois audience is that it is unreliable, untrustworthy, politically adventurist, and opportunist, not to be trusted."

Stanley waited. He would have to go to New York sometime and go over Jake's head.

"Now, what must you do with a petit-bourgeois audience? You must educate it. How must you educate it? Through the weapon of the Party press."

"Yes, but I think it was best not to push them too fast."

"Stanley, you're not so afraid of the Party press, you're not infected with Goldsteinism, are you, that you are ashamed of our Party press?"

"Jake, you know me better than that," Stanley said.

"Yes, I think it was just a mistake in tactics. And then, point two, Stanley. You didn't discuss social fascism."

"I thought about that. But what I decided was that it was better to make a positive and constructive speech. After all, what is the Socialist Party? Nothing. It doesn't amount to a row of pins. I thought I would point out positively what our Party stands for and not even dignify the Socialist Party and all the other social fascists by mentioning them," Stanley answered.

Jake shook his head slowly from side to side. Stanley waited. He was filled with hatred for the comrade facing him. He wondered how long Jake would remain in Chicago. But his hands were tied. Jake wielded power and authority. The Party was bigger than Jake and he had to serve the Party. It would one day test men like Jake and find them wanting.

Jake waved to the waiter and pointed for another cup of coffee.

"Stanley, I think you ought to lead a picket line," Jake said.

Stanley turned pale.

"What kind?"

"If you got arrested now before election, and got publicity, it would be a great help in our campaign. It would teach the workers of Chicago that the Party is the only one fighting for their demands, and that its standard bearers are out in the front line of the fight."

"What do the other people here think of the idea?"

"I told them. I explained the need to them, and, of course, they agreed."

Stanley waited for Jake to go on.

"Well, what do you think?"

"I just told you. If you lead, say, a rent strike in this district, and we can get publicity, it should be a dramatic example to the workers of this area."

"Yes."

"The idea, then, is to find a place where we can organize a rent strike," Jake said.

Stanley seemed absorbed in thought.

"You know this district. Where can we have a rent strike? How about your landlord?"

"He's pretty good."

"I know, but still he's a landlord. A landlord is always a landlord."

Stanley reflected that he himself was a landlord. He had lost two of his buildings in the depression already. But he still had a building. He couldn't, of course, lead a rent strike against himself. But, then, he hadn't thrown anyone out except one dirty social-fascist Socialist. He had thrown out that fellow Murkson, not because Murkson owed him four months rent; he'd thrown him out because Murkson was a social-fascist Norman-Thomasite Socialist betrayer.

"Yes, a landlord is always a landlord."

Stanley winced inwardly. He consoled himself with the assurance that he was now dedicating his life to the overthrow of the system of landlords.

"Barbara is pretty familiar with this neighborhood, and she's been canvassing. Perhaps she will know of a case," Stanley said.

"Swell. We got to organize this strike right and get a big turnout. We ought to have a mobilization and show the people being evicted that they have something to fall back on, someone on whom they can rely. Our Party."

"Yes."

"Is Barbara home now?"

"She might be."

"Well, we might try to get her and see about it now. We have to work fast."

Jake finished his coffee, and they got up from the table. Jake let Stanley pick up the checks.

XIV

Stanley paced the floor of his apartment. They had seen Barbara, and she was sure she could find a building where a good rent strike could be organized. The die was cast. He was going to cross the Rubicon. He wanted to do this, and he had to do it. It was something he wasn't afraid of doing, either. The only question in his own mind was whether or not it was advisable for him to be risked at this important juncture. If he were hospitalized by the cops because of the demonstration, or if he were put in jail for six months, why, then, yes, he would be a great martyr, but would he be as valuable to the Party? That was the question. And, of course, if he raised that question, Jake would misinterpret it. The point was that a live and free Bolshevik was more valuable to the Party than a dead or jailed or hospitalized Bolshevik.

He continued to pace the floor. He thought of his comrade, Otto Schmoll. Otto had been hit over the head by the cops in a rent strike in the Black Belt, and he had been in the hospital for three weeks with a concussion. Barbara had been in that one. Afterward, he had seen her shaking and in tears, and she had told him about Otto lying in a pool of his own blood.

But what kind of Bolshevik was he? He wasn't afraid. He would face what he would face. But it would be a serious mistake for the Party to risk him at this juncture of events, and if he could only get the Party to see it that way, get Jake to see it. Jake wasn't the kind of person you could talk to. Jake would use the most innocent thing you said for his own purpose. He would distort and twist it if it suited his purposes and his ambitions.

He paced the floor.

xv

"Stanley, I have to talk with you," Abe said, sitting down without taking off his hat and coat.

"Abe, you've come in on me just when I have to leave."

"What for?"

"That's confidential," Stanley said sharply.

"Stanley, I've been brought up before the Party on charges."

"Yes? What?"

"Charges of Goldsteinism."

"What do you mean?"

"Goldsteinism, they say, is a species of Trotskyism, and they accuse me of leading a faction, of backbiting comrades, destroying morale, wrecking Party spirit. I don't know. Stanley, you've got to stand by me. You know these charges aren't true. I've got to have worthy and loyal comrades like you defend me, stand up for me, help me to brand these charges as lies."

"I don't know anything about it."

"You know me, don't you? You've seen me working in the Party. You're my comrade."

Abe paused, a pleading expression on his face. He was waiting for Stanley to say something. Stanley said nothing but just looked at Abe impassively.

"Stanley, you can help me defend my honor, my Party honor. You know I've given everything to the Party and that I'm loyal to it."

"If you are, what are you worrying about?"

"I'll be expelled."

"What do you mean? If you are innocent, do you think the Party would commit such an injustice?"

"No. But . . ."

"But what?" Stanley asked coldly.

"But I am innocent."

"Well, what's the shooting about then?"

"I don't know. Only it's serious. I don't know what to do."

"Abe, don't set yourself against the Party."

"Stanley, I love the Party. The Party is my life."

"Then what is this little episode? You won't be expelled if you acknowledge what you did and accept Party discipline. They might put you on probation, but you can work yourself back into good standing."

"But what did I do? I tell you, I'm innocent."

"Do you think the Party would make serious charges against you if there wasn't some fire behind this smoke?"

"Are you with them?" Abe asked, glaring at Stanley.

"I'm with the Party, yes. I'm against no comrade. But I'm not a factionalist."

"What are you insinuating?"

"Abe, don't lose your head. You came to me for advice, didn't you?"

"I came to ask you to defend my honor and tell the truth, because you know the truth and can defend my honor. My enemies are using the Party to harm me, to get me expelled."

"Abe, I don't know a thing about this."

Stanley's emotions toward Abe were mixed. He was sorry for him, but he was annoyed with him. He felt a sudden contempt for Abe. Abe seemed weak, undecided, pathetic. He suddenly reflected that, whether or not Jake had done an injustice to Abe, the situation had revealed Abe as being of a weak character. Any man who seemed pathetic and made you feel sorry for him was weak. And if Abe was so weak, then maybe, yes, probably, it would be just as well if he were out of the Party. The Party tested a man's character in many ways. This was one way it was testing Abe's character.

Abe turned toward the door. Stanley wanted to say an encouraging word to him, but he didn't. And Abe walked out without saying good-by. Yes, he was sorry, but why should he stick his neck out? And even though Jake was behind it, Abe couldn't be in trouble with the Party this way if there weren't some basis for it.

Where there is smoke there is fire, Stanley reflected profoundly.

XVI

Stanley led a small group of pickets who marched in front of a gray stone building in the 5400 block on Harper Avenue. He was carrying a sign which read WE DEMAND A MORATORIUM ON RENT FOR THE UNEMPLOYED. Others marched behind him, shouting and making as much noise as they could. A small group of people watched the picket line on the sidewalk, and many people, mainly women, had their heads out of apartment windows, watching.

"We demand a moratorium on rents for the unemployed!" Stanley shouted.

"A rent moratorium for the unemployed," the other demonstrators shouted.

"Go back to Russia where you belong," a fat woman yelled from a window.

"Hands off China," one of the picketers shouted, and the others took up the cry.

The demonstrators were heterogeneous, young and old. Many of them were shabbily dressed. There were two colored men in the line. They marched back and forth in front of the building.

Stanley was nervous. The cops would be here in a moment. Then what would happen? At the same time that he was apprehensive, he felt a sense of unity, almost of losing himself in the group of his comrades who were marching with him. His fate was tied to theirs, and their fate was part of the fate of the Party, and the fate of the Party was part of the fate of the American working class.

"Hands off China!"

"Hands off China!"

The landlord, a small Jewish man, stood on the doorstep watching them, looking sadly from one to the other, his eyes moving as the line moved back and forth.

"You dirty Reds!" a woman yelled from a window.

Suddenly the landlord came forward. Stanley halted the line.

"Here, you give me my rent, and I keep my hands off China," the landlord said.

"Capitalist! Capitalist, landlord bloodsucker," someone yelled.

The landlord drew back.

"The cops! The cops! The cops!" a girl screamed.

The police wagon had come down the street and stopped. The marchers were moving in the same direction as the police auto, and when the policemen dashed out of the vehicle, clubs in hands, most of the marchers had their backs turned on them. As the demonstrators about-faced to meet the police, the first two policemen were on top of them, swinging clubs.

"Cossacks! Cossacks!"

The demonstrators ran in all directions, and the police followed them with swinging clubs. Stanley dropped his sign and ran down the street toward Fifty-third. He heard screams and footsteps behind him, but he didn't dare turn. He lost his wind and ran on out of fright. He turned the corner at Fifty-third and looked behind. Down the street the police were rounding up demonstrators. He saw several persons, male and female, stretched out with policemen bending over them.

A girl came screaming, and, with her, a comrade whose head was bleeding.

They hurried along Fifty-third Street, and pedestrians gazed at them.

XVII

"We have to make it a ringing denunciation. They'll put it on the front page of *The Fist*," Jake said.

"I denounce the Cossack cops of Chicago who battered down the workers defending their elementary rights," Stanley said, and paused a moment. "How's that for an opening sentence for my statement?"

"All right. Now, let's see. You ought to get in the landlords."

"Defending the bloodsucking landlords, the cops of Chicago acted like Cossacks. Wielding their clubs without mercy, they broke up a peaceful demonstration of workers who were defending an unemployed class brother from eviction," Stanley went on.

"That's good. Now I'll add the rest. Vote Communist in order to defend workers' rights and in order to defeat the bloody, hireling cops and the bosses who employ them to beat workers without mercy. Vote Communist to end police brutality in Chicago. . . . I'll go back to my room now and do the piece," Jake said.

He picked up his hat and coat and left.

XVIII

"Stan, how about getting some gin?" Al said when Stanley led him and Garfield into the apartment.

"Gee, Al, I'm sorry, but I don't feel like drinking," Stanley said.

Stanley shook his head. They sat down.

"Stanley, were you hurt in the riot?" asked Garfield.

"The cops rioted," Stanley said.

"All the more reason to have a drink. You must have had your nerves shattered yesterday," Al said.

Stanley thought these fellows were just Bohemian bums. Could they be regenerated by the Party? The Party regenerated worse than they, and it would one day regenerate the entire human race. If the Party could regenerate the entire human race, it ought to be able to regenerate Al and Garfield.

"We ought to do something to train our people," Garfield said.

"Our people. You're not a Party member," Al said.

"Neither are you, Al," Garfield replied.

"We ought to train our people to fight and to know the streets. Now, if the revolution comes, what about fighting out there in Cable Court?" Garfield said.

"The fighting won't be in a little half block," Stanley said.

Garfield thought for a moment.

"No, I guess it won't," he finally said.

"Well, fellows, I have work to do," Stanley said.

"Stan, can you let us take something for a bottle of gin?" Al asked.

"I'm sorry, fellows. I haven't got a cent."

"Well, we got to find someone else then."

"Don't forget to come to the protest meeting tomorrow night," Stanley said.

"We'll be there," Al said.

Garfield and he left.

The International Soviet shall be the human race.

The words of *The Internationale* kept running through Stanley's head. He thought of these words, and of Garfield and Al. Somehow they would never get serious about the Party. Perhaps if he got them to join, then the duties and discipline would regenerate them.

XIX

Comrade Mark Singer, usually called the American Gorky, was the guest of honor at the little gathering at Stanley's after the protest meeting. He was a tall man in his late thirties. He dressed like a worker, and had a charming and pleasant smile. His manner was shy. The comrades all sat grouped around him, with Stanley on his right.

"Gee, it feels good to get away from New York and to come out here among real people," Mark said.

Stanley was tempted to say something, but kept silent. He

thought that perhaps later, alone, he might be able to talk with Mark and sound him out about Jake.

"Well, there's no wasting time with us out here, Comrade Singer. We work hard for the Party," Stanley said.

"Hell, call me Mark. I can't stand these bourgeois formalities," Mark said.

"Isn't he simple for such a great writer?" Barbara whispered to Al.

Al said nothing. He got up and made himself a drink.

"Comrade Singer, what do you think of Sinclair Lewis?" a student from the University asked; she was a thin, ugly girl with bobbed hair.

"A bourgeois defeatist," Mark said.

"So do I. My professor in English talks of him as if he were the greatest living writer."

"What can you expect from bourgeois academicians?" Mark replied.

"That's what I feel like telling him."

Mark Singer seemed to become suddenly shy and embarrassed. He looked around the room, and then his eyes modestly fell to the floor.

"Aw, hell, I don't want to talk about literature. I'm tired of New York intellectuals with all their bourgeois abstractions. Out here you meet real people," he said, still seeming shy and modest.

Stanley grinned.

"We'll try to have you meet real people here, Mark," he said.

Barbara brought Mark a drink.

"We need good proletarian writers, writers who write of the blood and sweat of the workers," Mark said.

"How long are you going to be here, Comrade Singer?" a young fellow named Myers asked.

"Oh, hell, don't call me anything but Mark. I'm a proletarian writer," Mark said.

"That's what I have always felt. Of course, me, I'm an activist and not a writer," Stanley said.

"The party organizers, and the leaders like you—you write

your books with deeds. That's more important. What's important about the books we writers write compared with the deeds you write here in Chicago, in Kokomo, Carmody, in steel, in mines, in factories and sweatshops?" Mark said.

"It's such an inspiration to hear you talk like that, Comrade Sing. . . . Mark," Barbara said.

"Oh, come on, let's all have another drink," Al said.

Barbara took Mark's glass and mixed him another drink.

They raised their glasses and drank to Comrade Singer.

XX

"Jake Jackson, you know, has been here. He's leaving in the morning," Stanley said.

"That guy started writing a short story ten years ago. He's a four-flusher," Mark said.

"I thought he was in with the comrades on the Ninth Floor," Stanley said.

"I know it. You know, Stanley, politics is politics. And in politics for the Party, everyone has his uses, even the petit-bourgeois intellectual," Mark said.

Stanley listened, deciding he would be cautious.

"Yes, even Jake Jackson has his uses for the Party. And he is better as a Party member than he was before he joined the Party. Jake is a sonofabitch, but he's our sonofabitch," Mark said.

"You know, I feel that way. Take that fellow Al who got drunk here tonight. Well, now, if he hadn't come close to the Party, he'd be worse. If we get him to join the Party, perhaps we'll regenerate him," Stanley said.

"Yes, drunkenness is a petit-bourgeois vice. It's because a young fellow doesn't see a way out that he drinks. If we can teach a fellow like Al that the Party points the way out, he'll give up his booze," Mark said.

Stanley thought Mark Singer had very keen insight. It was a pleasure to talk to him, let alone be his host.

But then, Mark Singer was America's greatest proletarian writer. Having Mark here was almost like having Gorky in your home.

"Are you working on a new book?" Stanley asked.

"I'm going to. I'm going to write a novel about a proletarian, a sign painter. Say, have you got any sign painters in the Party here? I'd like to talk to one," Mark said.

"Let's see," Stanley replied. He pondered. "I don't know if we have or not. But I'll ask the comrades."

"Do," Mark said.

Mark began to yawn.

"You had a hard day. You better get yourself some sleep," Stanley said.

XXI

Charlotte came around at night.

"I've been trying to see you all day," she said to Stanley.

"I was out. I just got in. Mark Singer, my comrade, is staying with me, and I expect him in in a minute," Stanley said, hoping she'd be impressed by the name of this guest.

She seemed absorbed, worried.

"Has Jake been here?" she asked anxiously.

"He went back to New York this morning," Stanley said.

"He couldn't! He didn't! He couldn't do that to me," she said.

Stanley didn't say anything. He waited for her to speak.

"He couldn't have gone back without telling me."

Stanley still waited for her to say more.

"Where is he? He left his hotel. Where did he go?"

"Honest, Charlotte, he went to New York."

"What'll I do?"

"What's the matter?"

"Oh!" she exclaimed, suddenly stopping, and then she began to cry.

Stanley was tempted to put his arms around her and comfort

her. He didn't move. It really served her right. But he did feel sorry for her.

"Why did Jake do that to me?"

"What's the matter? Tell me, Charlotte. Perhaps I can help."

"I'm going to have a baby."

Stanley cautioned himself to be careful. Here was something he didn't want to get involved in. How old was she? He wasn't sure. She might be only seventeen. If she were, that was dangerous.

"Stanley, what'll I do?"

Stanley thought for a moment, his face grave.

"What can I do? I can't have a baby. I'll be disgraced."

Stanley again cautioned himself to be careful. He better not suggest anything. She might say he suggested it. And, anyway, he didn't know any doctors to whom to send her.

"I'll be expelled from school. I'll be disgraced. What'll my father say?"

"Are you sure about it?" Stanley asked.

She cried. Stanley wanted to comfort her; he didn't know what to do. He was hesitant about taking her in his arms to try to comfort her. He waited and did nothing.

She looked at him, her face pale.

"What kind of a Party is it? You talk about the workers and all the good you're going to do, and so does Jake, and he does this to me," she said.

"But, Charlotte—" Stanley began.

"Where's Jake?" she interrupted.

"I tell you I don't know. He left town this morning."

"What's his address? Give me his address."

"I haven't got it."

Stanley suddenly wondered—would she make all this public —wouldn't it be terrible to drag the name of the Party through the gutter press? She would have to be prevented from doing anything like that.

"Charlotte, what do you intend to do?"

She looked at him, blank-faced, helpless.

And suppose his name were dragged in? Jake met her at his apartment. Well, it wasn't his fault.

"Charlotte, this would be no tragedy for you if we had a decent form of society. If America were as civilized as the Soviet Union, why, this would be no problem."

"Where's Jake?"

"I don't know."

She suddenly put on her coat.

"Good-by," she said.

Stanley walked to the door with her.

"Brace up and be a brave girl," Stanley said.

"Yes!" she said absently.

Stanley squeezed her arm at the elbow. She walked off, and he closed the door.

XXII

"I have the report on the votes," Stanley said.

"How many did you get, Stanley?" Barbara asked.

"Forty."

"The robbers."

"That's capitalist politics for you. I know more than forty votes were cast for me."

"What'll we do? Let's have a demonstration," she said.

"I have to see what the Party decides. I already gave a statement for *The Fist* charging capitalist robbery."

"The Wall Street bandits," Barbara said.

"I made a good showing. And, of course, it's juridical cretinism to expect anything from the ballot," Stanley added.

He didn't say anything for a moment.

"Barbara, is there any news of Charlotte?"

"Oh, yes, she got fixed up. She'll be all right."

"I'm glad."

Stanley seemed reflective.

"Stanley, you weren't at the meeting when Abe was brought up on charges."

"I know it. I couldn't come. I gave an affidavit on his wrecking and factional activity," Stanley said.

"He was broken up. But, then, he should be—a renegade."

"He didn't defend himself well, did he?"

"How could he, the traitor."

"Barbara, the Party always tests your character, and if you're found wanting there's no place in the Party for you. The trouble with Abe was that he wanted to be a general instead of a humble worker in the ranks. That's what you have to expect from a petit-bourgeois college student," Stanley said.

"You took the words right out of my mouth," Barbara said.

"Say, I recruited Al for the Party. You know, the Party will regenerate him," Stanley said.

"Swell work," Barbara said.

"We're gaining. That's why they stole votes on me. They are afraid of us. We have a new president now, Barbara. Let me tell you, before Roosevelt, the agent of Wall Street, is finished with his first term, we'll be on the march," Stanley said.

"And our comrades will be on the march in Germany, Stanley, just think of it—the Revolution can happen in Germany now any day."

"Yes, after Hitler has his turn, ours will come. And Hitler's not going to last if the social-fascist Social-Democrats do put him in as Chancellor," Stanley said.

Barbara's face was shining.

"Oh, Stanley, we're really living history," she exclaimed in exaltation.

Barbara left. Stanley picked up Volume One of *Capital*. He read for a few minutes and then set the book down. He walked up and down the room in a reflective mood. Idly, he glanced at the manuscript of his unpublished novel. It might not be an important work of literature. And yet he remembered when he had written it out at the sand dunes. Finishing, he had had such an extraordinary sense of freedom. He missed this feeling. And yet, did he? He was not sure of his own emotions.

He paced the floor nervously, trying to think. Thoughts evaded him. He sat down again to work on his speech. He worked for a few moments and then put his papers away. He turned out the lights, lit his candles, and sat there in a dark corner. He was lonely.

Episode in a Dentist's Office

THE TWO YOUNG NUNS entered the anteroom of the dentist's office, sat down side by side, and waited. One was very beautiful; her cheeks were fresh and rosy, her skin was very fair, and her eyes blue and sparkling. The other nun was very plain, with a pointed nose and a sallow complexion. They did not speak.

The little girl went close to them. She was an attractive little child of about four or five. Her hair was blonde and curly, and she had an impishly charming face. She wore short socks and a blue dress with a light sweater over it.

"Hello," the plain nun said, a repressed smile on her face.

"I'm waiting for my mommy. She's in there," the girl said.

The plain nun stroked her hair. The beautiful nun smiled warmly.

"Are you ladies?" the little girl asked.

Both nuns smiled, through tense lips.

"Why do you dress so funny?" the girl asked.

"We don't dress funny," the plain nun said in a low and energetic tone of voice. It seemed that she was saying something she didn't want to say, and that she was holding back each syllable a moment before letting it escape from her throat.

"Yes, you are. You don't dress like me."

"What's your name?" the plain nun asked in an evasive manner and obviously with the intent of changing the subject of the conversation with the child.

"I have no name," the child said.

"But you must have a name," the beautiful nun said.

"I have no name. My mommy has no name. I have no name. Only my daddy has a name. What's your name?"

"You must have a name," the plain nun said.

"I have no name. My mommy has no name. I have no name. I have a daddy. My daddy has a name. Only my daddy has a name."

"What's your daddy's name?" the plain nun asked.

"I have no name. My daddy's name is Thomas."

"Thomas what?" asked the beautiful nun.

"Thomas Rucker. My daddy's name is Thomas Rucker. What's your daddy's name?"

"The same," the plain nun said in a restrained voice.

"What's your daddy's name?" the girl asked.

"Thomas Rucker," the plain nun answered.

"No, it isn't. That's my daddy's name. What's your daddy's name?"

"Thomas Rucker."

"What's your daddy's name?" the girl asked, this time more insistently.

"Thomas Rucker," the plain nun said, repressing a smile and speaking with a restraint which vaguely suggested an inner tension.

"What's your daddy's name?" the child asked the beautiful nun.

"The same."

"No, it isn't. Why do you wear that?" the girl asked, pointing to the starched white headpiece.

"We wear it," the plain nun said after a moment of hesitation.

"It's funny. Don't you have any hair?"

"Yes, we have hair."

"Where is it? I don't see your hair. See my hair," the girl said, pointing to her own hair.

Neither of the nuns spoke, and the plain one was visibly embarrassed.

The child moved off, turned around and faced the nuns again, and then came a little closer to them.

"Why do you wear black?" she asked.

"It's our dress."

"It's a funny dress. Why don't you dress like my mommy?"

"We dress this way."

"Why?"

"Because we dress this way."

"Why?"

"We do."

"Don't you take that black off?"

"Yes, we do."

"When?"

The nuns didn't answer. The plain one looked away from the girl.

"Is that cloth?" she asked, pointing at the headpiece.

"Yes," the nun said, embarrassed. The beautiful nun blushed.

"I don't like your clothes," the child said.

"Why?"

"I like my clothes. My clothes aren't black. See my dress. Why do you dress like that? I never saw anybody dress like you."

"Oh, you must have," the plain nun said.

"No, I never saw anybody dress like you. I never saw anyone. Why?"

"Because you didn't see them."

"Why?"

The plain nun didn't answer. The little girl turned to the beautiful nun and said:

"Why don't you talk more?"

"I talk," the nun said, her rosy cheeks still flushed.

"I don't hear you."

"I talk."

"Why?"

"How old are you?" the plain nun asked.

"How old are you?"

"I asked you first," the plain nun said.

"How old are you?" the child again asked.

"I don't know."

"Do you like the clothes you wear?"

"Oh, yes," the plain nun said.

"Do you?" the little girl asked the beautiful nun.

"Yes."

"I don't."

"Why?" asked the beautiful nun.

"I can't see your legs. Do you have legs?"

"Yes, of course," the plain nun said, again embarrassed.

"Where are your legs?" the girl asked.

The nuns didn't answer.

"Do you wear pants?"

The plain nun nodded, but didn't answer.

"Look," the little girl said, lifting her dress. "See my pants? I wear pants. I can't see your pants."

The nun gently put down the girl's dress.

"Don't do that. I want to show you my pants. Where are your pants?"

"We have them."

"I want to see them."

The nuns didn't answer.

"Can't you take that black off? I don't think you have pants. I have pants."

The girl lifted up her dress again.

"There, see, I have pants."

"Do you go to school?" the plain nun asked.

"Where are your pants?"

The beautiful nun smiled.

"What's your name?" the plain nun asked.

"I have no name. Why do you wear that? I can't see your pants," the little girl said.

The nuns looked off in different directions. Then the girl's mother came out. The girl said:

"Mommy, I don't see their pants."

"Shhh," the mother said, embarrassed, as she took the girl's hand.

The nuns smiled weakly. The girl and her mother left the office, and the girl was heard saying:

"I told the funny women that I have no name, Mommy."

The plain-faced nun went into the dentist's office. The beautiful one sat alone. She was visibly agitated, and nervously fingered her beads. When the plain nun had been treated, they left.

The two nuns walked along Fifth Avenue. It was crowded. The spring day was balmy. The beautiful nun looked at the people passing, and then down at the sidewalk. She was visibly agitated. The nuns didn't speak. The beautiful nun bit her lip, blushed, and looked at the well-dressed, chic women moving past her on Fifth Avenue.

Quest

ARTHUR, vice-president of a small but enterprising book-publishing firm, began to lose his hair at thirty-five. This was disturbing to him. Every morning he would look at himself in the mirror, hoping against hope that he would see no further signs of thinning hair. He had himself treated to a variety of oils, massages, and tonics by various barbers. These efforts were of no avail. He went to several doctors, also, but he got no help from them. He gorged on vitamin tablets, took quack medicines, tried a sundry assortment of hair oils and hair tonics advertised in newspapers and magazines, but all of this produced no results. He was losing his hair and began to grow very anxious.

Arthur had gone into the publishing business shortly after he had quit college in his senior year. His father, an oil man from California, did not know what to do with him and, above all, did not want him to go into the oil business. He considered Arthur the most stupid of his seven children and finally decided that he might as well become a book publisher. Arthur's main value to his firm was the money he brought it at a moment when the firm was on the brink of bankruptcy. Arthur considered the publishing business great fun. It gave him prestige. His name often appeared in the gossip columns and other sections of the newspapers. He went to many parties and met a number of seductive women. He married a girl with ravishing looks. She wrote graceful minor verse and was also the author of two novels, one a romantic tale of love on the

271

island of Capri and the other an equally romantic story of Italy and the Blessed Virgin Mary. Her name was Marie. Pretending to an esthetic interest in Catholicism, she was, in her personal life, pagan and sensuous. Many men envied Arthur because of his wife. Time had passed swiftly and pleasantly for Arthur. Now, at thirty-five, his thinning hair became an ominous warning.

It led to a whole series of seemingly minor changes in his life. He developed the habit of reading the obituary notices in the morning newspapers even before he turned to the book review or to the theatrical and motion picture page. He continually speculated as to how much space he would receive in his own obituary notice. He wondered what would be said of him and again and again, in fantasies, he wrote his own obituary. He began to look at men differently, to observe their hair and note whether or not they were growing bald or getting gray. He gazed at their faces like a conspirator in order to observe signs of aging, wrinkles and changes around the eyes. He looked at their abdomens, eager to see signs of paunches. He found comfort in the presence of older men, because he could feel much younger in their presence. But even while he gained comfort and security with older men, he was frightened. He would speculate as to how they were meeting the passage of the years. Were they unhappy? Sad? Disturbed? Frightened? And then he began to have stomach troubles and feared he had ulcers. Every morning he examined his stool for blood. Whenever he suffered from indigestion, he was stricken with terror. He became an insomniac and began taking sleeping pills. These made him drowsy in the daytime. Every day around five he would be heavy-lidded. In such a sluggish state, his expected evening of pleasure seemed burdensome. He lived for his pleasures, for parties, dates, first nights, evenings at night clubs. But, half-awake, he often did not know how he could get through his evenings. Heretofore, he had drunk moderately. Now, he began to drink heavily.

His symptoms multiplied, and his states of anxiety became more regular and more anguishing. He began to regard himself as an unhappily married man. His marriage seemed dull, excruciatingly dull. He was bored with Marie and convinced himself that she didn't understand him. And she, noticing these changes, was also growing disillusioned and cold to him. At the same time that Arthur was changing, she was becoming paralyzed at her desk. She had not written a novel for five years and feared that unless she wrote another one soon her name would be forgotten. She tried in vain to write. Angry with herself, she blamed Arthur. They quarreled with increasing frequency.

Arthur, in turn, became more resentful of his wife. His hostility to her became ever more pronounced. He feared that she was contemptuous of him because of his thinning hair and also because he did not exhibit as much sexual energy as he had when they were first married. Often he simulated desire merely because he feared that, unless he did so, she would think he was not a real man. He was suspicious of her. He was constantly on guard in order to protect himself from exposing his worries and anxieties to her. He sought to find evidence that she no longer loved him and then was sorry and condemned himself. He eyed her carefully and strangely in order to see if she were getting fat, or if signs of age were beginning to show in her face. He could no longer decide whether or not her body was beautiful. He often wondered what she would do after his death. Sometimes he imagined that she had died. He would then grow very disturbed. Neither of them had wanted children, and he secretly blamed her for their childlessness, although he was as opposed as she to the idea of having a child.

At his office, he became indecisive. He could not make up his mind, even about the smallest matters of detail. When he had read a manuscript submitted for publication, he could not make up his mind, and at editorial conferences he wasted everyone's time hemming and hawing in a way that meant neither yes he wanted the manuscript published nor no he didn't. He hesitated about making dates, delayed answering letters, lost reports, and held up the publication of books by his delays.

Although he did little work and took on few responsibilities, he convinced himself that he was overworked. He took a long vacation. When he returned, his hair was a little thinner, and he fell into the same routine of indecision, worry, delay, and evasiveness.

Finally he went to a psychiatrist, and after several visits the psychiatrist indicated that extramarital affairs might help him. On a few occasions Arthur spent passing and half-drunken nights with women, but when this had happened he was always ashamed of himself and fearful that Marie would find out. As a result he hated these women. He welcomed the idea of extramarital affairs as a means of salvation. But then he became afraid. He didn't want to tell Marie. He became non-communicative, and their domestic situation worsened. Marie was suspicious, fearing he was telling the psychiatrist about the intimacies of their relationship, and she became very sarcastic.

Then he broke two successive engagements with the psychiatrist. And he got drunker than he had ever been before. He feared he was going mad, and returned to the psychiatrist and told him he was fearful of telling his wife. The psychiatrist said he must tell her. So, after building up his courage all the way home in a cab, he burst in on her and told her the advice he had been given.

"I never heard of such a fool," she said.

They had a bitter quarrel during which Arthur defended the psychiatrist, and Marie described him as a fraud. He guessed that she loved him and he was upset. During the argument, he kept telling her,

"Marie, my health is at stake."

"If you want to, I won't and I can't stop you. But don't think that I'll want you if you go whoring all over New York."

He was in a quandary. Finally he brought Marie to see the psychiatrist, and, after a private talk with him, she assented to an arrangement whereby Arthur was free to have affairs.

Arthur went philandering, on what he accepted as medical instruction and the approval of his wife. He believed he was doing it as a duty to himself, as a means of preserving his mental health. But he didn't know what to do about managing affairs and several evenings, when he went out alone, he felt lost.

Marie never discussed his philanderings with him. She acted restrained and assumed something of the air of a martyr. She seemed to prefer not to mention the subject. Arthur went to his psychiatrist regularly and in time he found various girls with whom he had passing one-night relationships. Whenever he became nervous or disturbed, he thought of another girl. Marie was easily able to guess when he had been with a woman and when he hadn't. He was always beaming the morning after such an affair. She tried to sink herself in work but was more paralyzed than ever.

Then she decided to go to a psychiatrist herself. She found a German refugee who was highly recommended and had treated three of her friends with no tangible results. She quickly became attracted to him, and after several interviews she gathered from remarks of his that no sexual experience was completely satisfying unless, at the moment of fulfillment, one swooned into unconsciousness. She went home to her husband's arms and frantically tried to lose her consciousness. She failed. Nor did he become unconscious during these intimacies.

She now believed she had never had a satisfactory sexual experience in her entire life. She considered herself to be frustrated. That explained why she couldn't write. And Arthur was frustrated. She had a frank talk with him.

"Arthur, with any of the girls you've had—have you become unconscious?" she asked him in a strained and embarrassed tone of voice.

He hadn't. He wasn't sure she was right and planned to bring it up in his next interview with his own psychiatrist. But that very night the doctor was knocked unconscious by an automobile and died. Arthur felt lost. With his psychiatrist dead, he feared he would lose his sanity. Marie brought him to her doctor. After they had got together, Marie's doctor, who charged higher fees than had Arthur's, helped them to work out a schedule. On certain nights Arthur was to have the home for women, and on others, Marie, for men.

They worked on this schedule for several months, each of them seeking a succession of lovers who would help them to pass out. After each experience they would have breakfast the next morning and discuss the details. They enjoyed these discussions as much as they had the experiences and, whenever they had lovers, they always thought of each other and of how they would describe the affair over coffee, ham, and eggs the next morning.

But Marie was still unable to write. And Arthur's hair did not come back to him.

At the end of a year, they were divorced.

They agreed amicably on the divorce, and it was decided that Marie should go to Reno. But then they consulted the lawyers and a series of difficulties arose concerning the division of their personal property. Arthur wanted the bedroom set, and Marie wanted the living-room furniture. Arthur did not want to give her as much money as she suddenly demanded. When they discussed their library, which contained many books neither had ever read, their antagonism became really exacerbated. They had been living apart and had closed up their home pending the property settlement. They met one evening to settle who was to get what books.

"You never read a lot, Marie. Why not be sensible and not make such a fuss about the books?" Arthur urged.

"I like that. You didn't read—you merely published books on oil money."

"Is that so? If I couldn't read, would my firm be as successful as it is?"

"Because of your father's money."

"That's a fine statement to make after all these years," he said.

"Well, then, give me Proust."

"But I really think you ought to let me have Proust."

Thus the argument began, and from Proust it went to other matters. And they exhibited the bitterness they both felt. Each of them had passed from one bed to another. They were saturated with ennui. Marie had sought out males of all colors,

Negroes, Chinese, Italians, and even one Mohammedan, and still she had not been able to pass out in bed. Arthur had become a joke in the circles in which he traveled. His passes at girls, his efforts to seduce his telephone operator, his secretary, the bookkeeper, his flirtations with cigarette girls and hat-check girls in night clubs, all this had set going a whole stream of anecdotes.

They were both very unhappy. Neither could bear to be alone. When Marie was alone, she was in agony, and she smoked, drank, paced the floor, and became highly irritable. Night after night she went out, and she took benzedrine in order to keep awake, and then, when she came home, she took sedatives to put herself to sleep. Arthur was always jittery, always nervous, and his partners were discussing plans as to how they might tactfully eliminate him from the firm.

Now, they poured out on one another all of their bitterness, all of the saddening and terrifying unconscious shame which they felt. They raved and shouted.

"I was a goddamned fool to marry you," she screamed at him.

"You don't assume that I was a mountain of intelligence when I married a tramp like you?"

"So, I'm a tramp now?"

"I've heard stories about you. You've been chasing everything in pants all over town. Why don't you fornicate in Times Square with some newspaper photographers around?" he said with a sneer.

"What about you?"

"Have you had a lay that put you out yet?"

"You've got a filthy mind. You're a neurotic, and you always were, and you've almost put me in a madhouse."

"I wasted the best years of my manhood on you."

On and on, they talked and ranted. They said the most cruel and personal things about each other. Marie sobbed, and Arthur looked at her unmoved. Then she told him how bald he was getting. He retaliated by talking of her weight and her age, and remarking on how she had to wear a corset, wasted time in beauty parlors, and was fighting a ridiculous fight with old age. He told her she would one day be old and gray and wrinkled. And then he added:

"If you live that long."

"You'd be glad if I were dead."

"I don't wish you bad luck. I just hate you."

"And I detest you, you cad."

Finally they had said and repeated all they could say to each other, and they sat exhausted. His tie was loose, and he looked weary. Her hair was uncombed, and her nose was shiny. They looked like two tired people, approaching middle age. Around them were all the things they had accumulated, a large, unread, and expensive library, chromium lamps, modernistic furniture, an unplayed Baby Grand piano, pictures by Georgia O'Keefe for which they had paid heavily, an expensive radio, and shelves full of the kind of expensive and glittering junk that one picks up on tourist trips to Europe and Mexico. He was close to forty, and she was thirty-six. They said nothing now; they could no longer look each other in the eye.

Arthur thought of how he had once loved this woman, of how he had been so happy when they had first married. He remembered rather vaguely how they had been so inseparable, how they had held hands in corners like school children, remembered how shyly she had first given herself to him, how she had dressed and perfumed herself for him, waited in an agony of trembling excitement each day for him to come home from the office, and then flung herself wildly and ecstatically into his arms.

All this was past. Their memories were sour, curdled. They sat there for a short period amid their junk, their furniture, their meaningless and expensive collection of things, the distribution of which had led to the onset of these bitter recriminations. And these few minutes in which they sat silent, no longer daring to look each other in the eye, these minutes seemed to be very long.

"Well, you can see my lawyer," he said, rising wearily.

"I never want to see you as long as I live," she said.

He shrugged his shoulders and left the room, adjusting his tie. She ran to a mirror and looked at herself. She burst into tears. She could not believe that the face she saw was her own. It was puffed. Her eyes were swollen. There were circles under them. Her nose was shiny, and it seemed too long. She felt she was looking at a stranger. She turned away.

He returned, ready to leave.

"Take any goddamn thing you want. You need it. You can have it to comfort yourself in your old age," he said.

He walked out of the room. He slammed the front door.

Exhausted Marie sat down on a love seat. Again she looked around, remembering her life here. Then, in an agony of anger, she went through the house, breaking furniture, tearing books and throwing them on the floor, overturning furniture. As a final act, she smashed the set of Wedgwood which her mother, now dead, had given her as a wedding present. Then she powdered her face and left. In Washington Square she got a cab and had it take her quickly to a dinner engagement for which she was late. Riding up Fifth Avenue, she looked out at people passing on the street. Did they feel as she did? Did they surge with such bitterness? Were their lives ruined?

At the dinner, she got drunk and threw everyone into stitches telling them of her scene with Arthur.

In the meantime, Arthur had gone to his hotel, then to dinner, and then to a theater. Afterward he went to a night club and sat there with some newly found friends, sipping drinks until it closed. He went back to his hotel, feeling dreary.

Arthur and Marie did not see each other for five years. And then one day they passed each other in front of Saint Patrick's Cathedral. He was fat and bald now and he waddled along. She was overdressed and looked dissipated. She, too, had taken on weight, and her cheeks were puffy. There were rings under her eyes. They looked at each other, said hello, and passed on. Shortly after, he died of pneumonia. Marie, his divorced wife, went to court and gained control of the body, arranged the funeral, and got her picture into the papers. It was a big funeral. Many figures in the book world turned out for it. When Arthur's will was read, it was learned he had left his money to Marie. The will spoke for him beyond the grave, confessing his shame and humbly asking her forgiveness. Marie squandered most of the money in one, last, wild dipsomaniacal fling before middle age crushed her with corpulence and ultimately destroyed her looks. Night after night she was to be seen in taverns and night clubs, drunk. After one such night, she was knocked down by an automobile and killed. Her body lay in the morgue for three days before it was identified. She died without heirs, and what remained of the money she had inherited from Arthur went to the state.

Boyhood

I

STEPPING ON THE CRACKS IN THE SIDEWALK, Jim English asked Danny O'Neill when there was going to be a party. Danny, busy thinking his own thoughts and also stepping on sidewalk cracks, didn't hear Jim. He liked Jim, but felt sorry for him. Jim was poor, and everybody in the seventh-grade class thought he was goofy. Danny was sometimes treated badly by the other kids, but Jim was in a worse pickle then he. His father had run away and left him and his mother alone, and she did housework. The other kids all looked down on Jim, and Jim wasn't bright in classes. Sometimes, all you had to do to get a laugh was to use Jim's words. But Danny really liked him and felt sorry for him.

They walked along Indiana Avenue. Danny booted a tin can off the sidewalk into the withered, unkempt grass. Jim gave it a kick. They went out into the street and had a contest to see who could kick the can the farthest. Danny won. He was pleased. But then, it was easy to kick a tin can farther than poor Jim, just as it was easy to be less of a goof than Jim.

Danny kept kicking the tin can. He adjusted his gold-rimmed glasses.

Jim interrupted their silence by asking when there was going to be another party.

"I don't know. I don't *like* parties," Danny answered casually between swipes at the tin can.

"Why? You go to them, don't you?"

"Sometimes," Danny said noncommittally.

Jim looked at him, skeptical. "I don't believe you," he said, shaking his head sidewise.

"I'm not kiddin'. I really don't."

Jim laughed with friendly doubt.

"I don't believe it," he repeated, laughing a second time.

"I don't care if you do or if you don't. I know if I care a whole lot for parties or if I don't."

"No, but I think you're foolin'. I really think you're foolin' me. What about all those parties you used to give?"

"There wasn't so many of them. Once in a while I like a party. Once in a while. And anyway I only gave one."

"I think you're kiddin' me."

"I'm not kiddin' you, English. I only care about parties once in a while. I don't care so much about parties. I only like them now and then."

Danny started stepping on cracks again. He took three steps to a square, but it was difficult. Jim was silent at his side. Danny kept watching how vacant Jim's face was, and he missed several cracks. "Goofy," he muttered to himself.

Jim asked Danny if he didn't honestly know when there was going to be another party.

"Don't know."

Jim seemed hurt.

"You're not gonna get sore because I didn't believe you, are ya?" Jim said conciliatingly.

"Oh, no."

Danny lost interest in stepping on squares. He began touching the railings that enclosed the plots of dried grass in front of the buildings.

"Say, Roslyn Hayes is sort of a nice girl, isn't she?" Jim casually remarked.

"Hm . . . Yes."

Danny caught Jim suddenly dropping his face in confusion.

"Well, there ain't no more baseball games until the war's over," Jim said hurriedly.

"No, there ain't," Danny said, smiling to himself.

"Maybe not for years."

"But, Jim, what makes you so interested in Roslyn Hayes?" Danny asked, thrilled to mention her name, happy to be able to talk about her without giving away how much he loved her.

"I ain't. I just wondered about her. Do you think I'm interested?"

"I dunno. You asked me a lot of questions, and I wondered."

"I'm not. I'm not interested in girls."

"I just sort of wondered," Danny said.

"Rube Waddell's one of my favorite ball players of all times," Danny said.

"I never heard of him."

"Ain't you never heard of Rube Waddell? Honest?"

"No, who was he?"

"Rube Waddell was the world's greatest southpaw, except maybe for Eddie Plank."

"Who did he pitch for, Danny?"

"Philadelphia, the Browns, Minneapolis in the American Association. And I think he pitched in the National League before 1900, but he jumped when they started the American League."

"Why's he your favorite?" Jim asked.

"He's dead," Danny answered.

"Is that why he's your favorite?"

"No. He did anything he felt like doing. That's the way he was."

"Is he really dead?"

"Yes, Jim. I guess he drank himself to death."

"Was he really good?"

"He still holds the strike-out record in the American League."

"Honest?"

"Yeah. Haven't you ever heard about some of the things he used to do?"

"No. What?"

"Go off in the middle of the season without telling Connie Mack. He might even be pitching, and walk off in the fifth or sixth inning, and then maybe some scout or newspaperman would find him a week later, fishing by a country stream, or even pitching for some scrub team in a hick burg. When he

was feeling right, he would sometimes walk three men, and
then call the side in to sit around the pitching box while he
whiffed the next three batters. He could almost make a baseball
talk."

Jim didn't know whether or not he should believe Danny.

"Honestly, did they have a pitcher like that?"

"Yes."

Jim gaped, dubious.

"They're always remembering things like that about Rube
and writing them up."

Jim was still doubtful, wondering.

"Did you ever see a big-league game?" Danny asked.

Jim looked away, ashamed. Danny saw the queer, sad look
in Jim's eyes. He liked Jim. He wished he could make him
become something else besides the class goof.

"I seen enough," Jim said.

They came to Jim's home. It was a disheveled, unpainted,
slatternly wooden affair between Fifty-eighth and Fifty-ninth
on Indiana Avenue. They stood in front of it and didn't say
anything for a while.

"Listen, do you want to wait and go to the store with me?
It won't take me long, and then we can take a walk," Jim asked.

"No, I gotta hurry."

Jim looked disappointed.

"So long."

"So long."

Danny wandered on.

"Listen, Dan. . . ." Jim called after him.

"Yeah," unenthusiastically.

"Wanna go to a show on Hallowe'en night?"

"No, I can't get out."

Jim looked more disappointed.

II

Danny walked along. Jim didn't even know about Rube Waddell. Nobody liked Jim. He was too big a goof, and he was a string bean. He was sissified and threw a baseball and batted like a girl. He would get killed in a football game. But he felt sorry for Jim. He got a funny kind of feeling being sorry for Jim, as if it were his fault Jim was like he was.

Danny picked up a broken twig and swished it as he walked along. He remembered Jim's questions about Roslyn. Jim would like to go to the parties the kids had, and he would like to have Roslyn for his girl. He was an awful pest with his questions about Roslyn. Jim liked Roslyn. That was funny. A goof like Jim liking a girl like Roslyn. Danny had to laugh. He swished the twig and laughed again. Jim would give a whole lot to know the truth, to know that Roslyn liked Danny O'Neill. She did like him. She liked him, even if she did snub him sometimes. Glenn had said that she liked him.

Danny was very sorry about Jim. He knew that Jim was poor, and he felt sorry he had asked Jim how many big-league games he had ever seen. Yes, he felt sorry for Jim, but, then, Jim was an awful pest and was always asking the goofiest questions and expressing the battiest opinions. He was always saying crazy things about baseball and girls and everything. And he got poor marks in school. What could be battier than to want to go to a show on Hallowe'en?

Danny kept on walking, swishing the piece of dead branch.

III

There was going to be a Hallowe'en surprise party for Billy Morris. Billy was out with the kids—Danny, Dick Buckford, Ralph Borax, Glenn, Tommy O'Connor, Walter Regan, and Andy Houlihan. They had brought Fat Mulloy along, so he could be used as a pretext for running away and going up to

Billy's. They told Billy they'd ditch Fat and hide up at his house and have his mother make some hot chocolate, like she did on Hallowe'en last year. Then they said they would go out again and raise some more Cain.

They were straggling along a street. Danny felt creepy. He imagined he saw strange, funny things, witches the size of the Teenie Weenies in the Sunday *Clarion*, riding around the air on toothpick brooms, monstrous owls with fierce satanic eyes gleaming out of mysterious skies, demons from Hell dancing about fires like Indians on the warpath.

"You're a little goofy, aren't you, O'Neill?" Billy said.

He spoiled Danny's strange fancies.

"Not like you are, singing like a nut all day in school."

"Don't you wish you were able to?"

"Say, you guys, can that and let's do something," Fat Mulloy said.

"Let's kick in a window on George," Dick Buckford said.

"Let's not and say we did," Andy Houlihan said.

"Let's," several others said.

"But listen, you guys, we're liable to get in trouble doing that," Tom O'Connor said.

"Say, O'Connor, will you kindly go home and soak your head," Fat Mulloy bullied.

"Well, I don't wanna start out and land in jail," Tom said.

"You can't kick a window in on George. He's our janitor. We'll have to go someplace else," Ralph Borax said.

"What do you say about gettin' some rotten eggs or old tomatoes an' throwin' 'em in at the Chinks' laundry?" Billy Morris said.

"The Chinks are too mean and dangerous. They'll burn you with hot irons," Glenn said.

"What? Are all you guys yellow?" Fat asked.

No, they weren't yellow, they said, but—

"Well, then, let's do something," Fat said.

Everybody agreed with Fat. They straggled along.

"Wallio. . . . Walliwalli. . . . Wallioooooooooooooooooo," Billy sang monotonously.

"Morris, you better have your head examined," Danny said.

"All right, I'll do that. I sort of like your company anyway. We'll have a lot of fun at Kankakee."

"Let's do something," Fat said.

"Diz is Diz O'Neill is Diz O'Neill is Diz O'Neill is Diz O'Neill is Diz O'Neill is Diz O'Neill is Diz O'Neill," Billy droned in sing-song.

"Yeah, he is that way," Walter Regan said.

Danny ignored them, but he was disturbed.

Dick Buckford joined their chorus of raillery, saying that Goofy O'Neill's suit was a monkey suit because the coat didn't have any belt.

"Any of your business what kind of a suit I wear? Why don't you change your head? It's three times too big for you anyway," Danny said.

Several of the kids laughed at Dick.

"It's brains. You couldn't have a head this big," Dick said, and he laughed in that goofy way of his.

"Brains, hell. Your brains are in your slats," Danny said.

"You haven't even got any brains in your can," Dick said, grinning sheepishly.

"Damn it, let's quit goofing and do something. You guys are worse than my grandmother," Fat said.

"O'Neill is as dizzy as Jim English," Walter Regan said.

"I'm gonna paste somebody in the mouth tonight," Danny said.

"Diz O'Neill is as goofy as goofy as goofy as goofy as Jim English is as goofy as goofy as goofy as goofy as goofy as Diz O'Neill is," Billy sang drily.

"Goofier than English," Dick said.

Danny was hurt and angry. He wanted to be one of the kids like the rest of them, and not the goof of the gang. He did not know why they teased him so much. If he could ignore them, they would stop. But he couldn't. He always lost his temper and wanted to paste somebody. He was going off the handle now. He stepped forward, sneering.

"Damn you fellows."

"O'Neill is a crazy hot-headed Irishman, who is even goofier than Jim English," Billy Morris said.

Danny went for Billy, but Billy was too swift for him. He darted away, chased by leaden-footed Danny. Billy stood across the street, taunting Danny, who had stopped the chase. Dick joined Billy. They shouted at Danny, until he rushed toward them. They waited. Danny went at Dick and Billy with swinging fists, but he succeeded only in catching Billy with a glancing blow on the shoulder before they clinched. They tumbled; Billy was on the bottom and Dick on top. Billy kicked and squirmed and shouted and cursed, but all this effort failed to prevent Danny from rubbing Billy's face against the hard ground. Dick tugged at Danny, slowly dragging him off Billy. The rest of the kids, headed by Walter Regan, rushed across the street, shouting "Pile on." They all yelled, "Get off," "Le-go," "Le-go my ear." "Take your finger outta my eye," "Quit sockin'." Then the scramble quieted down as quickly as it started. They moved on aimlessly, and Billy started kidding Fat Mulloy.

Danny lost his resentment following the free-for-all and the shifting of Billy's attack to Mulloy. He thought of himself as one of the gang and of Fat Mulloy as an outsider. He was going to the party and decided that spoiling the night by his hot-headedness was silly. He was going to the party—and Roslyn would be there.

"Hello, fellows," Jim English said, approaching them from the rear.

They greeted him coldly.

"Where you all goin'?" Jim asked.

"Don't know," Billy said.

"We're going no place," Dick said.

"We're goin' to hell. You wanna come along?" Fat said.

"Say, all foolin' aside, can I go along with you fellahs?" Jim asked.

"We're gonna smash windows and set fires to gates and barns," Dick said.

"Are you really?"

"Yeah."

"An' we're gonna tear down fences," Billy said.

Jim gaped.

"Yeah, and we're gonna throw rotten eggs and tomatoes in at the Chinks in the laundry at Fifty-eight Street," Billy said.

"You better not come along. Soapin' windows is your speed, English," Walter said.

"Can't I come? But are you fellahs really gonna do all those things?"

"Yeah, you better not come along," Danny said.

"We don't want you," Walter Regan said.

"You can't come along. You're nothing but a big string bean," Dick said.

They were in front of the Episcopal Church. They left Jim there, speechless, telling him he would be safe in church. Danny thought he had seen a tear sliding down Jim's cheek. As he walked on, he felt sorry for Jim. But he couldn't do anything. Jim was a string bean and a goof, and they couldn't bring him along on Hallowe'en night. He didn't belong with the gang. Danny didn't know what he could do about Jim, because Jim didn't belong.

"We can't be letting fellows like English come along. We just can't," Danny said.

"No, we can't," Walter said.

We. That meant the bunch, Danny and the others. He was one of We. They only kidded him good-naturedly. We included him, soothed his bruised vanity.

They walked on, and they met a tough bunch of kids from another neighborhood.

"Don't nobody say anything to this bunch. We don't want any trouble with 'em," Walter said.

Tom O'Connor and Glenn said the same thing. Danny sensed what would happen quickly. In a fight, they would lose, and he didn't want to fight. But he knew that this tough gang would crack wise, and, if he didn't call them, he would feel that he was yellow like Dick. If they cracked wise, he would have to call them. Anyway, tough gangs weren't always so tough when you called their bluff. They might trim this gang in a free-for-all. Fat would fight. Billy and Ralph would stick. Walter was big but yellow, and in a tight place he might fight like a cornered rat. No matter what happened, Danny would be the hero. He would bear the brunt of the fighting, and, when they got to the party, Roslyn would hear of his bravery. That was worth several socks in the jaw. But he didn't want to fight unless— well, it would make things easier with Roslyn. She would see that he was something more than the rest of them.

"Hey, you guys tough?" one fellow shouted at them.

"Any of you guys lookin' fer a fight?" a second yelled.

"We eat guys what are tough," a third hollered.

They bragged and cursed among themselves.

Danny's breath came jerkily. He was afraid. He didn't want to call their bluff. If he didn't, none of the other fellows would. He was afraid. But if he kept still, he would be—yellow—and Roslyn at the party would like him better if he was brave— and sometimes a good fight was a lot of fun. He was afraid, and his breath came in jerks.

"Hey, any of youse guys tough?"

"Yes," Danny said loudly.

"What?" from several of the other gang.

Three of them rushed across the street. They looked very tough. One of them, the smallest and most cartoon-like in appearance, was chewing a huge wad of tobacco.

"Where's de guy what sez he's tough?" from the tobacco-chewer.

"Lemme getta poke at 'im," a second said.

"Listen, fellows, we're not looking for trouble or for any fight. We didn't do anything to you fellows and we're perfectly willing to mind our own business," Tom conciliated.

"Yah better not."

"We like 'em tough. Where's de guy what's tough? De tougher dey are, de harder dey fall."

"Yeah, and we're pretty tough. We're so tough dat when we spit, rivers overflow," the tobacco-chewer said, plopping a silver dollar's weight of tobacco juice onto the sidewalk.

There was a brief, tenuous silence. Then the tobacco-chewer repeated his question and clenched his fist. The rest of his gang, noisy, motley, profane, joined him. They outnumbered Danny and the kids, two to one. Several of them poised soot bags.

"Where's the guy?"

"Lemme at him."

"You the guy what spoke?"

"Here I am," Danny said with forced dignity.

He faced them with a scowl that he felt was like Jack Dempsey's scowl when he kayoed Fred Fulton. The tobacco-chewer stepped closer, and his gang crowded in.

"Who are yah? What makes yah think you're tough?"

Danny clenched his fists tightly.

"What's your name?"

"You might tell me yours first—Pug Nose," Danny said.

Fists were clenched and teeth gritted. Five of them surrounded Danny. The others picked men.

"Wait a minute, Spud! . . . wait . . . WAIT!" a tall kid said, stepping in front of Danny.

It was Tim Cleary, who used to sit in front of Danny in school but had moved away.

"I know these guys. They're all right. Friends of mine," Tim said.

"Well, dis wise guy says he's tough."

"He is," Tim said.

"Well, I chew nails."

"Forget it, Spud. These guys are all right."

"Well, if they're friends of yours—but I like 'em tough."

The tobacco-chewer spit again.

"I'm always ready to 'commodate guys what are tough," he said.

"Forget it, Spud. They're a good bunch."

"All right, Tim, but—"

"And what do you say, Dan?"

"It's all right, then, with me, Tim."

The two groups became vaguely friendly. They talked of their evening's braveries, real and imaginary.

"We put an old tree through a window," Dick said.

"We got shagged by de dicks. One of 'em shot at us. We were knockin' fences down," a member of the Cleary bunch said.

"We were almost made into chop suey by the Chinks. Threw tomatoes at 'em. One Chink got plumped in the face. Gee, it was funny. Dick here threw the tomato, an' it hit him in the face," Walter said.

"Yeah, it was a lucky shot," Dick said.

"We caused a blockade by piling boxes on de cartracks over our way on State Street. Cars were stretched along the whole block," Spud said.

Then they separated, mutually refusing offers of uniting.

"Gee, you're crazy," Billy said to Danny.

"Listen, Dizzy, you can't be pulling that stuff with us. Only for Cleary, we'd of had our blocks knocked off," Walter said.

"O'Neill's goofy. Just because he's gotta hard head, and you can't hurt him, he thinks everybody's like that," Billy said.

"Well, anyway, I was all ready to lam the guy that was chewing tobacco," Dick said.

Walter and Glenn also said that if it had come to a fight, they, too, would have done some lamming.

Danny defended himself by declaring that he would have been yellow if he hadn't called them, and that he wasn't yellow, like some guys.

They fooled away an hour, going up one street and down another, placing a few ticktocks on windows, ringing doorbells, planning adventurous ravages. At about nine o'clock they decided it was time to ditch Fat Mulloy. Walter whispered to Billy. The plan was to have Fat break a window, and then in the shag to outrun him. Tom O'Connor and Andy Houlihan, who were slower than Fat, said they were going home and left the bunch. Fat said it was good riddance.

Danny was pleased with himself, planning to cop all the honors at the party. He knew Roslyn would hear of his courage and admire him. She was going to like him. He was going to kiss Roslyn.

Danny knew he was going to kiss Roslyn, and that it would be different from all the other kisses he had ever had at parties.

"Fat, you're afraid to kick in one of the Hunky's windows," Billy said.

"No, I'm not."

"Yes, you are. You're afraid. You're yellow."

"Why don't one of you brave guys do it?"

"We will, but you're afraid to do it."

The others joined Billy in questioning Fat's courage, even Danny. He was one of the bunch and not a Fat Mulloy or— a Jim English.

"I'm gonna punch one of you guys in the snoot," Fat said.

They looked at Danny. He said nothing, walking along casually. Fat looked at Billy and stepped closer to him. Billy retreated.

"I'll sock you in the jaw," Fat bellowed.

"Yes, you might do that, but you're yellow when it comes to kickin' in one of the Hunky's windows," Billy answered.

"Am I?"

"Yes."

"Well, come on. Then I'm gonna lay one on you."

They went to the corner building at Sixtieth and Indiana. Fat walked up to one of the basement windows, and the others ranged themselves close by, ready to run. They were breathless. Fat looked at the window and then glared at Billy. Fat retreated but returned when Billy laughed at him. He kicked viciously, and the glass hit the basement floor with a metallic ring. They fled, soon followed by the Hunky, a swarthy man, who yelled after them in angry foreign accents. They turned corners, dashed up and down alleys, climbed fences, cut through dark gangways, flashed in and out of secret courtways. Danny fell and ripped his stockings. Billy tore his trousers. Ralph was almost hit by an automobile. And Fat lumbered at the rear, puffing, after the Hunky had given up the pursuit, yelling for them to wait. They ran on wildly. Danny lost the others in an alley. But he was happy. He knew the party would be lots of fun. He thought how Roslyn would kiss him and ad- mire him for his courage. He was going to have a good time at the party. Everybody would have some fun. They were all a good bunch of kids. They didn't mean anything by teasing each other. And he was one of the bunch, and not a Fat Mulloy or a Jim English. He was going to the party, a con- quering hero. He was going to the party—going—to—kiss— Roslyn.

IV

Danny arrived at the party. The others were playing tin-tin and paid no attention to him. He found a seat in a Morris chair over in a corner and sat there, alone and awkward. He looked at Roslyn. She sat on the piano stool at the other side of the parlor, dressed in a worn gray suit of Glenn's. Natalie O'Reedy sat next to Roslyn. Natalie was the prettiest girl at school. But Danny watched Roslyn. He gazed around at the other girls, Helen Scanlan, Loretta Lonigan, Cabby Devlin, and fat Marion Troy. His eyes turned back to Roslyn.

The tin-tin game grew dull, and they talked. But Danny had little to say. He was an utter failure at thinking up things to say when there were girls around, particularly Roslyn. He watched Roslyn, and slouched further down in the Morris chair. He wished they would talk of the meeting with Tim Cleary's bunch. Several times he hinted at it, but no one followed up his hints. He kept watching Roslyn, until she caught him and squelched his spirit with a glance. He sat slouched and miserable, losing the last tatters of the feeling he had had coming here. He attempted to start conversations with several of the fellows, baseball with Dick, grammar with Tom O'Connor, dogs with Glenn. But they all had other people to talk to. Danny slouched further down in the chair and felt even more miserable.

The party dragged on.

"Le's do something," Danny finally said.

Something, he hoped, would be post-office.

"What?" someone asked.

"I can't play any kissing games. My mother told me not to," Natalie O'Reedy said.

Danny was not alone in his disappointment when Natalie spoiled all hopes of post-office.

"Well, let's do something," Danny said.

"Maybe you'd like to start another fight," Walter answered.

"Listen, Regan, don't get snotty."

Billy told Danny that he couldn't allow any fighting in his house, and also that girls were present. Roslyn stared at Danny with sudden scorn. He said nothing; he couldn't think of anything to say. He slunk further down in the Morris chair.

Tom O'Connor suggested dancing. Marion Troy played the piano, and the fellows who knew how—Tom O'Connor, Glenn, Billy Morris, and Andy Houlihan—danced. The others looked on.

After about six dances, Roslyn said, "Let's sing."

She took Marion's place at the piano, and they all gathered around. Danny stood directly in back of her, with his arms around the shoulders of Dick and Ralph. He felt like one of the bunch again, as he stood looking at her in front of him. She was not only good and sweet and pretty, but also talented, and she could dance and recite and play at a party.

He watched her playing, her small slender hands sliding from key to key with a soft grace. Somehow it made him think of the seagulls flying over Lake Michigan off Jackson Park. Her hands impressed him that way.

They sang *Mickey* several times. Everybody liked it.

> "*Mickey, lovely Mickey,*
> *With your hair of raven hue,*
> *And your smilin' so beguilin',*
> *There's a bit of Killarney bit of the Blarney, too.*
> *Childhood in the wildwood,*
> *Like a wild sunflower you grew.*
> *Mickey, lovely Mickey,*
> *Can you blame anyone for falling in love with you?*"

They sang other songs: *Just a Baby's Prayer at Twilight, Over There, America, Here's My Boy, We'll Knock the 'Ell Out of Kelly.*

Danny sang throatily, unable to carry a tune. He thought that now his dreams would begin to come true. For a moment, it seemed as though Dick and Ralph next to him were not real any more. Everything seemed shadowy, except Roslyn's white hands. He kept watching her hands. They were so vivid, white, beautiful. Then he daydreamed. He thought of wartorn French roads and towns, of airplane fights, sea battles in uncharted waters. And through all these came Roslyn, the girl with the white hands, to kiss him. He watched those hands, the hands of a wisp of a wonderful girl in a boy's suit, sliding from key to key and making him think of the seagulls over Lake Michigan. Roslyn.

Suddenly he grew intensely lonely. He felt out of place at the party, a misfit. The girl before him, with the beautiful white hands, was a stranger. She was worse than a stranger. She was an enemy, ready to hurt him every time she could. And no one could hurt Danny O'Neill as much as Roslyn. The whole room was full of strangers, half-sneering strangers who were jealous of him, afraid of him, hating him. They were all friends, but he remained on the outside. He had to fight against them all the time, and he was tired of it. He wished his folks would move to a new neighborhood, where he could start all over again. He looked around from face to face. He wanted to punch them all, to go from person to person and bust each one—except Roslyn. He was lonely, and he didn't belong at parties where there were a lot of girls. He belonged on a baseball field or in a fight. He was lonely.

"*Just a baby's prayer at twilight*
For his daddy over there."

v

Mrs. Morris called them into the dining room for sandwiches and hot chocolate. Danny thought she was very gracious.

"Eats, eats, everybody," Billy said.

"Tie Buckford up so the rest of us'll get a chance," Andy Houlihan said.

"Yes, we better tie him up," Danny said.

He didn't feel so lonely now. The whole bunch was so good-natured. He liked them all.

"Go on, O'Neill! At my party you ate six sandwiches," Dick said.

Roslyn gave Danny a sudden, darting look.

"Now, line up, and each boy select his partner," Mrs. Morris said.

Danny wanted to walk across the room and take Roslyn's arm, but he couldn't. He stood in a corner and looked at the geranium-patterned wallpaper. Tommy O'Connor was near him, and Danny felt awkward, and so he started talking with Tommy about diagramming sentences. Tommy wasn't interested. He went over to where Dick was standing and asked Dick about his uncle, a minor-league ball player. Dick was busy talking with Helen Scanlan. Danny had been in love with her until he began to love Roslyn in the sixth grade. He looked around the room, shifted his weight from foot to foot, and felt completely miserable and unnecessary. He wished Roslyn would come over and stand next to him. He glanced at her, and she glanced the other way. He watched her, standing demure and possessed. He wanted her for a partner, and he was afraid to ask her. The other fellows seemed equally hesitant about selecting a partner. They stood about the room and waited.

"Come on now, boys. Line up with your partners," Mrs. Morris said.

Finally Billy Morris lined up beside Natalie. Glenn pulled Roslyn by the elbow, next to him, behind Billy and Natalie. The others rapidly found partners, except Danny. He marched into

the dining room at the end of the procession, feeling like a goof
and a dunce and wishing he hadn't come.

The table was set with small, yellow-ribboned baskets at
each plate, while orange streamers were draped from a pie in the
center. More orange streamers hung down from the chandelier.
Under each yellow paper napkin there was a favor.

They sat down and immediately began talking loudly.
Everyone was curious about everyone else's favor, except Danny's. Glenn pulled out a small whistle, which he futilely attempted to blow, and they all laughed. Roslyn displayed a
tiny automobile, which she rolled around her plate, and there
was more laughing. Billy held up a miniature washing board
and set the party into spasms when he rubbed on it with mock
vigor.

"Washing, washing today. I'm forced to take in washing by
my wife, Natalie." They all screamed with laughter. "She makes
me work, washing for a living. Washing. Washing," he said.

Danny's favor was a dunce cap of reduced size. He put it
on and grimaced awkwardly. No one noticed him. They continued to look at Billy, who was pretending to tear Dick's shirt
in the washing.

"Gotta go faster and faster. Life beats me when I loaf," Billy
said, rubbing vigorously, utilizing his entire body in movement.

They roared.

Danny envied Billy. He wished he could think of funny
things to say, like Billy did. He wished he could make people
laugh and like him, as Billy did. He wished he wasn't something
of a dunce. He never could think of anything to say. He sat
and played with his dunce cap and tried to think of something
funny, but couldn't. He played with his dunce cap and made
funny motions with his arms.

"Look-it," Marion Troy said, noticing him and causing everyone to give him a passing glance of attention.

They all seemed to be having a good time except Danny.
No one laughed at his jokes. The other fellows, particularly
Billy, could have said the same things and made everybody
laugh. Billy's description of how he brought Chinese laundry

checks to school was a scream. Danny tried to have a good time, and he laughed with all the effort of a man laboring. But he kept telling himself that he didn't belong at parties.

Several times, as Danny tried to repeat how goofy Jim English was, he was hit in the eye with a peanut. The fourth time he was hit, he started shooting peanuts back.

"Cut out slingin' peanuts, O'Neill. You're not home now," Billy said.

"Yes, this isn't a barn," Dick said.

Dick had started the peanut throwing.

Danny blushed. He imagined Roslyn staring at him, with eyes that bored into his soul. He was afraid to face her. His cheeks grew redder and redder. He wished he had never come to the party and vowed that next week at school he would paste every fellow present in the snoot.

VI

As the party was breaking up, Tom O'Connor, Walter Regan, Dick Buckford, and Glenn commenced fooling around and wrestling in the parlor. Danny was caught in between them. They were shoving and pushing, and he stepped aside. He didn't want to fool around. He stood aside, with his back to the four of them. Suddenly he was shoved violently from the rear and pitched forward. Everyone laughed, laughter that burned like streaks of flame. He got up, angry. His glasses fell off. He picked them up bent. When he tried to straighten them, they split in two. He was angry. He was sure that Wallie Regan had pushed him, but he couldn't prove it. He put his broken glasses into his pocket.

"Who pushed me?" he growled at Walter.

No one answered. Glenn and Walter snickered.

"If I find out who pushed me and broke my glasses, I'll kill him," he said to Walter.

"What are you lookin' at me for?" Walter asked blandly.

"Because you did it."

"I did not."

"You did, too."

"You're a liar."

"Who's a liar?"

"You are if you say I did it."

Danny stepped forward, and Walter retreated. Billy Morris moved between the two of them and said that they were in his house. He looked scornfully at Danny. Billy's mother was disturbed, and asked the boys please not to start a fight and break any of her furniture.

Outside, the kids would not allow them to fight. They haggled and argued.

"Regan'll kill you," Dick said.

"Come on an' let him try."

"Why, you're goofy. Look at how much bigger than you Regan is," Ralph said.

"Listen, he's goofy. You can't hurt him. What's the use of fighting with a guy like that?" Andy Houlihan said.

Danny closed in towards Andy.

"You little shrimp."

Ralph, Walter, and Dick crowded in between Danny and the cowering Andy Houlihan.

"Come on, Regan. I'll take you an' Houlihan."

"I gotta go home. I can't be hanging around fighting somebody who's as goofy as you."

Danny clenched his fists and went for Walter, but he was caught from behind by Ralph and Dick.

"Come on, Glenn, I can't be staying out all night to watch that roughneck start a fight. Take me home," Roslyn said.

Glenn and Roslyn started to leave. Walter and Andy joined them. Danny was crying as he shouted after them. He cursed Ralph and Dick, too. He crossed the street and went home alone.

He walked home slowly. The night was shivery and silent on Fifty-eighth Street. The moon was weird, like a witch. Danny cried and cursed.

VII

On the following Sunday, Danny went to a movie at the Prairie Theater at Fifty-eighth and Prairie Avenue with Fat Mulloy. Danny still felt humiliated about Billy's party. At school they had laughed at him.

After the show Danny and Fat stopped at a soda fountain next door to the show.

"Fat, do you like Regan?"

"No."

"I was wonderin'. I'm gonna get him."

Fat doubted Danny's ability to get Regan. Danny repeated that he would, and could, get Regan. He knew he could knock the hell out of Regan, but he was anxious. The bunch would all be with Regan. He was rich and could buy them sodas and candy. Sometimes he took them riding in his father's automobile. It was a big limousine with his father's initials on the door. Danny knew he would be out of the bunch if he fought with Regan. He knew he would lose any friendship that Glenn might have for him. Glenn was only a runt and even a sissy, but he was Roslyn's cousin. He loved Roslyn and thought he should remain friendly with Glenn. If he beat up Regan, he would be left out of parties, too. He would be lonely. But he had to get Regan. And he would.

Fat and Danny talked over their sodas. Suddenly Fat pointed out of the window and said, "There's Regan."

Danny turned to see Regan pass by. Danny was afraid.

"Here's your chance," Fat said.

Danny rushed out of the soda parlor and called after Regan in a mood of desperation.

"Listen, Regan, I want to see you."

"What for? I'm in a hurry."

Regan walked back slowly.

"What do you wanna see me for? I'm in a hurry."

"Commere an' I'll tell you."

Danny found himself calm now. He was calm and he hated

Regan. He hated Regan so much that he wanted to keep punching him and watch his face bleed.

"You shoved me."

"I didn't."

"You're a liar."

"I'm not a liar."

"You are. Now, listen. Will you fight?"

"I'm in a hurry. Anyway, I could lick you."

"Are you yellow or will you fight?"

"I'm in a hurry, and I can't now. Anyway, I could lick you."

"You *can*?"

"Can't I, Fat?"

Slap! The back of Danny's right hand snapped against Regan's lip, causing a thick trickle of blood. Danny was thrilled by the sight of Regan's blood.

"Damn you, will you fight now?"

"I can't now. I haven't the time, I tell you. But I'll get even with you for this. I'll settle with you."

Regan walked away.

"Yellow," Danny shouted after him.

"Yellow belly," Fat yelled.

VIII

"Are you going to Roslyn's party tonight?" Ralph asked Danny.

It was an autumn-weary day in the middle of November. Ralph and Danny were walking together on Indiana Avenue.

"No. I'm not invited."

"I don't think anyone was especially invited. She saw Billy and all of us the other day and asked us to come. Said she couldn't go up to everyone separately and ask them. She said she'd feel kind of funny if she did."

"Well, she never invited me. I saw her a couple of times last week, and she never invited me."

"Well, I know she meant that everybody should come."

"No, she never invited me."

"Well, I think she meant everybody. I know I'm goin', and I'm gonna have a good time."

"Hooray—Hooray—Giddap—Giddap—Bang, Bang, Bang —Look out, here I come on Pinto, chased by the sheriff, Fat Mulloy. Bang, Bang, Bang."

It was Billy Morris. He galloped past them, turned around, galloped back, and walked along at their side.

"Billy, in a way you're goofy," Ralph said.

Billy didn't say anything. They stopped in front of his home, a three-story, gray brick building.

"Where you going, Ralph?"

"Nowheres."

"And you?"

"Same place."

"Let's all go together. Or let's just sit here and talk for a while."

They sat down on Billy's front steps.

"I gotta go upstairs and take a bath for the party in a little while," Billy said.

Danny didn't want to sit, talking with them. It was one of those days when he wanted to be alone. But he thought that he might get them to go over to Roslyn's home and take a walk down around that neighborhood. Then maybe they would meet Roslyn, and she might invite him to her party. He knew Roslyn liked him despite everything. It was just pride that made her act like she did. Glenn once told him that she cared for him.

"Let's go up and see Glenn," Danny said.

"Glenn's gone downtown to get some favors for the party," Billy answered.

"We ought to have a good time tonight," Ralph said.

"Yeah, I always have a good time if Natalie is around. Gee, but she's a pip. She's got wonderful legs, too," Billy said.

"Yeah, she has, all right," Ralph said.

"She's more than all right. She's a pip," Billy said.

Danny envied Ralph and Billy. He was jealous of the easy

way in which they talked of girls, of their popularity, and of their invitations to Roslyn's party. He wished he could talk of, and to, girls as naturally, and that he could get along with them as well as Billy or Ralph did.

"Let's take a walk down and see Andy Houlihan. Maybe he'll have a good bonfire going in the prairie next to his house," Danny said.

Andy lived one block away from Roslyn. Maybe they would see her if they went around that neighborhood.

"It's too far. I gotta get ready for the party," Billy said.

"So do I," from Ralph.

"We don't have to stay long," Danny said.

"Helen Scanlan's going to be at the party tonight, isn't she?" Ralph asked.

"Yeah. Say, you kind of like her, don't you?" Billy asked.

"Yes, she's a nice kid," Ralph said.

"She's another pip, all right. She's got legs almost as good as Natalie's," Billy said, getting enthusiastic.

"Yes, she has."

"I wouldn't mind playing post-office tonight. Oh, boy! . . . with Natalie tonight. With some girls, too, but not Natalie, you can get 'em in the dark and cop a couple of feels," Billy said.

"Well, I wouldn't mind, either."

Danny wanted to protest against something, but he couldn't find any word that would tell him what that something was. He wanted to protest, because somewhere there was unfairness. He wanted to know why Ralph and Billy got along so much better than he did, and why people liked them better. He wanted to know why they should be invited to the party and not he. He could do almost everything better than either of them. He could fight, wrestle, play football better than they. They didn't even know the first thing about basketball. He got better marks in school, too. All Billy could do better than Danny was dance and make wisecracks. There was something unfair in the world somewhere, and he wanted to protest about it.

"Natalie and Helen are the best lookers in school," Billy

said, and Danny but half heard the remark. He sat pitying himself. There was something unfair, and he was being hurt because of unfairness and he wanted to fight, even though he was afraid of fighting.

"Yeah," Ralph said.

"Roslyn used to be, but she fixes her hair up funny now, and she's got skinny legs," Billy said.

Danny hated Billy for this remark. He looked at Billy, thinking of Billy's own toothpick legs, his ugly peanut of a head, his dirty brown skin. He hated Billy, and told himself that Roslyn was an angel.

"Billy, didn't Roslyn mean for everyone to come to her party?" Ralph asked.

"I guess so. Why?"

"I was telling Danny that, and he said it didn't mean him."

"She said she wanted everyone, but, then, she doesn't like him."

"Who wants to go to her damn party?" Danny said.

"I do. I expect to have some fun," Billy said.

A few minutes later Danny left, determined that Ralph, Billy, and Roslyn, too, could all roast in the hottest part of Hell. But he was glad the kids didn't know that he was so much in love with Roslyn. If they did, they'd never stop ragging him.

He had intended to go home. He walked down to Sixty-first and South Park and proceeded to go around the block several times. Each time he passed a lace-curtained window on the second floor of an ornate building in the middle of the block, he stopped and gazed up, as if interested in the stars that were just coming out.

A passer-by might have noticed that he was wistful as he gazed up past the lace curtains.

IX

Danny heard all about Roslyn's party. He was told that it was the best party ever given. They had played spin-the-bottle, post-office, wink, and tin-tin. Roslyn's father had played with them, and the kids said he was a regular fellow. And there had been all kinds of eats, too. Roslyn had called Andy Houlihan to the post-office a number of times, and Helen Scanlan had been sweet to Ralph. Glenn had copped off Natalie. He was a devil with the women. Billy Morris had been a scream. Every time he talked, he had made the whole party laugh. It had been a scream when he plopped the peanut into Dick's coffee.

And there were half-whispered conversations of what had been said and done in the post-office.

X

Danny met Ralph one afternoon about a week after Roslyn's party. He hadn't been playing with the bunch of late and was lonesome. He was glad to see Ralph and wanted to talk to him about a lot of things, particularly about Roslyn and her party. She had spoken to him, asking him why he hadn't come. He knew she liked him. He was glad to see Ralph, too, and wanted to talk about Roslyn.

"Hello, Ralph, how are you?"

"All right," Ralph answered with self-conscious casualness.

"Where you going?"

"No place."

"Let's go together," Danny said.

Ralph didn't answer. They walked slowly.

"You're kind of droopy. Do you know it?" Ralph said suddenly, following his remark with a scornful laugh.

Danny looked at Ralph.

"Yes, you're dizzy."

"How do you get that way?" Ralph asked, muffling his anger.

"Yes, you're dizzy."

"Well, what if I am?"

"Nothing. Only you're dizzy and a droopy drawers."

"Supposing I am?"

"Nothing."

Ralph laughed again.

"Yes, you're an old droop. Look at the way you walk."

"No, I'm not. I just walk—slow."

Ralph laughed again.

"You're not any too fast or straight when you walk," Danny said.

"I'm not a droopy drawers," Ralph said.

He laughed again.

"You're worse."

"I am?" Ralph asked. He was angry, and his voice throbbed.

"Yes, what are you gonna do about it?" Danny asked, arrogant.

"I am worse than a droopy drawers?"

"Yes."

"Well, what am I?" Ralph asked menacingly.

Danny couldn't think of anything more to say. He answered that Ralph was—just worse than a droopy drawers. That was all. He was worse.

They glowered, and Ralph cried slightly, from anger.

"Take that back," he demanded.

"Not unless you do."

"Take it back."

"No."

"I beat you once."

"That was in the fifth grade. But you can't do it again," Danny taunted.

"I beat you once. I punched the crap out of you. I can do it again if I want to."

"You're afraid to try it again."

"Remember that time you socked Billy Morris? Well, I licked you, didn't I?"

"Yes, but you can't now. Go get Morris, and I'll take the two of you."

"You know I can lick you if I want to."

"Wanna fight?" Danny asked.

"I licked you once. You just be careful about saying that I'm worse than an old droopy drawers."

"Then you watch what you say."

"Suppose I don't?"

"Then I won't."

"Don't forget that I beat you once."

"I can take you and Billy together now."

"You think you're tough, don't you?"

"No, but I'm tougher than you are," Danny said.

They walked for a block, silent. Then Ralph repeated that he once licked Danny, and Danny repeated that he could lick Ralph. Ralph repeated and Danny repeated.

"I can't play with you any more," Ralph suddenly said.

Danny ignored Ralph.

"I can't play with you any more, because my mother knows there's swearing in your house, and your aunt gets drunk."

"It isn't so," Danny said hotly.

"It is," Ralph said. "I don't care. My mother told me not to play with you any more. She says you'll grow up to be a bad influence."

"Well, don't walk with me," Danny said.

"You started walking with me," Ralph said.

"I'm walking this way, and I'm gonna keep walking," Danny said.

"So am I."

They strolled on side by side, without any further conversation.

XI

Walter Regan, Ralph, Billy, Dick, Glenn, Andy Houlihan, Fat Mulloy, a kid nicknamed Blackie, new at St. Patrick's, and Danny were all standing in front of school.

"Diz here is goofy," Dick said.

"He's crazy. Crazy people always have dreamy eyes like he got. You know, eyes that are always asleep," Billy said.

"What if I am?" Danny answered.

"No if about it," Dick said.

"Shut up, Buckford!"

Dick grinned foolishly.

"Gee, you're a hot-headed Irishman all right," Billy said.

"Well, Dick gives me a pain. If he wasn't yellow, I'd bust his mush for him."

"He's goofy with an ivory head. He's the kind of a guy you can't hurt. You keep hitting him until you get tired. He's got an ivory head," Dick said.

Glenn and Billy started poking each other in the ribs and wrestling. Then they ran around in circles, chasing each other, and shouting. Soon they were on the ground, wrestling. Walter Regan and Dick joined in with a whoop. Danny moved to do likewise.

"Who asked you in?" Walter asked.

"None of your damn business."

"It is, too, my business who I play with."

"And mine, too," Glenn said, getting up.

"And I don't wanna play with a roughneck Irishman who is always lookin' for a fight. Why, you're worse than the Germans," Walter said.

"Yes, and my mother told me to have nothing to do with him because there's always a lot of swearin' and cursin' goin' on at his house," Ralph said.

"Yes, and he hasn't any breeding. He's like a Hun, throwing peanuts at parties and starting fights in other people's houses," Billy said.

"He's goofy about my cousin, and she hates him," Glenn said.

They laughed at him.

The remarks had come so swiftly that Danny was without a reply. He stuttered in anger. Walter Regan invited the bunch to go with him, and they all accepted.

"You can't come," he said to Danny.

"Who wants to play with a yellow belly?"

"You can't."

They all left, laughing back at Danny, who stood, tearful and defiant, shaking his fists at them.

XII

Danny remained in front of the school for about five minutes. He was hurt and angry. Then he headed east along Sixty-first Street, planning to go for a walk all the way to Jackson Park. He was lonely and, whenever he felt that way, he took a long walk. He usually walked in Washington Park, but today he'd walk in Jackson Park. As he drooped along, he planned scenes bloody with the revenge he would wreak. When he grew up and became a great basketball player and a greater fighter than Benny Leonard, he would snub them. And the next time they needed him in a scrap, he wouldn't stick with them. He was through with them, and he could wait for his revenge until he became great. He was through with them, and all winter he would remain at home, reading.

He thought of Roslyn. He wondered if Glenn had told the truth. Did she hate him? If she did, well, the hell with her, too. Some day she, all of them, would feel sorry. If he met her he would snub her. He did meet her. She opened her mouth to speak. Danny didn't look at her. In fact, he didn't see her. After she passed, she turned around and yelled, "Funny face."

He came to his senses with a start and turned around.

"Funny face," she repeated.

"If I'm a Funny Face, you're one, too," he said.

She stuck up her small nose, turned her head pertly, and walked away.

He felt like a fool. He was sorry, and angry. He told himself that she could go to the devil, and for an entire block he imagined her burning in Hell.

When he came to Jackson Park, his mood changed. He became moody and lost in a vaporous sadness. There was a sadness about the park, half mellow with autumn, half bare with the wounds of the early winter winds. The park seemed to console him. He forgot all about the raggings he received from the bunch. He imagined himself alone, away from the world, a Robinson Crusoe on some distant sphere. Things seemed strange to him. He imagined that he was a soul in Purgatory, a soul cast there willy-nilly.

He walked. The park seemed bare, cold, strange, lonely; dusk covered it like a robe. Overhead, a frosty moon had blown the sun out of the sky, sinking it in the oblivion of another day. He saw etched against the distant sky the vague outlines of a human figure. He watched it approach slowly. It was bent and familiar. He looked at it, and then at the moon, alone and companionless in a sky empty of stars. He remembered all that had hurt him in the past weeks. He was lonely. The figure was upon him.

"Hello, Danny," it said.

"Hello, Jim."

"What are you doing here?" Danny asked.

"Oh, taking a walk," Jim said.

"So am I. I like Jackson Park better than Washington Park," Danny said.

"So do I," Jim said.

Danny wished he lived in the Jackson Park neighborhood and knew a new bunch of kids.

"Goin' home? It's late and it'll be a long walk."

"We can get a hitch on a truck," Danny said.

"Where were you going?" Jim said.

"Over to the lake."

Jim seemed moody, too. They walked on to the lake in silence and looked at it.

"Looks rough today," Jim said.

"It's always rough at this time of year. It's kind of cold, and the wind is coming up," Danny said.

"Yes, it is," Jim said.

"It's gray and kind of dirty," Danny said.

"Oh, boy, what whitecaps," Jim said.

"I like the noise it makes. I like it kind of wild," Danny said.

"I don't. You couldn't swim in it this way," Jim said.

"I'd like to. I'm going to try and swim in it against those waves some time."

"I don't believe you."

"I will some day," Danny said.

The two boys stood before the lake in the gathering darkness, looking at it, listening to the wild monotony of its slashing waves. Danny looked far, far out and saw the dark horizon. He looked and looked. He wanted to see the seagulls today, flying and crying in the darkness over the rough lake. He thought of Roslyn as a seagull. But he saw none. There was nothing but gray water, gray water and waves and foaming whitecaps on the lake. And there was no one around, no one in sight, only himself and Jim. They stood looking at the lake.

"Yes, it's better this way than when it's calm," Danny said.

They turned and walked back.

"Yes."

They walked along together.

"Where were the kids today?" Jim asked.

"I had a quarrel with 'em. They give me a pain, and none of them would fight."

"I don't like them either," Jim said.

Danny didn't answer.

"Was Glenn with 'em?" Jim asked.

"Yeah."

"Does he still tease his cousin?"

"He ought to. She's an old Funny Face. Worse than he is."

"I thought she was a nice girl."

"She gives me a pain."

"I kinda think she's all right," Jim said.

Danny changed the subject to baseball. And he had enough money to pay for both their carfares. They talked baseball all the way home on the car. They got off at Sixty-first and South Park. Danny looked up at Roslyn's window. It was lit up. He wished she'd look out and see him. They walked on.

Just as they were parting at Fifty-first and South Park, Danny said, "Listen, Jim, you come over to my house after school tomorrow?"

"Sure," Jim said.

"Danny, was that true what you told me about Rube Waddell?" Jim called after him.

"Yeah. I'll show you his records in the Spaulding and Reich guides tomorrow. I like a guy like him."

"So long, Danny."

"So long, Jim."